Roger Poulton was born in Plymouth in 1937 and was educated at the Royal Hospital School in Suffolk. He then served a Five Year Apprenticeship as an Engine Fitter in the Royal Dockyard at Chatham. Following six years in the Merchant Navy, he went into the Construction Industry, where he worked for more than forty years. He is now retired and lives in Gloucestershire.

A DOCKYARD MATEY

To my long-suffering wife Barbara, who has put up with my 'never-ending tales' over the past forty plus years.

RMJ Poulton

A DOCKYARD MATEY

AUSTIN MACAULEY
PUBLISHERS LTD.

A CIP catalogue record for this title is available from the British Library.

ISBN 978 184963 410 6

www.austinmacauley.com

First Published (2013)
Austin Macauley Publishers Ltd.
25 Canada Square
Canary Wharf
London
E14 5LB

Printed and bound in Great Britain

Acknowledgments

My grateful thanks to Mrs Carroll Beard, aka 'Blodwen Bach'; for her invaluable help and support in writing this book.

Thanks also to Mrs Clare Jayes, for her invaluable advice on my lack of knowledge of hymns and classical music.

Contents

Book 1: The First Year   18

Introduction   19

Chapter 1   21
    You've Got to Have a Trade

Chapter 2   27
    Confrontations

Chapter 3   33
    Early Training

Chapter 4   38
    Further Education

Chapter 5   43
    Christmas Capers

Chapter 6   48
    Dirty Work

Chapter 7   52
    Practice Makes Perfect

Chapter 8   56
    A Policeman's Lot

The Gate Pass – Poem   61

Chapter 9   63
    Young Love

Chapter 10   68
    A Painful Lesson

Chapter 11   73
    Happy Days

Chapter 12   78
    Lodgings

Chapter 13   83
    Never a Borrower

Chapter 14   88

Sporting Life

Chapter 15   93

Youthful Misdemeanours

Chapter 16   98

The Ultimate Trade Test

Book 2: The Second Year   102

Chapter 1   103

A New Dimension

Chapter 2   108

Fun and Games

Chapter 3   113

All Types of Valves

Chapter 4   117

More Schooling

Chapter 5   122

Waking Up

Chapter 6   127

A Right Pantomime

Chapter 7   132

Sharp Practice

Chapter 8   137

All Types of Engines

Chapter 9   142

Learning Fast

Chapter 10   147

Bolshie Billy

Chapter 11   152

Dirty Tricks

Chapter 12   157

Infernal Machines

Chapter 13   162

I Don't Want To Join the Army

Chapter 14   166
  The Tool Room

Chapter 15   172
  New Skills

Chapter 16   177
  The Last Few Weeks

Book 3: The Third Year   183

Chapter 1   184
  A New Year

Chapter 2   190
  Feet under the Table

Chapter 3   196
  Turning

Chapter 4   201
  The Maltese Connection

Chapter 5   207
  In Hot Water

Chapter 6   212
  Machining

Chapter 7   217
  Moya

Chapter 8   223
  Boredom

Chapter 9   228
  The Cellar Club

Chapter 10   233
  Shaping Up

Chapter 11   238
  Youthful Entertainment

Chapter 12   243
  The Perils Of Love

Chapter 13   248
  Something Different

Chapter 14   **254**

Domestic Strife

Chapter 15   **259**

The Social Scene

Chapter 16   **265**

The End of the Year

Book 4: The Fourth Year   **271**

Chapter 1   **272**

A Change for the Better

Chapter 2   **277**

Fun and Games

Chapter 3   **282**

Interesting Work

Chapter 4   **287**

The End of the Refit

Chapter 5   **293**

A Ceremonial Occasion

Chapter 6   **298**

Another Change

Chapter 7   **303**

More Discomfort

Chapter 8   **308**

Crane Maintenance

Chapter 9   **313**

Nobby Hall

Chapter 10   **319**

A Big Job

Chapter 11   **324**

Treasure Trove

Chapter 12   **329**

Personal Matters

Chapter 13   **335**

More Problems

Chapter 14   340

A Steady Slog

Chapter 15   345

A New Romance

Chapter 16   350

Another Year Completed

Book 5: The Fifth Year   355

Chapter 1   356

The Final Year

Chapter 2   362

A Dodgy Proposition

Chapter 3   368

A Fool and His Money

Chapter 4   373

Confrontations

Chapter 5   378

Hard Labour

Chapter 6   384

Lighter Moments

Chapter 7   389

Main Engines

Chapter 8   395

Pleasant Times

Chapter 9   401

Testing Systems

Chapter 10   406

Cold Work

Chapter 11   411

Under Pressure

Chapter 12   416

Perversity

Chapter 13   421

Interesting Jobs

Chapter 14   426

  Getting Some In

Chapter 15   430

  More Domestic Problems

Chapter 16   435

  The Last Lap

Book 1: The First Year

Introduction

In the years following the Second World War, the majority of British families suffered great hardship. Most of our cities and towns had been substantially damaged by enemy action and the cost and difficulties involved in the rebuilding of the infrastructure across the nation was enormous. Our heavy industry, which had manufactured armaments during the hostilities, was out-dated and soon became progressively redundant. Many companies, whose products had led the world through the previous hundred years or so, were deficient in design, quality and output and gradually, they went out of business. Years were to pass before some semblance of normality returned to a once prosperous nation.

The inevitable spiral of decline was accentuated by our inability to adjust to a rapidly changing world. The 'bright new dawn', for which we had so fervently fought, quickly degenerated and there was increasing International tension. In fact, the Cold War had started even before the hostilities had ended and the financial disaster which ensued resulted in severe cut-backs in government expenditure. The economy was rigidly controlled but, with the growing threat to our security, it was essential that the capability and integrity of the Armed Forces had to be maintained. There had been huge changes in the design and development of all manner of weaponry and a large part of the Royal Navy was both worn out and obsolete. It became a matter of great urgency then to reinforce the fleet with modern vessels.

For many years before the war, the Admiralty had built, re-fitted and maintained most of their Ships in the Royal Dockyards. With the coming of the uncertain peace, there was a pressing need to replace the employees lost to 'natural wastage', to ensure that the essential skills would be readily available in times of emergency. The Admiralty thus embarked on the education and training of large numbers of Trade Apprentices.

This book tells the story of a group of young men, who served their five year Apprenticeships in a Royal Dockyard in the nineteen fifties. They started work on the 31 August, 1953 and duly underwent five years of extensive training. The main character, Mike, is a fictional character whose story is made up of the experiences of many of the lads who served their time in those austere years. Of necessity, the names of individuals have been changed and if offence is caused by the author's rambling reminiscences, then any apologies called for will be freely given.

We have written about their everyday lives, both in and outside of work and their backgrounds, interests, pleasures and misdemeanours have been 'described' in some detail. They were a disparate bunch and some had great difficulty in coming to terms with each other. Life in Britain was very much different from what it is today and in looking back, we have recalled those days with humour, even though their experiences were at times anything but funny.

Over the past fifty years, the broad field of engineering has changed beyond description and the form of Apprenticeship as described in this book no longer exists. Computer-aided design and manufacture has yielded a very much higher standard, both in quality and finish, in all manner of mechanical and electrical components. What an 'old-time' Fitter took days or even weeks to make by hand is now turned-out, in very short time, by automated machines. Time is now increasingly of the essence and the 'Plant' must be brought on line as quickly as possible. Sometimes though, an old guy gets the opportunity to demonstrate his practical skills and by coming up with the answer to a difficult problem, he goes some way in justifying his existence. The reality is though, 'The world has moved on.'

Chapter 1

You've Got to Have a Trade

Mike's family lived in a village approximately seven miles from the town and like most working people, they struggled to maintain a basic existence. His father had completed twenty-two years' service in the Royal Marines by the end of the Second World War and following his 'demob', he had been shocked and depressed to find that jobs for 'unskilled workers' were exceedingly hard to come by. Hundreds of thousands of ex-servicemen had been looking for gainful employment. Prior to his discharge, he had been given basic training as a Scaffolder, and the job had great potential, following the wholesale destruction of our cities and towns. However, he neither liked working at heights nor relished the prospect of doing so on building sites.

After many weeks of fruitless searching, he had joined the Royal Marine Police, which put him back into a uniform similar to that which he had worn throughout his adult life. It involved shift-working and the mind-boggling monotony of 'guarding' the dockyard, alongside many other ex-Royal Marines. Compared to what he would have earned in the building trade, the pay was poor but fortunately, his service pension supplemented his income. The family budget was thus fixed, but it was a lot better than being on the dole. The consequence of him taking 'the easy option' was that he and his wife faced the difficult task of making ends meet and with three children, their chronic shortage of money adversely affected everyone. Like so very many others, their lives rapidly became little more than a miserable existence.

Mike was their younger son and he had been educated at a charitable boarding school since the age of eleven. When he left school at the end of the summer term in 1953, his intention had been to follow his father into the Royal Marines, but the old man had been definitely against the notion. In reply to all his son's arguments, he had doggedly maintained, 'You've got to have a trade'. He had previously made enquiries about the various trade apprenticeships available in the dockyard, even though the prospect of working there was not at all to Mike's liking. The old man insisted that he sat the written examination and having passed, he was invited for interview. He completed the aptitude test without difficulty and he was provisionally offered an Apprenticeship as an Engine Fitter and Turner. His lack of enthusiasm was most definitely not appreciated.

A letter came which duly confirmed the 'offer' and he was instructed to report to the dockyard for the routine prodding, poking and 'coughing' that made up the medical. The doctor pronounced him physically satisfactory in all respects bar one, his eyesight being deficient. The provision of spectacles was mandatory to his employment. Seeing his reluctance to proceed and that they were getting nowhere in their ill-tempered arguments, his parents tried a more reasonable tone. They made encouraging noises about how they wanted him to live at home and said that they would not want any money from him in the first year. In the second, they would only want a token payment towards his keep and having thus been assured, Mike's resistance collapsed.

His father was invited into the Yard for an interview and to sign the Indenture Agreement. When he returned home, he was most put out and grumbled at length about the responsibilities which had been 'forced' on him. The problem was his formal undertaking to financially support Mike throughout his Apprenticeship. He had not expected to have to keep him until he was twenty-one and he angrily told the lad that he should have let him join up. Having signed the indentures, there was nothing he could do to change the situation.

His wife tried to raise his spirits by saying that Mike could go into lodgings as soon as he was earning enough. It didn't help when the young blighter said that as he had signed a formal agreement, he would have to keep it. His father's anger rapidly grew into outright hostility, as the financial consequences of what he had accepted became clear. Since he was eleven years old, Mike had been freely educated, fed and clothed by his school and they had only looked after him during the holidays. The strains on the family budget would be sorely stretched, which didn't bode at all well for the future.

On the 31 August, 1953, the new Apprentices walked through the main gate for the first time and were shown down through the yard to the main canteen. There was a scene of total confusion when they arrived and in the general cacophony, there were loud calls for silence from the Supervisors. Names were called out and as the lads stepped forward, they were told to stand in groups of the various trades. There was a lot of laughing and derisory comments at the antics of the man in charge of the Engine Fitters, who was small in stature, probably in his early fifties. He was red in the face, sweating profusely and noisily clearing his throat as he tried to make himself heard above the din. He was standing precariously on a chair which wobbled alarmingly and after a long delay and a lot of bloody-mindedness by his charges, he gave up trying to maintain order.

There were forty-six Apprentices in the entry, and they had come from a broad variety of backgrounds. Some had been educated in the local Grammar Schools, others in the Technical Colleges and the remainder were mostly from the Secondary Moderns. Mike was the only one who had been to a Boarding School. A lot of the lads knew each other and they congregated in chattering, noisy groups, while they waited to be taken away to their place of work. There was a lot of banter between them, some of which was far from friendly. The first day had hardly started and there were already signs of hostility, with lads 'eyeing' others and making antagonistic comments.

After what seemed like an eternity, the Instructors formed their charges up outside the canteen, then took them off to the Factory building. The quarter mile walk was not without incident, with a lot of pushing and shoving in the ranks. At first, it was just high spirits, but there was a definite air of menace in the air. The loners were going to have to tread carefully, if they were to avoid the trouble for which the cretins were obviously looking. Mike had been warned by a lad in his village that it would pay to respect older apprentices, because any offence would bring quick retribution. But here, he was among a large number of new starters, mostly his own age and he had not expected any trouble quite so soon.

When they arrived, they were told to wait at the bottom of a stairway, which led up to a lecture room complex on the first floor. Without warning, Mike was roughly pushed from behind by a large, scowling youth, who was backed up by four sneering mates. The oaf loudly accused him of looking at him. One thing that a Boarding School gives a pupil is an intense dislike of bullies and Mike knew instinctively what he had to do. He was about to join battle when an Instructor, who had seen the confrontation brewing, hurried over to break it up. The lads were quickly shepherded up the stairs and into the lecture room.

They were soon called to order by the fussy little Senior Supervisor. He spoke in a slow, accentuated way and stressed each syllable of each word most carefully. 'H's were dropped, 'r's were not rolled, his 't's were soft and his 'th's were 'd's, 'f's or 'v's. He sometimes said 'you', to emphasise a point, but soon reverted to his normal 'yuh'. Grammar played no part in his speech and his 'local' accent was subtly different but similar to the Cockney as spoken in London, which was hard on the ear of an outsider. To this day, some Trade Union leaders, when interviewed on radio or television, give very good imitations of the man's discourse. He was po-faced and self-consciously puffed-up with the drama of the occasion and he wanted his audience to be greatly impressed by his importance. His whole demeanour demanded their instant obedience and respect.

'Right, you lot, my name is Brand and I'm your 'Seniah Hinstructah',' he said, by way of an opening. 'I don't like familiarity, so when you speaks to me, you calls me 'Mister Brand' or 'Sir'. You do what I says right away and you don't give me no arguments or back-chat, got it?'

Charlie, as he was known, was both confident and very experienced. He then went straight into a very long discourse of do's and don't's, culminating in the following dictum:

'Now, I'm a hard but fair man, who will not stand for any messing about. Me and your Instructors have been working with lads like you for more years than we can remember, so, if anyone thinks he can get one over on us, forget it. In our time, we have seen all the tricks, so be warned, you look for trouble with us and we'll come down on you like a ton of bricks. You play fair with me and I'll play fair with you. You don't play fair with me, then I won't play fair with you, then you'll be in the bloody shit-cart, won'tchah?'

Well, what did he expect? Here was a crowd of cocky young sods; each one thinking he was Jack the lad who knew it all. They didn't give a toss for the silly old sod who was so clearly bent on imposing his will on them. Nearly everyone fell about with loud shouts of laughter and hoots of derision and try as he might, Charlie failed in his frantic attempts to restore order. The door from the adjoining offices was flung open and into the room rushed another little man, who was dressed in a dark-blue suit. His face was flushed with outrage and he was screaming the most awful imprecations. It was their introduction to the redoubtable Mr Barry, the Inspector of Apprentices. The noise diminished, but not quickly enough to bring his voice to a normal level of pitch and volume.

'I'll not have this loutish behaviour,' he screamed. 'If you think you can behave like hooligans and get away with it, you're very much mistaken. Anyone who speaks out of turn, or misbehaves in any way from now on will regret it, that I can promise you. I'll have him out the gate so fast, his feet won't touch the ground. If you want to work here, you'll behave with courtesy and respect for your Instructors. Take heed, because there won't be any more warnings. Carry on, Mr Brand,' he said, and moved to one side, to allow Charlie to continue.

The lads were in no doubt about Barry's authority and they would soon come to fear the sound of his high-pitched voice. Everyone would quickly learn that his retribution, for any misdemeanour, would indeed be harsh. Clearly, no one should cross him, not if he had any sense. The first lesson had been learned the hard way and, in the modern vernacular, they were gob-smacked.

'Right, you lot,' said Charlie in a much softer voice, oozing respect and subservience for his doughty little boss, 'That was your introduction to Mr Barry, who is the Inspector who's in charge of all the Engine Fitter Apprentices. Make sure you pays attention to what he says at all times, or else!'

A wit later remarked that Barry had made a 'rat-like smile' at that, but no one thought of joining in any levity. He and his Senior Instructor had said everything necessary to establish their authority and they had effectively 'quelled the mutiny'. Charlie continued by formally introducing his co-Instructors, who were standing beside him.

'These two gentlemen are your other Instructors, namely Mister Greenwood and Mister Mortimore. We are three, hard-working souls and for our sins, we will be in charge of you for your first year. You can be sure that we'll be watching every move you make from now on. As I said earlier, you look for trouble with us and you'll find it, so don't say you weren't warned.'

The rest of the morning was spent with Charlie, outlining what he required from his Apprentices and what they were going to do in the immediate future. A more pleasant aspect, which Charlie spelt out at some length, was the issue of meal vouchers, which were provided for their dinners. He stressed that they could only be used by the person to whom they were issued; a point which had to be clearly understood. Any transgression, by 'dealing', would lead to immediate and severe retribution from the Management. There was apparently an active market in the purchase and sale of unwanted vouchers.

'The employer thinks it's important that their Apprentices are properly fed,' he said, with a syrupy smile. 'A nice hot dinner will be provided, which will help those of you who still have a bit of growing to do.' He probably thought that gem brought a little humour into the proceedings. 'The vouchers will be given out on a weekly basis, on a Monday morning and will be free to everyone that wants them. That concession is for the first year only and then small charges will be made, in increasing amounts, up to the end of your third year. By that time, you'll be earning enough to pay for your own dinners.'

The lads were then called forward and given their first week's vouchers. Charlie went on to explain that those who were living away from home, would enjoy a lodging-allowance, which he said was another example of the 'generosity and caring nature of the employer'.

He then returned to the matter of good order and discipline. There was to be no quarrelling and no-one was to 'interfere' with anyone else, which brought ribald comments from his audience. Fighting would most definitely not be tolerated and any violence would result in the culprits being brought up before Mr Barry for 'disciplining'. Personal effects were 'sacrosanct' and anyone caught with someone else's property would be severely dealt with. A Tradesman's tools were essential to his livelihood and it was a matter of honour that workmates didn't to steal from each other. In the light of what later transpired, he must have had his tongue in his cheek when he said that. Some of the lads had been warned that just by coming to work in the Yard, they were entering 'a den of thieves'. The reality was that anyone's property, no matter how small, was vulnerable to misappropriation by the 'tea-leafs' in their midst. Pilfering was both endemic and a long-standing practice throughout the Yard.

Learning the skills of a Fitter was not going to be easy, but their Instructors would always be there to help and advise them and everything would be properly explained as a matter of course. All that was needed was that they should knuckle-down, work hard and behave themselves. He was sure they would benefit greatly from their experience and skills. At the end of the morning session, everyone seemed to be well and truly demoralised and Mike was not alone in thinking, 'What the bloody hell have I let myself in for?' The old bugger had achieved his first objective. While there had been one or two quiet mutterings of 'I'm not putting-up with this shit,' most of the lads had sat glumly and silently staring at their tormentor.

The hooter sounded for the mid-day break and after being firmly instructed to be back by one o'clock sharp, they dispersed. Most went back to the main canteen to get their dinners and were pleasantly surprised by the range of dishes on offer. There were four different hot meals, with the additional option of a salad and four or so sweets. They were very impressed with the quality of the food and while tucking-in, they discussed the morning's events. Some older Apprentices sitting nearby listened to their tale of woe and openly laughed at their discomfort. One told them that they shouldn't take too much notice of 'that silly old sod, Charlie Brand.' The new lads were not too sure of the wisdom of his advice. The general feeling was very much to wait and see how things progressed.

'No, you'll be alright,' said another lad. 'Take no notice of him, 'cos his bark is worse than his bite, ain't that so, mates?' he asked those around him. 'I've had any number of run-ins with him and he don't scare me none,' he concluded smugly.

'One thing's for sure, we shan't go hungry,' one worthy remarked, with a big smile.

Their vouchers entitled them to a main-course and a sweet, and it went some way to make up for their torrid morning. When they had finished, a couple of the older lads said that they would walk back to the factory with them and they took a roundabout route around the dry docks. It gave the new lads some an idea as to what was going in the yard. With twenty minutes to spare, before they had to be back in the lecture room, there was plenty of time. In their innocent eyes, it really was a wonderland and they could see there was a lot of work in hand on the various Ships. When they arrived back, they excitedly discussed what they had seen. It had been a taste of what was in store for them in the future.

Chapter 2

Confrontations

They were peremptorily called to order as soon as they were seated in the lecture room and Charlie continued his discourse by talking about their training. He explained that the manual work would be supplemented by regular lectures, which would cover the theoretical aspects of their trade. He then went on to the safety aspects of working in the yard, which were of the greatest importance. They were not to wander aimlessly about, as it was a very dangerous place. There was also the need for personal cleanliness, particularly in washing their hands after finishing work. Facilities were provided, with hot and cold water and soap, for that purpose. All uneaten food had to be disposed of in the bins provided, to keep the vermin down. If they brought sandwiches, biscuits, tea, sugar or any perishable food in to work, they should bring a sealed tin to keep it in. It was sound advice indeed.

The lads were then ushered down to the stores to 'draw' their overalls. Two pairs were issued to each lad, along with hand-towels and cloths for personal use. Prior to going down, they had been firmly admonished to line up in an orderly queue and to keep silence while waiting to be served. Mike, who was standing about a third of the way along the queue became aware of pushing and shoving behind him. He turned to see what was happening and was dismayed to find the same lad was confronting him. He was obviously looking for trouble and as before, he was backed-up by his mates.

'You've pushed in front of me,' said the oaf, glaring at him malevolently. 'Come on, get back in place or else I'll have you.'

'I'm staying right here,' Mike retorted, 'so you can sod off.'

The lads around them backed away to make room for the impending 'set-to.' The oaf made a clumsy attempt to take a swing, but Mike stepped inside of the blow and brought his knee up into his assailant's stomach. The noise of the altercation and the cries of encouragement from those watching brought Charlie and the other Instructors running to intervene.

'Alright, alright, break it up,' he cried angrily. 'What's going on here, then?'

The oaf was on the ground, writhing and groaning in exaggerated pain. Seeing who was responsible for his discomfort, Charlie turned on Mike,

'You've been and gone and done it now, my lad,' he shouted. 'Don't say you weren't warned. You two come with me, straight up to see Mr Barry.'

He pulled the oaf to his feet and escorted both combatants back up the stairs to the office and soon after, they were called in to face the little man. He looked up at them sternly over the top of his glasses, as Charlie explained in dramatic terms that they had been fighting and needed to be taught a lesson. 'Pour encourager les autres,' perhaps? It was yet another opportunity for the inspector to demonstrate his authority and he asked each lad, in turn, what had happened.

The oaf sullenly told him that Mike had pushed in front of him and when he had politely asked him to get back in his place, he had become aggressive. The lads who had been around them would confirm it. He had not wanted any trouble, but Mike had been scowling at him all day and was to blame for what had happened. Mike then gave his version and accused the other lad of lying. The first he had known of the nonsense was when those behind him started pushing and making offensive comments. He had been struck on the back and when he turned, the oaf had threatened him and then tried to hit him. He had only defended himself.

It had been no more than a harmless spat, but Barry made his point again about their behaviour. If there was any more nonsense, it would result in severe punishment, dismissal if necessary. Seeing nothing further would be gained, he told them to wait outside. After a short break, during which they again exchanged veiled threats, they were called back into the office. They were each given a verbal warning about their behaviour, which would be put on their records. Any further trouble would lead to either suspension or the sack. They then went back to the Stores to pick up their kit.

Despite the dire warning, the oaf continued with his threats and Mike responded by calling him a lying sod. He offered to meet him outside work on his own to settle it. When they returned to the lecture room, they were greeted with ironic cheers and Charlie, who was still puffed-up with importance, loudly called for order. He again reminded everyone of the penalties for misbehaviour, with yet more threats of retribution in the event of any further trouble.

They were then instructed to go downstairs and form up in line, and were then led down through the Yard and into a large red brick building. There, they were greeted with loud cheers from the third-year Apprentices who were working on various lathes in one half of it. Despite loud cries for 'silence!' from the Instructors, there was a lot of calling and witty comments. A large area had been prepared as the 'First-year Training Centre' at the other end and, with due reference to his clip-board, Charlie allocated places at the work-benches. It was soon apparent that there were not enough benches to accommodate everyone.

He told them that the remaining benches would be delivered on the following day. Vices were bolted on the corners of each bench and under each one was a deep drawer, for the storage of personal effects. Bearing in mind the warnings about the thieves in their midst, it was an absolute necessity to keep everything securely locked away. Some of the lads had brought padlocks, though most of them were so poorly made that they could easily be broken. 'If something wasn't screwed down, it would 'walk,' certainly applied in that shop.

Their overalls were brand-new, stiff as boards and coloured a bright orange. With the lads being of different builds, it was some time before everyone had matching pairs which were roughly the correct size. Marking pens and bottles of Indian ink were handed out and they were told to write their names in large letters across the top of the left hand pocket and under the collar. Some ignored the instruction and did so in very small print, the object being to make identification more difficult. Charlie then spelled out as to how and when overalls should be donned and taken off, most definitely in respect of the latter.

'When you arrive in the morning, you will put your overalls on first thing after clocking on,' he cried, 'and then you don't take them off again until we says so. At dinner time and the end of the day, you stand quietly by your benches until we give you the word. Then and only then can you take them off, before going to the basins to wash up. Got it?'

Each lad was given a unique number, which he would keep until the end of his Apprenticeship. Charlie's ensuing instructions, which were detailed and lengthy, were about the regime of clocking on and off. He sonorously told them that the clock-cards were sacrosanct; a favoured word of his. The importance of clocking on before 07.00 hours, off again at noon, on again by 13.00 hours and finally off at 17.30 hours, was stressed with slow emphasis. If they clocked-on late, they would lose a quarter of an hour's pay, with no excuses being taken. Clocking off early without permission would be similarly punished. If anyone forgot to clock-on, a quarter of an hour's pay would be automatically stopped. Habitual lateness would not be tolerated and if it became regular, the offender would be suspended. In the event of further offences, he would be sacked.

'You do not, I repeat not, touch anyone else's clock-card, under any circumstances,' he warned. 'That is a strict rule, which is cast in stone. Anybody found messing with someone else's card will be severely dealt with. One more thing – you will keep proper order when in the clocking queue. I don't want no fighting, skylarking or any other nonsense or there'll be trouble from me.'

His final admonishment brought the first day to an end. It had been a very long day and most of the lads were more chastened than when they had first arrived that morning. Charlie was obviously convinced of the absolute necessity of imposing his authority, right from the start, His diatribes, which had gone on with numerous threats of retribution in the event of any offence, had been very clear. Any sign of weakness would surely be exploited to the full by the crafty, ill-intentioned young buggers in his charge. His was a heavy responsibility, which he carried with a steel-like determination. It was all part of his strategy for the maintenance of good order and discipline. So there it was, at the end of an eventful first day and with his charges in a subdued and apprehensive mood, they clocked off and made for the main gate.

When Mike arrived home, the first question from his mother was as expected.

'Well, how did you get on?' she demanded, with a piercing glare.

How could he tell her of the problems he had had? His reply was evasive and it provoked the inevitable reaction and the loud assertion that 'he needed someone to keep him under control. 'Such was life,' he mused as he sat down to eat his tea.

The next morning, everyone arrived on time and clocked on under the watchful eye of the Timekeeper. Mr Butler was a large, po-faced man, whose demeanour was devoid of either life or humour and it was his job was to supervise their daily attendance. What little confusion arose, such as cards being clocked upside down or the wrong way round was promptly dealt with. Each morning, he slowly counted up the cards then walked across to tell Charlie whether all of his Apprentices were present or not. A lot was said about his dead pan expression and the pedestrian way in which he carried out his duties. Having yet again been sternly warned about messing around, they accepted the odd manner in which he carried out his duties.

Charlie divided the lads into three groups, each under their specific Instructor. He had already noted the ones likely to cause problems and they were in his group. The remaining benches duly arrived and were noisily pushed into position by a gang of labourers. Despite having been given their places the previous day, the lads were all changed round to suit the new arrangement. For some, his lengthy explanations as to how he wanted things done and his dire warnings had gone in one ear and out the other. Mike was pleased to find that the few lads that he'd talked to the previous day were in his group.

Each one was given a brand-new wooden tool box, on which he white-stencilled his name and number. It was painted matt-black, was of robust construction and had rope lifting-handles on each end. A lot of the locks on the lid had the same pattern key, which necessitated an additional means of locking. Three files, two flat and one half-round, with a single wooden handle, a ball-peen hammer, a one inch flat cold chisel and a large screwdriver were also handed out. It was a time of severe austerity and Charlie told them that if anyone lost any of their tools, they would have to replace them at their own expense.

They were each given a small piece of mild steel, approximately four inches by four inches square and half an inch thick and were shown how to clamp it securely in a vice. The rest of the week was spent in basic instruction in the art of filing straight, flat and square edges on their pieces. They went on to make basic tools, which would be useful in the coming years, the first of which was a small pair of callipers. In the months that followed, they would progressively make more complex items. Among the tools put out for general use were set squares of different sizes, hacksaws and both inside- and outside-spring callipers. They intention was for them to be used as required, but it was not a satisfactory arrangement. Someone always wanted to use a tool when another person had it and the ensuing delays were frustrating and often caused tension between them.

Charlie told the lads of a long-standing arrangement, whereby they could buy various tools from the stores. They included vernier gauges, spanners and numerous other factory made tools, all of which were sold at generous discounts. After a number of pay days, some of the lads duly availed themselves of the facility, but others thought it easier to pick-up whatever they wanted. Having heeded the warnings, most of the lads were careful not to leave their tools on the bench or forget to lock them away but soon, 'losses' became 'the norm'. It had always been so and it remains a deep-seated practice throughout industry today. Another lesson quickly learned was the futility of lending anything. All too often, the borrower failed to return it, having either carelessly left it lying around or that he had had no intention of returning it in the first place.

Their lectures had commenced within days of starting work. They were given by different Instructors, who were Specialists in their particular fields. Their talks were both interesting and informative, with visual aids frequently used for clarification. They were mostly held in a relaxed and informal manner, with many discussions which covered a broad range of good Engineering Practice and the general design features of complex items of machinery. They were much appreciated and were mostly for two hour periods, in either the late morning or early afternoon. They broke the working day up nicely.

Some of the lads saw little point in paying attention and passed the time doodling or quietly talking to their mates. They even dozed-off during the films and slide-shows, which made up part of the lecture. A large part of the training would be concerned with the theoretical design of all types of engines, as well as various pumps, fans, and condensers, which were regularly used in Her Majesty's Ships. They also included the many ancillary fittings, which were mounted on boilers and machines, such as automatic feed-water control valves, fuel-control valves, and water-gauges.

Extensive reference was made to the large range of valves, used in both marine and shore-based applications. Large exercise books were issued, in which to make notes. They were told to sketch copies of the drawings, which were either pinned up on the wall or drawn on the blackboard as the lecturer talked. Various types of valves had been cut away, to reveal their internals, and they were handed round for examination and discussion. The operation of each one and how it was used in various applications of pressure and temperature control was discussed; also the practical uses of particular valves. The agenda included the different materials used in their manufacture, taking into account the chemical constituents of fluids and gases, which passed through them.

The operational parameters of two and four-stroke petrol and diesel engines were also gone into in great detail. Comparisons were made and the pros and cons of their specific applications were explored. They also covered the various types of engines, which were utilised for main propulsion, power-generation and ancillary machinery. Reciprocating steam engines were still used in many of the ships and would continue in service for many years to come. The various types of steam turbines, with the practical uses of both impulse and re-action types of rotor and casing blades were covered. They also looked into the practical aspects of the various types of auxiliary plant, such as condensers, vacuum pumps and other items of machinery.

It was intended that by the end of the first year, everyone would have benefited from their lectures and have a clear understanding of the relationship between the practical and theoretical aspects of their instruction. Many of their instructors were ex-Non-commissioned Officers, with very many years of service in the Royal Navy. What they didn't know about Engineering was not worth knowing, which perhaps made their lectures easy to understand and what was more, interesting. Certainly, there was little of the crass behaviour, which had already become a problem in the Dockyard School.

One evening, Mike came home to find himself in trouble. Contrary to his parents' previous assurances that they wanted him to live at home, the atmosphere in the house had quickly deteriorated. Everything he did was wrong and he was constantly subjected to increasing amounts of verbal abuse, with threats of physical violence from his father when he answered back.

'I found this in your bedroom,' his mother said, pointing angrily at a Mars bar wrapper on the table. She had obviously been through his pockets. There was also more than six shillings (30 pence) in your drawer. We didn't think you'd have money to spare from your wages, and you didn't think to share the chocolate with your sister, did you? Well, we're not going to have it. You're not going to go buying sweets, while we go short keeping you. From now on, you'll have to give me five shillings a week towards your keep.'

Mike was absolutely stunned, and it took him a minute or so to respond. 'But you said you didn't want any money from me in my first year,' he said. 'That was what we agreed.'

Despite his earnest protests that the money had come from his few days of doing odd jobs on the local farm and what had remained of the cash he had brought home from school, they were adamant, and the argument became heated. It was a clear indication of what was to come, and he was thus reduced to the same level of poverty as most of his workmates.

Chapter 3

Early Training

The weeks passed, and most of the lads gradually settled into their daily routine. There had though been great consternation among the Instructors, when halfway through the afternoon of first day, two of their new apprentices had told Charlie that they were leaving. They couldn't be talked round, and he had taken them over to see Mr Barry. As they had made up their minds, he didn't stand in their way. They were taken to the gate and were not seen again. That left a total of forty-two Apprentices and as it turned out, they all completed their time five years later.

Their initial practical instruction had been in the correct handling and use of the simple hand-tools with which had been issued. They were set to work on a succession of small pieces of half-inch thick, mild-steel plates similar to that already mentioned. They were shown how to mark them out, using 'scribers' and 'centre-pops' and then how to hand-cut them down to four inches square. The hacksaws which were old, with well-worn blades, resulted in sore hands and no end of grumbling. To the lads' frustration, there were only half a dozen saws available and with such a large number waiting to use them, there were interminable delays. Charlie nonchalantly told them that he couldn't do anything about it. He had indented for more saws, but they hadn't come through from the stores.

When a saw was available, the blade was usually completely worn away and totally useless. There was a scarcity of new blades, when they 'accidentally' got broken. A lot of time was wasted and the mischief makers made the situation worse by deliberately denying their use to others. The chronic situation led to arguments, which the instructors answered by repeating that they were doing their best to sort it out. As with all 'needs must' situations, a number of lads used their heads to overcome the problem. Some had the money to go to the stores and buy a saw. Others had contacts in the yard and were able to obtain them, complete with different types of blades that actually cut the steel.

Small amounts of money changed hands, with enterprising lads hiring out their saws for a few pence for a set time. Anyone foolish enough to leave one unattended suffered either its loss or the removal of the blade. It was a chaotic situation, which prevailed for a number of weeks. As they completed cutting-out the plates, they were set to work filing straight, square faces around the four edges. It was their first lesson along the long road of learning their trade and it was hard work. It took both time and effort, before a reasonable standard of finish was achieved. There was an uneasy peace in the shop, with the instructors continually going around their groups, patiently demonstrating the correct way to obtain the best results. After a number of weeks, the basic skills began to show, albeit in various levels of competence. Practice and the ready instruction brought improvement and Charlie was continually heard encouraging his charges.

'Don't worry, you'll soon get the hang of it.'

When most of them had reached an acceptable standard, they were issued with another piece of plate, which had been cut to 'near-size'. Their first task was to finish them to exact dimensions. Constant checks were made with callipers to achieve the parallel measurements and the squareness of the adjoining faces. Regular checks were also made on a 'bed-plate' to obtain the required standard of finish. It all took time but the lessons imparted gradually gave the lads the skills in the art of filing.

There are always clever buggers in any group and during the exercise, a couple of lads thought to pull a fast one. One knew an older Apprentice, who was working on a milling machine in the Factory. Thinking they were very smart, they took their plates over for machining and were smirking when they returned. Their plates needed little work to complete the job. As they'd not been apprehended when they returned to the shop, they must have thought they had got away with it. Charlie knew what they'd been up to. As he loudly proclaimed, he wasn't born yesterday and if they wanted to play silly beggars, that was their problem. They had been rumbled, and he laughed loudly when he confiscated their bright, shiny plates. Turning to the watching crowd, he then set about humiliating them.

'Well, well,' he cried with a broad grin, 'what have we here? Been 'acting the crack', have we lads? Well, we can't have that, can we? Are you so bloody stupid that you think that I'd fall for that? Come off it, I've seen it all before. Up 'til now, we've been very easy on you, but now you're going to see another side of our way of working.'

The bollocking which ensued delighted the rest of the lads and to further emphasise his point, Charlie moved them to a separate bench and gave them replacement pieces of plate and told them start again. In the next couple of weeks, he and his colleagues stood over them, to ensure they did the job properly. They came in for a lot of verbal abuse from their workmates, which greatly added to their discomfort. It was an important lesson, which most of the lads appreciated. Charlie had made a most telling point; that there were no short cuts in doing a job properly.

Not only was there a shortage of hacksaws and blades, files, wire brushes and emery cloth were also hard to come by. Full use had to be obtained from each item and the Instructors were assiduous in seeing that it was and the light-fingered activities of the small minority didn't help matters. In some instances, items disappeared from unlocked drawers, which led to angry arguments. The only way for some to replace their lost tools was to pinch them back from the buggers that had taken them. It was all very frustrating. Files had to be worn smooth, before a replacement could be obtained and an Instructor to would blandly draw his fore-finger across the proffered item, then say, without a flicker of emotion:

'There's still a bit of life left in that. Get on with it.'

If a new piece of emery cloth was needed, the old one had to be brought in exchange and to the increasing impatience of the supplicant, the instructor would examine it closely. The whole charade would be carried through with much 'humming and ha-ing', interspersed with severe glances at the lad. It was a usually a waste of time to try to con him, but occasionally, one would win. Generations of Apprentices had tried to pull fast ones and the Instructors had always ensured that they didn't! Only as a last resort would they hand-over a new piece and it was often in a worse condition than the one they'd been given.

The situation gave rise to an amusing incident, which proved a point. Charlie M gave the impression that he was hard of hearing, and someone suggested that a simple check would prove if he was kosher. Whenever he was approached, pretending deafness, he would ignore the supplicant and slowly walk away. If the lad persisted, he would then turn towards him, reach into his overall pocket and extract a well-worn piece of emery.

'That's all I've got. Do you want it or not?,' he would ask dolefully.

It was a no more than a ploy, but he was under a definite instruction to avoid waste. The stunt was set in motion and bets on the outcome were taken. The cunning plan was implemented the following day when, soon after the morning break, a lad approached him.

'Cigarette, Mr Mortimore?, he asked in a low voice.

Much to the amusement of those watching, Charlie M immediately turned and replied.

'Oh, that's very kind of you, lad, don't mind if I do.'

He took the proffered fag, a tailor-made one which had been specially purchased for the test. Then to their enjoyment, he said,

'Thanks for that, I'll save it for after dinner.'

He lodged the cigarette behind his ear and walked over to the caboosh with a sly smile on his face. The object of the demonstration had been achieved, though it didn't make any difference. Even though his deafness was a sham, it was best not to ask him for anything. He wouldn't hear what they were saying!

Ways had to be found to find, beg, borrow or steal what was needed for the job. The requisite items could be bought at a discount from the stores and all that was required was a note signed by an instructor. But only a few lads had the wherewithal to make such purchases. To buy the more expensive tools, such as set squares, spring callipers, micrometers and vernier-gauges, was out of the question. They would have to wait until they had more money. Small groups of lads went scavenging during their dinner breaks. The main places were in and around the workshops, beside the nearby dry-docks. Rich pickings could be had in the scrap skips by way of discarded tools and all kinds of disposables. If anyone was caught thieving, retribution could be painful. Under no circumstance were they allowed to board the ships, whether tied up alongside or in the dry docks. However, they had soon had the confidence to go further afield. Knowing what was going on, Charlie went on at length about the dangers of wandering about. He sternly spelt out the punishments which would come their way if they were caught. However, the booty to be gleaned too tempting for some and they came back with a variety of hammers, files, chisels and drills. A lot of what they found was of no further use; which was why it had been thrown away but occasionally, they did find some good quality tools.

The 'loot' was carefully cleaned, with the best bits retained for their own use. What wasn't wanted was sold off for a few pence. More sophisticated and better quality items were peddled by the older apprentices, where there was a ready outlet for their illicit wares. Several times, Charlie repeated his earlier dictum that: 'You do not steal another tradesman's tools, because they are crucial to his livelihood.'

Though most of his charges heeded his warnings, a few of the lads casually 'lifted' anything, whether it was useful or not. There had already been a small but definite relaxation of Charlie's strict regime, though some still complained about his constant level of control.

'It's like being in a bloody concentration camp,' one worthy opined mournfully.

Though many agreed with him, there were some that approved of the hold which their Senior Instructor maintained. It kept the lid on a lot of the inane nonsense, which always arose in any large group of young people. One rule that palled was that if anyone wanted to leave the shop during working hours, he had to ask permission. His departure was noted by the Instructors, to make sure that he was not indulging in the best loved British practice, that of 'skiving.' As if they would! Only in the direst need, could anyone go to the toilet outside of the breaks. They could come and go as they wished during the dinner hour, provided they didn't disturb the somnambulant enjoyment of their long-suffering Instructors.

There had to be a way of by-passing Charlie's eagle eye. The toilet block was located outside, at the east end of the Workshop and it epitomised completely the crude description of 'bogs'. It was in a deplorable state, although it was supposed to be cleaned every day, though rarely could the Management have checked if the cleaner was doing his job. The walls were covered in pornographic graffiti, with the most depraved depictions of the human anatomy and generations of Mateys, budding artists and poets to a man, had spent many happy hours expressing their talent for the dubious enjoyment of others. It would have taken weeks to read all that was on display and there were many scenes of helpless hilarity among the lads, following their visits.

Mike's parents often dreamed of the time when their financial problems would ease and they could again perhaps enjoy the comforts of the pre-war years. They talked about what they would do when their boat came in but, in truth, there was little prospect of that happening. Not long before, the few pounds which had come their way when Mike's maternal grandmother had died had soon gone. One evening, there was an air of great excitement in the house when the lad arrived home. A letter had come from a Solicitor, which informed his mother of the death of an uncle. She was highly excited about the prospects of 'her inheritance', despite her husband's urgings to 'calm down and wait and see'. Being unable to contain his mirth at her antics, Mike was roundly admonished as 'an ignorant sod' and sent out of the room.

Over the next week, the arrival of further news was eagerly awaited and the speculation continued unabated. They discussed the purchase of a 'nice little cottage', with a large garden, and perhaps a small car to round off their good fortune. Mike's sister would be able to go to a 'nice' school and they would be able to afford proper holidays. It went on and on and Mike was regularly upbraided when he said that her uncle had been a scruffy individual who had always been a scrounger and had never had two halfpennies to rub together. His mother countered, saying that 'dear old Uncle Albert' had been canny and must have had a bob or two hidden away. He would laugh on the other side of his face when her money came and she angrily told him that 'he wouldn't get a penny of it, so there.' His retort that he couldn't care less caused yet more ructions.

Uncle Bert had in fact died intestate, and his debts included many months' rent on the house, with substantial sums owed to the local tradesmen. In truth, there was no legacy. The crafty old bugger had always made out that he was 'comfortably off' and had regularly promised his many benefactors that they would be remembered in his will. The Solicitor noted in his further letter that he had written to all the old man's relatives, seeking funds from which he could pay off what was owed. Al duly wrote back that they hadn't seen their uncle for many years and that he and his wife would in no way be responsible for his debts. It brought an abrupt end to all of their excited chat and grandiose plans, and the family returned to a semblance of normality in watching closely how every penny was spent. As Mike thought wryly, it was funny how 'dear old Uncle Albert' had immediately changed to 'that old bugger Bert'!

Chapter 4

Further Education

The main Dockyards were situated in the towns of Chatham, Devonport, Portsmouth and Rosyth. There were also a large number of other, smaller Yards and Establishments, which were located throughout the Country. When one considers the huge number of Apprenticeships in progress at the time, the costs incurred in their training must have been very substantial. A very large number of skilled Craftsmen had worked way past their normal retirement age during the War and when it was over, were duly retired. They had had to be replaced and the Admiralty had trained Apprentices to meet the on-going requirements of their operations. The training programmes, which had been evolved over very many years, were constantly reviewed and updated to suit their current needs. Of necessity, the opportunities, for both academic and practical training, had to be as good as any on offer elsewhere.

With relatively few Apprentices being 'academically bright', the majority were only suitable for manual work in the yards. In their provision of the Dockyard Technical Colleges, the employer took that very much into account. A broad range of educational subjects gave each lad the opportunity to gain an Engineering qualification. His Indentures obliged him to attend with due diligence and it was an important part of his training. The College, (or School as it was called), was situated in very old buildings at the top-end of the Yard and it had served its purpose well for very many years. It was governed by a Principal and his Deputy, supported by a large number of Lecturers, most of whom had served their own time in the Yard.

Within a week of starting work, the lads had reported to the School to register and be allocated to their classes. That was based on the results of the written examination, which they had taken in the employment process. The Upper School lads were required to attend on two days per week and a further two evenings. They initially set out to study for the Ordinary National Certificate, with the course to be completed in two years. It was soon apparent that the work was too much for some lads, who had neither the ability nor commitment to keep up with the work. The brightest of those in the Lower School were also set to work on the ONC course, but it was to be completed in three years. The remainder were given the option of studying various City & Guilds courses, which were better suited to their limited abilities.

Mike was placed in the Upper School and right from the off, he struggled. His previous schooling did not meet with the demands of the course, particularly in mathematics. Trigonometric progressions/identities and calculus were an absolute mystery to him and he had little knowledge of mechanical drawing and had to start from scratch. He was thus very much at a disadvantage and he was soon aware that he wasn't going to make the grade. The other subjects, such as applied mathematics and chemistry, were not so demanding and he just about coped, but such was his depression, he made less and less effort. The pressure became even more demanding and at the end of the first term, he was told he could not possibly complete the course and was sent down to the Lower School.

He had initially been taken aback by the misbehaviour and lack of attention in the class. At his school, strict discipline had been maintained, with instant and painful retribution for anyone who stepped out of line. In the Dockyard School, 'messing about' was the norm and respect for the lecturers non-existent. Fool that he was, he had joined in the fun and had soon been as bad as the rest. Some Lecturers held their own, but others just walked out of the room and others were fair-game for the infantile amusement of their students. The nonsense got completely out of hand and it continued through the year. The weak Lecturers clearly didn't have the strength of character to control their classes and it hadn't been long before they had increasingly showed signs of stress.

An incident occurred which brought a temporary halt to the shenanigans. One of the worst offenders was a lad called Hartson, whose very size ominously threatened his classmates. All but a few gave him a wide berth and many of the seats around him were wisely left vacant. However, following his assault on another lad, two of them decided to teach him a lesson. He was in the regular habit of sloping-off to the toilets during a lesson, there to enjoy a smoke and a quiet read. One afternoon, when he went to be excused, he was closely followed out of the room. Minutes later, there was a loud, angry howl and the two clowns rushed back into the room. The proverbial then hit the fan. The door crashed open and Hartson stood there, wearing only his underpants, shoes and socks. He was bellowing with rage and covered from head to toe in grime.

The miscreants decided, in the modern parlance, to make a sharp exit and quickly moved to a window, jumped out and made off. They were followed by others, who thought it wise to get out as well. The rest of the class bunched around the sides of the room, to put as much space between themselves and the wounded party as possible. The Lecturer pressed the panic button, which had recently been installed under his desk, which brought reinforcements to his aid and he was escorted from the room. The class was then peremptorily ordered by the Senior Lecturer to return to their places and to 'keep silence'.

The outcome was that the three offenders were suspended for a week. In due course, the details of what had happened came out and it could have had serious consequences. When the duo had left the room, they had checked that their victim was in one of the cubicles and no one else was about. They had then lifted a very large and dirty coconut-mat, which was lying just inside the double-doors in the entrance hall and carried it to the cubicle and swung it up and over the top of the door. It had landed heavily on top of the hapless Hartson. With him being unable to open the door, they made good their escape. A lot of the ingrained filth in the mat had thus been transferred on to their victim. While the assault could not be condoned, it had the desired effect of bringing home to him that he couldn't get away with his anti-social behaviour.

On the first night class in January, a bomb-shell exploded in their midst. Their Lecturer had come up to the door in some trepidation and hearing the commotion, he had made a hasty retreat. The Principal was determined to resolve the problem of their behaviour and had moved the class to a room next to the Staff room and his Deputy, a Mr Fergus, was just the man to sort them out. The names of the main offenders were known to him and had been spoken to on a number of occasions. If they had known anything about the formidable Scot, they would have been aware of the very real dangers of messing with him. As it was, they were to find out that he had and fully warranted his most fearsome reputation.

The loud laughter and disorder continued unabated, when suddenly, the door crashed open and a heavily-accented Scottish voice bellowed for silence. Being young, stupid and full of themselves, the class was due for a rude awakening and the furious Jock came among them like a howling banshee. The sheer volume and profanity of his language was frightening; far worse than anyone could have had imagined. The commotion was cut-off short, but one lad, known for his lack of sense, loudly cried out 'hoots, mon!' and Fergie, full of menace and unbridled aggression, moved rapidly towards him. From time to time, we all say something and then immediately regret it. The lad wasn't quick enough to dodge his assailant and with a great roar, he picked him up and tossed across the room.

''Hoots mon', is it?' he yelled, apoplectic with rage. 'You take the piss out of me, laddie and I'll nail ye to the floor!' He paused momentarily and then went on. 'Is there anyone else who fancies having a go? He glared with wild eyes at anyone he thought was looking him in the eye, then told then, 'bloody well sit down, the lot of you'.

The assaulted lad had had collided with a radiator and was lying dazed on the floor. Those nearest the exit grabbed their belongings and rushed out of the room. The remainder were trapped and had retreated through the desks to stand against the wall. They made no effort to go back to their places, but sat in the nearest vacant desks. A few more edged over to the door and left the room. The wild man was not finished in venting his spleen, but the fun and games were most definitely at an end. If there was any more nonsense, he would deal with it personally and, having 'said his piece' and seeing that his assault had had the desired effect, he went to the dais at the front of the class. The lad groggily got up, went to his desk to pick-up his things, then walked unsteadily out of the room.

'Now let that be a lesson to you all,' Fergie said, with a malevolent glare, 'so pick up your things and get yourselves the hell out of here. When you come for your next lesson, I don't want to hear so much as a peep from any of you.'

The shock at what had happened knocked the stuffing out of everyone. The next day, what had happened was the talk of the Apprentices in the canteen. Those involved were certainly not looking forward to their next evening class and there was a lot of speculation about the retribution that would surely follow. Punishments were going to befall the silly sods involved, with fate worse than death being forecast for some with relish. The fateful evening came and there was none of the usual buzz as the lads made their way up to the School. It was with no little trepidation that they went into the classroom and they were not disappointed. They remained silent, apart from the odd whispers, with some speculating about whether or not they were going to get away with it.

The Principal, Fergie and their Lecturer came into the room, all of whom looked very sombre. Peering gravely over the top of his glasses, the boss opened the proceedings.

'Good evening, everyone. I'm sure you're all aware as to why we're here and know that we have a most regrettable task to perform. Your behaviour on Tuesday evening was not only deplorable but completely unacceptable and you know we have to address the problem. You have responsibilities, not only to yourselves but also to your families, the Staff in this College and of course, the Management of the Yard. We will not accept any further misbehaviour and if it doesn't stop, we shall have no option but to expel those involved. You must understand that we mean business and if you don't want to attend this College, come and see me. We've no interest in anyone who doesn't want to learn.'

He then read out the names of the Apprentices who had consistently disrupted their classes.

'Your names have been passed to the Management', he told them sternly, 'and no doubt, each one of you will be spoken to about what you will be doing from here on. That's all I have to say for now,' he concluded and he and his colleagues left the room.

Those named were 'carpeted' by their Managers, and given warnings about their future behaviour. It had the desired effect but it wasn't long before the indiscipline and nonsense slowly started to creep back. At first, animal noises were popular and then loud belching ensued, all of which the lecturers studiously ignored. Despite the growing problem, Fergie was not seen in the classroom again. Whether or not he was disciplined for physically assaulting a student was not known and notwithstanding their 'final' warnings, some of the class didn't heed what they'd been told. The Lecturers had told them many times that they would very much regret that they had not been more attentive to their studies. The most serious outcome was that the moronic behaviour of a few had seriously impeded the ones who had wanted to work, but were prevented from doing so.

The next mindless prank wasn't long in coming and the culprits were never caught. Most of the class looked askance at the two louts who had so effectively chastised Hartson, but they denied that they had had any part in it. While not serious, it was an act of unbridled stupidity, which caused no end of inconvenience to the hard-pressed Lecturers. The miscreants had entered the school early one evening and having taken bars of soap from the wash room, they went into their classroom and rubbed them over the surface of each blackboard. In doing so, they rendered them useless, which disrupted the functioning of the class for many weeks. Despite assiduous washing by the cleaners, they were unable to resolve the problem.

No one was accused of the deed, though everyone reckoned they knew who was responsible. After weeks of frustration, the blackboards were taken away and resurfaced. The Principal again visited the class to warn, yet again, that any repetition would lead to instant dismissal. The classrooms were kept locked out of class hours, which should have prevented any further nonsense. The students now had to wait around outside in the cold until their Lecturer arrived. However, a set of spare keys soon found their way into 'unauthorised' pockets. When the lecturer arrived one evening, he found his class sitting quietly in the room.

As the year progressed, the lads that wanted to work gradually gave up the struggle. Time and again, with monotonous regularity, the class was reminded that they would certainly 'rue the day' that they had not tried harder. Only a few heeded the warnings and as Spring passed on into Summer, there were other distractions for the reluctant students. In other words, there were girls and sporting activities and absenteeism became an additional problem. Instead of buckling down and working outside of school hours, they shut their minds to their studies. Those that had been sent down into the 'Lower School' after the first term should have done much better than they eventually did.

Chapter 5

Christmas Capers

In the weeks leading up to Christmas, the main topic of the lads' discussion was what they were going to do over the holiday period. Some of their parents would be hard-pushed to make something out of what little they had. In Mike's village, the local farms provided a ready source of root vegetables, which were 'clamped' in the fields. Greens could also be had, with the farmers' permission, (or without it!). Some of the village women were employed by them in December, picking and bagging up sprouts for the London markets. Work was also available on the fruit farms, grading and packing apples and pears, which had been in cold storage since the late summer. Some people also worked on the poultry farms, plucking turkeys, geese and chickens, but it was an unpleasant chore. When the work was all done and dusted on Christmas Eve, the farmers laid on a bit of a do, with food and beer for the men and port and sherry for the women.

Their farms invariably attracted the local villains, two of whom were 'Arry and Bert. The former was a very small, shifty-eyed little man, with a ready tongue and wit; a typical 'cockney sparrow'. His mate was a large, much younger man, with not much up top, and one was never seen without the other. 'Arry would usually stand watching Bert work, with his hands in his pockets and puffing gently on a malodorous hand-rolled fag. He had the knack of continuously moving it from one side of his mouth to the other with his tongue. Whether or not they were related was not known, but they lived in squalor in an old cottage about three miles from the village. Regular employment was not a part of their way of life, although in times of necessity, they often worked for the local council, on the bins or sweeping the streets. They mostly lived on 'Arry's wits and it was prudent to lock anything of value away if they were about.

For some years, 'Arry had put himself about as a small-time poultry-dealer, with a small circle of regular customers. Some of them were sufficiently well-off to have resisted his blandishments. However, he supplied cheap birds and the little bugger knew they could be trusted to 'keep schtum' about their origins. The farmers had to go to great lengths to protect their property, and were constantly out in the evenings in the week before Christmas. Every year, they put it about that they had poisoned some of their birds, so that the consumers would become very ill. Their stories were treated with contempt, because most country folk knew an unhealthy bird when they saw one. The festive season only came round once a year, and they were determined to enjoy it.

'Arry's scam had worked well for a number of years. As an additional precaution, he had a long-standing arrangement with a couple of the villagers, who kept a few chickens or ducks. When asked by the police if they had sold their birds to 'someone who was suspected of having possession of stolen goods', they would back him up without any hesitation. They would duly be rewarded with a drink in the Working Men's Club, usually a couple of pints accompanied by 'chasers', or tots of whiskey. It epitomised the splendid community spirit in the village! There was a potential problem though, since no-one kept geese or turkeys, both of which could be 'ordered'. More than one household kept their doors and windows tightly closed on Christmas morning, when their illicit birds were roasting in the oven. However, there was little chance of a 'Bobby' calling on that hallowed day.

Professional gangs also descended on the poultry farms at that time and were often in and out of the buildings, without the Farmer being aware anything was amiss. Their hauls were destined for London, where a large number of birds could be disposed of, with no questions asked. To their credit, the police occasionally foiled them and thus kept the thieving down to a tolerable level.

'Arry usually went around his customers in the second week in December. A soft knock would come at the back door and when it was opened, the shifty little man and his mate would be standing on the step. Father would be called and after being invited in, 'Arry would open the negotiation.

'Would you like to order a bird for Christmas this year, Al? I'll be having some nice ones in a couple of weeks, though they'll cost a little bit more than last year,' he would add hastily.

'How much do you think it'll be?' would be the all-important question.

'Fifteen shillings,' (75 pence), would be 'Arry's quick reply, accompanied by a shaking of his head, shuffling of his feet and a lot of self-conscious coughing, sighs and sucking of teeth.

A good quality chicken, bought from a reputable butcher, could cost in excess of thirty shillings, (around £1.50), which was a considerable sum to find for some families.

'No, that's a bit rich for me. I'll have to get ours from somebody else,' would be the riposte, it being all part of the charade.

'Nah, there's no need for that, old mate,' 'Arry would say, I'll do a bit better for you, seeing as how you're one of my regulars like.'

After a short discussion, with 'Arry making comments about 'how times were hard' and that 'good birds were not easy to come by,' reason would prevail.

'Alright, I'll tell you what I'll do. Twelve and six, (62.5 pence), but you'll have to keep 'schtum' about it, OK? I don't know,' he would add mournfully, 'I'll be lucky to get any Christmas dinner for myself this year.'

'Right-oh 'Arry, that's agreed then. When do you want your money?'

'On delivery, same as always, old mate,' would be the equally prompt reply.

'Arry' and his mate would then go off into the night, to continue their round. A new customer would only be accepted on the recommendation of an existing one and nothing was ever written down. He couldn't risk having compromising evidence on him in the event of having his collar felt. His cheap birds, (no pun intended), which he insisted were kosher, were usually delivered, un-plucked, on Christmas Eve.

When he returned to work after the holiday, Mike told his mates that things had gone very wrong with his father's 'deal'. Probably due to the diligence of the farmers and the bobbies, 'Arry had had difficulty in getting hold of the requisite number of birds. After a lot of anxiety in the house, the little man had eventually turned up very late on Christmas Eve.

'Where the bloody hell have you been, 'Arry? asked Al angrily. I've been worried sick, waiting for you to come with our bird. We thought you'd let us down.'

'Sorry, old mate,' said the little sod, being more shifty-eyed than normal. 'I've had a bit of a problem.'

It was odds on that the family was not going to enjoy their traditional Christmas dinner, and Al was loud in his angry abuse of the little man. 'Arry clearly didn't have his bird and a lively altercation ensued. Eventually, the little man capitulated.

'Alright, old mate,' he said, 'leave it with me. I'll make sure you get your bird.'

An hour or so later, there was another quiet knock, this time at the front door. It was 'Arry, and he was looking very harassed. On entering the living-room, he said to the old man,

'Sorry about the front door Al, but if you look out the back, you'll see we've got company.'

A quick peek from behind the curtains of a darkened upstairs window confirmed there was a bobby walking up and down in the lane outside.

'I've got you a bird, but it ain't a chicken,' 'Arry said glumly. 'Sorry about that.'

He then pulled a goose out from under his raincoat and laid it carefully on the table.

'There now old mate,' he said with a smile, 'that's as fine a bird as you could wish for.'

To the family's amazement, the bird was still warm!

'Bloody hell, 'Arry, what have you done?' said the old man, aghast. 'What am I supposed to do with that?'

'Don't ask,' 'Arry replied bleakly. 'Like I said, I've had a bit of a problem, but you'll be alright now, eh? Lovely bird that. You can soon pluck and draw it, then it'll be all ready for the oven in the morning.'

The cheeky little bugger then had the gall to ask for 'a bit of extra on account of all the bother he'd had in getting it'.

After more discussion, it was agreed that an extra half a crown was warranted. Mike rounded off his story by smugly saying that it had all turned out well.

'It's been bloody good eating in our house this year, and there's still lots left.'

A few days later, Mike learned why 'Arry had had a problem when a couple of lads, who lived at the top end of the village, gleefully told him about what had happened. Just after eight o'clock, they had been standing outside their house, when they saw 'Arry and Bert come scuttling down the hill from the farm. They were closely followed by the farmer, with two of his men. As soon as they'd gone, they had sauntered over to the gate and to their great delight, they found a sack which contained six chickens. They had thus come by their families' Christmas dinners and had sold the extra birds to their neighbours.

The majority of the villagers were honest citizens, who had nothing to do with any nefarious activities. However, the dealers were never short of customers. There had been a vigorous black market during the War, which had continued for some years after, and some of the crooks had prospered handsomely. One rogue sold meat – beef, lamb and pork – which was poorly butchered and delivered roughly-wrapped in newspaper. While it was 'dodgy', it was always a lot cheaper than could be bought in a butcher's shop. He continued in business until meat, which had been in short supply for so very long, became cheaper and more readily available.

From time to time, the police apprehended an illicit trader, but it only scratched the surface of the problem. Informing was taboo, and anyone who may have been tempted nearly always thought it prudent to 'keep schtum'. To do otherwise would have brought painful retribution, because nothing was ever a secret for long in such a small community. Hardly a week passed but the word went round that 'Billy', or some other dubious character, had something interesting for sale. If a watch, necklace or an item of jewellery was 'ordered', there would sometimes be a short wait before it was delivered. It was odds on that it was 'bent', or stolen. The buyer accepted the risk involved and in the event of disappointment, from faulty or sub-standard goods, he or she had little or no hope of redress. If someone was known to have been conned, the scorn among his or her neighbours was palpable, particularly if he or she had been bragging about their bargain.

Relations between the Farmers and villagers were often strained, with the former gravely threatening to prosecute anyone who trespassed on their land. Part of the problem was envy, because most of the farmers had become very prosperous, while their neighbours still struggled to eke out a living. They ostentatiously flaunted their new-found wealth and were arrogant and disdainful of them, some of whom they had known all their lives. They owned large cars and made much of sending their sons and daughters to private schools. Some aspired to 'Gentleman' status and no longer worked in their fields. They employed general foremen, to organise and run their farms, which they had done themselves for very many years. Their children had the same haughty attitude and inevitably, there was tension between their sons and the village lads, which often led to violence. Their whole attitude was deeply resented and stealing from them was an acceptable practice.

There was also an acute problem with shop lifting in the town. Anything with a re-sale value, was vulnerable to the depredations of the tea-leafs. Unlike the villages, where the men were the main culprits, the town women were often involved as well. One lad had a sister called Dawn, who was fifteen years old. She was a strikingly handsome lass, with a full figure and a fine head of dark red hair. One morning, she was apprehended, taken down to the local nick and charged with theft. When she came up in court, she was duly put on probation. He brother told his mates that she had only escaped being sent-down because of her previous good character. What he meant was; it was the first time she'd been caught! Illicit goods were often said to have fallen from 'off the back of a lorry' or were 'surplus' from factories or storage premises.

The problem of thieving remains as bad today as it was in the fifties. The main difference is that in our affluent society, the value of the items nicked is usually very much greater than back then. Goods are often stolen to raise funds to feed a drug-habit and the nerds involved have no compunction about assaulting and robbing the elderly or other vulnerable people. It is hard to understand the reluctance of the authorities to address the problem. When a burglar is brought into Court, a daft but wily Lawyer will often go to the height of inane verbosity to excuse his client's anti-social behaviour. The slob usually gets a light slap on the wrist from the magistrate or judge and is sent on a rehabilitation course. In today's politically-correct society, revenge is forbidden and any retribution exacted by a householder is treated far more seriously than the crime of theft. Sixty years ago, if someone caught a burglar, a sound thrashing was administered, without the involvement of the police. It was usually enough to deter any further problems.

Chapter 6

Dirty Work

Soon after they had started work, some of the lads had suffered sore, peeling hands, which had caused no end of discomfort. The change from the relative cleanliness of school life to a dirty manual job was the cause of their discomfort. Regular washing and careless drying of their hands probably exacerbated the problem. To the unbridled amusement of most of his charges, Charlie told them of his sure-fire cure.

'When you go to the toilet, pee over your hands and let it soak in for a minute or two, then wash them as normal. After you've dried them properly, put a bit of cream on them and rub it in well. You'll find it'll all clear up in a few days.'

His advice was greeted with hilarity and loud cries of derision. For a while, it was a matter of considerable debate and coarse embellishment. In time, their hands hardened, and it had obviously happened many times before. Charlie had procured a large tub of 'Rozalex', an industrial barrier cream, from the stores. It made washing easier and also protected their hands against infection. Cleanliness had been part of his initial briefing and many times, he had stressed the need to use the cream sparingly and to work it in well. Each lad had been issued with a rough-woven towel, with which to dry them properly. His comments about the vital necessity for personal cleanliness, particularly before eating or making drinks, had been sound advice indeed. The Yard was riddled with vermin and they had to be aware of the risk of contracting what was known as Weil's Disease.

The lads had soon become less intimidated by Charlie's threats and as his iron grip was relaxed, the atmosphere in the shop became less strained. The instructors 'caboosh', or hut, was made up of old packing cases and sheets of plywood and was sited in a corner of the Shop. Both electric lights and a heater had been installed. The Instructors had to have a modicum of privacy, away from the noisy buggers under their supervision and they retreated into it at break times, or whenever they needed a quiet smoke or a bit of a sit-down. The clowns who planned the nonsense had recently seen a war film about a prisoner of war camp and they made up a sign from a large, square piece of half-inch thick plywood. On it was painted the words 'Stalag Luft XV' in large letters and after a lot of dithering and impatient urgings to 'get on with it', they decided to put it up. During a break, a lad crept up to the caboosh and carefully placed the sign above the door, then scurried away.

His haste prompted a loud burst of laughter, which brought the Instructors rushing out to see what was happening. Poor old 'Pop' was first out and he banged the door open with such force, that it brought the sign down on his head. An ambulance was called and he was taken off to the medical centre for treatment. Charlie was absolutely livid and the lads were straight away marched over to the lecture room and brought before the furious Inspector. There they were sternly lectured at length about their crass behaviour and stern warnings were given about further mischief. It was a chastened bunch of lads that walked back to the Shop.

'Pop' didn't return to work for some days after his accident, and there was considerable anger among the more sensible lads about his injury. Those involved kept their heads down. He was both liked and respected by nearly everyone as a kindly and helpful old man. Those involved had been briefly suspended and had come into the Yard just before nine o'clock each morning and spent most of the time aimlessly wandering around. Luckily, no one asked what they were doing or where they worked. On the one wet afternoon, they had sat miserably inside a dockside crane and for the rest of the time, the weather had been fine. When they returned to work, one of them had the temerity to suggest that a whip-round should be made, to compensate them for their loss of earnings.

Another prank was when someone put a large twist of newspaper containing sulphur, into an old paint tin, then having lit it, he placed it in the caboosh and scarpered. The Instructors realised there was something amiss, when clouds of dense, acrid smoke was seen coming out of the door and the joints in the walls. Thinking their retreat was on fire, they panicked and amid much shouting and confusion, ordered everyone out of the building. The same lad saved the day when he went into the caboosh and brought the can out into the shop. A bucket of sand was poured over it and the fire was extinguished. Fortunately, the Dockyard fire crew had not been called and Charlie loudly vented his spleen in no uncertain terms. After he had calmed down, he again tried to explain that the workshop was not the place for sky-larking.

There were still minor instances of bullying, with the aforesaid oaf being one of the main antagonists. He and his mates would start by making snide comments to a lad they thought vulnerable and usually, their victims ignored them. Most of their mean tricks were childish. Tyres on bicycles were let down and belongings smeared with marking-blue or grease. Hiding a lad's kit provided more amusement and it was all petty and immature. In due course, their nonsense brought resistance and they were confronted. The old adage that 'a bully is a coward' was clearly true, and more than one slob learned a painful lesson, when he picked on the wrong lad.

It has always been a British trait to laugh, even in the most dreadful circumstances. We often do so at someone in authority or who is perhaps less fortunate or has suffered some minor set-back. 'Schadenfreud' has never been the sole property of our German cousins. Perhaps our oddest trait is the ability to laugh at ourselves, something that foreigners do not always understand. It plays an important part in our lives and right from the start, that was how it was with most of the lads. Good-natured banter and witty comments were at first confined within the small groups that knew each other, but that gradually changed. Some of the lads were more serious minded, perhaps being older and more academically inclined and were disdainful about their work mates' childish behaviour. In consequence, they were often subjected to comments, which were not always friendly.

The media had recently made much of the antics of a 'Lord of the Realm', who had been caught with his trousers down in the company of a humble airman. As the scandal unfolded, the articles had become increasingly histrionic, with lurid details published daily. At the time, homosexuals were fair game for persecution, and 'queer-bashing' was a normal practice. Almost inevitably, someone had to be nick-named after the noble Lord, and who better than one of the snotty brigade? He was christened 'Monty', and his soubriquet remained throughout his Apprenticeship. Other lads had nicknames for a variety of reasons. A lad's perceived 'rural' way of speech was thought amusing by most of his fellows and he was duly dubbed 'Percy the Ploughman', or 'Perce' for short. There was also Jock, Mac, Pat, Taff, and Geordie.

As already noted, there was an undercurrent of nastiness beneath the frivolity, with outright hostility between individuals, which was understandable in such a large number of boys. Though their humour was juvenile, laughter made their time at work pass more quickly. Anyone who was 'going steady' was often the butt of suggestive jokes. Comments such as 'being under the thumb' or, more crudely, 'getting it regular' were made. A favourite wind-up was for one lad to loudly pose a question to his mate.

'Did you have a nice weekend then, Bert, my old son?'

'Yeh, alright thanks', would be the reply. 'I saw you at the dance, chatting up the birds. How'd you get on? Did you get any?'

'No,' the sly bugger would answer, leering across the bench towards their intended victim. 'But our mate over there did. You had some, didn't you my old son?'

Norman, who was the oldest apprentice, was at first at a loss as to how to reply. He was engaged and, much to the delight of his teasers, he would blush furiously, which would only confirm his guilt to most of the grinning audience. After more ribbing and in increasing frustration, he would furiously deny that he had been 'sampling the goods' or 'tasting the forbidden fruits', as they so aptly put it. The silly charade would go on until he realised that it was best to say nothing.

The lad and his fiancée enjoyed a regular routine in their entertainment. Television was still very much in its infancy, and few families had a set. In 1953, the cinema was still the main source of pleasure for a lot of people. Every weekend, they sauntered along to one of the many cinemas in the town and once ensconced in their favourite seats, they would eagerly await the start of the show. There were often other friends present and there would be some good-natured calling until the lights were dimmed. After the show, they would either go back to 'his or hers', for tea. It was very much a matter of routine and they were comfortable with it.

That was not the end of the evening's entertainment. Over the next few days, each break would see Norman surrounded by his mates and he would loudly regale them with graphic dissertations of the films he had seen. The plots would be gone over in depth and the various scenes dramatically played out, word for word. There would be a lot of arm waving and play-acting of the most exciting bits. His audience would show their appreciation by noisily laughing and egging him on. If he couldn't complete his report in the one day, he would be sure to carry it over into the next, particularly if the film had been one of the epics. He provided a lot of enjoyment over very many weeks. Later, with the growth of television, the attractions of the cinema gradually declined. Whether or not Norm eventually became a professional film critic is not known, but he certainly missed his vocation if he didn't!

If a lad had been seen 'walking out' and had kept it very much to himself, it provided days of base amusement. He should not have reacted to the silly comments, but few had either the sense or experience of life to do otherwise. The more he denied the taunts or showed any embarrassment, the more he was teased. One called John, in responding to a seemingly innocuous question, foolishly admitted that he had never had a girlfriend. That gave rise to snide suggestions that he was a homosexual. The comments took on a more sinister tone and it soon got completely out of hand. He put up with their nonsense until one morning, he 'flipped' and angrily turned on his tormentors.

Charlie of course demanded to know the cause of the trouble. What had started as light-hearted ribbing had got to the point where the louts had been continually baiting the lad. The altercation had been the direct result of their offensive behaviour. He threatened that if there was any repetition of the nonsense, they would be for it. When he spoke to the victim, John told him he was fed up with all the nastiness and was going to leave. That would almost certainly result in questions about his supervision and he urged the lad not to go. Later on in the day, he told everyone that while their banter was 'all part of the game', he would not tolerate bullying. The tormentors duly apologised and that was the end of it.

As the lads reached a satisfactory standard in filing flat edges and faces, they were progressively moved on. The job was to make a one and a quarter inch square-hole in the centre of their plates. A large drawing was pinned to the wall and with exaggerated gestures and a few self-conscious coughs, the Instructor explained how to best do the job. The marking-out was done on a flat-topped, metal table, which had been specially set up for the purpose. Despite the advice of their instructors, the application of the marking ink was either applied too thickly or not enough and it was messy job. It got all over the hands and in some cases, their clothes as well. It was difficult to wash off and it indelibly stained anything it came into contact with.

Chapter 7

Practice Makes Perfect

As we've said, the horsing-around often went too far. Following the spats between Mike and the oaf, there had been a period of enforced peace, though angry glares and veiled threats were still exchanged. Mike chose to ignore him, but in the general fooling around, he knew that his antagonist was still looking for trouble. He was careful to lock his things away before leaving his bench, even for a short time. Other lads often returned to find their work had been liberally daubed with ink or, it had been splashed on to their personal belongings. It had the desired effect and he saw the oaf was watching his reaction, thinking perhaps there was little chance of retribution.

Mike had bought a new bike the week before he started work and of necessity, he was very protective about it, because the weekly payments took a large part of his wages. Its main use was to travel to and from work; a total distance of fourteen miles each day and the money saved by not travelling by bus was considerable. He was able to leave home a little later in the morning and his journey home after work was a lot easier. He didn't have to wait in long queues, for buses which were often late or didn't come at all. In the evening rush-hour, they were always crowded and there was no guarantee that one could get on them. Getting home after night-school was also a problem, because they were often cancelled and a seven mile walk in the late evening, sometimes in pouring rain, was not an enjoyable experience.

The main disadvantage was that when it rained, he got wet and he sometimes suffered greatly from the cold. He bought waterproof leggings, but they were cumbersome and of poor quality. The inside surfaces sweated due to the lack of in-built ventilation and he often arrived as wet as if he had not worn them. Due to a shortage of funds, he had not bought a cape or a 'sou'-wester', and it was some time before he could afford them. He often put his gear in the saddle-bag but didn't need it and on other days, he would leave it at home and then cycle home unprotected. One morning, he clocked-on with only seconds to spare and as he turned to hang his clothes above the radiators, he was regaled with a resounding chorus of 'The Fishermen of England'. While amusing, the noise annoyed the instructors, one of whom loudly yelled for silence.

There was an illicit market in which cycles could be bought at a substantial discount to the price of a legitimate machine. A suitable machine could be had for around a fiver, which could be paid over a number of weeks. When compared to the price of a new cycle, it was an attractive proposition. The bikes had been thoroughly checked and were adequate for getting to work. Though of dubious origin, there was rarely a problem. A buyer would be advised 'to put a lick o' paint on it, to suit yourself, like'.

What the seller meant was that it was 'iffy' and a change of colour would lessen the chances of the previous owner retrieving it.

One morning while Mike was changing, marking-blue was liberally sprinkled into his saddlebag, heavily staining his school books and pump. The shop fell silent as he walked over to confront the culprit.

'How'd you know it was me?,' the oaf asked with his usual sneer.

Seeing trouble brewing, Charlie intervened and warned them, yet again, about the perils of fighting. Soon after, the opportunity came for revenge, when Mike saw his antagonist going out of the shop on his own. He followed him down to the toilet block and they came face to face just inside the entrance.

'We've got some unfinished business,' Mike said angrily, and roughly pushed the oaf towards the urinals.

He grabbed the front of his overalls, kneed him in the stomach and turned and bundled him into a cubicle. He then upended him over a noisome toilet bowl and pulled the chain. The lad protested that that it had only been a bit of fun, which it might well have been. Mike dropped him in a heap on the floor, kicked him and warned him of further retribution if there was any more trouble. He then went back to the shop, hoping that his absence had gone unnoticed. A few minutes later, the dishevelled oaf came back into the shop, told Charlie he was feeling unwell and was going home. Revenge is unacceptable in our politically correct society but Mike's action had effectively put an end to what had become an intolerable situation.

To make the square hole in the centre of a plate, small holes had to be drilled on the inside edges of the lines to facilitate the removal the central core of metal. The edges were then filed down to complete the 'female' part of the job. Charlie had obtained a brand-new electric drilling machine, complete with a bench mounting kit. It was taken out of the box, mounted at the end of a work-bench, then plugged into a socket. Stern instructions were given about the need to use the machine with due care. A favourite was detailed off to operate it and no one else was to even touch it. The drilling work was a full-time job and the lad soon complained that he was unable to get on with his own job. A rota was then organised and the drillers were changed on a daily basis.

The system was unworkable and within days, that too was rescinded. The drillers had often been careless, with holes drilled over the lines which had been so carefully marked-out. They had also allowed their mates to jump the queue, and those waiting had become increasingly frustrated. There was yet another problem. One blighter had sought to make a bit on the side, by making a small charge for services rendered. His scam was angrily resisted by the lads, who threatened to sort him out. He had promptly resigned and there was a marked reluctance to accept the job. From then on, the lads were allowed to do their own drilling. As Charlie ruefully said, 'it was all too much bother'. The machine was clearly unsuitable for continuous operation and before long, a larger, free-standing one was brought in, which was much better.

As the plate was completed, a start was made on the 'male' piece. It was filed down to a nearly finished state, with the adjacent faces flat and square to each other. Then came the difficult job of fitting it into the hole in the plate. Judgements had to be made as to which edges were to be filed to achieve the best fit. Crude comments were made about the male and female interface, but the difficulty of the job put a damper on any exuberance. There were many cock-ups, with the instructors telling lads to start again, but they went to great lengths to demonstrate where their charges had gone wrong. The standard of work varied greatly. Some lads showed greater aptitude than others, but nearly everyone was willing and a spirit of competition set in.

'Don't worry lads, practice makes perfect. You'll soon get the hang of it,' cried Charlie.

With the job completed, a couple of weeks passed in making various tools. One, which would always be of great use, was a set-square and in time, different sizes were made. It was formed from pieces of mild-steel and took a lot of time to complete. The cutting and filing of the pieces for the handle, to be fitted on the shortest leg, were the most difficult. Great care was taken to obtain the best standard of work, both dimensionally and in finish. The next step was to assemble the pieces, by clamping them in a vice, then drilling and counter-sinking six small holes for the rivets. Welding rods were ideal for the rivets and the dockside provided the necessary material. Small, ball-peen hammers were used for riveting the assembly. The slightest slip ruined the job and it was frustrating to have to start all over again.

It was essential that only the end of a rivet was hit, when belling it over. Any indentations on the handle would spoil the entire job. A careless knock would also put the components out of 'true'. The lads practised on small pieces of scrap, before attempting to rivet their set-squares. Their initial efforts were dreadful, though most of them ultimately achieved a satisfactory finish. The most difficult job was to finish off the square, so that it was 'true' in all respects. Each face had to be filed flat and square to that adjacent. In time, the more adept lads made as many as three set-squares and when finished, they were oiled, wrapped in clean rags and put away in their tool-boxes.

One morning, Charlie called everyone together and told them they were ready for the next job. They were to make another plate with an 'L' shape in the middle, measuring two and a half by two inches. He talked at length about how they should go about it and was pleased to be asked a number of questions. Again, great care would have to be taken in cutting-out both the male and female pieces. Because of the narrow width of the female 'legs', the drilling and filing of the edges was difficult. Patience and concentration was called for, to ensure the accuracy of the work. Three weeks passed before most of the lads completed their plates and there was again a great variation in the finished items. They were coming along nicely.

Charlie had another trick up his sleeve. As each lad finished his 'L', he was given further pieces of plate and told to make a similar 'T' plate. There were rueful complaints that it was all go, but they still got on with it. The method of working was much the same as explained above and they were much quicker in completing the job. Their hard work was again followed by a couple of weeks of making personal tools. Some made small vices out of mild-steel blocks and plate. Charlie had a good supply of what he called 'closing-screws', which had been made by the third year Apprentices at the other end of the shop. When the components had been made, there was again some riveting to do in the assembly of their vices. They were finally polished, before being mounted on to blocks of wood.

The least popular tools made were spanners, which were inevitably of poor quality, when compared with manufactured ones. To be of practical use, they had to be case-hardened in the Blacksmiths' shop and were usually returned badly distorted from the heating process. Some were of the view that the damage had been caused deliberately and there was the usual scam in place. For 'a bit of extra care', a small contribution had to be paid. The offending Blacksmith was a large, malodorous young man who, it was said, was 'a bit mental' and when a lad mentioned the problem to Charlie, he wasn't interested.

'Oh dear! What a pity, never mind,' he said sarcastically. 'Now don't you go up the Boiler Shop causing trouble. I've got enough problems as it is.'

It was often possible to straighten a spanner with a hammer, using the bench as an anvil. It was then dressed on a fine grinding wheel and, if not thrown in the bin, it was put away. Everyone agreed spanners were not worth the trouble and they carried on working on other tools. Charlie told them they would need a variety of metal scrapers in the future, principally for the 'bedding-in' of bearings. His most useful tip was to grind down an old file, to form the scraping edge, but care had to be taken not to lose the temper in the metal. The business end was finished on a flat emery block, which gave the necessary cutting-edge. The fitting of a proper (new) file handle completed the job.

The formation of the bend in a curved scraper had to be done by the Smiths, which again meant coughing up. Assistance came from one lad's father, who was the Foreman of the shop next to the Smithy. If anyone wanted any tempering done, he took the job to him and he ensured that it was done properly. His kindness was very much appreciated and when the scrapers came back, the instructors helped with the grinding. The risks involved in using the machine were very real and they had to be sure that their charges always worked safely. Few scrapers were successfully completed and later, most of the lads bought them. Charlie did his best to ensure everyone learned all aspects of their trade and while it was obvious to most of his lads, some didn't appreciate his constant nagging.

One morning, after cycling to work in heavy rain, Mike went over to the basins and held his head under a tap. It being a cold January morning, it caused a buzz of amusement among his workmates. Seeing he was the centre of attention, Charlie loudly demanded to know what was going on. The lad explained that he had met with an unfortunate accident, which had necessitated washing his hair. Thinking the cheeky young bugger was having him on, he gruffly ordered him to get on with his work. A few minutes later, Mike told his mates what had happened. When riding along the High Street, a seagull had dropped a large dollop, which had landed on top of his head. The rain had washed most of it away, but what was left had necessitated a quick rinse as soon as he had clocked-on. Later in the week, he won the first prize in the Factory raffle. Was his good luck a co-incidence?

Chapter 8

A Policeman's Lot

The Dockyard Police were responsible for the security of the Yard; their main duty being to prevent the employees from misappropriating the Admiralty's property. Approximately fourteen thousand men and women came in to work each day and they had their work cut out to control their 'criminal activities'. Though they worked closely with the Civil Police, each Force jealously guarded their authority against incursion by the other. Permission to enter the Yard was only reluctantly given to allow them to investigate a crime and then, only after agreed procedures had been fulfilled. In consequence, their relationship was often strained.

The Yard Officers worked hard in carrying out their duties and operated under a lot of pressure. Had the ingenuity of the 'Mateys', in frustrating them, been channelled into their work, the efficiency and output of the Yard would have been substantially increased. The number employed could have been substantially reduced and the working conditions and practices of those that remained very much improved. As it was, the sheer scale of the work involved in the apprehension of the crooks was a never ending grind. Despite their limitations, they stuck tenaciously to their task and regularly enjoyed more than a modicum of success.

Their operation was run in close co-operation with Her Majesty's Customs and Excise, the objective being to control the traffic in contraband goods, such as tobacco, cigarettes, spirits, and watches. Depending on the number of Ships which arrived from overseas, there were many desirable items which could be obtained from their crews. The first Mateys to go on board a newly arrived Vessel would often search through her dead spaces and find items, which had been stashed by the crew for later collection. The Customs Officers, being canny, always had a thorough 'rummage' through a Ship before the Mateys were allowed on board. What they missed was often purposely left as bait.

The intention was to catch the finders red-handed and their Officers would make daily visits to that end. They resorted to crafty, but well known ruses, such as wearing dockyard overalls and while the Mateys knew the score, there was always someone who was daft enough to ignore the dangers of apprehension. It was not unknown for him to be stopped, when coming ashore at the end of the day, with the loot in his tool bag. A body search confirmed his guilt. Possession was taken as proof of ownership, despite loud protestations of innocence. Often, a Matey would say that he had only just found whatever and was on his way over to the Foreman's Office to hand it in.

There was a ready market in Naval 'kit', which had either been lifted from the barracks or ships' stores. Cold weather gear, such as Submariners' woolly jumpers and socks, was much sought after by those lucky enough to be sent on board the Vessels in commission. The penalty for buying, selling or being in unauthorised possession of illicit goods could be severe and over the years, a succession of ne'er do wells had suffered due punishment for their misdemeanours. Offending almost certainly resulted in either suspension from work or in serious cases, instant dismissal, with no appeal allowed. Everyone knew the risks and it was no use complaining when caught. Sympathy was not always forthcoming from their peers.

One of the duties of a patrolling Bobby was to apprehend anyone who was absent from their place of work, or skiving. Apprentices would often go for a walk on fine days, to have a 'butcher's' at the Ships which were tied up alongside. They might also visit mates working in other areas. When out and about, whether on legitimate business or not, it paid to be both polite and respectful to the Officer(s) who stopped them. The 'Plods' instinctively knew if the individual(s) weren't kosher, particularly if they were not relaxed in answering their questions. One well-worn ruse was to tow a small hand-cart or carry a tool-bag containing a valve and a few tools and fixings. One always had to have a ready reply and whenever possible, a work 'chit'.

'Oh, good morning, Officer, we are just on our way to such and such a building or Ship, to do a small job,' would be the opening gambit.

If in doubt, the Policeman might ask to see the chit, which detailed the replacement of the valve or whatever. Altering the date on one was something of an art. The ruses used to confuse the issue were both varied and numerous, as well as 'well-worn'. One can imagine the exasperation of an Officer, who had no way of making a quick check of what he had been told. In those days, there were no personal radios or cell-phones and his only means of communication was by using the network of internal telephones placed around the Yard. If dissatisfied, he would tell the lad(s) to 'wait there, while I check'. It was adds on that they would have legged it when he came back, very much to his frustration.

With the first-year Apprentices still being confined to the shop, the skiving and mischief was largely among the third-year lads. The youngsters contact with the Police was limited; being mostly at the gates, when entering or leaving the Yard. It was some time before they were confident enough to amble around on their own. The dangers of roaming were then very real and in the first six months or so, their walks were usually limited to the dry-dock facilities, between the Factory and their workshop. As they became bolder, they often walked up and down the jetty on the side of the No. 1 basin during the dinner hour. There, a large liner, which had been converted into an auxiliary depot ship during the War, was undergoing a long refit.

Another dry-dock was located directly across the basin, into which a succession of large Cruisers were brought for the maintenance of their hulls. Despite all the warnings, it was a regular occurrence for a couple of sheepish looking lads to be brought back into the shop by a 'rozzer', to be roundly bollocked for wandering off. Charlie always made much of the drama, by effusively thanking the Officer for his assistance in apprehending them.

'Thank you, Officer,' he would say, with a syrupy smile on his face. 'You can be sure I'll make an example of them. Then, turning to the lads, he would proceed to make his point.

'Now then, you little sods, you're for the high jump this time,' he would shout as the Officer went out of the shop.

Most of the Constables had seen service in the Forces and had an aggressive confidence, which intimidated the average Matey, even when innocent of any misdemeanour. The most feared were the plain-clothes Officers, who were usually referred to as 'the dicks'. It was a matter of honour to try to pull one over on them and individuals were often heard bragging about their successes, most of which was patently false. Their tales inevitably grew in the telling and they were often caught out. The active level of policing could in no way stop all the unlawful activity but in truth, it kept it down to a tolerable level.

Part of the Police strategy was the random personal searches at the end of the day and information was often passed to them by individuals, who snitched on their workmates. Once branded as a 'Copper's nark', it was difficult to live it down. After clocking off, the Mateys made their way across the yard to one of the three gates. There were always two or three officers standing across the road, who were coldly scrutinising the crowd walking past. Individuals were singled out and directed into a small building to be searched. Selection was usually done by an Officer glaring at a Matey, then cocking his thumb towards the building and uttering the word 'get', meaning 'get inside'.

Another Officer was supposed to ensure that those sent over didn't slope off into the crowd. Sometimes, someone would purposely position himself to be pulled out and thereby shield a mate from apprehension. Another might look furtively around and avoid making eye contact, which would surely attract their attention. Small groups would deliberately cause a disturbance, which would be enough to allow the felon(s) to go through unimpeded. Another ploy was to 'act thick' or argue with an Officer. For example, the person told to 'get' would answer back in mock outrage.

'Don't swear at me, mate. I'm not 'a git,' or, 'This is the third time this week I've been sent for searching. Are you picking on me, or what?'

To complain was a waste of time and deaf ears were the Coppers' prerogative. While the ruses often worked, the clowns would often realise with dismay that they knew there was something up. If someone was thought to be acting the crack, he would be taken to one side and his search delayed until the main rush was over. The Police enjoyed regular success in countering the wily tricks of the buggers who tried to buck the system. The ones that were caught would disappear for a time or, in the more serious cases, altogether. To a lot of the Mateys, it was all part of the game and there was little or no shame in being apprehended. By long-standing tradition, the Police were fair game for all manner of stunts, though the risks of getting involved with them were very real.

As the second half of the year progressed, the strict regime of confining the first year lads in the shop gradually relaxed. That was on the understanding that no one took liberties. It brought the inevitable nonsense, and the third year lads took every opportunity to exert their corrupting influence on their younger mates. After much discussion, a classic stunt was set up. The plan was to ambush the Officers who regularly patrolled the rail marshalling yard, outside the shop and given the serious nature of the stunt, it had to be properly thought out. The risk of failure was high and the retribution which would surely follow any cock-up, would be very heavy. Everyone was sworn to secrecy and only the ones that could be trusted were given the full details of what was planned.

Due to the very large number of Apprentices in that part of the Yard, it was impossible to maintain their constant supervision. Any Policemen walking through the area in the early afternoon would be almost sure to find miscreants, who had skived off from their workplace. In the Summer months, the favourite places for a quiet smoke were inside the open railway trucks. It had long been a problem and despite their considerable efforts, the Officers had not been very successful. A lookout was usually stationed on the fire escape, high on the gable end of the Factory, his purpose being to warn his mates if a Copper was in the vicinity. Ultimately, the Police decided to mount a raid in numbers, with the objective of apprehending as many Apprentices as possible. However, their plans had become known, hence the stunt.

One of their number was the father of a first year lad and he had warned him not to be in the area when the raid took place. The warning was duly passed on to the plotters. Just before the end of the dinner-break on the day, the Police came on to the west end of the yard in numbers, then moved in a broad line down through the wagons, looking into each one as they passed. To their disappointment, the trucks were empty. The Inspector had just called his men together when a large number of youths came out of the Factory to jeer and shout insults at them and as the Police went over to confront them, they disappeared back into the building. A meeting later the same day failed to ascertain how their cunning plan had come adrift. The inspector should have known that the leak had come from within his own ranks.

Following their abortive raid, plain clothes Officers were drafted in and they were seen skulking around. The conspirators' plan, which had been to ambush the uniformed Officers, was thus modified. They would now set about the dicks, with even more drastic effect. At the start and finish of each day and to mark the beginning and the end of the dinner-hour, the Dockyard siren was sounded and it was so loud, it could be heard for many miles around. The 'rozzers' had noted that on successive days, a small number of lads were tardy in going back to work, sometimes by as much as ten minutes and as always, when pursued, they had gone back into one of the nearby buildings. After failing to catch anyone, they increased their numbers and that was just what the lads wanted. Their cunning plan was put into action.

A comprehensive fire fighting system was installed in the area, with hydrants running at regular intervals along the length of the rail-tracks and around the perimeter of the sidings. Rolls of hose pipe, complete with nozzles, were stashed in numerous fire points. Having gone over their plan carefully, including their lines of escape, the Apprentices set the operation for the following Friday afternoon. As anticipated, the Officers formed their line and set off on their search and were clearly confident that they were going to catch the young sods that had plagued them for so long. When they were about a third of the way along the tracks, a loud cry signalled the start of the ambush. The water hydrants were opened and the hoses turned on the hapless Officers. The high-pressure jets drenched the officers and a couple were bowled over. In the ensuing chaos, the lads whooped with joy and leaving the hoses still turned on, they ran back to their workshops.

The Instructors had become more lax in coming out of their caboosh after the dinner break and those involved slunk back into the shop unnoticed. For once, everyone was working away industriously, without having had to be told to get on with it. A few minutes later, uniformed Policemen entered the shop and confronted Charlie and the other Senior Instructor, with loud accusations about their charges. Being quick-witted and very much to his credit, Charlie hotly disputed their allegations. With the assistance of the Timekeeper, he referred to the clock cards and demonstrated that everyone was present at the time the incident took place. The Coppers were not entirely convinced, but they had to accept what he said. Glowering as they looked around, they left the shop with what could only be described as bad grace.

Charlie, who had clearly smelt a rat, looked sternly around the smirking assembly.

'I don't know how you did it, and I don't want to, either,' he said mournfully then, softening his countenance, he went on with a wry smile on his face, 'You sods will get me bloody hanged one of these days'.

Nothing more was said about the incident, nor were there any repercussions from Management. The skiving in the railway trucks ceased by the middle of October, as it was no longer comfortable to sit outside though the Police were still seen skulking around for some weeks after, which caused no end of merriment and ribald comments. However, the Officers had achieved their objective, albeit at some cost to their dignity. The lads involved in the ambush enjoyed notoriety for its successful outcome and it was the subject of lively discussion in the canteen for some time. While he knew there had been some skulduggery with the clock cards, Charlie let the matter 'die a natural'. To have done otherwise would have drawn attention to his own shortcomings, and that would never have done.

The Gate Pass – Poem

The sky was grey and overcast
When through the gate a Matey passed.
A Copper pounced and with a shout
Demanded, 'Where's your pass, you lout?'

The Matey cringed and turned in fear,
And agitated, dropped his gear.
His mates all laughed as they came past,
'Go on Johnny, show your pass.'

'Come on,' he heard the Copper say
'I can't be waiting here all day.
Just hand it over, then we'll see
If you're who you're supposed to be.'

The lad went through his pockets fast,
But couldn't find his missing pass.
'I've got it somewhere, P C Plod'
'None of your lip, you cheeky sod.'

He cringed beneath the Copper's stare,
Hostile, with an angry glare,
Poor Johnny knew he had to act,
He was in trouble, time for tact?

But then, from down the road there came
The noise of argument and blame.
T'was Johnny's mates, whose plan innate
Was help release their troubled mate.

'Don't go away, just you wait here,'
The Copper ran to join his peers
To quell the row and move them on,
When he returned, our lad had gone.

He'd done a runner, took his chance
Scarpered from predicament,
Away from anger, retribution,
He'd lost his pass, no quick solution.

From that day on, he took great care,
To dodge the Copper, whenever there,
Standing glumly at the gate,
Though still upset and most irate.

Chapter 9

Young Love

A sardonic wit had unkindly nick-named one of his workmates 'Sexy Rex' and being of a quiet disposition; the lad had been subjected to a lot of teasing. He hadn't though taken much notice of anything said to him and in time, his tormentors had tired of his lack of response and looked elsewhere for their entertainment. However, Rex turned out to be a dark horse, which caused no end of hilarity. He was tall, very thin and had narrow, round shoulders. He was further burdened with a sallow and extremely spotty complexion and, to make things even worse, he had a toneless, drawling voice. He couldn't be described as the epitome of youthful, masculine vigour, who would cause the opposite sex any disconcertion.

One morning, he was very down in the dumps and when asked why, it all came tumbling out. He gravely informed his mates that he was in serious trouble. He had been quietly enjoying the amorous company of a young lady called Betty. Their friendship had started while they were still at school and had blossomed after he started work. Not being as daft as he looked, Rex had said nothing about it and no-one had had any idea that he was courting. As he explained, his predicament had come about because he and his beloved had been indulging in passionate activities of a carnal nature. Her father, being of a strict and serious mien, had closely watched them right from the start. They must have known that playing at home was very risky and that sooner or later, they would be found out.

They had in fact been caught 'in flagrante-delecto', when her parents had returned home unexpectedly the previous Saturday evening. Her father had gone ape and had thrown Rex out of the house, with the furious admonishment not to come back. The details, told mournfully in his deadpan voice, were savoured to the full by his workmates. There was a lot of sympathetic clucking in what was barely suppressed mirth. One individual, who was thought likely to spoil the show, was angrily turned on and told to shut-it. It was not so funny for Rex, who was in the depths of despair. He had trooped disconsolately round to his erstwhile lover's house the next morning, to try to put things right. Despite his profuse apologies, her parents had been deaf to his plea that they had only done it the once.

They had angrily refused to let Rex into the house, telling him in no uncertain terms to clear off. In those days, much was said by adults about maintaining 'decent standards' of behaviour, though many didn't always practice what they preached. Rex had always been warmly welcomed his girlfriend's home but now, he had well and truly 'shit it'. Both parents had been very pleased when he and Betty had started going steady and had quickly become very friendly, with regular, cosy visits to each other's homes. How could it all have gone so badly wrong?

Around midday on the Sunday morning, her parents had turned up at Rex's house with a tearful Betty in tow. They were full of righteous indignation at what they said was her seduction. To re-enforce their tirade and with a sense of high drama, Betty's mother had taken Rex's underpants from her handbag and laid them on the table. With a loud sniff to emphasise her disgust, she said that she had found them at the bottom of their daughter's bed. His parents were speechless with embarrassment for the first few minutes. Their son had kept schtum about the crisis, and they were aghast when told of what he had been up to. In an effort to calm the situation, Rex's mother suggested that they should sit down over a nice cup of tea to talk things over.

'Let's try to sort things out,' she said reasonably. 'We're not going to get anywhere by shouting at each other.'

She was absolutely right. The discussion continued in a more sensible manner, though there were further angry outbursts from Betty's parents. Rex's father had become increasingly resentful of his wife's quiet response to their verbal assault. He suddenly blurted out that 'it took two to tango' and it couldn't be all his son's' fault. Another lively exchange followed until they again agreed to tone it down. After a lengthy discussion, it was agreed that 'what was done was done and couldn't be undone'. The loving couple, both of whom were very contrite, would be allowed to continue to see each other, but only with their parents present. It would be on the strict understanding that there would be no more hanky panky. They could hardly believe that they had got away with it so easily.

If all went well – 'with no more nonsense mind' – they would be allowed to get engaged on Betty's seventeenth birthday and perhaps get married a year or so later. However, it has always been sod's law that if something can go wrong, it will inevitably do so. That duly kicked in and the couple's troubles became even worse. Only a few weeks later, Rex was again in a right old state and he forlornly admitted that he had well and truly done the dirty deed. Betty was with child – 'podded', 'up the duff' – or, as generally referred to in the most favoured idiom of the day, 'in the pudding-club'. While a lot of the lads were amused by his predicament, the general feeling was one of genuine sympathy. One lad asked Rex how it had happened.

'Didn't you use a johnny, old mate?'

Rex looked at him in some amazement, before blushing and replying angrily. 'No I didn't! I wouldn't insult my Betty by using one of them filthy things.'

Somewhat taken aback, his mates exchanged a mixture of knowing and baffled looks.

'I don't understand,' said his inquisitor, winking slyly to the other lads. 'What are you on about? What's wrong with using a johnny?'

The exchange had all the signs of a very entertaining few minutes and the audience, which had swollen to at least half the lads in the shop, raptly hung on to his every word.

"Cos they're only supposed to be used when you go with prostitutes, to stop you catching something horrible,' replied Rex, crimson with embarrassment. 'Ain't they?' he added lamely and looking around forlornly. That's what my dad told me.

It was all too much for his listeners, most of who fell about in helpless laughter. An angry shout from Charlie restored order and perhaps a little consideration from his mates. It was obvious the daft young sod hadn't got a clue and truth to tell, neither had a good many of the ones that were laughing at him. They were not going to let-on about their own ignorance.

'Bloody hell,' said the questioner, 'don't you know anything, my old son? Everybody knows a johnny is supposed to prevent you getting a dose, but it also stops you getting into the mess you're in. It's got nothing to do with insulting your bird. You've done that by putting her in the club.'

In common with the other know-it-alls, some of whom would in time fall into the same trap, Rex had had no previous experience. Compared with these enlightened times, there were no practical demonstrations of the correct application of that most useful comestible. Furthermore, sex was rarely mentioned in the home. Whatever exchanges took place were usually among peers, or in groups of similarly aged lads, who were generally ill-informed as each other. Some of them knew a little and often tried to impress others with their knowledge and experience. The truth was, they were as ignorant as everyone else. An indication of just how little they knew was demonstrated in the same discussion. During one of those moments when the talking had died down, one lad made a striking comment.

'My sister wears a 'Dutch Cap,' he said in a loud voice.

'We're not talking about bloody hats,' said a droll voice from behind a newspaper, a comment which brought renewed laughter.

'No, said the lad, 'it's what she uses to stop her having any more kids. You should see it; it's an odd looking thing. I don't know how it works or anything, but she swears by it,' he concluded.

It seems you don't know much about anything, you daft sod,' said the other lad, returning to his paper.

A general discussion ensued about contraceptives and how to get hold of them. To most young men, they were expensive and buying them was a problem. Chemists and Barbers stocked them, but most young men were reluctant to ask for 'a packet of three'. Some boasted that they had no problem, which resulted in further banter. One clown was taken up on his bragging and was urged to demonstrate how he did it on the following Saturday morning. Wagers were made and on the day, after a number of false starts, he went into a chemist's shop. He quickly came out again, red with embarrassment and without the goods. To cover his failure, he loudly complained that a po-faced old biddy had served him and he'd had to cut and run.

He then tried a Barber's shop but, as it was full of people who knew him, the outcome was that he failed miserably and duly paid his debt for doing so.

A bloke in the Factory sold them but again, there was the chance that the purchaser might be rumbled. This will seem very strange but as we've already said, things were so very different then. Young couples were just as red-blooded as they are today and they often walked down the aisle or into the Registry Office, with the bride 'in the family way'. If a lad got a girl podded, he was expected to marry her. Nowadays, if a loving couple don't want to get hitched, they just live together. In statistical terms, the number of unwanted pregnancies hasn't changed much, and marriage is now very much a matter of choice. Gone is the stigma and hypocrisy which was once attached to 'getting into trouble'. Not long after, the happy couple, supported with forced smiles by their families, attended the Registry Office to be married. Rex was the first in the entry to fall.

Most young men surrendered dumbly and without much enthusiasm to their fate. One can only wonder with no little sardonic humour at the many old folk, who look so disapprovingly at today's beautiful young people. They mutter sanctimonious and hypocritical epithets about how very much standards of behaviour have fallen 'from when we were young'. One recalls hearing of one August matron, who had been a magistrate in her mature years and had regularly lectured street girls on the folly of their ways. It was said by others of her age that in her youth, she had been free with her favours and on occasions had not been above accepting payment for them. A case perhaps of 'Don't do as I did, do as I say!' – At least she was talking from experience!

Due to their chronic lack of funds and with suitable accommodation being both in short supply and expensive, the majority of newlyweds moved in with their parents. They thus had the opportunity to live cheaply and save every spare penny towards a home of their own. Woe betide the young hubby who was tempted to go out with his pals for a pint. He would certainly get it in the neck from both his wife and her parents. Their situation often led to problems, with regular rows and the young couple's moral would soon hit rock-bottom. When the baby arrived, their home life, which had seemed as bad as it could get, would often get even worse. Many families lived a hand-to-mouth existence in small, crowded houses, with few mod-cons. There was little privacy and unless they were very fortunate, there was constant friction. Any complaint or rueful comment would be answered by an angry retort.

'You should have thought of the consequences, before getting yourselves into trouble.' 'Don't say you weren't warned,' and so on.

Almost all the lads that fell had problems, and they had to unburden themselves to someone. The workshop was probably the only place where they could get some sympathy for their trials and tribulations. The advice from their contemporaries wasn't much use, particularly when spouted by a juvenile sage. Basking in their own smug complacency, they had no idea of the misery in which their mate was living. 'Tell him to piss-off, the stupid old bastard' or 'She's got no right to speak to you like that. Don't you have it my old son', he would be gravely told.

That was the limit of their sound advice, and a fat lot of good it did. A family row sometimes got out of hand and ended in violence, with the poor sod getting a beating, either from his father in law and/or his wife's brothers. Unless he had support from his own family or friends, he was very much on his tod. Her brothers would sometimes suffer painful retribution from his workmates. The misery endured by some young men and to be fair, their wives as well, which had been the outcome of a few minutes of dubious pleasure as care-free singles, was at times a salutary lesson. It was strange that so few young men learned from their mates' sad fates.

There was a slow trickle of despondent young men, who tied the knot in haste, but it was not always a disaster. There had to be exceptions and one was Ron, a third-year apprentice. More by luck than judgement, he had landed on his feet. In stark contrast to his long-suffering mates, he had found himself living in a large, warm, comfortable home, with very caring in-laws and plenty of good food on the table.

'Her mother thinks the world of me, and she's a smashing cook', he said, with a self-satisfied smirk. 'The old man's a decent sort as well and is very generous, when we go down the pub of an evening. I couldn't be happier with my lovely girl, and that's a fact.'

His bragging was succinctly answered by the same comic who, without looking up from his paper, remarked that that was because her folks were so grateful for having got shut of their bloody, ugly daughter.

'You lot can laugh, but it's the best thing that could have happened to me,' came the quick reply.

The fact was that those blissful oases of comfort were indeed few and far between. Mostly, if a young couple fell, it was well and truly into the mire and it could be years before they were able to save enough money to secure their independence and make something of their lives. With National Service looming, their situation did nothing to lighten their burden. In looking back, at least half the nuptials in Mike's village were what were called, shot-gun weddings. We can only wonder how many married couples have, with the passage of time, conveniently forgotten the circumstances of their own marriages. Do they, as intimated above, now adopt the moral high ground, as so many do where the sexual antics of their grandchildren are concerned?

'There was no permissive society in our day. We were expected to behave ourselves', is often heard.

Like most teenagers from time immemorial, it was a 'racing cert' that they didn't behave either! Time makes great amnesiacs and, worse still, hypocrites of us all. Many young people did though conform with the perceived morals of the time. They went through the steps of going steady, got engaged and eventually married, with none of the problems that so many couples faced at the time.

Chapter 10

A Painful Lesson

One morning, Charlie called the lads together and told them they were going to embark on the next phase of their training. They would use the same plates in which they had formed a one inch square hole. Seeing him in such good humour and with the other Instructors grinning, he obviously had something awful in mind. He went on to explain that they were going to make one inch square, 'male' plugs and fit them into their plates. He held up a piece of round bar, one and a half inches in diameter and two inches long and after showing them a completed plug, each lad was given a piece on which to work. They were in for a rude awakening in that it would be a difficult and painful lesson, which would most definitely not be appreciated.

They were, he said, going to learn how to chip excess metal' away from the edges of the round bar, by using a hammer and a one inch, cold chisel. The tools were already in their boxes and with some apprehension, they got them out.

'Alright, you lot,' Charlie cried after a few minutes of noisy speculation, 'gather round. I shall now demonstrate the proper way to do it, which I am sure you'll all enjoy very much.'

The objective was to cut a consistently thin, continuous strip of metal from across the top of the bar. It was, he said, a relatively quick way of removing the surplus metal and as he assured them wryly, it was much easier said than done. The bar had to be put into the vice, lengthwise and be firmly clamped. That was a problem for some, because a lot of their vices were in poor condition. If the piece wasn't held firmly, it would almost certainly 'gain a mind of its own' and fly out of the vice, when impacted by the chisel. It would then be hazardous to both the chipper and his immediate neighbours.

Charlie put his bar into the vice and after ensuring it was square and level, he tightened it up. He then filed a shallow, forty-five degree bevel across the top of the edge facing him. With an exaggerated squaring of his shoulders and a dramatic flourish of the hammer and chisel, he proceeded to demonstrate 'the art of chipping'. He started with careful, gentle taps and when satisfied with the thickness of the metal being cut, he gradually increased his tempo. A succession of firm hits followed as he steadily worked the chisel along the top of the bar. He ended up with a relatively flat surface and a neat little coil of mild steel. Turning to his audience with a big grin, he capped his performance with a cocky comment.

'There you are, my lads,' he said, holding it up between forefinger and thumb, 'there's nothing to it. As I said, it's a very handy way of quickly removing surplus metal from a block, when you don't have access to a machine.

When I was in the desert with the Army during the War, we had to do it all the time. There were no little luxuries of life for us there, I can tell you.'

To confirm the technique, he then cut another pass across the top of the bar, saying at regular intervals, 'Easy, in'it?'

It was essential that the cutting-edge of the chisel was sharp. By hitting it with just the right amount of force and at the right angle, he had steadily moved right along the bar. When the lads tried to do it, they found it was not as easy as it had seemed. The chisel either bit into the metal, with the displaced sliver becoming steadily thicker or it broke free, which meant restarting the cut. Occasionally, shards of metal flew through the air, evoking loud protests from those working nearby. Prolonged practice would give most of them the aptitude for the job, but not without many problems along the way.

Charlie had a good supply of the bars, having known exactly what was going to happen. It was a hazardous exercise of which most of his charges had not been forewarned. Perhaps the older Apprentices had taken some twisted pleasure in anticipation of the sufferings of their chums? Certainly, the Instructors made it look easy, but they had many years of experience behind them. For most of the lads, it was a difficult and dangerous chore, which caused them no end of pain. Some were more adept than others and they loudly agreed with Charlie, saying it didn't seem to be too difficult. However, within minutes of starting work, there had been a continual round of loud, anguished yells, bad language and angry complaints as the lads failed to hit the ends of their chisels. Many hands were soon bruised and swollen, in some cases with the skin broken and bleeding. The Instructors watched with wry amusement, saying repeatedly,

'Keep trying lads, you'll soon get the hang of it.'

In comparison with these more enlightened times, there was little concern for health and safety in the shop. The serious hazard of flying shards, would surely have stopped the job in today's workplace. There were no method statements or risk assessments, though the hazards were clear for all to see. No protective gloves or goggles were available, to mitigate them either. Some lads bound their hands with pieces of cloth, but their efforts were clearly ineffective. As the time passed, the incidence of injuries declined and by the end of the second week, most of them had mastered hitting the chisel. Whether or not they appreciated it was debatable, but they had learned a valuable lesson, from which they would benefit handsomely later.

When the square section had been formed, the faces had to be filed flat and square to each other. It was a laborious job and there was the usual grumbling about their Instructors' pernickity attitude. Some craftily took their pieces over to the Factory to have the surplus metal machined-off to within a few thousanths' of an inch of the required dimensions. It gave the instructors no end of pleasure, when they ambushed them as they came back into the shop. With great drama and angry shouts, Charlie berated them, much to the amusement of their workmates. He confiscated their bars and they were told to start again.

Despite having been caught, some clowns still sought to get away with it. There had to be a way by which someone could avoid the instructors' beady eyes. They had soon tired of waiting by the door, whenever someone was absent. They also became careless and left confiscated pieces on their desks in the caboosh and the crafty buggers seized their opportunities to redeem them. It was not difficult to liberate a piece, when the instructors were out in the shop and if a lad was lucky, it would be the one that he'd previously had machined.

Another rumpus ensued when a lad brought a piece of steel back from the factory. When apprehended, he indignantly and loudly pleaded his innocence.

'I don't know what you're talking about, Mister Brand,' he protested, when accused of cheating. Taking the kosher block from his pocket, he went on. 'This is my piece and I keep it on me all the time. I don't leave it around in case somebody nicks it.'

It was hardly likely anyone would have done so, but the lad had thought his ploy through. Knowing the boss would be waiting, he had left his machined replacement outside, to be collected later. There wasn't much sympathy, but there was grudging admiration of the way he had got one over on Charlie. The instructors knew some of their charges were still dodging the job, but they took the view that they would be the losers. They were spurning the chance to learn a valuable skill. As long as the work was progressing and knowing that most of their charges were 'legit', they gradually let things go.

Trade Union membership was the hot topic of conversation one morning and it gave rise to a lively debate. No one had given any thought to it until a couple of older Apprentices had come into the shop the previous afternoon. They had told Charlie they were representatives of the Engineering Union and asked his leave to go round and hand out membership application forms. He had no hesitation in giving his permission. Their friendly demeanour changed abruptly, as soon as he and his colleagues went back into their caboosh. They were stiff and formal and said there was no choice, as all Apprentices had to be in the Union. Each lad was given a form and told to have it completed, together with their first subscription, on Friday afternoon. There would be a weekly collection of the subs every pay-day from then on.

When asked for his advice, Charlie was very helpful, saying that there were many advantages to be had from Union membership. A Joint Council of the Unions negotiated the pay and conditions for everyone employed in the Yard, though membership was not compulsory. It was for each lad to think about it and make up his own mind as to whether or not he wished to join. He declined to say if he and the other Instructors were in a Union. There was a lot of lively discussion, with a three-way split of opinion. Some said they would join, because their fathers were active members of their Unions. 'Fair enough,' their mates replied. Others were open to persuasion and didn't mind, one way or the other. The remainder resented the pressure from the older lads, who had lied when they had said that membership was compulsory.

The first year Apprentice's subscription was only six old pence (2.5p, equivalently) per week, which was a small price to pay for the benefits that membership brought. The issue caused an increasingly bad-tempered argument, which Charlie quickly broke up. He repeated that it was for each lad to make up his own mind and he wanted no argy-bargy about it. The following Friday, the 'reps' returned and again, after asking for permission to do so, they went around and spoke to each lad. When rejected, they were even more obnoxious and in some cases, they resorted to veiled threats. They insisted that joining the Union was compulsory and they wouldn't take 'no' for an answer. In pressing their point, they annoyed two of the biggest lads, who were more than capable of standing up to them.

When other lads saw the heated arguments, albeit 'sotto-voce', they abruptly changed their minds and wanted no part in it. The sum total of new members recruited was in the order of a dozen or so, out of the forty-two lads present. It was by no means a successful haul and the Reps left without the courtesy of thanking Charlie for his co-operation. When he heard what had happened, Charlie said that he couldn't understand what was going on as the Unions had always been very relaxed in their recruitment of Apprentices. From time to time in the past, a senior Official had spoken to them as a group, but never in their first year. He was sure that membership was voluntary, though he certainly wasn't going to get into any arguments about it.

Over the next couple of weeks, the Reps duly collected subscriptions from their new members. Some lads had changed their minds and joined, while others dropped out. A third rep came along to force the waverers to 'toe the line' and a few mornings later, it all became clear. A lad had told his father about the problem and like Charlie, he'd smelt a rat. When asked, the Convener confirmed that the Union was not actively recruiting Apprentices, though if someone wanted to join, he would be very welcome. Their discussion had let the cat out of the bag and what transpired gave rise to quite a row.

The so-called Reps had set up a lucrative scam; the ring leader being the Convener's nephew. Having lifted some application forms from his uncle's office, he and his mates had liberally distributed them around the first and second year Apprentices. They had then collected and pocketed their subscriptions. The Convener came down to the shop to discuss what had happened with Charlie and offered to answer questions from his lads. Probably with the intention of off-loading some of the blame, one of his questions was very pointed.

'Didn't you ask to see their credentials, Charlie? You must have known how the Union recruits its members; that we wouldn't send other lads to do it for us.'

Charlie ruefully admitted that he hadn't and apologised, both to the Convener and the lads who had been taken-in. In his anxiety to avoid upsetting anyone, he had sat on the fence. The Convener was not without blame, in that his nephew had regularly collected subscriptions, in breach of Union rules. He had enjoyed ready access to his uncle's office and had taken due advantage. The Convener assured them that neither he nor his fellow shop-stewards had had any idea of what had been going on. He went on to speak about the importance of a strong negotiating base in his dealings with the employers, which most of his listeners agreed with. He also spoke about the benefits available, including health and sickness payments, which were very important to working people. His discourse was warm and friendly and at total variance with the attitude of the three rogues.

Charlie was very upset because he should have known that something was amiss, particularly when the fraudsters had insisted that membership was compulsory. It was some days before he was back to his normal bossy self, and some of his charges were not slow to take advantage. His rigid control of those who wanted to leave the shop had gradually diminished and there was a more relaxed atmosphere. The reprobates' punishment was not seen as severe enough, by those who had been conned and they vowed that in due course, retribution would be exacted.

Returning to the job, the chipping of the male pieces was duly completed, and then came the really hard part. Long days were spent diligently filing the interfaces, to obtain the requisite close fit within the plates. It had been a valuable exercise and the Instructors had played their part by regularly speaking to each lad about how to achieve the best possible finish. The end results varied, but there were signs that some of the lads were beginning to acquire the skills of fine fitting. Others though were dismissive about what their instructors were seeking to achieve. They were content to amble along, doing as little work as possible and generally being a nuisance.

Chapter 11

Happy Days

Humour plays a large part in our lives, and is a fundamental part of the British character. While it was prevalent in most of the lads, some of them were of a more serious and responsible nature. The tension of the early days had softened and the stand offs had become less frequent. Some of the unpleasantness had been due to personality clashes, which often arise when people of different backgrounds are brought together in a strange environment. A pecking order had been established, with lads either tolerating or ignoring their adversaries altogether. Some of the enmities made in the first few weeks, lasted throughout the five years and in some cases, for long after. Amusing incidents happened from time to time, which helped to improve matters and the atmosphere in the shop was much more relaxed.

In most walks of life, one learns something new every day. However, we don't always learn from our mistakes and all too often, we will do anything rather than admit to our own shortcomings. There has always been a tendency to blame someone else for one's own foolishness and errors. That has inevitably led to an overly defensive attitude in our approach to life, which is not always to our advantage. Charlie went to great lengths to guide his charges along the straight and narrow, but he didn't always get the desired results. He always insisted that each lad was responsible for everything he did and had to be a limit as to what was acceptable. The lads respected him for it and in making his position clear, he regularly promised every help to his charges. Almost daily, he and his colleagues demonstrated their commitment to their welfare.

A large number of Warships and Auxiliary Vessels were in the Yard, either tied up around the basins or set down in the dry docks. Some remained in commission, being only in for short-term maintenance or repairs. Others were undergoing refits and, as completion approached, Royal Navy personnel were seen on board in increasing numbers. The Mateys were convinced that having been handed a Warship in pristine condition, the Navy was often careless of their very expensive equipment.

Most sailors had a supercilious attitude and a hearty dislike of the 'bloody Mateys' and were often heard loudly holding them to be 'lazy, useless bastards' to a man. Their view has often been demonstrated by the authors of both historical and fictional publications about the Royal Navy. Inevitably, the 'Andrew' is stacked out with patriotic heroes, all of whom have been thoroughly trained and are highly competent in everything they do. The reality is perhaps something different.

'On no account do you get involved with the Navy,' Charlie had told his lads many times. 'They don't like you, and you won't like them, so be warned.'

There were many small incidents which clearly demonstrated the extent of the problem, and they were not all amusing. One occurred, when Jim had skived off out of the shop for a quiet smoke. He was happily perched on a mooring bollard on the sea wall, when he was rudely startled by a loud shout.

'You thah,' said a very posh voice, which brought him abruptly back to the land of the living, 'What do you think you're doing?'

He turned and saw a diminutive Naval Officer, the lower sleeves of whose jacket were covered with four thick rings of gold-braid. He was very grandly topped off by a large brass hat, which made him look ridiculous; more like a commissionaire than a Naval Officer.

'Who, me?,' Jim replied, and then, less civilly, 'I'm having a smoke. What's it to you?'

'Don't you bloody well answer me back, you cheeky young buggah,' shouted the officer, being full of indignation and very much on his dignity. 'What's your name and where are you supposed to be working?'

'None of your business,' replied said cheeky young bugger.

He then dropped his fag and ran off, hotly pursued by the little man. In the chase, the officer dropped his hat and very wisely went back to retrieve it. Jim got clean away and ran around to the other side of the building, then into the shop and breathlessly returned to his bench.

'Here, what have you been up to?,' cried Charlie. 'No bloody good, that's for sure.'

'Nothing Mr Brand, honest,' replied Jim, smiling as if butter wouldn't melt in his mouth. 'I just nipped out to the toilet and came back as quickly as I could, that's all.'

At that point, the main door was thrown open and the Officer, red-faced with anger, came rushing into the shop.

'Are you in charge he'ah?' he demanded of Charlie, once more suitably adorned with his brass hat and clearly full of unbridled indignation. 'I'm the Engineer Captain of the Yard, and I've just been cheeked and insulted by one of your Apprentices, who was loafing around outside. I want him identified and severely dealt with. He was wearing a black beret and orange overalls, so you should be able to pick him out quite easily.'

'Now just a minute,' said Charlie, purposely neglecting to call him Sir. 'You've got no right coming in here making accusations. All my lads is present and correct and I can say, without fear of contradiction, none of them has been out of this shop in the last half hour. Ain't that right?' he said to the other Instructors.

'Yes, that's right,' they replied dutifully.

The Captain looked around and saw forty-odd Apprentices, most of whom were grinning like Cheshire cats and enjoying the drama enormously. Knowing he wasn't going to get anywhere, he turned and went rapidly towards the door. When there, he turned again and shouted.

'This won't be the last you've heard of this, I can tell you!'

He then left the building, loudly banging the door behind him and it was the last that anyone heard of the incident. Charlie pointed sternly to the offender, then dramatically at his feet.

'Come here, you little sod,' he cried angrily, to the great delight of the watching yobs. You've got a black beret, haven't you? Come on, own up. It was you loafing around outside, wasn't it? Keep bloody quiet you lot,' he bellowed at the noisy crowd.

'No Mister Brand, it weren't me,' the little sod lied then, with a quick change of mind, he owned-up. 'Well, yes it was me, but I didn't cheek him, honest. 'He just came up as I came out of the toilets and started shouting at me, so I ran off.'

'Right, I've told you time and again about keeping clear of the Navy, haven't I,' said Charlie, looking around severely. 'Just you remember what I've said and let that be a lesson to you all. Now get on with your work and let's have no more bloody nonsense.'

He then turned and, with the other Instructors smiling broadly, they went back into their caboosh.

The altercation was not an isolated incident. A few days later, during the dinner hour, a group of lads was walking along the roadway, which separated the dry docks from the adjacent basin. All four docks had ships in them, each undergoing hull repairs and or propeller maintenance. There was the usual tomfoolery among them and one picked up a large onion, which was lying in the gutter. He held back, then threw it at of one of his mates and missed his target by a considerable margin. The missile sailed over the top of the lads and struck the back of an RN Lieutenant, who was walking in front of them. He stumbled and fell, much to the amusement of a small working party of Matelots standing nearby. Their Petty Officer was alert and quickly led his troops away from the potential trouble.

The lads had stopped and stared at the Officer with apprehension and, as he picked himself up, he gave vent to his anger in choice, un-gentlemanly language. To avoid certain retribution, they legged it away. Fortunately, they had the sense to run into the Factory and not directly towards their workshop and once inside, they dispersed among the machines to lay low. The Officer followed and just inside the door, he asked an operator if he had seen the youths that had come in a few moments before. Of course he hadn't and, realising he had no chance of catching them, he gave up and went back out. With the coast clear, the lads made their exit from the bottom end of the building and went back to the shop. Much to their amazement, Charlie had already heard about the incident and he again warned them about the perils of 'messing around with the Navy'.

The Mateys were careful to give most of the Sailors and, particularly the Royal Marines, a wide berth. Their targets were the ones that presented the least threat, but the risks of buggering about were very real, because the ensuing punishment would be drastic. It would be wrong to say that there was no co-operation between the two camps because, when there was an urgent job on, the hostility was set aside. There was a determination and close co-operation to get it done and long hours were worked, sometimes in very difficult conditions. It often rankled with the 'Tars', that the Mateys were paid extra for overtime, shift-working, dirty-conditions, working at heights, etc, while they were not. Generally speaking, the Mateys had to put up with a lot of boorish arrogance and antagonism and, when the opportunity arose to redress the issue, it was usually taken up with enthusiasm.

With the coming of Spring, the time passed more quickly and most of the lads were becoming more skilful in their work. Charlie was no longer the stern martinet and the incidence of indiscipline had markedly declined. There was always a kerfuffle when Mr Barry or some other Manager came down to the workshop, sometimes with visitors. Having been given due notice, the shop would be swept and tidied and when the party arrived, all the Apprentices would be seen to be working diligently at their benches.

The Royal Navy trained their Artificer Apprentices in much the same way as the Yard and the end of year trade test was said to be common to both parties. Whereas the civilians spent the whole of their five years in the Yard, the Navy lads were shore-bound for three years, with the remaining two spent for the most part completing their training on board Ship. Being mindful that the last weeks of their first year would be taken up with the test, Charlie decided that his charges would continue their exercises, in preparation for what would be a demanding examination. With the usual drama, he called them together one Monday morning to explain what he wanted. This time, there would be a lot more close work in fitting an 'E' shape into the plates. It would measure two and a half inches high, by two inches wide and be fitted into their existing L' plates. He stressed that even greater care and concentration would be necessary to obtain the finish that he required. The time for the job would be considerably less than allowed previously.

'You've had it far too easy, and it's time you lot learned what working to a tight schedule is all about,' he said, nodding and grinning as he looked around.

His comments were greeted with a lot of exaggerated groans, but everyone knew it wouldn't be a difficult job. They had benefited greatly from their tuition and were mostly confident of doing the forthcoming test well. The practice gained and the various tools used, had given them a firm grounding in the art of fitting. All but a few would have no difficulty in completing the exercise to his satisfaction. Their work-rate had also been improved by an unspoken spirit of competition. It was a matter of pride to do a better job than a mate. Their hard work was bearing fruit and when it came, they were confident they would pass the final test.

The erstwhile shortage of hand tools had gradually diminished and whatever they needed was mostly forthcoming. Even emery cloth, which had caused no end of inconvenience, had ceased to be a problem. A number of rolls of different grades were hanging from nails outside of the caboosh. A used large piece, in good condition, was still a prized possession for the final polishing process. By then, the lads were familiar with the various sections in the Factory and most of what they needed could be drawn from the stores anyway. The storekeepers, with many years of experience of the wily tricks of the young buggers, would often check to ensure that the docket being offered was legit and so, they had everything they needed.

Work started on the 'E' plates and having marked-out and cut the edges, they concentrated on their squareness. Despite all the previous nonsense about cheating, some lads still sloped-off to get their plates machined. The instructors said nothing for a few days but one morning, several plates were confiscated and the miscreants gruffly told to start again. The lads were constantly checking the work and aping the instructors, they made much exaggerated 'humming and ha-ing' over the fine details of their plates. As soon as they were completed, they went on to the cutting out the male 'E'.

The fitting of the 'E' into the plate was difficult, due to its small size and forming the internal corners was tricky. There was often frustration when things didn't go well but the time passed quickly, with pieces being finished and submitted to the Instructors for their inspection. In the end, there were perhaps three or four Apprentices who had not completed their work in the time allowed. As before, the standard of fitting achieved varied greatly, though most lads had made a tolerably good job. Ideally, the 'E' had to fit 'all ways', i.e. from both sides of the plate and inverted, to completely satisfy their Instructors. No one managed to achieve that most difficult task. Charlie seemed pleased with their efforts though and he and his colleagues spent a lot of time discussing the merits of his work with each lad.

'All in all,' he said, 'things were going along very nicely.'

Chapter 12

Lodgings

Many of the lads were very much aware of their developing masculinity, and often boasted about their sexual exploits. Some hadn't even had a steady girlfriend, but that didn't deter them from talking about 'it'. They regaled each other with the crude details of all kinds of affairs, some of which were real but mostly, they were imaginary. When he was obviously lying, a teller would be roundly castigated as a 'bull-shitter' and bluntly told how little he knew. The truth was, most of them didn't know much about women. Those that did kept quiet about it, to avoid the coarse ribbing which would surely follow. What was generally known was usually gleaned from talking to older lads or from 'mucky' books, which by modern standards were poor fare indeed.

The whole situation was fraught with danger and it caused a lot of problems. Some adults were only too willing to assist the young men's education and there was certainly a desire to learn. For a lot of them, practical experience in the age-old pleasures of life would come much later. Within weeks of starting work, Jim had had reason to complain about the digs, which the Employer had found for him and another lad. Their homes were too far away to travel to and from work each day and they only went home at weekends. When asked what the problem was, Jim told his mates a hilarious story. Being short of cash, he and his mate had stayed in their digs over the previous weekend. He stressed that the landlady was kind and had made a genuine effort to ensure their comfort and their shared room, though plainly furnished, was warm and clean and the food she provided was of good quality.

'So what are you complaining about?' asked another lad.

Jim replied that lately, the good lady had been showing amorous intentions and had said several times that she liked a little bit of fun. 'I like a bit of a laugh,' he said, mimicking her voice, which brought loud laughter from his audience and a shout for silence from the caboosh. The merriment died and Jim continued. After their meal on the Friday evening, he had opened his pay-packet to give her the rent and had dropped a shilling on the floor. The coin was quickly scooped up and slipped down the front of her dress and smiling broadly, she then invited him to come over and find it. He tried to make out that he didn't know what she meant, though he was quick to assure his mates that he did.

'Come over here Jimmy and I'll show you,' she had said, reaching to pull him closer.

To her annoyance, he had fled the room.

'What's the matter with him? she had asked Henry, who had been quietly watching. 'Don't he like a bit of fun?'

It hadn't ended there. The following night, when his mate was out, Jim asked if he could have a bath. The water was heated by a boiler in the kitchen and it was some time before it was hot enough. After running the water and checking the temperature, she remained in the bathroom and Jim had asked her to leave. He got undressed and had only just got into the bath, when she came back in again, saying that she would wash his back. Only with great difficulty did he convince her that he didn't need any help. Later, when he'd gone to bed, she had come into his room and made to get in with him. She'd been most reluctant to go away and not before she had taken a firm hold of his 'what's-it'.

'What's that?' cried a lad, knowing full well what he meant.

'You know,' Jim replied, red with embarrassment, 'my thing.'

By then, everyone was laughing, much to his discomfort.

'Didn't you let her hold it?' he was asked and, before he could reply, the lad said, 'Cor, I would have.'

At that point, Charlie came out to see what all the noise was about and was told, with great relish, about what had happened. Seeing Jim was upset, he put his arm around his shoulders and said:

'Don't pay any attention to this mucky lot, my old son, I'll soon sort it.'

He went back into his caboosh and was heard talking loudly to someone on the phone. He then called the lad over and told him to go over to the Personnel Office, where he would be given help and advice. After he had gone, Charlie had another call from the Officer who looked after the welfare of the Apprentices and was asked if the other lad wanted to move as well. Henry was quick to decline the offer, saying they were good digs and that the lady hadn't bothered him. Jim moved out the same evening. The lesson learned was to keep 'schtum' about any such problems, because Jim's workmates teased him about his amorous adventure for some time after. When the Officer went to see her, the landlady insisted it had all been a misunderstanding.

'I can't see what he's complained about,' she said. 'I admit teasing him, but it was only a bit of fun. I've had any number of lads in my house over the years and nobody else has ever complained.

Suggestive comments were made about Henry's decision to stay with her. He was a large, easy-going lad, who took no part in the banter; nothing bothered him and he seemed to be quietly contented with his lot. A lengthy discussion about the pros and cons of living in digs ensued. One lad opined that if Jim's experience was anything to go by, he was going to leave home right away. Those who were in digs were quick to tell him that living in someone else's house was not all it was cracked up to be. A few were satisfied, but there were others whose accommodation could in no way be described as a 'home from home'. As another lad succinctly put it, 'you paid your rent and took your chance.'

'I've got smashing digs,' Colin smugly told his mates, 'and the family I'm with can't do enough for me. The food's good, with plenty of it and I've got a nice, warm room all to myself. I come and go as I want, with my own key to the front door. Oh yes, my feet are really under the table, and you should see the daughter. Seventeen, she is, and gorgeous. Fancies me rotten, she does.'

He caught their interest and over the next few days, he embellished his story. He told a good tale and had his audience hanging on to every word as he boasted of a number of amorous advances from the daughter. He was expecting a whole lot more, when her parents were next out for the evening. As is nearly always the case, the truth of the matter was somewhat different. His life was humdrum, to say the least and his story nothing more than the ramblings of a vivid imagination. His downfall came when he was seen out shopping after work one evening. An older lad asked him if he was lodging with Mrs Giordino. A highly embarrassed Colin admitted, much to the delight of his jeering mates, that he was and that he was going to move as soon as he could find another place.

His landlady had lost her husband, an ex-Italian prisoner of war, about a year before. She was not very particular about hygiene, and according to him, 'she stank something rotten'. Her favourite form of relaxation was in the regular supping of a stout (or two), preferably when bought by someone else! She swore fluently, having completed her education in the 'WAAFs' during the war. They had been the best years of her life. She had married Marco soon after the hostilities had ended, and theirs hadn't always been a happy union. She had been saddled with her husband's teenage son, who had come over from Italy.

According to her colourful description, he was a lazy little grunt, 'just like all bloody I-ties'. All he was interested in was eating her out of house and home and tinkering with his 'bloody motorbike'. He had no intention of doing any work and was waiting for her to pop-off, so he could get his hands on what little money she had. Colin was obviously well versed in her personal history.

She had owned an Italian restaurant in the nearby town, but the locals had had had no appetite for her husband's cuisine. They sold it and bought a transport 'caff', which had made good money but, just as it was doing well, 'the silly bugger had snuffed it'. Being unable to continue on her own, she had soon sold up. Their house had belonged to her parents and that was how she came to be running a lodging house. The lads agreed that considering how poor her food was, it was a wonder that her 'caff' had been so successful. Colin was roundly chastised as a lying sod, which put an end to his clever wheeze.

The tales about lodgings, good and bad, gave Mike food for thought. Having been away for much of his school days, his life at home had become very unpleasant. What had initially seemed to be a good arrangement had rapidly deteriorated into a most unhappy existence, with both his parents constantly on at him. They continually made it clear he was not welcome and he was regularly told it would be better for everyone if he left and went into lodgings. The problem was, he didn't have the wherewithal to go and it would be a long time before he would be able to do so. He just had to 'grin and bear it' and put up with the never ending nonsense which went for family life at home.

John lodged with a lady who dearly loved her two Pekinese dogs, and they were doted on to such a degree that her lodgers resented them. Much to his annoyance, he was often asked to take them for walkies, while she was cooking the evening meal. The problem was that she would not allow them both out at the same time, because 'something dreadful might happen'. Every evening, he had to take first one, then the other out and was given strict orders to keep them on the lead at all times. He was further instructed as to where they were to be taken and was forbidden from going into the local pub. When asked why he put up with her bloody imposition, John replied that his digs were clean and comfortable and the meals were always appetising and freshly cooked. He also enjoyed a room to himself and for all that, he paid a most reasonable rent. Helping her with her dogs was a small price to pay.

His good fortune was not destined to last. He got up one morning and walked along the landing to the bathroom in his bare feet. To his great consternation, he stepped into a neat little pile of dog shit, which he said, softly and warmly came up through his toes.

His shouts of outrage, spiced with choice expletives, scared the hell out of the mutt, who yelped loudly and fled down the stairs. His mistress found him lying in a crumpled heap at the bottom. In floods of tears, she loudly accused John of hurting her baby and told him to leave. Before he left, he apologised for what had happened but, it didn't change anything and he left his digs feeling very badly done to.

Most of the lodgings were plain and simple, but good value. Some of the landladies had cared for a succession of Apprentices over many years, and serious problems rarely occurred. When they did, it was often down to the misbehaviour of the lads. Some though only provided the minimum of comfort and were always on the lookout for ways to maximise their income. One lad, when asked why he had moved out of the digs allocated to him, had explained that he had been given mince and tatties for his tea, followed by half a banana with cold custard on all five nights he was there. For the most part though, the hosts were kind and genuinely concerned for the welfare of their young guests. Some of them had stayed on throughout their time and became one of the family. They remained in contact and made periodic visits to their hosts, long after they had completed their Apprenticeships.

Mike was out with a friend one afternoon, when they were accosted by four lads from another village. They were clearly looking for trouble. One of them, who was known as 'Anger, (as in coat-'anger'), accused Keith of bullying his brother and it was clear he was in for a duffing. Keith protested his innocence but the accuser, who was much bigger than him, was in no mood to listen. When Mike intervened, he was turned on by one of the other lads and pinned against a wall, at which point a very large young man and two other lads appeared.

'What's happening here, then?' he asked crossly. 'A spot of bullying, is it? Well, if you lads are looking for trouble, you can try me for size,' he told them and roughly cuffed 'Anger several times about the head.

Mumbling that they had only been larking about, 'Anger and his pals made off. When Mike later asked Keith who the bloke was, he replied that he was called Martin and he lived in the same village as 'Anger. He was about twenty-five years old and had been leading a local youth club for some time. A week or so later, they saw Mart and some other lads playing cricket. He was very well-built and his main interests were weightlifting, boxing and wrestling. He regularly took part in amateur bouts in the local halls and being a fitness fanatic, he and his members often ran around the surrounding countryside. Like so many athletes, he was of a quiet disposition but could be dangerous when riled, which was why 'Anger and his mates had beaten such a hasty retreat.

Keith told Mike it was rumoured that Mart had not 'developed normally'. In other words, he hadn't got what most young men took for granted. When Mike pressed him to explain further, he declined, saying that it was only a rumour and he didn't want anything he said getting back to the man.

Over the next few weeks, they went to see Mart several times. He rented a dilapidated cottage in a row of four, which was owned by an old woman, who had often been the object of unkindness from her neighbours. He had put an end to her persecution. He had also taken pity on a young widow, with four young children, who had been evicted from her home and she had moved into one of the other cottages. His pride and joy was an old SS Jaguar, a classic car which was about thirty years old. It was parked under wraps at the side of his cottage, and he readily accepted Mike's offer to help him with the engine. Keith wasn't interested and he stopped coming over with him. When asked why, he said that some people thought that Mart was queer, and he didn't want to get involved in that sort of thing. When Mike said that he hadn't given him that impression, Keith replied that 'there was no smoke without fire'.

Mike's pleasant sojourns with Mart and the other lads ended abruptly during a boxing lesson. He had hated boxing at school and after some coaching, he had made good progress. That was until a smart right-cross flattened him. Mart had told him many times to keep his guard up and it should have been an object lesson, but it put him right off the noble art. When he arrived home, his mother demanded to know what he'd been up to. He stubbornly refused to answer, saying that if he took part in sport, he had to put up with the odd injury. He was alarmed when his father said that he would have a word with the local Bobby. While what Keith had said about Mart had caused him concern, even though the man had not bothered him. He went to bed in some dudgeon and by the following evening, the matter was forgotten.

A few weeks later, he heard that Mart had been sacked from his job. Keith surmised that it might have something to do with what people had been saying about him. Apparently, he had roughed someone up at work, gone home, packed his things and had left the area as mysteriously as he had arrived. When Mike spoke to the old lady, all she would say was that he had gone and she didn't know where. Those that had spoken so unkindly had caused him great injury. When Mike discussed him with some of the other lads he had met at his house, they all said there had never been anything dirty about him. He had been driven out of his home by lies and covert suggestions that he couldn't be trusted. Blind prejudice perhaps? Nothing has changed in that respect.

Chapter 13

Never a Borrower

Money, or the lack of it, has always been a problem for most young people. The first year Apprentices' pay packets were always eagerly awaited, even though they contained little enough cash. The first-year weekly rate was set at two pounds, four shillings and nine pence (£2.22 approximately), out of which, the National Insurance contribution and a modicum of income tax was deducted. That reduced it to two pounds, one shilling and four pence (£2.07). In addition to their keep, they had travelling expenses, schoolbooks, pens, pencils and other miscellany. For the ones that smoked, it was hard to make ends meet. By the following Monday morning, most of them were broke and the next pay-packet, on Friday, was a long way away. Mike was able to supplement his earnings by working on the farm above the village for a while, but for most of his mates, their poverty was very real.

There has always been someone with an eye for making a quick buck, who takes every opportunity to exploit other people. Among the apprentices, there was a lad called Budd and he was both devious and unscrupulous. Outwardly, he was presentable and well-spoken and his parents were, he said proudly, 'professional people'. He was of medium height and rather thickset, with thick, black hair and eyebrows. He was seen as comfortably off, was comparably well-dressed and he always had money in his pocket. That he regularly smoked branded cigarettes, which he kept to himself, was indication enough of his affluence. Any request to 'give us a fag until Friday, old mate' was inevitably met with a most definite refusal.

'I don't 'give' anything to anyone, so don't ask,' he would reply. 'If you want something in this life, you have to pay for it.'

Budd soon started to benefit from his work-mates' penury. His first scam was to exploit their dire tobacco shortage, by selling single cigarettes for a few pence each. Credit was given until midday on Friday, when his customers were paid. As the demand picked up, he duly extended the service and every sale was carefully noted in a little black book. Anyone who didn't pay promptly was refused further credit until he did so. Budd's little business quickly became very profitable, given that the cost of a packet of twenty was well beyond the means of the majority of his customers. As they couldn't afford the luxury of manufactured fags, they were eagerly looked forward to and very much enjoyed. Their usual smokes consisted of a few strands of tobacco, carefully rolled, then shared by up to half a dozen lads.

The next situation to be exploited was their chronic shortage of cash. Budd started by lending small amounts, on the same payment conditions as his cigarettes. He charged 10% interest on the sums borrowed and a defaulter suffered a further 10% penalty for every week the debt remained outstanding. He soon expanded his enterprise into the ranks of the second and third year Apprentices. His little black book was replaced by a larger, hard-covered one and on Friday afternoons, he was very busy collecting his dues. He would disappear during the dinner break and be away for a couple of hours. Charlie must have been aware of what was going on, but did nothing about it. With work finishing at four o'clock, the shop was usually more relaxed and as long as there were no disturbances, the lads were often left alone.

Budd was doing very well, until the proverbial hit the fan. The first indication of trouble was when he was ambushed on his way back from the Factory and the altercation brought Supervisors running to break it up. No one admitted the reason for it and after their names had been taken, they were sent back to work. The Senior Instructors were told to make further enquiries. Someone gave the information for which they were looking and Budd was summoned into the presence of the Manager. Being adept at saving his skin, he admitted his part in, but not the reason for the confrontation. He was told that his conduct was most unsatisfactory and he would be subjected to disciplinary action. When asked if he had anything more to say, he insisted it wasn't his fault.

When pressed, he later admitted that he had tried to help his fellows out by lending them small amounts of money to tide them over until payday. He could not have known that the demand for his assistance would grow to such an extent that he would lose control of it. When older Apprentices had heard of his loans, they had tried to muscle in on it. He apologised profusely for the misunderstanding and pleaded for another chance. His excuses appeared to fall on deaf ears, though Mr Barry must have been impressed by his eloquence. The scam could well have back-fired on himself, as well as his Instructors. Budd agreed to cease lending money, with the outstanding debts to be written-off.

Was his attitude changed by his close shave with the heavy hand of authority? Not one bit. When he returned to the shop, he was just the same cocky young sod as before. He apologised to Charlie for the embarrassment and trouble he had caused and having done so, he had more pressing business to attend to. He sat by his bench and studied his book, then quietly went around the lads who had been involved in his usury. Despite his assurance to Management, they would still have to pay back what was owed. With no knowledge of his agreement with Mr Barry, most of them duly repaid their debts. Having got that out of the way, Budd tried to do the same thing among the older lads, but was not entirely successful. He wisely dropped the idea.

The loss of one's tools remained a serious problem. Anything left unattended 'walked' and had to be replaced, at the loser's his expense. Budd set up another kind of business. If a workmate was in need of a set square and couldn't afford one from the stores, he moved in. He would sidle up and quietly say that he had some second-hand squares for sale, which had been given to him by an uncle and were in good condition. If the lad showed interest, he was invited over to his bench and shown the squares, which were usually still in their original boxes. His prices were not much less than the cost of new ones and there was usually a bit of half-hearted haggling. After having been solemnly assured that the squares were kosher, the deal was struck. The buyer would pay for his square, with interest added on, over an agreed period of a few weeks.

Budd steadily acquired a stock of good quality, second-hand tools and no matter what was wanted, he could supply it. His stock was maintained from a number of sources. If he had a need for a particular tool, he would tell his supplier(s) and, in due course, it became available, having almost certainly been 'liberated' from elsewhere in the Yard. Ultimately, his greed for ever increasing returns was his undoing; a small set of chrome-vanadium spanners was his nemesis. A light-fingered Matey had seen them lying on a workbench on a Destroyer, pocketed them and quickly left the scene. The Matelot reported his loss through the Ship's office to the Dockyard Police. An informant blabbed after he was offered the spanners by the felon, but couldn't afford the price demanded. They had eventually come down to Budd.

He somehow learned that he was being watched and prudently disposed of them. One morning, everyone was told to stand by their benches and a search was made of the shop. After the Instructors had gone through their charges' drawers and tool boxes, they concluded that there were no stolen tools in their domain. Budd had got away with it by the skin of his teeth, and his dealing ended. It wasn't in his nature to lie-low for long and he was soon involved in another cunning stunt. Despite the dire warnings about the buying and selling of meal vouchers, he got involved. Yet again, Management became aware of what was going on and Budd had to accept that the profits gained were not worth the risks involved. He was a natural born entrepreneur and, if there was money to be made with minimal effort and an acceptable level of risk, then he was all for it.

An amusing tale came from Stan, a lad who lived a couple of miles away from Mike. He told his mates that a middle-aged woman in his village had been 'taking the local lads in hand'. His proud boast that had 'lost his cherry' to the randy lady immediately sent him up in their esteem. A social evening, or dance, was held in the village hall once a fortnight and the younger generation always spent part of the evening larking about outside. When inside the hall, they were under the beady eyes of either their parents or neighbours, which always 'cramped their style'.

When she was on the prowl, Mrs H would slip out of a side-door and if a suitable 'victim' was available, he would be led down the side of the tennis courts for a little bit of fun. Her forays had initially been confined to the more mature lads, but in time, she took to initiating the younger ones as well. Once she had had her way with a lad, she swore him to secrecy, and then promptly lost interest in him.

With so many of the youngsters aware of her depredations, it was perhaps odd that she was never taken to task. Despite having promised not to say anything, her victims always discussed their trysts with their pals. Some of the girls sniffily said that it was disgusting, but no one ever complained about his initiation, because it was generally agreed that the lady was providing a valuable service. There was though a suspicion that Stan had not been entirely truthful in his account. Someone suggested it would be a good idea to go to the next dance as a group, which he instantly rejected. His spluttering reaction confirmed that he had been having them on and he ruefully admitted his downfall was all in his imagination.

Friction and discord was the norm in most families in the village. A father would maintain his dominance by exacting violence on his wife, sons and in some cases, his daughters as well. He was free with his fists or his leather belt, sometimes with the buckle-end being used to quell any challenge. Some families suffered great hardship, due to their fathers spending so much of their money on drink. When in his cups, father would often be in an ugly mood and clearly looking for trouble. All hell would break loose until he had vented his spleen' and gone to sleep it off. More problems arose if he also had a gambling habit. The families so afflicted would regularly lose what little money they had and his wife would have to resort to desperate means to keep her family together. With so much hardship about, it was little wonder that their children often grew up into anti-social adults.

Life in the fifties was so very different from how it is now. Until a lad was eighteen, he was very much answerable to his parents as to where he went, what he did and who he did it with. From then on, their control was gradually relaxed, though there was always the prospect of him getting into trouble. Like Mike's parents, a lot were keen be shut of their sons as soon as possible. They would be constantly encouraged to settle down, with a nice girl and hopefully, wedding bells would ring before they reached their twenty-first birthdays. However, an increasing number of lads refused to conform to their parents' wishes.

A daughter was even more closely controlled and it often lasted right up until she got married. Her parents would be very anxious that she shouldn't miss the boat and if she wasn't going steady by her eighteenth birthday, they wanted to know why. If she hadn't tied the knot by her twenty-first, there was often real concern that she might be left on the shelf. Career girls were rare, but with the economy rapidly improving, some young lasses were increasingly determined to do their own thing. If they were bright, they would leave home and go away to college, take up nursing or join the Armed Forces. Some lasses though endured a miserable existence, which was only brought to an end when they married. They often 'jumped out of the frying-pan into the fire'.

The line between petting and outright passion has always been very fine and when forbidden, its attractions are magnified and much more pleasurable. Like anything so eminently enjoyable, pre-marital sex carried the risk of a penalty, which could be both onerous and painful. It was especially so in the days before the efficient means of contraception became readily available. The results of illicit liaisons were all too plain to see and many girls went off to the Church or Registry Office with a bun in the oven. Despite their constant vigilance, some families watched helplessly as their daughters fell, one by one, into the honey-trap that led to an early marriage.

Margaret lived a few doors away from Mike and there was no end of malicious gossip, when it became known that she was in trouble. Whenever asked out by a local lad, she had always declined, saying she had things to do. Since leaving school, she had made a sustained effort to better herself, by working hard and passing secretarial examinations in shorthand and typing. She enjoyed rapid progress in the Insurance Company for which she worked. When still only nineteen years of age, she became the Managing Director's Secretary, a position of great responsibility. Her parents boasted about the long hours that she worked and how very well paid she was and everyone agreed she was very much to be admired. As well as being bright and industrious, she had grown into a very attractive and confident young woman.

What had started as a good turn in taking her home after working late had changed when her boss regularly parked his car in a gateway on the outskirts of the village. Nothing is secret for long in a small community and people were soon talking about what was going on. It was hard to believe just how silly Margaret was by doing it on her own doorstep. The outcome of their trysts was devastating and when it came, there was little sympathy for her predicament. When she told her lover she was pregnant, he promptly dispensed with her services and 'buggered-off'. What had been a bright, vibrant young woman became an object of disdain and some pity.

The lasses that walked up the aisle, allegedly 'unblemished', inevitably adopted a superior attitude to those that had 'fallen'. It mattered not that they had been regularly indulging in the forbidden fruits in the months leading up to their marriage. Most engaged couples did what came naturally and few could honestly say that they had abstained. Often, a new hubby would have his leg rigorously pulled by his mates for 'sampling the goods before buying'. The received wisdom was that it was a lot better before marriage than after. The arrival of the first child was broadly held to be an effective means of contraception. One recalls a wit saying that if newlyweds set up a blackboard and chalked up a mark every time they had it in their first year, they would spend the rest of their married lives wiping them off.

Chapter 14

Sporting Life

Britain has always been a sport-loving Nation and in the years that followed the War, we enjoyed considerable, though diminishing success in International competition. By 1953, numerous other Countries were challenging for the honours and we suffered many defeats on the field of play. On occasions, out teams failed to achieve, equal and maintain the best standards of performance in most major sports. Our few successes were due to the natural talent and personal commitment and dedication of our sportsmen and women who sacrificed everything to achieve the ever-rising levels of excellence needed to compete on the World stage. There had to be reasons for our spiral of decline and there was much speculation in the press as to what they were. It had to be more than the impoverished state of the economy and while the reasons proffered varied greatly, one stood out like a sore thumb.

Despite the social changes, there was still a hard core of profound snobbery and exclusivity present in so many of our sports. It was to be many years before the problem diminished to a tolerable level. In other Countries, if a person had potential, he or she was given every facility to develop and attain the highest standards. Many countries thought that sporting success enhanced their National image, particularly Australia, New Zealand and the United States of America. The pursuit of excellence of the Soviets and the 'East European block' was still some way off, but the early signs of their determination were becoming evident. For many years, we ignored the pressing need to change and we failed to match their progress. Their success and our lack of it would in time make it imperative to follow their example and slowly but surely, we started along the hard road of change.

Football, or soccer, was our most popular sport, but the steady decline from our pre-eminent position before the War was clear. The league clubs were well supported, but the money pouring into their coffers was not always re-invested. The grounds were antiquated, with only basic facilities being provided for players and fans. Modernisation/redevelopment became a matter of urgent necessity. The Chairmen and Directors lined their pockets and the players were paid what could only be described as a pittance. The standard of football played was declining and interest in the game had started to melt away. Nationally, we fell on hard times and other countries regularly demonstrated that we were no longer the top dogs. At the time of which we are writing, the Apprentices had no idea about what was happening and tended to see the early disasters as little more than temporary blips.

Football was their main interest, and it was indeed an obsession for some, with a large part of their working day spent discussing all aspects of the game. The fortunes of the big Clubs were closely followed and rarely did a discussion take place without spirited arguments. Some supported their local Club, which had only recently been elected to the Football League. There was rarely any trouble at matches, even though the spectators were crammed into the grounds. Despite the exploitation of the players, one or two of the lads had hopes of making the grade as Professional Footballers and were on the books of the various major Clubs. The majority just enjoyed the game and what they lacked in skill was made up for by their enthusiasm. During the dinner breaks, there was usually a kick-about outside the shop and if they didn't have a ball, some other suitable object would be found to kick around.

The home Nations, including France and Ireland, enjoyed considerable success on the Rugby field and there were many wonderful games. As today, the more consistent teams came from south of the equator; from Australia, New Zealand and South Africa. The larger English Clubs were exclusive and joining them was beyond the means of most young men. In Ireland, Scotland and Wales, there was a more enlightened attitude and working men played at all levels. A lot of the minor Clubs had difficulty in attracting sufficient players and their standard of play had markedly declined. The 'old school-tie' syndrome still prevailed, probably because the game was mostly played by public and grammar schools but by the mid-fifties, they were encouraging young men from all backgrounds to join their ranks.

The Cricket season was in full swing at the start of the first year and the Aussies were, as usual, causing us problems. There was always great excitement at the prospect of seeing Don Bradman, Lindsey Hassett and Ray Lindwall playing. Denis Compton, Len Hutton, Cyril Washbrook and Tom Graveney could turn an aggressive bat for England and our other heroes were Godfrey Evans and the young Colin Cowdrey. We also had very good bowlers, such as the Bedser twins and Trevor Bailey, who played consistently well. County cricket was very well supported and there were many elite Clubs right across the Country. However, an aspiring player's social standing was often more important than his ability, providing he could afford the considerable expense, which membership entailed.

Local Clubs organised gala festivals and weekends over the Bank Holidays, when they played teams from outside of the immediate area. Everything was done to ensure that they were shown in the best possible light and the pitch and outfield was carefully prepared. The pavilion was thoroughly cleaned and re-decorated and coloured lights and bunting completed the titivation. The members' 'ladies' attended to the catering and ensured that the visitors were well-fed. It was vital that they went away suitably impressed with their hosts' hospitality. During the matches, the nets would be opened to casual visitors, who would pay a small charge to either bat or bowl against the club's players. Occasionally, it would throw up a young man with potential and if he was deemed as acceptable, he would be invited for a trial.

Mark told his mates about how he had been sorely disappointed and it aptly demonstrated how the system operated. He had paid a shilling to bowl an 'over' and had set about making a fine impression. With his first ball, he took the batsman's middle stump out, much to the delight of those watching. The man loudly proclaimed it as a fluke and shaped up for the lad to bowl again. Two balls later, he was again clean-bowled and, after ribald comments from his team-mates, he walked away with a distinct lack of grace. The lad was duly invited to attend a practice session but despite having been invited by the Captain, he had felt uncomfortable throughout the evening.

The following Sunday, he was asked to score, as the regular man hadn't turned up. He was pleased to oblige, seeing it as a fortuitous means of entry through the hallowed doors of the pavilion. He drooled at the thought of enjoying tea with the players, but it was not to be. When the umpires lifted the bails, he made to follow them into the building, only to find an elderly gentleman barring his way.

'Where do you think you're going?' he demanded, and before the lad had time to reply, he said crossly, 'Go on, clear off, we don't want your sort in here.'

Mark tried to explain that he was the scorer and had been invited in by the Captain, but to no avail, the old boy was adamant that his entry was denied. He felt both anger and deep disappointment at his treatment as he walked away. A week or so later, he was stopped in the village by the Captain and given a right bollocking for letting the club down. When asked why he had done so, he told him that he had been stopped from going into the pavilion by Major 'W' and, being very upset, he had gone home. The Captain apologised and said it was high time that someone sorted the old bugger out. It turned out some time later that the 'Major' was a fraud, having not attained a commissioned rank in the Army. He had been a Sergeant Clerk in the headquarters of his Regiment and had not seen any overseas service. Not long after, he left the village.

The exclusive policy of the Club in Mike's village inevitably led to anti-social behaviour and the local youths often were a nuisance during matches. Their noisy fooling about and vandalism caused no end of bother. One prank, which caused great annoyance, was when the heavy roller was trundled across the outfield and left in the centre of the carefully prepared wicket, which left a large indentation. Another time, they removed key nuts and bolts from the sight-screen, so that when it was moved into position for the next match, it collapsed. A group of dolts copiously and naturally watered one end of the pitch one evening, having read that a damp patch would greatly assist the bowlers. The members didn't bother with the local Bobby to 'sort-out' the troublemakers and they were duly chastised.

During one game, some youngsters were larking about on the boundary and there was anger and irritation among the other spectators. Ultimately, they were told to keep it down or leave. All was quiet for a while until a small mongrel came among them. He was teased and became excited, with a lot of yapping and growling and trying to 'nip' his tormentors. One of the lads was quietly snoozing with his head on his girlfriend's lap and the mutt went over to them. After sniffing the recumbent lad, he cocked his leg and urinated on him. His mate, who was lying prone nearby, was helpless with laughter and rolling about on the grass. Much to the delight of everyone else, the dog then went over and peed on him as well. At that point the official came over again and they were escorted off the ground.

A lad told his mates that when he had first come to the village, he was given an old racket and a few balls by a neighbour. Being keen, he went to see the lady that ran the Tennis Club and she kindly gave him and some other children basic coaching. Her husband died soon after and when she left the village, the Club folded. It re-opened the following summer, when some newcomers started it up again. When the children asked if they could join, they were snottily told that membership was by invitation only and in the ensuing weeks, they regularly barracked the players on the courts, most of who were from 'away'. Although the land had been given to the village some years before, the committee adamantly maintained that they had the right to choose their members. The ensuing dispute got out of hand and after furious arguments, the Club again folded and the courts again fell into disuse.

Had the parents, who were so critical and vociferous in their criticism, offered to contribute to the cost of running the Club or helped with the maintenance? Like cleaning the changing rooms, mowing the grass, marking out and tidying the courts, weeding the paths, mending the fences? Did their children have proper rackets and balls and proper kit? The answer to all these points was an emphatic 'no', but the complainants insisted that they had been acting on principle. As if! The ones that had made the most noise had had no intention of paying subscriptions, or of doing anything to support the Club. They had caused the argument, either to try to get 'something for nothing' or just to cause mischief.

Athletics had always been the pastime of the 'well-off', but there was a more progressive attitude coming into being. Young people were increasingly encouraged to succeed, on the track and field. Having both talent and commitment, they were often given financial help to train and thereby improved their performances. Despite the decline of sport in the Schools, we managed to produce a steady but small stream of World and Olympic champions. In due course, very many of our top athletes would come from the ethnic minorities, most of whom succeeded by their own sheer effort and determination. However, over the last fifty years, it hasn't helped that Local Authorities have regularly sold off their playing fields, even when the land had been generously given to the community by long-dead benefactors.

For most people, their only access to the Golf Clubs was when they walked on the rights of way which crossed the fairways. As with the Cricket Clubs, their kids often caused great annoyance to the golfers. Membership was for the select, affluent few and the Clubs remained bastions of exclusivity for many years. That situation no longer applies and if anyone wishes to play golf and can afford the expense of playing regularly, then membership is widely available. A lot of young people play golf, some of whom achieve very low handicaps, which indicates just how things have changed. As a result, the general standard of play has improved considerably and only a small number of Clubs remain exclusive. The last hurdle has to be with full membership status for women and the wheel is turning inexorably towards equality.

As today, there was no shortage of 'expert' opinion in the media on all aspects of the failure of British sport. Individuals, who had never achieved anything of note, regularly wrote highly critical articles about what was wrong. They were adamant that there would not be any improvement until we completely changed our teaching and training methods. Schoolteachers were already becoming increasingly reluctant to devote their time to sports and the problem appertained right across the board. How to halt the ever increasing spiral of decline was a matter of considerable concern. Little has changed.

Chapter 15

Youthful Misdemeanours

Earlier reference has already been made to the criminal tendencies of some of the villagers. Most of it was no more than petty theft, which to some extent supplemented their meagre incomes. A young lad called Maurice, or 'Morry', as he was better known, bought some cheap chickens from a man in another village and he waxed eloquent as he excitedly told his pals that they were 'on the point of lay'. Fresh eggs were relatively expensive and a number of the villagers kept a few hens. A local farmer and his men had recently been busy in the nearby woods, their intention being to contain the pheasants that he had reared. Through the winter, 'shoots' would be held on his land, which would give him much-needed income. With the accommodation of his birds in mind, Morry embarked on a campaign of systematic pilfering.

Soon after the enclosure had been completed, he and his brother moved in and they dismantled and carried away a fifty-yard length of chicken wire fencing, including the supporting posts and wire. They had already 'knocked up' a hen-house, from the remains of a neighbour's old garden shed and a few wooden planks and some roofing felt, which they had purloined from a building site on the edge of the village. They duly put the run up and when it was finished, it looked a 'puckah' job. To add insult to injury, the thieving sods then helped themselves to corn, which had been left in a bin in the woods for feeding the pheasants.

While most of the people knew what he had done, Morry was not called to account for his larceny. He was a shiftless individual and with his chickens not laying, he soon lost interest and sold them on. The hen house and the run were duly disposed of as a job lot and he even managed to sell the surplus wire-netting and posts. The proceeds didn't fully compensate him for all the effort he had put in but, as he nonchalantly said, he had still made a few bob out of it.

He later committed another crime, which had serious ramifications for the whole village. One afternoon, he ambled down to the Post Office/shop, which was approximately a mile away. While hanging around outside, an Army Dispatch Rider pulled up and left his motorcycle on the stand, with the engine ticking over. Probably without much thought, Morry climbed on to the machine and rode off, hotly pursued for a few yards by the frantic Squaddie. Knowing all the tracks and footpaths in the area, he by-passed the village and took the bike to the top of the hill. There, he dumped it in a ditch, covered it with brushwood and walked home. On the way, he passed the time of day with the Constable, who was standing outside the main gate of the Depot. The Officer later confirmed to the Civil Police that he had seen and spoken to Morry, which effectively gave the lad an alibi.

For some days, the area was crawling with the Civil and Military Police, who were looking for the missing machine. Their enquiries drew a blank, because no one had a clue as to what Morry had done. The first that Mike knew about it was when the lad called at his house to ask if he knew anything about four-stroke engines. The engine on the bike had been in good working order, but after a bit of tinkering, he had been unable to start it. Having sworn Mike to secrecy, they walked up the hill to look at the machine. After Mike had reset the timing, he soon had the engine running smoothly again. Grinning slyly, Morry tried to persuade 'his old mate to lend him a couple of bob', to buy some petrol.

Being mindful of the risks of getting involved with him, Mike declined to cough up and the ingratiating smile promptly vanished and he was angrily warned 'to keep his mouth shut'. A week or so later, the sound of an engine was again heard in the woods and Mike and his mate went to investigate. Morry and his brother had cleared a circular track and were having great fun in furiously riding the bike around it. It had been painted silver and with the number plates and mud-guards removed, it was hard to recognise it as the missing machine. The brothers were far from pleased to see their visitors, but the clown was quick to seize an opportunity. He again suggested that a contribution towards the cost of the sorely needed petrol would be rewarded with 'goes on the bike'.

Mike again refused, saying he wanted nothing to do with it. The brothers regularly rode the machine in the woods until one day, it was driven into a tree and that was the end of their fun and games. The Authorities never did learn of its fate. Mike's workmates were firmly of the view that the Dispatch Rider merited sympathy, because he had probably been court-martialled for losing the machine. The villain who had stolen both the fencing and the motorbike was eighteen years old and came from a relatively well-off family. Both he and his brother were seen as a bad lot by a lot of the adults in the village and were disliked by most of the youngsters. He was rarely called to account for his antisocial stunts.

The lad was a talented musician and his mother, thinking perhaps to divert him from mischief, bought him a piano. A young lady was engaged to give him lessons. He quickly became very adept on the keyboard and was soon playing popular songs and melodies in the Working Man's Club. He was very much in demand, seemingly being able to play any piece of music which he'd heard on the radio. A 'wag' joked that when he asked him if he knew 'his flies were undone', Morry had replied that if he hummed it, he would play it! Many thought his musical talent was wasted on such a worthless individual.

It wasn't long before he had a serious problem, which came from the generosity of his audiences. Through an evening, pints of bitter would be lined up along the top of the piano by a succession of happy punters. However, Morry's capacity for alcohol was limited and it became a matter of great amusement to bet on how long he would last. Wagers were made as to when his playing would deteriorate and the time he would fall off of his stool. When drunk, he could be both aggressive and 'maudling' and he inevitably complained loudly that everyone was against him. In the end, he would burst into tears, be violently sick and be put out of the door by the people that had hired him.

His family also complained that he hadn't been paid, ignoring the fact that he had ruined the evening for many of the revellers. While his behaviour was hilarious to some, the social evenings often ended with angry confrontations. Soon after his twenty-first birthday and amid great celebrations by his family, he got married. It lasted only a few weeks. Despite having dodged his National Service, he then joined the Army, and his parents boasted proudly that 'it would make a man of him'. Within weeks, he was discharged and he returned to the village as if nothing of any consequence had happened. Social scientists would have a name for his problems, but most people thought that he was little more than 'a pain in the arse'.

Hostility had always prevailed between the young men who lived in the surrounding villages, particularly at dances. They were not all blessed with common sense and from time to time, someone would get into trouble. An unusual incident involved Alan, whose father's farm was a couple of miles from Mike's village. Having been given a car for his eighteenth birthday, he was greatly envied but, he was adamant in his refusal to allow any of the local lads in it. One evening, just after the pubs closed, he had an accident and put his car in a ditch. He was well and truly 'sozzled' and could hardly stand and when the Sergeant arrived on the scene, he was very solicitous and gruffly ordered the crowd of onlookers to clear off. In due course, he took the lad home.

Alan was not prosecuted and that caused great indignation in the village. A local man had recently been prosecuted for riding his bike without lights and fined ten shillings (50p). It was a clear example of how there was one form of justice for the rich and one for the poor. Not long after, a more serious incident occurred, which involved some of the village youths. The local Bobby had not long come into the area and right from the off, he had clearly had a point to make. He antagonised a lot of people, including some of the residents who prided themselves on being law-abiding citizens. His aggressive, ill-humoured behaviour particularly upset the young men and when he verbally chastised them for hanging around one evening, they decided to teach him a lesson.

Later that week, they set up an ambush, by tying-off a rope at chest height between two trees across the road. After draping a handkerchief across it, they made off through the woods. A few minutes later, there was a loud crash as the Officer skidded and came off his bike. They were all safely indoors by the time the proverbial hit the fan. Luckily, he wasn't hurt, because he had seen the obstruction in time and had avoided it. He summoned the assistance of his Sergeant and they went straight away to apprehend one of the suspected culprits. In their haste, they accused the wrong person. His family and a neighbour, who was in the house when they arrived, insisted that their lad had not been out that evening and could not have been part of the mischief.

The Sergeant apologised, then asked him if he had any idea who might have been responsible and that gave his father the opportunity for which he had been waiting. He complained at length about the aggressive nastiness of the Constable and cited several recent incidents as examples of his harassment of the village youths. The Sergeant was taken aback at his vehemence and left with the assurance that he would look into the matter.

He must have done so, because the Constable was moved on to another area not long after. While one could not condone antagonism and violence, particularly towards the Police, the incident demonstrated a clear need for sensitivity in their relations with the public. Even today, that is not always so. The Sergeant had a very different attitude and patrolled the area for some weeks after in his car. If there was a problem, he dealt with it in a firm, quiet way, without any drama or threats. While always courteous, he enjoyed the reputation of being 'hard but fair' and no one took liberties. Another example of his discretion arose out of an altercation between some lads on a Sunday afternoon.

A Farmer's son, Martin, was out shooting rabbits with a pal on his father's land, which lay close by the village. When asked what he was going to do when he left school, he had smugly replied that he was going to 'help his father run the farm'. That caused no end of amusement and the village lads taunted him for being 'cheap labour'. Hard work was not one of his strong points and if he could avoid it, he happily did so. Despite the many changes and improvements in agriculture, a lot of the Farmers were still working manually on their land. Not all of them were well-off and some continually struggled to eke out a living. His was said to be strapped for cash, because he had recently paid-off a couple of his hands, which had caused a lot of resentment.

The trouble arose when Keith and a mate realised that their dog, a mongrel which they affectionately described as a 'Manchester Terrier', was missing. Only very rarely did he wander off and hearing gunshots in the field, they were concerned for his safety. They ran over to the road and found him cowering in the ditch. They picked him up, looked him over and were relieved that he was unhurt. An examination of the hedge revealed gunshot damage and they assumed that whoever was in the field had deliberately shot at their dog. As they walked back along the road, they were confronted by the two 'hunters', who came through a hole in the hedge.

'Is that bloody dog yours?', demanded Martin, with his habitual sneer, to which Keith replied that it was. 'We've got the right to shoot any dog that worries our stock,' Martin told him. 'If I see him in our field again, I'll shoot him.'

'Like hell you will' Keith shouted angrily. 'You do and I'll have you, you bastard. How can he worry your stock if there isn't any in the field?'

Martin must have realised his mistake in confronting the lads and in his confusion, he had raised the gun and pointed it at his adversary. Keith was alarmed and wrenched it away from him and on 'breaking' it, he was horrified to find it was loaded. He ejected the cartridges then in blind anger, he smashed the butt on the road and threw the main pieces over the hedge. He then went for Martin, but was pulled away by his mate. Martin backed off and after hastily picking-up the debris, he and his mate beat a hasty retreat through the hedge and made off across the field.

An hour or so later, the Sergeant turned up at Keith's house. Keith explained that he and his mate were on their way home with their dog, when they were stopped by Martin. In the ensuing argument, he had pointed a shotgun at him.

When he took it from him, he had found it was loaded and in his anger, he had smashed it. The Sergeant had been given a different story by Martin, which had been corroborated by his friend. He said that they had been walking down the road and had been set on by the two lads and Keith had destroyed the gun out of spite. The Farmer had demanded that they be charged with assault and criminal damage.

Keith's father pointed out that the incident had taken place on a public road and that a number of offences had been committed. A sixteen year old boy couldn't hold a shotgun licence and having a loaded gun in a public place and pointing at someone were both serious offences. He had also discharged it through the hedge and could well have injured a passer-by on the road. If any charges were to be brought, they should be on the Farmer and his son.

Nothing was heard about the incident until a week later, when the Sergeant called to say that no further action would be taken. Martin's friend had changed his story, after having been reminded that lying about what had happened was a very serious matter. His revised account had confirmed what Keith had said. He had then spoken to the Farmer and made his own responsibilities clear. It had been agreed that his son would not be allowed to go out shooting unsupervised in the future. Keith's father was angry that it had all been so conveniently covered up, because had his lad and his mate been the miscreants, the Sergeant would have had them in court. In fact, the Officer had dealt with a difficult situation with his usual tact. To have made an issue out of what had been a spat between the young lads would not have been in anyone's interest.

Chapter 16

The Ultimate Trade Test

With the 'E' plates completed, many of the lads had time on their hands and they looked for ways in which to gainfully pass the time. Charlie suggested they should make another plate, with a letter 'H' in it. To save time, they shouldn't bother to dress the edges and faces of the plate. His other suggestion was to do a more difficult job, by cutting-out and fitting a hexagon instead. That would be a little more challenging, particularly if the plug was fitted in all possible ways. Nearly half of the apprentices chose and finished the easier option and thus gained yet more valuable experience in good fitting practice.

One morning, Charlie announced that the time had come for them take the end of year trade test. Everyone gathered around a large drawing as he explained what was required. The test piece was to be made up of a block, strap, and gib and cotter arrangement. The strap would be a square, horse-shoe shape, with internal slots to accommodate the block inside it. A square hole would then be cut at right-angles through the two pieces, to allow the gib and cotter to be inserted. They would each have a five degree taper on their contact faces, to provide a means of locking when the whole piece was put together. The arrangement had many uses, in steam engines and other engineering applications and the test would be a true reflection of their skills.

'Right, you lot,' he cried, 'this looks a lot harder than it is. If you go about it in the right way, you'll do it with no bother at all. Now, I'm going to remind you of my basic rules. Never mind jeering,' he shouted impatiently at his interrupters. I know I'm repeating myself, but it's hand-tools only, apart from the drilling. We don't want any cunning stunts or crafty wheezes, because we've seen them all before. If you're caught acting the crack, or cheating, for want of a better word, then you'll lose marks. We'll be keeping a close watch to ensure that everything is above board and done proper, so watch it. There'll be no messing around or interfering with other people who want to get on. Anyone that steps out of line will answer to me.'

'Straight up to Mr Barry,' a lad quipped to a great roar of laughter.

'Yeh and you'd better believe it, cocker,' replied Charlie hotly. 'This is your trade test, so put your backs into it. When you've finished, your pieces will be marked by other instructors, to ensure that everything is fair and above board. I can't say better than that, can I? Right-oh, back to your benches and get on with it.'

He had not spoken to them like that for quite some time and they soon settled down. Over the next couple of weeks, the shop was quiet and there was a definite air of determination abroad. There was still some idle chatting and banter, but the instructors were constantly moving among them and were quick to subdue any frivolity. There was a job to be done and it had to be done right.

The pieces of mild steel to be used for the straps, had been machined to close tolerances, which meant only minimal work had to be done on the external faces. In checking the square and flatness of the adjoining faces, they still mimicked their instructors' gestures, which caused some hilarity among them. There was a lot of exaggerated holding-up of pieces and flourishing of set-squares, as individuals expressed their satisfaction at the way the job was progressing. Some tried to hide their frustration by making stupid comments and despite Charlie's warnings, there were the odd noisy arguments.

'Come on, you lot, keep it down. Let's get on with it, shall we?' the instructors shouted.

A lot of metal had to be to cut out from the centre of the strap and an impatient queue was soon waiting to use the drilling machine. There had to be other ways of doing it. Mike made a series of cuts down through the metal with his hacksaw; a laborious chore, but it had its advantages. By using rough-toothed blades and working steadily, it saved a lot of time. There was less metal to file away than if he had used the drill. Only a single hole was needed in each corner and the leaves of metal were easily broken away. He completed the face across the bottom with ease. When asked by an Instructor as to why he had done the job in that manner, he explained his reasoning, which was accepted. Whatever impediments arose, the lads had to use their ingenuity to legitimately overcome them.

The next step was to make the block and fit it into the strap and it was hard work to reduce the faces, to enable the two pieces to be brought together. Then the slot was formed to accommodate the gib and cotter. Due to the small size of the hole, it was even more difficult and many days of tedious work passed before it was completed. Some lads had their own micrometers and no longer had to rely on the communal instruments, as supplied by the Instructors. They were often tampered with, which as usual led to noisy arguments. It was particularly annoying when a lad didn't notice what had been done and his work was adversely affected.

'Private' instruments had still to be securely locked away and were rarely lent to anyone else. It was seen as mean by the ones who could not afford to buy them, but that was their hard luck because looking after one's own interests was essential. With the slot completed, the fabrication of the gib and cotter followed. A four inch long plug was made from a piece of bar then, after it was fitted in the hole, it was carefully cut through the middle to achieve the matching five degree angles on the contact faces. In a modern workshop, such painstaking fitting is not needed. A laser machine can cut a hole through a block of steel more accurately and infinitely quicker than by hand.

All that remained was to finally close-fit the pieces into a composite unit and finish off the external surfaces. Some lads finished well ahead of their mates and spent the remainder of the time titivating their work. At 14.00 hours on the final day, Charlie came out into the shop and brought a most welcome end to the proceedings. Despite all the pessimism, which had been so evident at the start, the majority of the lads had completed the test within the allotted time. Those that hadn't put on brave faces and covered their shortcomings with an air of indifference.

The test pieces were collected up and labelled, with the owner's name and number applied in indelible ink, then taken away for marking. A week later, the results were pinned up outside the caboosh. After all the histrionics that the lads had endured in doing the test, it was an anti-climax. The Instructors stood back and watched with sardonic grins as the lads pushed and shoved to find out how well, or badly, they had done. Having been increasingly concerned about his problems of the past year, Mike was very surprised to find that he had done much better than he could possibly have expected. It was a mystery, particularly when he was unsure as to whether or not he wanted to carry on with his Apprenticeship.

Nearly two weeks remained before the annual shut-down for the Summer holiday and the days were spent in a relaxed atmosphere. Some passed the time in cleaning the contents of their tool-boxes, but most were content take things easy. A succession of long, sunny days ensued and much enjoyment was had sitting on the river wall during the breaks. Charlie spent a lot of his time in the Factory, probably writing up their annual reports. After dinner on the last day, he called everyone together and with no little sense of drama, he handed each lad his test piece. The instructors then discussed how individuals had either gained or lost marks. After the break, the shop was tidied and swept out and when it was to his satisfaction, Charlie again called them together.

'Right, you lot,' he shouted, smiling broadly. 'I've got one or two things to say, before you go off on your holidays. When you come back, you'll be leaving our tender, loving care and we will be more than happy to see the last of you. Let me give you a word of warning. Just because you've had it nice and easy with us, don't think it's going to be the same with your new Instructors. They'll have different ways of working, to keep you in order, so you'll have to watch it. Not everybody's as easy going as us.'

His humour was rewarded with a loud roar of laughter and ribald comments. After again calling for silence, he continued.

'Alright, alright, keep it down. As I was just going to say before I was so rudely interrupted, when you come back, you'll be moving over to the second year Apprentices' fitting shop, alongside the Factory.'

'Bloody good job too,' shouted someone, who was loudly cheered for his cheek.

Others pretended to cry, with exaggerated wipes at their eyes with grubby handkerchiefs. There was a lot of noise and comments about how glad they would be to see the last of the old bugger.

'Now then, you cheeky sods,' he shouted. 'As I was just going to tell you, you'll clock-on here when you come back. After the Timekeeper has confirmed everyone is all present and correct, you'll move your gear over to your new shop and you'll report to Mr Thompson, who is your new senior instructor. One last thing and I'm serious for a moment. The last year has been very enjoyable, despite all your buggering about and getting us into all sorts of trouble. We hope that you'll make the most of our training and come to appreciate everything you've learnt. We've put in a lot of effort into trying to make you into some sort of tradesmen, so we hope it hasn't all been in vain.'

The lads could hardly believe that the dewy-eyed old bugger was the same man who had spent the first couple óf months continually shouting and threatening them. Queues formed to thank each Instructor and then to more loud cheers, Charlie made his time-honoured cry for the last time.

'Right you lot, overalls off,' he cried and in response to his charges' back-chat, he shouted, 'Don't do anything I wouldn't do in the next couple of weeks.'

There was the usual melee at the basins as the lads washed their hands, though there was none of the nastiness that had been prevalent in the past. They were in the best of spirits and excited about their forthcoming holiday. For most, going away was way beyond their means, but that didn't matter. With the past week's pay and two further weeks of holiday money in their pockets, they had some money to spend.

As he cycled home, Mike thought about how the first year had gone. After his early problems, he had settled down and the recent trade-test had confirmed that he had the ability to qualify as a fitter. The academic side had been little short of a disaster and he had totally lost interest in his studies. Living at home was his main problem and he had thought many times about moving out. Apart from a few short visits, his brother had not lived there since he'd left school. Mike knew that he wouldn't be able to leave for some time and the fact was, he had nowhere else to go. He was still dependent on his parents and that wouldn't change for at least a couple of years. Their demands for him to leave had come out of their chronic lack of money and one less mouth to feed would have improved their lot considerably.

He had been told many times by his mates that he should have buggered off long since, which was easy for them to say. They could not possibly imagine how bad it had been. All he could do was to save as much as he could over the next few years, then find a place of his own. It would be a long haul, but it would give him something to look forward to. In the meantime, he would just have to put up with all the unpleasantness and avoid the confrontations as much as possible. The one positive thing was that following their last bust-up, his father had stopped assaulting him, but it hadn't stopped him from regularly threatening the lad. The ill-treatment of his childhood had though taken its toll and it had turned Mike into a selfish, introverted youth, who was instinctively hostile to most of the people he met.

Book 2: The Second Year

Chapter 1

A New Dimension

When the lads returned to work after their holiday, they clocked-on, then sat quietly on their toolboxes to await their Instructors' pleasure. The time-keeper slowly ambled across to the caboosh to report that they were all present and correct. The only person late that morning was Charlie, their senior instructor. It was more than half an hour before he came hurrying into the shop, red in the face and looking exceedingly harassed. He was greeted with loud cheers from both ends of the shop, despite his shouts to keep it down. The lads were itching to be off and after a short discussion with his Colleagues, Charlie came out and stood on a wooden crate to address them.

'Right you lot, pay attention,' he cried. 'Alright, alright, keep silence,' he added angrily, in response to their ribald jeers.

When he had their attention, he gave them their instructions, preceded and interrupted by the usual throat clearing and self-conscious coughing.

'As I told you before you went off on your holidays, you're going to move over to the shop in the annex on the side of the Factory. You'll be working there for the next three months or so. Outside, you'll find some hand trolleys, which you can use to take your personal effects over and when you arrive, you'll report to Mister Thompson, who is your new Senior Instructor. That's it, so bugger off. Don't leave anything behind and remember, no messing about on the way.'

Gone was the soppy sentimentality of a fortnight before. As to be expected, their admonition about not messing about had fallen on deaf ears. All sorts of shenanigans took place on the way up the road, with toolboxes falling from upset carts and loud altercations. One group fell afoul of a Policeman, who took grave exception to their larking about and he sternly lectured them before sending them on their way. The more sensible ones ignored the boisterous antics of the minority and balanced their toolboxes on their bikes as they pushed them up the road. Others paired-up and carried them between them. When the early birds got there, their new Instructors were taking their ease in the office; a brick-built edifice with large windows and proper heating and lighting. They were miffed when told to wait out in the shop until everyone had arrived.

The Instructors were obviously easy-going and not given to constantly emphasising their authority. When the lads clocked -off at midday, they did so without supervision and on their return, it was the same. The afternoon passed in a very relaxed way and it was well after the tea break before Mr Thompson came out of the office and called for them to gather round. After he had introduced the other Instructors, he briefly outlined the work they would be doing, which was to refurbish all types of valves. The lectures, which had covered all manner of practical and theoretical instruction in their first year would be resumed, which was broadly welcomed.

The lads relished their new-found freedom and soon settled down. They were no longer subjected to the constant stream of orders and threats, to which they had previously become so accustomed. They were left very much to their own devices, with their Instructors sitting in their office for most of the day. In the mornings, it was rare for them to come out before 07.30 and sometimes, it was even later. It was the same at dinner time and the morning and afternoon breaks. With it all being so lax, some of them sloped off to see their mates or went for walks around the nearby dry-docks and basins. Someone had to be caught and one afternoon, two lads were brought back into the shop by a plain-clothes Policemen, who had 'h'apprehended' them over by the No. 2 basin'. With Tommo absent, one of the other Instructors had to sort it out.

'There's no problem,' he told the Officer. 'We sent these lads to pick up some internal mail from the main offices and they must have got lost.'

'Yeah, that's right,' said the brighter of the two wanderers. 'We turned left at the top of the road, instead of right like you told us. Sorry about that Sir.' He then turned to the Officer and said, 'We tried to explain that when you stopped us, but you wouldn't listen.'

The Officer replied that if that was the case, then there was no problem. However, he had to have the last word and solemnly reminded the Instructor about his responsibilities.

'You need to be more careful when you send lads out into the yard,' he said sonorously. It's a very dangerous place and they can soon get into serious trouble.'

Having said his piece, he left. Later, when Tommo came back, he came out of the office and called for the lads to gather round. He then set out the ground rules for going for a walk.

'Right lads,' he said, 'we only just got away with that, didn't we? We know you're bored with nothing to do, but it's not our fault. We ordered a supply of valves for you to start working on weeks ago, but they haven't arrived. Now, if any of you go out of the shop, keep a weather eye open for the Bobbies and don't get caught like those two silly sods today. You can easily spot the plain-clothes ones because they nearly always go around in pairs and wear 'gaberdine' raincoats. (also known as 'flasher-macs' in the vulgar vernacular). If they stop you, make out you're out on a job or failing that, run like hell in the other direction. Always carry a few bits and pieces in a tool-bag or box and have your excuse ready. Use your heads and most important, don't drop us in it. Life's too short for bloody scares like that.

The Instructors went back into their office and as they walked back down the shop, the lads discussed what had happened. Some couldn't believe how slack the supervision was, particularly after the iron rule of that old bugger Charlie. They agreed that the Instructor was right. No one wanted to spoil what was clearly a cushy number. It was hard doing nothing and the more industrious ones spent time polishing and making improvements to the tools they had made. Others went out on hunts to see what they could find. Some played cards or read, with one or two quietly studying. Tommo's advice was heeded and no one else was picked-up. A basic lesson had been learned which would stand them in good stead in the years to come. You didn't get punished for doing wrong, but you did for getting caught!

Towards the end of the second week, Tommo called half a dozen lads into his office to tell them about a memo he had received from the management. Due to their poor performance in the Dockyard School, they were to be given additional instruction in mechanical drawing. Mike was one who had failed miserably, having not always paid close attention to the Lecturer. Having started from scratch was the main reason, though he could have done much better. A Senior Draughtsman, from the main drawing office, was going to take the class and it was a valuable opportunity to make up for lost time.

The following Wednesday morning, they started their extra tuition and their Tutor introduced himself as 'Richard, or Dick to his friends'. He was a small, genial looking man, probably in his mid-forties and after telling them he would start from basics, he discussed his problems with each lad in turn. He was scathing about the Lecturer who, he said caustically, didn't know 'his ear from his elbow', or something like that. He had a supply of pencils, rubbers and basic materials and talked at length about their practical uses for different types of work. He showed them how to sharpen a pencil, saying that everyone should always have a pen-knife for that purpose. He stressed the importance of decent drawing instruments, which could be bought second-hand and cheaply from the drawing office. Mike's brother had recently suffered a financial crisis and he had conveniently relieved him of his instruments, which would be more than adequate for the job.

When explaining the need for a soft or delicate touch, an Engineer will often use the analogy of 'gently caressing' a part of a woman's anatomy. Dick did so and amused his pupils greatly in talking about 'the art of drawing'. He went on to explain the workings and functions of a drawing board and how to set it up to provide the necessary comfort in working. He demonstrated how to attach the sheet of paper to the board and listed the basic principles on a blackboard.

'Like anything else,' he said 'when you're interested in what you're doing, your time at work will always pass quickly.'

He brought the first session to an end just before the mid-day break. He told them that they would attend two morning sessions each week for the next month and he hoped they would benefit from his tuition. Their next one was to be on Friday morning, starting at nine o'clock sharp. When they came back into the shop after dinner, the re-action of their mates was mixed. Some took the superior view that they were thick sods, who weren't worth bothering about. Despite that, there was a fair bit of interest in what Dick had said, particularly that his talk had been very interesting. There had been no comparison with the instruction they had been given at the College. Could their crassness not have been the sole reason for their poor performance? Time would tell.

The lessons continued and were both interesting and beneficial and it was not long before they were showing a marked improvement. Dick covered all the basic techniques and they were soon exploring the complexities of third-angle projection. They drew various types of valves and he was both patient and encouraging in his tuition. He thought nothing of going over a particular point several times, if it was a problem. Their improvement was dramatic, though Dick laughingly said, 'they would never make 'draughtsmen'.

'Just remember,' he told them on the last day, 'always do your best and everything will be alright. Don't worry too much about it,' he said as an afterthought. 'If you're a practical man, then you only need to know the basics to enable you to pass your exams. To tell you the truth, I'm bloody hopeless at anything mechanical or doing jobs at home. When there is decorating to do or shelves to be put up, we have to pay someone to come in and do it. A skilled draughtsman is born to the job, with a natural eye for detail and an inherent sense of proportion and scale. He will have spent many years honing his skills and no matter how experienced he is, he learns something new every day. Isn't that the way of things in all walks of life?'

His pupils would in time have cause to be grateful to Dick for his patience and sensible advice.

Three large, wooden crates, which contained valves of various functions and sizes, were delivered to the shop for refurbishment. While the lack of work had at first been enjoyable, it hadn't been long before their enforced idleness had begun to pall and the lads had become increasingly restless. There was an immediate change in their moral and the contents were quickly 'sorted' into different categories. Tommo's helpers were chosen in the time-honoured Naval way, when his first request for help had fallen' on deaf ears.

'I said I wanted six volunteers,' he had called out loudly. 'Right then, I'll have you, you, you,' and so on.

Ribald comments were aimed at the lads who had been asked to help. The valves were sorted and those without labels were placed in separate piles. They were then broken down into groups of steam, water, oil and air valves, the details of each one being recorded on clipboards. Notes were added about the type, size, function and main dimensions. Other lads were told to make identification tallies and attach them to the handles of the unmarked valves. When they'd all been catalogued, the Instructors handed them out for refurbishment. There was a distinct reluctance to work on the fuel-oil valves as most of them were filthy, being liberally covered in dirt and black oil. However, the boss had already decided who would be doing what.

In contrast to the previous year, there were numerous tools in the form of spanners, hammers, cold-chisels and scrapers available. It wasn't long before the valves were being energetically stripped-down and the parts were laid out on the benches. The Instructors were just as pleased as their charges to be getting on. The air, water and lubricating-oil valves, a lot of which were made of brass or phosphor-bronze, gave the least problems. However, the steam-valves required a lot of hard work, because the fixings, i.e. nuts, bolts and washers, were mostly 'frozen', due to long-term exposure to high temperatures. They had to be chipped-off, by the use of the dreaded hammer and cold chisel and there were still the odd accidents, caused by careless blows to the heads of the chisels.

The fuel valves contained residual black and diesel oil. There was no problem in stripping one down but, if both flanges had been plugged, then when the cover-joint was broken, an inordinate amount of gunge poured out. Before long, those working on them were covered in the oil and smelt very strongly of it. The usual banter ensued, with silly comments being made about the state of their mates. Thinking that it might all get out of hand, Tommo intervened.

'It's alright lads,' he said, 'have your fun but it'll be your turn soon, so don't be too cocky.'

A forty-five gallon drum had been split in half down the middle, longitudinally and the halves were set up on trestles and partially filled with paraffin. Sacks of rags and cotton-waste were placed alongside, which provided the means of cleaning away the filth. Another drum was provided, complete with a large funnel, for the waste oil to be collected.

Chapter 2

Fun and Games

The foundry 'Messenger-boy' came into the shop twice a day to deliver internal mail and parcels. He was a tall, thin elderly man, with an unsmiling demeanour and he was often the butt of juvenile pranks. One wag likened the old lad to a 'split-pin', which amused his mates greatly. Ted was seen as an easy victim and it wasn't long before silly japes were played, like nipping outside and hiding his bike around the corner while he was in the office. The machine was a veritable beast, being of sturdy construction, with a large carrier affixed to the front. Ted worked very hard to ride it and was fortunate that his round was mostly on level ground. He wouldn't have had the strength to make it up any but the most gentle of slopes.

With their nonsense not having the desired effect, the clowns decided on more drastic action. A nearby dry-dock was full, awaiting the arrival of the next ship and two of them took his bike over and made to lower it on a rope into the water. Being happily engrossed in their prank, they didn't see him come out of the shop. Their mates, who were watching through the windows, saw Ted rapidly bear down on them and were powerless to warn them of the impending confrontation. Having tied off the bike, the pranksters only looked up when he was almost on top of them. One managed to jump clear and he scrambled away, but the other lad was too slow. Much to the delight of the audience, Ted kicked him hard on the top of his leg and left him writhing in agony on the ground. He then retrieved his bike and calmly wheeled it away. When the injured lad hobbled back into the Shop, he was met by one of the Instructors, who couldn't resist having a go at him.

'Now then, my old son,' he said with a grin, 'been having a bit of fun with old Ted have you? We should have told you that he's an old Marine and it's really best not to mess with him because he can get a bit stroppy when he's upset. Don't even think of complaining; you asked for it, so get back to your bench. Come on lads,' he shouted to the rest of the Apprentices, as he walked down the shop, 'the fun's over, so let's get on.'

Some people never learn. with painful lessons soon forgotten and the same mistakes are made, time and again. He or she will do the daftest thing and then blame someone else for their folly. Having been warned about Ted, the lads should have had the sense to leave him alone but, barely a week later, they were again up to their tricks, including the fool who had been so painfully chastised. Three of them went outside and loosened the nuts which secured his saddle, the wheels and the handlebars to the frame. When the old lad came out and got on his machine, it fell apart and dumped him on the ground. The clowns were well clear and luckily, the poor old lad was only shaken up by his fall. When he came back into the shop to complain, the Instructors sent the culprits out to re-assemble his machine.

A few days later, the same dolts had yet another go at the poor old sod outside of the foundry main-door. They somehow rendered his bike totally immobile; exactly how is lost in the mists of time. When he came out, he turned the bike to get on and found the pedals were jammed. The next morning, Tommo called everyone up to the front of the shop to tell them that he had received a snotty memo from the Foundry Manager about the damage to the bicycle. In making his point, he had noted that it was 'Admiralty Property'.

'When we get into trouble because you silly sods have been acting the goat, we draw the line,' he told them gravely. 'The Manager has demanded the names of those responsible, so they can be charged for either repairing or replacing the bike. I've a bloody good mind to tell him,' he went on, eyeing the culprits. 'Now, you've had your fun, so let that be the end of it. Just leave Ted alone or you'll have me to answer to.'

A few days later, when Ted arrived with the mail, he was mounted on a brand, spanking new bicycle, which was painted bright red. After carefully securing it with a padlock and chain, he came into the shop and balefully looked around, then went into the office. When he had gone, the Senior Instructor, who had walked to the door with him, turned and looked pointedly at his lads.

'Some good has come out of your stupid tricks,' he said loudly. 'Ted's been asking for a new bike for ages and now he's got one.'

Someone remarked he was sure 'Old Ted' had been smiling as he had slowly ridden away.

Jack lived about fifteen miles from the yard and one morning, he announced that he and his pals had joined the local Rugby Club. It caused a bit of a stir, because most of the lads had thought the game was not for the likes of them. Apparently, the Club had been having problems in putting out four sides each week. Mike had played rugby at school and had liked it more than football and after a discussion, he decided to go along to see a committee member who was an Estate Agent in the town. He was well-received and assured that he would be welcome to join the Club. There were a number of problems though, before he could do so, not least of which was the cost of buying the kit. There was also the annual subscription and a 'match fee' of half a crown each week, with a similar amount required for the beer kitty after the match. The cost of travelling to the ground and back meant that he would be very hard-pushed financially. There was no chance of any support from his parents and the first question his Mother asked, when he told her about it, added to his problems.

'Who's going to wash your kit? Don't expect me to do it,' she told him crossly.

Fortunately, the local farmer stopped Mike one evening to ask if he wanted to earn a bit of extra cash. Until recently, his son had been working on the Farm for not much more than his keep, which was not unusual. He had not applied to be excused from his National Service, as agricultural workers were entitled to be, and had opted to join the Royal Air Force on a three-year engagement. In normal times, his father managed to struggle along with three full-time labourers but, during hay-making and harvest times, he had to hire in additional labour. The loss of his son had created a problem, which was only partially resolved by Mike's pressing financial need. In the next month, by working most evenings and at weekends, he was able to put together sufficient funds to buy his kit.

The Club held their trials on the first Saturday in September and on the day, Mike met Jack in the town. When they arrived at the ground, they and a number of other lads changed and stood on the touchline. It was late on in the afternoon before they were given the chance to show what they could do. After being asked what position he played, which was either full-back or on the wing, Mike ran on to the field. It was all a bit chaotic, with most of the young lads having little idea of what the game was about. One of Mike's strengths was his ability to catch and kick the ball. At the end of the short game, the aspiring players were told that they would be informed if they were wanted in due course.

A post card duly arrived, which informed Mike that he had been selected to play for the 'B' fifteen. It was the junior side and he was pleased that he would know some of the other lads. His lack of cash and how it might stop him from playing was conveniently forgotten. On his way home one evening, he went to a sports shop and bought a new pair of boots and a club shirt. The purchase of the matching shorts and socks would have to wait. A neighbour very kindly gave him those very items, which had belonged to her son and although they were well-worn, Mike gratefully accepted them.

The wherewithal required to complete the purchase of his kit, did not to come easily. The Farmer was a crafty sod, with a reputation for not paying his labourers promptly. For the first couple of weeks, there was no difficulty in getting his money, but that didn't last. When Mike went to collect his wages, the man told him that he had not had time to get to the bank and he'd have to wait until the following week. The lad had already decided that if that happened, he would insist on being paid, because at least three weeks money was sorely needed. He also wanted a rugby ball to practice kicking and a hold-all in which to carry his kit. Money would have to be put by for the 'match-fees' etc. It was all a bit fraught and he thought many times of calling the whole thing off. The following week, when he went for his pay, the Farmer looked at his time sheet and re-acted aggressively, saying that it couldn't possibly be right.

'You've never worked all those hours,' he shouted angrily. 'I'm not paying you for all that lot.'

Mike explained that they included two weeks of evening work, Mondays to Fridays and the Sunday before, as well as the Saturday morning he had just worked. He came away empty handed. On the Sunday morning, the man had the effrontery to come knocking at his door in mid-morning to ask why he hadn't turned up for work. Mike bluntly told him that he wouldn't work for him again until he was paid what was owed. A bad-tempered argument ensued until he realised that Mike wasn't going to budge. He put his hand in his pocket, pulled out a wad of notes and paid him in full. As he turned away, he couldn't resist having the last word.

'You realise I've paid you more than the going rate and I should have made some deductions, for tax and things,' he said angrily. 'Now bloody well come on, we've got work to do.'

Half an hour later, Mike climbed up on to the combine harvester and they went out into a field of barley. It was an old machine, with a platform on the side for a man to stand on to fill the sacks, tie them off and drop them down a chute to the ground. It was noisy and dirty work, with noxious fumes coming out of the corroded exhaust pipe. When Mike asked why his men were not working, he was told that they didn't want to work overtime. That was strange, because Farm workers were so poorly paid, they usually jumped at the chance of a few extra hours, because the cash was always sorely needed by their families. The weather had recently been exceptionally cool, with rainfall well above average and only a few hot, sunny days. The quality and yield of the grain was poor and the situation was made worse by the time the sacks were left in the fields. The Farmer was very keen to get finished as quickly as possible and by driving the combine himself, he was at least making some money.

When Mike saw the Foreman one evening, he apologised for coming between the boss and his men but was told not to worry, because they were leaving anyway. They had also been accused of booking more hours than they had worked and the 'Guv'nor' had refused to pay them. If they had walked out on him at harvest time, they would have had great difficulty in getting another job, so they just worked normal hours. There was one last twist to Mike's problem and it came about the following Saturday morning. When he told the man he was playing rugby that afternoon and had to be away by noon, he made unpleasant comments about his unreliability. 'That Dockyard had buggered what could have been a bloody good lad,' he grumbled to the Foreman.

Mike decided he no longer wished to work for the man. One evening in the following week, he bought his socks, shorts, shin pads and a brand-new rugby ball. He had achieved his primary objectives. Until only recently, the balls had been made out of leather which, unless copiously 'dubbined', they quickly absorbed moisture. They were heavy to handle and kick but the new ball was only recently on the market and was considerably lighter, with water-proofing built in. His new pill was just the job and in the following weeks, he spent many happy hours practising kicking it.

The matter of washing his kit had become a serious issue with his mother and she was adamant that she wouldn't do it. Not having a machine, she did her washing by hand, which was very hard graft. Knowing the state it would get into in the coming months, Mike had to find some other way of getting it washed. Salvation came out of the blue, when he was talking to Tony, who lived three doors away. He said he might be able to work something out if the half-crown, which Mike had offered his own mother, came his way. His mum had a 'twin-tub' and it had lightened her job considerably. There was a lot of envy among her neighbours and her son had clearly seen the chance to make a bit on the side. Mike decided to approach the good lady directly and risk the older boy's ire.

When he said that her Tony had suggested she might wash his kit, she replied that he had already spoken to her. She would be pleased to oblige, providing his mother didn't object. Mike told her that there would be no problem, because she had categorically refused to have anything to do with it. They agreed that she would wash his kit, providing that he rinsed it out before bringing it to her and would pay her half a crown when he collected it. Mike was delighted to have done the deal so easily, though his mother was furious when she heard about it. She accused him of showing her up in front of the neighbours and his protestations that she had refused to help him fell on deaf ears. She shouted that 'when his cosy little arrangement fell apart, he need not come running to her.'

Tony's mum was as good as her word and Mike turned out in clean kit every week, something that didn't apply to everyone in the team. As expected, her lad had been miffed that Mike had spoken to her directly, which Mike countered by saying that it was what had been agreed. He asked him if he had been trying to pull a fast one on his mother, which he hotly denied. Mike ended the argument by saying how grateful he was and after a couple of pints, peace was restored.

Initially, he played in the 'B' fifteen for half a dozen matches and enjoyed them very much, though the standard of play was poor. When promoted to the 'Extra 'A's', it was a different game, with the teams being more skilful and fitter. He still took the goal and penalty kicks and scored a lot of points. His money problem though caused him a lot of embarrassment, particularly after away matches. He got out of it at the home games, by sidling off straight after he had cleaned-up. There was nothing for it but to discuss his situation with the Captain, which he did at the first opportunity. In self-consciously explaining how things were, he was surprised to get a sympathetic hearing and was told that others were 'in the same boat'.

It was a heartening response, but some of the other players were not quite so understanding. One loudly berated Mike and said that that if he couldn't afford to pay his 'dues', he shouldn't have joined the club. The Captain hasty intervened and told him it was none of his business. He was more concerned with keeping his team together, particularly as they were winning matches. Not long after, Mike was promoted to the 'A' team, which made his predicament even worse. Being a veritable bean-pole, he struggled to cope with the pace of the games and soon lost confidence. His request to go back down to the Extra 'A's' was conveniently ignored. The lads at work regularly discussed 'the hooligan's game played by gentlemen', (rugby), as opposed to the 'gentlemen's game played by hooligans', (soccer). It was an apt description, and one which has stood the test of time.

Chapter 3

All Types of Valves

The lads soon settled down to refurbishing the valves and regular deliveries were made to keep them going. They took turns in working on the 'dirty' valves, with no exceptions made, and as the more vulgar sages observed, they got 'shitted-up'. The hydraulic valves were just as unpleasant to work on because the fluid, phosphate-ester, was obnoxious. Great care had to be taken to wash one's hands properly and to use a barrier cream to protect them. Cuts and grazes had to be properly cleaned and protected against infection. Those from the lubrication systems were much better, in that they were relatively clean. The high-pressure steam-valves enabled the instructors to demonstrate how to scrape the surfaces on the connecting flanges. It was a laborious task, if one was to achieve the ideal 80 to 90% spread of 'flatness' across the inside faces. The lads were schooled in all types of screw-down and non-return valves and many new 'tricks' were learned.

One morning, everyone clocked on as normal and settled down to wait for their Instructors to come out of the office. The shop was unusually quiet, which should have aroused their suspicions that something was amiss but, as long as their charges were behaving themselves, why put themselves out? It was a good half hour before they turned them to and there was a definite undercurrent of excitement in the shop. All soon became clear., which could not be said for the air they were breathing. Although the lads had received a pay rise of ten shillings or so per week (50 pence), at the start of the year, it had not been enough to change anything. Their lack of cash remained a problem and most of them were still broke on Monday morning. Small groups of the smokers among them often shared a hand-rolled cigarette, which contained a few meagre strands of 'iffy' tobacco.

The difference was that the smokers were ostentatiously puffing away on 'tailor-made fags', i.e. manufactured cigarettes. Some had two, three and in some cases, four lit up and were grinning inanely at their mates. The atmosphere in the shop was thick with smoke, which caused grave discomfort to the non-smokers. The Instructors were soon included in the enjoyment of the quality ciggies, thinking perhaps it was someone's birthday. A large trembler-bell, which was mounted above the office door, sent one of them back into the office to answer the phone. It was just after ten-thirty and thirty seconds later, he came rushing back out into the shop in a state of great agitation.

'I don't know what you sods have been up to,' he yelled, 'but the bloody Police are on their way down here.'

At that, the shop erupted into a hive of frantic activity. The ones that had been so ostentatiously enjoying their smokes stubbed them out and everyone set to work, brushing-down the benches and clearing away the debris. The duck boards on the floor were lifted and the floor under and around the benches was swept clean. The rubbish was taken to a skip outside the shop and numerous boxes and cartons, some of which were full of cigarettes, were put into a large cardboard box. Coats and overall pockets were emptied, as were bench drawers and toolboxes, to ensure that no incriminating evidence was left in them. The instructors also cleared their office, so that nothing remained to show that they had been involved in the skulduggery. The air extractor fans in the roof were turned up to full power and the windows opened

The clean-up was completed and the box, by then three parts full, was taken out through the fire-door for disposal. When the atmosphere was free of smoke, the fans were switched back down to low power. Not long after, the Dockyard Police came through the door and went straight into the office. Had they looked down the shop, they would have seen everyone diligently working away, with the Instructors moving around attending to their duties. The shop was the essence of normality as Tommo strolled up the gangway to greet them.

'Can I help you, Officers?' he called out, with a pleasant smile on his face.

He went into the office with the Senior Officers and they were joined a few minutes later by Mr Barry. After some minutes, Tommo came out and called his colleagues into the office and when they eventually came out again, he was insisting loudly that none of his lads could possibly have been involved in anything untoward.

'I'm telling you, nobody has been out of this shop this morning. We haven't seen anything out of the ordinary and if you want to search the place, go ahead.'

That was exactly what the Police did and in the next hour, they systematically searched everyone and everything in the shop. Drawers and toolboxes were turned out and they even looked under the benches. Dustbins and cupboards were opened and even the valve-cleaning tanks were inspected. Nothing was found, but the Officers didn't leave empty-handed. Two of the lads were called into the office and then taken away for questioning.

It later transpired that they and some older Apprentices had paid a nocturnal visit to a store in the town and made off with a large quantity of cigarettes. The Police had already arrested the other lads and probably acting on 'information received,' they had known who they were looking for. Later the same day, a third lad was taken away from the shop, though he had not actually been involved in the burglary. Apparently, he had 'taken possession' of a considerable part of the haul and was charged with 'receiving'. The delinquents duly appeared before the Magistrates and were put on probation. Curiously, in its reports, the local 'rag' made no mention of the extent of the haul or even how much of it, if any, had been recovered.

When the reprobates came back to work, they were hailed as heroes, such being the perversity of the British psyche. Why so many people think that those who steal from businesses are to be admired is beyond reason. It is a sentiment which holds as true today as it did then. When later asked as to what they had done with the large box of cartons, the thieves said they had dropped it into the adjacent dock. No one had seen them do it and when the dock was later pumped out, there was no sign of the box. Following all the excitement, life in the workshop soon got back to normal, with most of the smokers reverting to sharing their smelly fags. The Instructors had handled a most difficult situation very well and they had given every support to their charges, even though some of them could only be described as criminals.

'Tommo' was an Ex-RN Chief Engine room Artificer, (CERA), and his lectures were both interesting and greatly appreciated. They extensively covered the functions and design parameters of numerous types of valves, which regulated and controlled all manner of fluid systems. Their operation at varying pressures and temperatures were analysed and discussed in detail. Particular emphasis given to the necessity of ensuring that a valve was in all respects fit for purpose. He also stressed the need for every valve to be sited for effective operation and maintenance. Just as important was its means of isolation, whereby it could be de-pressurised and drained before being opened-up 'in-situ'. When they eventually went on board a ship, they would find a lot of valves where the Installers had not taken that into account.

There had to be a limit to the number of valves in a circuit, either for practical reasons such as confined space or cost implications. He made a pertinent point when he held up a wheel-spanner. In a perfect world, its use in opening or closing a valve would be unnecessary. But no one lived in that happy state and when ill-used, the tool very often caused serious damage to a valve. No ship could ever operate without them, because even in normal use, a lot of valves became difficult to turn and seal.

'You'll always have a need for a wheel-spanner when you're on watch', he went on, 'and not only because of the difficulty in closing a hand-wheel. Very often, some silly sod has over-tightened it and you need to open it in a hurry. When you complain, they usually get 'cobby' (angry).'

He went on to explain about the damage which could be caused, particularly to gate-valves. Holding one up, he stressed that it should never be jammed shut. He handed round the body of a valve where the seats had been fractured. In another, the spindle had been sheared off and on another, the spindle-bridge had been broken. If that type of valve was leaking, no amount of tightening would seal it off. It was an object lesson for his listeners. He drew system diagrams on the blackboard, to demonstrate how to achieve the best isolation of critical valves. His attention to detail, about the design and workings of the various types of safety and feed-check valves was the most interesting. Some of his lads' questions sounded daft, but he always answered them clearly and concisely.

Interesting discussions regularly took place among the lads and they soon became adept in deciding what was needed to bring a valve back to good working order. Sometimes, the cover studs were in poor condition or perhaps one had been broken off. A hole would be drilled in the centre of the stub and it was removed with an extractor. The fixings on the steam valves always had to be replaced with new during an overhaul. The exterior surfaces were always cleaned and the rough edges filed off to finish the job.

The different kinds of joints used when installing valves in pipe work was also well-covered in their lectures. New gaskets were made from sheets of the appropriate material. They also learned about the many types of packing used for the various operating conditions and the correct way in which to strip out and re-pack the stuffing boxes. The Instructors were constantly heard trotting out the Navy dictum, that 'half-doing a job' was not an option. The lads had become increasingly adept in the use of their tools, with fewer cuts and bruises on their hands. A completed valve would be critically examined, with pertinent points being made and there was always a measure of pride when it was to his satisfaction.

Fund-raising, for social and welfare schemes, was organised in the Factory, which provided for care in the event of accidents or illness. The fund was maintained by weekly contributions and events such as concerts, dances/social evenings, prize-draws were regularly on offer. Trips were arranged to exhibitions, shows and sporting functions in London and there were outings to the seaside. 'Sweeps' and 'draws', linked to the football results and principal race meetings were regular features. The same people would often go around the various departments, to collect on behalf of sick workmates or in the event of a death, for their dependents. Membership was open to everyone and the organisers put a lot of time into their good works. The second-year Apprentices had come into a new world, where genuine care for others was a part of everyday life.

Their comfortable sojourn had to end and one Friday morning, Tommo called the lads down for the last time and told them that on the following Monday morning, they were going to move on. When they had first arrived, he had said that they would only be there for three months and that was how it had worked out. Due to his relaxed way of running the shop, nearly everyone had been much happier than in their first year and they had responded accordingly. Their attitudes had subtly changed and when there had been work to be done, they had willingly 'turned to'. The Instructors had encouraged them in a friendly and good-humoured way, with none of the shouting and/or threats which had previously been the norm.

Their pride in the job had clearly rubbed-off on to their charges, despite the many stunts, most of which had been brainless. The Instructors had regularly stood up for them, even when they had risked getting into trouble themselves. Their efforts and the help and support which they had given had been very much appreciated and all the hard work and commitment had borne fruit. There was a buzz of excitement when the lads were told where they would be working in the following week.

Chapter 4

More Schooling

When the apprentices had returned to the College at the start of the year, the Upper School lads continued on their two days and three evenings a week basis and had started right away on the Higher National Certificate Course, (HNC). It was an onerous task, which would require a great deal of commitment and aptitude to complete. Some of them though had not done as well as had been expected in their year-end exams and were sent down to the Lower School. Their failure was, as before, due to a combination of circumstances, not least of which had been their inattention in the classroom. They continued with the Ordinary National Certificate Course, (ONC) and would attend the school on one day and two evenings a week. The ones who had shown sense and responsibility would tread a very different path to those that were left behind.

Their ones that had failed accepted their demotion with nonchalance, thinking perhaps that they hadn't got the necessary capability and so didn't have to bother. They were not alone in their folly and any cry from the Lecturers to 'get on' was greeted with loud derision. The 'messing around' was resumed, which caused great disruption in the classroom. Their nonsense was made worse by the inanity of animal noises, most commonly imitations of farmyard sounds. There were loud woofs, neighs, moos, baas, quacks and cock-a-doodle-do's coming from all quarters, while the Lecturer was writing on the blackboard. It was juvenile and tedious and he didn't help matters by trying to humour the clowns by naming them without turning around. A wrong name led to loud laughter but he occasionally struck lucky. With great severity and no little drama, or as much as he could manage, he pointed to the door.

'I think you should leave the room, don't you?' he said mournfully, then bellowed in sudden rage, 'Get out!.'

The crass behaviour in the classroom got steadily worse and it wasn't long before the Principal again moved to regain control. The worst offenders cannily got thrown out fifteen minutes or so before the end of the evening and went home that much earlier. It worked a few times but when the Lecturer realised he was 'being had,' he refused to co-operate. A regular victim of the nonsense was a large, good-natured man whose middle name was Chisholm, which someone had found out by nosing around in the Principal's office. There had recently been a western film in the cinemas of that title and his students couldn't pass up the chance of teasing him. Their banal nonsense went on and on until they found something else to amuse themselves. While the pranks were innocuous, it was annoying to be continually harassed by buggers who had no intention of doing any work.

John, who had taken no part in the nonsense, suffered a particularly nasty prank. One morning, the lad behind him industriously scraped at sticks of chalk with a pen-knife and carefully collected the dust into a paper bag. The class didn't have long to wait to find out what he had in mind. Early in the afternoon, he stood up and brought the half-full bag down on to the back of the head of his unfortunate victim. Most of the class laughed loudly as John stood up with the back of his head and shoulders covered in the dust. The Lecturer turned and to everyone's amazement, he pointed at John and angrily told him to 'get out'. The lad tried to tell him that he had been assaulted, but to no avail. There was an ominous silence, with a lot of the students fearful of the retribution which would follow, but all the Lecturer did was to bemoan the mess around John's desk.

'Don't worry, Sir,' said the bugger who had done the dastardly deed, 'I'll soon clear it up.'

He and his mate went out into the corridor to fetch a vacuum cleaner and noisily brought it back into the room. After they had cleared up most of the dust, they put it back in the cupboard and returned to their seats, which was too much for the ones who had had more than enough of the inanity. They were loudly branded as hypocrites. Not wanting to be chastised, the culprit thought it prudent to leave as well. From then on, John sat as far away from him as possible. There was nothing he could do to redress the situation. Most of the class had been in fear of the lad and his mate up until then but, as often happens, that had changed.

Further mischief involved another Lecturer. Mr Brade was a small, mild-mannered man, whose object was to drum the principles of Applied Mathematics into their thick skulls. From the first evening, he was the object of silly comments by the idiots, who made a play on his name. Unfortunately, another film was going the rounds, the main theme of which was the suffering of slaves in the Deep South during the American Civil War. He was christened 'Massa Brady' and it stuck. No matter how hard he tried, he could not hold their attention and the nonsense got progressively worse. It was one long tirade of verbal abuse and the poor blighter became more and more stressed. Eventually, he had to find a way of ending his suffering.

Mr Brade applied for and secured an appointment as a Lecturer at the Royal Dockyard in Malta. No formal announcement was made, but it was common knowledge on the very day that he learned of his appointment. The class found out about it by the same means as before, i.e. by unauthorised snooping in the Principal's office. While awaiting his arrival, it was agreed that some sort of stunt was called for to mark the occasion. When he came into the room, he knew right away that something untoward was afoot. The room was all sweetness and light and he was aghast when heartily congratulated on his impending appointment. As he slowly made his way to the front of the room, he was treated to a loud round of applause from his appreciative class.

'How the hell did you find out?' he asked crossly. 'I only heard about it myself this afternoon and it was meant to be confidential. I should have known better; nothing is ever a secret for long in this bloody place.'

An intrepid pair had arrived at the College well before the appointed time and being 'at a loose end', they had looked around to see if there was anything of interest. The door of the office was ajar and being nosy buggers, they had looked inside. The Secretary, who was well known for her humourless, terse ways, had gone home and there was no sign of 'the boss'. While one lad had kept watch, the other had taken a quick 'butchers' (a butcher's hook, or look in the common rhyming slang) at the papers on his desk and a copy of Brady's letter of appointment was near the top of the pile. Having read it, they beat a hasty retreat to the classroom. The cat was out of the bag!

By the next evening class, his students had collected a large number of empty boxes of a popular chocolate confectionery. During the short break in mid-evening, they decorated the top of the blackboard and his desk with the boxes. When he came back, Brady had to laugh. He again appealed to them to treat his appointment with discretion, as he didn't want to 'get it in the ear' from the principal. He was wasting his time, and there was further ribbing from his class. They had him cold and weren't going to let him off that easily.

'I'll be going out in approximately six weeks' time,' he told them. 'Who will take my place hasn't been decided yet, but I've heard Mr Fergus's name mentioned.'

That was one up to him, and it abruptly shut them up. There was a stunned silence, broken intermittently by loud groans from individuals who were dramatically holding their heads in horror.

'Got you, you buggers,' he cried with glee. 'The truth is, I don't know who'll be coming in but I couldn't pass that one up, could I? One thing for sure, I'll be very glad to get shot of you lot.'

To his great surprise, at the end of his last evening, he was presented with a neatly wrapped parcel. He declined to open it, despite much urging to do so. There were no flies on the man and looking around, he told them he knew what was inside.

'Thank you all very much for this much appreciated gift,' he said. 'We haven't had what could be described as a fruitful relationship, but there's no doubt in my mind, I shall remember you all for a very long time to come. If any of you come out to Malta, please don't look me up.' Then, looking at the parcel, he said, 'My wife will be pleased. She's very fond of Maltesers!'

It was the last that they saw of a very able Lecturer, whom they had cruelly tormented. Life went on but their antics under the new man were nowhere near as bad as they had been. Could it have been that their behaviour was at last moderating to a more acceptable level?

One evening, while they were waiting for their Lecturer to arrive, Mike told his class mates about the previous Sunday afternoon. He had been sitting under a tree at the top of the hill above his village, looking out across the farmlands along the south side of the River Thames. When disturbed by a slight noise, he looked around and saw a young girl was watching him from behind a bush. When he spoke to her, she turned away and he called out that she had nothing to be afraid of.

Rhona and her family lived in the nearby woods and had camped there over many years and worked for the local Farmers during the summer months, picking fruit and lifting potatoes. They also tended his hedges and ditches and kept his woodland tidy, which gave them with a frugal living through the winter months. When not working on the land, they collected scrap and sold logs and kindling, clothes pegs and other assortments. Being largely unwelcome in the surrounding communities, they kept very much to themselves.

She told Mike that she had never been to school, but could read and write. She was a very pretty girl, perhaps fourteen or fifteen years old, with dark eyes, a full figure and jet black hair. Contrary to the misconceptions and prejudices of the locals, she was clean and tidy, though her dress was old and frayed. They had only been talking for a few minutes when she suddenly looked over towards the woods, then ran off. Moments later, two men approached and Mike, sensing trouble, made to go as well. He was intercepted and after having been aggressively asked what he was up to, he was roughly pushed through the woods by a short but powerfully-built young man. His appearance was made even more frightening by his scowling countenance and penetrating eyes. He was known as a bit of an oddity in that he was massively built above the waist but his body from there down was short and stumpy, almost as though he had been given the wrong pair of legs.

Mike had seen him before and knew of his reputation. He couldn't help thinking that the bugger really did look like a gorilla, but he wasn't going to say so. When they arrived at the camp, he was stood in front of an equally unfriendly older man who, in a few short sentences and in no uncertain terms, told him that his attentions to his daughter were not welcome.

'For a start, she's spoken for. Just you remember, boy, our ways are not yours and you've got nothing for us. We don't want trouble with you or anybody else around here, so just clear off and leave us alone. If you've got any sense,' he concluded angrily, 'you'll not come back.'

Mike apologised for his intrusion and told him he had not meant any disrespect. He had only been friendly, as he would have been to anyone he met when out for a walk. The old man grudgingly accepted his apology and told him to 'clear-orf' once again. When he got back to the village, some of his pals saw that he was a 'bit put out' and asked him why. He told them about his little 'bit of bother with the Gyppos', because he had spoken to their girl. One or two of them were all for 'going up to 'sort them out', or so they bravely said. The reality was quite different, because of the hard reputation of the 'gorilla'. It was generally agreed that Mike should have had more sense than to go near them in the first place.

There had always been problems between the Travellers and local people, most of which were due to their different cultures. The villagers insisted that they were unwashed, filthy even and totally dishonest and that it was wise to keep everything under lock and key when they were about. The family was thought to be true Romany, though they were often disparagingly called 'Diddicoys' by the ignorant buggers in the village. That they wanted nothing more than to live their lives in their own way and in peace counted for nothing in their eyes. Nothing has changed and such people still suffer from the same ignorance and prejudice, as indeed they have done from time immemorial.

Returning to the classroom, the consequences of the disorder were already becoming apparent. Everyone must have realised they were wasting their time and that there would be a price to pay for their inanity. Most people apply themselves to their jobs with diligence, if they want to get on. Some have faced incredible hardship in their careers and their success has often been immense. Despite starting their businesses with very little, they have become immensely rich through sheer hard work and determination. They have provided jobs and security, for hundreds and at times, thousands of other people. One of the strengths of this Country has been our willingness to absorb generations of people from all over the world, which has been and remains very much to our advantage.

For some years after the War, there had been a widespread crisis of confidence and a lack of ambition among a lot of the British people. There was a strongly held attitude of envy and resentment against those in authority or anyone who was perceived to be 'better off' than they were. It was clearly evident in many of the lads in Mike's entry though, as already mentioned, some were determined get on. When the exam results had been published at the year end, many of them had ruefully admitted that they could have done much better. The old chestnut of 'blaming someone else for one's own folly' was angrily raised by one or two but if they were honest, they had only themselves to blame for their failure. As the saying went, there was no substitute for hard work; an altruism that is as valid today as it was then.

Chapter 5

Waking Up

One advantage of the workshop was its proximity to the Canteen, and a quick dash across the yard would bring a breathless bunch of lads through the door only minutes after the hooter had sounded. Cynics often joked that it was the only time that a Matey 'shifted himself', and there was an element of truth in that. There was a popular rugby song at the time, which was sung with gusto in the bar after matches, the first verse of which went:

> 'Can a Dockyard Matey run?
> Yes he can, I've seen it done.
> When he hears that dinner bell,
> You should see him RUN LIKE HELL.'

It was sung to the tune of the Christmas carol *See amid the Winter Snow*, with loud shouts and stamping of feet accompanying the last three words.

The Canteen was very well patronised, and unless he got there quickly, it could be about fifteen minutes before a hungry lad was served. Mike and his mates usually arrived well ahead of the hoards and it was the same on night-school evenings. They were allowed to clock off at half-past four to go and go to avail themselves of sandwiches, cakes and hot mugs of tea. Anyone who has had Canteen tea will confirm, it did not keep its fresh-made taste for long. While not exotic by today's standards, the food at dinner-time was wholesome and substantial and was always piping hot, which was very much appreciated through the cold Winter months. There was also a lot of good-natured banter between the serving ladies and their customers, which was amusing.

The most 'classy' girls in the Yard worked in the Main Administration Building, particularly in the Wages Department. They used their own Canteen, where manual workers were most certainly not welcome. Entry was controlled by a doorman, who had no hesitation in asking a suspected intruder to show him his pass. The discriminatory practice of keeping office workers, ('white-collar'), apart was common sense, though it did encourage a measure of snobbery. 'The Staff', as they liked to be called, came to work in clean clothes and were not be expected to rub shoulders with grubby manual workers. In the main Canteen, there was a defined clean clothes area, which was used by the Apprentices when they were at school.

One lady who worked there literally stood out from the other women. She was petite and very shapely, with long blond hair, which cascaded down almost to her waist. Her substantial bust was always well-hoisted and tantalisingly contained in a low cut, snow-white blouse. One lad opined that she could balance a couple of pints of beer on her 'knockers', while another graphically described her as a 'ship in full sail'. Dora was a magnificent sight in their lustful eyes, and she nearly always wore a very tight, short black skirt, which fully accentuated her curves. She was liberal with her makeup, almost to the point of spoiling her undoubted attractions. Mascara, rouge and face powder were generously applied, and knowing she had 'got it', she 'flaunted it'.

She provided a lot of pleasure to the 'dirty little sods' who, if truth be told, she could have eaten for breakfast. Though popular with the men, she didn't enjoy the same level of regard from her own kind. There was inevitably a long queue awaiting her attention and it always raised a laugh when one or other of the other ladies called crossly across to them with impatience.

'Can I help you, lads? Come on, stop gawping, we can't wait here all day.'

The lady revelled in their attention and she easily dealt with their teasing and the younger men were often treated to a friendly quip. However, there was a line over which no-one was allowed to step.

One dinner time, she bent to pick something off of the floor and in doing so exposed rather more of her voluptuous flesh than normal. As she straightened up, she looked straight into the leering eyes of a spotty Apprentice who had leaned over the counter to get a better view. Quick as a flash, she picked up a large ladle and caught him a smart blow on the top of the head. He fell back among his mates and there was a huge roar of laughter, which brought the Supervisor over.

'What's going on here then,' he cried and, seeing the lad rubbing his head, he asked the lady if there was any trouble.

'Nothing that I can't handle, George,' she replied, tossing her tresses and smiling archly.

'That's alright then,' he said as he walked away.

The lad was scarlet with embarrassment, when he was pushed back to the front of the queue. Without any prompting, he had the good sense to apologise and his gesture was accepted.

'As long as we know where we stand,' Dora said, sniffing haughtily and then with a big smile, she added, 'or where we shouldn't stand, I should say!'

She had handled the situation well. In the modern vogue of political correctness, the lad would probably have been disciplined. As it was, she had effectively taught him a lesson and at the same time, increased the regard of her young admirers. The limit of what was acceptable had been clearly defined. Her attractions continued to be discussed, as they had probably been for years. Boys will always be boys and their common sense has always been inversely proportional to the degree of lust in their minds and what they had in their pants.

A Fitter sitting at the same table as our lads tried to pour cold water on their talk, by pointing out the risks involved in ogling her.

'I'd be a bit careful of what you say in here,' he said seriously. 'Her old man's a Foreman and I wouldn't go upsetting him if I was you. He can be a right bad bugger, and no mistake.'

One morning, Billy told his mates about his journey home the night before. He had seen Dora walking up the road and after passing through the gate, he followed her on to a bus. He sat down next to her but his pleasure was short-lived, when she looked over her shoulder, then asked him to move. When he stood up, he looked straight into the eyes of a very large and unsmiling Matey. His mannerly gesture was not even acknowledged and when the bus moved off, he had to be content with standing in the crush of the overcrowded aisle and looking down her cleavage.

To his dismay, the bus went straight on down to the Town Hall, without stopping and he had difficulty in pushing his way through the crush to get off. When he looked up at the number at the back, he saw that he had got on the wrong bus. To make matters worse, he then had to wait half an hour for another one and was late home. His mother had given him a right bollocking and had put her finger right on the button when she said she supposed that he'd been chasing after some bit of skirt.

'Why didn't you tell Dora's old man to show some manners, Billy?,' asked one of his mates.

'You should see the bloody size of him,' replied the worthy lad. 'Do me a favour. As Fred said the other day, you don't want to get on the wrong side of that bugger.' The lady was middle aged and was desperately hanging on to her attractions, with few of the beauty aids that women now have and she must have put a lot of effort into her appearance. Overhearing their discussion, another Fitter aptly summed up the situation.

'The trouble is, women like her are not all ladies, and some of them can be a bit rough', he told them gravely. It was an understatement if ever there was one.

As the pop song went, 'Growing up was very hard to do' and in general terms, the lads were nervous in female company. Girls of their own age were not a problem, but their mothers frightened the life out of them. Most of them had not had a steady girlfriend but as the second year passed, there was a steady change. It was all very juvenile, but it became increasingly important for a lad to lose his virginity, or 'cherry', as it was called. Those that were engaged or going steady were assumed to be 'getting it regular', something which had little basis in truth. The remainder were assumed to be 'virgo-intacta', until such times as they were able to convince their mates that they had scored.

A small group discussed the problem and concluded that there was only one way to do it, without getting caught. i.e. by putting a girl 'in the club'. Their idea was to obtain the services of a 'professional lady'. While it had some merit, no one had the foggiest notion about to how to go about it. A foray into the arms of a local lady was not on, so they would have to find their salvation away from the town. The possibility of being rumbled was the problem. Someone suggested a trip up to London as the best option and his mates readily agreed. Those listening thought it all a bit corny and suspected the buggers were up to no good.

There was more discussion, but their perennial lack of money was the biggest hindrance. No one knew how much it would cost and discreet questions among the men didn't help. Most were married and if they had ever been with a prostitute, they weren't going to admit it. One lad suggested that 'ten pounds should do it' and, having nothing better to go on, they took that as the basis of their calculations. With only four of them, they might get 'a special deal'. If it could be arranged without any embarrassment, that would be fine. Other things had to be considered. They had to include for their rail fares, for something to eat and a few beers to celebrate their achievement. They would need at least twenty pounds per man and it was reluctantly agreed that the venture would have to shelved, until they had saved what was required.

One of them had a bright idea and suggested that if everyone made a modest contribution, they could put their plan into action. They lost no time in sounding out their workmates as to whether or not they would contribute. It would be great fun and everyone would get a good laugh out of it. Mike and his mates told them to bugger off, but a fair number of lads were taken in. How they were so gullible was beyond belief. Quite a bit of money was collected on the basis of earnest promises to tell them 'all about it' on their return. Some weeks later, the rogues announced that Saturday was to be the day on which they would carry it through. They loudly crowed about how they were at long last to become men and their detractors were roundly berated for not entering into the spirit of the thing.

There was a buzz in the shop on the following Monday morning and the four 'heroes' were pressed to tell all. Slowly, with a great sense of drama, their story unfolded. They had gone up to London early and had approached a number of girls. Some had expressed interest in helping them and ultimately, a young lady had said she'd be happy to oblige, providing there was no 'messing around'. She was a 'right smasher with a lovely figure, big tits and all'. Her offer was accepted and the deal was struck. The graphic details of their copulation were less than convincing and a growing number of those that had handed over their hard-earned cash suspected that they had been had. The rogues were adamant that they had done what they had set out to do.

The next morning, Norman, who had been off the day before, loudly confirmed what the contributors had been dreading. They had indeed been the victims of a scam and he gleefully spilled the beans.

'According to you lot, you enjoyed the services of the young lady on Saturday afternoon,' he said. 'Well, how is it that I saw the three of you watching the match at White Hart Lane, eh? You were about four rows down from where me and my dad was standing on the north terrace. You've been caught out, you scheming sods.'

At that, all hell broke loose and the crooks were surrounded by their furious workmates. Amid loud demands for their money back, there were raucous laughs from those who had not been involved. With it all getting out of hand, the Instructors hurried to calm things down. Later, the truth came out and it was most amusing. One lad had 'cried-off' and the other three went up to London without him. When they arrived, they had made a bee-line for Soho, but no-one had had the courage to procure the services of the requisite lady and they had abandoned their plan and beat a hasty retreat into a pub. They then decided that they couldn't waste their day out and it was agreed that a football match was the best way to enjoy the afternoon. As Norman had said, they had gone along to watch the Spurs. They spent part of the evening looking around the West End and, after a few beers and a bite to eat, they had caught the last train home.

Knowing they were going to be closely questioned, they had made out that everything had gone to plan. Their cruel luck was that Norman had seen them and blabbed, otherwise no one would have been any the wiser. In placating the ones they had duped, the cretins solemnly promised to repay all the money they had extorted. Mike didn't help by pointing out that as they were permanently broke, it was most unlikely anyone would see their money again. The lousy buggers had had no intention of playing the game and they should have known better. They would just have to put their losses down to experience. It wasn't what the victims wanted to hear. Not a penny was repaid and truth to tell, the less than popular trio remained 'unblemished' for quite some time.

Chapter 6

A Right Pantomime

For many years, the villagers had enjoyed regular outings, one of which usually took place on the second Saturday afternoon in January. It was meant to be a family occasion, but was arranged mainly for the children. The treat was a matinee performance of the pantomime in the only Theatre in the Town, followed by a tea in an adjacent café. The show was considered a bit daft by the teenagers, but it gave them the opportunity for a bit of fun. They could be relied on to misbehave and in the past, the outcome had often been highly amusing. Despite having been told the previous year that they wouldn't be allowed to go, most of them got on the buses which were parked at the top end of the village. There was the usual chaos in getting everyone on board and the antics of those in charge set the tone for what promised to be a most enjoyable outing.

Stewards were appointed to keep the punters in order and on one bus, it was Fred Smith. How he relished bossing everyone about and with an air of great po-faced importance, he ticked-off their names as the people arrived, with regular licks of his pencil as he did so. Having lived in the village for years, he knew them all well, so it should have been an easy task but, he made a complete cock-up of the whole thing. He kept everyone waiting in a queue and they soon became impatient and were increasingly reluctant to do as they were told. Fred countered their grumbling by saying that they would only get on the bus when he said so and not before. He was bluntly told he was a useless bugger, for making them stand around in the freezing cold and was then swept aside by a rush of half a dozen irate mums, followed closely their noisy, excited kids. That put paid to Fred's intention of 'having a bit of order'.

The bus was full to busting and the driver, who had been laughing at Fred's discomfort, became alarmed at the antics of the unruly teenagers at the back. Kids were climbing over the seats, fighting, shouting and laughing, so much so that the noise was excruciating. Poor old Fred was in a flat spin trying to make himself heard. As a wag pointed out, he looked like a bloody goldfish, continually opening and closing his mouth in exasperation. After a few minutes, the organiser, who was a Sergeant in the Depot known as 'Rat' Grand, came storming on board and bellowed for silence. He was a tall, thin faced man, with very dark, almost black eyes and had a reputation for being an irascible character. The bus wouldn't leave until everyone had shut up, sat down and been accounted for.

With a semblance of order restored, he told Fred to check that everyone was in their allocated seat, which of course they weren't. Being conscious of the nonsense of previous years, the committee had told the parents in advance as to which bus and seats they had been allocated and it should have worked well. However, the perversity of the British psyche, when faced with assumed authority, was plain to see. The first bus was overfull and the second was occupied by the families 'who knew how to behave themselves'. Most of them were glaring angrily through the windows at those that obviously didn't. The third bus had only a very few punters on board and there was quite a crowd still milling around outside, unable to decide which bus they should be on. The Rat and his stewards tried to sort it all out, but with little success. Twenty or so punters were ordered off the first bus and told to board the third one. Family groups were split up and individuals were left sitting next to someone they didn't like. Eventually, angry words were exchanged between the stewards and the adults and threats were made to some of the teenage lads, which led to still more chaos.

The Rat ultimately gained control, when he shouted that he was cancelling the outing and that no refunds would be made. That did the trick, but what ensued clearly demonstrated the lack of regard in which the villagers held him. After many arguments and angry protests, everyone was at last seated and with ironic cheers, the buses moved off. It wasn't the end of the argy bargy and when they pulled-up outside the theatre, there were yet more problems. A Constable strode across in front of the first bus and peremptorily ordered the driver to move on, as he was causing an obstruction. While he was arguing with the 'plod', someone opened the door and everybody piled out. The other buses promptly followed suit. There followed a lot of angry shouting between all three drivers and the Policeman, with loud threats of prosecution being made by the hapless Officer.

'What the hell can I do about it?,' shouted the first driver, with the other two both nodding vigorously. 'No bugger takes any notice of me and I couldn't move away with them getting off, could I? You'd better speak to him over there,' he said, pointing at Sergeant Grand who, when he was confronted, was for once lost for words.

The buses departed and the excited punters noisily made their way into the foyer, only to be confronted by the grim-faced Manager. He curtly told them that they were too late, the curtain was due to go up and they couldn't come in. More shouting and jostling ensued and he was roughly pushed aside and the crowd rushed up the stairs, through the double swing-doors and down on to the balcony. Their seats were in a broad swathe across the width and the front ones were quickly filled by the youths, just as the lights were dimmed. One idiot had bought and opened an ice-cream and, after carefully placing it on the balustrade, he turned to take his coat off. When he went to retrieve his treat, he clumsily knocked it over the edge. It fell on to the occupants of the seats below, much to their loudly expressed annoyance.

The confection came in a paper tub, when bought in a cinema or theatre and while it was hard when taken from the fridge, it soon melted and had to be eaten quickly. The people who had been sitting directly below the balcony must have been liberally splashed with the gooey mess. Such was the commotion in the stalls, the cast stopped the opening scene and looked with dismay at the people who were angrily milling around. The Manager came on to the stage, bellowing for the curtain to be lowered and much to the audience's amusement, he was 'hopping mad'. He announced that until the culprit who was responsible for dropping the ice-cream owned up, the show would not go on. The Rat, followed closely by the other three stalwarts, marched to the front of the balcony and peremptorily ordered the dozen or so lads and lasses in the front row to vacate their seats.

Despite their loud protestations, they were taken to the back to await the arrival of the Manager. Seeking to ingratiate himself, the Rat told him that he would soon sort things out. He had intended all along for the 'little ones' to have the seats in the front row, which was well received by their angry parents. After yet more argument, it was agreed that the dropping of the ice-cream may have been accidental. The lads could stay, providing they remained seated under the close supervision of the stewards. Any further nonsense and they would be out on their ears.

The reaction of the villagers varied widely, from outright indignation and hostility to veiled sympathy. There were a lot of sniggers and snide comments, that 'boys will be boys'. The silly buggers were soon bored by the inanity of the panto and started yawning loudly and making rude comments about the questionable attributes of both the Principal-boy and the Dame. Each digression was answered with loud 'shushes' from those in front and growls of warning from the hapless Fred, who had been detailed off to mind them. The end of the show didn't come too quickly.

When the party came out of the Theatre, they were shepherded across the street and up some stairs into a large room above the cafe. The lads were held back until the adults and their broods were settled, then they were escorted up to be seated with their parents. That didn't please them one bit but as often happens, out of the darkness came a small beam of light. Mike found himself sitting next to a very pretty girl. She was a pleasant lass who said that she had enjoyed the antics of him and his mates. Jo was the youngest daughter of a colleague of his father's and it wasn't long before there were knowing looks from the other diners. Before them was a light tea of 'wet plastic' ham and stale bread, with 'butter' and a jam of dubious origin. It was supplemented by pieces of dry-looking plain cake and limp biscuits, all of which had obviously been laid out for some time. With everyone seated, the waitresses poured cups of well-stewed tea from large kettles.

Jo lived in the town and, before leaving, she asked Mike if he would like to come to tea on the following Sunday. He accepted her invitation with a lot of self-conscious blushing and irritating sniggers from those sitting nearby. He knew he would come in for a lot of ribbing on the way home. As it happened, he had put his mate Keith's nose very much out of joint. He angrily complained that he had been thinking of taking Jo to the pictures. Now, she had been taken from under his nose by that silly sod Mike. The journey home was thus made in silence, something the other passengers were grateful for.

There was a moment of light relief when one of the men loudly suggested that they should 'stop for a wet', which brought a murmur of approval from most of the men but was hotly shouted down by their wives. They weren't going to be left hanging around outside a pub on a cold bus, while their 'lordships' were drinking their fill. They had been caught like that before. When they arrived back in the village, one of the crafty sods announced that the men had been called to a meeting in the canteen, to discuss the problems. It was of course just an excuse for what was colourfully described by one doughty matron as 'a piss-up'.

What should have been an enjoyable trip had yet again been quite the opposite, and not only because of antics of the youths. Some of the women had loudly expressed their displeasure to the committee, and vowed that they would not be caught out again. To their obvious discomfort, another one loudly vouchsafed that 'they couldn't organise a party in a brewery'. Mike's romance didn't last long; only a couple of weeks in fact and when he told his mates that Jo had 'given him the push', they wanted to know why. The truth was that he had been in a bit of a fix, when she had suggested that instead of him calling for her on the second Sunday afternoon, they should go to the pictures.

Money, or rather the lack of it, was the problem but, the truth was he had already lost interest in the lass and when he told his mates about it, they hadn't passed-up the chance for some light relief at his expense. Each comment had been accompanied by the usual sly winks and loud laughter and there was no point in listening to their advice. When he had told Jo that he didn't like the pictures, she was clearly miffed and to make matters worse, he had then talked for most of the afternoon with her elder brother, who had been at the same school as himself. He had also sat through a 'family tiff', when Jo vented her anger at being ignored on her sister. His lack of enthusiasm clearly indicated that they were going nowhere, and she had been quick to act.

That was not the end of the story. When Keith heard that Mike's romance had ended, he jumped on his bike and rode into town to see her. His intention was to seize the unexpected opportunity to get his own back. His rival, having been told to 'sling his hook', had given him the chance to shine. Mike bumped into them, with her sister in tow, in the High Street on the following Saturday afternoon and where were they heading? To the cinema, of course, which was strange as Keith was usually as broke as he was. There was no point in being rude and he declined the offer to join them. That would have cost him, because he would have had to pay for Jo's sister. He heard nothing more until a week or so later, when late one evening, there was a loud knock at the back door.

'I wonder who that could be?' said his mother.

The old man replied that she would have to answer it to find out, but his droll attempt at humour fell on stony ground. When Mike opened the door, he was surprised to see Jo's father and it was clear that the man was very put out. He immediately launched into a tirade at the lad, the main point of which was that he would not tolerate his daughter being kept out at all hours. Knowing he was not responsible, Mike waited for the chance to respond.

'I'm sorry Mister Easton, but you've come to the wrong house,' he said politely. 'I haven't seen Josephine for at least a couple of weeks.'

Jo's father was clearly taken aback that he'd been barking up the wrong tree.

'I was sure she'd been out with you,' he went on. Last Saturday night it was, and she didn't get home until after eleven.'

'No, she wasn't with me,' replied Mike, having difficulty in hiding his pleasure at being innocent for once. 'I went to the dance in the village that evening. She must have been out with someone else.'

His parents confirmed that was true and their visitor, after mumbling an apology, gruffly said 'goodnight' and left. A couple of evenings later, Mike saw Keith and the lad was again far from pleased.

'You bloody-well dropped me right in it, you lousy sod,' he accused.

Mike told him about Mr Easton's visit and everything that had been said with some relish. He assured Keith that his name had not been mentioned and if he didn't believe him, he could go and ask his parents. He couldn't resist pushing the knife in further.

'If you've got trouble with her old man, it's your own fault for keeping her out late. It's got nothing to do with me.'

Keith had blithely gone to the girl's house earlier that day and had walked straight into a 'king-sized' bollocking. Her father, having got the truth from his daughter, had 'torn a strip off him', then told him not to bother calling again. That was the end of their amorous episode, which was hard on both the lad and the girl. Unlike Mike, Keith had really liked the lass and they had got on well until they had aroused her father's ire. He was right that the streets, particularly late on in a Winter's evening, were no place for a sixteen year old girl. Keith consoled himself by admitting that he didn't have the money to spend on girls anyway, and their rivalry was soon forgotten.

Chapter 7

Sharp Practice

Mike was always ready to earn some extra cash, but the opportunities to do so were few and far between. When a lad did a job for a 'grown-up', he or she would often find cause for complaint and refuse to pay him. A neighbour told Mike that he could do with a bit of help in his garden, which was overgrown with grass and weeds and suggested that he might like to earn a few bob by turning it over for him. The plot measured approximately forty by six yards square, and Bill assured him that he would 'see him alright for digging it'. He thought a couple of weeks should do it, which grossly understated the extent of the work. The next day, Mike and his pal Geoff went see him and offered to do the job for the princely sum of a pound each, which was reasonable for what was involved. Bill spluttered with mock indignation and said he was only trying to help them to do something useful. He could get the job done for half the price. After discussing it further, they agreed to dig his plot for a pound between them, and he would provide the tools.

Digging is a laborious chore, and the ground had not only to be cleared of the accumulated rubbish but the soil was on the heavy side. It was clear that they had been well and truly turned over but, having agreed to do the job, they had no option but to turn-to. They started work the following Saturday morning and there was an immediate problem.

'You're going to have to do it properly,' Bill told them crossly. 'I want the first two spits to be dug out and barrowed to the top of the garden. Then you'll have to break up the sub-soil as you move along the row. I'll get some manure from the Farm for you to dig in as you go.'

In other words, the crafty bugger wanted the ground double-digging and manuring, which was a lot more than had originally been agreed. They started work and it was very hard going and two hours later, after struggling manfully with his broken-down old wheelbarrow, they had just about cleared the first couple of metres. They then spent more than an hour moving the two spits to the top end of the garden, with one lad pushing the barrow and the other pulling it along with an old piece of rope. Unfortunately, they had broken one of his spades and when he came out to check their progress, he was outraged.

'Bloody hell,' he said. 'You haven't done much have you? I could have done much more myself.'

The lads looked at each other with dismay and Mike suggested that if that was the case, he'd better get on with it. There was more to come. When he saw his spade with a broken haft, he really lost his temper.

'You clumsy young buggers,' he stormed. 'I should have known better than to expect you to take care of my tools. Look what you've done to my spade. The cost of having it repaired will have to come out of your money.'

Geoff picked up the handle and pointed out that it was very old, worm-eaten, and rotten at the bottom. It was little wonder it had broken. Bill was really incensed and angrily shouted that he wasn't having any of their bloody cheek. He continued berating them in front of a growing audience of his neighbours, all listening intently to the one-sided altercation. Some sympathised with the lads, while others thought it was all very funny. Loud were their laughs at the antics of their irate neighbour and the evident discomfort of the two lads. They all knew that Bill was a sly bugger and there could only be one outcome, which wasn't long coming. Both lads had had more than enough of his nonsense.

'We're sorry you're not happy, Mr Clinton,' said Geoff, who was always polite when speaking to an adult, 'but if that's the way that you feel, you'd better do the job yourself.'

They walked away to murmurs of encouragement from the crowd but, as they did so, Bill had the last word.

'You pair of sods haven't heard the last of this, I can tell you,' he shouted. 'I'll be round to see your fathers, you see if I don't.'

But of course he didn't. When Mike had told his old man about what had happened, all he said was that everyone knew what Bill was like. He should have known better than to have got involved with him.

It was too cold to be hanging around the village and on wet evenings, Mike, Keith and some of the other lads often went into the Police Canteen early on, in the hope that the snooker table was free. After payment of the princely sum of sixpence, (2.5 pence), to the Steward, they were allowed to set up the table. If it was past seven-thirty, there was always a chance that members would come in, before they had finished their game and they had to give way immediately and so ran the risk of losing their 'tanner'. If the Steward was in a good mood and they had only been playing for a few minutes, they got it back, but he would usually keep it. Morry and his brother were both 'tasty' at the game, due to the amount of time they spent practising and very often, they did odd jobs for the Steward, such as clearing away the empties and sweeping up outside, which usually brought the desired reward.

Morry was often encouraged to 'take-on' an adult, particularly if he was a new member. The nonsense delighted the old-hands and they would suggest 'a little bit of a wager' to the unsuspecting victim. One would say loudly that he was backing the lad and with a dramatic flourish, put his half-crown on the side of the table. Almost inevitably, the man would look at his opponent and think that he would win with no problem. He would then match the bet and that was quickly followed by others, who mostly bet against him. The suggestions that they had only put a 'few bob' on the lad 'for interest's sake' did not alert the victim to what was going on. Fifteen minutes or so later, unless he was very lucky, the man would be obliged to hand over sufficient cash to buy Morry's backers their beer for the rest of the evening. The odd pint was put aside for the lad for good measure.

One member, who was quite skilled on the table, was the aforesaid Bill Clinton. He would often have quite an audience who, sensing the opportunity for a bit of fun, would split into his and the other player's supporters. Bill had an asset which stood out against all and sundry, and that was his amazing luck. Time and again, when he had run into a 'dry-patch' of missed or foul shots, he would give the cue ball an almighty smack. It would hit the target ball with some force and it then careered around the table, sometimes hitting seven or eight cushions before dropping, almost as a last resort, into a pocket. Such flukes, when played by others, were always referred to as 'Clinton' shots. Sometimes he would aimlessly strike the cue ball, and it would end up leaving his opponent with a difficult snooker. There would always be a sardonic cheer, and Bill would look around in mock affront.

'What's the matter?' he would ask. 'That was a good shot that was, just as I intended.'

While working on the Farm, Mike had been befriended by a young labourer, whose main job was to look after the sheep. Len always had his dog with him and he spent many hours in patiently training it. He was a very large, fit lad, who was perhaps in his mid-twenties. To demonstrate his strength, he liked to lift and carry a two-hundredweight sack of grain through the barn. He could also toss a bale of hay on to a trailer without any effort. He had a great liking for chocolate and was rarely without a large bar in his coat pocket. Like a lot of big men, he was a kind and friendly chap, who believed in working hard and more importantly, doing his job well. His diligence should have been greatly appreciated by the farmer, but that wasn't always the case.

One evening, he asked Mike what he did in the evenings. He replied that, apart from going to night-school, he usually hung around the village with the other lads. Len was clearly unimpressed and Mike then went on to tell him about his interest in playing rugby and that he was in training to build up his fitness. Len then told him there was a Youth Club in a village that was approximately three miles away, and suggested that it might be of interest to him. It was open on two evenings a week and there were regular dances throughout the year. There were also social contacts and sporting activities with other youth clubs. They agreed to go over one evening, when there was no work on the Farm and in the following weeks, their work was interspersed by press ups and the lifting of weights. Mike also ran behind the trailer, when they were returning to the yard. Len made one stipulation about joining the Club, which was that Mike didn't go blabbing about it in the village.

The Farmer's son, Mark, also bent his ear about keeping quiet. They had previously fallen out when Mike and his mates had sabotaged a group of carol singers the previous Christmas. He had been sweet on one of the village girls at the time, and the clowns' antics had led to an angry confrontation. Their relationship had not improved with time. The first visit to the youth club went well and everyone was friendly. With pop music in its ascendancy, a lot of the recent record releases were played and there were the usual games of table tennis, billiards, and darts. It was most enjoyable but, on the ride back, angry words were again exchanged between Mark and Mike. The argument ended when Mark told Len that he wouldn't be going to the Club again. Being mindful that he worked for his father, Len replied that he was a bit too old for it too, so he wouldn't be going again either.

Mike would have to go 'on his Todd', but he welcomed the chance to make new friends. The Club was run by a small team of enthusiastic and dedicated adults and it turned out to be as good as Len had said. In addition to the social side, there were training sessions in the school hall on Thursday evenings and on the sports ground on Sunday mornings. They were held mainly for the village football teams and included energetic work-outs and coaching routines. It was just what Mike needed, and he soon got to know the lads. Cross-country runs around the village added yet more interest.

In contrast to the problems that regularly arose between the youths of the local villages, the club was very relaxed. Mike had soon taken a fancy to Debbie, but their friendship got no further than a few dances on club nights. He completely forgot the promise he had made to Len about keeping quiet when he was asked where he had got to the previous evening. He graphically described the female attractions and not surprisingly, the maligned brothers were very interested. They had been to the same school as most of the girls he mentioned and decided to go to the next dance. Mike had been wrong to even discuss it, but it was too late for any regrets. He hoped they would forget all about it and didn't mention it again, but they didn't and he was to very much rue his folly.

They arrived at the club much too early, the time being only just after seven o'clock. It wasn't due to start until an hour later and it wouldn't warm-up until well after that. Mike had stupidly thought it would start at the same time as the normal club evenings. Morry was a pragmatic character and was always quick to act upon any situation to his advantage. Scruples were foreign to his nature and he decided that the free hour would enable him to go for a few beers. The three lads rode back down the road to the pub, where the lad quickly downed several pints. He was soon in full voice about how he was going to take the dance by storm, saying that he fancied a girl in the village, though whether or not she liked him was a different matter. He would soon be put right on that small point.

The problem was, Morry couldn't hold his drink and he became increasingly loud as they rode back to the hall. In less than half an hour, he was involved in a spat with some other lads and then much to Mike's dismay, he then insulted both Debbie and her friend Heather, which brought an abrupt end to their friendship. Not long after, the brothers were ejected following a heated argument with the club leader. Mike stayed on, but was left to reflect on his stupidity. As he was riding home, he thought about the words of a well-liked teacher, who had been very much a gentleman of the 'old school'. He had once told his class that people always judged a person by the company he kept and just how right that wise old man had been was amply demonstrated. Debbie never spoke to him again.

Worse was to come when the Farmer sent Mike out to give Len a hand. He had heard about the shenanigans at the dance and was furious that Mike had broken his promise. He felt very strongly that the antics of the brothers had reflected badly on himself.

135

'You've let me down,' he said angrily. 'You promised not to go telling them where you were going and if that's how you are, then I don't want anything more to do with you.'

Despite Mike's apologies, the damage had been done and his relationship with Len was irreparably marred. The only one who gained satisfaction about the whole charade was Mark and he took great pleasure in repeatedly saying 'I told you so' to Len. He didn't miss any opportunity to stir it, when Mike was around. With the hay-making well in hand, Mike didn't have time to go out of the village and his visits to the club ceased for a while. Jiving was the 'in' mode of dancing at the time and young people took every opportunity to leap around the floor. They often incurred the displeasure of the dedicated ballroom dancers and were often pointedly asked to desist, particularly when over enthusiastic. There was no such impediment in the Club. Some brought their latest records for the enjoyment of everyone and the sessions were continually devoted to learning the new dance. Even the most awkward lad could be persuaded on to the floor by a light-footed lass.

Jenny was one of the best dancers and she was always dressed simply in a plain white, short-sleeved blouse and a flared floral skirt, with two or three petticoats beneath. The pony-tail hair-style was popular and there was a lot of competition among the girls to be the best turned-out. A young man called Jake had recently bought his first motorbike, a 250 cc, 'single-pot' BSA. It was second-hand, but in good nick and when he rode it down to the Club, a lot of the lads and lasses were very impressed. At the end of the evening, he rode off proudly with a cheery wave and a lot of noise. A week or so later, an incident occurred which caused a lot of heartache among the members.

No one knew how Jake persuaded Jenny to let him to give her a lift home, but she accepted his offer. Less than a mile from the Club and on a sharp bend, the lad lost control of his machine and they came off it. Jenny was tragically killed. Someone later said that Jake had been more concerned about the damage to his bike, than the poor lass lying in the road. Only a few weeks later, he turned up at the club as though nothing untoward had happened. Most of the members had had a genuine affection for the girl and were angry and resentful about his lack of concern. From then on, motorbikes were off the agenda, and when Jake went home, he did so on his own.

Chapter 8

All Types of Engines

On a Friday morning, the lads were called to the front of the office and told where they were to report the following Monday morning. There was a lot of talk about how the changes would affect them personally. More than half of them were going to a small workshop on the first floor of the small complex in the Factory, which included the lecture room. Moving on didn't appeal to everyone and there was a lot of talk about how the new workplace would compare with their present one. When they later discussed it over dinner, an older lad told them that their new Instructors would be 'a bit different' to Tommo and his colleagues. One, who was disdainfully referred to one as 'Mad Marsh', was said to be both aggressive and volatile. While the lads listened with trepidation, some were of the view that their informant was only trying to 'put the wind up them'. They would have to face up to any trouble, if and when it came. There was no point worrying about it.

There was the usual hustle and bustle as the lads collected their belongings together. As they went out of the door, most of them thanked the Instructors and noisily said goodbye to their mates who were going elsewhere. When they arrived at their new shop, they had to carry their toolboxes up two flights of stairs and were relieved to find there were no Instructors waiting for them. It was much the same as three months before. The tea break came and went and everyone sat about waiting to be told what to do.

Eventually, the door which separated the offices from the shop opened and three Instructors walked in. Despite the fact that there hadn't been any undue noise, Mr Marsh shouted for silence. They didn't respond quickly enough, because he exploded into a rage, picked up a large hammer and threw it with some force across the shop. It thudded against a wall, having narrowly missed two of the lads. One of them picked it up and threw it back with equal force and the Instructors quickly retreated back into their office.

There was a stunned silence, then someone suggested that the lad should get lost, to avoid almost certain retribution. They didn't have long to wait before Mr Barry walked in, followed closely by his indignant Instructors. He called for attention, then lectured them at length about the need for strict discipline and the dangers of throwing tools about. It was a sentiment with which they all agreed. He then demanded that the Apprentice who had thrown the hammer step forward. Having 'thought as much' at the identity of the culprit, he told them they would hear more about it later and that the Instructors would take the name of anyone who stepped out of line.

The atmosphere in the shop was tense as Marsh, the Senior Instructor, told them about what they were going to do. His discourse was given in a curt manner; so very different to what they had been used to. One thing was sure, they were determined to protect the lad under threat. Two lads said they would go to see Mr Barry, because he had to know exactly what had happened. There had been a lively discussion about what had happened during the dinner hour and on their way back to the shop, they had called in to seek Tommo's advice.

'You know I can't get involved in any bother,' he'd replied. 'The Management might think I had something to do with it and then I'd be for it. If I'm asked about how you behaved when you were with me, that's different. My weekly reports will confirm that I had no trouble with anyone. If I were you, I'd go to see Mister Barry and explain what happened. Just tell it to him as you've told it to me. I'm sure he'll listen.'

They thanked him and had returned to tell their mates what he had said. When the Instructors came back into the shop, the reps politely asked to see Mr Barry. Marsh must have known he was in trouble, because he abruptly told them to get back to their benches.

'We're not going to have any barrack-room lawyers here, I can tell you,' he angrily replied.

The Apprentices stopped what they were doing and it was clear that nothing would be done until the problem was sorted. He had no alternative but to accede to their request and went into the office. When he returned, he sullenly told them that the Manager would see them right away. The reps looked apprehensively at each other and when they went into his office, Barry was sitting with his assistant and they were both looking very stern.

Sit down,' he said, pointing to the chairs in front of his desk. 'I'm told that you want to discuss this morning's disgraceful episode in the workshop. If it will clear the matter up, then I'll be pleased to hear what you have to say.'

Fred started by saying that when the Apprentices arrived in the shop, there was no one there and it had been some time after the morning break before their Instructors had appeared. The lads may have been talking, but they had quietened down when Mr Marsh had called for silence. Perhaps it had not been quickly enough because he had lost his temper and had thrown a large hammer across the shop. Had it hit anyone, it would have seriously injured him. As it was, it had knocked a large piece of plaster off the wall. Barry looked pointedly at his assistant and it was obvious that they were unaware of all the facts.

'There can be no excuse for anyone throwing hammers about,' Fred went on. Everyone is sorry to complain, but we cannot accept that an Instructor could do something so dangerous.'

Barry interrupted him by saying that they had to maintain discipline. There had been numerous incidents in the past year, when things had got out of hand. Fred pointed out that Mr Marsh had a bad reputation among the Apprentices and his action that morning had gone beyond normal discipline. There may have been misbehaviour in the past but in this instance, no one had done anything wrong. Barry replied that he had heard enough and would make further inquiries and speak to them again after he had done so.

On their return, Marsh headed off any discussion by blandly telling Fred and his mate to return to their benches. Having overstepped the mark, he was perhaps trying to make up for it by being reasonable. It was clearly not the 'Mad Marsh' that everyone knew and disliked.

Three small diesel driven mobile air-compressors had been brought into the shop and he started off by explaining their functions. He gave them examples of the many uses to which they could be put, particularly when part of a ship's equipment. The lads were then split into three working parties, each one to strip-down a unit under their Instructors' supervision. There was a lot of excited chat, though three machines between more than twenty lads indicated that they were not going to be unduly stretched.

The next morning, the Instructors were again late coming into the shop and when they did, Marsh was not with them. The lads were still very subdued, with none of the usual chatter and laughter. Mr Barry had sent for Marsh soon after he had clocked on, because his inquiries had apparently opened 'a whole can of worms'. His Supervisor's belligerent attitude to his Apprentices had at last been exposed. When there had been complaints in the past, he had assumed that they had come from malcontents intent on causing trouble for an Instructor, who was trying to run a tight ship. After talking to the reps, he had spoken to the other Supervisors in turn and had been told that it hadn't been an isolated incident. Having established the truth, he had taken the necessary action.

Marsh was 'moved' to another job. No doubt, he had been helped on his way by his colleagues, who had seen an opportunity to get rid of him. In any working environment, there are always those who look for the chance to stab someone else in the back, usually when he or she is vulnerable. It often provides the means for a move up the ladder. With Marsh gone, there was a marked improvement in the moral of the apprentices. Their Instructors were much more relaxed, and they went out of their way to give their charges every help in what they were doing. A week or so later, they were moved to a new working area on the ground floor of the Factory under a new Senior Instructor.

There was a large range of old engines and machines there and Dan and Mike were told to overhaul a petrol-driven lawn mower. It was powered by a four-stroke engine, which gave them the opportunity to put into practice the lessons learned in the lecture room. The engine was soon stripped down and the components laid out on their bench. Their first lesson was in the correct method of replacing the old piston rings. The piston was cleaned and the diameter checked to gauge the wear which had taken place. The fitting of the new rings was a fiddly job and their Instructor used a square of very thin, shim steel, which was wrapped around the piston. When the rings were passed over it, they were expanded sufficiently to be inserted into the grooves below. The cylinder was also inspected and the bore measured along its length. The wear was minimal, with no further action needed.

The cleaning of the carburettor led to a heated argument, with Dan saying that the outside should be properly cleaned and not just wiped-off. Even though it was off an old machine, the job still had to be done properly. He was right and it was soon again in pristine condition. The cutting cylinder and end-bearings needed attention because two of the six blades, which ran diagonally around it, had been damaged. It was wire-brushed, then sent over to the welding shop for repair. From there, it went on to the machine shop for grinding around its circumference. The grinding was done in an adapted lathe to form a smooth, even and parallel cylinder.

The cutting blade had been also been removed from the bottom of the machine and lightly reground. With both components replaced, the cutting function was set up and the instructor used a cigarette paper to check it. If it cut the very thin paper cleanly, then it would cut grass. After having been reassembled, the engine unit was then reinstalled in the frame. The drive-chains, cogs and clutch were then refitted, followed by the carburettor and petrol tank. The controls were reconnected, the ignition timing checked and the points set. The tank was filled with petrol and after several attempts, the engine was started. It promptly emitted clouds of acrid, blue smoke, much to the discomfort of their workmates. The last job was to tweak the fuel/air mixture and the engine was soon running as smooth as silk.

A small group were working on a large, eight cylinder diesel generator, the parts of which were in numerous boxes lying around the shop. They were under the instruction of an old Fitter, a portly little man called Ted. His bottle-bottom 'granny' glasses gave him an exaggerated, vacant expression, which amused them greatly. He was a bit odd, for he daubed his face with rouge, a thick coating of face powder and a liberal application of lipstick. The poor old fellow had become unbalanced after the death of his wife and had taken to wearing her underclothes and makeup to work. They were asked to show him a bit of consideration and let him be. Despite his odd ways, Ted was a very good tradesman and they would learn a lot from him. He was a quiet, unassuming man who would amuse them greatly with his tales of his seafaring days.

The lads quietly eyed up their new boss and concluded that he was completely away with the birds. The old fellow spent most of his time day-dreaming, staring sightlessly into space and quietly humming to himself. He was probably reliving happier days, before old age and illness had deprived him of his wife. Although a few funny comments were made, no one took advantage or was in any way unpleasant to him. As the Instructor had said, he was soon amusing them with tales of his years of service in the 'Andrew'. He yearned for the good old days of the coal-fired Ships, on which he had served in the West Indies. He wasn't shooting a line, because he had indeed served as a Chief ERA in the Royal Navy for many years.

Ted and his team went over the main block and, over the ensuing weeks, they carried out the refurbishment of most of the engine's components. The most interesting job was the overhaul of the pistons and connecting rods, including the bottom-end bearings. Ted may have been a bit funny, but he knew what he was doing. He would accept no half measures, or 'naffing the pig', as he so quaintly put it in a passing moment of lucidity. If something was not to his satisfaction, he quietly said so. There was no argument and having made a point, he would walk away. With all eight piston assemblies stripped down to basics, the components were thoroughly cleaned then laid out on a bench to await reassembly. Their next job was to fit the bottom end bearings, a key stage in the overhaul, and Ted explained at length about how best to go about it.

Seeing something special going on, other lads came over to listen to what the old Fitter had to say. Work on the crankshaft had already been completed and it had been set up on two large wooden 'vee-blocks' and covered with a large square of cloth. Ted was pleased to have an audience and he puffed away contentedly on his malodorous pipe as he applied a very light cover of blue to the surface of the first journal. He put the shells into the bottom end and brought the two halves together, then nipped-up the fixings. A single turn of the shaft was sufficient to mark the shells and having taken them out again, they were in turn put in a vice and he deftly scraped away the high spots. After wiping off most of the blue, he replaced the bottom-end for a final check. When he opened it up again, his audience saw that both shells were marked right across the full faces of the bearing surfaces.

'That's how it's done,' he said to his lads, now you do the other ones.'

He then crossed the shop, sat down, and continued puffing gently on his pipe.

Chapter 9

Learning Fast

A valuable lesson had been learned and it would, in time, prove to be an indispensable part of their trade. The old adage that one should 'never judge a book by its cover' was never more apt. As they'd been told, Ted was indeed a craftsman of great experience. Their Instructors made the most of his skills, by regularly changing the Apprentices who worked with him. What he had to tell the youngsters, including his tall stories, would almost certainly bear fruit in later years. One morning, the old fellow spun a yarn which not only caused great amusement but, in their unanimous view, it really 'took the biscuit'. With them steadily working, he settled down and after lighting up his pipe, he 'got under way.

'Many years ago, in the West Indies,' he said, with a faraway look in his rheumy eyes, I was Chief ERA on an old four-stacker Turtle-back. She was a natural draught, coal-burning, up an' downer.' To anyone else, this would have been known as a four-funnelled, coal-burning Destroyer, with reciprocating main-engines and natural draft boilers.

'It was as hot as hell down below, and she was always breaking-down. At times, we were hard put to keep her going. One morning, we had a bottom end go in the starboard engine and with heavy weather brewing, the Old Man, (the Captain), was in a right state. We had to get under way as quickly as possible. I took one look at the bearing and thought, 's'truth, this is a pearler'. An oil-way was blocked, which caused the bearing to overheat and the white metal lining had melted. There was a fair bit of scoring on the journal, so we were in a right a fix.

'Seeing the extent of the damage and being short of time, normal scrapers weren't any good and we were stuck about how best to tackle the job. I soon sussed what had to be done and I said to my mate, there's just the thing in the stores. I went down and picked up a house-brick, what I'd seen lying on a shelf some time before. I put it straight into the shell and rubbed away and it was just the job. We soon had the bearing fixed and were under way again before the storm broke. Yeh, that was a good job, that was.'

Being unsure as to whether or not he was having them on, the lads stifled the urge to laugh. The old lad wandered off and they couldn't hold their mirth any longer. Another of his tales, again told with a straight face, had the same effect. It was about how he and his hardy band of Stokers had replaced a lost 'screw' (a propeller) while anchored in a lagoon. Luckily, there was a replacement on the upper deck and after Jimmy, (the First Lieutenant), had ballasted the ship down by the head, they rigged the propeller over the side and on to the end of the shaft 'as quick as you like'. Was it an impossible day dream? Well, maybe. When they told the older lads about the tale, they laughingly replied that they had heard it all before and had believed every word.

'I've always known that Old Ted knows a thing or two,' the Instructor said, 'but I reckon the crafty old sod's been having you on, and not for the first time, either.'

The lads working on the engine had been split into two groups, with the first reinstalling the crankshaft. The second was attaching the matching connecting rods to the pistons. Each piston had already been fitted with new rings, which had been done under Ted's close supervision and with particular care. With the crankshaft installed into the main bearings, the pistons were in turn dropped into their cylinders. As each one was boxed up, the engine was barred over, ready for the insertion of the next one. It was steady, interesting work and those involved were enviously watched by the lads who had more mundane jobs to do.

Everyone was clearly enjoying the work. There were all sorts of engines being worked on, some of the most interesting being the single and double-acting steam reciprocating pump-units. The majority of Warships and auxiliary vessels were still steam-driven, and turbines were used for the main propulsion. A range of rotary and 'up and down' engines catered for the auxiliary applications. The reciprocating engine had given very many years of sterling service, though many of the more compact multi-stage pumps were powered by electric motors. On the more modern Vessels, the principle units often had steam turbines as emergency back-ups. Despite their arduous duties, the old 'up and downers' were the most reliable and it would be some years before they were eventually replaced.

The engines in the shop were very suitable for practical instruction purposes and the various functions easily explained by the instructors. The design parameters had already been covered in the lecture room. Good lessons were learned from working on the century-old technology. Returning to the lads working with Ted, the rebuilding of the engine progressed steadily. With the installation of the pistons completed, the cylinder heads were replaced and hardened down. Ted demonstrated how to properly adjust the tappets and each lad had a go. The rocker covers were then loosely placed on top.

Ted sent Geoff and Mark down to the test house to collect the injectors, which had been sent for either refurbishment or replacement. They were issued on a 'new for old' basis and were readily available from stock. Sensing the opportunity for a skive, they gleefully went off to a chorus of ribald comments. On arrival, they reported to the charge-hand and he handed over the injectors without comment. That was not what they wanted and they looked for an excuse to delay their return to the shop. Geoff told him that they were very interested in diesel engines and had a particular interest in the testing of the pumps and injectors. They would very much like to look around his test house, to pick up a few points. He must have known what they were up to but he told them to talk to his assistant, Derek, who was a fifth year Apprentice and he seemed pleased to see them.

He readily explained how he dismantled, cleaned and reassembled the various components, then set them up on rigs for testing and calibration. To their dismay, he was finished in less than half an hour. They had to drag things out and with no one else to question their presence, it wasn't difficult.

They spent a very relaxed couple of hours in the shop, yarning about everything but work. Derek had a new Triumph Tiger 21, which was a 350cc, twin-cylinder motorcycle; a beautiful machine and his pride and joy. With the job being so 'cushy', he had indeed been fortunate to have been there for nearly six months. The general rule was that each Apprentice spent approximately three months in each Department. However, Derek was a bright lad, who had successfully passed through the Upper School and was destined for much better things than most of his mates. He was industrious and having carried out his work very much to the satisfaction of his Manager, strings had obviously been pulled.

The design and quality of British motorcycles at the time was poor, by modern standards and most of the traditional manufacturers had either gone or were going out of business. Their competitors were mostly Japanese and they had seized their opportunity to take over as world leaders in the field. They designed, built and marketed machines which completely eclipsed the British models. Derek's bike was only a few months old and it was already showing signs of deterioration, particularly on the chromed fittings. He had taken advantage of a nearby facility and was well along the road in re-chroming numerous parts. When asked how he found the time, he replied that he got on with his work in the mornings, which left the afternoons free for his other little jobs. It was illegal, but his Charge-hand turned a blind eye, providing that he didn't do work for anyone else.

When Geoff and Mark got back to the shop, they said nothing about what they had seen and they ignored their mates' silly comments. After dinner, the injectors were fitted into the engine, again under the rheumy eyes of the fitter. The fuel pump and filters had already been installed on the side of the engine and the fuel tank was bolted on top. The system was then completed, with various copper pipes being renewed as necessary. The next morning, the lubricating oil system was installed. After the exhaust manifold and silencer had been fitted, the crank-case was closely inspected and the doors finally replaced. Only the governor and the throttle linkage remained to be fitted and that was followed by 'timing' of the engine.

The generator had been overhauled in the electrical shop, and its return caused a buzz of interest. It was offloaded by a 'rigger, who huffily ordered everyone to stand clear. As he attached the straps to the casing, he stressed the importance of always using certified lifting gear and that the paperwork had to be in order – all of the test certificates had to be valid. He lifted the generator off the truck, swung it round and it was lowered on to the skid. The holding down bolts were inserted and nipped, then the half-couplings were aligned. It was the Apprentices' first introduction to the use of double clock-gauges, which were the best way of aligning shafts and couplings. The holding down bolts were then hardened down, and a final check ensured that nothing had moved. The coupling was then boxed up and the 'rocker-covers' bolted-on.

The next morning, the fuel tank was filled with diesel and the sump with lubricating oil, following which, the starting battery was installed. The engine was ready for a light test-run and the exhaust was connected to a flexible pipe, which passed up out through the roof. The run lasted for less than quarter of an hour, with a couple of the lads recording the temperatures and pressures indicated by the gauges, which were mounted at the non-drive end of the engine. The generator was then connected to a 'test-rig' and a further run was overseen by an electrical fitter and his mate. They confirmed that all was in order and with a final flourish, Ted shut it down. The next day, the unit was loaded on to a lorry and taken away.

A steam engine is a most beautiful creation, with a very smooth, almost silky movement. Three lads were working on a vertical, double-acting machine, the type of which was used for pumping feed water, fuel and lubricating oils. It had given many lads practical training in how to service both steam and pumping ends. Because it had been taken apart so many times, the fixings were easily undone, which would rarely be the case with one which had been in prolonged service. In addition to a travelling three tons capacity electric, overhead crane, which ran the length of the shop, there were two beams, which were attached to main columns and rigged with chain blocks. They provided an additional means of handling components which were too heavy to move by hand.

It was a simple task to lift the cover off the steam end, then disconnect and remove the piston from the cylinder. Similarly, there was no problem in dismantling the pump end and the services of the rigger were not required for such light work. The components were laid out on a bench and the instructor oversaw the removal of the old rings and the fitting of new ones. He discussed the functions of the shuttle valve and the water-end valve box with many of his lads. The former controlled the ingress of steam into the cylinder and the latter, the passage of water through the pump. Both functions had been covered in the lecture room, but with the 'animals' in front of them, their workings were that much clearer.

The components were clean, with only workshop grime to be wiped away. Where damaged, the 'non-bright' surfaces were wire-brushed and given a lick of paint. They had already been told many times that the moving components of an engine should never be painted. The linkages always had a bright finish, with a light covering of oil regularly applied to preclude rust discolouration. The refurbishment of the various parts took some time, then a start was made on the reassembly of the machine.

There was a bit of spat amongst some of the lads one dinner time, which caused some excitement. Someone had brought a battered football to work for a kick- about in the road outside the shop. Dave was a big lad and was probably a better player than any of his mates. However, he was 'a clogger', a term which was generally used by football critics to describe anyone who was overly-aggressive and lacked finesse in his play. Despite the games being light-hearted, he always ran about in the same manic way as when he was playing in a proper match. The altercation arose because his mates wore light shoes, while he sported a pair of hob-nailed boots. A succession of lads suffered painfully from his enthusiastic depredations.

He had been told a number of times to tone it down a bit, because they didn't appreciate having the skin taken off their shins or their ankles bruised. Dave took no notice and when a lad was unceremoniously upended on the hard surface, he lost his temper, jumped to his feet and kicked the legs from under his aggressor. His mates quickly intervened to calm things down. The next day, the answer to the problem came from Dave himself. He had a way of trapping the ball by stamping on it with some force and most times, he controlled the ball but often, it shot away at an angle from his foot. Dave insisted that the only proper way was to 'kill it', and he did just that. The ball burst, and that was the end of the dinner time kick-abouts.

Chapter 10

Bolshie Billy

All too soon, their stint in the engine shop was over and it was time to move on. Four of the lads, including Mike, were sent to a fitting facility at the top end of the factory. They were pleased when told that they would be doing assembly work, as the Foreman explained what the job entailed. He stressed the need for their diligence and to do exactly as they were told, then took them over to the workbenches. He pointed out the Fitters with whom they would be working, naming each one as he did so. Mike's eager optimism was promptly shattered, when he walked over to introduce himself to Billy, who looked him up and down and turned away without speaking. He was in his mid to late fifties, very small in stature, thin to the point of gauntness and as bald as a coot. His granny glasses, through which he peered malevolently, gave him a sinister look. Mike took umbrage.

'Excuse me,' he said, 'I was told to report to you. You might have the good manners to reply.'

The little man turned around and quietly replied, carefully enunciating every word. He spoke very much like Wilfred Bramble, the actor who played the old man in the television comedy series, 'Steptoe and Son' and he was quivering with outrage at the lad's impertinence.

'When you speak to me, sonny,' he said and curling his lip in contempt, 'you do it with a bit of respect. Let me tell you right away, I hate mouthy, bloody Apprentices, particularly cheeky sods like you. I've heard all about you and if I had any say, I wouldn't have anything to do with you, so don't come in here throwing your weight about. There's your vice; go and stand by it until I give you something to do.'

His belligerent reaction took Mike aback and for a moment or two, he was nonplussed. He should have kept his mouth shut, because older lads had already warned him about the problems with some of the Fitters.

'Now just hold on, Mister,' he said, louder than he should have. 'I only wanted to say hello and didn't expect to get a bollocking for it. Bloody hell, what's the matter with you? If you don't want me to work with you, I'll ask the Foreman to put me with someone else.

'You do what you bloody well like,' shouted the little man. 'One thing's for sure, you're not working with me and that's final.' He then turned away again.

'You are a silly sod, Mike,' said Mal, one of the other Apprentices. 'You've really upset him by answering back. You should have just kept quiet and it would have sorted itself out. You'll have to go over and apologise, when he's cooled down.'

Mike was so angry, he certainly wasn't going to apologise to the horrible little bugger. He walked over to the office and after knocking on the door, he went in and told him about what had happened. After listening to most of his story, the Foreman interrupted him.

'Look lad, everyone knows what Billy is like and most people take no notice of him. I'm not bothered that he doesn't want you to work with him, because it's happened before. You'll just have go and work with Cyril. I'll tell one of the other lads to work with Billy, then we'll all be happy. I'd be interested to find out though why he objects to you. Off you go and tell Mal I'd like a word.'

Mike went back to his place and after pointing the lad in the foreman's direction, he went over to introduce himself to Cyril. He was also elderly, but was short and rotund and he had a welcoming smile when he replied. He made no reference to Mike's altercation, but merely nodded towards some boxes of machined parts, which were lying on the floor. He told him that he could start by 'de-burring' them. Mike picked up a box and carried it over to his bench. In doing so, he noticed that the other apprentices were doing the same job. There was a large number of chain sprockets, of various sizes, the fettling of which would provide them with weeks of work. When he returned, Mal was far from pleased.

'You've dropped me in it,' he complained bitterly. 'Why couldn't you just keep your mouth shut for once?'

Having had enough argument for one day, Mike ignored the rebuke and turned to his Fitter to ask what the sprockets were for. Cyril explained that they were to be installed in a number of large chain-driven units, which were to be assembled in the shop. They were destined for two Aircraft Carriers, which were under construction in a Civil Shipyard. When in operation, they would move an aircraft across the deck to position it in line with a steam catapult, which would assist it in 'take-off'. More than three hundred and fifty sprockets had to be de-burred, to ensure their free movement in operation. Each one had been machined from solid steel-bar, with the bore splined to close tolerance dimensions, to give a sliding fit on its shaft. The cutting of the teeth had been done on a milling-machine, which had left sharp burrs on the edges.

There was a lot of grumbling about the job when they were discussing it over their dinner and their mates were highly amused when told about Mike's run-in with 'Bolshie Billy'. Some of the lads had landed in 'cushy numbers' and were smugly looking forward to the next three months. They could hardly contain their mirth, winking and grinning slyly at each other and making daft comments.

'It's all very well for you lot to laugh', said John, 'you don't have to put up with all the shit. You should see the awful job we've been given, bloody sprockets covered in cutting oil and grease, with sharp edges you could shave with.'

After dinner, Mike walked back to the Factory with Jim, who was in his third year. He laughed loudly about Mike's problem and shouted to some other lads, who were walking in the same direction.

'Hey you lot, come and listen to this. This poor sod has only gone to work with Billie Murtell, hasn't he? I'm sorry old mate,' he said to Mike and laughing loudly, 'but you really have got the shitty end of the stick this time, ain't he lads?'

They duly commiserated, but a lad called Al looked distinctly unimpressed. He told Mike that he had worked in the same shop during his second year and he was most scathing about Billy.

'I don't suppose you know he was one of the buggers that was sent away from the Yard during the War, because of their politics,' he said glumly. 'Not many people remember it now, but its right enough, because my old man knows him well. Don't you worry about him, the horrible little bastard,' he went on. 'He's a really nasty piece of work. Like many of his kind, he's all wind and piss, shouting the odds about brotherly love and workers' rights one minute, then being nasty to everybody around him the next. He's not worth bothering about.'

After they had clocked on, the lads quietly talked about how best to cope with the unpleasantness. They agreed that it was no good looking for trouble and they would just have to get on with the job. Only a few minutes later, there was a bustle behind them and they were verbally assailed by Billy, who was obviously still very put out.

'Come on you lazy sods,' he cried, 'you haven't got time to stand about yarning. You've been told what to do, so get on with it. This job's on a price, so the sooner it's finished, the more we'll earn.'

If there was one form of persuasion which spurred the average Matey into action, it was the chance to earn extra money. While his productivity was often less than desired, the magic word 'bonus' could be guaranteed to put a spring in his step. The lads were soon speculating about their potential rewards and they set to with a will. Having had no previous experience of piece-work, they were perhaps over-optimistic that they too had fallen on their feet. They beavered away, with none of the back-chat and bawdy humour which was the norm. The breaks came without being dragged out and it was a thoughtful bunch of lads that queued to clock-off on the following Friday afternoon. Mal summed up the situation when he said that the week hadn't been all that bad after all. In reply, John again made the point that the atmosphere in the Shop was most definitely not what it ought to be.

'Haven't you noticed that the Fitters don't have much to say, when Billy's around? It's almost as if they're afraid of stepping out of line. Something is bloody wrong here.'

Mal agreed it was 'a bit subdued', but it was none of their business and he doubted if there was anything untoward going on. During the next week, the lads soldiered on, in diligently taking the burrs off, then cleaning and oiling the sprockets before putting them back in the boxes. The work was hard on their hands and a moment of carelessness often resulted in cuts and abrasions. To make things worse, the residual cutting-oil, which had been used in the machining process, was obnoxious. Initially, they had washed each sprocket in paraffin before starting work, but that had been discarded as a waste of time. Some of their cuts became infected and were treated by the Factory first aider. Wearing gloves was unknown, and anyone who did so would have soon been accused by his workmates of being soft.

The low morale in the shop was the main topic of conversation in the canteen for some days and when they were asked about it, the older Apprentices said it had been like it for a long time.

'I'll tell you what it is,' said Al, earnestly looking round at the others. 'It's that Billy Murtell. They're all shit-scared of him, the nasty little bugger.'

'Go on with you,' said another lad. 'How do you make that out?'

'It's because he's a Shop Steward, and he's also on the works council. He's got a lot of irons in the fire and what's more, he's as thick as thieves with the convener. They've got things tightly sewn up and most people think it best not to cross them. Everyone is shit-scared, and that's why they keep to themselves. Like a lot of little men in positions of power, Billy likes to throw his weight about. I'll say no more,' he concluded dramatically.

His audience was taken aback by his vehemence and he was reminded of the need to keep his voice down. They didn't want what anything to get back to Billy, because it would only make things worse. One ploy, which they decided on, was to try to butter up their Fitters. Malcom and Pete remained of the view that they should stop messing about and just get on with the job.

'You would say that, what with working with him and all,' quipped Mike, smiling craftily.

The lad wasn't going to fall for that and he bluntly told Mike he was wasting his time trying to include him in his devious nonsense.

Gradually, the pieces of the enigma fell into place and it was just as Al had said. Billy's only authority was his undeniable influence in all matters Union. Between them, he and the convener wielded a considerable power in the factory and would go to any lengths to deal with anyone who crossed them. The Dockyard was a designated Strategic Defence Establishment, where industrial action was forbidden by law. Disputes were always settled in line with laid-down procedures. It was very different from the major industries in the private sector. There, the workers were constantly in confrontation with their employers and were regularly either 'working to rule' or on strike. Disruption had become an accepted way of life and would remain so until the late 1970's.

The long-standing agreement with management about the recruitment of apprentices still appertained. Many lads remained averse to joining the Union and they deeply resented any pressure to do so, real or imaginary. Within a few days of their arrival, Billy started his subtle campaign by discussing it with Mal. He didn't have much patience for the finer points of persuasion or accept that the young people in his care had a choice in the matter. Mike and John were typical of the 'antis' and were aggressive to anyone who threatened them. In contrast, the other two lads were more mature and they resisted Billy's blandishments in a more subtle way.

Mal was a member of the 'Young Conservatives' and had a keen interest in politics. He and Billy had numerous discussions about the Union movement and the man realised that he had met his match. The lad was very aware of what was going on and easily countered a lot of the man's socialist assertions. They sensibly discussed the suffering of the people living under the yoke of communism and were soon on friendly terms. The hostility that Billy habitually showed to Apprentices was noticeably absent with Mal and to a lesser extent, his pal Pete. That goodwill did not extend to Mike and John and one morning, after making a few petty, critical comments to them, he came to the point.

'Neither of you are in the Union, are you?,' he asked the balefully.

They looked at each other with mock concern. They had known it would only be a matter of time before they were confronted, and Mike was ready with his answer. He replied that they were thinking about it and would let him know when they'd made up their minds. That wasn't good enough and with a flush of anger rising in his face, the little man blew again. Mike and John stood their ground in facing up to, or rather, looking down on him. Older lads, who had worked in the shop in the past, were of the view that he was a toothless tiger and quietly staring him out was the best way to get him to sod off. Both lads were careful not to raise their voices, but Billy was determined they would not get the better of him.

'I'll have you know,' he said dolefully, 'that generations of working people fought so that buggers like you could enjoy all the benefits you have today. You're typical of today's youth. You're shiftless and couldn't care less about what others have suffered on your behalf. All you can do is look out for yourselves and you make me sick. If I had my way, everyone would be in the Union; then we wouldn't have to work with the likes of you.'

Everyone else had stopped work, in the expectation that there was going to be yet another row. They were disappointed, because the lads turned back to their work and ignored him. A few minutes later, they saw their adversary going into the convener's cabin, where he remained for nearly half an hour. On his return, he went straight to his bench and stood there in angry silence, glowering at the two lads.

Chapter 11

Dirty Tricks

One morning, Mike showed Cyril a sprocket, which had a small blemish on the outside of a tooth. After he had looked at it closely, the fitter agreed it was defective and put it to one side. While they were talking, Mike asked him what he thought about Union membership and was taken aback by the vehemence of his reaction.

'Now lad, don't bring me into your silly arguments,' he replied sternly, because whether or not you join the Union is entirely up to you. I keep myself to myself and I don't get involved. I'll tell you though, before someone else does, I'm a lay preacher, and I'm not obliged to join the Union.'

He had neatly dodged the issue. Another Fitter called Ron, who was working nearby and had overheard them talking, was more forthcoming. Seeing Billy was out of the shop, he beckoned the lads over to his bench.

'I couldn't help overhearing what you asked Cyril,' he said quietly. 'Just a word of caution, be very careful about what you say in this shop.' He lowered his voice, so that they had to stand very close to hear what he was saying. 'Some people get a lot of pleasure from stirring it, if you know what I mean. You've probably noticed that the atmosphere around here is not what you'd call relaxed. I'm one of those that joined the Union because I had to. After twenty-two years in the Andrew, I never thought the day would come when I would be dictated to by a bunch of bastards like them,' he said, nodding pointedly towards the Convener's hut.

Like so many ex-servicemen, he was not sympathetic to the concepts of solidarity and brotherly love. He told them they should 'stand by their guns' and only join when it suited them. Mike said he had no intention of doing so at that time, though he would probably do so in the future. He had only been awkward with Billy after he was so offensive and was 'buggered' if he would fall into line.

'That's up to you lad, but just remember, he's a crafty little sod and he won't give up easily, you mark my words.'

Later, when he was again talking to Cyril, Mike asked him about his church activities. He replied that he and his wife were committed Methodists and it was their main interest. Both their families had a long history of service to their chapel and their only regret was that they had not been blessed with children, to carry on after them. He went on to say that he always kept his preaching very much apart from his work, but was only too pleased to help if someone was genuinely interested or had a problem. Mike then remarked that he had seen him driving a new Standard Vanguard. It was a large car for such a small man, though he had the tact not to say so. It was unusual for a Matey to own a car, let alone a new model, which was luxurious in comparison to a lot of the old bangers on the roads. That gave Cyril his chance to make another point.

'Yes, it's my one weakness,' he said solemnly, 'and I've got a strict rule about it. I don't give other people lifts and the like, so if you're dropping hints, don't. Then I won't have to say no, will I? The car cost us a lot of money and it's for our sole use and pleasure. It's not there for the convenience of other people.'

'I'm not dropping hints,' Mike replied quickly. 'I've a good bike and I'm happy to make my own way to and from work. Anyway, I live seven miles out in the sticks and I don't think you go my way anyhow.'

He knew what the old fellow meant. There was always someone who, seeing another person with something they envied, were quick to seek to get some advantage from it. When rebuffed, they were inevitably put-out. Later, when they were talking about Cyril, Mike suggested to his mates that they should moderate their language and Mal, who was 'ear-wigging', looked at him in surprise.

'Don't tell me you're beginning to think about other people's feelings, he remarked sarcastically. That's not the Mike that we've all come to dislike so much.'

When Billy was away from his bench, the Fitters were more relaxed and he must have been aware of it. There was also a fair bit of 'crawling' going on and whenever the Foreman appeared, certain individuals would always find a reason to sidle up to him. 'There's a bit of a problem with this here part, which I'd like you to have a look at, 'guvnor.' The request would usually be accompanied by a fawning 'dog-like' look of servility. The boss didn't always react favourably to the intrusion and he was often clearly reluctant to even consider the problem. When the 'sniveller' was sent packing, his workmates would be beside themselves with mirth, and the smarmy git would be subjected to scornful comments for his pains. There wasn't much by way of camaraderie or team-spirit about.

What irked the people most was when Management disciplined someone on the basis of information received. The problem of sneaking was widespread in that there was always someone carrying tales. The surprising thing was that the very ones that complained bitterly about the practice of back-stabbing were usually the worst offenders. Things haven't changed much and in any workplace, the problem is as prevalent now as it was then.

Four large prefabricated casings, which measured approximately sixteen feet long, by six feet wide and two feet in depth, were delivered into the shop. They were off-loaded and placed on trestles and, after they had been levelled, Billy explained to the apprentices that they were to be thoroughly cleaned, internally and externally. The debris from the previous welding and machining stages were still in the boxes and it would take a lot of time and effort to clean them out. Smiling malevolently, Billy pointed to a drum of diesel oil and a sack of rags and curtly told them to get on with it. Before they could start work, the noon-day hooter sounded and Mike and John hot-footed it over to the canteen.

'They should have been properly cleaned before they left the machine shop,' one lad told them, as they were discussing the problem over their dinners. Tell the old bugger that it's a job for the Labourers and that you shouldn't be used for that sort of work.

'Yeah, that's right,' his mate interjected, nodding vigorously. 'Don't you have it. Just tell him you're not doing it and if he won't listen, go and complain to the foreman.'

'No, no, that's not the way to go about it,' came back Al, 'You've got to be a bit craftier than that. You've got to say, 'Excuse me, Mr Murtell, but will we be getting a bit of extra, for doing all this cleaning work?' Just act all innocent like and he'll be lost for words. Like as not, he'll say, 'I'll speak to the Foreman and come back to you.' You then say, 'Oh alright then, we'll wait for his answer by our benches.'

'That'll fettle him, because the crafty little sod will have already been in and agreed how many extra hours he'll be getting for it, including 'uncas.' (unclean condition payments). No doubt, he'll keep them and you'll be very lucky to get anything. He'll come back later and tell you that it's all been settled and you're to get on with it. That's when you say, nicely mind, 'Oh thank you very much, Mr Murtell, we'll thank Mr Jones as well when we see him.' You'll have him then, the lousy little bugger.'

The lads laughed out loud at Al's strategy. It would have to be carried through exactly as he had said, if there was to be any chance of success. Billy wasn't born yesterday and whoever spoke to him would have to be very much on his toes. John and Mike were resourceful lads and as they walked back to the shop, they discussed how they would go about it. A few minutes after they had clocked on, they turned to their vices and continued with their work. Their hearts sank when Billy didn't come back and they assumed he'd be away all afternoon. They wouldn't be able to speak to him until the next morning, by when the whole thing may well have gone cold. However, at about twenty past one, he came out of the Convener's office and as he approached his bench, they went over to speak to him.

The next few minutes were very amusing to those who were covertly watching the drama. Billy was suspicious about their motives and knew right away they were up to no good. As Mike played through Al's strategy, the little man became increasingly agitated. Al must have known him very well, because the discussion went exactly as he had predicted. He balefully told them he would 'speak to the Foreman on their behalf' and, knowing he was in his office, Mike asked him to do so right away. The blood drained from his face and coloured up in outrage. Everyone had stopped working and some of the men were openly smirking at his discomfort. The discussion came to an abrupt end.

'You've really got up my nose,' he shouted angrily. 'You're buggering me about, that's what. Well, we'll see about that. You can leave the bloody job alone and I'll get somebody else to do it. You cheeky sods,' he went on, 'I'm not going to put up with your bloody nonsense and if there's any more, I'll make a formal complaint to the Management. Now piss off back to your benches and get on with your work, before I get really upset. Cocky young bastards,' he muttered angrily as they walked away.

The next morning, a cleaning gang arrived and after looking at the casings, they asked Billy the very same question – what hours had been allocated to the job, including 'uncas'? The little man's reaction was comical, with those watching revelling in his discomfort. After telling them to 'come with me', they went to the end of the shop where they had what appeared to be a lively discussion. They eventually reached agreement, although from his demeanour, it wasn't altogether to the Billy's satisfaction. One of the Fitters remarked that he had probably given away more than he had bargained for. As Al had said, he had tried to organise the job to his own advantage, by getting the Apprentices to do it. It all worked out well and the gang, suitably motivated, thoroughly cleaned the casings over the next couple of days.

Another problem arose when late on in the day, a youth came over to speak to Billy. It was the same lad that had worked the Union membership scam in their first year. He had frequently been reminded of his outstanding obligations and threatened that recriminations would ensue if he didn't settle-up. The Convener was said to use his undoubted power, either formally or by some other means, when the need arose and that was why his nephew had not suffered any retribution up until then. After thanking the messenger, Billy walked across and told Mike and John that he wanted a word with them. When they showed no immediate inclination to go to see him, Billy smiled in his snake-like way.

'I'd go right away if I was you,' he said in his flat voice. 'It doesn't pay to keep Mr Barnes waiting.'

'Discretion being the better part of valour,' they walked across from the shop and went into the Convener's office. When they went in, he looked balefully at them and it was definitely not a time to be clever.

'I hear you've been acting the goat with Mr Murtell,' he said quietly, by way of an opening. 'I thought perhaps it would be helpful if we had a few words, just to clear up any misunderstanding like. Billy has served our Union well over a great many years and you should be aware that we don't take kindly to people mucking him about. You may think you're very clever, but we have ways and means of dealing with people like you, should the need arise. Know what I mean? Course you do. Now,' he said, lowering his voice almost to a whisper, 'you may or may not want to join the Union, that's up to you. As I said, you're not obliged to do so, but that may change before too long. Just be warned; a word to the wise as it were. We won't stand for any piss-taking where any of our officials are concerned. Think on lads, because I won't tell you again. Now get out.'

Mike was outraged at his implied threat, but for once, he showed some sense in making his reply.

'Is that your nephew out there, grinning like a Cheshire cat?,' he asked quietly.

The Convenor started and the angry colour drained from his face. Mike's meaning was abundantly clear and there was no need to say anything else. The lads left the office and as they walked back to their bench, they saw Donny was still slyly grinning from behind a column. Had he had some hand in the warning that they'd just received? Mike was all for going over to speak to him but was dissuaded from doing so. They were in enough trouble as it was.

'Take no notice,' said John, 'we can always sort him out some other time.'

The next day, they were working quietly when Ron came across for another chat. After talking about what they were doing, he started reminiscing about his time in the Navy. He had enjoyed his life on board the various Ships on which he had served and the places that he had visited, some of which the lads had never heard of. It had been a good life, he said, which had been well-paid and had brought a nice little gratuity at the end of his engagement.

'If it was that good, what made you leave?' John asked impertinently.

'The same old story,' the man replied sheepishly, 'the wife. We had only been married for three years and for a lot of the time, I was in the barracks. During that time, we lived with her mum and dad and I must say, after not having had a home life for so long, it was very nice to have a comfortable place to hang my hat. They lived in a big house, with plenty of room and we were one, big happy family. With all of us working, there was plenty of money coming in and we lived very well, very well indeed actually.

'The problems started when I was drafted to a Cruiser, on which I'd been standing by. She'd just completed a long refit and after her sea trials, we sailed out to the Med. Not many weeks later, the wife wrote to say she was expecting and the baby was born while I was away. By the time I came home, he was three months old. I suppose it was a bit hard on her, even though she'd had her parents with her when he was born. When my time was up, I was thinking of signing on for another five years, but she put her foot down. She probably had her mind on my gratuity, because she had started on about a place of our own in her letters. So that was that, I came out and promptly landed in the shit in this bloody place. I keep looking for another job but there's not much going that I fancy. If you're thinking of joining up when you finish your time, the Andrew is as good a life as you can get, providing you're still single!'

They talked for a while about the merits of a sea-going life and it was Ron that sowed the first seed of doubt in Mike's mind about joining the Royal Marines. At the end of his Apprenticeship, he would have a valuable trade and there wasn't much call for fitting skills in the Commandos.

'If you don't fancy the Navy, you could do worse than join the Royal Engineers,' he went on. 'They have a couple of Landing Ships and you could probably get in on one of those. You'd automatically get an NCOs rank, same as you would in the Andrew.'

Their cosy chat ended when the Foreman came down the shop, with a Naval Officer in tow. The lads turned back to their work and some minutes later, they came up to their bench and each picked up a sprocket. After making minor comments about the need to ensure that the teeth were properly de-burred, they went to look over the casings. The Lieutenant was the Naval Inspector for the job and it was from him that they learned more about the machines. As they had been told, they were to be installed as part of the aircraft launching systems on two new Carriers, one British and one Canadian. They were roller beds, which would be electrically and steam driven, to laterally move an aircraft across the deck. When positioned, the aircraft would be hooked on to the steam catapult and assisted in take-off. It was the first order that the Yard had been given for the manufacture of such machines and was probably why the Foreman was so keen to make a good job.

Chapter 12

Infernal Machines

Firm dates had been set for the delivery of the machines, with the first four units destined for a British Carrier. The other four, to be installed on a Canadian Ship, would not be required until six weeks later. Obviously, time was tight; the delivery dates had to be met and pressure was now on for their completion. Just as the assembly work was about to start, the Foreman noticed that the spec called for both the internal and external surfaces of the boxes to be painted and they were sent right away over to the paint shop. Billy had a set of the drawings in his bench drawer and he was tersely told by the boss that they should have been put up for general information. It was essential, he said loudly, that everyone was aware of the finer details of the machines. From then on, Billy regularly walked around, loudly urging everyone to put their backs into it but, made no mention of the bonus to be paid on completion of the job.

With the fettling work completed, each sprocket was tapped and a grub-screw inserted, to lock it on its shaft. The lads then worked on the preparation of the rollers, which were made in stainless steel. They were approximately three feet long, with deep grooves cut longitudinally around their circumference and along their full length. The shaft through the middle had been fitted by the Manufacturer and the ends were splined, to accept the sprockets. They were also reduced to fit into the supporting bearings, located in pre-sealed housings. As each roller was completed, a unique number was written on the end in indelible ink. When the boxes came back from the paint shop, they were again set up and a start was made on the installation work. Mounting-brackets were affixed along the sides of each box and the bearings installed. They had been previously pre-packed with grease, to protect them against the ingress of water and dirt.

The 'driving' and 'free-end' main shafts were similarly supported by large, heavy-duty bearings and after being fitted, they were closely checked to ensure ease of movement. The drive-chains were then pulled through the casings. Great care had to be taken to maintain the internal cleanliness of the machines as the work progressed. The chain tensioning equipment was fitted to the non-drive-end of each casing, then the free ends were brought together, the fastenings fitted and the chains tensioned. Cyril and Mike fitted the drive-shafts' half-couplings, with the lad doing the keys. They had to be a firm, sliding-fit, to ease future removal. A hole was drilled and tapped in the outer end to allow a length of screwed round-bar to be inserted. A small plate, with a hole drilled in the centre, two nuts, a flat-washer and two square metal blocks completed the withdrawing kit. Three more sets were made for despatch with the machines.

There was to be yet more unpleasantness from Billy. He and Mal had continued their lively discussions about the benefits of communism over capitalism and vice-versa, with each one countering the other's points with no little skill. The trouble came when Mike interrupted them by scorning the whole concept of communism, saying that more than twenty million people had died following the revolution in Russia. A far greater number had been killed during and after that in China. He didn't have the wit to stop there and went on to say that the red propaganda about the Spanish Civil War was nothing more than a cynical distortion of the truth. Communism was a cruel myth; there was no such thing as 'equality for all'; in fact, it was all a bloody great lie, from start to finish. John, who couldn't resist putting his oar in, called across that he was of the same view. Billy rounded on them in fury.

'I've told you before to shut your stupid bloody mouths,' he screamed. 'You don't know what you're talking about. You're nothing more than cheeky, snotty-nosed kids, still wet behind the ears, think you know it all and believe everything you read. There's going to be no more argument because I don't even want to speak to you, so sod off.'

Cyril leaned across the bench and quietly told Mike to 'pack it in'. The lad protested that he'd only wanted to make a point and hadn't been looking for a confrontation with the horrible little bastard. Billy heard Mike's epithet quite clearly and knew that others in the shop agreed. The discussions ceased and Mal was clearly upset. He angrily told Mike that by his crass interference, he had spoilt things by antagonising Billy, just for the sake of it. Mike replied that he didn't want any more arguments either.

The assembly work on the first four machines went well and other trades were called in to do their part of the job. The drive motors were mounted on the side of each machine and the couplings aligned. The electric cables were run between the motors and their junction-boxes and the ends were 'glanded' and 'made-off'. Cables were installed to connect the junction boxes to a temporary switch box for test and running purposes. The Copper-smiths installed the permanent lubrication pipework, which distributed grease to each bearing. A manual pump and manifold was mounted on the end of each machine and the system feeding the bearings was connected up. When they had finished, the systems were primed with grease and the system checked for leaks.

The half-couplings on the motors had been left disconnected, for direction checks and when they were 'flicked', they all turned the wrong way. It has always been a mystery that, when power is first applied to a newly-installed motor, only rarely does turn in the right direction. The junction box covers were removed and the wires changed over then, after a lot of muttering and a number of blown fuses, the 'Leckies' got things right. The couplings were finally adjusted and boxed up then, after a last look around, the machines were ready for their first runs under power. Each unit was run in turn for a few minutes, under the critical eyes of the Foreman and then for an hour in both directions. After a few minor adjustments, they were deemed to be satisfactory.

The machines were at a designated inspection point and the RN Engineer Lieutenant was joined by a Lieutenant Commander. When they had completed their visual checks, each unit was started up and again run in each direction. The official proving runs, which followed over the next few days, were carried out in the presence of both the Yard's Design Engineers and representatives of the Shipyard. It was sod's law that there had to be another electrical problem, which took time to resolve. Billy became increasingly agitated and repeatedly told the Apprentices to stand clear and not get in the way. The bearings were checked for overheating, particularly on the main drive-shafts and ultimately, the machines were passed as fit for purpose.

In the meantime, Mike had unwittingly caused another kerfuffle while they had been running. He had been talking to the Lieutenant and had asked him about how they would be installed on board the ship. The Officer explained that the top of the plates would sit flush with the deck, thus giving the rollers a couple of inches projection above that level. That would be sufficient to give them firm contact with the wheels of the aircraft and facilitate its lateral movement across the deck. Mike then asked about the conditions under which the machines would be working. He already knew that trouble-free running, in all weather conditions, tropical to arctic, was an absolute necessity. That was why chain drives had been chosen as the preferred method of motivation. Seeing the lad was concerned, the officer asked him what was bothering him.

'I was wondering if the conditions on deck are ever very wet?' Mike replied.

'Well yes, very much so at times,' the officer replied. 'The crew are often soaked through, despite wearing their heavy weather gear. I've known green ones come over the bows and sweep along the deck during storms, even on the largest ships.'

'Because of the clearance between the plates and the rollers, the machine will not be waterproof, will it?,' the lad continued. 'What will happen to all the water which will fall into the machine and fill up the inner space? With it sloshing about, the shafts and bearings will soon get rusty, unless they're heavily greased.'

The Lieutenant looked at him, somewhat taken aback.

'Oh, bloody hell,' he said, 'I think you've got something there. The drawings don't show any drainage points and to be honest, I hadn't thought about that. I'll get it checked, so please don't say anything for the time being.'

The next day, the Design Engineers confirmed that the lack of drainage had been an oversight. Any ingress of water would have to be continuously drained away, with outlets provided at all four corners of each machine. The draughtsman had provided triangular cut-outs in the internal bracings, but had not detailed the drainage connections and pipework required, to take the water away. The problem was resolved by fitting three-inch flanged-connectors into the bottoms of the casings at each end. A couple of Pipe-fitters duly arrived to fabricate the pipework, in galvanised mild-steel, and the arrangement was terminated in a large manifold under each machine.

Following the discovery of the omission, Mike had been feeling pleased with himself, but that was not to last, because Billy was hopping mad. How dare a mere Apprentice deign to intrude into the 'glory', which was his by inalienable right? Further unpleasantness was inevitable and it quickly followed.

'You think you're very clever, don't you?' he sneered. 'You know what I think? You knew that something was wrong and being an awkward bugger, you didn't say anything. Now you've embarrassed everyone in front of the Navy and I'm going to show you up for what you are. You're a nasty piece of work, you are.'

Mike was too taken aback to have a ready response and to answer him back would only have made things worse. Others in the shop seemed to be in agreement with what Billy had said. Further criticism was not long in coming and he was 'sent for' soon after. When he entered the office, he was greeted by the stern-faced Foreman, who had been well wound up by his charge-hand.

'Is it true that you knew all along about the problem, but didn't say anything? Well?' he demanded angrily, 'what have you got to say for yourself?'

'I can honestly say I didn't notice anything, until we were doing the test-runs,' Mike replied. It was only while I was looking inside a machine, to make sure we'd not left anything in it, that I thought something could perhaps be wrong. Later, when I was talking to the Lieutenant about what conditions were like on the deck, when the ship was at sea, I realised there could be a problem with water inside the box. He said he would look into it.'

'Why did you discuss it with him and not with Billy, or me for that matter?' You should have nothing to say to the Navy, about anything. You work for me, not for them.'

'I'm sorry Mr Jones, but you know that whenever I speak to Billy, I always get my head bitten off,' replied Mike. 'It's been the same ever since I came to work in this section. It makes no difference what I say or do, it's always wrong and I'm bloody sick and tired of it. Even now, when I'm in the right, I'm still in the shit and all because he can't stop having a go at me. If I'd kept quiet and said nothing and it had all come out later that I'd known about the problem, then I'd have been in even more trouble. There's no pleasing some people. As it is, it was noticed in good time and it has been put right.

'Alright, lad,' replied the Foreman, mellowing somewhat. 'I can see what you mean. All I'm saying is that when you first thought something was amiss, you should have said so. Let's leave it at that shall we? I'll have another word with Billy, to smooth things out. As you know, your time here is nearly up and you'll be moving on. Just try to keep out of trouble between now and then, will you? Off you go. Well done by the way; for spotting the problem. I'm sure we all appreciate it,' he added by way of an afterthought

Billy's good humour at the successful outcome of the test runs was only fleeting. How could it be otherwise? When he came back from seeing the visitors off, he accused the Apprentices of slackness. He was referring to the small number of faults, which had been found during the inspection, none of which had been significant. All four machines had been signed off. The last job was to lay and secure the non-slip decking plates across the top of the casings. Each one had been profiled to allow the tops of the rollers to protrude through and it should not have been much of a job. However, the fabricators had forgotten to hard stamp the identification number on each plate in accordance with drawing. They had to be offered up, then the lads painted the numbers on the underside of each plate before bolting them down. The job took twice as long as it should have, which didn't please their impatient tormentor.

160

After all the hard work that the fitters and their lads had put into the first four machines, the pressure was suddenly very much off. The atmosphere in the shop was more relaxed and the assembly of the second batch was duly completed in good time. The Painters made good the damage caused during the assembly stage and the copper pipework was liberally daubed, to give it protection against the elements. The last job was to attach the identification plates, inscribed with all the relevant information, to each unit. The packing of the machines, including the spares, then ensued. From past experience, the packers knew that they had to keep a very close watch on their kit and materials. Mal and Pete recorded what was put into each crate and their notes were sent over to the drawing office for typing into packing lists.

It brought to an end to a most interesting job. In the last few days, there was a lot of talk as to how the lads were going to broach the ticklish question about the bonus they had earned with Billy. However, due to Mal's insistence, they did nothing about it before they were sent elsewhere.

Chapter 13

I Don't Want To Join the Army

With many of the lads nearing their eighteenth birthdays, they often discussed their future obligation to Queen and Country, i.e. their impending National Service, which involved serving a minimum of two years in the Armed Forces. With military commitments all over the world, the Country had a pressing need for manpower and in the event of an emergency, the period of conscription could be extended above the mandatory two years. Theoretically, the call up appertained to every young man of sound body and mind, but the reality was somewhat different. Certain categories were deemed to be in 'reserved occupations'. For example, those working in the agricultural or coal industry were exempted from service, as were those who were in the Merchant Navy. Others, in the Police Force or Fire Service, or in a job which was of National importance, could apply for exemption. Any request, which was supported a potential conscript's employer was considered, though not always sympathetically.

Deferment of his service could be obtained if a lad was serving a fully-indentured apprenticeship. Students in higher education could also delay their call up until they had finished their courses. There were also numerous ways by which a reluctant conscript could dodge his responsibilities, including string pulling, whereby someone could avoid his call up, for the most specious of reasons. Anyone who suffered from a mental or physical disability or was considered to be medically unfit was not required. Flat feet were unacceptable, a shortcoming which opened the door for all kinds of frivolous nonsense. The local adjudicators must have heard all manner of reasons as to why the reprobates who appeared before them should not be obliged to 'get some in'.

It was a waste of time to try to con the Doctor when attending the mandatory medical, because he would instinctively know if a lad was acting the crack. However, the British male can be crafty and there was a steady stream of reluctant conscripts who tried it on. The general rule was, you had to go, unless you were fortunate enough to have either the influence or luck to buck the system. A few bright sparks buggered-off abroad, which was often problematical. In some Countries, such as Australia and New Zealand, there was a similar obligation for military service. As each lad neared his eighteenth birthday, he duly received a letter which formally advised him of his impending call up. He was then summoned to report to the Labour Exchange to 'register'. It was a matter of great concern and when someone got his letter, he was often subjected to silly comments, either from those that had already registered or had already served their time.

A lad would be advised to be very careful about what he said to the Registrar, because it was not a time to be clever, and a bit of respect was essential. He had to be sure that the Registrar clearly understood that he was serving an Indentured Apprenticeship. When asked if he wanted his service to be deferred, the answer had to be 'Yes please, Sir'. Notes would be made of his personal details, such as anticipated academic qualifications, interests, hobbies and sports played and at what level. With the interview over, a 'thank you very much for your help, Sir,' was called for. There had been a number of instances when 'silly buggers' had been too clever and had duly suffered the consequences. Their Apprenticeships had been interrupted and they had had to complete their time after they had been discharged. Third, fourth and fifth year wages, when in their early twenties, didn't bear thinking about. Most young men of that age had family commitments and their lives were hard enough, without the added burden of poor pay.

On his designated day, Mike cycled into the town and duly reported to reception. He was greeted by a fussy little man who, much to his annoyance, called him by his surname. He bit his tongue and went into an adjacent room, where three other lads from his entry were waiting. There was a subdued discussion about what they wanted to do while they were waiting. One lad said he had 'no intention of joining the bloody Army', but they were not in the mood to listen to his nonsense. They waited for nearly an hour before the interviews started and wry comments were made that the organisation wasn't up to much. Eventually, they were called into an office in alphabetical order, where they were dealt with quickly and efficiently.

The Registrar was very friendly, not at all like the po-faced blighter downstairs. He stood up and they shook hands, then he smilingly pointed to a chair in front of his desk and his first questions confirmed Mike's name, address, date of birth and National Insurance number. He explained how the various stages would be carried out, whereby each young man would be brought into what he humorously referred to as the tender, loving care of the Her Majesty's Armed Forces. They then discussed Mike's Apprenticeship and his application for deferment was noted. The lad was relieved to be told that 'there shouldn't be any problem there'. When asked if he had a preference, Mike replied that he would like to join the Royal Engineers. His interview went well and he was soon on his way back to work.

The conversation during the dinner hour was about how things had gone and what questions had been asked. A week or so later, Mike received confirmation of his deferment, which was valid until he had completed his time. He was not against joining-up, which surprised some of the other lads. The idea of doing something different and going overseas appealed to him. However, in time, he would become increasingly thankful that his father had been so adamant about him not joining-up when he had left school. His wisdom about having a trade would be very much borne out in the years to come. Progressively, Mike became convinced that a military life was not an option he would willingly take and like so many others, he became firm in his determination to dodge his National Service.

The deferment would lapse at the end of his time, unless there was a good reason for extending it further. Within a matter of weeks, the lad would report to his designated barracks and after basic training, he would be assigned to his slot in the military machine. As a tradesman, he would perhaps enjoy a marginally better life than the average conscript. In the Army, he would likely go to one of the Engineer Regiments and shortly be promoted to Corporal. If in the Royal Navy, he would similarly assume the rank of Petty Officer. He would usually not make any further progress during the remainder of his service, unless he was of exceptional ability. Conscripts were paid a pittance, in comparison with their mates in 'civvy-street' and the only option was to 'sign-on' for a regular engagement, which would bring the chance of further promotion, with more pay.

There was a definite stigma attached to a lad, if he was perceived to be reluctant to serve his Country. Many families had lost close relatives in the War and the memory of their sacrifice was still very fresh in their minds. There was a sense of patriotism in the community, which demanded that every young man did his bit and he was regularly reminded of his obligation. Joining the Merchant Navy was an acceptable alternative, perhaps because of the huge contribution made by the sea-going fraternity in the War. However, the owners were only too aware of the situation and they exploited it to the full. With hundreds of young men regularly coming out of their time, there was no shortage of job applicants.

Some of the Fitters had done their National Service and returned to work in the Yard. The tales they told were interesting and often hilarious. Sometimes they were so incredible that the raconteur would be roundly accused of 'bullshitting'. While some stressed the positive aspects of their service, some had sobering tales to tell. One of them told Mike that he had suffered greatly under his first Petty Officer in the Royal Navy. He had been a mean-minded, loud-mouthed shit and apparently, 'a right pain in the arse'. For many weeks, he had come among them at odd times of the day and night, upending lockers, overturning beds and screaming with rage. He would in no way be challenged and their time under his instruction had been an absolute nightmare.

Much to his listeners' surprise, Ron softened his account somewhat. His watch had completed their initial training as the best in the entry and it was only after they had joyfully said their goodbyes did they realise that their P.O. had carried through his regime with great cunning. His reputation was legendary and he had enjoyed great success over many years in turning a motley bunch of unfit, idle and nondescript youths into a very smart body of men, who accepted their discipline without question. They had benefited very much in that they were clean, tidy and methodical in everything they did. On the day they passed out, their tormentor beamed and said loudly that they had been the best 'lot' he'd ever had.

Stan told them that his Corporal in the Army had been totally different. He had been a mild, quietly spoken man, with none of the unbridled aggression of his contemporaries. However, Drill Sergeant Duncan was ramrod straight and always immaculately turned out. His uniform looked as if it had just been sponged and pressed and his boots were always shined to perfection. It was he that set the standards in the platoon and he never accepted anything less than maximum effort. Everything was done 'at the double' and they spent many hours being roundly chastised for all manner of offences, imagined and otherwise. Dunc was so formidable that even the cockiest, loud-mouthed slobs shook, whenever his beady eye fell on them. Their main problem was his way of screaming his orders. 'Attention' and 'Stand at ease' bore little relation to the actual words, but they had soon cottoned on. As with Ron's P.O., only at the end of their training did they realise they'd been had.

Jim had only recently returned to the Yard, and his service had been an interesting experience. When he'd registered, he'd been asked if his father had been in the Armed Forces and he'd replied that he had been a regular in a Scottish Regiment. He had gone through most of the War on active service and had come through it without as a scratch. After his demob, he had returned to his home in Glasgow but being unable to find a suitable job, he'd gone to live and work in England. To his great alarm, Jim had been sent to serve in his dad's old Regiment.

He laughed when he told the lads that during the bitter winter months, he'd found the kilt extremely draughty. Although his father was a Scot, he had suffered at the hands of his comrades, particularly from a young man who later became his 'oppo', i.e. best-friend. He was an 'English bastard' throughout the time he was stationed in that bonny land and there lies perhaps the true definition of the word 'Sassenach', which is often spoken with venom by our Scottish cousins. His biggest problem was the distance between his barracks and home, particularly when his short 'leaves' came round. His hardship had been mitigated by his father's kindly sisters, to whom he affectionately referred as 'Big Maggie' and 'Wee Effie'. They had kept open house throughout his time in Stirling and had made his life very much more bearable.

Before he went to 'get some in', Martin had completed a seven year Apprenticeship as a silversmith with a large Firm of Jewellers in London. After his basic training, he was sent to serve in a prestigious Regiment and because of his tradesman's status, two, then three stripes soon came his way. The tapes on his arms smoothed his path into a leisurely life, compared to that of most conscripts. Further promotion would have entailed a lot more responsibility and that would not have done. He had spent most of his two years living in the relative luxury of a Barracks in the centre of London, which was less than an hour from his home. He in time had cultivated a serious drinking habit, usually at someone else's expense. His main occupation had been in the repair and maintenance of the large quantity of splendid silverware, which belonged to the Regiment. Apart from that, his service to the Crown had been a complete waste of time.

Apparently, he had taken advantage of every situation which could be exploited, with a lot of private commissions from those he served. Most of the work had been in the restoration of damaged items of antique silver. They were brought in by Officers, who were either caring for their inheritances, or selling them off to provide the additional means to subsidise their high standard of living. It had to be said that Martin had not benefited physically from his service. In fact, his appearance had declined markedly from when he first went in. He was a very poor specimen of manhood indeed and, in that respect, he was very much the exception to the rule.

Chapter 14

The Tool Room

The final 'change-over' of the year came and for John and Mike, it wasn't a minute too soon and when they arrived at the Tool Room, they found other lads from their entry already there. The Foreman told Mike he would be working with Len, in the 'non-destructive test room'. It was a small facility in an annex off the main section and he went straight over, only to find it was unlit and the door was locked. Someone told him that his new boss was 'on-leave' and would not be back until the following Monday. His informant went on to say that Len could be a bit difficult at times, and that he always kept the door locked when no-one was working there. There was expensive equipment inside and a lot of thieving sods about. He went back to the Fitting-shop to collect his belongings, then stowed his box in the Tool Room until his new boss came back.

During the morning break, the lads sat by the door and were joined by others, who were working nearby. They were well apart from the Fitters, who jealously guarded their places against any intrusion. Anyone who has worked in a Tool Room will know that the Tradesmen are a race apart. There was an air of hierarchical deference, with the most highly-skilled men being very much looked up to by their workmates. Mere Apprentices had to know their place and show courtesy and respect for the men they were working with. Being new to the place, they were on their best behaviour and not a little apprehensive about what was in store.

'Who're you with, Mac?,' asked one of the lads, winking slyly. He already knew and had sensed had the opportunity for some mischief.

'Bloke called Ted Blount,' replied our worthy and not sounding very happy about it.

'Hey, he's supposed to be a bit of a bugger to work for,' said another lad. 'From what I've heard, he's a stickler for having things right, a proper old woman by all accounts. If something ain't to his liking, he'll make you do it over again until it's right, no matter how many times you have to do it. You'll have to watch it, old mate, because he won't have any messing about.'

Someone remarked that most of the Fitters were 'tarred by the same brush' and demanded too much from their Apprentices. A lad, who had just moved out of the Tool Room, said that Ted was one of the worst and he often commented that they had to be 'kept in their place'. Mac didn't see the surreptitious winks passing between the blighters who were sitting around him. A wind-up was in progress, and he was the hapless victim, which augured well for a good laugh. He was not the brightest of the bunch and being just as apprehensive as everyone else, he rose to the bait.

'He'd better not come it with me, because I won't bloody-well have it,' he replied testily.

'That's right, you stick up for yourself, my old son,' said John and winking slyly. 'Tell him to piss-off if he starts taking liberties.'

There was no doubt in anyone's mind that they would have to be very careful. It was all very well talking, but no-one had any intention of sticking his neck out, just to make a useless point. There were some hard buggers among the men, who thought that any lip was best sorted by a clip around the ear. They would just have to do exactly as they were told. However, Mac still hadn't cottoned-on to that he was being had, and another lad chipped-in.

'They say Ted's very particular about how his Apprentice makes his drinks.'

'Well, he needn't expect me to wait on him, hand and foot,' their victim retorted angrily. 'He can make his own bloody drinks.'

When the bell went, they went over to their Fitters and Ted angrily demanded to know where Mac had been. He loudly accused him of neglecting his duties and he was obviously determined to gain the upper hand.

'What have you forgotten to do?' he asked, looking balefully at the frowning young man.

The men nearby had stopped what they were doing and were ear-wigging the exchange. They had heard many different responses from reluctant lads in the past so, if Mac objected, an altercation would surely ensue.

'I haven't forgotten anything,' the lad replied stiffly, then after a pause, he asked lamely, 'have I?'

Despite his earlier brave comments, he was clearly backing off. Having the courage to face-up to his angry fitter was not on, even though he would come in for some stick later.

'Yes, you have,' said Ted in a low voice, which added to his menace. You didn't make my drink, did you? That's your job, every break and what's more, you do it exactly like I tell you, got it?'

What remained of Mac's bravado crumbled.

'I'm sorry Ted, I didn't know anything about it,' he replied. 'You didn't say anything earlier.'

'That's alright, as long as you don't forget,' replied the crafty old sod. 'Now, let's get things straight, so's you know exactly what I want. I 'as cocoa in the morning, 'an I don't want no lumps, get it? You take this mug,' he went on and pulling the odious object from his workbench drawer, 'and after making sure it's nice an' clean, you put a spoon and a half of cocoa and two spoons of sugar in it. You go to the boiler over there and pour a small amount of water into the mug and mix it all up, taking care to stir it well so that there ain't no lumps. You then fill the mug to about half an inch from the top and give it a good stir. When you come back, you add a spoon and a half of condensed milk from the tin and stir it in well, before bringing it to me, nice and hot. That's what I want and what I'm going to get,' he concluded.

Mac nodded dumbly as Ted then went on to explain exactly how he wanted his tea to be made later in the day. The watching lads were nearly beside themselves with laughter, though the fitters saw nothing funny about what was going on. It was such a simple chore, which any lad should have been able to do.

167

With principle at stake, Ted was intent on imposing his authority on what was potentially an awkward Apprentice. He spelled it all out, so there was no doubt in anyone's mind as to who was the boss. The odd thing was though, most of the fitters made their own drinks. They knew from past experience that in doing so, they avoided the risk of someone acting the crack at their expense. The chore of waiting on them had apparently been resented by generations of Apprentices.

Cocoa and tea were the usual drinks, though a few brave souls made coffee from the noisome 'ersatz' bottled liquid, which was based on chicory essence. There were no refinements in the packaging and the quality of the contents was not always good. The cocoa tended to go lumpy if not kept dry, and no little care had to be taken in making up a drink. The mixing should have been done with a little cold water but, in his ignorance, Mac assumed that Ted had meant hot water. His instruction to make sure that the mug was clean was laughable, because most of them were inevitably 'iffy'. Most were heavily stained and corroded, from many years of use and their washing was usually perfunctory. They were usually of a pint capacity and made from enamelled steel. Caution had to be taken with the first few sips, otherwise burnt lips would ensue.

Some of the men had billy-cans, with wire-handles for ease of carrying. A tight-fitting lid conserved the heat inside and prevented spillage. Some of the men were malodorous, with neither knowledge nor care about personal hygiene. It was said that they only bathed on high days and holidays and it was best to stand well up-wind of them. A few brought fresh milk to work, but most used either condensed or evaporated milk, bought from the traders. They also bought their cocoa, coffee, sugar and tea, meat and fruit pies, biscuits and chocolate bars from them. The state of the milk cans, which languished in their drawers or tool boxes, was at times disgusting. Being of a careful nature, they had to extract every last drop, before buying a new can.

When he was later taken to task, Mac insisted that he wouldn't be making Ted's drinks for long, which was greeted with hoots of derision. The next day, at the morning break, he was in the boiler queue and looking decidedly sheepish. Being roundly abused for his cowardice, he tried to mitigate his surrender by pointing out that none of his tormentors had had the guts to say no to their fitters. That wasn't going to wash and he disconsolately made his way back to his bench. Early the following morning, he told his mates he was going to fettle the old bugger, when he made his cocoa. He looked decidedly shifty, when he sat down, which aroused everybody's curiosity.

'Come on, you bugger, tell us what you've done?' one lad said.

'That's for me to know and you to find out,' Mac replied tersely.

'You can't keep it to yourself, can he lads?' the lad retorted. If you've been acting the crack, you've got to say. We're your mates,' he added for good effect.

Mac then dramatically gave them the hairy details of his prank. He'd gone to the boiler and made Ted's cocoa as instructed. When he came back, he spooned in the milk and sugar and, seeing that Ted was not watching, he had dipped the spoon into a tin of 'Stag' jointing compound and stirred that in as well. His mates recoiled at the very thought as it was a foul-smelling brown paste, with a paint-like consistency. He went on to say that when he handed Ted his drink, he'd stood watching as he tasted it. He had expected the man to spit it out but much to his amazement, Ted loudly complimented him.

'By heck lad, that's a nice cup of cocoa. I can see we're going to get on just fine, thanks very much.'

His audience fell about with laughter, which brought loud calls from the men to pipe down. Mac was very smug about his prank, even though most of his mates didn't believe a word of it.

Just before the noon siren, there was a kerfuffle around Ted's bench and the old man rapidly ran off in the direction of the toilets. While waiting to clock off, Mac gleefully told his mates that his boss had been complaining all morning about his guts. He must have been violently sick, because when he came back, he put his kit away, locked his drawer and after going into the Foreman's office, he went home.

'Bloody hell Mac, you've poisoned him,' someone said in a shocked voice. 'If anyone finds out, you're going to be well and truly in the shit.'

'Then just you keep your bloody mouth shut,' replied Mac, turning on him fiercely.

Pranks played outside of their own circle were hazardous and everyone had to keep schtum. How it all turned out was even more hilarious, though there could have been serious consequences. When Ted returned after more than a week off, he still looked far from well and a lot of sympathetic comments were made by his colleagues. Looking exceedingly mournful, he took pleasure in telling them in great detail about how very ill he'd been. At one time, he said, it had been 'touch an' go', with the doctor having been very concerned about his condition. To Mac's clear relief, Ted had no idea of what he had done and he certainly wasn't going to tell him. Ted went on to say that his tinned fish sandwiches, which his wife had packed-up for some days previously, were thought to have been the cause of his 'food poisoning'.

'I told the wife that the sandwiches were a bit funny, but she put it down to my poor sense of taste,' he said. 'I've always been very fond of "errins-in,' (Herrings in tomato sauce – an old Navy favourite), and I've never had any problem up 'til now. What was left in the tin must have been a bit off, that's the only reason I can think of.'

Mac had been as solicitous as the rest of the Mateys and later, when he went to take Ted's mug from the drawer, he was peremptorily brought to an abrupt halt.

'Never mind about that,' the old man said. 'I'll do it myself. After what I've been through, the doctor says that I've got to be a bit careful about what I eat and drink.'

He then took a brand new mug from his bag and after taking his tin of cocoa from the drawer, he went over to the boiler to make his drink. Mac was 'cock-a-hoop' as he sat down with his mates and they were again beside themselves with laughter. He was very much the man of the day.

'Told you I'd fettle him,' he crowed, smiling broadly, 'I don't have to get his drinks any more and I only said I wouldn't, didn't I?'

The fact that he'd been so very lucky was not lost on his workmates and nothing more was said about his stunt. He had, in the time-honoured saying, got away with it.

The bonus money, outstanding from the Fitting-shop, had still not been paid and it had become a matter of great concern. Malcom said that he would go over to see Billy, though Mike cynically said that all he would get out of him was that it hadn't yet been decided and he'd let him know. And that was exactly how it turned out. Two weeks later and with still no action, they were very angry. Mike tried to get a feel for the situation by going over and quietly discussing it with Cyril, but he was less than helpful.

'Don't involve me in your arguments,' he again replied crossly. 'I'm keeping well out of it.'

From what the older lads had told them, they were supposed to have received 20% of the bonus paid, but the skulduggery was widespread and it was never easy to sort. Billy was the sole arbiter about who should receive what and it was very unlikely he would cough up. Mike and John were all for confronting him, but Malcom was still convinced of the need to show a bit of sense. He strongly maintained that a mannerly approach was much more likely to yield a positive result. It was agreed that he would talk to Billy again at the earliest opportunity. After many days of dithering, in the vain hope of catching the little man in a good mood, he went over to see him. When he came back, he was clearly upset and as they had thought, he was empty-handed.

'The job had taken too long to complete, so there was no bonus,' he explained disconsolately. 'If we had put our backs into it, then we would have got something. As it is, he can't do anything about it.'

'Bloody won't, more like,' retorted John angrily. 'The old bastard's cheated us. It wouldn't be so bad if what he said was true, but we flogged our bollocks off on those machines and now, as we thought all along, we've got nothing out of it. I've a bloody good mind to tell him what I think of him.'

For once, Mike was giving the matter serious thought.

'There's something not right here,' he said. 'How could a job like that not make money? No one, other than Billy, ever complained about us not working. You'd have thought the Foreman would have said something, if we hadn't been pulling our weight. If the job was targeted properly, then what could have gone wrong?

Someone suggested that perhaps Billy had booked the hours that he'd been absent from the shop 'on business' against the job. Had the Apprentices' hours been booked in full or had they been discounted to say, 20%, in line with their intended payments. Again, his mates shook their heads, saying that they didn't understand it either. Mike then said that there was only one way forward and that was to go and see the Foreman. He went off feeling less confident than he looked.

When he went into the office, Mr Jones looked up and asked what he could do for him, which was encouraging. He had expected a brusque greeting and after listening for a couple of minutes, the Foreman cut him off short.

'Look lad, he said angrily, I can't believe what I'm hearing. It's not for you to come in here and question me about the bonus or anything else for that matter.

I won't have that from any Apprentice and certainly not from you. If you've got problems, sort it out with your Fitter and don't come bothering me. Now bugger off before I lose my temper.'

Mike left him feeling very much as Malcom had done after he had been to see Billy. When he told his mates what the foreman had said, they had to accept that nothing more could be done to remedy the situation. The older lads had warned them that apprentices were generally exploited, with only a few Fitters being decent enough to acknowledge their contribution to their earnings. Some of those that did often only handed over a few measly shillings with reluctance. Mike was bitterly disappointed with Cyril who, despite his protestations of Faith, was not above cheating. He went back over to see him and before the man could say anything, Mike told him he now knew what had happened.

'You say you're a Christian,' he said angrily, 'but like the rest, you pick and choose which commandments you obey.'

'Don't shout at me,' Cyril replied indignantly. 'You know how things are here. I have to do as I'm told, same as everybody else.'

There really was nothing more to be said.

Chapter 15

New Skills

Len returned on Monday morning and, hoping to make a good impression, Mike reported to him soon after he'd clocked on. To his dismay, he was greeted in an off-hand manner. He said nothing to his mates, having decided to keep his mouth shut and do exactly as he was told, then perhaps things would improve once they got to know each other. He had been told that his new boss was a serious minded young man, with no time for levity. In telling the lad about the work he would be doing, Len stressed the importance of always doing it properly. He then sonorously told him that he was married and had recently become a father. He had few interests, apart from those which directly affected him and his family. In short, he was as dull as ditch-water, and it was clear that he wanted to keep Mike very much at arm's length.

After showing him where he could put his things, he took him over to a bench on which was stacked a large number of small square steel plates. They were test pieces which were to be subjected to Brunel testing, to determine the inherent hardness of the metal. Each piece had to be firmly clamped into a vice and then, with a ball bearing inserted into the bottom of a machine, a pre-calibrated load was exerted on to the plate to form a circular indentation in the metal. The diameter was carefully measured under a microscope and the applied load noted. A simple calculation gave the resultant hardness factor, which was recorded on a test-sheet. It was a simple job but, with more than a hundred pieces to be tested, it could not be described as interesting work. Having demonstrated what was required, Len asked Mike if he had any questions and then disappeared.

Over the next few days, he was only rarely in the Test Room. When he had completed all of the pieces, Mike made a fair copy of the record sheets and in due course handed them to his boss. He put them to one side without even looking at them and apparently, his disinterest was nothing out of the ordinary. No matter how hard a lad tried, there was no pleasing some Fitters. It seemed that he would rather not have had the responsibility of an apprentice. When Mike later asked if he wanted to go over the sheets, Len blandly said he had already sent the results over to the laboratory. The object of the exercise had been to give Mike training in the technique of doing the tests. He then took him over to another machine and, after showing him how to use it, he set him to work. It involved calculating the shear stress factors of another pile of test pieces. He then again left Mike, who was by then feeling very depressed, to his own devices.

One morning, Len was more cheerful than hitherto and as he pottered about, he was quietly singing. There was a popular song on the hit parade, an inanity called 'The Naughty Lady of Shady Lane' and this had evidently struck a chord with the proud young dad. The theme was based on the gift of a baby to a blissfully happy young couple. It was an immediate hit and in a matter of weeks, it was followed by another equally daft song, the opening words being, 'Twenty Tiny Fingers, Twenty Tiny Toes'. One morning, after having had a perfunctory look at what Mike was doing, he pulled out a large envelope containing photographs of his wife, baby and their boxer dog. Over the next half-hour, each one was lovingly pored over and all the circumstances appertaining were explored at length. It seemed to be never-ending to the hapless lad, who had no interest at all in wives, babies or dogs. At long last, Len completed his expose and as he put them back into the envelope, he told Mike exactly how he felt.

'I can see you're not interested in my snaps,' he said angrily. 'I didn't expect you would be, but you could have made more effort. Go and get on with your work.'

Mike had 'shit it' and when he mentioned it over dinner, there was a lot of laughter. Being in their teens and single, no one had any interest in domestic matters and would not have behaved differently. Some though had older siblings with young families and they were most scathing about the inordinate attention which was lavished on the new arrivals by their parents. Mike learned soon after that Len had run into difficulties. His situation at home, which had previously been all 'sweetness and light', had turned into one where he and his wife were under increasing pressure to move out. A serious minded young man had turned into a despondent one, who had all the cares of the world on his shoulders. The inevitable sleepless nights, coupled with the never ending grumbles from his in-laws, had become almost unbearable. It was little wonder he had been so detached, when Mike had first arrived and the lad soon got his chance to redeem himself, quicker than he had thought possible.

Len had found a small flat, near the town centre and although it was far from ideal, it would suit their purpose until he and his wife could afford something better. The problem was, the previous tenants had left it in a bit of a state. His wife had gone to see it, burst into tears and flatly refused to have anything to do with it. Mike offered to give him a hand and when they heard about the problem, some of his mates offered their help as well. Mike told Len that he could give him two or three evenings, but made no mention of the other lads. One of the lads was a third-year Shipwright and, seeing that the front door and some of the windows were broken, he made a note of what was needed. The next evening, he appeared complete with tools, pieces of wood, glass and a large ball of putty, all of which had come from the Joiners' shop. A new lock was fitted on the main door and inside bolts as well. The windows were repaired and new sash cords added to the security of the place.

A couple of the lads repaired the brickwork and tiles around the sitting room fireplace and others washed and sanded down the old paintwork. There were none of the high quality emulsion and gloss paints of today and what was casually referred to as 'distemper', which was only available in a few basic colours, was slapped on the ceilings and walls. Lights and power points were stripped and made good and loose and damaged floorboards were either repaired or replaced. By the end of the second evening, Len was a changed man and was smiling from ear to ear. When they had finished, he was profuse in his thanks to everyone for all their help and he assured them that he could easily complete the outstanding work over the coming weekend. A few drinks in a nearby pub put the seal on a job well done.

The following Monday morning, Len brought Mike up to date. Without saying what had been done, he had managed to persuade his wife to have another look at it and when she had seen the clean, bright flat, she had changed her mind and agreed that once they had got a few bits and pieces together, it would suit them very nicely. Len had spoken to the landlord, who was also very pleased at their efforts and he had given them the free use of the courtyard at the back, which would be very handy for both the baby and the dog. The next day, her parents had come over to see where their young family would be living and had made their contribution by giving pieces of furniture, curtains and bedding etc. Their new-found independence was, Len said, largely due to Mike and his mates, who had rallied round when he had so desperately needed help.

One morning, there was an air of excitement in the Factory and when the bell sounded for the break, there was a rapid exodus outside. A large Destroyer had been brought in for repair. She was a large, modern vessel, probably no more than two years old, and she was in a dire state. As the water was pumped out of the dry-dock, the full extent of the damage became increasingly evident. Her bows were extensively smashed, the damage going back for a distance of approximately thirty five feet from her stem. The Navy had been very fortunate to have brought her safely back to port. The incident had not been reported in the press, though it soon became known that she had been in collision with a Cruiser, while on exercise in the North Atlantic. Nothing was known about the other Vessel or where she had been taken.

There was an urgency in repairing her and the job was put in hand with rare fervour. Working day and night, her 'forrad' end was a hive of activity and the Apprentices saw for the first time just how the Yard responded to a critical situation. The damaged section was cut back to a secure bulkhead and completely rebuilt. Large, pre-rolled steel joists were delivered, then lowered into position and welded into place. The complete bow-end arrived one morning, having been pre-fabricated, with the anchor hawse-holes already in place. It was rigged, sent down, positioned and fixed in place in very quick time. With all the connections installed, the plates were welded on and within weeks, the hull was completed. Work was already well in hand on the reconstruction of the internal bulkheads and decks.

The Painters came on board and with the hull was back in pristine condition. the installation of the deck machinery was followed by that of the internal equipment, including the electrical cabling. The superstructure was painted and the fixtures and fittings mounted on the upper deck. All in all, the reconstruction was carried through in less than two months and well ahead of schedule. Even to the most cynical observers, it demonstrated that when needed, the Dockyard was equal to any task. The Ship was re-floated, moved out through the basins, then soon after, she was re-commissioned and returned to operational service.

After all the excitement of moving into his flat, Len had soon reverted to much the same demeanour as previously. In common with the majority of young married men, his financial situation was tight and it would remain so for some years to come. He was still regularly absent from the test room and Mike had no idea where he spent his time. Providing everything that required testing was done promptly, no one was any the wiser. Mike duly learned that he had a secure hidey-hole and had been studying for his forthcoming HNC examinations. Following his discharge from the Army, he had gone to the local 'College of Knowledge', to make up for lost time. Like many others, he had failed his exams during his Apprenticeship and had woken up to his urgent need of qualifications. The untimely arrival of the infant had nearly put an end to his good intentions.

Doing non-destructive tests on samples was a tedious chore and there always had to be someone in the room, in case an urgent job came in. Len had been working overtime and had hastened to point out that Apprentices were not allowed to do so before their fourth year. The extra pay earned had been very welcome and the only time Mike made a useful contribution was when there was an urgent batch of shear and tensile tests to be carried out. The time dragged by, week by dreary week and when he asked Len if there was anything else he could do, he was gruffly told to get on with his revision. If Mike had had an ounce of gumption, he would have responded positively to that suggestion. Much of his time was spent yarning to other lads, many of whom were also less than gainfully employed.

One morning, Len told Mike that he would be away for a couple of weeks and that he was to work with another Fitter. As it turned out, he didn't see the man and spent the whole of the fortnight doing nothing. His mates were not busy either, but surprisingly, Mac had become an object of envy. He had accepted that nothing could be gained by being awkward and despite their ribbing, he had applied himself well to a number of jobs. The one which made his day was when he was told to mind a small, flat-bedded grinding machine. Having not received any previous instruction, he watched Ted set the piece up on the magnetic bed-plate and start the grinding off the top surface. All he had to do was to keep an eye on it and tell his boss when it was nearing the end of the pass.

Ted was clearly breaking the rules, but Mac was on cloud nine. He made much of how the man trusted him and of the responsibility involved. He had become very scathing, saying about his mates that they were lazy sods. Ted had, in fact, played a 'canny card' in that he could keep an eye on the blighter, while he got on with his other work. With their noses clearly out of joint, his mates insisted that the old bugger was having him on.

'Piss-off,' Mac replied crossly. 'You're only bloody jealous.'

Despite being keen to learn, they were given simple jobs and then only under close supervision. Marking out, drilling and tapping very small, threaded holes was interesting, but it was some time before they were given more difficult things to do. They were under-employed and as long as they didn't make a noise or acted the goat, they were mostly left to their own devices. They often discussed what they would do when they were earning good money. Some of the older lads had 'got' into trouble and in some cases, they had reluctantly married the objects of their irrepressible carnal desires. The only way to their future prosperity was to avoid matrimony. One lad was saving for a new motor-bike, while another day-dreamed of buying a car. Nick liked sailing and was intent on getting his own dinghy. When Mike was asked what he wanted, he replied that his ambition was to own his own home, which was seen as a bit odd. He replied that he was determined not to live from hand to mouth, like his parents.

With their second year drawing to a close, they were very much looking forward to their summer holiday. The Yard would be closed during the last two weeks in July and on their return, they would start their third year. As they reached their eighteenth birthdays, they were given a substantial rise in wages, which always made the day. When added to the increase they would get at the beginning of the third year, their financial situation would be greatly improved and they would be well on the way to self-sufficiency.

The end of year exams in the Dockyard School had to be faced first and for some, it was a daunting prospect. While the Upper School lads were confident that they would easily cope, some of the Lower School ones suffered no little trepidation about the trials ahead. They knew that they should have worked harder, as their lecturers had constantly urged all through the year. There was no shortage of clever buggers among the men in the factory either. They took great pleasure in prognosticating about the rocky path which lay ahead for those that squandered their chances. For the most part, their less than well-meaning advice was ignored, but no one doubted the truth of what they said.

Despite the problems at the start of the year and lately with Billy in the Assembly shop, Mike had enjoyed his second year. The depression he had felt at the end of the previous year had soon passed and all the intensive training, practical and theoretical, had put him and his mates well on the road to becoming competent Fitters. They were under no illusions that the road ahead would be difficult and at times, they would still struggle. Their older mates had talked a lot about what they would be doing when they returned to work and bearing in mind their improved finances, the future looked a lot brighter. They went off on their summer holidays in a happy frame of mind.

Chapter 16

The Last Few Weeks

The lads had mostly been employed in the various Departments in the Factory throughout their second year. The objective had been to give them broad practical experience in the many types of fitting work. Some though had worked in the Locomotive shed, which was adjacent to the north-western side of the building. There, they had learned about the maintenance and repair of the numerous locomotives, used in the movement of goods around the Yard. They were mainly steam-driven tank engines, but there were also a number of diesel-driven units. During the winter months, it was a shitty job and there were long faces when they were sent there. Few of the 'locos' were repaired under cover, and those which were, were parked outside provided a trying experience. No matter how well wrapped up against the cold they were, the lads had chapped hands and chilblains. Their suffering was partially alleviated when they took components inside the shed, where there was a number of large, pot-bellied stoves, supplemented by waste-oil burning heaters.

The locos were always dirty, much more than the more modern diesels. When one came in for repair, it was inevitably covered in a noisome gunge, made up of oil, grease and coal dust. The filth was everywhere in the shop, both on the floors and across the work surfaces. The coming of spring brought some respite, but nothing could be done about the dirt. The only compensation was that the work was interesting, with regular opportunities to put into practice the skills that they had already learned. The Fitters were mostly in their late forties and very experienced in all things engines. They were also very canny in the supervision of their Apprentices and were very willing to impart their skills. To a man, they reckoned they knew all there was to know about their charges' silly stunts.

The shed measured perhaps eighty feet long by thirty feet wide, with a double run of rail tracks running through the whole length. It provided for most of the work to be carried out 'under cover' and there were large sliding doors at each end. Along one side were a dozen or so benches, with a small machining facility to one side, made up of lathes, drilling and shaping machines and a mechanical saw. An electrically-driven, overhead crane and a couple of swinging lifting beams, rigged with chain blocks gave the means of lifting heavy objects. There was also a large, electrically-heated 'oil-bath' at the end of the shop which provided the means of 'shrinking' couplings and wheels on to their shafts.

The lads were soon introduced to the 'art' of scraping large phosphor-bronze bearings, most of which had been cast in the foundry. Having been machined to a close tolerance to the shaft diameter, they were taken over to the benches for 'close-fitting'. After being de-burred, each half-shell was set up in a vice, with the crowns uppermost and carefully marked-off. The runnels, which were needed for grease distribution across the bearing surfaces, were then cut out. A lad would work under the close supervision until he was thought to have picked up the basics. A specially prepared cold-chisel was used to chip the metal diagonally in four directions away from the grease inlet hole. When completed, the shells were offered up to the journal, which was lightly covered in engineers' blue, and the bearing assembled. The high spots were highlighted and scraped away. The object was to achieve a contact area of approximately 80% across the bearing surfaces.

Learning the skill was harder for some than for others and the fitters offered tips about how to best do what was required. The 'clearance tolerances' were then set, before finally boxing up the bearing. It was done by compressing lead-wire between the bearing surfaces and inserting metal-shims between the two halves. When the bearing was warm, it would work efficiently and give a prolonged duration of service. Practice made perfect and they soon could 'fit' a bearing to the satisfaction of their fitters. Modern manufacturing processes turn out bearing-shells which, in theory, negate the need to fit them in the manner as outlined above. However now and then, the old skills are still used to address a particular malfunction.

The method used in 'shrinking' a large-bore coupling or a wheel on to a shaft, had not changed in many years. The requisite expansion was achieved by immersing the female halves completely in hot oil, the temperature of which was evenly raised to a prescribed level by electric heaters. The resultant expansion of the metal allowed it to be slid easily over the shaft and when it cooled, firm contact between the mating surfaces made for a firm fit. The job had to be completed smartly, because the heat was soon lost. From time to time, it was not unknown for the part to be stuck half way on the shaft. The Fitters then had the ball-aching job of carefully reheating the assembly, using large gas torches, to pull it off again. It was a dirty, hazardous operation, with the inexperienced lads picking up a burn or two, as well as being covered in oil. There was only one way to do it and recriminations from the Foreman would surely follow any 'balls-up'.

Despite the dirt and discomfort, the Apprentices soon settled down and there was always an air of excitement when a locomotive raised steam, even after only a short refit. The lads were given the job of collecting the lighting up materials and after filling the water side of the boiler, the fire would be lit. With a head of steam up, the engine would be moved. The apprentices were strictly forbidden to drive an engine but, as with many rules, they were made to be broken. It was not unknown for a lad to craftily show an interest in how the controls worked and then get around the Driver to let him have a go.

One lad, much to the envy of his mates, was seen moving the engine fifty yards along the track, then bringing it back. All the time the Driver and his Fitter were on the footplate, he did exactly as he was told, but the temptation was too much and having been 'egged-on' during the dinner break, he proudly explained how it all worked to his mates. He then gave them a practical demonstration by moving the engine up and down a few yards either way. The Fitters were ensconced in their mess room and would remain so until the hooter sounded the end of the break, so Sod's Law dictated that what should have been harmless fun quickly turned into a dangerous stunt.

After a few short runs, he took the engine further down the track and in his confusion, went further than intended. The points at the bottom of the Marshalling-yard allowed the loco to carry on across the road and along the side of the basin. In his excitement, he had forgotten how to stop the engine and he ran it into a train of empty wagons, which sent them careering down a spur. One of his mates pulled on the steam whistle, which gave warning to pedestrians and thus alerted a Copper to their presence on the line. Soon after, they came to a gentle stop due to a rapid decline in the steam pressure and with no small sense of relief, they applied the brakes. With the Copper rapidly bearing down on them, they took off up the road back to the shed and safety, or so they thought.

Their come-uppance was not long in coming and they stood in front of the Foreman, looking most forlorn and on the end of a monumental bollocking. They offered no excuses and were soon back in the shed, where they were given further 'earache' from the Fitters. The Foreman then marched the main culprit back down the road to the lifeless engine and made him rake over the coals in the furnace to raise steam again. The Driver moved the engine down the track to retrieve the wagons and having brought them back, it was uncoupled and parked outside the shed.

When he had first heard about their prank, the Foreman had known that the young sods had put him in a bit of a fix, which would require a lot of explaining. Having constantly suffered the pranks of the young lads under his supervision over the years, the latest one was really no big deal. His main concern was that someone could have been hurt, when the loco had crossed the road. The Officer had been waiting when he came back into his office and he had already had his story ready.

He told him that following the overhaul of the engine, the safety devices had not been fully set up and tested. After offering him the time-honoured palliative of a mug of tea, he went on to say that following the test-run, the Driver had parked the engine by the shop but the throttle had gently leaked steam into the cylinders and the engine had eventually moved of its own accord. That was absolute nonsense, of course, but how was the Officer to know? He went on to say that only by the quick wits of the lads, who had been playing football nearby, had a very nasty accident been prevented. The Copper relaxed and said that as no real harm had been done, he would not report the incident. The Foreman later told his Apprentices that he would not tolerate any more messing about and any further transgression would bring immediate retribution.

Returning to the Tool Room, Len had gradually became more relaxed and he and Mike often talked about what they were going to do in their forthcoming holidays. His wife wanted them to go away with her parents but after all the unpleasantness, Len was firm that they shouldn't do so. Their flat had turned out to be just the job and he was both pleased and relieved with how well his wife had settled in. They had become friendly with their neighbours, some of whom were of their own age and they often went out for the evening together. An 'old girl', who was a retired children's nurse, was happy to oblige with regular baby-sitting and it was good that they were getting on so well. Len again told Mike that he and his wife had very much appreciated his support.

'It's not for me to advise anyone about marriage,' Len said soberly, 'but every young couple should avoid living with their parents. I didn't know that it could be so bloody awful. When I came out of the Army, I tried to tell Jen that we should wait a year or so before we got married, which would have given us the chance to put some money together, but she wouldn't have it. Egged-on by her mother, she demanded that we got wed as soon as possible and whenever I said that we should wait, she got angry and said she had waited long enough. If I had known what I know now, I would have stuck to my guns. When we were first married, we all got on well and it was very pleasant. Later, little niggles started and things slowly started to go downhill. Her father always insisted that we paid our way, which was only fair, but I soon felt that they were taking more from us than was right. Her old man often avoided paying when we went out for a drink and there were times when he could hardly be civil. After the baby came, he never stopped dripping about what a bloody nuisance we were.'

'Look Mike,' he went on, 'I know I wasn't friendly when you first came, but perhaps you can understand why. I was so bloody depressed by the way things had gone and I almost walked out. Our worst mistake was to start a family right away. Jen's a couple of years older than me and she wanted a baby more than anything. It was a miserable time and we always seemed to be arguing, something we'd hardly done before we were married. In the end, her mother was constantly finding fault with everything we did as well and she never missed an opportunity to remind us as to how grateful we should be. She used to walk into our room without knocking and when I mentioned it, she told me it was her house and she would do whatever she wanted. When she interfered in our personal matters, it really was the end. Now we're on our own, we are very much happier and as far as I'm concerned, the less we see of them, the better. The flat isn't all that good, but its better by far than living with them.'

Mike was taken aback at the lengthy account of the trials and tribulations of Len's domestic life. Having bottled it up for so long, he'd had to tell someone about it. Having no idea about marriage, Mike had been surprised at how quickly the 'sweetness and light' had ended. In rounding off his tale of woe, Len told him that many of his friends were suffering in the much the same way. The shortage of accommodation was chronic and whatever became available, either to buy or rent, was soon snapped up. He had been fortunate in finding the flat, even though it was in such a deplorable state and in a run-down part of the town. His parents, in contrast to hers, had never tried to interfere and when they moved in, they had given them a lot of the small essentials necessary for them to live in a modicum of comfort. Mike was to hear of many other similar situations.

Envy has always been a cardinal sin, of which we are all guilty of at one time or another and some people in Mike's village had to know everyone else's business. His parents were among them. He would often squirm inwardly when he heard them talking about someone's most intimate secrets, the source of his mother's information being usually from the gossips among their neighbours. No one was safe from their prying and at times, their spiel was both cruel and totally untrue. That in no way deterred them, despite a regular succession of inter-family rows, though many suffered the indignity of their personal affairs being aired in silence.

If a family's fortunes were 'on the up', their neighbours wanted to know why and if they couldn't find the reason, they would invent one. With most of their incomes being similar, any change for the better often became the subject of envious speculation. Similarly, if and when a lad got into trouble with the Police or a lass suffered an unwanted pregnancy, it yielded unbridled delight in some quarters. The gossips would split into two camps, one gloating and the other sympathetic to their predicament.

The most outrageous example of just how cruel people could be came when a family was said to have 'a dark secret'. The woman who started the rumour told a neighbour that her husband knew someone who had been in the Security Forces during the war. Apparently, a young man of the same name had been caught and executed for spying. Despite having being sworn to secrecy, the neighbour hadn't been able to resist blabbing and it was soon all over the village. Mike, not being the soul of discretion, took his mother to task one evening, for being part of the nonsense. She roundly turned on him in angry reply.

'You shut yer mouth,' she yelled at him. 'You don't know nothin'!'

Only a few weeks later, the victims packed up and left the village and a year or so later, the truth came out. There had, indeed, been a spy of the same name, who had been hung for treason, but he certainly hadn't been their son. They had in fact suffered the sad loss of both of their boys in the War; one at Dunkirk and the other while at sea in the Royal Navy. The odd thing was that among the unfeeling gossips were people who were always the first to 'rally-round' in support of anyone in difficulty; a death in the family or serious illness. Not a few of them hung their heads in shame when the truth became known.

Mike, being an awkward bugger, didn't let the matter rest. His mother had been anxiously waiting for him to say something further to her when it had all calmed down, but he hadn't done so. His opportunity to 'give the pot a stir' came when he saw the originators of the nonsense get off the bus one afternoon. He walked up behind them and told them that they should hang their heads in shame for what they'd done, which angered her husband greatly. It provoked a furious argument which the cheeky young bugger ended by telling the man that he was pathetic. He threatened to complain to Mike's parents, but they must have thought it best to drop the whole matter and nothing further was said.

From mid-June, the moral of the lads rose by the day. Most of them had benefited from the practical experience of working in the Factory during the past eleven months. The school year came to a most welcome end and everyone happily relaxed. As the days passed, they became increasingly excited at the prospect of their forthcoming holiday. It would be the last year that they would be required to take their annual leave in the last two weeks of July. In future, it would be taken when they wanted it. The Saturday morning shift had also gone and the shorter working week, with no loss in pay, pleased everyone. Better still, there had recently been a marked improvement in the financial health of the nation. At long last, it was recovering from the economic disaster which had been brought about by the War and there were more and better quality goods in the shops. Best of all, food rationing was well on its way to becoming a thing of the past.

On the last Friday before the shut-down, the Apprentices helped tidy up and sweep out the tool room. Following the disaster of staying in the caravan the previous year, Mike's parents had no intention of making the same mistake again. They were going to Cornwall to stay with relations, and he was most definitely not invited and being well able to look after himself, he would enjoy living on his own. The last afternoon was very relaxed, with most people chatting and little work being done and when the hooter sounded at four o'clock, they made their customary dash for the gate, with a lot of excited calling to each other as they went through.

It had been an interesting year and most of the lads were well on their way to becoming competent Fitters, though they still had a lot to learn. The coming year would bring a new challenge and their optimism was somewhat dented by their older advisers, who earnestly insisted that they had not enjoyed their third year. During that time, they had received comprehensive instruction in the operation of all types of metal-cutting machines and it had not all been plain sailing as some of them had been better at it than others. Their younger mates were solemnly warned that the sheer repetition of machining work, be it on lathes, borers or millers would try their patience to the full. Even when they became competent enough to do piecework, the extra money earned would all too often be hardly worth the effort. No one likes change and their unknown fate caused our lads some concern. Were the older lads winding them up, or were they just being truthful? The best thing to do was to wait to see how it turned out.

Book 3: The Third Year

Chapter 1

A New Year

At the start of the third year of his Apprenticeship and, as so eagerly anticipated, Mike was given a pay rise in addition to the one that he had received on his eighteenth birthday. Both payments were relatively substantial and he was very aware that he would now be earning almost as much as his father. It was something that would have to be kept very much to himself, with his payslips well hidden away from his mother's prying eyes. Despite having recently increased his 'lodge' payments, she would be sure want more and the difficult decision would be as to how much to give her, to satisfy her demands. He was not averse to paying his way in contributing to the family budget, which was only fair, but it still remained a pressing problem.

There was the same chaos in the Factory as there had been at the start of each of the previous two years and everyone was noisily milling about, as they moved their kit to their designated new places of work. Each lad had received a written instruction, which clearly informed him as to where he was to go, but there was still an air of confusion in the air. The 'chits', which been issued before their holidays, contained errors and the problems were exploited to the full, despite the strenuous efforts of the Timekeepers to clarify matters.

Some went to Departments which had no knowledge of them and promptly came back for redirection. Some of the chits had been written in pencil and were gleefully altered and swapped around but eventually, it was all sorted out and they gradually dispersed to report to their new bosses. It was all good fun and everything was back to normal by mid-morning. Most of Mike's entry was destined for the machine training area, where they would be working for the next three months. Having seen the same nonsense acted out many times before, their new Instructors initially ignored them then after nearly an hour, they came out into the shop and made a roll-call, which confirmed that everyone was present.

There had been the usual messing about and odd arguments, with some lads claiming the machines on which they would like to work. They needn't have bothered, because that had already been decided. The Senior Instructor, Mr Meredith, introduced his three colleagues and the lads were allocated to their groups. Their initial instruction would, he said, be very much concerned with 'Safety in Working' and no one would be allowed to operate a machine until he was adjudged competent to do so. That inevitably meant a delay, which gave rise to loud, exaggerated groans. The Instructors were unperturbed by their charges reaction and soon had their groups in some semblance of order.

After dinner, they went up to lecture room and Bill, as he was known, opened his discourse by stressing that it was very much in their interest to pay close attention to what he had to say and make notes in their books, for future reference. He looked solemnly at his charges and there wasn't a sound from them. He then relaxed and smiled, which brought a few witty comments and some exaggerated groans. Most of them realised though he had something important to say.

He said that there had been many accidents on such machines in the past, a lot of which would have been avoided if those involved had done as they'd been told. However, there were always some who couldn't be told anything for their own good. All he could do was to keep repeating the message and hope that most of what he was trying to put across would stick in their minds. Bill was a small, dapper man who, though quietly spoken, came across well. Like so many of his colleagues, he had also served in the Royal Navy for more than twenty years, latterly as a Chief Instructor. He clearly knew his business and he went on to outline the scope of their training in the operation of manufacturing machines. There would, he said, be a mixture of practical instruction in the workshop and regular sessions in the lecture room.

The objective was to turn them into first-class operators of the many types of machine which were currently in use in the Factory. Bill had an altogether different way of stating how things stood, from what they had experienced previously and the lads listened intently as he set down a number of 'hard and fast' rules.

'Working on machines is dangerous and if any of you get caught up in one, you'll find out exactly what I mean. I don't want to start off your training by making any threats but be warned, the machine shop is not the place for skylarking. The rules are in place for your own good and your instructors will neither accept nor tolerate anyone breaking them. I want you to clearly understand what I'm saying, so that we all know exactly where we stand.'

The discussion in the canteen over dinner was mostly about what they'd been told and the consensus was that it all seemed to make good sense. Perhaps at long last, they were beginning to accept that they also had responsibilities, not only to themselves but to others as well. The older Apprentices were unanimous when they said that Bill was a decent bloke and everyone should listen to what he had to say. However, one lad remarked that 'turning' wasn't all that interesting, when compared with the fitting work they'd been doing. With more than half of his charges wearing ties, Bill had taken the opportunity to make a pertinent point.

'Rule number one is, if you wear a tie, it's best to take it off before starting your machine. If it gets caught up in a moving part, you'll be in real trouble and it's most unlikely you'll get clear without being injured. You may well be badly hurt. If you don't want to take it off, then just ensure you tuck both ends well away inside your shirt or down your jumper. You can't be too careful where ties are concerned. As you can see, none of your Instructors is wearing one and that is because we have seen so many accidents. The watchword must be the old scouts' motto, 'be prepared'.

'Rule number two is, never leave your machine running unattended. If you have to do something else, even for only for a few minutes, then shut it down. If you're going to be away for some time, turn the power off at the main switch as well. Our main concern is to ensure that you don't wreck the machine, if it's left running unattended. You might also injure someone else, who may be working nearby.

'The next rule is that you do not interfere with anyone else's machine. We've had cases in the past where someone thought it very clever to play a trick on a workmate, either in fun or even to be downright nasty. When it all went pear-shaped, he denied responsibility for what had happened. Anyone caught 'having a laugh' in this way will be severely dealt with. Each one of you will be treated as an adult and you must behave accordingly. Management will not accept any excuses if a machine is badly damaged, as a direct result of someone larking about.

'Rule number four is that you must ensure that all guards are firmly fixed in place before you start the machine. That is what we call a copper-bottomed rule. Again, no excuses will be accepted if you cause an accident, either to yourself or to someone else, by not complying with it. Always be aware that there are real dangers to other people, as well as yourself, from an unguarded machine.

'Number five is not so important as the ones I've already mentioned but I want you all to remember, a clean and tidy machine is likely to be a safe one. When you go out into the shop, you'll see that the Turners, most of whom have been doing the job for many years, have a real pride in their machines. They wipe them down and clear away the debris on a regular basis. Don't leave bits of rag, metal, tools or anything else where they can fall into the machine. At the end of the day, clear away the swarf from on and around your machine and put it into the receptacles provided. You must always keep the immediate area tidy and clear of obstructions. Don't leave anything lying about where someone can trip over and injure himself.'

Bill went on with his list of 'do's and don'ts' for some considerable time and seeing his charges were becoming restless, he decided he had said enough for one day. Like most people when faced with a new experience, they were very anxious to get going.

'I'm sure you all realise the sense of what I have been saying,' he went on. 'We must do everything possible to prevent accidents. If you have any problems with anything I've said, or want further information, ask your Instructor. He'll be only too pleased to help. If you're in doubt about anything, shut the machine down and ask for help. Tomorrow, we'll discuss the basic principles of machine work, during which we shall see a couple of films. I'm sure you'll find them interesting. Over the next few weeks, your lectures will cover all aspects of machining. One last point, whenever you're working, always be ready to stop your machine, should the need arise. A safety handle is provided for that purpose and you should always keep your hand near or on it, when your machine is running.

After asking for any questions, which met with no response, he sent them back down to their workshop. About fifteen lads went off down to the same shop in which they had worked in their first year. Their Instructor was a tall, stern faced man of advanced years and as they trooped out, there were calls to 'give Charlie our love when you see him!'. The next morning, the lads in the Factory were allocated to their lathes and strictly instructed not to touch anything. It was frustrating, because they were itching to get started. Mike and his mates were in Bill's group and while waiting, they discussed their machines. Some of them had had done simple jobs on lathes at school but accepted they had to start again, like everyone else.

The Instructors busily went from lad to lad, to demonstrate how to check the machine before starting it up. Despite the clear instructions of the previous day, some of them had to be reminded to either take their ties off or to tuck them in. Because of the number of Apprentices under instruction, they had to be patient while waiting their turn. By the middle of the afternoon, everyone had been told exactly how it had to be done. They were then told, with no little drama, to 'make' the main switch and they turned their lathes, first one way, then the other. After all they'd been told, they were in no doubt about the inherent dangers to life and limb.

The next morning, each lad was issued with a short length of mild steel round-bar, which was an inch in diameter and six inches long. Even so, they were again strictly forbidden to switch on until told to do so. After what had seemed an interminable delay, they were at last going to do some machining. The first lesson was about how to set the piece up correctly, i.e. firmly and centrally in the four-jawed chuck. To the novice, it was not as easy as it looked. After a lot of prompting, most of them had the knack of it by the end of the day. Almost without exception, the lathes were in poor condition, due to their many years of service, before being given over to the apprentices' training. The instructors countered the grumbles by saying they were suitable for the job and would be for many years to come.

A lathe was lying in pieces on the floor at one side of the shop and over the next few days, the lads looked it over. There was extensive damage to a number of components and what would have to be done to return it to a serviceable condition was discussed in considerable detail. Apparently, an operator had left it running when he'd gone up the shop to make a cup of tea. On the way back, he'd stopped to talk to a mate and had completely forgotten about his machine. Having many years' experience, he should have known better and he'd been downgraded for his carelessness. When asked who it was, Bill said the man had suffered enough and shouldn't be the butt of teasing from 'green as grass' Apprentices.

The repairs would give the lads in-depth knowledge of the design of a lathe, as well as good experience in making the necessary parts. When completed, it would either be set up in his workshop or sent elsewhere. In his opinion, it had previously been a good machine, with many years of service still left in it. The 'saddle/tool-post' assembly, which moved the cutting tool across or along the piece of work, had come into contact with the chuck. Severe damage had been done to both the drive and the feed mechanisms, including the gear wheels, which were located on the end of the machine. It had not done the chuck much good either but, though in a battered condition, it could still be refurbished.

One of the lads asked why there was no safety device, which would have stopped the machine and prevented the damage. Bill replied that it was very old and no such device had been fitted. Taking them across the shop to a larger, more modern machine, he pointed out and demonstrated how such a device worked. He again repeated that his standing instruction was to never leave a machine unattended when it was running. Everyone had 'got the message', though whether they would keep it in mind remained to be seen.

Not everyone appreciated their Instructors' endless strictures. What was grinding was that throughout their first week, they had been continually lectured on little else but safety. By Friday dinner time, they had still not been allowed to actually make a cut and they were busting to do so. There was a bit of grumbling in the canteen and they made much of how their Instructors went on and on about it. They learned another lesson that day and it was nothing to do with turning. It was that in any public place, 'walls have ears'. What was said was overheard by others sitting nearby and someone must have had mischief in mind. On their return to the shop, they were confronted by their unsmiling Instructors and Bill staggered them by repeating, almost word for word, their complaints. He took the opportunity to launch into yet another list of home truths about working safely.

'I was hoping we could have avoided this sort of nonsense,' he told them tersely. 'Well, no matter, we may as well get everything out into the open, right at the start. Some of you may think you're very clever and that we're a bunch of old duffers, who have been put out to grass, while waiting for our retirement. Well, that's not so. What we've been trying to do for the past week is to drive into your thick skulls that you've got no option but to comply with the rules. You ignore what we've been telling you at your peril. Look about and you'll see that there are a number of people working in this Factory who have suffered injuries in the past. Go and speak to them. I'm sure they'll tell you to pay heed to what you're being told.'

Clearly, their Instructors took their responsibilities very seriously indeed. They were both angry and disappointed that some of their lads had been so disparaging about them and it was a chastened bunch of lads that sat in front of them and all because of a few ill-chosen comments, which had been overheard.

'Just one last thing,' Bill said, looking directly at Sid, one of those who had complained loudly, 'before we get on with the job. If you've been thinking I'm a bloody old woman, why didn't you tell me to my face? Perhaps if you'd discussed your complaints with us, instead of moaning in front of all and sundry, we could have sorted things out without all this unpleasantness. I'll finish by saying again that if you want to discuss anything at any time, speak to either your Instructor or to me. If it saves you from doing something silly, then you'll be the ones that benefit.'

At the end of the lecture, Sid and another lad stayed behind and shamefacedly owned up to their stupidity. They explained that without thinking, they had been grumbling to the other lads and it had got a bit out of hand. They hadn't meant any disrespect and were sorry it had got back to them in the way it did. They would certainly be more careful in the future, in the canteen or anywhere else for that matter. Bill, after listening to their apologies, was surprisingly generous.

'It's alright lads,' he said in a friendly voice, 'we've heard it all before and know exactly how you feel. Just try to remember, it's us that will catch it in the neck if any one of you comes a cropper. That's why we keep on and on at you about the need to work safely. Let's leave it at that, shall we?'

Chapter 2

Feet under the Table

The path of young love has always been fraught with hazards and the lads knew well the folly of admitting any interest in the opposite sex. Keeping a romance to oneself was difficult and when it became known, the lad was fair game for outrageous mickey-taking. Bill was a quiet lad, who got a lot of stick after being seen out one Sunday afternoon, when he had apparently been oblivious to everything and everyone, according to the snidy bugger that reported back. The lad and his beloved had been seen walking leisurely along the sea-front in Margate and being thirty miles from home, they must have thought they were safe from prying eyes. When he came into work the next day, he was completely unaware of what was to come. After donning his overalls, he sat down for a quick glance through his paper and was serenaded with a boisterous rendering of an old favourite song.

'Oh, I do like to be beside the seaside, I do like to be beside the sea,' his mates howled.

It was followed by a great roar of laughter and cheers for the lad. Much to his dismay and embarrassment, he had been rumbled. One of the Instructors, who were rudely disturbed by the noise, came out of the office.

'Cor blimey, you lot,' he shouted, 'keep it down. We ain't even woke up yet.'

With his amorous liaison outed, Bill's response to the inevitable leg-pulling was at first muted.

'I don't know what you're on about,' was his opening gambit, but that didn't wash.

He then made things worse by blushing furiously. Despite his earnest protestations of innocence, he was loudly derided by his workmates, with the mischievous sod who had blabbed to the fore. He told Bill that other people would confirm his romantic sojourn and he then made the most of the little he had seen by saying that it had all looked pretty serious.

'Holding hands and gazing lovingly into each other's eyes, they were. Her name's Maureen and she was in my class at school. She works in Boots now, on the cosmetics counter,' he added smugly.

'I thought for a minute it was my daughter you were talking about,' quipped an Instructor, who was clearly enjoying the banter and the obvious discomfort of the hapless victim. 'I wouldn't like an idle sod like you for a son in law, and that's a fact,' he concluded as he went back into the office.

The crack provided great entertainment and a humorous inquisition followed. How long had he known the lovely Maureen, and where did they

190

meet? Had he been to meet her folks yet? What was her mother like? Did they live in a nice house? Were they well off? Did he have a nice tea when they got home? Had he remembered his manners and not let his mum down, like someone else they could mention? One cheeky bugger even asked if she had a sister, who might be looking for a nice young man?

It went on and on and, if he'd had any sense, Bill would have ignored them. Like everyone else before, he was steadily lured into a detailed discussion about his budding romance and it wasn't long before he was bitterly regretting having said anything to the lousy buggers, who were intent on ribbing him. Sensing more to come, they pressed him again about how he had been received in her home. Bill suddenly thought of how another lad had neatly dodged a similar predicament by spinning the most outrageous tale. He had gone on at length about the warmth of his reception and the culinary delights on the table at his new girlfriend's house and had laid it on so thick that no one had believed him. The problem was, what he'd been given in Maureen's house could in no way be described as a lavish spread. The questioning had by then become increasingly more personal and crude.

'What's she like then, this Maureen; a bit of alright or what?' asked someone, winking and grinning at his mates.

'Have you had any yet?' asked another vulgar bugger, in an allusion to the more intimate side of the relationship.

Bill refused to answer any further questions and his tormentors soon tired of their little game.

Mike had become friendly with a lass called Doreen; their liaison having started during the youth club summer outing to 'Sarf'end', i.e. Southend. While past his eighteenth birthday, he was still a callow youth, a veritable bean pole. In contrast, Dot was a buxom red-head, of a substantially heavier build. He was her first real boyfriend, so her friends cattily said, and she had quickly become very proprietorial. He later found out, when it was all over, that she was quite a bit older than him as well. He had been sitting at the back of the coach and his interest was aroused when she sat next to him on the way back from the seaside. She was said to be of a 'very warm and loving nature' and with the irrepressible stirrings of lust in his loins, he had willingly succumbed to her blandishments.

Their relationship had quickly blossomed, with regular, passionate cuddles in her father's tool shed, after the youth club had closed. It was away from prying eyes, and they had 'snogged' in some semblance of comfort. With nothing being a secret for long, his dalliance became known to his mates at work, though how was a mystery. Despite days of interrogation, Mike was not forthcoming, which suggested to his inquisitors that it could be serious. Nothing could have been farther from the truth and in a moment of weakness, he ruefully admitted that he wasn't at all keen on the lass. Someone asked why he was still seeing her and then the truth then came out.

Bearing in mind our previous comments about the poor quality of food which most working people ate at the time, with it being neither plentiful nor very good quality, any addition to a young man's sustenance was very welcome. In fact, the crafty sod had, for once, landed on his feet. Though he had quickly become disillusioned with Dot's charms, he had given the matter some serious thought and had decided that a few weeks pretence about his affections would not be an undue hardship. In other words, he was a selfish, lying toe-rag who was stringing the poor lass along.

Dot's mum was known for her generous hospitality and she kept a most excellent table. Sunday tea was an experience as near to heaven as Mike had ever known. For some weeks, he was the centre of attention, due to his vivid descriptions of the meals he had enjoyed. Some of those listening accused him of exaggerating, while others loudly condemned him for his hypocrisy and his 'lack of decent feelings'. Most of the lads though congratulated him for 'suffering in a most noble cause'. Dot's father was a Foreman Fitter, in the local Cement Works, and his family enjoyed a much better standard of living than their neighbours. Arthur and Gladys spoke 'proper', which was somewhat different from their working class roots. Much to his mates' amusement, Mike unkindly imitated their conversations around the table.

'Have anotha' couple of ham san'widg'es or a piece of choc'lit cake, My'kal,' which was a very kind exhortation from the good lady.

'Oh no thank you Mrs S, I couldn't possibly eat another mouthful,' replied the lying sod, optimistically hoping she would insist, which she did.

'Oh go on with you. A big lad like you needs to keep his strength up, ain't that so Arthur?,' she went on, archly winking at him.

'That's right, my lad,' said the good man in his gravelly voice, 'we men never knows when we might need to be at our best.' Then, entering rather more than intended into the spirit of the badinage, he went on, 'particularly when we've got such big fine girls to look after.'

'Now then Arfur,' said Glad, forgetting for a moment her newly-acquired gentility, 'I'll give you big, fine girls, you see if I don't. There's no call for coarseness,' she went on, by way of further admonishment and blushing demurely in emphasising her point. 'Come on lad,' she continued to Mike, 'just a little piece more' and not taking no for an answer, she cut him another hefty slice of her most scrumptious chocolate, cream-filled cake. 'We can't have all this going to waste, can we?'

'That's right,' said Arthur unabashed, 'you just fill your boots, my old son; you're more than welcome. I'll just have a little piece more of the same, thank you my love,' he said, smiling broadly and carefully enunciating every syllable.

Dot's mum was highly delighted that her daughter had found a nice young man who, she probably thought, 'had prospects'. She and her husband did their best to ensure that the welcome was clearly on the mat, and the budding romance had their every encouragement. Arthur told Mike, when they were talking about work, that there were always opportunities for good tradesmen in his industry. When he finished his time, he would be pleased to help him to find a good job, if that suited him, of course. With his feet so very firmly under the table, Mike became increasingly nervous about his subterfuge. It would be very difficult to get out of what had become a very awkward situation. So what did the lousy bugger do? Nothing!

Over the next few weeks, he continued to tuck in enthusiastically, while at the same time dreading the inevitable sexual confrontation with the less than delectable Dot in the shed. The good lady even gave him what later became known as doggy bags, to take home, all generously filled with goodies from the tea table. Again, some of his audience were openly disdainful and they roundly accused him of bullshitting. That his recent 'pack-ups' had caused comments was not lost on them.

'The grub is always gratefully received,' he told them, 'and if you don't believe it, that's up to you.'

When someone asked for further proof of the good lady's largesse, Mike replied that he usually ate her 'pack-ups' away from home, to avoid problems with his parents. Like all good things, his trips into Glad's culinary heaven came to an abrupt end and not in the way he had anticipated. One evening, after having politely said goodnight to her parents and being reluctantly led down the path towards the shed, he clumsily tried to fob Dot off with the excuse of 'wanting to get home early'.

'I've still got some homework to finish, and I'll be in big trouble if I don't hand it in in the morning, he said lamely.

Dot wasn't born yesterday, and her immediate change in demeanour told him that she wasn't going to wear it. Her response was swift and to the point.

'I think you've gone off me,' she retorted angrily. 'You've hardly had a word to say all day. You don't just come over here to talk to my dad about work, you know. It's me you come to see.'

She then laid into him for the liar he was and ended her diatribe by saying 'he was a rotten sod and she didn't want to see him again'. And that was it. His epicurean romance was over! Not without some regret at what he was losing, he gave three mental cheers and quickly pedalled away. He was though no different from anyone else. As soon as someone has lost something that wasn't wanted, he or she can't help wondering if they have done the right thing. The little seeds of regret germinate into a sense of loss, even if it is only a small one. He was in fact glad that he had got rid of the lass, despite her having done the 'dirty deed' for him. Not long after, he found out the reason why she had 'given him the bullet'.

A machinist called Jack lived in the same village as Dot, and he worked near Mike and his mates in the Factory. He had been quietly ear-wigging the lads' inane discussions and, seeing a chance for mischief, he had 'blabbed' to his girlfriend about Mike's perfidy. She, more in nastiness than with any concern for Dot's feelings, had told the poor lass about Mike's less-than-honest intentions. To her credit, she had replied that Mike was a nice lad and he wouldn't be so unkind as to pull a stunt like that. However, the doubt had been sown and when he had made such a lousy excuse for going home early on the following Sunday evening, she had seen through him and had acted accordingly. He gave the youth club a miss for some time after but, when he did go again, he was disconcerted to find that none of the other girls would speak to him.

A ramification had come from his parents when, noting that he was no longer out at Sunday tea time, they wanted to know why. His father, being cynical of everything he did, guessed what had been going on and he roundly berated Mike for 'sponging' on other people. With his gourmet romance over, he came in for yet more criticism from his mates, though some thought he'd done well to make it last as long as it had.

Only a week or so later, Mike saw Jack in the town with Dot on a Saturday afternoon and he had obviously taken the opportunity to insinuate himself into her affections. When tackled about it, he glibly said he had always admired the girl and saw nothing wrong with calling round, when Mike was no longer involved. Being a decent sort of bloke, he had 'packed in' his girlfriend before doing so. It was unanimously held that he was a hypocrite and a rat for 'shitting' on a workmate. The man shrugged off the criticism, saying he didn't care what they thought and within a matter of months, the loving pair got engaged. They got married in the following Spring. Whether or not Jack later went to work with Arthur in the Cement Works is not known, but he had left the Yard by the end of the year.

Alongside the water heaters in the Factory was a range of four electric ovens, which were always switched on during working hours. They mainly heated the items of food that the men brought into work for their midday meals. Geoff had seen some of them heating cans of soup and beans for their delectation and thinking it a good idea, he followed suit. For a few days, his mates looked enviously on as he enjoyed what he described as 'something different' for his dinner and his example was followed by others, until it all went horribly wrong. Posted prominently above the ovens were notices which warned the users that they were very hot and great care had to be taken in their use. Only metal containers should be used, and all paper wrappers had to be removed before anyone put any food into an oven.

The arrangement had worked well for many years and each day, men would quietly walk down the shop, clutching their containers, to put them into an oven. There were cries of, 'wotcha got today then 'Arry?,' or Bert or whoever. The replies were always of interest, because the ingenuity of some of their wives provided many with a variety of tasty treats. One morning, Geoff walked up the shop clutching his can and stopped for a chat with a couple of pals on the way. When he came back, he was very much looking forward to his tomato soup, which was a new brand product, only recently in the shops. Someone sarcastically commented that he hoped he had taken the wrapper off the can, before putting it into the oven.

'Do me a favour,' came the sharp retort, 'what do you think I am, bloody daft?'

The answer was obvious to most of those present and they didn't have long to wait to have it confirmed. About five minutes to twelve, there was a loud 'crump', which was quickly followed by clouds of acrid, black smoke billowing from one of the ovens. The men nearby ran over to see what had happened and when one switched the oven off and opened the door, all was revealed. The inside was in one hell of a mess. Geoff's precious can of soup had exploded and its contents were liberally spread all over the other items of food which had been placed there with such loving care. There were cries of outrage and loud threats of retribution against the bloody fool who had 'done for' twenty or so different dinners. Geoff decided that discretion was called for, if he was to avoid due punishment.

The lads watched as the men hotly debated who was responsible. As usual, when someone fell afoul of them, the Apprentices kept schtum. No one identified him, which was very amusing, particularly when he later arrived in the canteen, 'for his dinner'. When asked about what had happened, he was dismissive of the fact that he had caused so much trouble.

'With you lot going on at me, I only forgot to punch a couple of holes in the can, didn't I? No matter, worse things happen at sea,' he said, with a foolish smile on his face. 'Anyway, I don't know what all the fuss is about. They only got a bit of extra gravy and where's the harm in that? I'll just have to keep clear of the ovens for the next few days, won't I?'

Cleaners came during the afternoon to clean out the oven and it was back in service by the following morning. There was no 'come-back' and Geoff, having got away with it, continued with his ignorant and selfish ways, as if nothing had happened.

Chapter 3

Turning

Monday mornings were usually spent in the lecture room, and the lectures were initially about cutting tools. They covered the many aspects of the design and application of the tools used in turning cast-iron, mild-steel, brass and bronze, all of which the lads would be machining in due course. They were interesting, with numerous films and slides provided to get over the most salient points. Most of the cutting tools were made in the Yard, using methods evolved over very many years. The everyday ones were hand-worked from forgings in many shapes and sizes by the turners. Special tools were made in the tool room, to suit specific jobs. Bill spent some time in defining the method of obtaining the correct cutting-edges, with particular reference to the angles needed to obtain the optimum cut. He stressed the importance of grinding the metal without losing the inherent 'temper' of the steel.

He made much of the need to look after the tools 'with tender, loving care' and his comments were discussed at some length, with a number of suggestions coming from his colleagues. He summed up by saying that the best place to learn the basic rules of turning was on the shop floor and that they would be given practical demonstrations to help them along. An entire lecture was devoted to the various types of grinding machines, used for sharpening the tools. There were numerous such machines throughout the factory and in workshops all over the Yard. He pointed out the many pit falls relating to their use and the over-riding need for concentration and due care at all times.

His main point was the critical need to always use eye protection, whenever they were doing any grinding. He then went on to the practical aspects of machining and stressed that the operator should always ensure that the tool was properly clamped in the tool post, which was mounted on the carriage of the lathe. It was as important as all the other rules that they had already been given. He cautioned them about the need for care when setting up a work-piece in the chuck. A tool or work-piece, which came 'adrift' during a machining operation, was one of the most dangerous situations that a Turner could face. Before closing his lecture, Bill reiterated that if anyone had any problems, his Instructor would always give practical assistance.

The next morning, the lads were allowed to run their machines under close supervision and the ones with previous experience of lathe work were more confident than their peers. Their cutting tools had already been sharpened and each lad was shown how to clamp it firmly in place and after setting up their pieces in the chuck, they were ready to go. The functions of starting, stopping and moving the tool manually along the face to be machined were practised until everyone was confident that he knew what he was doing. The Instructors went from machine to machine and their gems of advice were constantly heard.

'Get a feel for the controls lad and take your time.'

'Don't force the tool into the metal like that.'

'Steady, I said.'

'Move the cutter along the bar at a firm, but steady, rate.'

'Treat it the same as if you are stroking your girlfriend's hand.'

'Don't try to run before you can walk.'

'Slowly now, you've got all the time in the world.'

And of course, there was that old favourite: 'Don't worry, you'll soon get the hang of it.'

They were heard repeating their instructions time and again over the next few days. As they gained confidence, they were allowed to slip the long-travel feed into the automatic mode. The encouragement of the Instructors was beginning to bear fruit and with everyone absorbed in what they were doing, there was little levity or messing about. When ready to move on, each lad was shown how to make cuts across the end-face of the bar and then how to machine it at various angles. Within a short time and almost without exception, they were adjudged sufficiently competent to operate their machines without the constant supervision of their Instructors.

There was a lot of discussion in the canteen about what they were doing and the older lads, who had themselves gone through the whole rigmarole, adopted superior attitudes. One crowed about how he had been one of the best Turners in his entry and had soon been given the more difficult jobs to do. His mates derisively reminded him that he had been 'worse than bloody useless'. It was all good fun with everyone joining in, particularly when the clown admitted he had been exaggerating.

The lectures covered other aspects of machining, such as thread-cutting and boring, functions which was more precise in their application. When studied in the classroom, with films which demonstrated the various techniques, it all seemed to be straightforward. However, it was not as easy as it looked. Tables were pinned up on the blackboard, which explained the relationship between the cutting rates and the various arrangements of the gear wheels at the end of a machine. They enabled the cutting of the stipulated number of threads per inch. The data was copied into notebooks and fair copies were later made for ease of reference. The various profiles and angles of the threads were discussed and by the time they were ready to cut a single-start v-thread, they had received all the theoretical training required.

A piece of round-bar was set up in the chuck and a hole drilled in the outer end. The 'tail-stock' was brought it into firm contact, which gave the piece stability. It was carefully machined down to the required diameter and after checking that the machine-gears were correct for the number of threads to be cut, they made a start. The rough machining of the thread was completed with only half a dozen passes. It was then finished off with a 'chaser', which obtained a smooth finish along the length of the thread. Checks with a thread-gauge confirmed its completion.

They then went on to cut a matching female thread. Another piece of mild-steel was clamped in the chuck and the face machined off. The hole was made with a large twist-drill, which was inserted into the tail-stock. The one that Mike was given was in poor condition and he was shown how to sharpen it on the grinding-machine.

There were a lot of interjections from his Instructor such as: 'No. No. Not like that,' and: 'Bloody hell, be careful, you silly sod,' which amused those watching. It was an acquired skill which had to be worked at and truth to tell, some of the lads never did learn to sharpen a drill bit properly. High quality drills were only available to the experienced Turners and they jealously guarded them against their light-fingered neighbours.

Seeing that their charges were growing restless while waiting to use a drill, they were told to quietly read over the notes they had made in their lectures. Mr Barry was in the habit of walking through the shop at least once a day, and he usually chatted with one or other of the instructors. He gazed around sternly, ostensibly looking at the Apprentices beavering away and sometimes, he would approach a lad, his purpose being to make a telling point.

'Er laddie, what are you doing?,' he would ask in his peculiar, high-pitched voice.

Almost without exception, the lad would start as though alarmed, then reply respectfully. 'I'm just practicing cutting across this face, Sir,' or whatever he was doing.

'Good, good. That's the idea. Carry on,' the man would reply and walk on.

He might then loudly stress the need to pay close attention to his Instructor and as soon as he was gone, everyone would relax and carry on with what they had been doing before being so rudely interrupted.

For the most part, the atmosphere in the shop was very relaxed and unless they were waiting for instruction or to use a specific tool, the lads quietly enjoyed themselves. The Instructors were quick to remind them to keep it down, when the need arose. Most of their charges had taken to reading newspapers, books and magazines to pass the time. The instructors knew what was going on but thought that as long as they were quiet, they could do as they pleased.

One morning, all was quiet and Johnny was happily puffing on a fag, while looking at the *Daily Mirror when s*uddenly, a high-pitched voice came from the other side of his machine.

'Er laddie! What d'you think you're doing?'

Johnny shot up in panic, his paper was thrown down and the blood drained from his face. There was uproar in the shop, with loud laughter and even the Instructors joined in the fun. It was his mate, not Mr Barry that had caught him idling.

'You bloody bastard,' yelled Johnny, and picking up a handy spanner. 'You almost gave me a heart attack.'

The lad pretended to make off before he could retaliate, and their inanity lightened the mood in the shop for the rest of the day. The lectures and the practical work on the machines were already becoming less interesting, as they were neither difficult nor stimulating. The time dragged and soon there were increasing complaints about being bored. Until only recently, they had been kept busy in the various fitting sections and it was generally agreed that they didn't have the same interest in turning metal. They were clearly not looking forward to the months ahead, when they would be working on a succession of machines. Some of the older lads confirmed that turning was by no means the hardest of the skills that they would learn.

'You've only got to look around to see it's not a job for anyone with a brain,' said Johnny. 'How the hell anyone can work on a machine, doing the same thing week in, week out, year in, year out, I don't know.' They must all be bloody zombies or something.'

'You can't say it's all boring,' said another lad. 'Some of it is highly-skilled and must have taken years to learn.'

'Like what,' replied Johnny, sensing the chance for an argument.

'Well, like the very large machines at the end of the Factory; the ones that turn the shafts and propellers like. You can't tell me that isn't skilled, interesting work.'

'Yeah well, I suppose they do take a bit of operating,' conceded his mate, 'but all I'm saying is, I wouldn't want to be doing machining for the rest of my life.'

Never one to be serious for long, Ron chipped in that he'd been talking to a bloke who was operating a very large horizontal boring-machine. When he had asked him if he found it boring, the man, knowing he was taking the piss, had told him that if he didn't have anything intelligent to say, he could sod off.

Each lad was closely watched as he drilled the hole. It was essential not to overload the drill, break it and thus damage either the piece, the machine or himself. After inserting and checking that the boring tool moved through the hole at the optimum level, the cutting of the metal ensued. As their confidence grew, they quickly achieved the size of hole required. With so very many machines in the factory, the Apprentices very often talked to individual Turners, to discuss what they were doing. They were not always amenable and when Brian approached Sid, he was clearly not welcome. The man was said to be very experienced and competent at his job and what was more, he knew it. From the way that he looked at the lad, he didn't appreciate being interrupted.

'What d'you want?' he demanded crossly.

'I saw you were turning the inside of that valve and thought it was a difficult job. Perhaps you could give me a few tips about how it's done,' the lad said lamely.

'I'm not here for your benefit,' came the tart reply. 'If you've got any questions, ask your Instructors, that's what they're paid for. Now, naff off and let me get on with my work.'

'The miserable old sod,' said Brian as he walked back to his machine with one of his mates. 'I only wanted to ask a few questions about what he was doing.'

There was little sympathy when he grumbled about Sid's reaction. He should have known better than to even speak to the old bugger. Everyone knew that Apprentices were not popular with a lot of the men. Bill had warned them to be careful, because some of the Turners could be a bit funny.

Dave's father had told him that there was a lot of bad feeling among the turners, the reason being because of what had happened to them after the War. During the hostilities, the Dockyards had been under enormous pressure to repair and service the Fleet and with an acute shortage of labour, large numbers of semi-skilled workers had been made up to skilled status 'for the duration'. When it was over, a very large number of ex-Servicemen, who were 'time-served men', had returned to the Yard and most of the 'dilutees', as they were cynically called, had been down-graded back to their original occupations. They had willingly turned to during the War, but when it was over, they had been cast aside.

There was no doubt that they had been treated very badly. However, it would have been an even greater injustice if after their own sacrifices, the ex-Servicemen had been told there were no jobs for them. That had happened at the end of the First War and the Management had had no option but to re-employ them. It was generally held that those who had stayed at home in 'reserved occupations' during the War had 'lived the life of Reilly and had waxed fat', while they were away fighting for their Country. They therefore had nothing to complain about when the 'status-quo' had been restored. Many of the dilutees had become very skilled Tradesmen, while working as Fitters, Platers and Boilermakers and some had enjoyed accelerated promotion to Charge-hands and even to Foremen. Very few had been fortunate enough to maintain their exalted positions though.

Sid had suffered more than most, having been promoted to Senior Instructor, in charge of a large training facility. No one could deny that he had been of inestimable value to the Yard but he had been duly downgraded and had returned to work on a lathe. He had suffered a substantial reduction in pay and that was why he and so many like him were so bitter. Dave's dad, who was sympathetic to their plight, had told his lad that their resentment was understandable and a little respect was called for when talking to them. With the Royal Navy in an ever increasing spiral of decline, it didn't take much thought to realise that the problem of employment in the Yard was going to get a whole lot worse and no one could be absolutely sure of keeping his job in the future. The cold wind of change was already beginning to blow and it could only get worse.

Chapter 4

The Maltese Connection

For some lads, a measure of release from the boredom came from an unexpected development. One morning, a small group of eight or nine foreigners came to work in a small fitting shop at the bottom-end of the factory. Their Supervisor was a Mr Bellamy, or 'Bellers' as he was better known. He was one of the young, new breed of Instructors, who had recently been brought into the Apprentice Training Department. The visitors had come from the Royal Dockyard in Malta for 'special training' and being from a very different culture and background, they must have been nervous about how things would work out. As it happened, they need not have worried.

Three lads, led by 'Rob', went over during the afternoon and introduced themselves with broad smiles and welcoming hand-shakes all round. The lads from Valetta didn't speak very good English, or so they said. While it wasn't much of a problem to communicate with their new friends, they had no knowledge or appreciation of English 'humour', or the local accent. When Bellers saw that the lads had made friends with his charges, he must have thought it would make his own job that much easier. When told that he would be supervising the Maltese party, he had also been very apprehensive, because with similar visitors in the past, more than one instructor had 'come a cropper.'

It is a particular British habit to ridicule others or more crudely, 'take the piss' and our ability to laugh at ourselves has always been something of a mystery to foreigners. At first, the 'Malteasers', as they quickly became known, were rather bemused by their new friends. One of their Instructor's traits, which amused everyone, was his way of addressing his charges. Why so many people, when speaking to someone from another Country, think that they have to shout in a slow and sonorous way to make them-selves understood, is hard to comprehend. He enunciated every syllable, in a loud, flat voice and was clearly perturbed that very little of what he was telling them was not being taken in. His main concern was that Management might think that he was not up to the job.

Bellers had taken his charges over to the main canteen at dinner time, there to enjoy their first taste of English cuisine, but the culinary delights had not been at all to their liking. The hustle and bustle and the queues must have been so confusing and the menu boards had clearly been a problem for them. His well-meant gesture had not been the success he had hoped for and when help had come, in the form of the lads, he was then more than grateful.

'Am I glad to see you lot,' he said, smiling broadly. 'I've been having a bit of a problem explaining things to these chaps, so perhaps you could give me a hand to get things over to them.'

The lads were only too pleased to help out and, after offering their new mates their tobacco boxes for a friendly 'roll your own', they were soon amicably discussing how things were. The Maltese lads were in their early twenties and 'out of their time' and were delighted to be welcomed in such a friendly way. There was a lot of loud laughter when they were told what they were going to do, because most of them did in fact speak good English. They had been having their Instructor on and before the lads went back to their machines, Rob promised they would come over again the next day.

Bellers told the Manager about how the lads had helped him out and suggested that they should be allowed to mix with the visitors, for an hour or so each day, at least until his party had settled in. Mr Barry was a wily old campaigner, with many years' experience of his Apprentices' crafty ways and he had grave misgivings about their involvement, particularly in view of their previous behaviour. He bluntly told his subordinate that he was reluctant to let the young buggers anywhere near them. After a bit of persuasion, he agreed to give it a go, but solemnly warned him that he would be held personally responsible if anything went wrong.

As the days passed, the two groups got on even better and there was a marked improvement in the Maltese's' ability to understand their Instructor. The only drawback was that their new friends didn't speak the 'Queen's English'. A lot of what they said was interspersed with crudity and swear words, which was 'par for the course'. They saw nothing wrong in passing it on to their new friends and soon, they too were speaking in almost the same way as their tutors. It wasn't long before they were planning to go out together, in the evenings and at the weekend. There was a large fair in a park on the outskirts of the town and it was agreed that they would meet there. It was always well attended by young people, with a lot of the usual buggering about and they all looked forward to a most enjoyable evening.

Having met at the entrance, they walked around the rides and stalls for half-hour or so, then sauntered over to the shooting galleries. After listening to the blandishments of the stall holders, they settled on the one they thought was best. They were standing among a large number of prospective punters, many of whom were loudly bragging as to how they had come away last year with a splendid prize. Everyone knew it was nonsense but the banter and resultant noise added to their enjoyment. Individuals started to wind-up the attendants, initially by making critical examinations of their guns, peering down the sights and making derogatory comments.

'Come on,' the attendants cried crossly. 'D'yuh want ter shoot or not. We ain't got time to mess about with you lot, so get on with it'

One 'wind up merchant' tried a shot, then abruptly put the rifle down. After winking at his mates, he started to argue loudly about its poor state.

'You must think I'm bloody daft,' he said loudly. 'You couldn't hit a barnyard door with that bloody gun. Ain't you got anything better?'

With so many noisy youths milling around, the man called for help from his mates. The cheeky sod hadn't even paid him for the gun. Every evening, there was a stand-off between the fair-ground folk and the customers who were only interested in causing trouble. It happened in every town they visited. The disturbance quickly became unruly, when the man from the coconut shy came to his assistance. Intent on yet more mischief, one lad went over to his stall and inspected the coconuts on their stools. He had suspected that something dodgy was going on, and the absence of the attendant had given him the opportunity for a 'decko'. The coconuts were all firmly attached to their supports, with little chance of being dislodged.

When he told everyone about it, the crowd reacted even more noisily. The good humour evaporated and there was growing anger at the wily tricks of the fair-men. The shouting brought an immediate response and the shooting gallery men were quickly joined by most of the men working on the fairground. Three or four Coppers also came running across to see what the commotion was about. After ordering the crowd to stand away from the stalls, the Sergeant accused the stall-holder of 'getting up to his usual tricks'. The Officer was clearly 'playing to the gallery', and he got a loud cheer from the crowd. He told the man sternly that he wanted no further trouble and if they couldn't run their stalls in an orderly manner, he would have to 'sort them out'.

Soon after, he and his Officers had to intervene again when about a dozen youths had gone across to the dodgems and, ignoring the queue, had piled into the cars. The owner and his assistants panicked. Numerous notices stated that each ride would be for the duration of four minutes and there had already been complaints that only three minutes had been forthcoming. The punters' remonstrations had fallen on deaf ears. The owner had had no compunction in physically ejecting anyone who spoke out of turn and there was a lot of anger in the watching crowd. The troublemakers had climbed over the barriers on all four sides of the track and in an effort to forestall them, he had cut the power off, while his attendants tried to sort things out.

With peace restored, the lads duly proffered their shillings, some of which were purposely dropped on the floor. The ensuing scramble delayed the start of the run by at least five minutes, amid an increasing tirade of abuse from the crowd. Eventually, the attendants moved over to the sides from where they would control the proceedings. Other notices clearly stated that the cars were not to be used as bumper cars. When the power was switched on, there was a great cheer and shouts of encouragement from the crowd. The clowns immediately steered their cars across the track, their aim being to make violent contact with their mates.

The attendants rushed around furiously, shouting for them to knock it off, but no one took any notice. One of the men skipped across the floor, dodging in and out of the traffic, to intercept an offender but in his excitement, he picked on the wrong car. As he jumped on to grab the steering wheel, he was upended and pulled down across the car and it continued going around with him firmly held down and kicking his legs wildly in the air. This led to even more hilarity in the crowd and once again, the man operating the ride pulled the switch.

Further disorder ensued and some of the punters demanded their money back, insisting that they had not been involved in the misbehaviour. One of the lads went over to speak to the Policemen, who had retired to the main entrance for cups of tea from a mobile van. They must have thought they could keep an eye on what was going on, but made no effort to intervene in the fun. He told the

Sergeant that there was going to be serious trouble on the dodgems, because the buggers running them were short changing their customers, because the duration of the rides was considerably below that which was stated on the notice boards. The Sergeant slowly walked over to have another word with the owner, who had already laid hands on one of the lads.

As it happened, it was one of the Maltese, known as 'Sammy', who had been treating a girl to a ride on the dodgems. He had been caught up in the nonsense and when he was threatened, his mates went to his assistance. The Officers arrived just in time to prevent the whole 'shebang' from getting completely out of hand.

'Alright, alright, I'm not deaf,' the Sergeant shouted to the furious crowd and after telling them to calm down, he again confronted the owner.

The man was sternly told to unhand the lad and was then asked what the trouble was. The response from the crowd was immediate. Before he could answer, the lad who had approached the Sergeant stepped forward and repeated his complaint about the man's 'sharp practice'. The owner, who knew he was being stitched up, was spluttering with rage and loudly denied that he had been up to no good. His protestations fell on deaf ears.

'I've warned you a number of times about your crafty tricks, haven't I?' the Sergeant said angrily. 'Well, I'm telling you straight and for the last time, if there's any more complaints from the public, I'll take you and your motley crew down to the Station for a word with my Inspector. Now, give everybody back their money and be warned, no more funny business, or else.'

His comments were gleefully applauded, with various comments such as 'cheating bastards' and other epithets being shouted at the man and his attendants. After again calling for silence, the Sergeant turned and asked the owner why he had assaulted Sammy. He replied that a crowd of youths had been out of control on the track and he had done no more than 'apprehend one of the culprits'.

'I'm sick and tired of being blamed for something I ain't done,' he whined. 'Every night, it's always the same, they come down here looking for trouble and wreck my cars. When I ask them politely not to do it, I'm made out to be the villain and you lot come over and threaten me and my boys. We ain't been cheating nobody, despite the accusations against us. I've got a living to make and I just want to be allowed to get on with it, without all this bother,' he concluded indignantly.

Turning towards Sammy, he accused him of being one of those who had misbehaved and insisted that he had been right to detain him. That was hotly denied by those watching and after again calling for silence, the Sergeant asked Sammy if what the man had said was true.

'Ah'ma verra sorry meestah,' he said, having been advised by one of the lads to act dumb. 'Ah no speek'a de vera good Eengleesh. I'm a veesetor to your Cahntry an' I cahm tonight weeth thees yahng lidie for 'appy times. Ah don'a causa no trahble an' Ah don'a do anythin' wrong.'

The officer was somewhat taken aback and, turning to the crowd, he asked, 'Does anyone know this young man?'

There was a lot of shaking of heads and straight-faced lies that Sammy was a complete stranger. The girl tearfully told the Sergeant that they had only just met and she confirmed he hadn't done anything wrong. The crowd were highly amused when she said that he had been driving 'ever so slowly' and she had urged him more than once to get a move on. Someone had driven into them a couple of times, but he had not been in any way to blame.

'Right,' said the Sergeant, turning back to the sweating owner, 'I think you owe this young man an apology, don't you?; if he doesn't want to press charges, that is. While I'm thinking about it, I'd like to see your safety certificate, just to be sure that everything is in order.'

After he had shown the Officer the document, the man mumbled an apology and gave Sammy and some of the other rogues their money back. The Sergeant dispersed the crowd by loudly saying the fun was over and he didn't want any more trouble. Other punters also demanded and were given refunds and that was the last of the nonsense for the evening. As he was walking away, one of the lads suggested to the Sergeant that he should take a look at the coconut shy, and the shooting gallery too, while he was at it.

'You lot can bugger off and stop wasting my time,' the Sergeant retorted. 'You don't have to let these twisting sods see you off, do you?'

The next day, there was a lot of discussion and laughter during the morning tea break, with Sammy very much 'the hero of the hour'. In making out that he didn't speak English, he had capped their mischief better than they could possibly have hoped. The nonsense had by no means been an isolated incident. As the man had said, wherever they went, the local youths always arrived 'mob-handed', with the clear intention of causing as much trouble as possible. The provocation played out the previous evening could have turned nasty, violent even. The Sergeant must have known what they were up to no good, but had turned a blind eye to their antics.

It was common knowledge that the fairground folk were as crafty as a bag full of monkeys and up to all sorts of tricks. Irrespective of that, there was a lot of prejudice against them and the 'boys in blue' were often no different to anyone else in victimising them. In summary, the evening had turned out better fun than anyone could have hoped. A good laugh had been had, with no real harm having been done, except to the takings of the fairground. The Maltese lads were only recently 'out of their time' and had had been brought over primarily for training in the maintenance of Submarine diesel engines. There was a large workshop in which the engines were completely overhauled and it included a research and development section. From what they said, their Apprenticeships had had been much the same as those in the Yard and other Tradesmen from Malta had been selected for the same 'additional training'. Strangely, they had not done the standard Trade Test and when he was asked about it, Bellers said that they would probably do it after they had had further fitting practice.

The Maltese lads were a jolly lot, who got on well with everyone and they were clearly adept at manipulating any situation. Their initial comments about English food had been nonsense, because it was not so very different from what they had been used to at home. As with the Yard lads, the employer had found accommodation for them and they were paid a 'living allowance'. Within a matter of weeks, most of them had moved to more suitable digs. They often met up with the lads in the pubs, clubs and at dances and had soon integrated into what had at first been an alien society.

Some of them soon took up with local girls and one or two settled into serious romances. When seen out, they came in for the usual ribbing, and they quickly learned to say nothing about their courting activities. These days, much is made about the need to integrate people who have come to live in this Country and it is right that they should do so and be free from prejudice or discrimination from anyone. Their arrival had been a new development, to which the Apprentices had responded in a most positive manner. There was none of the tension and ill-feeling, which often prevailed among the English lads and their friendships lasted throughout their stay, with no edicts from above. Whether or not management was aware of the success of letting their Apprentices mix freely with their Maltese trainees was not known. Could it have been that they had unwittingly stumbled across a better way of controlling them? Perhaps, for once, the soft-touch yielded much better results than the heavy hand.

Chapter 5

In Hot Water

Most families in the village lived in basic accommodation, with few of the comforts which we now enjoy. They had cramped, unheated bathrooms in small annexes on the north side of their houses and their hot water came from a gas-fired 'geyser', which was mounted on the wall above the bath. In Mike's house, the water had to be liberally supplemented by pans of boiling water, which was heated on the gas cooker and brought through from the kitchen. The heater hadn't been serviced for years and in consequence, there was a two inch layer of very fine ash lying across the top of the burner elements. When Mike tried to explain that it was dangerous, the old man angrily told him to mind his own business and not to be so bloody clever.

On Saturday evenings, everyone in the family had a bath and a succession of bodies went 'through it' in turn. By the time the old man went in, the water was almost as dirty as he was. His only advantage was that there was almost a full bath, even if it wasn't very warm. They had none of the modern toiletries, such as the soaps and shampoos that we enjoy today. With the water being so 'hard', bubbles were only achieved by the liberal addition of washing powder. It couldn't have done much for the dermatological health of the bathers.

The main reason for the routine was one of economy. It cost a lot less to get everyone clean in one fell swoop, than by letting individuals have a bath when and as they pleased. When Mike told his mother that he needed more than one bath a week, she had her answer ready.

'We're not made of money, you know. I don't know what you'll think of next.'

By the middle of his third year, he was earning decent money and he got around the problem by paying her the princely sum of six old pence (approximately 2.5 pence), for the privilege of a mid-week soak. She was crafty though and took advantage whereby, as he was getting out of the bath and having already heated a couple of pans of water, she would knock loudly on the bathroom door and call to him.

'Don't let your water go, we might as well use it as waste it.'

In talking to his mates about the rigmarole at home, Mike learned that some of them had similar problems. Some families still heated their bath water in a 'copper', which was fired by either coal or wood. They then had to laboriously ladle it into a bucket, then poured it into a galvanised bath, conveniently placed in front of the fire in the living room. One wag commented wryly that he and his brothers were always sent out of the house, when their sisters were bathing. It had been the first intimation that they were growing up, and they had not been above peeping through a gap in the curtains. The lads who enjoyed more modern facilities couldn't believe that people were still living in such primitive conditions. As one ruefully said, his mum would have him bathing every night of the week if she could.

Len, who had heard Mike grumbling about the problem of getting hot water, said that he might be able to help him out. His brother worked for the Gas Board and he would ask him what could be done. The next morning, he told Mike that Joe had said it was common for such heaters to get very dirty and It could be easily fixed in less than an hour. The gas was a product of the 'coke-ovens' and despite being scrubbed, it was never as pure as it should have been. The burner probably needed adjustment as well. Even though the Gas Board urged their customers to have their gas appliances serviced at least once a year, few bothered to do, due to the cost.

He told Mike that Joe would be happy to come out to have a look at the heater, which gave him food for thought. Only a few 'bob' would be required, 'for the trouble like', so Mike duly accepted the offer. The opportunity came a few weeks later, when his parents went off to Cornwall to stay with relations. After the nonsense of the previous year, he would be left at home, to fend for himself. The prospect of a couple of weeks, free from all the tension, demands and frustrations of family life appealed enormously. It didn't occur to him that he would be doing anything wrong and he made the necessary arrangements for the 'service'.

On the Sunday morning, Joe arrived on his bike and Mike showed him to the bathroom, then went into the kitchen to make the obligatory cup of tea. When he came back a few minutes later, the lad had already removed the front of the heater and was looking at the inside of the appliance with some consternation.

'Bloody hell,' he exclaimed. 'When was this heater last serviced?'

'Buggered if I know,' Mike replied. 'Certainly not since we've been here and that's more than six years.'

'Well, it's in a hell of a state. I don't know that I should even touch it. I've never seen anything so bad. My boss would have a blue fit if he saw it.'

After a few minutes, he asked for something to put the ash in and he started work by scooping large handfuls of the ash into a hessian sack. With most of it removed, he then asked Mike if he had a vacuum cleaner.

'We haven't got one', Mike replied, 'but I'll see if I can borrow one.'

A few minutes later, he came back with a hoover and there was yet another problem. The cable was much too short to reach the only 13 amp 'point' in the living room, so he went off again to borrow an extension lead. It was but a few minutes job to clean the inside of the combustion chamber. Joe then removed the burner elements and, after poking out each hole with a pin and a final blow-through, he replaced them. A check then had to be made to ensure that the exhaust flue was clear. Having borrowed next door's washing line, Mike climbed on to the annex roof and pulled the sack up through the flue. With everything back in place, Joe lit the pilot light, then turned the hot tap on. The heater ignited and to Mike's delight, it produced very hot water. The job was completed.

After clearing up the bathroom, they went off down to the pub for a 'quick half'. The princely sum of 'Five bob' (25 pence), sealed the deal and Joe happily rode off back towards the town. When he returned home, Mike was horrified to find that the vacuum cleaner had gone from the back yard. He didn't have long to wait to find out where, because the owner came down a few minutes later and loudly berated him for not returning it, as promised.

'I'm very sorry, Mrs Burke,' he said meekly. 'I really do appreciate the loan of your cleaner and I was going to clean it out, before I brought it back. I had to see the Gas Fitter off first,' he added lamely. 'Thanks very much and let me know if there's anything I can do for you at any time.'

The lady was not altogether satisfied with his apology but, having given him a piece of her mind, she left it at that. He returned the washing line, but neglected to wipe it off before doing so. Later, having spent a couple of hours training on the recreation ground, he returned home for an eagerly anticipated bath. Compared with the lukewarm immersions of yore, it was luxury indeed and for the next hour or so, he happily soaked his body, adding to his enjoyment from time to time with regular runs of piping hot water. He thought how pleased his parents would be when they came home to find that he had solved the problem. He should have known better to even think that they might have appreciated anything he did.

When they arrived home, after a long, dirty and exhausting train journey from the depths of Cornwall, they were in no mood for talking and he said nothing of what he had done. After they had eaten their supper, an early night was called for but, a bath was imperative before they retired. Anyone who has travelled on a steam train will know just how dirty an experience it was. Mike's mother padded out into the annex to run the bath and she immediately set up such a howl that his father went running out to see what was wrong.

'Oh Al,' she wailed dramatically, 'he's been meddling with the geyser and I've nearly scalded myself.'

She had done nothing of the kind. When she'd turned the hot tap on, it had run very hot and in the coolness of the bathroom, it had given rise to clouds of vapour. Not to be outdone, the old man came back into the living room in a fury, demanding to know what the hell had gone on, while they were away. Mike tried to explain that he had merely cleaned and adjusted the heater to make it work properly and that sent the old man ballistic. Not so long before, it would have led to an outright physical assault on him, but the old man kept his fists to himself.

'You want to leave things what don't concern you alone,' he yelled. 'What'll I say if the bloody thing blows up? As it is, your mother has nearly burnt herself. You're a bloody nuisance, always interfering with things.'

Mike couldn't believe his ears. To say that the heater was more dangerous than before was nonsense and in the weeks ahead, the temperature of the water would surely decline. To avoid further argument, he left the house. Yet again, his mother had caused a row, just for the sake of doing so and he was inwardly seething. Over the next few days, nothing further was said about his 'interference', and baths were taken more regularly from then on.

While he was at work in the following week, Mrs Burke complained to his mother that he had ruined her hoover. When he got home, it was evident he was in for more 'aggro' and, relishing every moment, she told him of her neighbour's visit. She was demanding that he either got it fixed, or bought her a new machine. His father chipped in, by repeating that 'it was the result of meddling in what didn't concern him'. He went along to placate the irate lady and after she had explained what was wrong, he said that he would have a look at it. Contrary to what he'd been told, she was quite reasonable and said it wasn't 'sucking' very well. Mike re-assured her and she was quite relaxed about it.

It was an old machine, which was made up of a cylinder, with an integral fan motor at one end. At the other end, a flexible hose connected to the end-cover, which was secured by two clips. Easy access to the inside was given when they were released. A rubber ring secured the paper dust bag to the fan housing and when he opened it up, the cause of the problem was clearly evident. With her husband watching closely, Mike withdrew the bag and as he had expected, it was stuffed full of dirt. All that was required was to empty it. While he did so to a newspaper, he noticed something bright in the debris. He had found a ring, which the woman delightedly told him she had lost some time back. Mike had redeemed himself and he made matters even better by suggesting that they should check the rest of the contents to see if there was anything else of value.

As she didn't have a new bag, he put the old one back on to the spigot and boxed it up. When he switched the machine on, it worked better than it had done for a long time. After suggesting that a regular clean would keep it in good working order, Mike took his leave. He had been remiss in not having emptied and cleaned the bag, before taking it back, but she had beaten him to it. He left with her thanks and a couple of shillings, which she had insisted on pressing into his hand. It wasn't the outcome his mother had hoped for, but at least, it calmed her down.

On bath nights in the summer months, children and adults would come out of the houses looking well-scrubbed and wearing clean clothes. It was the one night of the week when a lot of families went out, to the canteen or the Working-men's Club. The regular dances and social evenings did much to brighten their lives. When there was no 'formal-do', tombola, bingo, or a whist drive took up the early part of the evening and it was followed by a sing-song around the piano. They were jolly events, which usually ended with some of the punters being the worse for wear. As the teenagers grew up, so the evenings with their parents palled and they sought their entertainment elsewhere.

Other villages had much the same facilities and groups of young people would often cycle over to their functions. The dances had become increasingly lively of late and the antics of some of the youths often spoiled what had been a pleasant evening's entertainment. The trouble-makers, having found it a bit tame, would seek to liven up the proceedings. Younger adults would often intervene, to 'sort out' the mischief-makers and then, it would get out of hand. Inter-family tensions also resulted in loud altercations and sometimes, violence and it was a rare night indeed when the proverbial didn't 'hit the fan'.

A Royal Marine had recently come on leave and was staying with his parents in the village. Lofty was a tall, powerfully built young man who was in his mid-twenties and he was the epitome of fitness. It was clear to most of the lads that he was not to be trifled with. One evening, a large oaf called Lou was obviously looking for trouble and he became increasingly bold. His reputation was such that most of the punters gave him a wide berth, particularly when he had been drinking. He'd 'ruled the roost' in the village for the last year or so, despite having been warned about his behaviour by the local Bobby. It had to be 'odds-on' that he would meet his match in time and that evening, he did just that. Someone quietly warned him to tread carefully, where Lofty was concerned, but it had clearly not penetrated his dim mind.

The weak often attach themselves to the strong and that was how it was at the dance. Lou stood at the end of the room, flanked by four of his mates and they stared belligerently at the dancers. He loudly bragged that he wasn't afraid of any 'bloody squaddy' and would soon sort things out. There was clearly going to be trouble and some of the punters left, to avoid the impending confrontation. Those that remained sat back to enjoy the fun. There followed a ritual, that had taken place several times before. While somewhat ungainly, Lou fancied himself as a natty dancer and a 'ladies' man'. He would point to a girl and send one of his 'side-kicks' to tell her he wanted to dance with her. Any protest from a boyfriend or brother often brought painful retribution. Many of the girls looked at the oaf with more than a little trepidation and they were always discomfited when dancing with him.

The girl who received the invitation that evening was heard to politely decline and the scene was set. Lou angrily confronted her and demanded to know why she didn't want to dance with him and when her boyfriend made to intervene, he was punched in the face for his cheek. Seeing a neighbour in trouble, Lofty walked over and tapped Lou on the shoulder. As he turned around, Lofty buried his fist into the pit of his stomach and all the aggression went out of the big man. He was roughly turned around and frog-marched to the exit then, assisted by the sole of Lofty's shoe, he left the building. The Marine then turned to Lou's mates, who were standing helplessly to one side and quietly told them to leave as well.

The next morning, there was a lot of talk about the battered state in which Lou had been found, in the early hours. According to his mother, he had been waylaid on his way home and severely beaten. It caused no little mirth when she tearfully said that her lad 'was a good boy, who wouldn't hurt a fly'. The truth was, he was an obnoxious, antisocial yob. The first person to be blamed was Lofty, but his parents quickly let it be known that he hadn't been involved in any way. They had still been up when came home and he'd definitely not gone out again. It was a mystery, which provoked a lot of gossip during the next week or so.

Chapter 6

Machining

As their training progressed, the Apprentices rapidly gained confidence and became adept in the various aspects of turning various metals. After all the early pressure about working safely, their close supervision had gradually diminished to a more tolerable level. The Instructors let their charges get on with their jobs, which were mostly making simple components, from specially prepared sketches. Their practical lessons had been extended into machining complete spindles, valve bodies and the covers which to accommodate them. There were the usual cock ups, but some of the lads thought they already had the makings of competent Turners. They were quickly told that it would take many years to achieve that exalted status. The lectures came to an end and in consequence, all their time was spent in the shop, which some found tedious.

Johnny had been closely watching the turners working just across the gangway and in common with many others, he had a particular dislike of Sid. The man had been so unpleasant to one of his mates only a few weeks previously and he was obviously looking to redress the situation. His first little game was childish, but it amused those watching. He silvered the head of a penny to resemble a half-crown, then drilled a small hole in it and screwed it to the wooden floor. He then sat in wait for a victim and he didn't wait long before Sid came past on his way back from the boilers. Seeing the coin, he stopped and looked around in a 'shifty 'way, then stooped to pick it up. Johnny and his mates loudly jeered and as Sid jumped in alarm, he dropped his mug of tea. He vented his spleen with a storm of verbal abuse at his tormentors. The jape wasn't going to trap more than the odd victim, because of the hilarity it produced.

Johnny then retrieved the coin and attached it to a length of cotton. During the afternoon break, he had three or four victims in as many minutes, including some of the men who were working nearby. His mischief came to an early end when the Senior Instructor came out to see what was going on.

'Come on, you noisy buggers,' he shouted. 'Keep it down. We'll have Mr Barry down here and then we'll all be in the rattle.' Turning to Johnny, he said, 'Stop your nonsense and do something useful.'

For a while, the lad was subdued, but he wasn't finished yet. He was obviously planning something far worse. Following his embarrassment with the coin, Sid had gone on at some length, saying loudly that 'the bloody Apprentices had no respect for their elders and needed to be taught some manners.' He clearly took a very jaundiced view of everybody and everything, while at work and his problems with the lads brought little sympathy from the other men. They knew that to react in any way to their nonsense was certain to draw attention to themselves.

Sid had great pride in his work and no matter how complicated the job, it was always done to the highest standards. He was the top Turner, who could always be relied on and for that reason, he was allowed to come and go as he pleased. Most of the Turners were closely watched to ensure that they didn't extend their breaks, but Sid suffered no such restriction. His most valued possession was his toolbox, which was a true work of art. The inside had been skilfully constructed with a series of trays and drawers and everything required for the job was neatly stowed in its allotted place. There were micrometers and vernier-gauges, adjustable squares and protractors, internal and external callipers and a comprehensive range of good quality cutting tools. Everything was thoroughly cleaned immediately after use, then securely locked away.

No one was allowed near his most hallowed possession and anyone who stopped to compliment him on it was given short-shrift. The lid was quickly closed and double-locked and the intruder told he was too busy to 'stand around talking'. If he was going to be away from the shop for any time, he always took it home or had it securely locked away in the stores. When he went to the water boilers, Sid would lock his box and balefully gaze around, as if daring anyone to go near it while he was away. When he came back, he would again look around, before unlocking it. His extreme caution had been brought about by the depredations of those around him, men and boys alike, over many years.

As already noted, Bill had warned the lads many times not to annoy the Machinists and, for the most part, they had taken heed. Johnny was perhaps less mature than most and he often went too far with his pranks. When taken to task, he would usually escape retribution by adopting an aggressive attitude. The bollockings he had received from successive supervisors should have sufficed, but they had never deterred him from his nonsense. One lunch time, Sid made a grave mistake, one that had not happened in a very long time. He went up the shop to make his drink but, for some inexplicable reason, he left his box open. In the few minutes he was away and in the rush to wash up ready for dinner, a vandal struck. Layers of black 'Bostick' – a contact-adhesive only recently on the market – were liberally smeared on the mating faces of the box.

The lads saw Sid hurrying back to his machine in some agitation and when he got there, he slammed the lid down and locked it. He then went back up the shop to clock out. At the end of the dinner break, he resumed working as if nothing untoward had happened. It was late in the afternoon before he tried to open the box, only to find that the lid was stuck fast and no amount of effort would open it. Looking closely, he saw some of the black stuff, which had oozed out of the gap and those watching saw what could only be described as an appalling sight.

With increasing agitation, he tried to force the lid open, which culminated in a desperate move. He went to a nearby fire point and took down the axe and with loud cries of angry frustration, he rained blows down on the top of the box, which was soon match wood. The poor old bugger had completely lost control and, having destroyed his pride and joy, he collapsed in a sobbing heap among the debris. The men were aghast at what had happened and it wasn't long before they were looking around for the culprit. Their accusations were mainly directed against the nearby apprentices, all of whom furiously denied any responsibility. Eventually, they decided that the only person who could possibly be responsible for the outrage was Johnny.

'Don't bloody look at me,' the lad cried out in alarm. 'I had nothing to do with it.'

Some of his mates believed him, because he had been with them while waiting to clock off. The Foreman came running down the shop, to see what all the commotion was about and when he saw the wreckage of Sid's toolbox and the state of the distressed man crying beside it, he loudly demanded to know who was responsible.

'I don't mind a bit of harmless sky-larking,' he cried ominously, 'but what I won't stand for is when someone gets hurt and has his property destroyed. I want the bugger that did this in my office, now.'

The outcome had been far worse than anyone could possibly have intended and no one stepped forward. After telling two of the men to give Sid a hand, the Foreman walked back to his office in disgust. They went over to Sid and picked up the pieces of his box but the man was inconsolable. His tools and 'knick-knacks' had been severely damaged, with a lot of them beyond repair. It was generally agreed that he had been treated abominably. When later discussing it, the Apprentices were convinced that none of them had been involved and that they would not take the blame. Two of them had spoken to Johnny and he had again strongly denied any involvement. He had invited them to look into his toolbox, which confirmed there was no Bostick in it.

Their Instructors came among the lads to make their own inquiries and looked into everyone's drawers and toolboxes, but nothing untoward was found. Over the years, there had been all manner of nonsense from their charges and they loudly stated it was the 'shittiest' trick they had ever seen. Having been solemnly assured that none of their lads was responsible, they had to fend off the angry accusations from the men. Bill had already threatened that if one of his Apprentices had been involved, he would come down on him like a 'ton of bricks'. He spoke to the Convenor, when he came to inquire about what had happened and for a time, it seemed likely that the situation was going to get out of hand.

Over the next week, the Factory was buzzing about the incident and relations between the two camps were as bad as they had been in a very long time. The poor old bugger, who had aged considerably since the incident, remained very depressed about it all. He forlornly took what remained of his toolbox and its contents home and didn't bring it back in to work again. His hostile demeanour and aggression towards all and sundry had been effectively stifled and he kept even more to himself from then on.

The lads, who had for so long been working under close supervision, had at last started to relax. There was a growing practice for small private tasks, which were completely illegal, to be done. An example was when Mike obliged a neighbour by making a new wheel-spindle for his wheelbarrow. He produced it, complete with washers and nuts and a matching liner for insertion into the hub of the wheel. When installed, the proffered half-crown was gratefully accepted and from then on, he was regularly asked to make something or other.

One lad found an old clothes drier, which consisted of half a dozen long wooden slats, which were held up by two ornate cast-iron frames, one at each end. It was made to be suspended from the ceiling, above an open fire and was moved up and down by a long length of rope, threaded through a system of pulleys. Fred turned new ones from of a piece of brass round-bar and his mother was highly delighted with his initiative. Small items were regularly turned and no end of discarded utensils were retrieved, refurbished and put back into use. There was hardly anyone in the shop, including the Instructors, who didn't at some time do such jobs.

The Instructors allowed the 'Government jobs' to be done because there were not enough legitimate tasks to gainfully make use of their time at work. Refurbishing valve spindles and 'chasing' the threads didn't take more than a few minutes to complete. Rather more care had to be taken in re-facing flanges, particularly those from high-pressure steam systems. Some of the lads were set to work in turning new components for the wrecked lathe. New bushes were made for the bearings and gearwheels and the drive-shaft was set up in a machine and straightened by one of the Instructors. The thread, which ran along most of its length, was carefully refurbished, as were the ends of the shaft.

The reassembly of the machine gave the boss the opportunity to explain the workings of the various parts, which was of great interest. As they completed their basic instruction, the lads were gradually moved out into the main shop, with each one assigned to a Turner, the object being for him to gain practical experience. It was not something that they had looked forward to, due to the on-going hostility of many of the men, most of whom were engaged in regular patterns of work. Some were not averse to giving their lads difficult jobs, in the hope that they would make a mess of them then, they were able to ostentatiously sort it out and at the same time, demonstrate that the lad was a dolt, who knew bugger all about turning.

Their criticism was at times justified, but in a lot of cases, it was no more than sheer, bloody-mindedness. Mike soon fell foul of his boss, who complained to the Foreman when he slipped away for a few minutes. It was an inauspicious start and he suffered no end of 'bollockings' in the first couple of weeks. As he grumbled to his mates, he could do nothing right for Archie. The man was uncommunicative about any of the jobs he gave him and he continually rejected his finished work, without giving it more than a cursory glance.

The lad put up with his nonsense but one particular job caused him no end of problems. It involved the machining of a shuttle-valve for a steam-driven pump. It would not have been difficult for an experienced Turner, but it became a bone of contention between them. To minimise the metal to be machined off, the valve had been cast very close to the finished dimensions and it called for great care in setting it up. Knowing he was in trouble, Mike asked Archie for help, only to be roundly berated as 'bloody useless'. In a long-suffering voice, the man loudly proclaimed that, if he wanted the job doing properly, he would have to do it himself.

When the Foreman came by, he said to Mike that he had heard he had messed up a simple job. Forgetting his determination to keep his mouth shut, the lad retorted that he was doing his best and a bit of help from his Turner wouldn't have gone amiss. He couldn't expect him to have the skill of a man, with many years of experience behind him. The Foreman was incensed at being answered back and told him in no uncertain terms to shut his mouth. He was there to learn the job, do what he was told and not be constantly complaining, when someone pointed out his errors. He warned him that he would be keeping his eye on him from then on. There was some small comfort later, when another lad told him that that the Foreman had taken Archie to task for giving the lad such a difficult job.

There was a heated argument at the water boilers one morning, between Geoff and a group of the men. He had been seen carefully tying cotton twine around an egg and after lifting the lid off a boiler, he'd suspended it in the boiling water to cook. He was angrily admonished and he made matters worse by insisting he was doing no harm. However, when he was rudely apprehended, he had jumped, let go of the twine and the egg was languishing at the bottom of the boiler. He bluntly told them 'to mind their own bloody business' and was immediately surrounded by an irate crowd of Mateys, who were equally incensed at what he had done. There were loud cries of 'You dirty bugger' and 'Get him out of here!'. With it all getting out of hand, Geoff walked away and red-faced with embarrassment, he abandoned his egg and returned to his lathe.

When his mates heard about the altercation, they were beside themselves with mirth. For a while, they kept up the pretence of verbally chastising him and the more they teased him, the angrier Geoff became. Not long after, Joe and the Foreman of the next section came down to see him and made it clear that what he had been doing was unhygienic and had to cease forthwith. There was little sympathy for him, because in the past year or so, he had become both self-centred and conceited, with little concern for anyone else. His confrontation with the men was a little bit of light relief, which had brightened everyone's day.

The lads spent approximately three months working with the Turners and, for most of them, it had not been a pleasant experience. They were greatly relieved, when told they were to move on. Working in the lathes section had become increasingly boring and the unending problems with the Turners had not helped. They had endured a lot of back biting and tale telling from the men, which had often led to angry confrontations. The atmosphere had thus become very tense, particularly after the incident with Sid's box. The culprit was never found and despite having been questioned a number of times, Johnny had consistently denied any part in it. Many of the men weren't convinced of his innocence and there were mutterings that 'the lousy bugger' had got away with it.

Chapter 7

Moya

In any young, male environment, be it at work or pleasure, the main subject of discussion is usually about women. There was a lot of talk about sex among the lads, or rather their lack of it and truth to tell, few of them knew much about it. As noted previously, they mostly still lived at home and generally conformed with their parent's rules and the socially accepted standards of the time. While mostly past their eighteenth birthdays, there were still some who hadn't even had a steady girlfriend, let alone experienced the nefarious delights of 'doing what came naturally'. Generally speaking, they reckoned they knew all about it, but few had put their grandiose theories into practice. The mating process certainly wasn't easy and, for some, it was the bane of their lives.

For some time, Mike had been enjoying the amorous embraces of Moira, the daughter of the Farmer for whom he worked in his spare time. After his problems in getting paid the previous year, he had gone further afield and had found a job on a farm two miles away from his home. 'Moya', as she insisted on being called, was in her late-twenties and was a qualified teacher. She had recently returned from Australia, to help her father run the Farm, after it had fallen on hard times. Bert had let it run down to such an extent that it was no longer a viable business. How it had happened was a mystery, because the land was a light loam, very fertile and, when properly husbanded, it was very productive.

Moya was a 'well-made' lass, with an air of aggressive self-confidence and she didn't suffer fools gladly. She took one look at Mike when they met and must have decided that she didn't like what she saw. Needless to say, the feeling was mutual. She was wearing very old clothes, the outer garments being a cut-down gabardine 'mac' and her father's old corduroy trousers. She wore a battered trilby on her head and her feet were encased in well worn, hob-nailed boots, which were several sizes too big. In Mike's eyes, she 'looked a sight', resembling what we now call a 'bag-lady'. From the start, she was curt and rude and neither spoke to nor looked at him, if she could avoid doing so. The common courtesies of life had no part in her agenda.

For the first few weeks, they regularly went out into the fields to load trailers with hay, which Bert had bailed. Her attitude didn't change and Mike was just as unpleasant to her as she was to him. One Saturday morning, the boss told her to 'take the lad' out to a barn, about a mile away; their job being to start a crawler tractor which had been stored there since the previous autumn and bring it back to the yard. When she asked why she had to take Mike, her father angrily told her to do as she was told. Moya grumbled continuously while she got her tractor and trailer ready and after loading what she thought was needed, they set off. The journey was made with regular glares and scowls from the woman in Mike's direction.

By the time they arrived, it was raining and water was copiously dripping down on to the tractor from the roof. When Mike suggested they should start by cleaning it down, then cover it with a waterproof sheet, she angrily told him that 'she was in charge', and he would do as she 'bloody-well' said. Although he was tempted to respond, Mike sensed an opportunity to put one over on 'the snotty cow'. The outlet of the exhaust pipe was blocked and he disconnected and cleared it with a broom-handle. He then checked the fuel-system and found it was contaminated with water. When he told Moya that they would have to drain and re-prime the system with fresh diesel oil, she grumbled loudly about having to go back to the yard for it.

While she was away, Mike drained the system, cleaned the filters, then removed and cleaned the injectors. He used the waste diesel to wash most of the filth off the engine and the top of the tractor. The lubricating oil in the sump was in reasonably good condition and he topped it up from the can they'd brought with them. An hour or so later, when she returned with a ten gallon can of diesel, they filled the tank, primed the system and checked it for leaks. He then found that the battery was flat and without asking her, he took the one from her tractor and put it in the crawler, which brought yet more black looks. On starting up the engine, it slowly turned over a few times, then 'coughed' and roared into life, which filled the barn with acrid smoke.

Just as they were going to move the tractor out of the barn, Bert arrived and he was delighted to see it was running well and there wasn't much more to be done. He then went back to the Farm to fetch another battery, which had been 'on charge'. Eventually, Moya drove the machine back to the yard, followed by a very happy Mike on the other tractor. He had been greatly amused to be sternly warned to 'take bloody good care of it, or else!'. When they arrived, her father was discussing the hire of the crawler with another Farmer and was stressing the merits of the machine and that it had to be looked after properly. He and his sour daughter seemed to have something about their tractors. As the man was leaving, Bert loudly thanked Mike for a good morning's work, which didn't please 'her Ladyship' one bit.

The other Farmer had a couple of large fields of strong land, which were very heavy to plough and with grain prices picking up, he was keen to bring them back into production. Being typical of his kind – always on the look-out for something for nothing – he had gone on a bit about having to pay for the loan of the machine, but Bert knew that his was the only tractor in the area which was powerful enough to do the job. A couple of weeks later, it was returned in good order and Bert was very happy with his extra cash, though nothing extra came Mike's way.

One evening, Moya and Mike were caught out in a hay-field in a thunderstorm. After hurriedly throwing a sheet over the partly-loaded trailer, they'd 'legged-it' over to a nearby barn to shelter from the rain and while they were standing just inside the door, he became aware that she was very upset. He must have sounded less than sympathetic, when he asked her why she was 'greeting'. It was enough to tip her over the edge and she rounded on him in fury, screaming that he should mind his own bloody business. Being just as angry, he told her she was a stupid, bloody cow who had no manners, and then he moved away to avoid further argument.

Not long after, she was still in tears and he went over and apologised for losing his temper. Her anger had gone as well, and she mumbled that she was sorry too.

'I don't mean to take it out on you,' she said miserably, 'but I'm just so bloody fed up. Just look at me, I'm an educated young woman and what you see is a raggedy-assed, smelly slut and I don't like it. I'm working all day, every day and I get no thanks from the old man. He thinks it's my place to be here and he constantly bemoans the fact I wasn't born a boy. All I am to him is the son he never had and I'm sick and bloody tired of it. It's not my fault his men left, but he should have looked after them better.

'It wouldn't be so bad if he paid me, but all I get is my keep and the few shillings my mum gives me. While it's her farm, he makes her life a misery and he has no thought for anyone but himself. I wouldn't mind so much if he was hard-up, but he isn't, he just doesn't like parting with his money. Well, I've had it with all this shit and I'm going back to Australia, as soon as I can.'

Having blurted it all out, Moya started crying again, with floods of tears. Mike didn't know what to do, but he put his hand on her arm and repeated that he was sorry for what he had said. She moved closer and he put his arms around her shoulders and gently hugged her. Within a few minutes, she had calmed down and regained her composure. The ice between them had been broken and, much to Mike's relief, their animosity was at an end.

'Look,' he said, 'I'd no idea that you were so unhappy at home. I thought it was just me you didn't like.'

He went on to say that there was only one way to solve her problem and that was to tell her father exactly how she felt. Although it had little relevance, he told her about what had happened to him and his mates regarding Billy and their bonus and how the sensible option, as put forward by one of his mates, had yielded 'bugger-all'. If you had a problem, it had to be sorted and if there was unpleasantness, then it had to be faced. Left to fester, it would only get worse, so she had to sort it out. For the first time, Moya looked at him in a friendly way.

'I think you really understand just how I feel,' she said. 'You're right, it's no use getting upset and howling about it. We're going to have to have it out.'

'I suggest you do it quietly, without losing your temper,' said Mike. 'If he loses his rag, walk away and say you'll speak to him again when he's calmed down. In the meantime, you could refuse to do any more work until you've come to an agreement and make sure to ask for your back-pay, to cover all the hours you've worked since you came home.'

The rain had stopped and after Mike had solemnly agreed not tell anyone about her problem, they went back out into the field. They couldn't load wet bales, so they secured the trailer and took it back to the yard. After they had unloaded the half-load, Mike went home and thought no more about it. From then on, their friendship steadily grew to a very much more pleasant level. One evening, they had only been able to load two layers of bales when again, the heavens opened. Having loosely thrown a sheet over the load, they spent the next hour underneath the wagon. The thunder and lightning was not only above them! Mike lost his last tenuous link with boyhood that evening and when he went home, his feet weren't touching the ground. In the weeks that followed, they became even closer and many pleasant evenings were spent happily canoodling.

While he had been tempted to tell his workmates about his loss of virtue, he had kept schtum; a sound decision and one he wouldn't regret. He was acutely aware of the way the other lads expounded on every detail, real and imaginary, about their exploits with women. They had no thought for the harm they were doing and there was nearly always be someone about who knew the lass. To blacken her name, all too often on the most specious of grounds, was most definitely not on. Was there not an element of hypocrisy there?

A month or so after he had finished working for Bert, he was surprised to be accosted in the town, one Saturday morning. He didn't recognise the smart young woman at first and couldn't believe it was the same person. Moya was smartly dressed in a dark suit and was wearing high-heeled shoes, which made her as tall as he was. Her makeup was skilfully applied; her hair was shining and neatly 'cropped' and she looked absolutely stunning. After a few minutes chatting, she suggested that they went for a drink in a nearby hotel and that was followed by lunch in the restaurant. It was the first time Mike had eaten in a Hotel and it was made all the more enjoyable by the fact that Moya was happy and very excited.

'I'm going back to Sydney next week,' she told him, 'and am I looking forward to it! I've been offered my old job in the same school and I'm going to have a room in my friend's house. I'll be able to take up my sports again and hopefully, the social life will be just like it was before. Remember your advice about dad? Well, I did it just as you said and it couldn't have worked out better. We've now got a working foreman and couple of men and I only work when I feel like it. Dad's paid me in full and, what's more, mum's her old self now as well. I've spent most of my time doing his paperwork, because his office was in a hell of a mess. Letters were unanswered, bills not paid and there were all sorts of grants and payments that he could have claimed for and hadn't. We've now got a woman from the village to take over from me and if you go over to the Farm, you'll find a much different place to how it was. Anyway, that's enough about me, how have you been getting along?'

'Not so bad,' replied Mike. 'I usually play rugby on a Saturday afternoon, but I've got a sore knee. Like as not, I'll be off for a couple of weeks. Apart from that, I'm doing pretty well.'

'Are you going out with anyone at the moment?' Moya asked, with a coy smile on her face.

Mike would have preferred to have done without that question and she must have known why. After their intimacy, the local girls had not been as attractive as they had seemed before. On more than one occasion, he had been tempted to go over to see her, but hadn't done so, because she had specifically asked him not to. They had discussed their relationship and agreed that their age difference was too much for them to go any further. Their parting had been painful, though he knew exactly what she had meant. Now, sitting in the Hotel, he knew she had been just as fond of him as he had been of her. Before he could answer, she reached across the table and took his hand.

'We got on really well, didn't we?' she said softly. 'It was something special for me too and I shall always remember our lovely times together. You were there when I desperately needed someone and it has meant a lot to me. I was so horrible to you, I'll never know how you put up with me.'

'You were a bit of a tartar,' replied Mike, 'but I probably gave as good as I got. You're right though, it was lovely while it lasted, even if it couldn't be. I won't forget you either and that's a promise.'

It was on that moist-eyed note that they said their goodbyes a few minutes later. Having taken note of his address, Moya promised to write once she had settled in. As Mike reflected later, she had been both kind and considerate and for that, he was to become increasingly grateful. Some time later, he went over to the youth club but came away again early. It had lost the attraction it had once held, as so many things do. On his way home, he stopped off at a pub and saw Bert sitting in a corner and after offering to get him a drink, which was declined, Mike sat down and asked him how he and his family were getting along.

'I thought you'd ask,' the old man replied. 'I don't know if you've heard but Moira has buggered off back to Australia and we don't hear from her much. We get the odd card from time to time, but no doubt she's back in her old routine and enjoying herself. She'll write when she wants something, he mused. The wife wants to go out to see her sometime, but I don't know, it's an awful long way to go just for a few weeks. I tell her that we'll just have to see.'

Mike didn't mention their lunch. The fact was, he still missed Moya and was sincere when he told her dad that he wished her well. There is nearly always a sense of loss, when a relationship ends and that was very much how it had been for him. He hadn't coped as well emotionally as he would have done in later life. He couldn't blame Moya, because she had clearly stated her intention to return down under and he had been a willing partner as she had patiently introduced him to the delights of physical love. It had been a salutary lesson that he couldn't always have what he wanted and it was quite some time before he took up with anyone else. He had kept his promise that he would not mention their liaison to anyone. His stated intention to save his money for the future was taken by his mates as his reason for his lack of interest in women and he was content for them to see it that way.

Mike didn't drink much alcohol at the time, being usually content with either half a pint of cider or perhaps a small glass of shandy. He had seen the dreadful state that so many young people got themselves into, when they'd had 'a sniff of the barmaid's apron'. The intensity of the hangover after drinking a bottle of wine with two mates the previous Christmas had also put him off. There was no merit in suffering so badly, particularly after doing something that he didn't particularly like. In the late Summer and early Autumn, he often cycled long distances, thinking nothing of covering ten miles or more in an evening and sometimes even longer at the weekend. His bike was still in in good condition and he had both the energy and fitness to explore the surrounding countryside. His life at home had also been more bearable of late, but that wouldn't last.

He only received one letter from Moya and as usual, his mother had opened it before he got home. How thankful he was that he'd told her of his mother's predilection for opening his mail and had asked her to only write about how she was getting on. Her letter contained nothing which could have caused any further problem. She asked him to go over see her mother and that he was pleased to do, because he had always got on well with the lady. He promised to return in the Spring, to turn her vegetable patch over and while they were talking and much to his surprise, she had casually remarked that he and her daughter had 'got on better than we thought at the time'. Mike was lost for words and had blushed with embarrassment.

'Don't worry lad,' she said kindly, 'I knew something was happening when she suddenly stopped going on about you. A mother usually knows these things. She came home one evening in a right 'tiz' and tore into her father. As it happened, they sorted out their problems and it all turned out for the better. Bert wasn't very happy about her going back to Australia, but it was what she wanted. She's always been very strong-minded and now she's a grown woman, she makes her own decisions.'

And that was how it was left.

Chapter 8

Boredom

As the time progressed, the lads gradually moved on to different sections to work on other types of machines. Nothing changed, because the Machinists still had no time for them, with little instruction being forthcoming. Was that perhaps due to the fate of their workmate, Sid? Probably, for most of the lads, the work was extremely tedious and with time hanging very heavily, they either gathered in groups or sat quietly reading. That didn't always suit their mentors, who were quick to point out that their place was at their machines. If they skived-off they were often reported to the Foreman, which didn't make for happy relationships. Meal breaks were extended to the maximum that could be got away with and any legitimate excuse for absence was exploited to the full.

Their attendance at the Dockyard School was down to one day and two evenings a week, for most of the lads. With no one calling the register, some didn't even bother to turn up for their classes. As they had been warned, so many times before, they were playing a silly game and without qualifications, their progress up the ladder in the Engineering Industry would be both slow and limited. A lot of the younger men, with whom they worked, were attending night-classes at the local Technical College. When asked why, they readily admitted that they too had not listened to their elders, when they were Apprentices. Most of them had young families and they were paying dearly for their immature stupidity.

The football season was in full swing and some of the lads were very concerned about their personal fitness. Those that lived in the town could train at their clubs but, living out in the countryside, Mike had to make do with the local recreation field and running along the lanes around his village. There was an extensive complex of playing-fields in the Yard, which was used by the Naval personnel in the barracks and it provided an ideal facility, which could be used in the dinner hour. When they first went along, a grounds-man questioned their right to be there but after politely telling him that they were in training, he didn't object to their exercises and running a few laps of the track. Most of them made do with sandwiches for their dinner, either brought from home or bought in the canteen. As often as not, they were quickly devoured after they came back from their runs.

Weather permitting, Mike ran in the evenings during the week and there was rarely a problem. There was little traffic and the only impediment was that on mild evenings, he sweated profusely. His shirt and shorts necessitated a regular quick rinse through, after his parents had gone to bed. He left them in front of the fire to dry overnight and when his mother found them one morning, there was yet another row. A kindly neighbour gave him a pair of football shorts and a shirt, which had belonged to her son and from then on, he added them to his weekly laundry. It amused his mates greatly that he still had to ask permission to do the most simple of things.

Their theoretical training had been intended to be supplemented by instruction from the Machinists, though most of them only 'went through the motions'. Each lad was regularly moved to a different machine which, in addition to the various types of lathes, included large drilling and milling machines, planers, shapers and horizontal and vertical borers. Their progress was supposed to be closely monitored by the various Foremen, though little was said about it. They seemed to be more concerned with their charges' behaviour. Some of the men though actually welcomed their lads' assistance and the additional responsibility gave them an extra interest. If their jobs were done on piecework, then a lad could often make a useful contribution. The ones that didn't had almost certainly had to put up with all sorts of nonsense in the past. Like the Turners, they were quick to describe their charges as 'not interested' and for the most part, 'downright bloody lazy'.

One morning, Mike was moved over to work alongside a diminutive, elderly Scotsman, whose demeanour was cold and unwelcoming. As they had walked down the shop, the Foreman had clearly explained how things were with his new mentor.

'Now lad, it's well known that Mac's a bit of an awkward bugger and you should bear that in mind. I don't want him coming into my office and bitching about you all the time, O.K? On no account do you speak to him when you get into work first thing in the morning. Don't even think about it, because he'll go berserk if you do. Sometime around nine o'clock and not before, you'll see him moving about and when he looks over towards you, just say 'Good morning Mac' and nothing else. Like as not, he'll return your greeting and from then on, you'll be alright. As I've said, you've got to tread very carefully with him so don't get in any arguments and don't play any silly bloody tricks. Do as I say and you'll be alright.'

Mike was soon warned by others about the little man, particularly the lad who had preceded him. Not long before, there had been a serious incident involving a young Machinist called Jones. He had not been working directly with Mac, but had been operating a vertical borer near to him and despite having been similarly warned about the wee man, he had decided to have some fun. Being much bigger than his intended victim, he must have thought he would be able to 'take the piss' with impunity. As it turned out, it was a decision which could have resulted in his injury and perhaps, it may have been even more serious.

Just after seven one morning, he had carefully placed an empty, galvanised bucket behind Mac's machine. He then silently went back a few minutes later and kicked it over, the loud clatter of which greatly startled his victim. Mac had jumped up and down in fury and screamed foul imprecations at his tormentor, which was exactly what he'd set out to achieve.

'Oh shut up, you stupid old sod,' Jones had shouted back. It's only a bit of fun, and we can do without your bloody tantrums at this time of the morning.'

He very quickly regretted his folly, because his response fanned the flames of Mac's fury to an even greater intensity. The wee man picked up a large ball-peen hammer and came running towards the lad, swearing profusely and with the clear intention of doing him the maximum bodily harm.

'Ye bloody bastard, yeh,' he had howled. Realising he had over-stepped the mark, Jones had rapidly made off up the shop, closely pursued by his angry assailant. Other men intervened by catching and telling the apoplectic Scot to 'hold-fast' and 'calm down'. When the Foreman came running to find out what all the fuss was about, he was also very angry and he went after Jones. He apprehended him outside the building and roundly bollocked him for his stupidity. To avoid any further unpleasantness, he moved him to another section.

Mike decided to play the man along and, over the next few days, he did exactly as he had been told. His discretion was greatly appreciated and despite the knowing prognostications from his mates, he had no problem with his new boss. As it happened, he soon made his mark with him. First thing, he quietly got on with whatever job he was doing and sometime around nine o'clock, Mac was as relaxed and forthcoming as anyone else. He was of a serious disposition, being perhaps what Scottish folk called 'dour' though in essence, he was a quiet, kindly man, who liked to be left alone. It wasn't long before Mike sussed exactly what was required and if he was in any difficulty, Mac always helped him, providing the request was made after nine o'clock!

He had been thrown in at the deep end and certainly needed all the help he could get in learning how to work the small horizontal borer. It was a complex machine for someone with so little experience and he had to pick it up as he went along. Setting up the piece was nearly always difficult, but the actual machining only took a few minutes and within a few weeks, he was able to tackle most of the work that came his way with some confidence. When a job was finished, he would complete the docket, then take it over to the despatch area. If the next job wasn't to hand, he would clean down the machine and await Mac's pleasure. At the morning breaks, he would wash their mugs, then go on to make their drinks, which brought a lot of sly comments from his mates. Having established good relations with his boss, he wasn't going to put them in jeopardy, just to amuse them.

His main difficulty was in setting up the various jobs to the necessary line and level. Some of the pieces were oddly shaped and it often took a lot of time and patience. His chore was made easier when Mac gave him access to a cupboard which contained all manner of brackets, clamps, packers and lengths of screwed rod, complete with nuts and washers. When Mike was singing Mac's praises in the canteen one dinner time, his mates were very cutting in their derision.

Mike regularly bought the *Daily Telegraph*, which was much more interesting than the other papers and the sports section was the best part of it. Mac was a keen crossword buff, so the lad's last task of the day was to tear out the main one from his paper and hand it to him.

'When I was working with him,' said Cyril, 'it was as much as he could do to even speak to me, let alone help me with anything. A right miserable old sod he was and I was glad when I left him.'

Other lads had had similar experiences and couldn't understand how Mike was getting on so well.

'Perhaps you didn't go about it the right way,' he replied with a smug grin. 'I show a bit of respect and it has worked well. At least I know where I stand, unlike some of the buggers we've had to work with.'

'You're a snivelling git,' retorted one of his mates, a view with which most of them concurred.

There was quite a bit of interest in Mike's rugby and his mates often asked him how the last game had gone. After only a few matches in the 'B' fifteen, he had been moved-up to the extra 'A' team, where the games were of a better standard. He had already contributed to his team's efforts by taking penalties and conversions, when tries were scored. Among the nearby machinists was a man who regularly worked on the biggest machines. 'Lou' was a very large Yorkshireman from 'Ull', (Hull), who had played rugby league in his younger days. He was passionate about the sport and Mike often went over to talk to him. Their discussions were about diet, training and more importantly, tactics.

'Don't have a bath the night before a match,' he soberly advised, 'because it'll sap thee strength. Get some good fish or meat down you, early in the week. A couple of meat-pies will do, if you've nothing better. Keep off fish and chips later in the week though; there's nowt by way of goodness in all that fat and batter. Don't overload your stomach before a match. Get out early and stretch your muscles and warm-up properly, before you go on the pitch. Do some short, sharp runs to top it off and you'll be soon be away. One last thing, keep off the pop (beer) until after the match, when you'll need to replace your body fluids. How's your drop-kicking? The points gained from a well-aimed kick can often win the game. With the final whistle nigh and only a couple of points in it, ask the scrum-half for the ball, straight back from the scrum. Bang! Three points 'in the bag.''

When Mike told him that his kicking had recently fallen off, Lou suggested he should spend more time practicing, from all distances and angles and he should keep at it until it all came right again. He also suggested doing a light run, before doing any kicking, which would loosen up his leg muscles and clear any minor injury from the last game. The tactics discussed opened up a whole new dimension to Mike's game. It wasn't long before he was promoted to the 'A' team. It turned out to be a promotion too far and he soon lost confidence. The game was a lot faster and his team-mates were less forgiving about his mistakes. He spoke to the Captain about it and, after some encouraging comments about soon settling down, he did start to play a better game.

The full-back is the last line of defence and if the opposing three-quarters are in any way 'tasty', then it's unlikely he can hold-out fast running opponents on his own. After coming in for a lot of criticism from a team-mate, his self-control snapped. Throughout the match, his tormentor had been continually 'needling' him and after Mike told him 'to get off my bloody back', there was an angry confrontation. While no blows had been exchanged, the Captain reported the incident to the Committee and Mike was dropped from the team. What really upset him was that the other lad got off 'scot-free'.

When Mike later tried to explain that he had been provoked, the Captain had been in no mood to listen. He also 'got no joy' when he complained to a member of the Committee that he had been unfairly treated. All the man could say was that he didn't see what he was complaining about. From what he had heard, he had insulted the other lad and despite having been told to calm down, he had refused to let the matter drop. The club would not accept their players quarrelling on the field, no matter what it was about. His biggest disappointment was that he had scored two penalty goals in the game, which it ended with a win of six points to three for his team. When he discussed it with Lou, the man was quite blunt.

'Eh lad, the folly of youth,' he said soberly. 'You can't complain about what's happened, though I suppose they should have treated the two of you the same. If I'd have been the Captain, I would have told him to get on with his own game and leave you to yours. As it was, you shouldn't have reacted. You should have walked away, when it all got a bit heated. You should never play any sport, if you can't take a bit of criticism. How else are you to know how you're doing and what to do to improve thee game? One thing's for sure lad, it'll be a long road back, if my experience is anything to go by.

Mike had to accept that what his mentor had said was sound. As it was, some of his new team-mates were soon aggravating him in much the same way. A surprising development came when he unexpectedly met his original critic outside the clubhouse before a game. The lad approached him and after saying he very much regretted what had happened, he apologised. He had owned-up to the Committee about his part in it and told them that they had treated Mike unfairly. They shook hands and agreed that the matter was closed. After all the coaching by Lou and his regular training, he had become very much fitter and as he came off after a match in which he had played with enthusiasm, he was complimented by the club Captain.

The Club celebrated the end of the season by entering teams in the local 'seven-a-side' tournament. Clubs from all over the county competed for the various trophies and the event was always eagerly looked forward to. When the Captain asked Mike if he would like a place in the junior squad, the bloody fool turned him down. The brusqueness of his reply was not appreciated and it caused yet more resentment among the players who had overheard their conversation. He had been offered an olive-branch, and his stupidity had finally destroyed any chance of redemption. When he later went to the Club for the trials being held in advance of the new season, he wasn't even invited on to the pitch. For the first few games, he turned up on match days hoping to play, but often turned out for opposing sides. After being roughed up by his previous team-mates, his rugby career came to an abrupt end.

Chapter 9

The Cellar Club

There was a local 'entrepreneur', or, to be more accurate, a 'wide boy' called Fred Jones in the town. When he'd been demobbed after the War, he had looked for ways by which he could not only make a comfortable, secure living and also 'better' himself socially. He had initially set up as a trader, with stalls in the local markets and, through a lot of wheeling and dealing, he had prospered. In a few short years, he had become a businessman of some note, with his fingers in a lot of pies. He and his wife, Rose, lived in a style which differed greatly from their humble beginnings. They had a large house at the top of the town and she took the comforts of life very much for granted.

Fred had noticed the success of recently opened 'coffee bars' in London and set out to open one in the high street. It would be the first in the area and to get it off the ground was going to be fraught with problems. The Council was unenthusiastic, particularly when told that the customers would mostly be from the younger generation. Similar bars elsewhere were by no means havens of peace and good behaviour. The press took the opportunity to exaggerate the extent of the difficulties and Fred had problem after problem and raising the necessary capital was the most serious. It was essential to get it up and running as quickly as possible, if a decent level of profit on his investment was to be gained.

His plan was to appeal to 'the better class of clientele', and that meant that he had to discourage the trouble-makers and 'riff-raff'. For planning permission to be granted, he had to agree that no additional burden would be placed on the police by the anti-social behaviour of his customers. His bar would have to be strictly managed and that meant he would have to employ a doorman, provisions for which had not been included in his sums. His first concern though was how to convert a derelict building into a bright, attractive venue, without it costing him 'an arm and a leg'. It would have to be tastefully decorated and fitted-out with the latest Italian equipment, which was very expensive.

Rose was a very smart lady and they had a beautiful daughter called Jeanette, who was eighteen years old. Thinking them to be very much part of the local 'teenage scene', Fred enlisted the help of her and her boyfriend to advise him. They duly went up to London to look around some of the 'up-market' coffee bars and learn about the problems in running them. They came back full of enthusiasm and bright ideas and talked the old man into providing additional facilities which, they assured him, would ensure the success in his venture. His budget was put under more pressure and for a time, it was touch and go as to whether or not his project would go ahead.

After many delays and frustrations, Fred duly completed the new coffee bar and it opened in a blaze of publicity. For the first couple of nights, it was jam-packed with eager young punters. Gaining entry was difficult, due to the large number of complimentary invitations that had been given out and there was little room for the paying customers. The proud owner was delighted, forgetting that most of the clientele were freely enjoying their coffees and cakes etc at his expense. With the espresso machine working flat-out, everyone had a wonderful time. At the end of the evening, Jeanette had no difficulty in persuading her father about the success of his enterprise.

The same thing happened the next evening, with the place really 'stomping' and Fred must have thought that he had 'a nice little earner' going. On the third night, it was little more than half-full and the takings were well below breaking even. When he discussed it with his young advisers, they didn't know what was wrong. A few days later, he was grumbling loudly that he was getting poorer by the minute. His daughter's friends had told her that the prices in the bar were too expensive and one even had the cheek to say that the cakes and biscuits, which she had freely scoffed, were 'a bit stale'.

The prices charged in London had no relevance to Fred's coffee bar, though he had pitched them somewhere near. He cut them, at least until it was all 'up and running'. He had in fact 'pulled a fast one' when he bought his consumables; the first two deliveries being job lots from a fellow market-trader. His daughter had known nothing about that and she was very put out when she learned what he had done. Fred angrily retorted that her boyfriend, Keith, had not been much use to him and in the ensuing row, the loving couple's relationship was brought to an abrupt end. Fred doted on his lass and he was very careful to say that he didn't blame her for the debacle.

A few weeks later, the coffee bar was still less than half-full most evenings and, not making anything near the desired amount of 'dosh', Fred then had another bright idea which was to convert the very large cellar underneath the building into a club where his customers could enjoy 'piped' music, and dance. Jeanette was told to ask around her friends to see if they thought it would catch on. She reported back that they would welcome the opportunity to meet in warm, friendly surroundings, instead of hanging around in dance halls and pubs. While no longer part of the family, Keith still kept his ear to the ground. He was nice to Jeanette and was still making clandestine visits to see Rose, who was very fond of him.

Despite all the comforts and luxuries provided by her husband, she was often very scathing about his 'airy-fairy' projects and d disdainfully said that few of them had ever achieved much success, which wasn't true. Keith was a valuable source of 'intelligence' when Mike and his mates met him, one Saturday evening, at the refreshment kiosk near the railway station.

'The club will be for members only,' he told them loftily. 'I have it on good authority that there'll be no chance of you lot being allowed to join. Only the select and chosen few will be allowed in, people like me, who've got a bit o' class'.

'I thought she'd given you the elbow,' said Mike, referring to the lovely Jeanette and winking slyly at his mates. 'How come you know so much anyway?'

'That's for me to know an' you to find out,' Keith replied smugly, tapping the side of his nose.

'Here, Keith,' another lad interjected, 'you're not still popping round to see her mum while Fred's out on business are you? Bloody hell, you'll be for it if he catches you.'

From Keith's reaction, there was more than a grain of truth in what he had said. He furiously denied any such liaison and their ensuing howl of laughter brought about his early departure.

Posters were put up in the coffee bar which informed the customers of the impending opening of the 'Cellar Club' and inviting applications for membership. The opening night was just as crowded as that of the coffee bar and the ensuing chaos was exacerbated by those with mischief in mind. The only way of gaining entry was through the bar and down the stairs in the far corner. A continuous stream of punters passed through the tables, which caused no end of noisy arguments. Fred had installed more tables and chairs than originally intended, which had narrowed the spaces between them to the point where anyone who walked between them came into contact with someone sitting down.

The doorman was a dour, po-faced individual, who was probably in his mid-fifties and he had little by way of natural charm. His was a difficult job and, come what may, he was determined to do it. It was agreed among the watching 'nerds' that he contributed in no small way to the chaos that evening. His unyielding attitude resulted in a long queue of irate customers up the stairs, through the bar and out on to the street. The Police arrived and pushed the noisy crowd, who were milling around outside, back on to the pavement. The Sergeant went inside to speak to Fred, who was beside himself with rage and having got little sense out of him, the Officer asked everyone to leave. The opening night had turned into a shambles.

A lot of people had been put off by the cost of joining the club, which disappointed Fred greatly. Once more, he was heading into deep water and was soon was showing signs of panic. He made another attempt to open and with far fewer people trying to get in, he enjoyed more success. A couple of waitresses served the customers in the Cellar, as well as in the bar above, but it was not a success. The punters declined to fork out for 'being served by some daft girl' and with few tips being received, the girls became slower and surlier in their demeanour. There were complaints about the poor service and when the coffee eventually came, it was mostly cold. Fred took no notice and did nothing about it.

Down below, the atmosphere was anything but lively. The music came from two speakers, which were linked to the Juke-box up in the bar. Fred had avoided having to splash out on another machine, at least until he was making the sort of money for which he was becoming increasingly anxious. The atmosphere was dead and his customers sat around miserably grumbling to each other. Their entertainment relied on others feeding the machine upstairs. The 'yossils', who were waiting outside, soon cottoned on to a way of causing additional excitement. Some of them had been excluded and with nothing better to do, winding the doorman up was an attractive proposition. Having noted that Fred and his minders were absent, they noisily made their way downstairs.

'Good evening, Mister Campbell,' the 'spokesman' said politely, when he opened the door. 'Could we have some membership forms to fill-in?'

The man being canny knew he was being set up for a confrontation.

'No, you bloody well can't,' he retorted. 'Don't think for one moment that you can come down here to pull the wool over my eyes. I know all about your wee games and I know a trouble-maker when I see one. Oh yes, I've met buggers like you many times in my career and I know exactly how to deal with you. Now take my advice, laddie and get yourselves back up those stairs before I throw you out on your ear.'

As it happened, one of the 'King Teds' was on the pavement outside and seeing the nonsense going on, he decided to intervene. 'Jacko' was a short, very well-built young man, with an imposing presence, arrogance even. He was dressed up to the nines and sported an expensive camel-hair overcoat, which was casually draped across his broad shoulders. He must have thought 'a bit of aggro' would enhance his reputation but as he went in, someone went across the road to the Pub to warn Fred. Jacko, flanked by his three 'oppos', made their way down the stairs and rapped loudly on the door. Some of the customers in the bar, sensing trouble, deemed it wise to make a quick exit. The cellar door was thrown open and the startled doorman loudly demanded to know what the hell all the noise was about.

'We've heard there's a new club down here, so we thought we'd come and have a butchers,' Jacko said, glaring malevolently at the doorman, who was barring his way.

'Well, you've wasted your time,' he replied. 'We don't want your sort in here, so take yourselves back up those stairs and leave, before I have you thrown out.'

'What d'you mean, our sort?' yelled the angry Ted. 'I'm going to have to teach you some bloody manners, you ignorant bastard.'

With that he roughly pushed the man aside and entered the Cellar, followed closely by his mates. The twenty or so members present moved to the back, with the lads standing protectively in front of their girls.

'It's alright folks,' said Jacko, smiling like a malevolent snake, 'Don't mind me, I ain't got nothing against you lot.'

At that moment, the cavalry arrived in the form of a clearly incensed Fred, flanked by his 'heavies'.

'Now what's going on here then?,' he shouted angrily.

'These bloody louts have just forced their way in and threatened me,' replied the doorman indignantly. 'I've told them to get out, but they won't go.'

'Oh won't they?,' said Fred in a menacing voice. 'So you're looking for a bit of bother, my old son,' he said to Jacko. 'Well, we can oblige you,' he went on and nodding pointedly to his companions, who were glaring belligerently at the discomfited Ted.

The Teds realised that they had bitten off more than they could chew and shuffled their feet in embarrassment.

'No, we weren't looking for no trouble, Mister Jones,' Jacko replied, with more than a hint of respect. 'We only came down to have a look at your Club and this old sod wouldn't let us in. He insulted us, ain't that right lads?'

'Well, he was acting on my orders,' replied Fred. 'Now, get the hell out of here and don't come back, got it? As for you,' he said, poking Jacko roughly in the chest, 'I've a good mind to give you a slap. Go on, piss off, before I lose my bloody temper.'

Jacko and his mates beat a hasty retreat up the stairs and out of the building. They should have known better than to 'act the crack', where Fred was concerned. He had been there when needed and they'd been scared witless, when the tables had been turned on them. Fred had a reputation as a bit of hard-man and few young men were brave enough to confront him. Having somehow got wind of Jacko's intention, he and his heavies had gone over to the pub opposite to await developments. Having seen them enter the building, they had followed them down into the cellar. The doorman's brave front had been put on in the certain knowledge of his boss's support.

Chapter 10

Shaping Up

Mike had gained valuable experience, while working on the horizontal borer, in working on a broad range of items, including many types of large valve-bodies in cast-iron, brass and phosphor-bronze. Once he had the knack of setting up the machine, the work had been interesting and satisfying and his three months with Mac had passed quickly. When the Foreman came and told him that he was to move on the following Monday morning, he had mixed feelings. Knowing he wouldn't be able to do so on the day, he went over to say goodbye and thank his boss for all his help and advice. He appreciated all that the 'wee man' had done for him. Mac was very pleased and wished him all the best in his new job. As he was packing up, a lad came by to say he had been detailed off to work on his machine. Having been warned about the lousy bugger with whom he would be working, he was feeling very apprehensive. Mike readily assured him that he would have no problems, provided he 'played the game'.

Mike also went and said goodbye to Lou, who had been so helpful about playing rugby.

That's alright lad,' the man said, when he thanked him, 'I'm always pleased to help in any way I can. Just remember to put your brain in gear afore opening your mouth in future. What's said can never be unsaid, so it's best not to say it in the first place.'

It was yet another gem of sound advice. Mike hadn't had the courage to tell him about his latest act of stupidity, particularly when he had gone out of his way to coach him on the finer points of the game. He had made a complete mess of things and had already had to endure a lot of criticism from his workmates.

On Monday morning, he reported to the Foreman at the 'top end' of the Factory, which contained a large number of different shapers, which could be used to either cut or plane metal, in either the vertical or horizontal plane. His machine was old and well-worn, a description which appertained to so many of them. The modern ones in the Tool Room were expensive and only operated by skilled hands. He was told to get some bits of steel plate from a waste skip and set them up as practice pieces. He would thus get some practice in operating the machine and learn the basics of shaping. With the help of another Apprentice, who had been working in the section for some time, he started work.

The cutting tool was the much same as on a lathe and after his previous experience, there was not much of a problem in setting it up. He scribed a line along the side of the piece and clamped it square and level in the vice. As with the borer, the machining only took a few minutes. After completing half a dozen pieces, he was able to start working on the more simple jobs. George, who was

Mike's mentor, was working nearby and for the first few days, he took no interest in what the lad was doing. On the Friday afternoon, he came across to look at a square block of mild-steel, which Mike had rough machined on all six faces to rough dimensions. While it looked alright to the lads, he thought otherwise and bluntly said so.

'You'll have to do a lot better than that,' he said scornfully. 'Look at it, it's all over the place. My boy's still at school and he could have done better.'

Mike didn't argue about it, though he mentally asked himself what the old bugger expected from someone who had only just started working on the bloody machine. If he had taken some interest in what he was doing, he may have done a bit better. As it was, he let George 'rabbit on' in silence.

He took Mike over to a pile of six-inch square, by one and a half inches thick blocks of mild-steel, which had been roughly sawn from 'black bar'. He was to machine them down to stipulated sizes and thicknesses, in the numbers required. The dimensions were checked by the simple use of callipers and a steel rule. The way to obtain the best finish was by regularly sharpening the cutting tool. With practice and by discussing the job with John, he soon produced what was wanted. They were part of a batch of 'machined-packers', which would be used in the setting up of a large machine on board a Ship; a main engine or a steam turbine or a gearbox.

When completed, the packers were taken away to another section. Each piece would be hard-stamped, with an identification number, then drilled and fine-machined in a horizontal grinder. The whole batch would then go on for final assembly and packing. After he had completed a couple of dozen packers, Mike went over to see how the rough packers were being ground off, to close tolerance dimensions. His mate Lennie was watching the horizontal grinder and was just as pissed-off with the monotony of the job as Mike. After setting one up, he sat by the machine, while the abrasive wheel made its way slowly across the surface. It was known as a wet machine, as the fine grinding was aided by a copious amount of water, which acted as a coolant. In contrast to when they had been working on the lathes and shapers, no one seemed to take any notice as to whether or not they were actually working. It was all very laid back and if someone decided to slope off, he did so knowing no one would bother him when he returned.

The increase in pay they'd received at the start of the third year had greatly improved the lot of the lads. Even so, by Friday dinner time, the majority were eagerly awaiting the arrival of their pay packets. The necessity of sharing a single, hand-rolled cigarette had gone, though most of the smokers rarely bought tailor-mades during the week. They rolled their own while at work and. to a non-smoker, their 'ciggies' had an obnoxious smell. When near them, they constantly complained, but it made no difference, since they were very much in the minority. The commonly held view was that if someone wanted to breathe fresh air, he could take himself outside. When asked why he smoked, one individual replied that it was a social habit, which he very much enjoyed and it always broke the ice whenever he met a stranger.

Being well aware of the lads' lack of interest, the foreman used the only incentive available. When jobs were suitable, he put them on piece work. He set his targets at a level which gave the lad the opportunity to earn 'a little bit of extra'. After years of combating their crafty ploys, he was well versed in getting the hours 'something like'. Les had been working that way for some considerable time and he maintained that he was making tidy sums of extra cash. His mates cynically thought he was related to the boss, because he always got the best jobs. He retorted that he was given the same targets as everyone else and it wasn't his concern if other people were a lot slower than him. In fact, he not only worked hard, but consistently produced the quality of finish demanded by the Inspectors.

He was one of the few lads who owned a decent motor bike. His first had been a BSA 250cc 'single-pot' machine, which had caused no end of envy among his peers. His father had a general store and Les had regularly delivered papers, groceries etc since even before he left school. Having steadily saved his money, he had eventually had enough to buy his bike. A couple of years later, he had traded it in and bought a brand, spanking new Matchless 500cc, twin-cylinder machine. He was then seen as a pre-eminent motor-cyclist among the apprentices and it went to his head. Most of his contemporaries were riding small BSA Bantams or Francis Barnetts, with 125, 150 or 175cc, two-stroke engines. They had little power, compared with the larger, more sophisticated bikes, which were always described as mean machines.

The Dockyard Police were soon after him and the unfolding drama became a matter of great interest. One morning, a 'po-faced plod' came into the Factory looking for the owner of the motor-bike which was parked outside the door. Having identified Les, he insisted that it be moved immediately. With a parking area provided local to the Factory for cycles, motor cycles and the few cars that were brought in to work, there was no need to park in the road outside. The access doors had to be kept clear at all times, for safety reasons. The green-eyed cynics reckoned that Les only put his machine there, so that he could go out to look adoringly and pat it 'now and then'.

A couple of days later, the Officer again came into the shop, this time to warn Les about the way he had ridden through the Yard that morning. To the lad's annoyance and embarrassment, he demanded to see his driving licence and insurance certificate. He then compounded the offence by going out and inspecting the tax disc. In reply to the lad's complaint, the Officer said that he was only being thorough in the 'h'exicution of 'is dooty'. Les was outraged when, after finding nothing wrong, the Officer loudly warned him again about his riding and sternly told him that he would be 'watching out' for him.

The relationship between Les and the Police deteriorated steadily from then on. Other Officers often chastised him about his riding and each time, he loudly protested that he was being victimised. Having had several final warnings, he should have known he had to toe the line. Common sense dictated that he had gone far enough. He also came under pressure from the shop stewards and some of the men in the Factory. To weave in and out of the very large number of Mateys, at anything other than a slow crawl, was extremely dangerous and it was compounded by the large network of railway lines, which ran all over the Yard. The rails at the road crossings were very slippery, when wet and someone may well have been injured had he had lost control. Ultimately, he decided to be more sensible.

He had to get his adrenalin fix elsewhere and that was when he left work in the evening. On the open road, he was a 'hell-rider', who cared nothing for speed limits or other road users. Access into and out of the Yard was through three very large gates, with the largest located in the middle. With approximately fourteen thousand Employees, the Officers had their work cut out to control them in an orderly manner. They didn't separate the traffic from the pedestrians, probably because there was rarely a problem. As a direct result, motor cyclists suffered little impedance to their movements. The motorists fared rather differently, in that they were regularly pulled over to have their vehicles searched.

As soon as he was through the gate and notwithstanding the huge crowd of Mateys crossing the road, Les weaved in and out of them at an ever increasing speed. When clear, he 'let her rip' up the hill and away, 'like a robber's dog'. His manic behaviour soon attracted the attentions of the Civil Police and they tried to apprehend him, but without success. The Officers on foot had no chance, because he spotted them as he came out of the gate. Their next move was to have two motor cyclists waiting at the foot of the hill with their engines running, to clock his speed and pull him over. Their machines were standard issue Velocettes which, while adequate for patrolling the town, were not built for speed. In consequence, Les escaped before they had even got going.

Les made monkeys out of the 'boys in blue' for quite some time and his reputation among his workmates soared. It had to come to an end, however, and when it did, it was a bit of an anti-climax. One evening, there was no sign of the Police when he came out of the gate and he happily roared off up the hill. Just over the brow, he had to brake hard and was fortunate the road was dry. About fifty yards down the other side was a road block and with great glee, the Officers pounced. He was charged with dangerous driving and a few days later, he came up before the Magistrates. Following a lengthy account of his misdemeanours by the Prosecuting Officer, he was fined and banned from driving.

The lad had got his come-uppance, for which he was to enjoy a lot of sympathy and when he returned to work the next day, he was loudly cheered. There has always been something in the British psyche which has dictated that, anyone who comes into confrontation with the 'Law' is a bloody good bloke, a hero even. As it was, the Officers had removed a very real menace from the road outside the Yard. The old French adage 'pour encourager les autres' very much appertained, because those that had thought to 'ape' the antics of the fool were deterred by the severity of his punishment. The odd thing was that when it was all over, Les promptly sold his bike and reverted to his normal polite and easy going self.

It was around that time that something untoward had happened to one of the lads' erstwhile Instructors. It was said, but never substantiated, that he had been disciplined by management, moved to another job and was no longer involved in the Apprentices' training. It was strange that no one was able to find out the details, despite diligent inquiries as to what he had done. Everyone knew he had occasionally worked on what were euphemistically called 'Government jobs', but they had never been anything more than of a very minor nature. He had always stressed that 'the rules' were there for the orderly progression of the job and had been very much liked and respected. Most of his former charges were very concerned to hear that he had been in trouble.

Mike's work on the shaping machines dragged on interminably until one morning, he was told by the Foreman to work on a milling machine. Its function was similar to that of the shaper, in that it efficiently removed various thicknesses of metal, but the cutting was done by a rotating multi-bladed head, instead of a fixed tool. It produced a much better standard of finish and in a quicker time. After talking to the men, who were working on more sophisticated machines, he accepted that it was all part of his training. Some of the jobs they were doing were complex and called for no little degree of skill and attention.

Chapter 11

Youthful Entertainment

By the middle of 1955, there was an air of increasing optimism among the people of this Country and a lot of young men and women had money to spend and were wearing smart clothes. Some of the older women made a few bob, by doing sewing and alterations to clothing and they were greatly appreciated in their communities. Their skills had mostly been passed on within their families. Suits and dresses were altered to suit the new fashions and some of their efforts were most impressive. Young women made their own wedding dresses, very often from those given by their relations or friends. Nothing was wasted and, with only bits and pieces to buy, it saved them a lot of money. A new trend had caught on among the younger generation and it was dubbed the 'Edwardian' look, which was noticeably different from the mode of dressing in vogue at the time and it gave rise to the term 'Teddy boy or Girl'.

The male Teds wore black suits, the jackets of which had black velvet collars and came down to knee-level. Their trousers were called 'drain-pipes', being tight-fitting around the legs. They wore white shirts, with high collars with shoe string ties and high-buttoned waistcoats. Their only concession to colour was their 'day-glow' socks, in bright green, orange or red. Their hair was longer than had been the norm for many years and it had to be most carefully styled by a competent barber. Thick rubber-soled shoes, usually referred to as 'brothel creepers', completed their outfits. In comparison with most other young men, the Teds cut something of a dash and the best dressed ones were seen as 'well-off'. They additionally sported light-brown, 'camel hair' overcoats, which were casually draped across their shoulders, which demonstrated their class among their contemporaries. Most of them were in their early twenties and more mature than the average 'oik'.

The 'Teddy Girls' were slower to get off the ground, but their numbers increased steadily as the craze caught on. Like their 'fellahs', the best dressed ones had the funds to fully indulge in the full Edwardian mode. They wore black costumes, the coats of which were tight-fitting, with small, accentuated waists and high busts. Their skirts were cut well below the knee and in some cases, came right down to the ankles. They wore beautifully laced and embroidered blouses, with high necks and their outfits adorned by large pieces of either antique or imitation cameo jewellery. Exotic earrings were highly popular, as were numerous bracelets on each wrist. They wore black net stockings and shoes or boots in the pre-World War I style, the fastenings of which were made by buttons.

Their hair was piled up ornately on the top of their heads in the 'Queen Alexandra' style and held secure by tortoiseshell combs and ornately headed silver pins. Because of the need to accentuate their curves, stays and girdles were a fundamental part of their outfits and the skills of the 'corsetieres' were very much in demand. Their makeup was not always skilfully applied but the end result could sometimes be absolutely stunning. The most sophisticated girls used an ivory cigarette holder and a few even sported 'lorgnettes'. Their outfits were often topped off by very ornate parasols or umbrellas.

As some wit commented about a Teddy Girl called Celia, 'she was divine until she opened her mouth'. She was perhaps five feet eight inches tall with an excellent figure and she made the most of her attributes. 'Cel', pronounced 'seal', was the girlfriend of Jacko White, the 'King-Ted' who had recently been ejected from the Cellar Club. When riled, she could be just as obnoxious and foul-mouthed as he was but at other times, she could be absolutely charming. Mike saw her coming out of 'Marks' one Saturday morning and he went over and asked if she needed a hand with her shopping. She graciously accepted and was very chatty as they walked down to the bus stop. Jacko was clearly miffed when he saw Mike and when he told him to 'get lost', Cel was quick to bend his ear. If he hadn't been in the pub with his mates, there would have been no need for the lad to have helped her. Jacko was suitably abashed and grudgingly apologized to the lad, with the blackest of scowls.

'Don't take any notice of him,' the good lady said, nodding towards her beau. 'He's all mouth and no trousers, he is.'

'That's not what I've heard,' retorted Mike; then, thinking on his toes, he turned to Jacko. 'Sorry for any offence, mate,' he said lamely. 'No disrespect intended.'

That went down a bundle and, with honour satisfied, he quickly walked away.

When out on the Town, Cel often carried a very ornate, frilly black parasol, an appurtenance of great beauty. It was best to keep well clear if she'd had a few, because she was prone to use it on anyone who raised her ire. Her 'brolly' had a sharp point at the bottom-end and when wielded in anger, it could cause serious injury to the object of her aggression. While it was unusual for her to be directly involved in any violence, she would often make a timely intervention in support of 'her lads'. Ladies like Cel were best avoided, when the proverbial 'hit the fan'.

According to the older people, the behaviour of the younger generation had got very much worse since the end of War. In their view, the advent of the Edwardian craze accentuated the decline even further. The media piled in and printed grave articles about 'falling standards' and they were soon joined by commentators on the radio. Minor incidents were described in histrionic terms as a grave threat to society. Politicians jumped on the band wagon and expounded how disgraceful it all was. Social 'experts' (who were anything but) were regularly consulted to no avail. They made a deteriorating situation considerably worse, with their graphic spiels about the growing disorder. Solid citizens indignantly wrote to the papers, to give vent to their outrage and demanded that corporal punishment be brought back without delay.

Some of the buffoons blamed the behaviour of the young for the Country's problems, which was ridiculous. Given the scale of the opprobrium that they faced, it was inevitable that the Teds came into increasing conflict with the authorities. The Police didn't always help matters, when faced with a large number of unruly youths and if some of them were wearing drain pipes, they were Teddy boys, who had to be dealt with drastically. Whether or not they were actually involved in the trouble didn't matter. Many confrontations got out of hand due to the over-reaction of the 'Bobbies' to situations which could have been better handled. Senior 'po-faced plods' were often heard sanctimoniously expounding to the media that they were not going to tolerate young people disturbing the peace. Of course they weren't, that was what they were so very well paid for.

When a forthcoming dance or concert was thought likely to be a 'lively' event, every 'bone-head' in the area made a bee-line for it. Most of the trouble came from the 'hangers-on' who conveniently attached themselves to the Teds. The Kings and their Queens were more concerned with looking after their expensive gear and getting involved in a brawl was definitely not on. They usually withdrew back through the ranks as soon as the proverbial 'hit the fan'. Their minders were said to carry various weapons, such as knuckle dusters, coshes and sometimes knives or razors, with which they assaulted and/or intimidated other people. The aggression shown would have been comical, had they not presented such a serious threat.

The Teds would usually stand in a group in the dance hall and glare malevolently at whoever they thought was vulnerable. Many would be smoking, holding their hand-rolled fags enclosed in the palms of their hands and chewing gum with open mouths, like the American gangsters they had seen in films. Other young men, being very much in the majority, resented their nonsense and welcomed the opportunity to do battle with them and in many of the confrontations, affronted civilians were joined by Servicemen in 'sorting them out'.

The growing aversion to authority had come from a number of sources. At the end of the War, a very large number of young men had come back from the Forces and they had not always been welcomed back into the society which they had served so well. They had a deep-seated contempt for anyone who perceived him or herself as 'their betters'; or of a 'superior class'. A lot of the new generation of snobs had come from humble beginnings, but had somehow conveniently dodged their War-time service. Many of them had waxed fat, compared to most working folk and were generally despised as parasites. The trendy, anti-social influences, which had become so prevalent among the younger element, had its origins in the United States, with all sorts of 'naff' behaviour being regularly seen in cinemas. Films, such as 'The Blackboard Jungle' and 'West Side Story', added fuel to the nonsense and the young people 'aped' the antics of their cousins on the other side of the pond.

Although things were changing, traditional family values still largely remained intact. Most teenagers accepted their parental control and kept clear of trouble, but they no longer had to contribute as much of their income to their families' budgets. As well as buying new clothes, they indulged themselves in all manner of luxuries, such as radios and gramophones etc. The quality of broadcasting had gradually improved and a whole new world of pop music was opening up. Radio Luxembourg provided late night enjoyment and private broadcasters, which were illegal at the time, were starting-up transmissions from off shore. For many years, the older generation (those above thirty years of age) had enjoyed both modern and what was called 'old-time' music and dancing. The local musicians energetically copied the style and hits of the big bands in the local dance halls.

Music had also come from the West Indies and South America, and the calypsos and sambas became increasingly popular. There was a marked change in the air and pop music, as we know it today, was born. New technology was increasingly being used in the manufacture of gramophone records, which were made in plastic, instead of 'bakelite'. They became cheaper, and 'Hit Parades' were printed and commented on in numerous musical publications. In time, the old seventy-eight rpm records were gradually replaced by the more compact forty-five discs and they in turn were supplemented by the 'long-playing record'. 'Skiffle', which was first heard in the cellar of a London pub, rapidly caught on. The main exponents were Chas. McDevitt and Lonnie Donegan and in many venues, a group would be heard grinding out 'Freight Train', 'My Ol' Man's a Dustman' or 'The Rock Island Line'. Their obvious lack of musical talent didn't seem to matter.

Up until then, guitars could be bought for a few pounds in any junk shop but that abruptly changed, due to the pressing needs of the young men who were forming their own groups. Despite only being able to play a few chords, they thought they were going places and their instruments became increasingly expensive and hard to find. Old ladies profited handsomely when they sold one, which had belonged to their late husbands or a son who had left home. A group of 'skifflers' would consist of a couple of lads strumming on their guitars, with two other lads providing the 'backing'. One would be bashing out the rhythm on a washboard by rubbing the serrations up and down with his fingers, on the ends of which were metal thimbles. The other lad strummed the beat on a 'double-bass' made out of an old tea-chest, a broom handle and a length of rough twine. The result was often painful on the ears.

The American Forces had brought the jitter bug and jiving to Britain during the War, but until now it hadn't really caught on. Most mature adults preferred the more sedate waltzes, foxtrots, quicksteps and tangos of ballroom dancing which were regularly interspersed with the 'old-time' waltz, military two-step, valeta and, dare we say it?, The Gay Gordons'. They often loudly complained about the jivers antics, saying smugly that their mode of dancing was much better than 'all this new-fangled nonsense'. Middle-aged people liked the 'crooning' of the War-time favourites, such as Gracy Fields, Vera Lynn and Bing Crosby.

The new crazes were fully exploited by the music industry. There was a popular demand for ballads, which were sung by Pat Boon, Connie Francis, Frankie Laine and Frank Sinatra. Swing music was still popular and it enjoyed a renewed interest with a succession of American big bands coming over to perform in Britain and Europe. They played mostly in the style of Glen Miller, who had been so very popular until his tragic death in the War. They were supplemented by 'home-grown' bands, such as Ted Heath, Eric Delaney, Johnny Dankworth and Joe Loss, who performed in subtly different ways. Each band had their devoted fans.

Another form of music, which had been on the scene for many years, was traditional jazz. Louis Armstrong, with his fabulous interpretations of the old classics, was without doubt its greatest exponent. His band was world famous and it also made regular tours around the main cities of Europe. Their concerts were always sold out at all the major venues. Kenny Ball and his jazzmen and Humphrey Littleton and his band played to large audiences and regularly provided a high standard of musical entertainment on the radio. In turn, their most popular numbers were reproduced by many of the small local bands and heard in all sorts of venues. In direct contrast to the skiffle groups, they were mostly competent musicians, with the best of them having devoted followers of their own. They zealously copied the dress, mannerisms and speech of the 'greats' and aped the exaggerated way in which they played their instruments.

Modern jazz also had its adherents, with large concerts held live and broadcast on the radio by the leading exponents. They also went on tour from time to time. Count Basie, Benny Goodman and Ronnie Scott were at the forefront, with their bands regularly playing in the select clubs in the metropolis. As we have said, It was a time of great change, where popular music was very much part of the everyday lives of the modern youth. Classical music still had its place, with adherents attending regular concerts by the many large, full-time orchestras. Gilbert and Sullivan operas were still very popular as well, either performed by the full-time professional companies or by local Societies. In summing up, there was music for everyone in the nineteen fifties and it did so very much to lift the moral of the people, after the hard times which had gone on for so long.

Chapter 12

The Perils Of Love

Returning to the story of the Maltese lads, an incident occurred one weekend which was absolutely hilarious. The 'dark-horse' in their midst was none other than the aforesaid Sammy, the lad who had met a young lady at the fair. Their friendship had blossomed and, knowing his mates ribbed each other in the same way as the apprentices, he had wisely kept it to himself. The crafty bugger had managed to do so by going to places where they were unlikely to be seen. By the time his perfidy was uncovered, he had 'had his feet under the table' for some time. He had been warmly welcomed by her parents, with them probably seeing him as a prospective son in law. Could it also have been that he was from a beautiful Mediterranean island, and the thought of cheap family holidays in the sun in the years ahead was a pleasant prospect? A cynic might have thought so. Sammy was not going to disabuse them while he was enjoying their cordial hospitality.

Following a dance on a Saturday evening, the lads usually met up at the coffee stall near the railway station. Just after midnight one evening, as they were enjoying their mugs of coffee and eating their hot meat pies, there was suddenly a surge of excitement from those standing near the road. Everyone turned to see what was going on and they watched the unfolding drama with incredulity and increasing mirth. Legging it down the road, and being hotly pursued by an older man, who was shouting dire threats and imprecations, was a young man. He was running hard to out-pace his pursuer and was clad solely in his socks and underpants, with his trousers and shirt tightly grasped in one hand. Much to the lads' unbridled delight, it was none other than their friend Sammy. Three or four of them quickly moved into the road and intercepted the man, who was outraged to see his quarry escaping down the hill. After having been solemnly warned about 'assaulting one of our mates', the poor old bugger turned away and disconsolately trudged back up the road.

When they arrived at work on the following Monday, everyone was busting to hear the details of what had gone on. When he came into the shop, Sammy was given a loud cheer, which he answered with a rueful smile.

'Hey, come on Sammy, tell us what you've been up to,' he was urged.

Knowing he would be teased unmercifully, he refused to say anything about it. 'You can all a-bugger off an' mind'a your own beez'ness,' he replied tersely, but it all soon became clear.

On the Saturday evening, he had gone to his girlfriend's house and had been warmly greeted as usual. It was their regular practice to go down to their local for a few drinks and he had enjoyed many very pleasant evenings there before he and Sandra went off to a dance. The lass told her father that she 'had a bit of a headache' and, if they didn't mind, she and Sammy would stay behind for a quiet hour in front of the telly. They would perhaps join them later. Mum duly set out a plate of sarnies and some slices of cake, before she and her husband left the house.

The young couple didn't waste any time in making their way upstairs for a more salubrious means of enjoying their embraces. The time passed more quickly than they had realised and much to their alarm, they heard the key in the front door and her mum and dad came into the house. Finding they were not in the sitting room and hearing frantic scuffling from above, Ernie sussed what had been going on and he ran up the stairs. When the bedroom door crashed open Sammy, with great presence of mind, went through the open window and jumped down to the ground below.

'Bloody hell Sammy,' said one of his listeners, 'you might have broken something doing that.

He was loudly told to 'shut-it' and Sammy was urged to continue. He had been caught on the job and, hearing Ernie coming up the stairs, there had only been time to don his pants. To a roar of laughter, he told them that luckily, he had kept his socks on. He had grabbed his shirt and trousers but had not been able to find his shoes and his only means of escape was out of the bedroom window. Luckily, the room below had a bay-type window and he had been able to step out on to the flat roof, before jumping down into the garden. He had then made off down the road past the station and the coffee stall. With Ernie gaining on him, he had fortuitously been rescued by the lads' quick-witted intercession and had got away. The next morning, one of his mates had called at the girl's house to collect his shoes and the rest of his clothes and they had been abruptly thrust out by her mother and the door had been slammed in his face.

'I didn't have time to say sorry for my cousin,' Ali said mournfully, much to the amusement of everyone. 'You Eengleesh should'a be more unnerstanding, heh?'

Only a couple of weeks later, two of the lads saw Sandra at a dance with another young man and, thinking themselves very witty, they gravely advised him to keep his trousers handy at all times. He was nonplussed and angrily demanded to know what the hell had been going on 'while he was away'. They were later confronted by the angry young lady and she roundly berated them for the upset they had caused. She had been going steady with a soldier while he had been stationed in the local barracks. And when he had been posted to Germany, she had got fed up with staying in. Sammy had been a welcome diversion. When her soldier returned, they had 'picked-up' where they'd left off and the two daft sods had messed it all up. The last they saw of her that evening, she was getting into a taxi with some other bloke!

Few of the lads had had a steady girlfriend when they had first started work but by the middle of their third year, the unattached ones were well in the minority. The possibility that their offspring might 'get into trouble' was a matter of serious concern for many parents and, in consequence, they kept them under a very tight rein. That usually appertained until they either got engaged or reached their twenty-first birthday. If a daughter had not settled down by then, they would think perhaps there was something wrong with her. No one wanted their daughter 'left on the shelf' and often, a spot of match-making would be called for. While their sons were not so rigidly constrained, they would also come under pressure if mum and dad thought they were not shaping-up to the inevitable. The 'key of the door' – i.e. their twenty-first birthdays – meant that it was time for them to make their own way in the world. Very few families wanted their unmarried sons living with them indefinitely.

Most of the lads, who were still living at home, were content to abide by their parents' rules. Their 'outdoor' activities had to be accounted for and often, they had to be home in the evenings by a stipulated time. Breaking the curfew, either accidentally or on purpose, could be harsh for some. Families inevitably suffered the ultimate indignity and perceived shame, if their children 'got into trouble', as so many did. When a daughter became pregnant, or a son had 'got a girl into trouble', it was little short of a disaster. Their already-tight budget would be stretched to breaking point and both families would suffer as a direct result of a few minutes of illicit passion. When the unfortunate couple married, they usually moved in with her parents and unless they were very fortunate indeed, it almost certainly led to yet more problems.

When a lad started 'seeing' a girl regularly, they came under the close scrutiny of their families and they would be solemnly warned about the perils of getting into trouble. It was a situation which had appertained since the beginning of time, but it seemed to make little difference. Going steady usually led to a growing intimacy and if they weren't 'at it' when they were courting, then their engagement usually brought about what every young couple like doing best.

When they first heard of a budding friendship, some parents would object, saying 'snootily' that the other family were a bad lot or were in some way, 'beneath' them. When a lass was satisfied that her suitor had honourable intentions, he would be brought home to be formally introduced to her family, even if and when they were neighbours. The mandatory ritual had to be played out, usually by the expedient of the traditional Sunday afternoon tea.

The budding relationship often brought a new dimension to both families' lives and her parents were usually keen to do the job properly. The primary objective was to formally confirm that the lad was acceptable. If all went well, it put the necessary mark of respectability on the romance. That first visit could be a traumatic experience for the lad in that he had to be on his best behaviour and treat her parents with the necessary respect. It was not unusual for close relations to be invited over to meet him as well and their presence often made the inquisition that much harder to bear. Any reluctance to conform was inevitably perceived as a snub and her parents would 'take umbrage'. The relationship would then be discouraged or, in extreme cases, be banned altogether.

As he explained in some detail, Fred's problem had been with his mother and the charade which he described amused his workmates greatly. His suit was pressed and his only decent shirt was washed and carefully ironed. Clean underclothes were provided, despite having been changed the evening before. His socks were washed and darned and his shoes cleaned several times. With them being in need of repair, he was firmly told to keep both feet on the floor, to hide the hole in the sole of one of them. His father's tie was sponged and pressed and a clean handkerchief was produced, with strict instructions as to its proper use. Before he dressed, he was closely inspected to ensure that he had washed his neck and behind his ears. Spots and blackheads were 'popped' and the few whiskers on his chin removed. His hands and nails were scrubbed until they were sore. At the last minute, his hair was deemed to be too long, so he was sent round to a neighbour for a crop.

It had all been carried through, despite his protests that her parents were hardly likely to look at him that closely. When mum was finished, he had been cleaned to such an extent that he didn't know if he was 'coming, going, been or went'. All in all, she had done a thorough job and had turned him into someone his mates found hard to visualise. He was, they said, 'a scruffy bugger', with little chance of cutting a dash in polite society, no matter how hard his mum tried. Others had gone through similar treatment from their own mothers and some of those that hadn't would probably do so in due course. Appearances and first impressions, no matter how false, mattered and it was appreciated when a lad turned up 'all spick and span'. In summing up his ordeal, Fred said that near the end of her campaign, his mum had made a telling point about the importance of the occasion.

'I'm not having you letting me down and them looking down their noses at us. I wouldn't know where to show my face,' she had said dramatically.

She had then gone on at length about the finer points of behaviour and what was essentially the norm in company, particularly when eating. All her nonsense had culminated in her final instructions and how his mates laughed when he mimicked her in a falsetto voice.

'Don't eat everything in sight. Just you show how well you've been brought up, by saying when asked if you'd like something more. 'No thenk you very much, Hi've had quite sufficient.' Oh! And don't sniff, use your hankie and not your sleeve like you usually do, you dirty little bugger.'

'So how'd it all go then?,' asked Bert. Though bursting with mirth, he was pretending to be concerned.

'Alright, I suppose,' Fred replied, knowing what was going on and being reluctant to admit it had been anything but.

Bert had heard that he had left the girl's house much sooner than he could possibly have imagined. The reaction of her parents to their daughter's first hesitant and shy introduction had firmly placed Fred on the back foot. Not only were they less than welcoming, her brothers and sisters had coldly stared at him throughout his time in their house. It was, he said later 'as if she'd brought something nasty in from the street'.

'Well she had,' chorused his audience, jostling him and laughing loudly. 'What did you get to eat, Fred?,' asked another lad, when the noise died down.

'That's the worse part,' came the terse reply. 'I didn't stay long enough to get anything. It didn't matter though. I didn't think much of her to start with and now I've met her bloody family, what more can I say? My problem was what I was going to say to my mum, after all the trouble she'd been to in getting me ready. She went up the wall alright when I told her, but not in the way I'd thought.'

'So you told her the truth, my old son,' said Bert, with more sympathy. 'It's not as if it was your fault that they're a lot of stuck-up sods, though knowing them, I don't know what they've got to be so snotty about.'

That was the end of Fred's little foray into a loving relationship. His mum hadn't made anything like the fuss he had imagined. She had listened to his indignant tale and had then said, resignedly, 'Never mind, it's probably for the best.'

Fred's experience was by no means an isolated occurrence. If a girl had siblings, who knew her new boyfriend, his first visit could be very unpleasant and her brother(s) would often jostle him, or give him a 'duffing' to deter his amorous intentions. Many budding relationships foundered on the rocks of Sunday afternoon tea, with the lad or lass quickly shown the door. If seen walking out later, they were usually stiff-faced and blushingly self-consciously. Having cleared the first hurdle, their families would become friendly, with regular visits to each other's homes. They would often say what a lovely couple they were and archly tease them. The path of true love has never been smooth and rarely was a new relationship free from stress. Things haven't changed much in that respect.

The good relationship between the families was tenuous and could soon be broken, if and when the lovers split up. It was a matter of pride for them to tell their friends that he or she had 'packed him or her in'. Recriminations would ensue, with the parents saying that he or she wasn't good enough for her lass or lad etc. The comedian Les Dawson and his 'oppo' Roy Kinnear, so amply lampooned the typicality of such ladies in their television comedy sketches of two 'old biddies' gossiping over the garden wall. They would sniff loudly in disdain and adjust their accoutrements, before making cutting comments in cynical criticism of the objects of their denigration. There was always someone who, having heard that the couple had parted, would gleefully 'give the pot a stir'. The ensuing row would often develop into an all-out feud, which sometimes deteriorated into violence.

It was even worse if the lad was thought to have 'taken advantage' of the lass. Most families were conscious of their social position and any slight, real or imaginary, would cause grave offence and lead to all sorts of trouble. If they were poor, all they had was their pride and it was perhaps understandable that they fought like hell for it. Modern sociologists like to refer to the sense of 'community' in the old days, but it is no more than a myth. People don't change much, only their personal circumstances do. Life for most people was anything but the friendly and peaceful idyll that some of them would have us believe. Despite the massive improvement in their standard of living, most people maintain a perception of pride and respect.

Chapter 13

Something Different

One Monday morning, Mike packed up his toolbox and decamped again for pastures new. The Foreman had instructed him to report to a workshop at the top of the Yard, where he would be working on a special assignment. He must have had his tongue firmly in his cheek because, when he arrived, there was little being done. The shop was about two hundred yards from the main gate, which pleased him greatly, because it made for a shorter journey to and from work. The shop contained a number of machines including a couple of lathes, a vertical drilling machine, a shaper and the usual grinding-machine. It was intended to be a self-contained facility for finishing off numerous valves, of all shapes, sizes and functions. The Submarine, for which they were destined, was under construction on a nearby slipway, inside very large, old wooden building. The work would be similar to what they had done in the valve shop, but without the mess and grime which came from fittings that had already been in service.

The Foreman told the lads to sort themselves out around a large work bench, which stood on one side of the shop. As was usual, they were sternly advised to behave themselves and told that the charge-hand would give them work to do in due course. The dinner-hour came and went, without anyone else acknowledging their presence and by the middle of the afternoon, they were becoming increasingly restless. The first intimation that they were disturbing anyone came when an angry bellow emanated from behind the large screen, which separated them from the Fitters. When a lad answered back, a very large spanner was lobbed over the screen and it hit the wall near him with a loud thud. Someone was determined that the Foreman's instruction about being quiet had to be obeyed and a few minutes later, a tall, thin Fitter with an angry glint in his eye came over.

'You've got my spanner,' he said quietly and then glaring balefully around him, 'I think you've got my message as well. I don't expect I'll have to send it over again, will I? After all, it's dangerous to throw things about, and somebody might get hurt next time.'

This was their introduction to Sarge, which they would long remember. He was the charge-hand to which the Foreman had referred and he had the reputation of being a most irascible and aggressive character. When he gave someone a job, he expected it to be done right away and without any mucking about. There was no ambiguity about him; he was in charge and if they knew what was good for them, they would do as they were told, first time and with no argument. The man was said to be 'a martinet', who was both helpful and instructive, provided that things went his way. Only when he wasn't obeyed did he become unstable.

They soon learned that Sarge had been made that way by his service in the Army. He had been conscripted soon after the defeat at Dunkirk and had taken to military life like a duck to water. Promotion to full Sergeant had quickly ensued and he had been at El Alamein, the invasions of Sicily and Salerno and then up through Italy. With the War going so much better than in the early years, he had been recalled to the home front and had parachuted into Normandy as part of the D-Day landings. He had been among the first troops to cross the Rhine and had remained in Germany for some months after the cessation of hostilities. For all the horrendous experiences that he had endured, he was a modest man who was dismissive of his own efforts and he always maximised the sacrifices and exploits of others.

After their initial spat, the lads glumly accepted that they were working with a formidable character. He explained that the shop had only just been set up and that everything that passed through was to be carefully checked and inspected, before being installed in the new Submarine.

'At the moment, we haven't got much to do,' he told them, 'but what work there is, I want done properly and without any bother. Just remember, each fitting that you handle will have a vital function in the system into which it is installed. Men's lives will depend on you doing the job properly. Any job, no matter how small, has to be done with care and attention to detail. There will be no half-measures here, so just you heed what I say. I'm not one for bull-shitting, so do your best while you're working here and we'll get along just fine.'

Mike took an immediate liking to the man, and it wasn't long before they were yarning about some of the situations that he had come through in the War. After seeing what some of the German units had done to the civilians in Italy and Northern France, he had had no truck with the Gestapo and SS. He maintained that the vast majority of the 'Wehrmacht' had been decent, honourable soldiers, who had had a rotten job to do. They had fought well over a very long time and often in terrible conditions. However, the SS had been a totally different kettle of fish. While the Allies had been ordered to treat their prisoners with humanity, the SS troops they had captured had often been shot out of hand. Mike was appalled by his admission, but Sarge was adamant that he and his pals had done nothing more than rid the earth of what he cynically called 'vermin'.

'We entered a village one morning and, unlike the other places that we'd liberated, no one came out of the houses to greet us. We soon learned why, because most of the people had been wiped out, including the women and children. Their bodies had been taken into the church during the night, probably by the Resistance and when we arrived, the stench was sickening. It's something that I'll never forget as long as I live. Later we made contact with what remained of the local men and gave them what arms we could; mostly rifles and ammunition that we'd captured or picked up from dead Krauts. Later on that day, we caught up with the bastards that had done it. As we thought, they were SS and we shot every last one of them. Our young Lieutenant tried to stop it, but there was no getting in the way of the Frenchmen. Their vengeance was very sweet.'

The above tale will probably give the reader the impression that Sarge was little better that those he killed. However, his compassionate side was borne out by another of his tales. Months later, his platoon had relieved another unit who had lost a lot of their men to snipers. When they came under fire, his troop had dislodged them by the use of hand grenades and a friendly tank. A group of 'Gerries' came up out of a cellar to surrender and he and his men were astounded to find that they were mostly boys of about fourteen or fifteen years of age. Although he had been told to take them back as Prisoners of War, Sarge took the youngsters to their homes. The SS had rounded-up them up the day before and had given each lad a cap and a great-coat, then shown them how to fire a rifle. Their duty was to fight and die for the Reich. After it was all over, Sarge and his companions called at the home of two of the lads and were welcomed with open arms by their parents. In the years that had passed since then, he had regularly visited them and been delighted to see what fine young men their lads had become.

'There's no glory in War,' he said quietly, 'and I should know, I've seen enough of it. It's a never-ending nightmare of pain, misery and suffering and the World isn't any better for all the poor buggers that died or had their lives destroyed. We had a job to do but I wouldn't want to go through it all again.'

The weeks passed quickly, even though the lads could have been better employed. The training that they had previously received in overhauling valves stood them in good stead and it was rare for anyone to have any complaints about their work. There was no misbehaviour, though many situations were enjoyed to the full. Spring gave way to Summer and with their working environment being so relaxed, they were mostly content. One morning though, Danny cause 'a rumpus', when he raised the matter of piece-work with Sarge. From his reaction, one would have thought that he had mouthed the gravest of insults, because the man immediately exploded.

'I've bloody well told you how this job is, haven't I, cocker?,' he yelled. 'Are you taking the piss or what? If you are, I'll have your bloody guts for garters. I've been watching you and I don't like what I've seen. You're a bloody idler and no mistake, so how you reckon you're going to earn anything on piece-work is beyond me. You know there isn't much for us to do, so what are you on about, eh?.'

The lad could have curled up and died because, by the time Sarge finished with him, he didn't know whether he'd been 'punched, bored, drilled or reamed'. The only excuse for his indiscretion was that he had become bored with the inactivity and had sought to relieve it by provoking someone else. In picking on the charge-hand, he'd chosen the wrong man. Later, when the boss had calmed-down, he went over and apologised.

'It's alright lad,' he was told, 'if it wasn't you, it'd probably be some other stupid sod asking daft questions. It happens all the time, so I suppose I should be used to it by now.'

Not long after, Mike was sent to report to a Foreman down in the Yard and was told to work with Malcom. He was based in a small workshop, alongside a dry-dock and he serviced refrigeration equipment. He was cold and distant but the lad knew that respect was imperative, when starting with a new mentor. The man commented that he had taken his time coming over, it being well past eleven when he arrived. He briefly explained what the job entailed, and then bluntly told him that he could either pay attention and learn, or he couldn't, the choice was his. He handed over a refrigeration manual and then disappeared for the rest of the day. Anyone who is experienced in such circuits will know that to a novice, they are incomprehensible. A fridge plant is complicated and practical tuition is a valuable part of the learning process. Malc was not at all happy about imparting it to a mere apprentice.

In the first week, Mike docilely followed him about, carrying the tools and fetching anything he required. One morning, they went to a canteen to service the main fridge unit which had a meat and a veg room, with the former being in need of attention. He straightaway asked Mike questions about what could be wrong with it, which amply demonstrated that the lad had absolutely no idea. After a few minutes, he told him he was 'thick and bloody useless', like so many other of the daft sods who'd been sent to work with him. Mike protested that he was interested in the job, but knew absolutely nothing about refrigeration to which Malc retorted that he had given him a manual and demanded to know why he hadn't read it. He then sent Mike to fetch a bottle of Freon from the shop.

On his way back, Mike bumped into Phil and the lad told him it was best to ignore Malc's moods and just do what he was told. He had worked with him some months previously and had suffered the same sort of treatment. In time, he had thawed, and they had had a normal relationship. Mike went back on board in a happier frame of mind and was determined to follow his mate's advice. Malc connected the bottle to the system, with a short length of copper-pipe and while he was recharging the refrigerant, Mike had a look at the manual. His boss took a small blow-lamp from his tool bag and showed him how to check if a compression joint was tight and in fact, he had already renewed some faulty fittings. He then sat back, took his paper out of his pocket and told Mike carry on checking the external pipework.

He then went on to make a similar inspection of the pipework inside both rooms. With all checks completed, Malc started up the compressor and with everything in order, the job was completed. They spent the remainder of the day resting and when Mike asked what they were going to do next, he was told to keep quiet and study the manual. The next morning, he was surprised to hear his boss tell the Foreman that the job was well on, with just a few small items remaining to clear. The truth of the matter didn't come into it. A couple of days later, Malc announced that he wouldn't be in the shop for a couple of days, as he was going to do a job at Herstmonceaux. The lad had no idea as to where or what the place was and he optimistically thought he would be going on the jolly as well. He was quickly disillusioned.

'Oh, no!,' said his boss with mock severity, 'Apprentices are not allowed to go on overnight trips. Don't worry though, I'll leave a list of jobs for you to do while I'm away, so you won't get bored.'

A number of large houses inside the Yard were occupied by Senior Naval Officers and one had reported that their fridge wasn't working. Mike was told to go and have a look at it and when he arrived, he committed the cardinal sin of knocking at the front door. It was eventually opened by a rather grand and exceedingly posh lady, who peremptorily told him that 'the Tradesmen's entrance was around the back'. The back door was opened by the Officer's manservant and he took the lad through to the pantry to show him the offending unit. While they were discussing it, a bell on the wall rang and the man went upstairs to answer 'Her Ladyship's' summons. He could hardly contain his mirth when he came back, because she was greatly offended at Mike's audacity in calling at the front door. It was, he said, beneath her dignity to even speak to a common workman.

Mike saw right away that there was a loose connection in the pipework and that the gas charge had leaked away. He told the man he'd report back to the office and would return the next day to fix it. The next morning, he went back up the Yard, with a labourer towing a hand trolley. Their instruction was to pick up the fridge and take it back to the shop. Not having a replacement unit, they would service it and return it as quickly as possible. The servant grumbled that he would 'get it in the neck', when her Ladyship found out. Back in the shop, the defective fittings were replaced and the system recharged. After testing, it was taken back to the house and by the end of the day, it had been reinstalled and was working normally. When he returned to the shop, the Foreman admonished Mike for his 'faux-pas' in calling at the front door. Obviously, some bugger had complained.

'Bloody hell, lad,' he said with a hint of a smile, 'that's the best one I've heard for a long time. I don't think anyone has done that before. Just remember, when you are sent to one of the Senior Officers' houses, you go to the back door and don't forget to tip your forelock, if the resident speaks to you.'

It was not the last that Mike heard of the incident. When Malc returned and was told about what he had done, he was very critical of the lad's lack of tact.

'I'd have thought that you would have known better than to have pulled a stunt like that,' he complained at some length. That's the trouble with you Apprentices, you never think about what you're doing.'

A week or so later, they were sent to do the annual service of the refrigeration plant at a Galley in the Royal Marine Barracks, which was located outside the Yard. While getting their tools and equipment together, confirmation as to just how much of a 'funny bugger' Malc was became evident. One of the things he did was to transfer a charge of Freon gas from a large to a much smaller bottle. When Mike asked him what he was doing, he was off-hand but, when pressed, he explained.

'Oh, we don't to haul that bloody great bottle about,' the man replied. 'A small one will be more than sufficient for the job we're going to do.'

'You could have said that when you sent me back to the shop on my first day,' retorted the lad. 'I lugged that bloody great bottle across the Yard just to please you.'

'That's your hard luck,' responded Malc with a sardonic grin. 'If you'd had your wits about you, you would have seen the smaller one on the bench and brought that.'

While they were walking up the hill towards the barracks, Mike remembered what Charlie had said during the first few weeks of his Apprenticeship. 'Under no circumstance should anyone 'mess' with the Royal Marines', so good behaviour was most definitely called for. When they arrived, Malc reported to the Chief Cook and they were taken over to the cold rooms. After checking everything was switched off and it was safe to enter them, they set to work to check out each unit. Some time later, Mike became aware that something untoward was happening. His boss had disappeared and he was inspecting the coils inside the veg room when he was joined by a very large Wren Cook. She had carefully closed the door behind her as she came in and smirking suggestively, she asked him 'if he wanted a bit of fun'. Having heard of the pranks played on Apprentices while out on jobs, he neatly turned the tables on the lass.

'I should say so,' he replied, with a broad grin. 'Come on then.'

As he moved towards her, the smirk disappeared and she quickly went back out through the door. There was a loud cheer from her mates and when he followed her out, he was told by one of them that he had well and truly 'fettled her'. Later, as they were making their way back to the Yard, Malc explained that the same woman had taken the piss out of a succession of his lads and it was the first time anyone had called her bluff. He doubted she would try her tricks again.

Chapter 14

Domestic Strife

As noted previously, the parents of the teenagers in the village often indulged in match making, if they thought that some help was called for along the matrimonial way. It was fraught with problems, because if either party rejected their potential partner, grave offence could be caused to the other family. If it all came apart later, serious recriminations would often ensue.

When Mike told his mates about his mother's latest antics, they were in fits of laughter. Unbeknown to him, she had been discussing such a match with a woman in the same street and their cosy little chats, over a nice cup of tea, had gone well. When she told him what had been agreed, he rejected it out of hand. His mother was crestfallen and angrily berated him for an ungrateful sod, saying she only had his best interests at heart. She then changed tack, saying what a lovely girl his intended was and that he wouldn't get the same chance again.

The argument went on until in exasperation, she loudly demanded to know what she was going to say to Mrs Turner.

'I don't care what you tell her,' Mike replied. 'Her Jean is a fat lump and as dull as ditch water. I'm not surprised she's so desperate to get shut of her.'

'I don't know why you bother with the cocky young sod,' interrupted his father. 'He's far too big for his boots and thinks he's much too good for any girl around here. If you ask me, she'll be only too pleased not to have anything to do with him,' he added contemptuously. There was more than a grain of truth in his comments.

Mike ignored him and after a few more 'what am I going to tell her mother?'s', the argument ended. The next day, she told him that Jean's mother was 'very upset', when she'd told her of Mike's lack of interest. A few days later, he met the woman coming out of the post office and when he spoke to her, she glared at him and said that she had nothing to say to him. He persisted and quietly explained that he intended to go away to sea when he finished his time. It wouldn't be right to get married, then leave his wife at home for months at a time.

'I've known your Jean for a long time and I'm sure she'll understand,' he went on. 'She's a lovely lass and will make a good wife for some lucky chap.'

He was relieved when the lady replied that she understood only too well his reasons for not wanting to settle down. She had put up with years of loneliness, while her husband had been at sea and she wouldn't wish that on her daughter. They parted on good terms. Some days later, his mother told him that she had seen Mrs Turner and she hadn't seemed to be all that bothered by his rejection. Mike didn't enlighten her as to the reason why.

There was yet another upset at home, due to his mother's intrusive attitude. Despite his long-standing and numerous protests, she still had no thought for his privacy and when he arrived home one evening, she told him with a smirk that there was a letter for him on the sideboard. When he picked it up, he saw it had been opened and promptly 'blew his top'.

'Why have you opened my letter?' he cried furiously. 'It's private and none of your business.'

'Don't you speak to your mother like that,' interrupted his father angrily. 'You'll shut your trap when you're in this house and if you don't like it, then get your bloody letters sent elsewhere.'

'Nobody ever writes to me,' his mother wailed. 'I never get any letters and anyhow, you're only eighteen and I've got a right to know what you're up to. If you don't like it, you can always go into lodgings,' she said, sniffing loudly and looking abjectly at the old man for support.

It was rare for the house to be in any semblance of normality and each time his mother looked for trouble, all the old man could say was that if he didn't like it, he could bugger off.

Another incident, which caused ructions, was when he came home to find his mother sitting 'bolt upright' at the table, which had been cleared of everything but a single object which she had positioned exactly in the centre.

'What's this,' she demanded, rigid with righteous indignation and pointing dramatically with a vertical digit at the offending object.

'A johnny,' replied the cheeky young sod.

'Don't you speak to me like that,' she shouted angrily. 'I won't stand for it.'

'I wouldn't have to, if you didn't go through my pockets,' he retorted angrily.

His father intervened in much the same vein as before and later, Mike tried to explain that if she had asked him quietly, he would have told her that there was no 'big deal' to the offending object. One of his workmates had 'half-inched' (stolen) a box of Durex from a barber's shop and had brought it into work. He had only bought one, to avoid being different, because not have done so would have brought scorn from the other lads. He had put it in his pocket and forgotten all about it and there it had remained until his mother had found it.

'I've asked you time and again not to go through my pockets,' Mike said, this time in a much more reasonable tone, 'but you still take no notice.'

The old man replied that he would have to put up with it, while he remained in his house, as he couldn't be trusted to keep out of trouble. The thing was, Mike had never been in any trouble, apart from the odd incidents of nonsense with the village Bobby, but that cut no ice. He was tempted to say that the best way to keep out of trouble with a girl was to use a johnny, but wisely didn't do so.

'Just remember that when you signed my indentures,' he said to his father, 'you agreed to give me a home for the duration of my Apprenticeship, so let's have no more rubbish about my leaving.'

'You'd be much better off in lodgings,' chipped in his mother, who was determined to keep the argument going. If the old man was venting his spleen on Mike, then at least he was leaving her alone.

'I'll go in my own good time and not before,' Mike replied stiffly and walked out.

When he arrived at work one morning, his right hand was strapped up and his mates sensed that there was something wrong. They knew he had had a miserable childhood, but they hadn't appreciated the extent of the violence which his father had regularly perpetrated on him. There had always been tension in the house, which he had resolved by physically assaulting either his wife or son. From a very early age, the lad had regularly been confined in a dark, cold bedroom and had often thought that the loneliness and despair was worse than being beaten. The rows had got progressively worse of late and the previous evening, when the old man had advanced on him with his fists clenched, something had snapped and he had reacted without thought.

'You mean to say you hit him?,' said one of his mates in a shocked voice.

'Yes,' Mike replied. 'I just couldn't take it anymore.'

His admission was discussed at some length and someone remarked that no matter what his father did to him, he would never retaliate.

'Have you got any idea what it's been like all these years?,' Mike asked him. 'I've been regularly beaten and ill-treated and have lived in constant fear of what he was going to do to me. It's been a life of hell and I've had enough of it.'

One of the lads said his father had never laid a hand on him and he couldn't imagine living like that. Others said they had endured similar treatment, though they were quick to say it had not been as bad as what they'd just heard. Mike told them that the root of his problem was that his father had always denied his paternity. Throughout his childhood, he had either ignored or ill-treated him. His elder brother had at a very early age assumed that he could chastise him as well. Being constantly told that 'you're not one of us' and 'you're not wanted here' had been unbearable at times. Mike had thus grown into an introverted and anti-social youth, who didn't make friends easily. Some of the lads were sympathetic, but they were also firmly convinced that he should just leave home. However, some good came out of the latest confrontation. The old man's aggression and ill-treatment declined markedly from then on. He had realised that the defenceless lad, that he had beaten with impunity for so long, would no longer tolerate his mindless violence.

Not all of Mike's tales were dismal and he had his mates in fits of laughter one dinnertime, when he told them about 'their bloody dog'. Some months before, his father had been given what he blandly described as a Labrador pup. The mutt was nothing of the kind, it being a cross between that august animal and something out of the back streets of hell. At nine months old, nothing was safe from his depredations and if anything remotely chewable was left unattended, it was fair game. 'Nicky' was very adept at knocking over milk bottles left on doorsteps, dislodging the caps and lapping-up the milk. One afternoon, the butcher was seen angrily pursuing him down the back alley; the bloody dog having entered his van and made off with a string of sausages. Mike's old man, ignorant bugger that he was, told the man it was his own fault for leaving the van unattended. He reluctantly paid for the sausages, then told his wife that 'they would do' for their tea. His philosophy in life was governed by the principles of 'waste not, want not' and the basic tenets of hygiene were definitely not his most pressing concern.

One morning, the dog came into the house with a package in his mouth. When he was violently sick a few minutes later, they saw that he had stolen a half-pound block of margarine from a neighbour's house. Another trick he pulled was when he went into their back yard and 'lifted' a joint of beef, which had been left on the doorstep by the butcher. It was wrapped in newspaper and was looking very much worse for wear, when the dog brought it in. The old man nonchalantly took it from him, wiped it over with a dirty tea-towel, re-wrapped it in the same paper and put it back on their doorstep. As nothing more was heard about it, the Bodens must have enjoyed their Sunday dinner in complete ignorance of what had happened to their joint.

One evening, Al had an altercation in the pub with a man who crossly complained that the dog had chewed his hat. He had left it on the floor by his chair and their ensuing argument went as follows:

'Your bloody dog has chewed my hat,' shouted the furious owner.

'How d'you know it was my dog?' retorted Al, who knew bloody well what the mutt had done.

'Because I took it off him,' replied the owner. 'You want to keep him under control.'

'Well, you shouldn't have left it on the floor,' said Al, conscious of the snickering in their audience.

'I don't like your attitude,' snarled the owner.

'It's not my 'at 'e chewed, it's yours,' countered Al, to a great roar of laughter.

With 'fisticuffs' imminent, the landlord came from behind the bar and broke up the altercation. The old man must have decided that enough was enough and when another customer, who had clearly enjoyed the argument, said that he would take Nikki 'off his hands', he accepted the offer with alacrity. The family was greatly relieved that the bloody dog had gone out of their lives. A few weeks later, the man told Mike that he had settled in well with his family and they all thought the world of him. After having been taken to the bus stop to meet his daughters off the school bus a few times, Nicky now went off on his own to greet them. Obviously, his new home suited him and he had responded accordingly. It was hard to believe it was the same dog.

Al was 'a light-fingered magpie' and he regularly 'lifted' things, not all of which were useful. Being a policeman in no way inhibited him from helping himself to other people's property, whenever the opportunity arose. He came by various hand-tools, which he said he'd found lying around. He really surpassed himself when he brought home a ten gallon can of chocolate-brown paint and promptly set to work painting every piece of wood in the house. He couldn't give it away and ultimately, what was left was buried in the garden.

Another stunt was almost beyond belief. He had 'palmed' a screwdriver, which a carpenter had left in the police-post in which he was on duty. For some time after, he studiously removed a large number of brass screws from a huge pile of empty ammunition boxes, which were stacked nearby. Every time he came home, he would empty his pockets of dozens of assorted screws. In a couple of months, they added up to a wooden box full, which weighed perhaps fourteen pounds or more. One afternoon, 'Arry and Bert came by and, seeing the box of screws, the little man made an offer for it.

'I'll give you 'arf a dollar for that bit o' brass, Al,' he said craftily.

'Like hell you will,' came the indignant reply. I've been collecting those screws for the past two months, and a lot of hard work has gone into it as well.,

After a noisy argument, they settled on the princely sum of seven shillings and sixpence (37.5 pence) and they were both well pleased with their bargain.

Some time later Fred, from two doors away, was heard complaining to another neighbour that he had bought a load of old ammunition boxes for firewood and when they were delivered, most of the screws were missing. Previous loads had yielded him sufficient money to pay for the wood, but this time, he was going to be 'well out of pocket'. Mike could have told him who the 'tea-leaf' was. Al thought himself very clever in pulling one over on the old bugger, even though the gain had been hardly worth the effort.

Chapter 15

The Social Scene

Public houses and Working Men's Clubs provided all manner of leisure facilities for many people. The larger companies in the town had extensive recreational facilities, which were provided for the benefit of their Employees. Some had beautifully maintained sports grounds, which were used for football, cricket, tennis and the many other outdoor activities which were popular. The bars in the Social Clubs sold beer and spirits at a considerable discount to the pubs and they had very large rooms in which social evenings, dances, whist drives and a new craze, bingo sessions were held. Billiards and snooker, darts were also catered for. Educational or cultural facilities were often well supported, and plays and concerts put on. Not all their workers used the facilities, perhaps that being due to the cost of socialising being beyond their means.

The Clubs regularly arranged outings to the seaside or to the London theatres and main sporting events. In general, they catered for whatever took their members' fancies. However, family life was changing and the disciplines and values, which had held sway for so very many years, were being slowly eroded away. They were increasingly seen by the younger generation as having little relevance to what was termed as 'the modern scene'. Parents and grandparents were often heard bemoaning the fact that their off-spring had little respect for their elders, their complaints being usually accompanied with rueful comments. Had anything changed since they were young?

'Young people don't behave like we did,' they went on. 'They think they can do anything they like, with no thought for anyone else. When we were young, we had to do as we were told or we got what for.'

The lot of most working folk had recently started to improve and the more some people had, the more they wanted. The social changes, which should have followed the misery and suffering of the First World War, had not materialised, but they had certainly done so after the Second. As the workers got the taste of the better things in life, they increasingly demanded a fairer share of the fruits of their labour. Who would now put up with cold, fat-back bacon and a raw onion for dinner or a slice or two of bread and beef-dripping for tea, while their 'betters' lived off the fat of the land? One of the main reasons for the steady improvement was full-employment and with skilled labour being in short supply, the Unions flexed their muscles and were prepared to fight for a better standard of living for their members. There was an air of militancy abroad, which they exploited to the full.

'We're no longer content to scrabble around under the table and meekly pick up the few crumbs the management grudgingly puts our way,' one Steward was heard to say. 'What we want is a slice of the cake and what's more, we want some of the cream off the top as well!'

Another Steward aptly summed up the general attitude by saying,

'You should always see the Employer as a sack full of pennies, with a small hole in the bottom. You've got to be just as determined as he is and shake and shake the bloody sack and pick up the pennies, one by one, as they fall out.'

When asked what should be done when the sack was empty, he lugubriously replied, 'You drop it and pick up another one.'

The grinding poverty, which had endured among the working people for so long, was rapidly becoming a thing of the past. A lot of them had money to spend for the first time in their lives and they were determined to enjoy it to the full. Social commentators often refer to the politically motivated, 'mindless' militancy, which in time became the norm for so many years. If we are honest, we must admit that things did get out of hand, with prolonged strikes, 'works to rule' and bans on overtime. On the other hand, there had always been large-scale corporate greed, with Directors of Companies helping themselves to huge salaries and outrageous emoluments while at the same time, cynically limiting the pay of their workers to the absolute minimum. Such greed was just as prevalent then as it remains today.

As Mi8ke was so poi8ntedly told, we owe a debt of gratitude to the legions of men and women who suffered great hardship, over many years, in their fight for better pay and working conditions. Nowhere was their suffering more amply demonstrated than in the agricultural industry where, in general terms, the rise in Farmers' incomes had been meteoric. They had recently enjoyed a standard of living which only a few years before would have been unimaginable. Most of them benefited hugely from the substantial increases of prices and the many subsidies which appertained to their crops and after their own years of relative poverty, many became very well off. Few of them had either the thought or decency to give their workers more than they were obliged to do under the Minimum Agricultural Wage Agreement. While they had waxed fat, their workers remained at the bottom of the wage league for very many years.

Woe betides the man who had the temerity to complain or was suspected of agitating in the common cause. It was not unusual for him to be sacked and promptly evicted from his 'tied' cottage. Many farmers would not have members of the Agricultural Union working for them. As British industry recovered, large numbers of labourers left the land to work in the factories and on construction sites. Rapid strides were being made in the design and operating functions of all manner of farm machines and it wasn't long before there was a growing shortage of men, with the requisite skills and experience, to work them. Only when their pay and conditions became more generous, did the lot of the men improve but even then, the additional benefits they received did not compare with those enjoyed by skilled workers in other industries.

By the late fifties, many families went away in the summer for a week or odd days at the seaside. Few could afford to stay in a hotel, so they went either to a boarding house or a caravan near a beach. On their return, they would tell their neighbours about their experiences and their accounts were often boring to those who still couldn't afford to go away. The stories they told were varied, with some having had 'a wonderful time' in clean, comfortable digs, good food and with a friendly landlady. There were also dreadful tales of where it had all gone badly wrong. The weather had been awful and the rooms were cold and dirty, with 'bloody awful' food. The teller would indignantly inform his listener(s) that 'they would not be going back there again'.

That they had been able to afford a holiday for the first time was a matter of pride and some would never admit that it had been a complete disaster and usually, it was their kids that 'blabbed'. Holidays were a growing trend and soon, more and more people were going much further afield than hitherto.

The coming of television in the early fifties changed the whole way of family life for the majority of people and they gradually became more 'insular' and took less part in their community activities. The word 'community' no longer appertains in many of our towns and villages, as it once did and half a century later, people's aspirations are very much different from what they once were. The pursuit of pleasure though has not changed in that it has always been an important part of people's lives, particularly when they are young. In those days, the cinema still played a large part in their entertainment and even poor families went to 'the pictures' regularly.

British made War films were very popular and depicted the heroic deeds of the Armed Forces and our Allies in their monumental struggle against oppression. The Americans made many more, nearly all of which demonstrated how they had won the War on their own. Their manipulation of the historical facts often provoked comments in the Press and there were loud jeers from the ex-Servicemen present. They ignored the plain truth that we would have most certainly lost the War, without the Americans support, which had started even before they entered the conflict. Children regularly went to Saturday morning matinees, to see cartoons, cowboy and adventure films, which were mostly American-made. In its heyday, the cinema was a relatively cheap means of entertainment, but as we've said, the advent of television was already beginning to change things.

The main pleasure for the young males was sport, either playing or watching it. Apart from the most pressing need to procreate, there was the age-old need to compete with one's peers. The Apprentices' interests were broadly based and the extent of their differences was amply demonstrated by one lad, who had signed on for a well-known football club, while another was learning Russian! It is a popular misconception that life today is more violent and that we live in a less honest society than in the past. However, the general pattern of crime has changed and is worse in some respects than it used to be. There is more sexual and domestic crime, (rape, indecent assault and burglary) and the curse of mugging is a serious problem.

As a Society, we have become more selfish and individual greed has grown inexorably, apace with the vast improvements in the standard of living. Some aspects of our lives have improved though. For example, wife-beating and the ill-treatment of children was once a generally accepted practice for a lot of people. 'Spare the rod and spoil the child' was often the dictum and the results were plain to see. While it still goes on, it doesn't seem to be quite so widespread as it once was.

The problem of drug abuse is the one dreadful development in this modern age. In the fifties, the only people who 'did them' were the ones with plenty of money. Most people had barely enough to live on, let alone buy drugs. 'Beer and baccy' and, to a lesser extent, minor gambling, were the main vices of most working people. While crime statistics may indicate otherwise, comparisons are very difficult to make. Statistics mostly relate to the offences that actually come to Court. These days, we have a large number of highly-paid academics, lethargically loafing about in the Universities at great cost to the taxpayer, with the time and expensive computer facilities to enable them to produce useless surveys and analyses. All too often, their findings are based on their politically prejudiced assimilation of the so-called facts.

Regarding burglary, there was little point in 'turning over' the vast majority of houses, because the residents had little worth stealing and besides, any such incident was promptly dealt with, either by the families involved or others living nearby. You didn't steal from your own and the Police were not involved if it could possibly be avoided. Retribution then was often swift and drastic and there was no point in the burglar(s) complaining that they had been assaulted, as happens so very often today. The local Bobby was content to let people sort things out for themselves. So very often, the old and vulnerable are now viciously beaten and often cruelly injured, sexually assaulted and murdered even, by the morons who are intent on robbing them. Such animal behaviour was not tolerated and nor should it be now.

The current tendency is to do everything possible to 'help and rehabilitate' criminals and, all too often, to ignore the interests of the injured parties. Householders are regularly charged with assaulting a felon, while the low life is allowed to walk away scot-free. One only has to consider the case of Tony Martin, who was cynically prosecuted and imprisoned for protecting his property, to appreciate just how serious the problem has become. There is a growing frustration at the inability of successive Governments, the Police and the Courts to tackle the problem. In the fifties, there was perhaps a little more 'common courtesy' and respect for others among ordinary working people and it's true that people didn't have lock their doors and bar the windows of their homes but having said that, it was often wise to do so.

As we have said, violence in the home, on the streets and in public places, such as dance halls, clubs, pubs was just as serious a problem as it is now. Youngsters would often turn up in force at a dance and following a 'set-to', it would come to an early end. One spat would beget another one soon after, where those that had been bested sought their revenge. Alcohol was the basis of their courage, which was needed for the fun and games and the opposing factions would initially line up facing each other across the hall. The next half hour would see an increase in both noise and tension, despite the frantic efforts of the organisers to keep the peace. The girls would be among their lads, egging them on and making disparaging remarks about the virtue of the lasses standing opposite. Before the 'proverbial' hit the fan, the girls on both sides would retire behind their lads and without any more ado, all hell would break loose.

Around Christmas time, the organisers would try to ensure that their 'knees-ups' would be trouble-free, by making their functions 'all-ticket'. Known troublemakers, who somehow came by their tickets, would be turned away at the door. There would be an immediate problem, if the officious bugger in charge refused to reimburse their money. Their strategy often worked but, the ingenuity and persistence of their unwanted patrons was often difficult to overcome. Forged tickets were used to gain entry and a couple could gain entry by someone else purchasing their tickets by 'bone-fide' means. They would then go immediately into a back room, open a window and pass their half-tickets, which had been retained as 'pass-outs', to their mates. Ultimately, those in charge would become aware that they had far more revellers than had been planned.

It could be a serious problem in a large hall, with three to four hundred people present; the maximum to be allowed in would have been previously agreed with the authorities. When the organisers went to evict the intruders, things could quickly get out of hand, particularly if they were heavy-handed. If the ensuing rumpus spilled out on to the street, it caused yet more problems for the Policemen, who had been sent to maintain order. It was not unknown for some of the patrons to be carrying knives, razors or knuckle dusters and if things weren't going their way, they were not always loathe to use them. The funniest incident occurred one evening when a highly excited yob pulled out a pistol and excitedly waved it around, shouting dire threats to those around him. The punters, who had been shaping up well for the 'set-to', saw it was a fake and fell about laughing. That was the end of that particular bit of trouble.

Nita was a regular at the dances in the Town Hall and she was in her mid-twenties, short in stature and 'well made'. Being a very competent dancer, she was never short of partners to trip her way through the evening's proceedings. She always held them closely, with regular contact being made with the insides of her most ample thighs. One evening, Barry came back from a waltz and he was shaking with laughter. Apparently, the lass had felt something hard in their contact area and had asked him what he had in his pocket. Seeing him 'lost for words', she had asked him again, just as the music ended and her voice carried across the floor.

'Here, what've you got in your pocket? You're not one of them there cosh-boys we've been hearing about, are you?'

There was a loud outburst of laughing among his mates, which momentarily stilled the buzz of conversation in the rest of the hall. They had all enjoyed the same sensation while dancing with the buxom lass.

Itinerant workers, who were employed on the big new Power Stations and Oil Refineries under construction in the area, also frequented the dances. The weekend was when they let their hair down, which they did with gusto and where better than in the nearby towns and villages? The locals soon became aware of the threat to 'their women' and reacted accordingly. The Irish lads were among them usually most sociable, but were only too willing to 'mix-it' with anyone who was 'looking for it'. 'With the drink taken', they were formidable opponents and many of the locals, who had thought themselves 'hard', learned a painful lesson. They had cash in their pockets and, more importantly, they were willing to spend it. In contrast, the locals kept a tight hold on their money. Some of the girls transferred their affections and it wasn't long before their beaus visited their homes. Inevitably, some of them found themselves 'booked' for an early marriage, which caused great mirth when 'the Father' was seen visiting a family with a crestfallen Paddy in tow.

Chapter 16

The End of the Year

One morning, Malcom and Mike were sent to service a fridge in an Officer's house. On arrival, the lady of the house let them in and told Malc she had to go out for an hour or so. When they were finished, he was to be sure to lock the door and to leave the key under a pot outside. That gave him the welcome opportunity to skive off and as long as Mike didn't go back to the shop, he would be in the clear. It should have been the end of the matter but of course, it wasn't. The lad had been sitting comfortably in the kitchen, reading his paper, when the lady came back. He told her that they had just finished and his boss had gone off to do another small job. She remarked that one of the rings on her electric cooker wasn't working and asked him to have a look at it. Though a job for an electrician, he found the fault and reattached the power lead, which had come adrift from the ring. Having then accepted her offer of a cup of tea, he spent the best part of the next hour chatting to her.

When his boss returned, he was far from pleased and after making a final check of the fridge, they took their leave. The lady told Mike she had enjoyed their chat and he should 'call-in' anytime to see her again.

'Like hell you will,' said Malc crossly, as they made their way down the Yard. 'You'll get us both shot by messing about like that. What if her old man had come home to find the pair of you chatting so cosily? You bloody well watch it in future and don't do that again.'

He was well aware of the ramifications to him personally, had her husband had cause to complain. It mattered not that nothing untoward had happened and he was dismissive of Mike's suggestion that she was a bit lonely and had just needed someone to talk to.

'I've told you before, when we're working in the Navy's houses, we have to be very careful,' Malc went on. 'You've got to be discreet and not put yourself in a situation which could be open to misinterpretation. More to the point, you might get me into bloody trouble as well, by looking at jobs which don't concern us.'

He then made Mike laugh so much, that tears ran down his cheeks. With his usual deadpan expression, he explained at some length the etiquette of using the toilet in an Officer's house. It was, he said, something which had to be avoided if at all possible.

'It's best if you can hold on to it, but if you're caught short, never ask permission from the lady of the house. Her servant, if she has one, may let you use the one below stairs,' he went on sonorously but, if you've been on the beer the night before and have made a bit of a smell, then you'll have a problem.

There are things you can to do, though only as a last resort. It's a well-known fact that if you strike a match in the bowl, the gas will burn off and the smell will disappear, like magic.'

'That's no use to me,' interrupted Mike, 'I don't have any matches, because I don't smoke.'

'Well, if that's the case,' replied his Fitter, 'you'll just have to take deep breaths, until it's all gone.'

Mike could contain himself no longer and he roared with laughter.

'You really have missed your vocation,' he said to his grinning mentor, who was highly amused at his own wit. 'By heck, you really had me going there.'

For most of their time together, Malc had been both serious and unsmiling. However, when in the mood, he had a dry and cynical wit about life. Mike never did find out where he disappeared to, when he went AWOL, which had happened regularly. It couldn't have been a woman, because he had not shown any interest in the opposite sex. Most of the Fitters were only too pleased to talk about their lives outside of work, but Malc had told him nothing about his home and interests. His private life was just that and in summary, he was an enigma, who was easy to work with and the jobs they did were both interesting and varied.

The beginning of July came and with it, the last few weeks of Mike's third year. The start of the fourth would see him and his mates working out in the Yard and in addition to a substantial increase in their basic pay, they would get further emoluments, from overtime and adverse condition payments. There would also be the opportunity to work on bonus jobs and in discussing it all, the lads were reiterated their determination not be exploited, as so many other Apprentices had been. For the first time, they would be well paid and they were looking forward to that very much. There was also a lot of talk about what they were going to do in their forthcoming holidays. While some would be going away, most would still be spending their time at home and plans were made to meet up and perhaps go to a County Cricket match or have a day out at the seaside. As before, Mike was going to work on a Farm and thereby put a bit more money aside for the future. As last year, his parents and sister were going down to Cornwall and he would again be looking after himself and while he was telling them about it, one of the lads had a bright idea.

'We could have a bit of a do at your place,' he cried. 'An all-night party would be just the job. We'd have a kitty for the beer and soft drinks and the girls would provide the food, or we could send out for fish and chips. I reckon that's a smashing idea, don't you lads?'

'You can bloody-well forget that,' Mike said hotly. 'I've heard what your parties are like and there's no way I'm going to be cleaning-up after you wreck the place. My old man would have a fit if he knew I'd let you lot into the house. No, you can bugger off. Besides, when I've been out at work all day, I'll be too tired for a party.'

'You're always telling us you're putting money away for a rainy day, Mike,' said another lad. 'What's that all about? When are you going to spend it and what on?'

Mike was reluctant to explain but when pressed, he told them of his plans to own his own house. It brought jeers from some, though others thought there was no harm in dreaming. His aim was, he said, to finish his time, then 'strike-out' on his own. That would resolve the problem with his parents for once and for all. In the meantime, living at home remained a matter of convenience, which was not altogether understood by his mates.

'You're a silly sod, if you ask me,' said one lad. 'You put up with all the rows and unpleasantness, just to save a few bob? I'm buggered if I'd do it.'

Mike had recently been looking at the flats which were advertised in the local paper and in Estate Agents' windows and had estimated that he would need at least three hundred pounds before he could even think of making a move. He'd have to rent a furnished flat initially, then perhaps buy a larger, more permanent place with a mortgage later. He was steadily adding to his savings and the start of the fourth year would increase them substantially. They laughed when he told them that he had had to find somewhere secure to stash his pass-book, due to his mother's systematic rummages. He had recently done so under the wardrobe in her bedroom, which meant he could only retrieve it when she was out of the house. He was called a devious sod and someone said it was little wonder he had so many problems.

Just before they finished work and were tidying up the shop, Mike was pleasantly surprised when Malcolm gave him a small, buff envelope.

'Here you are lad,' he said, 'something by way of a little bit extra for your holiday.'

'What's this?' Mike asked with a grin. 'You're not having me on again are you?'

'No, no,' said his boss, smiling broadly. 'What I didn't tell you was that most of our jobs have been done on a price. A lot of them were so small, they were hardly worth bothering about, so I agreed with the Foreman that we'd let them all add up until the holiday break. Your share, which I agreed with Bill when you first started, is twenty-five per cent. Don't spend it all at once. Oh and another thing,' he went on, 'don't go blabbing to your mates about it, 'cos I don't want it getting around that I'm a soft touch. I'd only get it in the ear from the other Fitters, so least said and all that jazz eh?'

You could have knocked Mike down with the proverbial feather. Throughout the Yard, the Fitters' shady tricks, re: their 'piece-work' earnings, was a fact of life. He and his mates had suffered at the hands of the ubiquitous Billy in his second year and they had no hope of changing the system. The Apprentices were expected to pull their weight, but it was a long established practice for the Fitters to choose whether or not to give them anything. Some lads had learned a painful lesson, when they'd had the temerity to protest about the unfairness of it all. The stock answer was, the system had worked very well for many years and no changes were necessary. They would all benefit when they were Fitters and should stop 'bitching and get on with the bloody job'.

Malc had 'played the game' without being asked, and Mike had been fortunate to have worked with him. That he had behaved himself had obviously struck a chord. There had been numerous times when his boss had been uncommunicative, sullen even, but Mike had always done as he was told. He couldn't understand how they had made any money, because they had never put themselves out. Now that their time together was at an end, he could only say that he had met a lot worse Fitters. When he later opened the packet, he was delighted to find the princely sum of two pounds, fifteen shillings and sixpence, (£2.775). It was a considerable sum and the following morning, he retrieved his pass-book and went into Town to put it in the bank.

As he had cycled home the previous evening, Mike had been in a good frame of mind because back in the Spring, when he had gone over to see Bert, he had been dismayed when told that he 'wouldn't be required this year'. In fact, the man had been a bit gruff when he explained that he had enough labour for the work ahead. However, all was not lost, because on his way home, he had called in at the pub and spoken to the Farmer who had hired Bert's crawler the year before.

'I was hoping to see you, lad,' Mr Fredericks told him. 'I've heard that you're a handy mechanic and I wondered if you'd like to come and do some work for me?'

They agreed the rate of pay, which was rather more than Bert had paid him and in the ensuing weeks, Mike had worked regular evenings and weekends for him and he would be doing so full-time during his two weeks holiday. He had very much enjoyed working on his Farm and had done all sorts of jobs on tractors and various implements, as well as in the fields. Like last year, the early Summer months had been cool, with a lot of rain, which had delayed the hay-making. Fine weather in the next two weeks would help the job along, though they would have to pull out all the stops, if they were to get the remaining hay in before it spoiled.

When Mike returned home, his mother went on at length about her forthcoming holiday, with a whole list of 'do's and' don't's'. Rather than get into yet another argument, he kept quiet but was mortified when she said she had asked Mrs Cole; the woman next door, to keep an eye on him. As usual, he let it all go in one ear and out the other. Two weeks of peace and quiet was going to be sheer bliss, compared to the nonsense he had to endure, for most of the time. He decided that he would do everything possible to forestall the old busy-body. She had the most annoying habit of walking straight into the house, without knocking and he would have to be constantly on the ball, to ensure she couldn't do so. The back door would be kept locked at all times and he would use the front one to enter and leave the house. He would also keep the curtains drawn, to prevent her from disturbing him and providing he kept a low profile, he would have no problems.

The next morning, his parents left just before eight o'clock and were driven to the station by someone who lived in the village. Soon after, he cycled over the hill, then down across the tracks to the Farm. Just as he arrived, it started to rain heavily. There was work to do in the barn and he joined the men in sorting and bundling a huge pile of old sacks into bundles. It was a dirty job, made all the more difficult by the confined space in which they were working. The boss had bought the sacks as a job lot from a dealer, to facilitate the transportation of his potatoes, which were nearly ready for lifting. Mike was relieved when the Foreman said he would not be required the next day and when he got home, his main thought was for a long, hot soak in the bath and then after a rest, he would go to the fish and chip shop for his dinner.

Being happily ensconced in the bath, his peace of mind was shattered by a loud hammering on the back door, accompanied by increasingly indignant shouts of frustration.

'Come on, open up,' the old girl from next door cried angrily, 'I know you're in there and I want to know what you're up to.'

The racket went on for some time before Mike got out of the bath and opened the bathroom window. He angrily told her that he was in the bath and would be most grateful if she would bugger off and mind her own bloody business. The woman went away, complaining loudly that she wasn't used to being spoken to like that and his mother would certainly hear about it, the minute she came home. Mike closed the window and resumed his ablutions. His adversary was a very determined lady though and she made several more attempts to gain entry, during the next few days. Each time, she was thwarted by the simple expedient of being locked out and ignored. When Mike saw her husband in his garden, he apologised for being rude to his wife, but was surprised when the man was completely unperturbed.

'Don't worry about it, lad,' he said. 'I've told her time and again about interfering and if you've put her right, then it's no more than she deserves.'

There was no further problem and his time on his own passed very pleasantly. The weather cleared up and the hay-making was resumed. Two of the men didn't drive and Mike mostly drove a tractor and trailer out to bring the bales back into the yard. When he called to see Moya's mother, on his way home, there was no sign of the Ferguson tractor. Apparently, Bert had sold it. At the end of the first week, the hay-making was over for the year and his boss had been in a pretty good mood. When Mike asked him if he would be needed on Monday morning, he replied that he would be going to see what was what over the weekend. With a 'bit o' luck', they would be 'taderin' – i.e. 'lifting the potatoes'.

When Mike arrived, the men were busy cleaning the digging machine and making it ready for the job. At nine o'clock, a lorry rolled into the yard with about thirty women on board and a bossy little man in charge. A few minutes of quiet negotiation settled the rate for the job and the work was soon underway. The first field was staked out, row by row, to give each woman an equal opportunity to earn her money and before long, the men were loading the sacks on to the lorry which, when completed, went straight off to the London Market. At the end of the day, more than half the field had been 'lifted' and by the end of the week, all three fields of 'earlies' had been cleared.

On the last Friday afternoon, Mike cycled into the town to pay his cash into the Bank and do a bit of shopping. The fortnight had gone very quickly and he had very much enjoyed the physical work and the change had been as good as a rest. As it happened, he spent a small part of his earnings on a large slice of rump-steak, which he had not had at home before. When he asked the Butcher about the best way to cook it, he had received a number of odd looks from the other customer and was told to lightly salt and pepper the meat on both sides, then to fry it gently in some beef fat, taking care to leave the middle rare. The man even gave him a small piece of dripping to help him on his way. Having bought some chips on the way home, it was the most enjoyable meal he had had for a very long time.

Book 4: The Fourth Year

Chapter 1

A Change for the Better

As anticipated, the fourth year brought a marked change in the lads' working environment. Whereas in the past two years, they had worked in the comfort of the Factory, they were now dispersed around the various Departments across the Yard. They would either be working on the Ships, which were undergoing refits or repairs, or in one of the many Fitting-shops which were situated alongside the basins and dry-docks. Their pay had been substantially increased, to reflect the contribution they would be making to the Sections in which they were working and each lad was given a 'chit', which allocated him to a Foreman, with clear directions to his office. The older lads, who were bent on mischief, had tried to spread alarm and despondency among the lads and they were very apprehensive about how it was all going to turn out.

The prospect of enhancing their earnings, by piece-work, had been very much on their minds for some time and as previously noted, their Fitters would expect them to pitch in and make positive contributions to their efforts. They had been repeatedly warned that some of them could be very aggressive and were not averse to reacting violently when upset. There was also the prospect of being paid for working in abnormal conditions – for example, dirty and confined spaces or on temporary scaffolding. The 'uncas', (unclean conditions payments), were said to be the most readily available and in summary, they were going to be treated as adults and it all made for an exciting time ahead.

There was a lot of excited discussion as they prepared to leave the Factory, but they were not all going out into the Yard. The Upper School lads, who were destined for better things, were continuing with their expert tuition in the warmth and comfort of the Drawing Office. It is a human trait to day dream and Mike had spent many hours in the preceding weeks speculating about what he would be doing. He might as well not have bothered, because in the light of what transpired, it all came as an unpleasant surprise. The Management had kept close tabs on the troublemakers and the ramifications of what they had or had not done was about to be brought home. While some lads found their way into 'cushy' jobs, many others were sent into the dirt and excruciating noise of the working Shipyard, which was not at all to their liking.

Mike and a lad called Dan went over to an office on the side of the No. 1 Dry-dock to report to a Mr MacArthur. He was the Engine-room Foreman on a Frigate, which was undergoing a long refit. It had been well after nine o'clock before they had been given their slips and they had had difficulty in finding a sack-barrow, with which to move their toolboxes and when they arrived, they were greeted by an extremely loud little man, whose stream of invective disconcerted them greatly. He had been 'naffing' waiting for them 'since half-past seven' and 'where the bloody hell had they been?' Mike tried to explain, but it 'cut no ice' with the furious Foreman.

He was widely known as a 'martinet' among the Apprentices and he was having 'none of their bloody excuses'.

'Don't answer me back, you little bastard,' he shouted at Mike, who was head and shoulders taller than he was. 'I'm the bloody Foreman and don't' you naffing well forget it. Don't think for one moment that you can get one over on me, laddie because I'll not have it. Just be warned, the two of you, you're going to have to shift yourselves in my Section. I've been warned about you,' he shouted at Mike, 'and you needn't think I'm going to put up with any of your bloody bullshit.'

It was all too much for the lad. He should have kept his mouth shut, walked out even, and made a complaint to the Manager but, not having the sense to ride the storm of abuse, he interrupted the little man in the full flow of his invective and angrily shouted back at him. Worse still, he was stupid enough to give the man the impression that he was threatening him.

'Don't you call me a bastard, you cantankerous old git,' he retorted angrily. 'You may treat other people like that, but not me. We've not done anything wrong and until we do, you've got no reason to bollock us.'

It was the last thing that the Foreman expected. No one answered him back like that and his face, which had been flushed with anger, drained of blood. He turned away, picked up the telephone and informed his Manager that he had been threatened by an Apprentice. When he put the phone down, he turned to the lads and said, 'I've nothing more to say to you. Wait outside.'

A couple of minutes later, the Manager came hurrying to the office with two other men and curtly asked them if they were the ones who had threatened Mr MacArthur.

'I haven't threatened anyone,' cried Dan in alarm, and he ran off along the side of the dock, heedless of the cries from the Manager to 'come back here.'

The man then turned to Mike and glared angrily at him.

'Follow me,' he said, and they went over to the Factory and up to Barry's office. He told the lad to wait, then went into the office to tell the boss about what had happened. Being close to the door and with the man shouting angrily, the lad heard all that was said.

'If that lout thinks he can get away with threatening my Foreman, then the sooner he learns he won't be working in my Department the better. His behaviour has been completely unacceptable and I'm sure that you'll have something to say to him.'

Mr Barry wasted no time in calling Mike into the office and, when he saw who it was, he exploded in outraged indignation.

'So laddie, despite all the previous advice and warnings, you're in trouble again. You don't seem to have taken any of them in and I might as well not have wasted my breath. To my certain knowledge, this is not the first time you've threatened to assault someone. Well, we've reached the point of no return where you're concerned. You have obviously have no intention of behaving in a civilised way and we have no option but to dispense with your services. Have you anything to say for yourself?,' he asked by way of an afterthought.

'Yes sir, I have,' replied a very chastened Mike. 'When we arrived, the Foreman said that he had been waiting for us since half-past seven and he gave us no chance to explain why we were so late reporting to him. He set about us, shouting and swearing and he refused to listen to anything we had to say. I've never minded a bollocking when I've done something wrong, but we really did report to him as soon as we could. I'm sorry it all got out of hand, but I didn't threaten him in any way. I'm not that daft. He was so angry, effing and blinding and insulting us and with it being so unfair, I admit I lost my temper.'

'How do you mean, you were insulted?,' interrupted Barry.

'He called us bastards, sir, and I don't accept that from anyone.'

At that point, there was a knock on the door, which the Dock Manager answered and Dan's dad came in, with his son close behind. With very many years of service in the Yard, he was greatly respected and seeing who it was, Barry said to him,

'Oh it's you, Fred,' he said. 'As you can see, we're rather busy at the moment.'

'Morning Mr Barry,' Fred replied mournfully. 'My lad here has come to me in some distress about what has gone on this morning and I thought I should come over right away to see if we can sort things out.'

'Ah, you're the other lad are you?,' said Barry to Dan, who nodded dumbly.

He told Mike to wait outside and it must have been a good ten minutes before Dan and his dad came out. With barely controlled anger, he sternly told him to go back into the office and quietly advised him 'to keep his mouth shut'.

'You're a bloody lunatic,' hissed Dan angrily. 'Why couldn't you keep quiet, instead of getting us into this mess?'

'Never mind that for now, Daniel,' said his dad. 'Come on, let's get out of here.'

Mike went back into the office with great trepidation. Both managers were sitting behind Barry's desk and he stood dejectedly before them. Barry, looked sternly over his glasses, and told him that he had just heard Dan's account of what had happened. Contrary to his initial reaction, he now understood that the case was not as straightforward as it had first appeared.

'We've decided against sacking you, but I want to make it perfectly clear. No matter what the provocation, you will not under any circumstance assault or threaten anyone. Your behaviour today will not be tolerated but, because you've said you're sorry about what happened, which is all that can be said for you, we'll give you another chance. With Mr Johnson's agreement, I'm giving you a final warning, which will be confirmed in writing and remain on your record until the end of your Apprenticeship.

'Now, get out and report back to your Foreman and don't let me hear of any more nonsense or you'll very much regret it. There'll be no more chances; that I can promise. You might wish to apologise to Mr McArthur. It's the least you can do.'

Mike was very relieved that the outcome had not been much worse, even though he had been the victim of circumstances. As Barry had said, he had been very lucky and would have to stay out of trouble over the next two years. When he arrived at the office, he met Mr MacArthur coming out and as instructed, he apologised for his behaviour. Dan was standing beside him and it was clear that he had nothing more to say.

'I don't want your bloody apology,' he snarled. 'Just get yourself down below on yon Ship and report to Sam Snaith, who you'll be working with. One more thing laddie, just think on. I'll be watching you closely from now on and I'll not have any more of your bloody nonsense, I'm telling you.'

With that, he turned and stalked off up the road towards the Factory.

The lads put their boxes in the workshop, and then made their way on board the Ship. Mike had quite a job finding his Fitter, because all he knew was that he was working in the after Engine-room. After asking many times, he was directed down into the dark depths but even then, no-one seemed to know where Sam was. He eventually found him under the bottom floor-plates. His new boss was small and wiry in stature, with a shock of unruly light brown hair and a bushy moustache. Mike was greatly relieved when looked up from what he was doing and smilingly greeted him.

'Hello, old mate,' he said, 'where've you been? I've been waiting all morning for you. He then winked at his discomfited Apprentice and went on. 'You've had a bit of bother with old Mac, from what I've heard.'

He grinned widely and the ice was broken. The lad felt the tension go out as he looked at the amiable little man and with a rush of bonhomie, he shook hands with him and said he was very pleased to meet him.

'I'm sorry I'm late,' Mike went on. 'As you say, I've had a bit of bother. By heck, you've got a right bugger there, haven't you? I'm going to have to watch my step with him.'

'Yeah, you could say that' Sam replied. 'He can be a bit of a tartar at times, but we tend to keep out of his way if we can. Some Foremen have a reputation for being a bit awkward, but ours is like that all the time. That's why some people call him 'the poison dwarf', not a 'Scots git', by the way,' he said, again smiling broadly and winking. 'I'm much too respectful to call him anything but Mr McArthur. Anyhow, what got you into his bad books so quick? It's not a very good way to start in a new Department, if I may say so.'

'I think least said, in this case,' replied Mike. 'I'm in enough trouble as it is and I don't want to make things any worse if I can help it.'

'Alright, my old son,' said Sam, 'fair enough. Look, I'll show you what we're doing. See, this drawing? It lists all the underwater valves on the Ship and our job is to open up and inspect each one and where necessary, fix it. Some valves need a lot of work, some don't, but then you'll know all about valves won't you? Actually, I've nearly finished the job, so we should be able to clear it all up by the end of next week. There's plenty of time left on the target and we can get to know each other as we go along. I think we'll keep you well away from Mack, for the time being. We don't want any more problems, do we? When he comes down, say nothing and try to look busy. If he speaks to you, answer with a bit of respect. Anything for a quiet life', he concluded.

And that was how it was left. In a few hours, Mike had gone from being in a very good frame of mind into the depths of despair and then back to some semblance of happiness again. With the ship in dry-dock, there was no problem in stripping whole valves out and taking them up to the Fitting shop on the jetty for refurbishment. The ones that could be done 'in-situ' were quickly dealt with. Later, Sam confirmed what another Fitter had told him and that was, when a ship was at sea, the failure of a valve could have serious consequences. The important thing was that he was both easy-going and friendly and he obviously knew what he was doing.

All the large cooling water inlet and outlet valves, to and from the main and auxiliary condensers, had already been overhauled and from the way he spoke, Sam knew all the dodges and was adept at making the most of any difficulties. The slightest problem had him hot-footing it to the office to make a claim for extra hours, even though the job was awash with time. He explained that when the estimators 'priced' a job, they didn't always take the difficulties fully into account. They were nearly all mean sods, who were always reluctant to give anything away and would never admit it, when they underestimated a job. Very occasionally, they would over-price the work and by keeping quiet about it, the Fitter would make up for the ones that were short. Actually, it's all 'swings and roundabouts', Sam quipped with a big smile.

Chapter 2

Fun and Games

Another lesson was confirmed in Mike's first week with Sam and that was whenever a Draughtsman located a valve in a system, he didn't always consider the access needed for its operation and maintenance. It was a particular problem with the ones which either connected directly on to the Ship's hull or were mounted directly on an internal bulkhead. In mitigation, they had to make the maximum use of all available space, which in most Ships was very restricted. If a valve was located high on a bulkhead and within the webs of two stiffening struts, an internal inspection in situ was impossible. There were any number of valves which, with a little bit of thought, could have been a lot easier to work on and Sam answered Mike's many questions, as they quietly discussed the various systems on which they worked. When they completed a valve, it was checked for smooth operation and 'the nip' was taken off the newly packed gland.

The excruciating noise which the caulkers and riveters made on board was intolerable and Mike suffered a series of chronic headaches. With the hull modifications nearing completion, there was a huge amount of internal work in progress and whole sections were being modified and replaced, with new bulkheads being installed and the requisite holes and doorways being cut out in situ. In contrast to these modern times, there was no Computer Aided Design (CAD) capability in the Drawing Office or laser cutting machines in the Plate shop. The work was done manually by the caulkers and the resultant din was unbearable. Hearing protection, which is now taken as a norm, was not available and Mike often went up to the first aid post for some aspirins and cotton wool to put in his ears.

It was sod's law that Mac would catch him away from the job and one morning, he was intercepted as he was coming back on board.

'What are you doing up here?' he demanded angrily. 'I told you to stay on the bloody job, didn't I?'

'Yes, Mr MacArthur,' replied Mike meekly. 'I've got a splitting headache and Sam sent me to the first aider for some aspirins. I'm just on my way back.'

'Aye, well, you'd better get a shift on and just remember, I'm watching you,' replied the stern-faced boss. 'On your way then, get yourself down below.'

In the meantime, Sam had gone off to attend to other business in the Factory and when he returned, he was grinning widely. After asking the lad how he was, he said that he'd heard he'd been in trouble with Mac again. Mike told him that he had caught him coming back from the first aid post.

'Yeh, I told him you were suffering a bit with your head,' Sam replied. 'He wasn't very sympathetic though, the miserable old sod. Anyway, next time you want to go off the job, you're to call at the office. Oh, and while I remember, I've heard that he's been carpeted for swearing at you on your first day. Apparently, he had a right bollocking, so I reckon that's why we ain't seen much of him, these past few days.'

A week or so later, when Sam reported that he had completed the job, he was told to shift his gear over to another Ship. Mike was to be allocated to another Fitter, which was terrible news. After a stern warning from Sam to be respectful, he went up to the office to see the Foreman. Mac quietly listened to what he had to say about having been unwell with headaches, but hadn't said anything before because he didn't want to be a nuisance. After a few bad-tempered comments about how he should have said something and how 'today's generation were soft', he abruptly changed his mind and told him to continue working with Sam.

Soon after clocking on on the following Monday morning, they went over to a large Cruiser whose refit was at an advanced stage and there was said to be an urgent need for her to be back at sea. Apparently, time was increasingly of the essence and Sam gleefully told the lad that plenty of 'ovies' – overtime working – would almost certainly be coming their way. It would only be weekday evenings at first, but perhaps a weekend or two would be worked in the final stages of the refit. Mike was pleased, because it would give him a most welcome opportunity to enhance his savings. After speaking to some of his mates, Sam laid claim to a small cubby-hole on the upper deck and he solemnly warned the lad that clean habits and quiet behaviour were essential, if they were not to be ejected from the comfort it provided.

A number of RN Officers and their men were already working on board and might have need of the cabin. He found a 'gash-can' – a rubbish bin – and borrowed a broom to sweep it out. When seated comfortably during their first break, he explained that the Naval personnel would soon be coming on board in ever increasing numbers and it was therefore essential that they were always respectful to them. He had no time for the banal nonsense, which often went on between the Mateys and the Navy. He had a bunch of keys, from which he extracted one which fitted the lock on the door and when Mike asked where he'd got them, he tapped the side of his nose and with a grin, he gave the time-honoured reply.

'That's for me to know, my old son. You don't need to.'

Perhaps a Matelot, while attending to a pressing job, had put the keys down somewhere and 'lost' them. No doubt, he had been most explicit in his venomous outpouring of hatred for 'those thieving bloody Mateys'. An enterprising soul must have slipped them into his pocket, then scarpered before they were missed. Having adroitly dodged his Apprentice's question, Sam went on to spell out further rules, which would govern their occupancy of the cabin.

'If an Officer or a Chief P. O. comes in and I'm not here, you speak very politely and with a bit of respect. They will then, like as not, leave us alone and we can continue to have a little bit of comfort to lighten our days. With a bit o' luck, we'll have some evenings as well.'

He later came back with a most useful item, a small electric hot-water heater, which he connected to a power socket on the bulkhead. It was an essential requirement for their brew ups and they would have to keep mum about their good fortune, to preclude others from either using or stealing it. It was difficult to say which would be worse. He also 'came by' a couple of old leather cushions for them to sit on. A few days later, he was proved right in his presumption that someone would question their occupancy of the space and he had his explanation ready. It was one of the Commissioned Engineers who came in and Sam's spiel went as follows:

'Oh, good morning Sir,' which was a very good start. Plenty of respect, and the Officer was clearly impressed. 'We've been detailed off to overhaul the manoeuvring valves in the Boiler-rooms and with it being a finicky job, we've had to find somewhere secure to stow our gear. The Foreman said it would be alright if we moved in here temporarily, as long as we left it like we found it and moved out right away when told to.'

The items of 'equipment' which he showed to the Officer were comprised of a small electric vacuum cleaner, a bag containing spanners and hammers, a bale of cotton waste and a quantity of lint-free cloths. The Lieutenant must have been satisfied with his explanation because, after saying that it wasn't to become a refuge for idle Dockyard men and being laughingly assured by Sam that it wouldn't be, he left them in peace. It was a valuable lesson.

The job involved opening up and inspecting the valves which regulated the volume of high-pressure steam, which passed from the boilers to the main turbines and they were mounted in a row on the forrad bulkhead, near the top level in each Boiler-room. It was an interesting job, which would keep them busy for some weeks. There was rarely a problem with them, as they would have been previously maintained to the best standards. Being the most important valves on the ship, strict clean working conditions were essential and on no account could a dismantled valve be left unattended. The third member of the team was an old rigger called Joe. He was long and thin and always had an unlit dog-end in the corner of his mouth and a 'dew-drop' on the end of his nose. He duly arrived with a set of one ton chain blocks and an assortment of slings, shackles and lifting eyes. His was the responsibility to ensure that the components were handled with the greatest of care.

Sam warned Mike not to try it on with the old lad, because he was a decent bloke and would make a significant contribution to the job. He was also the 'gofor'. If they wanted anything from the stores, he went and he was not averse to going for their sandwiches and cakes. They started work by disconnecting the remote operating linkage on the first three valves, then released the top cover of the first one and lifted it off to expose the internals. The fixings were cleaned and after being oiled they were stowed away in a box. The chamber was closely inspected and the valve was taken off the spindle. The whole operation was discussed with the Ship's Engineer and nothing untoward was found. A light lapping in of the valve to its seat was all that was necessary. Sam brought a smile to his lad's face when he said what he had already been told elsewhere.

'You always have to be soft an' gentle, when you're lapping-in a valve, just as if you're caressing a woman's thigh,' he said, with a faux-dreamy look in his eyes.

After vacuuming the inside of the valve and wiping the exposed surfaces with lint-free cloths, they reattached the valve to the spindle. A new gasket was fitted to the cover and the assembly was boxed up. The operating linkage was reconnected and the ball-joints greased, following which, they opened and closed the valve a few times to confirm its smooth operation. With the first valve overhauled to his satisfaction, the Engineer was content thereafter to visit the job periodically. There were eight such valves in each boiler room and the method to be used was identical for each one. As already noted, the work had to be done with great care and over the ensuing days, they worked away steadily.

Sam had already obtained the hours allocated 'to this most important and difficult job' and when he had come back from the office, he had been gleefully rubbing his hands.

'Overs 'till eight o'clock, weekdays,' he crowed. 'Lovely grub, and I got us a few more hours on the target as well,' he added.

'How'd you manage that?,' asked Mike.

'Never you mind, my old son,' Sam replied and again tapping his nose. 'The more we get, the better. We'll have to keep well on top of this job though, if we're to make any money.'

More unpleasantness came that evening, when the Foreman came below not long after they had resumed work. When he saw the lad, he flushed with anger.

'What's he doing here?' he cried. 'I never said he could work overtime.'

Sam had anticipated his reaction and had warned Mike to say nothing.

'Now then Mac, you know Joe doesn't work overtime and you can't expect me to do a difficult job like this on my own. It's a two-man job and the greatest of care has to be taken at all times. Besides, he has worked really hard since coming over to me and I've been keeping him at it, just like you said. If he can't stay, then you'd better send someone down to give me a hand.'

'Alright, alright, I hear what you're saying. Just get on with it, will you?,' the Foreman replied testily as he turned away and went back up the ladder. 'I don't know why I bloody bother; no bugger ever takes any notice of me.'

They didn't see him again for a few days and when they did, he made no further objection to Mike working overtime. During the following week, he came down to tell Sam about an urgent job which needed doing. A small valve in the double-bottom of the Ship had been missed when she was in dry-dock and the gland might have been leaking into the enclosed space. The culture of blame in the workplace was very much as it is today, though who was responsible for the omission was not known.

Sam and Mike went down through the decks to the bottom plates under a magazine and unbolted and lifted a manhole cover to gain access to the valve. After getting permission to enter the space, an electrician rigged a temporary light and a small ventilation fan. Access was difficult because they had to crawl through a small hole in a main hull strut to get to it. Sam checked the extended spindle, which went up through the plating into the space above and it turn turned easily. They added a turn of packing to each gland and a liberal greasing of the spindle completed the job. After boxing up the manhole, they went back up to the caboosh.

In the weeks that followed, the Mac became less antagonistic towards Mike, though he was always careful to be working whenever he was around. They made steady progress on the valves, with Sam constantly checking it was in accordance with his 'schedule' – in other words, 'to meet his pecuniary expectations'. Mike was indeed very fortunate to be working with such an easy-going Fitter, after all of the previous unpleasantness. To lighten their days, daft 'incidents' occurred in the Boiler-room, with a lot of them being at the Andrew's expense. Numerous working parties were on board, the principal reason being for the crew to become thoroughly familiar with the Ship's plant and equipment. She was a large Vessel and when in commission, she would have a crew of approximately eight hundred or so Officers and men.

Chapter 3

Interesting Work

A party of Stokers had come down into the stokehold to clear away the dirt and rubbish which had accumulated in the space during the refit. They steadily worked their way across the tops of the Boilers and along the landings, walkways and platforms and after thoroughly cleaning the bottom plates, they ended up in the bilges, which were in a most dreadful state. Loud were their complaints about the filthy 'bloody Mateys' and how they should be made to clear up their own 'sodding mess'. P.O. Stewart was in charge, and he was a typical long-service NCO, being both aggressive and loud. Respect for others was not his strong point and his Stokers and the Mateys with whom he came into contact were all addressed in the same forthright manner.

Mike noticed that the Chiefs and P.O.s had a peculiar way in which they addressed their Officers. To his ears, it bordered very close to but never crossed the line of the time-honoured military crime of 'dumb insolence'. They were in no way offensive and they certainly didn't disobey any orders but nevertheless, they always seemed to have a deadpan expression on their faces and a flat way of replying to anything an Officer said. Their attitude had been inculcated into them over many years and was accepted as the norm. P.O. Stewart was a very experienced NCO, who knew his job and he did it with the minimum of effort and he didn't need anyone, who was much less experienced than himself, to tell him what to do. His attitude to his men was simply the same as with so many other NCOs. 'When I says jump, you jump,' and Lord help anyone who didn't do so quickly enough!

The ship's broadcasting system – the tannoy – was re-commissioned and manned throughout the day. A Bosun's Mate would twitter his call (whistle) and intone a succession of messages to the Jolly Jacks and individuals would be summoned by name and rank and instructed as to whom and where they should report. It made interesting listening and was highly amusing to the Mateys. A benefit of being on board was the canteen, which was initially set up on the jetty in a mobile galley, (kitchen) and it negated the need for the crew to return to the barracks during the day. Though denied the use of the facility, Sam somehow got their sandwiches there for the princely sum of a 'bob' each (5 pence). Mike had never seen anything like the veritable 'door steps', which were made up of two large slices of freshly baked bread, liberally spread with 'marge', with a thick slab of either corned beef or tinned ham inside. Mustard was liberally spread on the meat to aid consumption.

In due course, the food was prepared on board and again, the Mateys were denied access. Sam still regularly sloped off during the morning break or just before dinner time and came back with the requisite goodies. A vivid memory is of the doughnuts, which were sold for sixpence each (2.5 pence). Being roughly the size of a cricket ball, they had a thick wedge of 'ersatz' cream in the slit across the middle. They were a deep, golden-brown in colour, crispy on the outside and the dough had a creamy consistency of mouth-watering amplitude. It was indeed a delightful confection and the Ship's cooks who made them must have been true artists indeed.

The platform on which Sam and Mike were working was one level down from the double access doors, at the top of the after stoke hold. Ladders connecting the various levels ran from top to bottom at each end, so they saw everyone who was either going up or coming down. They had rigged a large tarpaulin above the valves, which kept falling debris and dirt away from their internals. Sam was soon on good terms with P.O. Stewart and they regularly yarned, talking about the Warships they'd served in and the ports they'd visited. The P.O. took an active interest in the job, often looking inside the valves and knowledgeably discussing what was being done. When the Engineer was needed to inspect a valve, he was only too pleased to send a Stoker to find him.

His instructions to his men were unambiguous and whenever they approached the platform, Sam and Mike were always 'busy'. The harmonious atmosphere which Sam had been so determined to build didn't last, due to the inanity of two fifth year Apprentices who were fitting gauges to the Boilers. A large, stainless steel fascia board had been erected across the front of them and, to be fair, it was a difficult job. It would have been very much easier, had the board been made in aluminium and assembled in the workshop because each gauge was inserted into a pre-cut hole and secured by four screws. The drilling and tapping of the fixing holes caused the less-than-active duo great problems and they soon got bored and were looking for mischief. Who better to have fun with than the Matelots, who were working in the bilges below?

One morning, there was a loud call from the top level for P.O. Stewart, to tell him he was 'wanted up top'. 'Right oh,' came the reply, and soon after he came puffing up the ladders, through the air lock and out on to the upper deck. He came back down again almost right away.

'I'm sure somebody called me, but there's no one there,' he said to Sam.

Sam and Mike had only just come down below and were unable to comment, but no sooner had the P.O. reached the bottom plates, when another call came from above.

'P.O. Stewart! Come on, you're wanted up top. Shift yourself.'

He again laboriously made his way up the ladders and out of the Boiler-room. Two minutes or so later, he came down again and was obviously very put out.

'Some bugger is playing games and I'm not happy,' he said to Sam.

'We don't know what's going on, George,' he replied, 'but we'll keep a lookout for you.'

Soon after, there came yet another call, this time urging greater effort on the part of the incensed P. O., telling him it was the third time he'd been called. It was all too much and with a great deal of cursing and swearing, he came up yet again. This time, as he paused for breath on the manoeuvring platform, he looked enquiringly at Sam.

'We know who it is, George,' said Sam. 'It's those stupid gits who're supposed to be working on the gauge panel. It's them that are playing silly buggers.

P.O. Stewart went up the remaining ladder at a rate of knots. When he came back, he was smiling broadly and as he passed, he winked at Sam.

'Thanks mate. I don't think that silly sod will be bothering me again, or his mate if it comes to that.'

He then went on down to where his men were working and after telling them 'it was all sorted', they resumed work. As they came up after being piped 'hands to dinner', one of them took a flying-kick at one of the pranksters' tool bags. Later, the clowns came down to collect their gear and while they were on their way back up, one of them said to Sam that they didn't understand how the P.O. had found out that they had pulled the stunt. As he had said, he had effectively ended their little game.

'Serves you bloody right,' said Sam, who had been just as angry as his pal. 'You should have had more sense than to mess with a three-badge P.O., particularly a Stoker. If you got thick ears for your pains, that's no more than you deserved, you daft pair of sods.'

P.O. Stewart later explained how he had sprung his trap. When the third call came, he had already sent his 'killick' – his Leading Stoker – and another hand up ahead of him. They had gone on to the deck and having spotted the miscreants, they had quietly moved in behind them. When the P.O. appeared, the clowns tried to slip away but found the two burly stokers barring their way and had suffered accordingly. When they came back, they quietly got on with their work.

Soon after, the valves in the after Boiler-room were completed and all that remained was for the 'Laggers' to make good the insulation. The stokers cleaned up the platform and applied liberal coats of paint to make everything look 'tiddly', or neat and tidy. The transformation that P.O. Stewart and his men had made in only a few short weeks was amazing and Sam told Mike that he hadn't seen anything yet. The entire space was 'spick and span', with the transformation in the bilges being the greatest improvement. As he said, 'you could eat your dinner off of them there deck-plates'. Some of the Stokers were still busy painting the ancillary machinery and pipework and others were vigorously polishing the 'bright-work', such as the copper pipes and handrails. Other Matelots stripped, cleaned and tested the lights. When they had finished, the Boiler-room was in all respects ready for re-commissioning.

The overhaul of the forrad Boiler-room valves was nearing completion, when Sam was told to take charge of a gang. Their job was to lift the top cover on the port main-drive gearbox, which was in the forrad Engine-room. An odd noise had been heard coming from it when the Ship was last underway and an investigation would perhaps identify the cause. Clean conditions would again apply and the immediate area was sealed off. With steam due to be raised, it was essential to complete the work without delay. Overtime would be worked in the evenings, with a weekend if necessary. The noise was unlikely to have come from any of the bearings, but they were opened up and closely inspected. A systematic check was then made of the lubrication system, to ensure that all the oil-ways were clear.

While that was in progress, a problem arose with a couple of the Engine-room artificers, (ERAs), who were taking an interest in the job. Mike spoke to them a couple of times, but they had no time for lesser mortals like him. Their disdain did not extend to their C.P.O., to whom they spoke only when spoken to and then with great respect. Like Mike, they were in the fourth year of their Apprenticeships and were 'as green as grass' about the mechanical workings of the Ship. When they had first come below, they had gone straight over to the gearbox and as they had lifted the dust sheet, Mike advised them to be careful. He was contemptuously told to mind his own bloody business. Undeterred, he pointed out that the work was being done under clean conditions and as they were wearing standard overalls, they were not complying with the regulations.

'Piss off!,' one of them shouted angrily. 'We don't need a bloody Dockyard Matey to tell us what to do.'

When the Fitters came down, Mike told Sam what had transpired and he was unperturbed.

'Never mind, old mate, you've tried to tell them what's what. Don't bother any more.'

Later in the day, the two 'Jacks' were again looking into the gearbox, but this time with great consternation and Sam and the other Fitter went over and asked them what the problem was. One of them replied that he had been leaning over the top of the box, when a small spanner had slipped out of his pocket and fallen inside.

'Bloody hell,' said Sam in his inimitable, bland way, 'that's torn it!'

He called the rest of the team away and told them to do nothing further on the gearbox until the problem was sorted. Turning to the Jacks, he sternly told them how things were.

'We'll keep out of the way until you find it and by heck if you don't, you're going to be in the bloody rattle,' he said to them quietly. 'You were warned by my mate about looking over the gearbox in them overalls and you didn't take any notice. Well, it's your own fault and you've got to sort it out.'

With the weekend nigh, it could not have happened on a worse day and they weren't going to get any help from the Mateys. They hurried off to fetch some torches, balls of string, magnets and mirrors on extension rods. Their intention was to make a thorough search of the gearbox and hopefully retrieve the spanner. As soon as they were gone, Sam got his team around the unit, to see if they could locate it. Only a few minutes later, he was called him down to an inspection door on the inboard side.

'I think I've found something,' the man cried excitedly, 'It's lodged just above the door, on a web plate.'

'Well, don't knock it off,' Sam replied. 'We may not find it again. Here, let me have a decko.'

After fumbling around inside for a minute or so, he gave up. 'No, I can't reach it. Here, you've got longer arms than me,' he said to Mike. 'See if you can get a hold of whatever is there.'

The lad reached inside and, after moving position several times, and with a lot of grunting and stretching, he eventually brought out a small, black shifting spanner.

'Got the bugger!' he cried triumphantly.

'Well done, lad,' replied Sam. 'Now then,' he said to the others, 'we'll say nothing to them cocky young gits when they come back. I think a short, sharp shock is called for.'

He put the spanner in his pocket and went back up to the top of the box. When the gang came down the next morning, the Tiffies were slumped down beside the gearbox, in the depths of despair and were sick with worry about the consequences of what they had done.

'We're just going to have to report it,' one said mournfully to the other.

Hearing that, Sam put on his most solicitous smile.

'Alright, we'll give you a hand. You go up top and get a bit of breakfast and some rest and we'll see what we can do.'

His intention was that they should be made to sweat a little longer, to teach them a lesson they wouldn't forget.

Chapter 4

The End of the Refit

When the Tiffies came back a couple of hours later, Sam spoke to them again and they were much more communicative. They showed him where they had looked and confirmed that they had found nothing untoward. Much to his surprise, they had not looked inside of the door through which Mike had searched.

'Have you had any luck? Have you found anything?' one of them asked eagerly.

'Yes my son, we've found a small shifting-spanner,' he said, holding it up. 'Is this the one you lost?'

The Tiffies looked at each other in utter disbelief and their relief was palpable and they couldn't thank Sam enough for his help. It never occurred to them to ask exactly where and when it had been found and Sam was certainly not going to tell them. He then asked them again if they were absolutely sure it was their spanner, which they immediately confirmed.

'Well, I'm sure you'll understand that I've reported this incident to my Foreman, because I don't want any come back on me and my mates later,' he said. 'If you've dropped anything else, you'd better say so.'

The Tiffies were most insistent that they had not and Sam took their word for it. He then went off to discuss what had happened with Mac. Within a couple of hours, the Engine-room was a hive of activity and the Engineer Lieutenant came down with the Commander and a couple of stern looking Chief ERAs. The Tiffies, who were standing apart, were getting regular black looks from them. Even P.O. Stewart came below to see what all the fuss was about. Mac arrived with the Manager and two 'gearbox specialists' from the Design Office. None of them had the proper protective clothing and so as not to be outdone in such august company, Sam asked them to stand well clear.

'We don't want any more accidents, do we?,' he asked – a sentiment with which they all concurred.

He then went through what had happened with 'the bosses' and what had been done to retrieve the situation. The Commander closely questioned the 'Tiffies' and sarcastically concluded by asking them if the spanner was all they had dropped. They assured him it was and it was agreed that the gearbox should be boxed up as quickly as possible, before which, the gang would make a final search through all the access doors, with the Engineer Lieutenant and his Chiefs present. Before he left, the Commander thanked the Manager for his men's assistance and said he would make his appreciation known elsewhere. Sam was literally purring with delight. He had agreed with Mac for a 'job and finish', which meant that the gang would work all the hours necessary to complete the job in a single operation.

With the main lubricating oil system re-commissioned, the gearbox was turned over by the barring gear – a small, electrically driven machine which was mounted on the engine casing. The gears were slowly inched round to allow the close inspection of all the contact surfaces of the wheels and pinions and apart from minor marks on the leading edges of the teeth, nothing untoward was found. With everything in order, the top cover was replaced and bolted up. Mike and the other Apprentice had been sent under the plates with flogging spanners and heavy hammers to check that all the holding-down bolts were tight. The cause of the intermittent noise remained a mystery and the gearbox was once again in a secure state. Valuable lessons had been learned and the nonsense was soon forgotten.

Sam and Mike returned to the forrad Boiler-room to finish off the manoeuvring valves. The next day, Mac told them that, as nothing untoward had been found, they could leave the valves that remained and finish the job by re-packing the glands and greasing the remote linkages. The ease of movement was demonstrated to the Engineer, both from on the platform and the deck above and his signature brought an end to a most interesting job. When Sam had first come into the forrad space, he had been approached by another P.O. stoker; a young man with only a single stripe under his crossed anchors and he was clearly finding his way in his new job. Similar cleaning had been going on apace and it was nearly finished. All P.O. Brown wanted was for Sam to ensure that all the rubbish and debris from his job would be properly cleared away when he was finished.

'You need have no worries there, P.O.,' Sam told him. 'You won't even know we've been here.'

'When on board a commissioned Ship,' Sam explained, 'the moral of the crew is of the greatest importance. A busy Ship is a happy one, so what the Officers do is to create a spirit of competition between the various sections. What's been going on is that the Stokers, who've been working in the Boiler and Engine rooms, have been up against each other to make the best job. When it's all finished, the Chief Engineer will inspect each space and decide who has won and the winners will be sitting pretty, because there will have been a lot of wagers made. While gambling is strictly forbidden, there are times when discretion is called for and the Matelots set great store in winning and hanging on to their trophies, in the face of fierce competition. It'll be interesting to hear what the Chief's decision is and they'll all be off ashore after, that's for sure.'

Their next job was both arduous and difficult. When steam had been raised, a small leak was seen coming from the flange of a main isolating valve. In the normal course of events, such valves were hardly ever shut and a leaking flange was rare. With commissioning well in hand, it would have to be fixed as quickly as possible, which meant replacing the gasket. Had it had failed at sea, it would have meant shutting down both a boiler and a main engine. The valve was located high on the starboard side of the engine room, affixed to the after bulkhead and close to the deck-head above. Access was difficult and when the scaffolding was rigged, the lagging was stripped away to expose the fixings.

The glands/spindles on high-pressure steam valves nearly always have a build-up of residual boiler chemicals on the outside and due to the temperature of the metal, it is often a waste of time to lubricate them. A regular turn or two usually keeps the valve operable, but the one in question was seized solidly and had obviously not been operated for many months. Joe rigged his tackle in the space above, then dropped a sling through the extended spindle hole in the deck, to allow the valve to be taken out. The breaking of the down-stream flange was easy, with only a quick application of a hammer and cold chisel to break the nuts. The other flange was much more difficult because access was obstructed by the body of the valve and its proximity to the bulkhead and deckhead stiffeners. Mike spent most of an afternoon trying to break 'that last bloody nut' and early the following morning, the valve was still not out when Mac came below.

'Here,' he said crossly, 'give me the bloody hammer and chisel.'

With that, he placed the tip into the gouge which Mike had made and gave the chisel a sharp tap. The nut split with a crack and the pieces dropped to the deck. Sod's law, one might say? Mike was miffed, particularly when Sam laughed at his frustration.

'There you are, laddie,' Mac said, smiling broadly for once. 'That's the way to do it.'

Joe straight away took the valve to the Factory for refurbishing. The flange on the pipe only needed wire brushing and a brief scrape and the mounting-plate on the bulkhead was similarly cleaned. The valve came back late the following day, having been completely overhauled and sand-blasted. A bag tied to the handle contained a new set of fixings, together with two spiral-wound gaskets. By then, the Engineers were anxious to 'flash-up' again, so its re-installation was most urgent. An hour or so later, the job was completed and the Laggers quickly made good the insulation and the scaffolding was taken down.

Shortly after, the Cruiser was moved to a berth in the No. 1 basin. A number of jobs, which were mostly minor defects and omissions, remained to be done. Mike was no longer constantly looking over his shoulder whenever the Foreman was on board. Overtime in the evenings was still being worked, but the eagerly-anticipated weekends hadn't materialised. A C.P.O. came into the caboosh one morning and told Sam it was needed and he and his lad cleaned it and moved out right away. A large number of Sailors were working on board and with more arriving each day, the mess-decks were filling up rapidly. Steam was raised, the Boiler safety valves were 'floated' and the ancillary machinery run-up. The upper decks were systematically cleaned down by the seamen, with thick coats of grey paint being applied to the upper works, including the funnels. Sam aptly summed-up the situation.

'Don't stand about when you're up top, old mate,' he said sagely, 'because if you do, the Matelots will paint you, as well as everything else. Their motto has always been, 'If it don't move, paint it.''

The First Lieutenant, or 'Jimmy the One', as he was affectionately known, decided to test the steam siren and, to his great disappointment, it didn't work. There was a steady discharge of brown sludge, which ran down the front of the newly painted forrad funnel. Not a sound came out, even when it was warmed up and he testily referred it to the Manager. Sam was detailed off to investigate. Up until then, Joe had been very protective of his role as the rigger but the job was clearly an exception. Access was up a vertical ladder, which was attached to the funnel and he refused to climb up to the platform, which was about twenty five feet above the deck. There was no point arguing about it. It was a cold, windy day, with rain in the air and Mike was not best pleased as he went up alone with the necessary tackle. When he removed the end cover from the siren, he saw that the steam chamber was blocked and he disconnected the whole unit and lowered it to the deck.

The siren was immediately despatched to the Factory and while it was away, the supply line was purged. Again, the gunge displaced ran down the funnel and liberally spattered the deck to the rear of the bridge structure. The upper deck Chief was incensed about the spoiling of his new paintwork. When the siren came back, it was immediately reinstalled and just before knocking off time, it was tested. Mike had never heard a Warship's siren before and the noise was excruciating. He had been expecting something altogether different, like a mournful bellow but it was more like a triumphant 'whoop', which was both effective and impressive.

The anchor windlass in the bows and the mooring-winches at various points around the deck, had not been included in the refit. When steam was applied to the windlass, it struggled to lift the port anchor, which had been dropped by ten feet or so. The cause of the problem was soon evident in that a lock-nut in the valve gear had come loose and the timing of the steam into the cylinder had slipped. Sam made the necessary adjustment and the machine was operated without further problem. One of the watching Mateys knowingly commented that the Navy must have known about it and Sam, who was always quick to defend his late shipmates, pointed out that a Warship was usually tied up to a buoy or alongside a jetty. It could be months between the use of the anchors and no one would have been aware of the problem. He told him angrily that if he didn't have something sensible to say, he should 'bugger off'.

With the refit almost completed, there was little gainful work to do and the few remaining jobs were being quickly completed. Sam and Mike spent their time clearing minor defects, which had become apparent, as the auxiliary machinery was re-commissioned. A leaking joint here, or a valve-gland weeping there. To the Apprentice, it seemed to be 'all hell and no notion', but Sam was again quick to put him right.

'The crew is led by a large number of very experienced hands, with many years of service,' he said solemnly. 'The remainder are usually made up of a lot of young lads, with limited service and some who have not been to sea before. Like you, they've got a heck of a lot to learn. The Officers know exactly what they're doing and what needs to be done and with attention to detail and a lot of hard work, everything will gradually fall into place. When she's ready, this Ship'll go out into the North Sea to work up and they'll soon have her running like a well-oiled machine. It can't really be otherwise can it?'

Over the past year, Mike had often travelled to and from work by bus and in doing so had suffered many frustrations due to regular delays and cancellations. To add to his discomfort, he had suffered an embarrassing problem. As soon as he sat down, he had become sexually aroused and hiding it had been difficult. It was very embarrassing and he often carried his raincoat to cover the protuberance. To make matters worse, he'd even been asked why he always carried his mac, even when the weather was fine. His mother had also made her usual song and dance about it and the more he fretted about the problem, the worse it became. It had got so bad that he had recently stopped using the bus altogether, unless it was absolutely necessary.

He often cycled over for a drink in 'The Windmill', a pub which was about two miles from his village and one evening, he told a couple that he was looking for alternative accommodation. The husband was a retired regular Naval Officer, who worked at the Admiralty in London. He had a twenty-eight foot yacht and spent most of his spare time working on her and sailing up and down the east coast. He told Mike that he was always on the lookout for suitable crew, if he was interested and had the time. He was perhaps in his fifties and his wife, Joy, was perhaps in her early forties. She was a very attractive woman, with a trim figure and a striking head of deep-red hair. Sailing, she said, was not at all to her liking, particularly when the weather was cold and the sea rough. She liked her home comforts, though she always went with him when he ventured over to the Continent.

Over the ensuing weeks, Mike saw them regularly and they became friendly. On New Year's Eve, he spent a very pleasant evening imbibing and from time to time, he was aware that the woman was smiling at him. He went over to ask how they were and if they had enjoyed their Christmas. When everyone went outside to 'see the New Year in', Joy came across and offered her cheek for a friendly peck. As he put his hands on her arms, she unbuttoned his jacket and closely embraced him. She then gave him a most passionate kiss and when she released him, she whispered that there were more of those to come when he needed them. Her passion had had the desired effect and experienced woman that she was, she must have noticed.

Not long after, she told him about a vacant flat, the owner of which was abroad and needed someone to look after it while she was away. She offered to 'show him round' and they agreed to meet in the Town on the following Saturday morning. When he arrived, Mike was surprised that Malcolm was not with her and what ensued was completely unexpected. It turned out to be a most enjoyable experience.

After a cursory look at the lounge, the lady led him into the bedroom and, without any preamble, pulled him down on to the bed. As he had thought, she was a most passionate woman and she obviously had a great need of physical love. The next hour or so was the most pleasurable that he had ever known for quite some time and in taking her leave, she asked him to be discreet about what had happened. He readily gave her the necessary assurance.

When he next saw Joy and her husband, she asked him straightaway if he was going to look after the flat. Mike replied that to be honest, he couldn't afford it and it was not what he was looking for. He politely thanked her and said he hoped that he hadn't put her to any inconvenience. He was surprised when only a few minutes later, they left the pub.

He didn't go to there again for a couple of weeks and when he did, Malcolm and his gorgeous wife were not there. The landlord told him that they hadn't been in for some time, then asked him if that had anything to do with him. Mike surmised that he must have seen their passionate embrace and put two and two together but, whatever it was, he didn't let on about what had gone on!

Chapter 5

A Ceremonial Occasion

The last job of the refit had to be the complete refurbishment of the quarterdeck. All the damaged planks had already been lifted and replaced and the seams between them were caulked with hemp and sealed with tar. The high spots were planed off and then the whole area was sanded down. The Navy was always extremely pernickety about their quarterdecks and it had to be absolutely right before the Ship was re-commissioned. The upper deck had been cleared of all plant, tackle and detritus and the area abaft the funnels was roped off to deny the Mateys any further access. Woe betide anyone who strayed on to their hallowed ground. The painting of the upper works was finished and the deck lights cleaned and re-commissioned. The brass fixtures, including the ship's bell, name boards and gun tompions, were all polished and re-placed. The deck awnings were erected and the gratings and decorative boxes, which covered the machinery, were titivated and put in place. After a lot of drama, everything was at long last finished.

A working party of Jolly Jacks had cleaned the jetty and the mooring bollards were wire-brushed and given a lick of black paint. The mooring ropes were renewed, complete with 'rat guards', which some Jacks laughingly said were there to keep the bloody Mateys from sneaking back on board. The ensign staffs were made ready for when the Ship would proudly fly her colours again. The commissioning of the beautiful Cruiser was imminent and everyone was very busy preparing for the big day. When the Navy had a traditional function to perform, they did it with panache and style and the crew was assembled on the jetty and painstakingly rehearsed through each stage of the ceremony. The sessions were carried through under the eagle-eye of the Commander, who loudly controlled them in a very 'upper class' voice. Initially, he stood on a bollard, but after a small dais was put in place, he used it to address his troops. The Sailors provided the Guard of Honour and the Royal Marine Band the accompanying music.

A new 'brow', or gangway, which had canvas 'dodgers' with the ship's name and crest along each side, was rigged between the jetty and the quarterdeck. It provided a single, guarded access and was manned continually by an Officer and his side party. The upper deck was a hive of activity, with the gun turrets constantly moving on their mountings, as they were trained up, down and around. The Boilers and the ancillary plant below were in the final stages of running tests and what had until only recently been chaos had, as Sam said it would, become orderly and efficient. The Ship had been systematically gone through from stem to stern to ensure that she was in all respects ready for her Captain's inspection.

Some of the jobs, which had been completed during the refit, still required further attention and one of them fell to Sam to sort out. The gland of a large valve in the upper deck fire-main leaked copiously, when the line was pressure-tested and the Seaman C.P.O. took it as a personal affront. He was scathing about the 'Dockyard Mateys' bloody incompetence and lackadaisical attitude' for which, he loudly complained, they were very highly and unjustifiably paid. When the lads came to fix it, a resounding bollocking was administered which went something like as follows:

'You lot are bloody useless. Can't you do anything right first time? This bloody valve has leaked all over my nice, clean deck. Now look at it. I've a bloody good mind to make you clear it up, though I couldn't trust you to do that properly, could I?'

His tirade greatly amused a group of Matelots, who were standing nearby and pretending to be busy. Sam didn't respond to the 'song and dance' about what was a trivial matter and he shook his head at Mike, to warn him not to say anything either. When the Chief had exhausted his stream of invective, Sam tried to placate him.

'I'm sorry about that Chief,' he replied amenably. 'You're quite right, it shouldn't have happened. We'll attend to it right away and soon have it fixed. You go for a wet (a drink of tea), and I'll come and give you a shout as soon as it's done.'

With the main shut down and isolated, the gland was released and the old packing was taken out and renewed. The spindle was cleaned and given a liberal coating of grease, then opened and shut a few times. The surrounding area was wiped down with cotton-waste, to remove greasy marks from the paintwork, then Mike cleared away the tools. The valve was then demonstrated under pressure to the Chief's satisfaction, following which, he walked away with a deadpan expression on his face. Later, a fresh coat of paint was applied to the small damaged area and that was the end of the matter.

A very amusing incident occurred on the jetty while Sam and Mike were standing on the upper deck during a morning break. The Royal Marine Band was drawn up in their intended position and was practising the musical items, which they would be playing on the big day. All went well until they came to a piece, which we believe is from the 'Soldiers' Chorus' in the Faust Opera. The Bandmaster was not satisfied with the opening bars and after a number of attempts, he became somewhat impatient.

'No, No, it's still not right,' he cried. 'Your timing is all over the place. I want it to go like this.'

He took a deep breath and waving his arms in time, he sang out loudly,

'Soldiers like bloody great hunks of dough.' (pronounced 'duff' – Navy parlance for cake).

Amid a lot of laughter and spontaneous applause from those watching, the Band 'got the message' and played it to his satisfaction.

A full dress-rehearsal of the ceremony took place and there was great excitement in the air as it got under way. The Commander was flanked by his

Senior Officers and he was clearly in a state of agitation. Sam and Mike watched what was happening from the upper deck and they were in for the biggest laugh yet. The crew was drawn up in their divisions, with the Band and Guard of Honour standing in front of them. They were all wearing their 'Number Ones', (best uniforms, complete with gold badges and medals). The proceedings opened with a pep-talk and the Commander spoke at some length, from time to time, as the ceremony was carried through. The older men among the Mateys had seen it all before and took pleasure in explaining what was going on to the ignorant youths in their midst.

As per long-held tradition, a 'lady of distinction' was to be the Guest of Honour and he gravely informed the crew of her name and title. So that they would get it exactly right on the day, they would rehearse the three cheers, to which she would be treated on the completion of her duties. That wasn't altogether to the liking of many of the Jacks, who were stood shivering in the cold wind. There was a lot of muttering and shuffling of feet and their impatience was regularly quelled by the dulcet tones of the Chiefs and P.O's standing in front of them. Only when he had their full attention did the Commander proceed with his rehearsal. It was getting on towards knocking off time and the Jacks were becoming increasingly anxious to return, either to the barracks or on board, to prepare for their coming evening in the flesh-pots of the Town. However, the chance of having a laugh at their Senior Officer's expense could not be resisted by some.

'Three cheers', when given by Servicemen, is always accompanied by the raising and replacing of their headgear and it was practised a few times, with loud cries of 'off caps' and 'on caps' and the Commander was soon satisfied. Then came the matter of the three cheers and the watching Mateys couldn't believe their ears, when he loudly announced that it would be carried through exactly as per his instructions.

'Now, pay attention,' he cried. 'When giving three cheers, Awficers will shout 'hurrah' and NCOs and other ranks 'hooray'. Now, that's not difficult, so let's get it right first time, shall we? Right, three cheers for Lady Browne, Hip, hip, hip...'

'Hooray, hurrah, hooray.' came back the loud disjointed cry from the assembled ranks.

'Now, that wasn't very good was it?' shouted the Commander. 'I want it done crisply and altogether, so let's try it again. Hip, hip, hip...'

'Hurrah, hooray, hurrah,' they shouted, this time even louder and more in unison, but still not to his satisfaction.

'No! No! No!' he bellowed, 'it's still not right. You're far too ragged down at the end there and some people are shouting hurrah, who should be shouting hooray. We can't have that so let's try it again.'

And so it went on for the next quarter of an hour, with the Commander growing increasingly frustrated and flushed with anger. With his loud cries of 'No! No! No!' the watching Mateys could hardly contain their mirth. Some parts of the crew were still shouting the wrong words and there hadn't been much improvement in their cohesion either. Eventually, he looked pointedly at his watch and saw that it was well past the normal knocking-off time. It must have suddenly clicked that the crew were messing him about and he wasn't having that, oh no! He was more than a match for the lower deck and if they wanted to play silly beggars, then he would do likewise.

'Ah,' he said, looking round balefully and very slowly, with his hands on his hips. 'It's like that is it? Well, I'm not going ashore this evening, am I?'

He glared around for a minute or so longer and it was clear to even the thickest Jack exactly what he meant. So, they tried again and surprise, surprise, they got it right, exactly right and to his complete satisfaction. A further call for 'three cheers' was made and it was perfect. With that, he smiled grimly and strode off the dais. As he passed along in front of the men towards the brow, he called out,

'Right-oh Master-at-Arms, that's enough for today. Carry on, when you're ready.'

And that was that.

'In all my years in the Andrew, I never saw anything like that bloody nonsense,' Sam said, with tears running down his cheeks. 'That takes the bloody biscuit, that does.'

Despite all their hard work on the Cruiser, the last few Mateys on board didn't get to watch the commissioning ceremony. By the day, they had been moved to another Warship in the adjacent basin and had to be content to listen to the music being played across the other side. They heard the twittering of the bosun's calls as Senior Officers were piped aboard on arrival at the jetty. Their main purpose was probably to imbibe a few less than well-earned 'pink-gins' or 'horses' necks' (gin and angostura bitters or brandy and dry ginger ales) in the wardroom after it was all over. The ceremony apparently went well and very much to the satisfaction of all concerned.

Sam and some of the other Fitters went on board the Cruiser again a few days later, without their Apprentices, to supplement her Crew as she went out into the North Sea for her sea trials. It was always a most enjoyable few days away from the Yard and when she returned, the defects they found were quickly attended to. Within a few days, she was ready to finally leave the Yard. One of the defects had been the unsatisfactory state of the lubricating oil which circulated through the main drive-units in the after Engine-room. With steam-driven turbines, water inevitably finds its way into the oil, mainly from the leaks on the steam side through the LP casings' gland seals. It is removed by passing the oil through purifiers; i.e. centrifugal filters which remove the traces of emulsification/water and any suspended solids present in the oil.

Sam suspected that they were not working properly and he went to see the Chief ERA, who explained that they were run daily and it was unlikely that they were not performing properly. Having inspected the oil samples and noted their cloudy appearance, it was obvious that something was wrong and if Sam wanted to have a look at them, that was alright with him. Just to be sure, he would send a couple of Tiffies down with him. Sam and Mike made their way directly down to the machines, which were installed on the bottom level, between the main condensers. Under the watchful eyes of the ERAs, he released the cover of the first unit and saw right away that all was not well. An 'O' ring seal was missing from the top cover and the rotating filter unit had been wrongly assembled. The rotating part of the machine was made up of a large number of conical plates, which interlocked with each other in a column, to form a fine filter.

Several plates were missing, perhaps having been damaged and discarded during cleaning. While the principle of the machine was simple, care had to be taken in its assembly and clearly, that had not been done. When he opened up the second machine, he found a similar state of affairs and being ever the diplomat when talking to the Naval personnel, he suggested there was no point in making a fuss about it. The Chief agreed and went off to find the instruction manual and see what spares were in the store. Having discussed the instructions, they agreed that Sam would demonstrate how to do the job properly. The Tiffies watched closely as both machines were thoroughly cleaned and re-assembled with replacement plates and new sealing rings. When they were started up, they sounded a lot better than previously and it was soon apparent that the oil discharge was much clearer than before.

The Chief moved his men away from the Mateys to instruct them and when he came back, he grimly thanked Sam for resolving the problem. Sam, not to be outdone, turned to Mike and told him sternly that he hoped that he had also learned from what he had seen. When they went to see the Chief the following morning, he was very pleased that the oil in the tanks was crystal clear. Not for the first time, Sam had been right to insist that half-measures were not acceptable and doing the job right, first time, was the only way. Considering the length of time that the Cruiser had spent at sea, the number of defects found in her main propulsion and auxiliary plant were relatively few. No problem had been reported with the lub oil in the forrad Engine room, but the Chief Engineer was said to be determined to preclude similar problems in the future.

A tube-leak, which had been found in one of the Boilers during the trials was given the urgent attention of the Boilermakers. The remaining defects were remedied and signed off by the EngSneer, following which, the Mateys left the Ship. On a bright, breezy morning early in the following week, the tugs moved her slowly across the basin and into the lock and at high tide, the sea-board gate was opened and she moved out into the river. She was going out into the North Sea to 'work-up', before re-joining the Fleet and she looked a magnificent sight as she slipped her tug and got under way.

The next day, the Mac sent for Sam and from his demeanour when he returned, he had some important news. When he had entered the office, Mac had invited him to take a seat, then had told him that the Management had been impressed with how well he had been working. He was to be promoted to Charge-hand and though completely taken aback by the news, he was absolutely delighted. When Mike had first started working with him, he had appreciated right away that he was a cut above the normal run of the mill Fitter and he richly deserved his promotion. His skills were exceptional, compared with most of his contemporaries and the lad was sincere when he thanked him for all his help.

'Yeah, well, thanks very much,' replied Sam in some embarrassment, 'though some of our mates won't be so pleased when they hear, I can tell you. Never mind, they can either 'like it or lump it' as far as I'm concerned. The extra money will be very welcome.'

It couldn't have happened to a better man.

Chapter 6

Another Change

In the meantime, another Light Cruiser had arrived for a 'short refit' and was initially tied up on the east side of the No. 3 basin. Most of her complement went off on leave, with only a skeleton crew left on board for security purposes. She was similar to the one cruiser that had just left, in that she was also nearing the end of her service life. The paintwork around her hull was much the worse for wear, with a large indentation down the starboard side running towards the stern. She had probably scraped her side when coming alongside a quay or perhaps had been in a minor collision. The Sailors were not forthcoming and a few days later, she was moved up through the basins and into a dry-dock where the damage was found to be more extensive than had first been thought. A large piece had been broken out of one of the blades of the starboard outer propeller and there was also damage to a number of hull-plates beneath the waterline. Several hull struts had been also bent and would have to be repaired.

Soon after she was put into the dock, Sam, with Mike in tow, was sent to down to work on her main engines. There had apparently been problems in maintaining the vacuum at the low pressure end of the starboard after engine and he straightaway went to see the Chief ERA, perhaps thinking he would get more sense out him than from the Engineer. The Chief told him that they had first noticed the problem about a month previously and it had got steadily worse. He suspected that some of the main condenser tubes were leaking, because Boiler samples had indicated contamination of the feed-water. The steam to the LP cylinder gland-seals had been increased, which had caused a further problem with the lubricating oil in the engine. They discussed the problem for quite some time, before Sam went off to report back to Mac. When he returned, he was very pleased with himself. He told Mike that as the Ship was urgently needed back at sea, overtime was to be worked on the job.

When the main condenser was opened up, it was clear that all was not well, with both the inlet and outlet cooling-water boxes in a filthy state. A lot of the tube ends were damaged and some of the tubes were blocked. Cleaners were set to work and a couple of days later, a more detailed inspection was carried out. Each bank of tubes was rodded through, then washed out with high-pressure hoses. The steam side was filled with feed water, with a dye colorant added and as suspected, numerous leaks were found in the tube ends. The water was drained off and new ferrules and grommets fitted. The leaks had probably been resultant from careless tightening of the ferrules during the last re-fit and the contamination of the feed-water had been a direct result. As Sam was quick to point out, it wasn't the Andrew's fault.

The remedial work was duly completed and the condenser was re-filled with water and tested. A broken gauge connection was found on the low-pressure turbine-outlet casing, which connected the LP cylinder to the top of the condenser, which had probably been the main cause of the loss of vacuum. In the circumstances, it was decided to open up, clean and survey the other condensers, including the auxiliaries. In discussing them, Mike asked Sam how the ship's Engineers had let them get into such a state. He was bluntly told not make stupid comments, which might be overheard and construed as unfair criticism.

'I've told you before that you've got a lot to learn,' he said tersely. 'All the muck in the condensers was probably sucked in when she was out in the estuary or maybe when she was coming up river. If she'd gone back out into clear water, it would have all been flushed out again, so don't be acting so bloody clever. It's our job to put things right, not to point the finger at other people and anyway, when a Ship's in commission, you're never in port long enough to start messing about with the engines, unless it's absolutely necessary. The Engineers on this old girl will have had more than enough to do, just to keep her going and don't you forget, we benefit from their problems, so shut it and let's get on with the job.'

While the cleaning was in hand, they helped a Fitter who had come out from the Factory. Ron was a specialist in the maintenance of steam turbines and he also had a reputation for being very thorough in everything he did. He stripped out the labyrinth seals at each end of the LP cylinder and having found them in what he said was 'poor condition', he ordered new ones. They should have been replaced during the last refit, but had probably been left as a cost-saving measure. With the Yard still operating on an austerity basis, all such expenditure was strictly controlled. The new seals were fitted after Ron had checked and carefully burnished the surfaces of the shafts, by the deft use of fine whet stones.

The Dock Foreman had been told that the shafts would be inched round from time to time, when the main bearings were opened up. They were in very good condition, considering the many thousands of miles which the Ship had steamed since they were last surveyed. Lead clearances were taken and the data was carefully recorded for posterity. Great care was taken to ensure that no further problems would arise when the Ship returned to sea. It was at that point that Mac informed Mike that his time with Sam was up and, on the following Monday, he was to be sent elsewhere. The lad was pleased when the old bugger, who had given him such a hard time in the first few weeks, made appreciative remarks about his work and he was even more surprised when he said that he would also inform his Manager. When Mike told Sam what Mac had said, his mentor was just as pleased.

'There you are', he said warmly, 'you can now appreciate what I've been telling you all along. Mac is a decent bloke and when he's treated with a bit of respect, you don't have any bother with him. You have to bear in mind, he's got a lot on his plate and has no time for being mucked about by some cocky young sod. As I've said all along, you play it straight with him and you'll be fine. I've worked for him for quite some time and he looks after me very well. Take it as a lesson in life, my old son.'

After collecting his gear, Mike didn't have far to go on the Monday morning but yet again, it was like going from heaven to hell. He was sent to work with a fitter called Sonny, also known as 'Sonny Jim', who was working in the dry-dock gang who were removing the damaged propeller from the same Ship. Anyone who has worked in a dry-dock, particularly late on in the year, will know just how cold and miserable a job it can be. The weather was dreadful and the work was both dirty and arduous and the only concession to the conditions was the free issue of wellington boots. There was none of the warm, protective clothing of these more enlightened times. The Mateys had to wear whatever they could find to keep dry and warm. There were several waterproof jackets and trousers in an old railway truck parked on the jetty and they were filthy and smelt disgusting. At lunch time, he went to see Sam to ask if he had any suggestions, and he was most helpful.

'That's alright, my old son,' he replied in his usual friendly manner, 'you've done right to come back to me. Now, I reckon I can get hold of some decent waterproofs for you. Whatever you do, don't put on any of those old wellies. You never know what dirty buggers have had them on before, so we'll get you some new ones, also some Submariner's socks and perhaps a jersey as well. They'll cost a few bob, mind. We'd better see about some neck-cloths and a couple of pairs of waterproof gloves as well. With all that lot, you'll be nice and snug and looking tiddly eh?'

Mike handed over a couple of pounds with no qualms, being greatly relieved that his former mentor was disposed to help him out. Sam sternly advised him to keep out of the dock until he had got his gear and said that he'd have a word with Sonny, who was an old mate.

'Just make sure you stow your clobber away securely in a locker, with a good padlock on the door. You know what a thieving shower of bastards we've got round here, don't you? Don't leave anything lying around or some lousy sod will pinch it. Come back tomorrow afternoon and I'll have your gear.'

The next day, Mike went back and collected his bits and pieces and as he handed them over, Sam had a few more helpful comments. He spoke mainly about the need for personal cleanliness, saying that the water in the docks was contaminated by all sorts of 'nasties'. For that reason, he was very specific in his instructions.

'Always wear your gloves when you're working and wash your hands well every time you come up top, especially before eating or going for a 'Jimmy', (a Jimmy riddle – rhyming slang). Make sure to keep your cap on and always wear a neckerchief. You can't be too careful, because you can catch all sorts of things in a dock. You should also have a bath every evening. I wouldn't use the showers in the amenities if I was you 'cos there's a lot of odd buggers about,' he said, winking slyly. 'You won't have to worry about Sonny, but watch out for some of the other ones in the gang. Just say that if anyone touches your gear, you'll thump him and with your reputation, that'll be more than enough.'

Mike felt a lot better about going to work in the dock and he went down below in a good frame of mind. There, he was critically examined and suffered daft comments about what he was wearing. Knowing his critics were green with envy, he took no notice.

The removal of the screw and tail-shaft took just over a week to complete and in addition to working until eight o'clock each evening, they worked through the following weekend, which did much to make up for the discomfort. Sonny took Mike into the Factory to see the shaft being straightened in the huge lathe, by his old mate Lou and they also looked at the repairs in progress on the damaged screw. The broken blade had already had a piece cut out and a new one was in the process of being brazed into it. Sonny explained that the Section was in constant demand for that sort of work and they regularly did repairs for other Yards. A couple of days later, they went back to watch the Operators dynamically balancing the propeller; a very complicated process which required great care.

Mike soon got into the rhythm of working in the dock and was again impressed with the skills of the Riggers, who were working under the stern of the Vessel. One of them was called Will and he was a grizzled old man who was not exactly friendly to Apprentices, having often been the butt of juvenile pranks in the past. He seemed impervious to the rigorous working conditions and was by far the most energetic member of the gang, particularly with the really heavy work. While the Fitters and their lads struggled to swing a fourteen-pound hammer, the old man handled it with effortless ease. He was a veritable giant, with heavily muscled arms like a professional weightlifter and the gang seemed to have a great deal of respect for him. However, there was an insidious mole in their midst, with evil intentions of vindictive mischief in mind and it wasn't long before he played his hand.

The gang worked steadily in fitting the new bearing-liners into their housings, which were located in the hull and in the 'A' frame beneath the stern. The latter provided the support which enabled the propeller to rotate clear of the hull. It was hard and difficult work, which called for a fair degree of skill. With the bearings installed, the tail-shaft was brought back from the Factory, off-loaded, then lowered into the dock. The riggers used numerous sets of chain blocks to slowly feed it through the bearings and into the hull. When it was almost home, a messenger came to tell Will that the Foreman wanted to see him in his office right away and there was some light-hearted banter that 'the old bugger was for it now', as he climbed down off the scaffolding.

About half an hour later, he came back down into the dock and made his way slowly back up to the platform. He stood in front of his workmates, with tears streaming down his cheeks, and it was some minutes before he could tell them what had happened. Despite the unending profanity from those working around him, Mike had never heard Will swear and although a bit gruff at times, he had come across as a gentle, kindly old man, who worked as hard, if not harder than anyone else in the team. They pressed him to tell them what had happened.

When he'd gone into the office, the Foreman had picked up a piece of paper, passed it across the desk and asked him if the contents were true. The memo had stated that Will was well past the age of retirement and should not still be working in the Yard. He had reluctantly confirmed that was correct, but couldn't believe what he had just read. Someone, who either worked with or near him, had turned him in. The tip-off had come in the form of an anonymous letter, addressed directly to the Manager. The Foreman had received a 'right bollocking', as he should have been aware of the situation and ensured that the Yard's rules were properly upheld. He had told Will to go and 'pick up his things' and then he would be escorted to the gate. His dismissal was, in the modern parlance, 'instant'.

'Who could have done such a thing?,' the old lad asked mournfully. 'I've never harmed nobody, and I've always worked just as hard as anyone else. Now what's to become of me?'

His workmates self-consciously stood around him and shuffled their feet and some tried to console him, but were unable to do so. One of them went up out of the dock to find Dolly Gray, the Shop Steward and when he came down a few minutes later, he explained that while he felt very sorry for Will, given the circumstances, there was nothing the Union could do about it. The rule was that everybody had to retire on their sixty-fifth birthday, with no exceptions made. The Unions had fought over very many years to get that concession from the Employers and turning to Will, he made his point.

'You must have known you should have gone when you was sixty-five,' he told him. 'You've been very lucky to have got away with it for so long and to be frank, Will, I don't know how the hell you've managed it. All we can do now is to see that you are treated with a little bit of respect, but you're going to have to go, old mate, there ain't nothing we can do about that.'

'I've worked here, man an' boy, for more than sixty years and I've always done my best,' Will replied sadly. 'I suppose you're right, Mister Gray. I've got to go, but what hurts me more than anything is that a workmate has done me harm in such a nasty way. I just don't understand it, whoever he is. Why didn't he speak to me direct, if he wanted my job so much? I could have gone quietly and none of this would have happened.'

One of the Fitters then quietly asked Will how old he was.

'I shall be seventy-three in a couple of months' time,' he replied, with a note of defiance in his voice.

He then picked up his bag and in company with the Shop Steward, he went up out of the dock for the last time. The Charge-hand, who was equally as taciturn, turned to his workmates once Will was out of earshot and angrily told them just how he felt about 'the whole bloody issue'.

'I don't know what's gone on among you lot, but be warned, whoever has done the dirty on that poor old sod had better not let me find him. He ought to be bloody well ashamed of himself.'

It was a sentiment with which they all agreed, or so they said. What had been a tight-knit gang had suddenly changed into a sullen group of men, all of whom suspected each other of treachery. While no one was actually accused of the dirty deed, one or two were thought of as the most likely culprits. As Sonny amply put it, 'If you can't rely on your workmates, who the bloody hell can you trust?'

Chapter 7

More Discomfort

Nothing more was heard about the old lad until about a month later. The gang was working on the screws of a Frigate in another dry-dock and a Rigger, who coughed self-consciously, made an announcement during the morning tea break.

'I thought I'd just mention that Will died yesterday, the poor old bugger.'

His workmates looked at him in a stunned silence and then disconsolately at each another. They had not found out who had done the dirty on him, although some still had their suspicions. The most likely ones had been closely watched but whoever the guilty swine was, he had had the good sense to keep schtum. In the week after the old man's departure, the shaft had been coupled up and the propeller put back on. Mike's suspicions were brought into focus when he had been sent down into the stern-chamber to help another Fitter to assemble the muff-coupling, which connected the tail-shaft with the next section inboard.

Ken was a bit of a clever git, being curt in his speech and cocky in his manner and it wasn't long before they fell out. They struggled with what was normally a straightforward job which, while awkward due to the confined space, should have been completed within a day. After badly distorting the forrad bulkhead of the chamber, by the injudicious use of a hydraulic jack, Ken angrily shouted at Mike, when the wooden packing under it collapsed. He told the lad in no uncertain terms to 'piss-off', saying he would finish the job himself. The lad went straight back to Sonny and told him what had happened.

'Don't take any notice of him,' his Fitter said. 'He's a queer sod at the best of times and I only sent you to give him a hand, to see what fitting the coupling was like. Come on, we've got another job to do back over on the Cruiser.'

Their task was to assist two test engineers in a survey of the steering gear, which had been reported as 'playing up'. The engine had been inspected and the rudder and its supports were to be closely examined. Apart from moving a wheeled, scaffold platform from time to time, to give the 'boffins' access, their assistance was little more than minimal.

While the survey was in progress, Sonny and Mike walked along under the full length of the hull, up one side and down the other. What they saw confirmed that the Jolly Jacks had indeed been careless in conning their vessel. The hull had been extensively damaged beneath the waterline, which indicated that she had been aground on more than one occasion. There were signs of scuffing along the bottom edge of the rudder, though it was otherwise in good condition. Following the submission of the Engineers' report, a decision would be made as to what remedial work was necessary to ensure the free movement of the entire system.

Back on board the Frigate, there was a serious problem. After Ken had completed the assembly of the muff coupling, he had started to re-pack the stern gland but for some reason, he had left the job only half-done. The Foreman and or hid clerk should have been aware of the situation, because the job card had not been signed off and returned to his office. While the dock was being refilled, Ken should have gone back down to check that all was in order, with only perhaps a minimal adjustment of the gland ring being necessary. Only a small flow of water was required to lubricate the tail-end bearing but, there had been an inrush of water into the enclosing chamber and it had flooded. The dock had had to be pumped out to a level below that of the shaft and there was one hell of a rumpus. Ken was sent elsewhere to work, which caused no end of mirth among his erstwhile mates.

Due to the overtime that Mike had worked and his regular receipt of conditional payments, he had been earning considerably more than his father for quite some time. He had kept the extent of his new-found wealth to himself and had regularly changed the place where he kept his pass-book hidden. On a number of occasions, he had tried to buy his mother off, by putting a bit of extra into the family budget but to no avail as the more he gave her, the more she wanted. His purchases of clothing, books and other luxuries, caused angry resentment and the hostile atmosphere in the house had grown steadily worse. She had continued rummaging through his belongings and opening his mail and his angry protests were always answered by their equally angry retorts that, 'if he didn't like it, he knew what he could do'.

He was reluctant to burden others with his problem but at times, he had to get it off his chest and hearing of his predicament, a Fitter told him about some 'super' digs, which he described as warm and friendly. Mike was very tempted but after thinking hard about the whole situation, he decided he had to stick it out at home. When the overtime came to an end, as it surely would, his wages would be substantially reduced and limit the extent of his saving. A more mature young man would have grasped the nettle but as we've noted previously, the courage to do so was lacking. The root cause of his troubles remained in the old man's long-held and vehement insistence that he was not his father. There was nothing he could do about it and it would continue to cause him grief until the end of his Apprenticeship.

His life was not all doom and gloom. He enjoyed long bike rides around the surrounding countryside and when the weather was settled, he would often cycle as much as ten miles. From the beginning of his fourth year, he had been able to afford to buy meals in the many tea shops and 'caffs', which specialised in high teas of ham and eggs and chips. While no longer teetotal, he only imbibed a small shandy or a glass of cider now and then. He had made new friends and often went with them to watch cricket or football matches. There was a Plymouth Brethren meeting house approximately a mile from the village and after a lad had invited him to a meeting, Mike went along one Sunday evening. He soon came away when another young man abruptly told him that he wasn't welcome. He had apparently seen Mike coming out of the local pub and in the ensuing argument, an adult confirmed what the lad had said.

He regularly went to the dances at the Town Hall on Saturday evenings, though tickets were often expensive and hard to come by. If they were bought legitimately, the halves could be retained as 'pass outs' and could be handed out to mates through the gents' toilet windows. Other dancers also gave them their halves, so entry was easily illicitly gained, though the lads had to be careful not to draw attention to themselves and their scam worked well, even for the gala evenings. Because of potential problems, they were usually 'all-ticket', with the known troublemakers excluded. Despite the organisers' best efforts, they were regularly infiltrated by the riff-raff and brought to a premature end by their rowdy behaviour. Time and again, they thought they had nipped the problem in the bud, only to find that soon after the second session started, all hell broke loose.

The Management must have sussed what had been happening and the windows and catches in the gents' and ladies' toilets were repaired. However, when one door closed, another opened and when an enterprising lad went to the cloakroom one evening, he saw that the attendant was elsewhere. He couldn't believe his luck when he found a key on a board, which was clearly labelled for a door at the back of the building. It was conveniently located down an unlit corridor and later, when the lock was changed, they could still hand out tickets through the letter box, It was all so easy to buck the system and the lads benefited greatly for some considerable time.

Going to a dance meant dressing up – in most cases, a bath, shave, suit, shirt and tie – and it brought the usual probing questions from Mike's mother. His journeys were not without problems, because the last bus had recently been 'taken off' due to the misbehaviour of some of the passengers. Now it went at half-past ten, which was far too early to leave a dance and it meant that he and his mates had to walk home. It was inevitable that they were caught out by the weather and they were often soaked to the skin. One wet evening, he 'found' an umbrella and he used it for some weeks after until someone else 'half-inched' it.

Sunday evenings in the Cellar Club were mostly happy and relaxed, with none of the problems which occurred elsewhere. In the months that had passed since it opened, it had gained a regular clientelle and the small group that Mike went with was mainly made up of lads from work and their girlfriends. Most of the girls were dressed in the current mode, which consisted of white blouses and very wide skirts, which were pushed out by numerous petticoats. Dave was more 'with it' than most of his friends and he favoured the Edwardian style. He didn't dance much but when he did, he remained rooted to the spot, while his lass rotated, first one way and then the other around him. It was all a bit droll but he was only aping the real Teds. He was of a more serious disposition and though friendly enough, he was always quick to inform someone of his displeasure.

One evening, he was seen speaking angrily to a lad from another group and he ended it by saying loudly, 'I'll not bloody tell you again, you daft bugger!'

The object of his ire was a lanky youth, whose very large feet were contained in a pair of soft leather shoes. They were colourfully referred to as brothel creepers and had inch thick soles. His partner, Jackie, was a petite and pretty girl, with lustrous black hair, which she usually had tied back in a pony-tail. She was an elegant dancer and she skipped and glided beautifully as she performed her pirouettes. Her boyfriend was not as well accomplished and must have thought the admiring comments were meant for him as well. Dave had been happily 'doing his thing', when a bloody great foot suddenly kicked out near his head, which disconcerted him greatly. That was the reason for his quiet word with, 'that long streak of piss', as he so eloquently described him. Despite the warning, it happened again soon after and the youth found himself on the floor in a dazed condition. Dave had 'clocked him one' and it was a minute or so before the doorman realised that something was wrong. When he asked what was going on, a quick-witted reply was forthcoming.

'It's bloody hot down here and the poor lad must have fainted, or something.'

Everyone laughed at his effrontery. While Jackie and her friends helped her boyfriend away up the stairs, others joined in the fun and told the man that something had to be done about the ventilation. The following Saturday afternoon, when Mike saw Jackie in the Town, she was most apologetic about what had happened. She had spoken to Norman about 'kicking-out' a number of times and he had ignored her warnings that it was dangerous. Unfortunately, he had come unstuck with Dave and been duly chastised. In the following week, a couple of ducts were installed to bring fresh-air down into and out of the cellar. It made for a great improvement in the atmosphere, which had previously been full of cigarette smoke. The long-legged oaf was not seen again and, much to the lads' disappointment, neither was Jackie.

Bill had recently been going to a Methodist Church on Sunday evenings; his main reason being on account of the 'crumpet' in the congregation. After the Service, the young people met in a large room under the building for a social end to the evening, with cups of tea, sandwiches and cakes being freely provided. Music and dancing were prohibited, but it was all very cordial and Bill had soon made new friends. The rule was that everyone had to attend the Service, which wasn't at all to his liking. Mike, always game for another facet to his entertainment, agreed to meet him there the following Sunday. It was a cold, wet evening when they arrived and the Service was still in progress.

The answer to their problem lay just across the road in another Christian organisation, which had a facility whereby Servicemen were assured of a warm welcome and an appetising meal at a most reasonable price. The objective was to keep them away from the dubious attractions of the numerous pubs in the town. After telling Mike to let him do the talking, they went into a large hall where Bill ordered a veritable feast, which consisted of bacon, egg, sausage and chips, with bread and butter and large mugs of tea to wash it all down. Nearly an hour later, replete and in very good humour, they made their way back across the road and down into the room below the Church. They were warmly welcomed and Bill introduced Mike as another potential 'customer'. He had been right about the 'talent' and they both had a very pleasant time.

Their visits to the Servicemen's Mission became was a regular part of their Sunday evening' entertainment. However, they were destined to be thwarted when a member of the staff asked Bill which Service he was in. The lad told him that he was in the Navy and was 'standing-by' a Frigate in the Yard. His questioner was unimpressed and crossly told him he was talking nonsense. If he had to tell lies, he should at least get his story right. The ship he had named was in the Mediterranean and it was obvious he was not in the Navy. He bluntly told the lads not come in again and to leave as soon as they had finished their meal.

The following week, they were confronted by two members of the youth committee, one of whom was an apprentice in the Yard. He had noticed that they had not attended any services, nor made any financial contributions to the Church. He had spoken to one of the Elders and been told to tell them that they had to 'toe the line'. He had also seen them going into the King's Head Hotel, on the previous Saturday evening. Mike, as usual, couldn't keep his mouth shut and told him it was immature to 'tell-tales'. As they walked up the hill afterwards with a small group, he was confronted by the lad who had had so much to say. He had taken exception to what had been said and in the ensuing spat, Mike lashed out and the lad fell to the ground. His friends were outraged and the unlikely pair were told in no uncertain terms to go away and leave them in peace.

The next day, the injured party saw Mike in the canteen and, after assuring him that he had no intention of resuming their argument, he apologised for his part in it. They shook hands and that was the end of the matter. When he had gone, Mike thought glumly about the stupidity of what he had done. He was still getting into scraps which he could so easily have avoided. It was high time that he grew up and learned to behave in a civilised way because it could only be a matter of time before he would either meet his match or find himself in serious trouble.

Chapter 8

Crane Maintenance

Mike continued working in the dry-docks until the end of January. It had been a very cold Winter and he'd often been glad to take refuge in the dockside workshop, where there had been in some semblance of warmth. As mentioned earlier, the racket in the dock could be excruciating in its intensity, particularly when the hull-plates of a Ship were being replaced or internal bulkheads reconstructed. He was very relieved when he was told to report to the Manager of the Cranes Department on the following Monday. At long last, he was leaving the cold, dirt and discomfort of the docks and in his new place of work, he would be involved in the overhaul and maintenance of a broad range of lifting equipment. One thing was certain, he would be working in more salubrious conditions, or so he thought.

Having spent six months working on interesting jobs, with Fitters with whom he had got on very well, he was understandably apprehensive about the move. Noting his unease, his mates were quick to give the pot a stir.

'Oh, bloody hell, not the Cranes,' one of them said, laughing loudly. 'I wouldn't like to be in your shoes, old mate. The Foreman's a right miserable sod and you don't want to be getting on the wrong side of him, that's for sure. Oh dear, oh dear, you're for it now.'

Mike knew better than to listen to his prattling, but the seed of doubt was firmly planted in his mind. He had been in more than enough trouble and he decided he would do exactly as he was told and see how it panned out. His previous complaints about headaches, which had yielded some respite, had resulted in a lot of unpleasantness at first and where had he ended up? Back working in a succession of dry-docks for more than the remainder of the time that he should have served in the first place. As someone pointedly remarked, 'you can't buck the system because they (whoever 'they' are) will always get you in the end.'

On the following Monday morning, he and Dave reported to the Cranes Foreman and were yet again disappointed with their reception because on their way over, he had assured the lad that he was absolutely determined to keep out of trouble. It wasn't as bad as with Mack, but 'with open arms' it most certainly wasn't. The man was po-faced and abrupt in his briefing, going on at length about safety and the need for good behaviour. No mucking about would be tolerated and they were to do exactly as they were told. It was the same old story. He then took them down into the shop, and they were introduced to their Fitters. Mike's first impression of Bert was favourable as he was a large, friendly old man, who smiled at him broadly. He was servicing a 15 ton capacity, diesel-engine driven, rail-mounted crane. It was a new machine, which had not done much work and it was parked at the top-end of the Rail Marshalling-yard. As they walked down the road, Mike optimistically thought that he might just have fallen into a cushy number. Most of the morning passed with the engine ticking-over, to warm it up ready for an oil-change. As it turned out, Bert had no intention of doing it that day and having warmed the cab, he took his ease in some semblance of comfort in the Driver's seat. An hour or so later, he sent Mike into the Factory to fill a large billy-can with hot water. When he came back, his boss placed it on the exhaust manifold to bring it back to the boil and he then made their tea.

He told Mike that had served in the tanks in the First World War, because he had been able to drive a lorry and knew a bit about engines. The luxury of a 'nice hot cup o' tea', during the bitter months of Winter on the Western Front, was his abiding memory. He had avoided the horrors of the trenches because the tanks had been kept in reserve for some time after they had landed in France. He then went on to tell the lad about how things were, between himself and the Foreman.

'We don't want to go back to the shop for our tea breaks because it takes up too much time. Besides, Jack will think we've been working through our break and like as not, we'll get a little bit of extra cash. It's all a bit of an act because he's as sharp as a razor and knows exactly what's going on but he'll leave us alone, as long as we don't take liberties.'

The tea break lasted longer than the normal fifteen minutes, with Mike being told to keep a 'weather-eye' out of the cab for 'visitors'. At about eleven o'clock, Bert decided to 'show willing', which was evidently one of his favourite terms. He then did something that Mike had heard about, but had never seen before and it certainly demonstrated his skill as a craftsman. He took the rocker-cover off, the top of the engine, then checked the tappets' clearances with feeler gauges and made minor adjustments with it still running. It may have been 'no big deal' to an experienced mechanic, but Mike was very impressed at his dexterity; a knack that had been acquired over very many years. With everything in order, the engine was shut down and Mike replaced the cover.

'Now about this job,' Bert said, gently puffing on his pipe. 'As I expect you know, we get a number of hours to do the work. We've got plenty of time, so we needn't rush to finish it too quickly. When it's done, I'll get a bit of bonus money and you'll get a quarter of it. Tomorrow, we'll check the timing and have a butcher's at the injectors, then we'll change the oil and filters and generally finish off. We'll also check the brakes, pump grease around the whole issue and do anything else we can think of. Not a bad job,' he said, taking out his malodorous pipe, nonchalantly re-lighting it and filling the cab with acrid smoke. The old lad was 'winding-down' to his retirement, it being only a matter of weeks before his sixty-fifth birthday and he was very much looking forward to working on his allotment, growing vegetables and a few flowers, with pom-pom Dahlias being his favourites.

'I don't want to get under the old woman's feet, so I shall be spending a lot of time down there,' he mused. 'I've got a nice little shed, with an old armchair and a pot-bellied stove inside, so I shall be very comfortable. There's always someone about, so I shan't be short of a bit of company.'

Because they were out of the way, they rarely saw the Foreman and when he did appear, he usually came at about the same time. With the job completed, an Inspector came to check and test the crane. A couple of Riggers made up the test- load and it was subjected to safe-working and overload tests. After having been driven up and down the track a few times, he signed it off as fit for service. When they returned to the workshop, Mike's thoughts were very much about how much extra cash he would get and with no overtime, it was an important consideration. The following Friday, he was handed his bonus money and he also received a number of hours 'uncas', which were paid at the princely rate of three pence an hour. Compared to the dry-dock, the maintenance of the crane had been a salubrious billet, to say the least.

Their next assignment turned out to be a disaster. They were sent over to a crane alongside the No. 2 basin, to carry out a hoist-rope change. The 'gang' was made up of two Fitters, their Apprentices, a Mate and a couple of Riggers. Soon after they arrived, Bert complained that 'he wasn't feeling a hundred per cent' and he went back to the shop. When the gang climbed up into the drive-house, they were shocked to see that both the cab and the power-room behind were in a right mess. Paper, uneaten scraps of food and noisome filth of a far worse nature lay on the deck and Bill, the Fitter, angrily described the Drivers as dirty sods, who hadn't even bothered to go down to the toilets on the jetty. The smell was disgusting and he went back to the Foreman, to ask for the mess to be cleaned away and the space disinfected.

When the Foreman came along, he brought the two scruffy individuals who had recently been driving the crane and he shouted that he was tempted to make them clean the bloody place out. However, a gang of cleaners duly arrived and they spent the rest of the day working in the enclosed space. The next morning was dry but bitterly cold, which made for arduous working conditions outside. There was no sign of Bert and with the poor old boy still 'out of sorts', Bill told the lads that they would have to give him a hand. They climbed up into the power house to prepare to unwind the old rope off the winch drum. A few turns of a long hemp rope were taken around it, with the short end attached to the old wire rope. He then told them to go out of the cab and climb up the jib, which was elevated at an angle of approximately forty-five degrees.

They were to ensure that the connection between the two ropes passed freely over the pulley at the top, as the rope was paid out and lowered away. It was no problem for Mike but Dave had no head for heights. Bill curtly told him to do as he was told. While he had been explaining what he wanted, the lad had been quietly, in metaphorical terms, 'shitting himself'. The very thought of climbing thirty or so feet up the frosted jib, the base of which was perhaps twenty five feet off of the ground, frightened the life out of him. However, he reluctantly followed Mike out through the cab window.

Mike climbed slowly up, with Dave following close behind. In starting off, he had remarked that it wasn't too bad, as there was a handrail up one side but as they made their way up, he fell behind, with Mike telling him several times to 'take it easy'. About half way up, he could go no further, nor could he retrace his steps back down again. They were in real trouble and Mike urged his mate to stay still and calm and he would help him down when he was ready to move. Bill, who had stayed in the cab, was loudly shouting advice out of the window, which was no bloody use at all. A small crowd of Mateys had gathered on the jetty, some of whom were shouting encouragement and making witty comments. Mike had to step over Dave, which caused the lad to panic and it was some time before he was able to move. Their progress down was painfully slow, with Mike patiently guiding his feet on to the rungs of ladder, one by one. At the bottom, the lad was in a right old state and Bill abruptly sent him down to help the Riggers on the jetty.

Mike went back up the jib with a hammer and a 'podger' (a single-ended spanner with a point on one end). The thought of what would have happened if he had come down to fetch them and had left Dave on the jib didn't bear thinking about. The tools were needed to force the joint in the ropes through the gap between the guard and the pulley, which was a difficult job for one man. When ensconced at the top of the jib, he waved to the driver to wind the wire rope off of the winch and down to the ground. As anticipated, the splice jammed and Mike waved frantically for the unwinding to stop. The jib gave a couple of bounces, which made him hang on grimly. He then took the hammer from his belt to force it through the gap and that was where he came unstuck. The rope was covered in thick, black grease and he was wearing industrial gloves, which impeded his grip on the hammer. After two or three blows, it slipped out of his hand and fell to the ground.

Mike looked down as it fell and was horrified to see the Foreman was standing underneath the head of the jib. He shouted a warning to 'look out below' and was relieved to see Smithy scramble clear just before the hammer hit the ground with some force and very near to where he had been standing.

'You bloody lunatic,' yelled the furious Foreman. 'Come down here, now!'

Mike went back down the jib, through the power house and down to the ground. Waiting for him was the incandescent Foreman, with Bill standing meekly beside him.

'You could have bloody-well killed me,' the man shouted angrily. 'Didn't you see me standing there?'

Mike, who was just as shocked by what had happened, made no reply. The Foreman's mood then changed and he glared malevolently at him.

'You did that on purpose, didn't you?' he accused. You tried to bloody well get me.' Then, he went on with increasing fury, 'You saw me standing underneath and you dropped your sodding hammer on purpose. Bloody hell, I'm not having that.'

He then strode rapidly away towards the shop. All the time that Mike was being berated by the Foreman, Bill had stood by and not said a word. He asked him why he hadn't spoken out, when he had been watching him from the cab and must have seen what had happened.

'Don't you stick up for your Apprentice, when he's wrongly accused?,' he shouted furiously. 'If the job was so bloody dangerous, why didn't you come up the jib, instead of skulking in the cab? And why wasn't the area under the crane roped off? You're the bugger that should have had the bollocking, not me.'

Bill was full of righteous indignation and angrily shouted back. 'That's it, blame me. It was you what dropped the hammer and I'm not going to have any part of it. Oh yes, we were warned about you before you came down here and what was said was right. You're bloody trouble, you are and no mistake.'

Despite having made a conscious effort to behave himself, Mike was once more well and truly 'in the shit'.

He was later called into the Manager's office, with the Foreman and Bill present. He listened in silence while Smithy gave his side of the story, which he ended by accusing Mike of intending to harm him. When asked what he had to say about it, Mike knew he had to keep his nerve. It had been an accident, nothing more and he said right away that he had no reason to hurt Mr Smith. In concentrating on the job, he had been unaware that anyone was standing beneath him and with Dave unable to go up the jib, he was up on his own. He had been wearing gloves to protect his hands and in trying to force the splice through the gap between the pulley and the guard, the hammer had slipped from his grasp and dropped to the ground. When he said that the area below the jib should have been roped off, to prevent anyone from straying into it, Mike saw right away that he had made a valid point. The Manager then asked Smithy why the job hadn't been carried out, as per standing instructions. It was all very well blaming the lad, but where was he in all this? Mike mentally breathed a huge sigh of relief.

"I've been told that this young man had to help the other Apprentice down off of the jib. Why were they sent up there without proper supervision? I've spoken to you many times before about safety and the lad is right, the area should have been roped off. You're blaming him for nearly causing a serious accident, but why did you walk under the jib in the first place? It seems to me that there are lessons to be learned here.'

At that, he broke off his outspoken criticism of the Foreman, thinking perhaps that he shouldn't have spoken so bluntly with subordinates present. Or was it that he was trying to make some valid points about safety in working, knowing full well that what he had said would find its way back down to the Shop floor? Bill and Mike were told to go back to the shop, leaving Smithy and his boss free to continue their one-sided conversation.

Chapter 9

Nobby Hall

When they arrived back in the shop, they were immediately surrounded by some of the men, all being curious to know what had happened. Mike couldn't believe his ears when he heard Bill tell them about his role in the Manager's office, especially when he said that he 'had told them straight'.

'So I said to Smithy, I said. Don't you bloody well have a go at me and the lad about what happened. You shouldn't have been standing under the crane, I said.'

Mike smiled grimly at the sheer effrontery of the man, but he had had enough trouble for one day. He wasn't going to get into another argument by setting the record straight. When Bill had been standing in front of the Manager, he had been deferential, obsequious even and there had definitely not been any 'So I said to Smithy, I said!' He was later told that Bill's sly ways were both well-known and despised by his workmates. One of the other Fitters came up to him some time later and tried to make light of the incident.

'I don't think you'll hear anything more about that little bit of bother,' he said quietly. 'One thing though, we're going to have to do something about your throwing skills. You need to improve your aim, then next time, you'll hit the old bugger. Keep trying my old son, keep trying!'

Mike had to laugh but, more to the point, he knew he had been accepted in the shop. After dinner, he and the rest of the gang went back to the crane and continued working. After the joint was forced through the pulley cover, the old hoist rope was wound off. A new one was pulled on and affixed to the winch drum and the hook was attached to the free end. Using the adjacent crane, the drive motor on the winch was taken out and dropped to the ground, and then a replacement was hoisted into position and installed. A drive-unit on a long-travel bogey was seized up and that was also replaced. With the job completed, the crane was given a similar statutory test to that on the diesel-crane and after a short run, it was put back in service.

One last point tested Mike's resolve to keep out of trouble. He had looked forward to getting a bonus payment from the job, but Bill had no intention of sharing it. When Mike tackled him, he was most indignant.

'You've got a bloody cheek, what with all the trouble you've caused,' he retorted angrily.

Not for the first time, the unfairness of the system was plain to see and to extract retribution on the sly dog would only have caused him yet more trouble. Despite having worked at a considerable height and in hazardous and very dirty conditions, he had received no other payments either. Bill, who had not done any of the arduous work, had kept the money which he should have shared. However because of the unfortunate incident with the Foreman, his work on the cranes in that part of the Yard was abruptly curtailed. Late on Friday afternoon, he was called into the office and curtly told to move his kit over to the Locks Maintenance Department.

On the following Monday morning, Mike cycled down the Yard to report to another Foreman. a Mr Manchester, who was in charge of the facility. His first impression was that the man was indeed the martinet that his mates had been at pains to warn him about. As well as the locks, which were the sole means of entering and exiting the Yard, he supervised the maintenance all the ancillary plant and machinery in the immediate area and also dockside cranes around the No. 3 basin. It was said that he ran a tight ship and he always dealt severely with anyone who messed him about. His was an onerous job and he clearly had more to do than many Foremen. Word of the lad's arrival had gone ahead of him, because when he went into the shop, no one answered when he asked where he could find the Foreman. One of the men merely nodded towards the office and sullenly continued with what he was doing.

When he knocked on the door and went in, Manchester looked up from some papers on his desk and curtly told him to wait. Some minutes later, he looked up again and asked what he wanted. Mike told him who he was and said that he had been instructed to report to him. The man looked at him balefully and said that he didn't know why he'd been 'lumbered' with him, which confirmed his worst suspicions. He held his tongue, knowing nothing would be gained by answering back and the Foreman went on to lay down the law about how things were done in his domain and how he expected everyone to work hard to produce the best results. Any laxity or messing about would not be tolerated. His lecture went on for some minutes until at last, he went to the door and called for someone to fetch Nobby Hall.

A few minutes later a large, stern looking man, who was wearing very dirty overalls and a greasy beret, put his head around the door and asked if he had sent for him.

You know bloody well he did, you daft old sod, Mike thought gloomily, as he stood impassively in front of the Foreman. It was the Fitter with whom he would be working and he also had a reputation of being a hard taskmaster. *Talk about falling on your feet*, he thought wryly.

'Come in, Nobby,' said the Foreman. 'I want to introduce you to your new Apprentice. From what I hear, he's a bit of a lad, so you'll have to keep him well under control. If he steps out of line at any time, you're to wheel him in here right away. You be warned my lad,' he said, turning once more to Mike, 'there'll be no second chance for you here.'

It was said with both men nodding at each other and warily looking the lad up and down. The Foreman then, to Mike's growing impatience, continued with what seemed to be a never-ending diatribe of 'do's and don't's', culminating eventually with a repeat of his stern instruction to Nobby that if he had any trouble with 'this bugger', he was 'to wheel him in here without a second thought.

Bugger me, the lad thought, as he followed Nobby out of the office, *I'm still in the shit. No matter what I do, it's wrong even before I do it!*

As they walked along the side of one of the locks, Nobby looked sternly at his new Apprentice and then said something completely unexpected. 'Don't take too much notice of what that bugger says, nobody else does round here. He's just got an obnoxious way of saying things and he's all wind and piss. You can't believe anything he tells you, because he's a bloody liar and can't to be trusted. Like so many others in this place, he's only got where he is today by dodging his responsibilities during the War. Be warned, he snivels like hell to the bosses at every opportunity.

'Now, lad, I don't want to know what you've done or for that matter, what you are supposed to have done. That's history as far as I'm concerned and none of my business. However, I've got to say that if you play the game with me and behave yourself, then we'll get along just fine.'

Mike could hardly believe his ears. His new boss had no time for the obnoxious Foreman and their relationship was frosty to say the least. He had served for many years in the Royal Navy and as with so many of his ilk, he had a deep-seated contempt for most of his fellow Mateys. They were crafty, lazy, scruffy and without any self-respect, which he said in a slow measured voice and a deadpan expression on his face. He had been in the Navy for nearly forty years and should have been pensioned off before the War, but had been retained 'for the duration'. He was discharged in 1946 and been 'dumped in civvy-street, with not so much as a bloody thank you'. The only job open to him had been 'as a bloody Fitter in this sodding place'. As a highly-skilled Tradesman, he was stuck in a dead-end workplace and in the ensuing months, Mike came to greatly respect him.

Nobby led Mike down the side of the pump house, through a side-door and along a passage into a small mess room. He preferred it, he said, to the one at the side of the workshop, because it was more private and nobody came bothering him. He went over to a locker, opened the door and told Mike that he could clean it out and stow his gear inside. The gesture was very much appreciated.

'Where's your gear?,' he asked, after sitting down and pulling a newspaper from his pocket.

Mike replied that it was still in the Cranes workshop and he would need to find a hand cart to fetch it. He was told where he could 'borrow' one and sternly instructed to put it back where he found it. The move took up most of the rest of the morning and when he came back, Nobby was nowhere to be seen. He spent the afternoon sorting and putting his gear away, then he swept out and tidied the mess room. The reason everyone was so dirty was due to a coal stockyard which was situated to the west of the locks, and everyone and everything was liberally covered with a fine dust. The next morning, Nobby took Mike around 'his patch'. He was in the middle of overhauling a rail-mounted, steam-driven crane, which was parked in a siding on the edge of the stockyard.

At the end of the previous day, they had stopped work early, about fifteen minutes before clocking off time. Nobby explained that as they worked in such filthy conditions, it was accepted that they could take some extra time for cleaning up. There was a large wash room in the pump house, complete with a shower cubicle and indeed, a luxury beyond belief; lashings of very hot water. After cautioning him to keep the place ship-shape, he told Mike that he could use it, but had to keep it to himself. The problem of having to go home to bath, with all the ensuing problems about the expense, was a thing of the past. All he had to do was to bring a towel, soap and some old clothes to work in and like his boss, he could change back into his clean clothes at the end of the day.

Nobby demonstrated his resourcefulness, while they were working on the crane. After checking the water level in the boiler, he flashed it up using wood and lumps of coal, which Mike had garnered from out in the yard. He soon had a good fire going and in consequence, their working conditions were that more tolerable. He told the lad that his jobs regularly yielded satisfactory amounts of extra cash and that he would be adequately compensated for his contribution. He was fortunate indeed to be working with a Fitter who, despite his contempt for most things in the Yard, still made his days interesting. Like others before him he disappeared from time to time, leaving his lad to get on with the job. It was some time before Mike found out the reason for his absences and in fact, it was no big deal.

In the pump house was a hydraulic-pumping system, powered by two coal-fired Lancashire boilers and a very large horizontal, compound steam engine. She was a beautiful piece of engineering, which turned over at eight revolutions per minute. A plate on the side of the LP cylinder indicated that she had given many years of service and in Mike's eyes, she was a magnificent sight. The steam end was coupled to a pair of large hydraulic pumps, which provided the motive-power for moving the lock-gates. Whenever a 'watch-keeper' was away on leave, sick or needed a break, Nobby was called upon to stand in. Then, he was in heaven; a situation which would have delighted any elderly engineer.

He greatly feared that 'someone', meaning Manchester, might take the job away from him. Mike was sternly warned that he always had to conduct himself with decorum when visiting the pump house and what was more, on no account should he go blabbing to his mates. He was also forbidden to bring anyone in to look at the engine. Having promised to behave, he was occasionally allowed to repair the odd valve or re-pack a gland while his boss was on duty. It was a toss-up as to which of them had the most oil and grease on, the man or the engine.

Nobby had tried to make his mark in the pump house many times over the years and Manchester had probably had a hand in his denial. He was convinced that he would remain a 'hairy-arsed' fitter for the rest of his working days; a fate on which he was always ready to expound.

'You'd think with all my years of service and qualifications, I would have been an ideal bloke for a permanent watch-keeper's job,' he said wistfully. 'I don't suppose it'll ever happen now, so it's all the more enjoyable when I get a few hours in and I certainly don't want anyone to bugger it up for me.'

There were other aspects of the man that Mike liked. A week or so after he'd arrived, they had started working overtime on three and sometimes four evenings a week and again, the lad was sternly warned to keep his mouth shut, where his mates were concerned. He couldn't think why others shouldn't know but, given the money he was earning, he did as he was told. His boss was a decent bloke and that was borne out by his regular receipts of both bonus and other payments. While Nobby had a relaxed way of going about his job, he always set to with a will when necessary and always insisted that it was done properly. He was a great raconteur and he amused the lad greatly with his tales of his exploits on the seven seas.

As a young man, he had been stationed 'out East', in Hong Kong and Shanghai, and his best runs ashore had been in Port Arthur, in farthest Russia, He had been a Chief ERA in an old four-stacker Cruiser and his greatest conquest had been a 'Russian Princess', who had desperately wanted to marry him. It mattered not to his listener that he was so obviously shooting a line. On most Thursday evenings, after clocking off at eight o'clock, they went 'for a wet' in a pub just outside the nearby gate and though they only ever had the one pint, it was very much appreciated. If the powers that be had thought that they were punishing Mike for his past misdemeanours, they were sadly remiss because he was happier working at the Locks than he had been in any other part of the Yard.

One morning, they were working on a coupling in the drive-house of a crane by the No. 3 basin and Mike was sent to fetch a spanner, which was part of a chrome-vanadium set, which Nobby had 'got hold of' with considerable difficulty. After being sternly admonished to be sure to double-lock the toolbox and thus thwart the evil intentions of 'those thieving bastards' in the shop, Mike set off without a care in the world. There were numerous Warships alongside, some of which were in commission and of great interest in passing. Time was taken up chatting to other lads along the way and he took far longer on the errand than was warranted. His boiler-suit had the usual front and side pockets, with a long, thin one down the outside of the right leg and he pushed the spanner into it. He made his way back to the crane by completing the circuit of the basin and it had taken him more than an hour and a half. It shouldn't have taken more than fifteen minutes and as he put a foot on to the bottom rung of the vertical ladder to climb up to the drive-house, a furious bellow greeted his tender ears.

'Where the bloody hell have you been?' demanded Nobby, glaring angrily down from the platform above. 'I told you I wanted to get this job done by dinner time and you've not taken any bloody notice. Get your arse up here, quick as you like.'

'I'm sorry, Nobby,' Mike shouted back. 'I've had one or two distractions along the way and I was caught short.'

He then started to climb up the ladder, two rungs at a time. and was almost at the top when the spanner slipped out of his pocket. In falling down the side of the crane, it hit a cross-bracing with a loud 'clang', then fell with a 'plop' into the basin. There was another bellow of rage from above, with threats of dire retribution on his person. Mike thought it prudent to make himself scarce for a couple of hours and only ventured back to face his boss well after the dinner break. He apologised profusely for his clumsiness and offered to pay for a new spanner but was both surprised and relieved when Nobby calmly assured him that it was alright; he'd already 'obtained' a replacement.

'Don't worry, lad,' he said, 'worse things happen at sea. I'm as just as much to blame, because I shouldn't have shouted when you were coming up the ladder.'

Other Fitters would have made a right song and dance about the loss of what was a valuable tool, but Nobby put it down as an accidental loss. That he had already procured a replacement spoke volumes for his ingenuity and working with him obviously had its compensations.

Chapter 10

A Big Job

Nothing more was said about the loss of the spanner, or Mike's absence and they duly completed the job. The following morning, they were again working on the crane in the stockyard but it was very much a 'fall-back' job, because whenever something else needed doing, they were sent to it. Their next job was a big one and it gave Nobby the opportunity to put one over on the other Fitters. All was not well in the low-pressure cylinder of the large engine in the Pump house and with no movement of the lock gates anticipated in the week ahead, Management had decided to take it out of service. Nobby was designated as the 'acting and unpaid' Charge-hand and the gang was made up of three Fitters, two Apprentices, two Labourers and a couple of Riggers. The plant was shut down over the weekend and work started promptly on the Monday morning. To Mike's delight, he was told that overtime would be worked through the evenings.

There was an air of purpose in the air as they got the job underway. The Riggers brought the overhead crane into position and rigged-up the requisite chain blocks, strops and shackles. The low-pressure cylinder top cover was attached to the hook, the weight was taken up and the peripheral nuts and bolts were slackened off. Nobby bustled around importantly and following their removal, the Apprentices were given the job of checking and refurbishing them. They started by thoroughly wire-brushing off the dirt and paint, then the 'burrs' were filed off the nuts and the threads were run down, to ensure ease of tightening when they were replaced. Due to the large number, the job took a couple of days to complete. Each set was reassembled and oiled, then stowed in a large wooden box. When Mike asked why each assembly had been hard-stamped with a number, he was told that they had to be replaced in the same holes, when the cover was put back on. The lads couldn't really see why that should be necessary.

The head was broken away from the cylinder, lifted clear and laid down on the floor with the internal face upwards. It was cleaned off, closely inspected and made ready for re-fitting with a new head gasket, which was made from asbestos tape and tied into position with twine. After removing the gland, they dismantled and removed the 'bottom' end cover, which was in two sections. The piston-rod was disconnected from the cross-head and the piston was pulled out of the cylinder. There lay the root of the problem. The rings were badly worn, with the main parts needing complete renewal. As someone ruefully commented, 'Nobby was as happy as a dog with two dicks'.

The Foreman let him get on with it, because after only a couple of cursory visits, he stayed in his office. Hostilities had been suspended for the duration of the job and from time to time, Nobby went over to report on progress. The work proceeded steadily and with the gang setting-to with a will, everyone was happy. The renewal of the piston-rings was followed by the 'tarting-up' of the piston rod, which had been disconnected and set up between two large wooden V blocks. That was followed by a similar job around the flange at the top of the cylinder. The Apprentices overhauled the lubrication system, but were often called to assist the Fitters, when another pair of hands was needed. The main job, which Nobby did personally, was the close inspection of the internal surfaces of the cylinder.

After a lot of 'humming and haa'-ing', he buffed off the worst of the marks by the deft use of a small hand held grinding-machine and then ground away the small 'lip', which had formed circumferentially around the top of the bore. That, he informed Mike gravely, would ensure that the piston would move smoothly over 'top dead-centre'. He then made a detailed survey of the dimensions of the cylinder, by using a specially-made length of half-inch plate, to which an internal micrometre had been attached. It involved measuring the diameter at regular intervals both circumferentially and along the length of stroke. Mike recorded the readings as his boss called them out and with the job completed, he was sent to the mess-room to make a fair copy for record purposes.

The bottom-end and cross-head bearings were opened up and found to be sound and when all of the refurbishing work had been completed, an immediate start was made on the reassembly of the engine. The piston was lifted off the floor, turned through ninety degrees and reattached to the rod, then eased back into the cylinder and re-connected to the cross-head. The bottom end cover was assembled and hardened-up and the gland 'stuffed' with new packing. The engine was then pulled over through three hundred and sixty degrees, by means of a long wire-rope, which was wound around the fly-wheel and with the other end attached to the crane, the piston was moved freely throughout its stroke. The cylinder-head was then replaced and hardened down. A plug was taken out and a vernier-gauge was inserted to confirm that the clearance between the top of the piston, at top dead-centre and the underside of the cover was correct. After pulling the engine over a couple of times, Nobby dramatically announced that it was spot-on.

In the meantime, the boilers had been cleaned and closely inspected. They were manually coal-fired Lancashire boilers and the Boilermakers completed their work in good time. Sarcastic comments from the Fitters implied that they had 'only half-done the job'. The boiler-mountings, such as the safety, main steam stop and water feed valves were all stripped and checked, then the gauge-glasses were refurbished, with the brass-work given a vigorous polish. At the other end, the blow-down valves were taken out and new internals fitted. The whole job took just seven days to complete, which was inside the original estimate. With everything boxed up, steam was raised and the safety valves on the Boiler were floated. The tools and tackle were cleared away and the working area cleaned down. When the cylinder had been warmed through, the head fixings were finally hardened down.

Nobby remained in the pump house to assist the Operators in putting the unit back into service. When Mike arrived next morning, his mentor was standing in front of the engine, which was turning over very smoothly. Looking very pleased with himself, he gave the impression that she was very much his 'baby'. Later, when he had come back down to earth, he told Mike that the Management was very pleased with the way the job, which had been done competently and with a minimum of fuss, had been completed. It had been the Apprentices' first experience of working on a large steam engine as up until then, they had only seen single-acting, reciprocating, steam pumps. They smugly thought they had 'a bit of crowing to do' to their mates.

Taking everything into account, Nobby should have been a full-time Charge-hand, but he was only given responsibility when it suited Manchester. Their feud, he maintained, had 'put the mockers' on his promotion, though obviously, there was antagonism and prejudice on both sides. He had competently taken the lead in the overhaul of the engine, during which time Manchester had been conspicuous by his absence. No doubt, with the job done, he had lost no time in reporting it to the Manager and blandly helped himself to the credit.

'I've-a' finished that job, George. No problems there. She's back on line and sweet as a nut.'

Who hasn't been incensed, at some time or other, when someone else with little or no input to a successfully completed job, has rushed to impart the good news to the boss. The Ivors of this world never pass up the chance to grab the kudos for themselves and things haven't changed much in that respect over the years.

Nobby and Mike continued working on a succession of cranes and with the coming of spring, their working conditions improved markedly. There were always interesting diversions, with the regular movement of Warships, Fleet Auxiliaries and Dockyard craft through the locks. It was particularly interesting if a large ship, such as a cruiser or even one of the new Daring Class destroyers came in or out. A Warship in commission was a wholly different entity to one that had been laid-up for many months. Despite the signs of wear and tear, most of the Ships were in good shape, which demonstrated the pride that their crews had in them. From time to time, foreign ships visited the Yard, a lot of which were decrepit in comparison. When a Ship came in to pay off, after her final voyage, she was stripped of any useful and valuable equipment, before being towed away for disposal or scrapping.

Dockyard Mateys were not allowed on board until a Ship was formally cleared by HM Customs. Many years of experience had given their Officers the 'edge', though it was a constant battle against the skulduggery of both the Matelots and the Mateys. They were heartily disliked and it probably spiced up their days no end when they caught someone up to no good. It could often be a week or more before they completed their work and relinquished control of a Vessel to the Yard. They were supported by the Dockyard Police, some of whose own Officers would often pose as bone-fide workmen. Everyone knew they had to be very careful, because a fortuitous find was inevitably contraband. Access was also strictly monitored if a Ship was modern, with highly classified equipment on board. Each workman was security-cleared and issued with an additional pass. They were often searched when they came ashore.

The Mateys had to be very careful that any finds hadn't been deliberately planted and it was also difficult to prevent some other bugger from making off with them. Anyone who was fortunate to find something of value had to keep it very much to himself. Trusting no-one was most definitely the best policy. Apprentices often ignored the warnings of their seniors and when caught 'in possession', they suffered accordingly. The majority of the Mateys wouldn't have anything to do with contraband, though when faced with temptation, it was often hard to resist. Utmost care had to be taken when 'moving' anything ashore, as there was often surveillance in place. Numerous felons had been caught over the years, by Constables lurking at the bottom of a Ship's gangway.

For the crook, the final hurdle to be overcome was in leaving the Yard. As previously noted, the Police presence at the gate was daunting and they were very adept at picking out offenders. They weren't as daft as some Mateys liked to make out and anyone who thought otherwise was in for an unpleasant shock because cocky behaviour was a sure way of getting caught. It has always been a human trait though to give the game away by looking guilty and the Mateys regularly did just that. Some could carry it off, but most couldn't and the Police knew it. A ruse which occasionally worked was to carry goods out after the evening school classes, when an apprentice would be laden with books. If he was stopped, the Copper was usually content to look in either his satchel and/or saddle-bag and not bother with a body search. Once through the gate, the villain was home and dry.

Some amusing incidents occurred when a Cruiser came into the Yard and was tied up at the 'Battery Corner'. Most of her crew left her during the day, leaving a small working party on board to complete the decommissioning work. That involved shifting a large amount of stores and equipment ashore, most of which would be needed when she was ready for sea again. Numerous crates and boxes were brought on to the jetty, loaded on to lorries and taken away to the barracks. The Yard supplied the Crane-drivers and 'Banks-men' and a Fitter and mate ensured that the cranes were kept in good working order. The crew's day finished at 16.00 hours and the Mateys in the workshop eagerly awaited their departure. Their intention was to pick-over the growing pile of rubbish on the jetty and glean anything of value. With so much valuable equipment on board, the sentries' presence was imperative.

It wasn't long before there was a lot of shouting from the deck and the Mateys rummaging came to an abrupt end. They returned to the shop with all sorts of knick-knacks such as pencils, notepads, rulers and rubbers, most of which bore the legend 'Admiralty Property'. Someone had picked-up a few bath and hand-towels, which they said only needed to be rinsed out to be as good as new. The toilet rolls they had found; soft for Officers and hard for Crew, caused great hilarity. The most prized items were red imitation leather cushions, most of which were split but still provided a degree of comfort. There were salt and pepper pots, knives, forks and spoons, all of which could be cleaned up and taken home. Many items were embellished with the ship's crest and were very attractive keepsakes. Just before packing-up time, a squad of RN Patrolmen arrived at the shop.

The Chief spoke gravely to Manchester, then he and his men retrieved nearly all of the 'booty', much to the disgust of the tea-leaves. To the Matelots' obvious delight, they also found items which had been half-inched in previous forages. It was Navy property and if anyone wanted 'to make something of it', he would call for the assistance of the Police. If anything else was removed from the jetty, the offenders would be prosecuted. 'Schadenfreud' was clearly in Nobby's reaction when he loudly told his workmates to keep their light-fingers to themselves. He, in turn, was told to 'go away' in the most basic terms, which cannot be recorded here.

Over the next few days, the Crew completed their work and the Cruiser was handed over to the Yard for a refit. The last job for the working party was the clearance of the pile of rubbish, which had grown to quite staggering proportions. Several lorries were loaded and after the jetty had been swept clean, they returned to the barracks. The Andrew would ensure that nothing, which could conceivably be of any further use, would be thrown away. As a wag so humorously put it, 'I bet they even insist that the Jacks use the bog paper on both sides!'

Chapter 11

Treasure Trove

The next day, a rail-mounted steam-crane fitted with a 'grab' puffed on to the jetty and was joined soon after by a locomotive with three open wagons in tow. Nobby was replacing a long-travel unit on one of the dockside cranes and being curious, he asked the driver what was going on. Apparently, when the tugs had moved the ship alongside, the mooring Master had thought she had 'touched bottom'. The basin had not been dredged for many years and they were amazed at what came up in the grab. All sorts of goodies had been dumped overboard by generations of Jolly Jacks. Rather than lug all the boxes of stores off the ship, they must have conveniently heaved some of them over the side.

There was a large amount of crockery, which had evidently not suffered unduly from being immersed in the malodourous basin over very many years. There were cups, saucers and plates of all shapes and sizes, also tureens, gravy boats and large meat dishes, in fact, examples of everything which had been used for the comfort and delectation of the Officers and their long-suffering 'Tars'. Much of it bore the crests of Warships, most of which had long gone, either to the bottom of the sea or to the breakers. Hundreds of Ships must have used the jetty over the years and what was recovered was a veritable treasure trove. Some of the items were truly antique and would today be of great interest to the collectors of relics of our once glorious Royal Navy. Despite his boss's warning, Mike had put a small pile of choice pieces aside, and when he went to collect them, a stern voice made him jump out of his skin.

'What d'you think you're doing?' asked an unsmiling Policeman, who was obviously very pleased to have caught someone up to no good.

'Oh, hello Officer,' said Mike, blushing furiously. 'I've just picked up one or two bits and pieces of crockery, for interest like.'

'Have you got permission to do it?' asked the Copper and without waiting for a reply, he went on. 'No, I thought as much.' He then he interjected, 'Here, don't I know you?'

'Yes, PC Turner,' admitted Mike. 'You've worked with my father, over at the Depot.'

'You know you shouldn't be taking anything off this jetty,' the Officer went on, 'so just put it all back on the pile and get off to where you're supposed to be working. And don't let me see you doing anything like that again. Go on, clear off.'

Mike walked disconsolately back to the workshop and before going in, he turned and looked back. He was not surprised to see the Copper putting something his saddle-bag. He had been a victim of the old adage, 'Do as I say, not as I do!'

Nobby took a week off in the first week in April and in his absence, Mike was told to work with Sid. He was the same man who had greeted him in silence when he had first arrived. When he asked Nobby about him, he said that he was a bit odd and most definitely couldn't be trusted. He had the unfortunate habit of criticising his workmates behind their backs and telling tales to the Foreman. It was thought that Manchester got a lot of his information about what was going on in the area from him. Sid also had a reputation among the Apprentices for being a tight old sod. Mike knew better than to listen to all that was said and decided to see how things worked out. Before he left, Nobby sternly advised him to watch him and be very careful of what he said in front of him.

On the Monday morning, Sid was no more pleased to see Mike than he was to see him. He balefully pointed at some large phosphor-bronze valves and told him to 'get on with them'. After working steadily, Mike had stripped them down by dinner time and had noted that the flange-faces and seats all needed attention. A small lathe in the workshop was in very poor condition and the Foreman wasn't about to ask what he should do with them. Initiative was called for so, after putting on a clean pair of overalls, he put the valve bodies on a hand trolley and took them over to the Factory. An Instructor in the Apprentices' shop readily agreed to get them machined and told Mike that they would be ready the following morning.

When he later told Sid what he'd done, the man didn't even reply, but turned and went straight away into the office. Mike followed him and was both dismayed and angered to hear the whining sod complaining to the Foreman. Manchester turned to Mike and without any hesitation, gave him a bollocking.

'It hasn't taken you long to upset people, has it?' he concluded angrily.

Mike couldn't understand what all the fuss was about and he explained that the lathe in the shop wasn't suitable for re-facing the valves. He'd used his initiative to get them machined in the Factory and if he'd been able to, he would have asked for his permission. As it was, the job was being done and the valves would be completed by the next morning. Sid had made a song and dance about his absence to cause trouble. He then suggested that the lathe should be repaired, which didn't impress either the Foreman or his snivelling Fitter. They were taken aback by his outburst and as had happened before, it turned out to be his best means of defence. Manchester told Sid that perhaps Mike had done the right thing, though the man, who was shifting from foot to foot, looking at the floor and sucking his teeth, was loathe to agree.

'If you want to leave the job,' said Manchester in a more reasonable tone, 'tell someone where you're going. Sid came looking for you because he needed a hand and that was all he was telling me. He was right, because you might have had an accident and been lying injured somewhere. You're right about that bloody lathe though. I've been meaning to get it fixed or replaced for ages, but being so busy, I haven't got round to it. I'll make a note to get it done. That's all for now, you can go back to work.'

The Foreman had made a valid point about his absence, but he was inwardly seething that Sid had been so quick to report him. What had made it all the more galling had been his clumsy attempt to justify the Fitter's snide action. He had though taken his time walking over to the Factory, joined his mates in the canteen and after dinner had loitered in making his way back to the shop. He went back to his bench and quietly carried on working and was soon aware that some of the other men were covertly whispering as they watched him. Despite having calmed down, he couldn't let Sid get away with his treachery. The problem was how to get his own back, without getting into more trouble with the boss. When Sid came down the shop a few minutes later, he came over to the bench and after listening to what he had to say about the valves, Mike made his point.

'I'd been warned you're a snidy git, who's always telling tales,' he said quietly. 'Now I know, don't I? I think a few words are necessary elsewhere, just so we can get things straight, don't you?'

Sid mumbled something about getting on with the job and not having time for arguments and as he walked away, he said crossly,

'As I said, I need a hand, so are you coming, or what? I ain't got all day.'

Mike followed him along the side of the lock to the back of the pump house. The cover-plates of a deep culvert, which contained large-bore pipework, had been 'lifted' and a number of valves, which were operated by extended spindles, had been taken out to give access to a large slide-valve. Sid explained that when he'd finished cleaning it internally, he had been unable to find the Rigger who had been working with him and finding that Mike was missing as well, he'd had no option but to tell the Foreman. As far as he was concerned, he had done nothing wrong. There seemed to be little point in prolonging the argument so Mike kept his reply short.

'In future, if you've got a problem with me, you come and discuss it and don't go snivelling to the bloody Foreman, OK? I expect you know what the other men say about you and I hope I don't have to speak to you again about your snide ways.'

Sid nodded glumly, mumbled that he was sorry and that was the end of the matter. With the help of the Rigger, it took them less than an hour to box the valve up and reconnect the spindle. The next morning, the valves were collected from the Factory by a Labourer, who'd been given a definite instruction to come straight back and not do a disappearing act, 'like someone else he could mention'. It was Manchester's idea of a humorous quip, but it fell on stony ground. When the man returned, it took Mike the rest of the day to grind in the seats and reassemble the valves and the next morning, they were re-installed in the culvert. The rest of the job was completed, without further complaint and after the usual pressure-test, the plant was put back into service.

When they were back in the workshop, Mike pointedly asked Sid about how much bonus, uncas and confined-space money he was going to get from the job. The man was taken aback by his cheek, particularly as he had been so obviously nailed in front of everyone else. There were knowing looks, winks and sly-nods from their audience and everyone stopped to hear Sid's reply. The devious bugger shifted from foot to foot, cleared his throat a few times, then mumbled that he would 'think about it'. Determined not to be fobbed-off, Mike made his point.

'Now come on Sid,' he said, 'you're not thinking of pulling a fast-one are you? That wouldn't be wise, would it? I wouldn't like to have to fall out with you all over again.'

Sid was aware of the sardonic grins from the other men and he knew he had been neatly put into a corner. 'I've already said I'll think about it, haven't I?' he replied testily. 'I'll let you know in the morning.'

Mike's cunning little plan kicked in and any show of anger on his part would only lead to more trouble. He had already enlisted the aid of Jim, the other Apprentice and just before knocking-off time, the lad sidled up to Sid to give the pot another stir.

'I just thought I'd mention it Sid, but you don't want to be messing Mike about,' he said slyly. 'He can be a bad bugger and you have to be a bit careful with him, know what I mean?'

He gleefully told Mike about the man's reaction as they were cycling up to the gate. 'You should have seen his face,' he said. 'I thought he was going to have kittens. What made it worse was when someone else said they'd also heard what a nasty bugger you are. Sid then said in a loud voice that he'd never had any intention of holding on to the bonus and anyhow, he always made a point of being 'straight down the middle' with his Apprentices.'

The next pay-day, Mike was very pleased when Sid handed over the money. He loudly thanked the man, saying that he hadn't really believed what he had heard about him and his sarcasm brought laughter from the other men in the shop.

One of the first things Nobby asked when he returned was how Mike had got on with Sid and when he told him about their problems, Nobby laughed out loud. He had in fact already been told about what had gone on by someone who was bent on causing further mischief.

Up until then, Mike had thought his boss was mostly of a serious nature, though that day, he was clearly in good humour. He heard him quietly singing a song, which he had not heard before. The first two lines went as follows:

'Lord it is my chief complaint
That this Dockyard's weak and faint.'

He sang on, with more words of his own, to the tune of the well-known Hymn No. 260 – 'Hark my Soul, It is the Lord'. It cheered the lad no end to be told that he had done the right thing with Sid. Later, he thought he heard Nobby was still singing when he came back from an errand, but perhaps not. The old bugger couldn't be that happy.

Mike's three months at the Locks came to an end, when Manchester told him he was to move to another Department. He was to report to a Mr James, the foreman on a couple of Ships which were tied-up in the No. 2 basin. As usual, he was a bit apprehensive about moving, but he recalled that his mates had made much about what an old bugger Manchester was and how 'the Locks' was the worst job in the Yard. It had turned out to be a load of old cods-wallop. He should have known better than to listen to them, having heard it all so many times before. Now, after enjoying his stint there and having learned so much, he was sorry to be moving on. It was a funny old life, he thought ruefully, because nothing was ever as bad as it seemed.

'Nil Carborundum Illegitimus', Nobby said sagely, which he obviously thought was Latin. When Mike asked him what it meant, he translated it as: 'Don't let the bastards grind you down!'

The old lad suggested that Mike should go down the Yard to speak to his new Foreman right away. He might also be able to find his Fitter and introduce himself, before some other bugger 'stirred-it'. On the way, he stopped off to see a couple of mates, to discuss the latest developments with them. They were working on a very large ocean-going tug which was tied-up in the No. 3 basin and when he arrived, they were discussing their impending moves. They were soon joined by another couple of lads and there was a lot of ribbing, particularly about the fate of the aforesaid Mac. Mike couldn't believe his ears when he mournfully said that he'd been told to report to Mr Manchester at the Locks. The other lads had a field day, saying it was his turn to get 'shitted-up to the eyebrows'.

'There's no way I'm going to work in those conditions,' Mac said vehemently, 'or for that old bastard. I shall tell the bloody Manager straight, I'm not doing it.'

His outburst was greeted with loud derision and as they went over to the canteen, Mike tried to bring some reason into the discussion. He pointed out that his stint had gone very well and it had had its compensations, particularly with the overtime and extra payments he had received. He told Mac to ask to work with Nobby, because he was the only decent bloke there but, as far the lad was concerned, he'd made up his mind and that was that. Mike mentally shrugged, because the cocky sod wasn't worth bothering about and after dinner, he went to the dockside office and introduced himself to Mr James.

'Oh yes,' said the Foreman, who was known to everyone as Jimmy. 'I've got your name here, along with three other lads.'

Mike asked him if he should fetch his toolbox that afternoon, so that he could make an early start on Monday morning, but Jimmy replied that it wasn't necessary. He could take his time in coming over.

'We're not exactly pushed for work at the moment, so there's no rush,' he said laconically.

As he cycled back to the Locks, Mike thought how very different it was from when he had reported to Mac at the start of the year. Many of his moves had caused some problem or other and moving was never easy. Since then, he had worked with some decent blokes and his time with them had been both enjoyable and lucrative. You had to take the rough with the smooth and get on with it, because everything usually turned out right in the end and if it didn't, so what?

Chapter 12

Personal Matters

The long, cold Winter had come to an end and the mellow days of Spring were more than welcome. Cycling to and from work was no longer the interminable chore that it had been and having finished at the Dockyard School, Mike no longer made evening journeys, unless he was working overtime. As so many Fitters had told him, engineering was changing drastically and whereas only a few years ago, it had been sufficient for a working man just to have a trade, that was no longer true. The ever-increasing pace in the advance of technology was becoming more demanding and without qualifications, a Fitter would in the future have difficulty in finding a well-paid job. In general terms, the lads that had applied themselves to their studies would have no such problems.

Nobby had shaken his head solemnly when Mike had admitted that he had not done as well as he should have. His attendance at the College had been a complete waste of time and as the man dolefully said, he would pay for it later.

'You'll regret messing about, when you should have been concentrating on your studies, not that it's anything to do with me. I've known any number of young men who couldn't be told, both in the Andrew and the Yard. Most of you have self-destruct mechanisms, which stop you from seeing what is blindingly obvious to older, more experienced men. You don't get on with your parents and they want to be shut of you, but have you ever stopped to think just how hard life has been for them? Like a heck of a lot of people, they've struggled to raise their family and when your father insisted you got a trade, he did you a great favour. He wanted to make sure that you didn't end up as he has, with few of the comforts of life.

'If you'd got any sense, you'd have resolved the problem with him long since. You're earning good money now, probably a lot more than he is. I was in the same sort of situation when I was your age, so I joined the Andrew and that was more than enough of a home for me.'

Nobby had not spoken much about his personal life before, but that morning, he had opened up. He had married late in life, with both of them in their early fifties by the time that they'd taken the plunge. His wife had been lumbered with caring for her mother long after her father had died and had eventually inherited their house, part of which she had let out. It was as her tenant that he had first met her. They had soon settled into a comfortable companionship, though they had little in common. Her interests were in music and amateur dramatics, while he was content with the quiet life. They got on well and their home was warm and comfortable and what was most important, she was a very good cook. All in all, his marriage was most satisfactory.

As with most of his contemporaries, the pursuit of the opposite sex was Mike's main interest. He had recently become friendly with a lass named Sue at the Town Hall dances. She was a well-endowed girl who, his mates unkindly said, was 'poured into her dress' and 'goofy' to boot. Mike thought she was vivacious, which caused them to jeer that he was a soft sod. She was a popular lass and often he was lucky if he got more than a couple of dances with her in an evening. He was though a poor dancer and when he apologised for his clumsiness, she curtly told him that she couldn't stand people who were constantly saying sorry for trivialities. It was a little flash of temper which indicated what sort of girl she was, but she soon forgave him.

One evening, he saw that she had not been caught up in the usual rush for partners when the last waltz was called and he quickly moved in. She snuggled up very closely and with the lights dimmed, he enjoyed a very pleasant few minutes, with the added pleasure of an occasional kiss. As the dance ended and thinking he was on to a good thing, he asked if he could see her home. He needn't have bothered, because she rebuffed him without hesitation.

'I don't know what you think, but if you imagine that I'm easy, you can forget it,' she replied with a sweet smile. 'I'm not interested in one night stands. I want more than just being 'pawed-about' by someone I've just met.'

He politely said goodnight and walked off. The next week, he saw Sue smiling at him and went over to speak to her. She was just as warm and friendly as before and while they were dancing, he said that he hoped he had not upset her the previous week. She assured him he hadn't and said that all she had wanted to do was to tell him how things were. Mike replied that he understood and with his tongue in his cheek, he assured her that he had had no ulterior motive. (the liar). Through the interval, they sat quietly talking in the hall, which amused Mike's mates greatly. When he'd asked her if she would like to go to the bar, she had declined saying that she didn't approve of drinking. Later on, when he suggested a date, she replied that she was not interested if he was not serious. If they were to 'go out', it had to be steady and she would want to see him every night. That was most definitely not on.

When he next saw Sue, they agreed to be just good friends and he told her that if she ever needed any help, she could count on him. It sounded pretentious but after the dance, she was waiting by the door and he was surprised to be asked if he would see her home. Apparently, a bloke had been pestering her and she was nervous about walking on her own. As they went along, he was very conscious of her body which was pressed firmly against him. With regular stops for a cuddle, he became increasingly optimistic about something more than the usual bit of 'slap and tickle'. It was not to be. After several attempts to explore 'the forbidden areas of delight', with which she was so abundantly blessed, he realised she was having him on and she pulled away, leaving him with a large lump in his trousers.

He went off to meet his mates at the coffee stall and ruefully told them what had happened. They laughed loudly, when someone said that Sue was a well-known 'prick-teaser'.

'We didn't like to say anything,' he went on, 'because you seemed to be very keen. Now you know, you'll perhaps be thinking about her a bit differently. I'd put it down to experience,' he concluded smugly, much to the amusement of the other lads.

Sue had adeptly thwarted his evil intentions and no real harm had been done. A lad called Willy, who was in the same 'entry' as Mike, came over for a bit of a chat one afternoon, which was odd as only a few weeks previously, he had brought an abrupt end to Mike's budding friendship with another girl called Janet. Initially, his behaviour had not been offensive as such; just that he was staring at them with a silly grin on his face while they were dancing. Mike had ultimately spoken to him about it and Willy had duly apologised and said he didn't want any 'bad-blood' between them.

The following week and with the apology forgotten, Willy had made another move. Mike had danced with Janet a number of times and towards the end of the evening, she had accepted his offer to walk her home. When the last dance was called, Willy smartly nipped in and took her on to the floor before Mike realised what was happening. After waiting outside for some time, he was dismayed to see her come out of the hall with him. They crossed the road and got into a car and Mike was left with his nose out of joint. When he saw the lass again, she told him that Willy had said that he had gone and had offered her a lift home. When they arrived, he had 'tried it on' and when she'd being pushed him away, he had reached across her, opened the door and angrily bundled her out of the car. She had been badly frightened and was still angry at the way he had treated her. Obviously, his sole intention had been to 'get one over' on Mike.

Following his brush with Sue, Mike thought as to how he could get his revenge on the obnoxious sod as he had seen the lad watching them with the same sardonic grin on his face as previously. During a waltz, he made sure that she snuggled up closely, to give him the impression that he was really keen. When he came out at the end of the dance, Willy was lurking at the side of the building. The following week, they again danced and he continued with his ploy and it was 'odds-on' that he was going to fall for it. When the last waltz was called, Mile saw Willy dancing with Sue and later, he watched them drive away. While standing at the coffee stall a few minutes later, he told his mates about what he had done.

On Monday morning, someone remarked that Willy looked as if he had been 'in some kind of bother'. He later saw him coming out of the canteen and he couldn't help laughing at his battered condition.

'So what happened then, Willy?,' he asked innocently.

'I'll tell you what happened,' the lad retorted angrily, 'that bloody cow of yours attacked me.'

That gave Mike the opportunity he'd been waiting for and he turned on him with some venom. 'So you've had your come-uppance, you lousy bastard. Well, it serves you right, doesn't it? I don't know what you did but if you'd had any sense, you wouldn't have acted the crack with Sue. Didn't anybody tell you she's more than capable of looking after herself? She's got a brown belt in judo, you stupid sod and you're lucky to have got off as lightly as you did.'

It was a lie, but Willy wasn't to know. Lowering his voice, Mike made a more pertinent point.

'That's twice you've shat on me and don't bother to deny it or I'll give you a slap as well. All that crap about bad-blood between us, eh? The next time you mess with me, you'll get a fat lip and that's a promise. You'd do well to give me a wide berth from now on, because I won't tell you again.'

Some time later, Mike met Sue in the Town and over coffee, she told him what had happened on the fateful night. They had stopped outside her house, and Willy had soon got a bit fresh. When she told him to stop, he became very annoyed, as he had with her friend Janet. He angrily accused her of being a tease and said that he was going to 'teach her a bloody lesson'. When he moved to grab her, she had lashed out and caught him a sharp blow on the nose, which put an abrupt end to his nonsense. She had not been back to the Town Hall since and probably wouldn't bother going again.

'Well, you have been leading blokes on a bit, haven't you, Sue?,' Mike said with a grin, adding wryly, 'me included.'

She replied that a woman had the right to 'say no'; a point with which Mike fully agreed and despite what had gone on, he didn't bear her any ill-will. As it happened, he didn't see her again, because the number of dances held in the town hall declined markedly in the summer months. Although he'd been right about Willy's perfidy, there was obviously a more sinister side to him. His behaviour in getting rough with both girls had shown that he was given to preying on women who he thought would be easy. If that was the case, it would only be a matter of time before he got into serious trouble.

Growing up had been a slow and at times, a painful process for Mike. As he'd been told so very often, his main problem was that he never knew when to keep it shut and it had often got him into trouble. Older people had told him about their early years, which they said mirrored his own and had he paid heed to what they said, valuable lessons could have been learned. Someone remarked that he was his own worst enemy and with a little effort, he could be a much nicer person. He was kind and considerate, when someone genuinely needed help, but he could also be cold and uncaring. He was aggressively intolerant of cruelty to children and animals, yet was unfeeling to any lass that took an interest in him. His salvation was definitely in his own hands and by the time he was twenty, he should have learned from his own experiences.

He regularly cycled around the countryside and one of his favourite rides was up to the top of the hill above the village. He would often look out over the flat lands that bordered the Thames and down on to the Farm on which he had worked. He thought about Moya from time to time, but the ache he had felt when she had returned to Australia had long gone. Sitting there and quietly reflecting, he thought about the village and all the altercations and dramas, which continually broke out among the residents. Some of his neighbours couldn't live without 'having a go' at someone else. It wasn't a large community and they should have been able to live happily with each other.

An incident the previous Saturday afternoon had sparked off his line of thought, which could have had serious consequences. Among the worst troublemakers was a couple who lived about six or seven doors along the street. David was a tall, thin man of uncertain moods and his wife, Renee, couldn't have been more different as her very size intimidated most of the other residents.

They were both very Welsh and from day they arrived, they made no effort to live in peace with their neighbours. They were contemptuous of all things English and it wasn't long before Renee made her presence felt by regularly upbraiding other people. Her 'war-cry' always included the words 'I'll wipe the bloody floor with you' and she was always given plenty of 'sea room' when in battle order. They had two sons, both as obnoxious as their parents, one being thirteen and the other ten years old. The elder lad was long and thin like his dad and his brother was just like his mother – a barrel of lard.

In truth, there was some justification for the family's attitude, because of the snide comments made about them. It was generally held that 'Dai bach', as he was called, was a thick sod, who wore wellies because of a predilection for sheep. They'd probably had to put up with it all the nastiness before and were determined to give as good as they got. Dai didn't help matters in the Working Men's Club one evening when he was craftily drawn into an argument with a couple of buggers, who were intent on winding him up.

He nearly brought the house down when he was heard to say loudly, 'It may be three quarters of a mile in your car boyo, but it's more than a mile on my bike.' That brought howls of laughter, which incensed the redoubtable Renee.

'You know bloody well what my Dafyd is trying to say, you ignorant English bastards,' she howled.

A brave soul at the back of the room loudly commented that he was sure that Dai, who was a Policeman in the Depot, was good at his job and would go far.

'Not bloody far enough,' someone else replied to more loud laughter.

One Saturday afternoon, Mike and his mates were watching the cricket on the 'rec' when they saw the older lad assaulting a smaller boy over by the pavilion. His brother ran across and roughly pulled the lout off his victim, who was bleeding from the nose. In his indignation, he lifted the assailant off the ground by the front of his shirt and threw him on his back so heavily that it winded him.

It wasn't long before the lads heard what sounded like a howling banshee. Charging towards them at a rate of knots was an extremely irate Renee and she was clearly intent on dire retribution. They should have legged it but for some reason, they stood their ground. The woman made straight for Rod and swung an arm the size of a ham at him, screaming her battle cry of 'I'll wipe the bloody floor with you!' He ducked and stepped smartly away out of her reach. The momentum of her intended blow caused her to lose balance and she fell heavily to the ground. A number of the villagers came rushing over to see what was happening. Most of them thought it very funny that Renee was lying on he back, with her legs in the air and showing, as someone cruelly observed, 'all she'd got'.

A 'berk' loudly commented on her 'granny's drawers', while another said that 'it was a wonder that Dai could 'find 'it' among all that fat'. Someone else muttered, 'I wouldn't let her on top and that's a fact', which provoked further hilarity. The humiliation completely knocked the stuffing out of the woman and she lay there sobbing. When Dai came running to her rescue, he knew better than to make anything of it.

'Come on my lovely,' he said dolefully. 'Take no notice of this ignorant lot, they're not bloody worth it.'

There were mixed feelings in the village about what had happened, with some of the residents being sympathetic to her. Others who had seen the intended assault Pere quick to put the record straight. Renee had tried to assault Rod, as she had done to others on numerous occasions and he had only dodged out of the way. They maintained it was high time she learned that she couldn't go around hitting and threatening other people. The lively discussion was interrupted by Sergeant 'Rat' Grand, who came striding up and demanded to know 'what the bloody hell was going on.' Getting no sense out anyone, he curtly ordered them to 'pack it in' and that was the end of the excitement.

There were no repercussions, despite Dai's angry threat to go to the Police. When his sons were sternly warned about their bullying antics, the elder lad said that he had already had an earful from his father and he readily promised to behave. His brother was lacking in gumption because, within a few days, he was soon up to his old tricks. Being big for his age, he was the 'king-kid' at the local primary school and despite numerous warnings and clips around the ear, the message didn't get across. It was only after an irate dad had accosted his father at work and threatened him personally, that his son's behaviour improved. Not long after, Dai told his neighbours that he and his wife had had enough of their bloody nonsense and were off back to Wales where people knew how to treat others 'with courtesy and respect'. It was a bit rich to say so, particularly after his wife's aggressive behaviour.

Chapter 13

More Problems

Mike arrived at work on Monday morning and, after clocking on, he pocketed his card to give to the Time-keeper at his new place of work. He donned his overalls, then went to say good-bye to Nobby but he wasn't in the shop and, being reluctant to disturb the Foreman, he asked a couple of the men if they had seen him. He got the usual negative response. The only place he could be was in the pump house and sure enough, Nobby was there, pacing up and down across the front of the engine. Due to the absence of the duty Attendant, who had rung in sick, the old lad was in his element.

'Morning Nobby,' he greeted his mentor. 'The way you're walking up and down must remind you of the days when you were pacing the quarterdeck. Takes you back, eh?'

'I've told you before, you cheeky young sod,' came the instant response, 'the quarterdeck was not for the likes of me. Chief ERAs always had far too much to do than spend their time idling on deck. We had real duties, unlike those 'poodle-fakers' who called themselves Officers, who knew sod all about the Ship and its mechanical workings.'

Mike laughed out loud, because he was obviously well on form. It was the Nobby that he had come to know so well and he was always at his sarcastic best first thing in the morning. From their many discussions, he knew he had little time for anyone who was not in the 'black-hand gang', as the engineers were so aptly known. He seemed to want to chat but Mike was itching to be off, despite what his new Foreman had said about there being no hurry. After thanking him for all he'd done for him, he took his leave then, in company with the other lad, he walked off down the road, with his toolbox on a hand-trolley. Another chapter in their Apprenticeship had come to an end.

When they arrived at the office, Jimmy sent Mike to report to Stuart, who was working in the engine room of a 'Loch Class' Frigate. She was tied up alongside the nearby jetty and when he went down into the engine-room, he saw two large triple-expansion steam engines, both of which were in the process of being stripped down. His new boss was a large man and probably in his mid-thirties. In a marked northern accent, he subjected the lad to a lot of 'do's and don'ts,' in a monotonous' toneless voice. He was not exactly 'full of the joys of spring' that morning and after he had finished, he didn't speak to the lad for the rest of the day. During the dinner hour, Mike was told that his last Apprentice had not got on at all well with him. Apparently, he hadn't pulled his weight and had stirred up trouble among the other lads.

When he asked the lad what the problem had been, he was told that the gang in which he'd been working were an odd lot. When he next visited the canteen, it was said that that the previous bunch of Apprentices had been cynically exploited. Anyone who has worked on a large marine engine will know that it is a dirty, heavy job and at first, they had worked as hard as their bosses, but had received little by way of appreciation for their efforts. Having turned-to with a will, they were dismayed when their bonus and condition payments had not been forthcoming and when they complained, they were told that they should 'just get on with the job and stop 'belly-aching''. They had then decided not co-operate with their Fitters until there was a change in their attitude.

Mike was determined to avoid any more arguments but clearly, something had to be done. One lad told him that he had been threatened and there followed a number of discussions about how they could resolve the problem and it was generally agreed that they would not get anywhere by angry confrontations. They decided to only go through the motions and do little gainful work. The first job that Stuart gave to Mike was to go under the floor plates and go round all the holding-down bolts on both engines. He was given a large flogging spanner and a heavy hammer and told to check that all the nuts on the two inch diameter bolts were tight. He was obviously being provoked, probably in the hope that he would refuse to do the job.

The bilges were in the most appalling condition, due to the unsavoury habits of the Mateys. Being of a lazy disposition, they regularly relieved themselves into the bilges and Mike looked his Fitter straight in the eye, then took the proffered tools and quietly made his point.

'I wasn't born yesterday, mate. I know what your game is and you'd better think on before 'acting the crack' with me. You've given me a job to do and I'll do it, but don't make a habit of taking the piss.'

'Are you threatening me or what?,' retorted Stuart, feigning righteous indignation and smirking at his watching mates.

'No, but just so we know how things are; we don't want any more unpleasantness, do we?' he concluded and still staring pointedly at him.

He lifted a floor-plate to get access but realised that if he left the hole unattended, someone might fall into it. He put the plate back and went to look for a length of rope to make a temporary barrier. In the 1950s, safety was not such an important issue as it is today but if anyone created a hazard or caused an accident, he would have had to account for it. When he came back, Stuart demanded to know where the hell he'd been. Mike explained that he had been to get a rope to put around the hole and his Fitter reacted even more angrily.

'I don't want any bloody excuses,' he stormed. 'Just get on with the naffing job.'

Mike held his tongue and after he'd roped off the area, he again lifted the plate and went down into the bilges. The stench was appalling and made him gag and despite having put on his waterproofs, he was soon covered in the gruesome slime. He stuck at the job and was about halfway around by the dinner break. To his surprise, he had not found any loose bolts and when he asked his mates about it, he learned why. Stuart had made Colin do the same job three months before. When he had finished, he had been told that he had not done it properly and had been sent down to go around the bolts again.

'So that's his bloody game,' said Mike. 'Well, we'll see about that.'

When got back to the Ship, he said nothing to the other Apprentices, but got straight on with the job. He finished the port engine, then went straight on the starboard one. By the end of the day, he had still not finished the job and he resumed work the following morning. Having finished, he came up from below and replaced the floor plate. He needn't have bothered, because he was immediately confronted by Stuart, who asked him how the job was going. Mike told him that he had gone over every nut and bolt and had found them all tight.

'Are you telling me you've done the job properly?, the man sneered.

'I don't give a bugger what you think,' Mike replied, 'but what I do know is that you're taking liberties. We've got some sorting out to do, haven't we?.'

'What do you mean?,' asked Stuart, still smirking. 'You do as you're told.'

'Yeah, that's right, but I'm not going to be buggered about by a silly, fat git like you,' Mike replied. 'The Foreman should be made aware about what's going on here.'

That's alright by me,' replied the Fitter, 'and we'll go to see him right away.'

They trooped off the Ship and when they entered the office, it was as if Jimmy had been expecting them. He looked up from what he was reading and spoke directly to Mike.

'And what appears to be your problem?' he asked, with a deadpan expression on his face.

'I've asked to come to see you, Mr James, because I'm unhappy with the way I'm being treated. Stuart here seems to have a point to make where I'm concerned. I don't mind what jobs I do, but I'm not going to be buggered about. He's had me working in the filthy bilges, doing the same job as was done by another lad three months ago and when I finished, he told me to do it again.'

'You do as you're told,' replied the Foreman sternly, repeating the words that Stuart had already said, 'and you'd better do so, if you know what's good for you.'

'Do you know what?,' interrupted Mike without raising his voice, 'I think you're in on this nonsense. Well, I want to see Mr Barry right away to make a formal complaint and I also want to discuss other matters with him, particularly the filthy condition of the Engine room bilges They must be a health hazard. Does it never occur to anyone to clean them up?'

He had put his case to good effect and from the darting glances that he had given Stuart, the Foreman was obviously unsure of himself.

'Now, don't let us be hasty,' he said in a more reasonable tone. 'Perhaps we've been a bit hard on you, but it's only for your own good. We wanted to know what sort of lad you were, didn't we Stuart? We didn't expect to be talking to a mess-deck lawyer, though I'll tell you what. Let's see if we can sort things out, shall we? You go back down below and we'll consider what you've said.'

'Suits me,' replied Mike and he turned and left the office.

As he went across the jetty, he realised that the crafty old sod had 'had him'. He had missed the clear opportunity to make a formal complaint, which would have brought the Apprentices' grievances to the Management's notice. Back on board, the other lads were impatient to know what had gone on and there was a stony silence from their mentors. When he later recounted what had been discussed, they berated him for not 'bringing things out into the open'. Someone caustically remarked that he was 'all mouth and no trousers' and Mike had to admit his naivety. However, he had learned the lesson that it was no use doing things by halves, because if he started something, it had to be seen through. However, the outcome of his confrontation was not as bad he had thought. The next day, a gang of men came down to clean the bilges and he was not told to do the job again.

The stripping of the engine went on steadily, with the lads working without enthusiasm amid constant 'carping' from their Fitters. They continually complained that the job was running late and their earnings would be down. It didn't occur to them that there was a simple answer and that was to play the game with their lads. When Mike reminded Stuart that he was due some uncas for working in the bilges, his reaction was off-hand and he bluntly told him that unless he got something out of it, he would go to see the Foreman again. The man grudgingly said that he would 'see what he could do' and in due course, he received the princely sum of six shillings (30 pence). The blighter then had the gall to tell him not to 'broadcast' his windfall to the other Apprentices but, while he was eating his dinner, he did just that.

Stuart's attitude changed somewhat after a dangerous incident. He and another man were standing on the floor-plates between the two engines, when a large baulk of timber fell near them with a loud crash. It caused them great alarm and they rushed about to find what had caused it to fall. Chris, who was the smallest Apprentice, came into the engine-room from the stoke-hold and was grabbed by the irate Stuart. He hotly denied any knowledge of what had happened and when Stuart raised his fist, Mike stepped in and roughly pushed him away.

'You keep your fists to yourself, you bastard,' he snarled, 'unless you want to settle it here and now.'

The altercation brought other men over and when everyone had calmed down, one of the Riggers brought some sense into the debate. He pointed the finger at the guilty party, who was none other than Stuart himself.

'It was you what left that timber on top of the engine,' he accused. 'I said to my mate at the time, didn't I 'Arry, that don't look very safe, sitting on the edge like that. You want to be more careful and not be blaming others for your bloody stupidity,' he went on. 'You could have caused a serious accident.'

Stuart was taken aback and it gave Mike the opportunity to tell the men that he and his mates wouldn't accept any lad being assaulted. As they turned away, Mike told Stuart that a word of apology to Chris would be appreciated. He mumbled he was sorry and normal working was resumed.

The top and bottom covers were rigged, unbolted and removed from the cylinders, and then the pistons were disconnected and lifted out. They were laid down on the bottom plates but, with space being limited, there was little room in which to work. It was made even worse when the connecting rods, the cross-head assemblies and the bottom-end bearings were taken out. To resolve the problem, a couple of deck-head plates were removed, to create an egress out on to the upper deck. The hard-marks on the components were checked, to ensure they would go back into the same position when the engine was re-assembled. They were then lifted off the ship, loaded on to a lorry and taken into the nearby workshop.

The bores of the cylinders were surveyed and the dimensions around the circumference and along their length recorded. It was a similar job to that which Nobby had carried out on the big compound engine at the locks. The pistons were closely inspected, as were the contact surfaces of the vertical cross-head guides. The bottom-ends, crankshaft bearings and journals and main bearings then followed. Notes were taken, with detailed references made to the overall condition of each piece. It was a most thorough exercise, which gave the lads a lot of information about the workings of large reciprocating engines. In their interest, they forgot the problems of the past few weeks and at times, they worked well.

The Ship was a small Frigate, which was nearing the end of her service life. Considering the many thousands of miles which she had steamed, her engines were in good condition, with most of the components only requiring minimal refurbishment. Some of the piston-rods though were heavily scored and were taken away for machining. It was very much a team effort, but the Fitters were continually moaning about their Apprentices. The tense atmosphere remained and it was clearly a stalemate which was going to take some breaking.

Chapter 14

A Steady Slog

With the main components out, the Fitters turned their attention to the air pumps, which were directly driven off each main shaft. When the Ship was under way, the pumps raised the vacuum in the condensers, to achieve the optimum mechanical efficiency of the engine. Each unit had a single piston, with integral non-return valves and like a lot of the other components, they were very large. No undue problems were found and they were quickly reassembled. In the meantime, Stuart and Mike had been checking the crankshaft main bearings and journals, which were also in good condition. The oil ways were checked, to ensure the free flow of lubricating oil through the bearings and when Mike pointed out that the dirty conditions in which they were working were not conducive to keeping the journals clean, Stuart lost his temper.

'Why don't you change the naffing record?' he shouted. 'You're always bitching about something and I'm sick and bloody tired of it. If you don't like the job, piss off and give the rest of us a bit of peace.'

His workmates laughed at his loss of temper and for a while, the mood of the gang lightened somewhat. The components, which had been sent ashore, were progressively brought back on board and the rebuilding the port engine commenced. The main bearings were boxed up and the bottom ends, connecting rods and cross-head assemblies followed. The pistons came back with their con-rods attached and were lowered directly into their cylinders, then the head and lower casings were replaced. It was some weeks before the port engine was completed and the work was repeated on the starboard unit.

The manoeuvring valves were remounted on the sides of both engines, following which, the Coppersmiths came below to install the pipework for the pressure indicating gauges and the automatic lubrication systems. They made a tidy job and their technique in grouping and securing the copper lines along and up the sides of the engines was most impressive. Whether or not their skills have been lost over the last fifty years is a matter of conjecture, but it is rare in these modern times to see such artistry in copper pipework. The last job was for the Laggers to replace the insulation and cladding around the cylinders and when they had finished, the rebuilt engines stood out well in the surrounding chaos of the engine-room.

Despite their co-operation over recent weeks, the lads' relations with the Fitters had not improved as the men were convinced that their earlier lack of effort had cost them dearly. In yet another heated argument, a lad pointed out that had they been more honest with them, the nonsense would not have got out of hand. He made no reference to their lack of effort, because it would never have done to have admitted they had not been working normally. If they were to succeed in their strategy, they had to be squeaky-clean. There was no doubt that the impasse had delayed the job but, as the Foreman had said when Mike first met him, they had not exactly been pressed for time.

Mike and his mates had regularly talked to the lads who were working in other Sections, though care had to be taken not to be overheard in the canteen. There were treacherous buggers about, who would have had no compunction about 'spilling the beans'. As previously noted, some of the Fitters could get physical, so to needlessly provoke them made no sense. Some lads were adamant that they would not be intimidated and that was a problem in itself. Given time and a fair wind, they would crack it and they just had to keep their heads and take their chances, when and as they arose. Their campaign was going to be one of attrition, rather than resisting the system, with no thought of the consequences. 'Slowly, slowly, catchy monkey' was very much the order of the day.

Mac came into the canteen with good news one dinner time. In the past week or so, he had been seen around the Yard in a very clean state and how he had managed it, given the conditions in which he was supposed to be working, had been a bit of a mystery. He told Mike that Manchester was 'had gone off sick' and that Nobby had been deputising for him. That morning, the arrangement had been formalised and he had been made up to 'Acting Foreman'. With congratulations in order, Mike decided to pay a visit. When he went back to work, he told Stuart that he was going to the first-aid post, to which Stuart retorted that he should ask Treatment if he could do something about his mouth while he was at it. Having called at the post for the record, Mike cycled down to the Locks and when he went into the office, Nobby was sitting at the desk.

The grimy old man of yore had been replaced by a smartly turned-out Foreman. He was pleased to see Mike and after shutting the door, he poured him a mug of well-stewed tea from a large teapot on the top of the filing cabinet. When they were sitting comfortably, he explained what had transpired. With Manchester said to be away indefinitely, he had been asked to 'hold the fort' and he had been only too pleased to stand in. That had given him the opportunity to make a few pertinent points and he must have played his cards well. In the ensuing discussion with the Manager, he had pointed out that the Department didn't have a Deputy Foreman as such and with eight Fitters, their Apprentices and an equal number of Mates and Labourers, the matter of an appointment had become urgent.

The running of the Locks Maintenance Shop had become too demanding for one man, particularly when he was so unwell. The Manager replied that Mr Manchester had been in good health until recently and they had long-since agreed that a Deputy was unnecessary. Nobby countered by saying that was clearly no longer the case and an early decision was imperative, so that everyone knew where they stood. The Fitters were unhappy with no one formally in charge and they clearly resented a fellow giving them orders. They agreed that the situation couldn't go on indefinitely and Mr Clarke said he would give the matter his full consideration.

It was exactly what the devious old bugger had wanted. When asked if he was putting himself forward for the job. Nobby had replied that he would be happy to be considered, but it was for Management to decide who the best man for the job was. Apparently, the Shop Steward had been in to see the Manager that morning and had said much the same. Taking that into account, he would inform the Fitters of his decision the following morning. When he'd returned to the shop, Nobby was aware that everybody knew where he'd been and there was a most definite resentment in the air. As he had so often said, he was contemptuous of most of the lazy buggers, so he had just ignored them. If one of them was made up, it was nothing to do with him, as long as his cushy little number continued in the Pump House.

The following morning, the Manager had come into the shop just before the morning break and called on Nobby to join him in the office. The outcome was that he was formally made up to Charge-hand right away and with Manchester likely to be off for some time, he was also to deputise as Acting Foreman. Both 'promotions' brought him a most welcome increase in pay, one permanent and the other temporary and he had been highly delighted to accept.

They had then gone out into the shop and the Manager told everyone about the arrangement. He had asked them to give Mr Hall their full support and since then, Nobby had been in full charge of the whole shebang. His first job had been to 'sort out' the Shop Steward, who he maintained was an officious little bugger. When Mike had finished his tea, he congratulated his old boss again, saying that if anyone deserved promotion, he did. When he got back to the Ship, he was told that the Foreman had sent the Fitters over to another Ship, which had just come in for repair. They would be assisted by their Mates and the Apprentices were to stay where they were. When someone had asked Stuart what they were to do in their absence, he couldn't resist making a jibe.

'That'll teach you clowns to bugger us about,' he had chortled. 'As a matter of fact, we've got a job to do on the main engines and the Foreman wants to avoid a repetition of all the bloody nonsense. We'll be earning a good few bob extra, so you lot can just get on with whatever he gives you to do.'

With that, he and the other men had trooped off the ship. Mike and his mates sat around yarning until the Foreman came on board. Pointing to an auxiliary condenser, he asked if any of them had worked on one before. No one had.

'Good,' said Jimmy, 'Take the end covers off, so that I can have a decko inside and give me a shout when you're ready.'

Bill and Ted went to fetch the tools from the store, while Mike and Chris made sure all the connecting valves were closed. It had all been secured when the Ship had come into the Yard and there was only residual water in the system. When the other lads came back, they made an immediate start on loosening the fixings and, by the end of the day, they were ready to remove a cover. They were still working on it when the foreman came on board the next morning and he wasn't pleased.

'Are you lot messing me about or what,' he asked crossly. 'You should have had both covers off by now.'

Bill responded and he 'upset the applecart', by asking him what hours had been allocated to the job.

'What d'you mean, hours,' Jimmy shouted angrily. 'When I give you a job, I expect it to be done, right away and with no questions asked. You only get to work on piecework when I say and not before. Now, bloody well get on with it before I really lose my temper and sort you lot out.'

He then took Mike along to the Engineer's store and they took out a large box which contained the necessary kit for cleaning the condenser. It consisted of various sizes of long, thin wire-brushes and various lengths of screwed rod with which to push and pull them through the tubes. When they came back to the engine-room, Bill was letting go the last few bolts. Looking up, the Foreman saw a set of one ton chain blocks was attached to a trolley mounted on the runway-beam above.

'Who rigged those blocks?' he asked.

'We did,' Mike replied, 'They were hanging loose over there and we thought they would be ideal for the job.'

His first thought was that he was going to get yet another bollocking. However, it was not given in the same aggressive way that they had become used to. Jimmy quietly but firmly made several points and what he said made good sense.

'Has no one told you that on no account do you interfere with lifting gear? Also, you don't do any rigging, unless it's under the close supervision of a qualified person? They're golden rules which everyone has to adhere to, because of the safety aspect. Fitters are allowed to rig up to one ton capacity blocks, but for anything larger, they must be put up by a Rigger. There are no exceptions for a very good reason and that is, 'Always safety-first in working,' got it?'

Mike duly apologised for their mistake. If they'd cast their minds back, they would have remembered the lectures in their first year, when they had been thoroughly instructed in all aspects of working safely. Charlie Brown had told them on numerous occasions.

'You can't be too careful, because the Yard's a bloody dangerous place. When you go out there and do a job, do it right first time and above all, do it safely.'

Jimmy had been pleased to make his point and no harm had been done. However, if there had been an accident, he would have had to 'carry the can'.

'Accidents never just happen,' he had told them sagely, 'they are always caused and my job is hard enough, without silly sods like you not taking enough care.'

The inside of the condenser was clean, with only a few tubes blocked and a little silt in the end-boxes. The Foreman examined the tube-ends for damage or signs of leaks and decided everything was sound. He told the lads to clear the blocked tubes and then put the covers back on. While they were working, he explained why he had not sent them with their Fitters and contrary to what Stuart had said, it wasn't because they had been misbehaving. Management had decided to delay the refit on the Frigate in favour of the Ship which had just arrived and a small gang had been sent to do the urgent work needed on a main engine. It was likely that they were going to be under-employed for the next few weeks and their time at work was going to pass very slowly.

There was a buzz on the upper deck one morning when the lads came up for the break. A Light Cruiser was in the process of being moved through to the No. 1 basin. She had been in a heavy collision with another Vessel and had been laid-up for quite some time. As she went past, there were a lot of comments about her dilapidated state, which was sad, given the usual immaculate appearance of Vessels of her class. Apparently, while on exercise in the North Atlantic, she had cut across the bows of a large, modern destroyer, the same ship that had come in, minus thirty feet or so of her bows, back in their second year. Their Crews must have had great difficulty in bringing both Ships safely back into port. The hole in the Cruiser's starboard side had been sealed and there must have been a great deal of deliberation in the 'corridors of power' before her future was decided. With capital expenditure so drastically curtailed, she had been laid-up until the decision had been made to scrap her.

It was difficult to imagine how the collision had happened, considering the scope of equipment on board. Mike had received some basic instruction in navigation while at school and he told his mates that when two Ships were in close proximity, the slightest error in judgement or delay in obeying an order could often have drastic results. The Senior Officers would have paid a heavy price for their misfortune. He amused them greatly when he recited a short ditty which had been used by his Instructor in getting the basics of safety at sea over to his juvenile charges.

'If on your starboard red appear,' he had intoned dolefully, as was his wont, 'it is your duty to keep clear. Two whites, red and green, dead in front, 'full ahead' and ram the 'grunt.''

After dinner, the lads walked down to where the Cruiser was moored, on the north side of the No. 1 basin. Any hope of going on board was stymied by a notice, which expressly forbade access without written permission. They had to be content to walk along her length on the jetty before going back to work. In her prime, she must have been an elegant sight, when steaming with 'a bone in her teeth'. She was now little more than a rusty old hulk and there must have been a lot of sadness in the minds of the old sailors who had served on board her in her 'heyday'. Not for the first time, the Navy had been less than careful with what had at one time been a very fine Ship.

Chapter 15

A New Romance

The prospect of not having much work to do, when compared with how busy they had been only recently, was not to the lads liking and in the following weeks, they only saw the Foreman infrequently. When Mike had called in the office, Jimmy had been too busy to speak to him.

'We're up to our ears with the rush job at the moment,' his Clerk had explained, which was reasonable enough. 'Just go back on board and I'll tell him you called.'

Mike thanked him and said that if he and his mates could be of any help, they'd be pleased to pitch in. That must have struck a chord with the Foreman, because when he saw Mike later, he was very amicable.

'Thanks for the offer, lad,' he said warmly, 'I'll let you know if I need you.'

Having decided to join the Merchant Navy when he finished his time, Mike spent a lot of his time looking around the engine-room. A friendly Fitter had done a trip 'deep-sea' on a motor ship (a diesel-driven Vessel) and had hated it so much that he had promptly come ashore again. He had then done his National Service in the Army, which he had enjoyed. After his demob he had got a job as an Engineer on a tug on the River Thames, but his wife had soon complained about the shifts and weekends that went with the job. The pay had been good, compared to that of a fitter, but she had insisted that she wanted to see more of him. He had caved in and gone straight back to square one. When he had handed in his notice, he had been offered an increase in pay and told that he would have had a secure future on the tugs. To make matters worse, his wife was pregnant and they were soon well and truly in the mire.

Tommy was servicing the emergency diesel generator, which was housed in a small enclosure on the upper deck. When Mike asked him if he could give him a hand, he explained that the hours allocated were barely sufficient for him alone. Anyway, he was still a journeyman and an Apprentice couldn't work with him until he had completed the requisite period of service, which was an additional two years. The term 'journeyman' related to the times when a newly fledged Tradesman travelled widely around the Country to broaden his experience. Mike explained that he wasn't interested in working with him, per-se, he just wanted something useful to do. When he saw him again a day or so later, Tommy repeated that he didn't need any help and he had completed the job and gone elsewhere by the end of the week.

Mike looked forward very much to the evenings and Monday and Tuesday were usually spent in a pub with his pals. From Wednesday on, there was always plenty to do. They were traditional jazz fans and would often go out of their area, to hear a live band playing. On Thursday, Mike sometimes went to the Cellar Club, though it was tame compared to when it had first opened. He had to be mindful of the last bus at half-past ten, because missing it meant a long walk home. He often went swimming at a Boy Scout facility on a Friday evening. Saturdays and Sundays were the best nights, with all manner of attractions. They roamed far and wide, by bike, bus, train and shanks' pony in pursuit of their entertainment and with money in their pockets, their enjoyment was guaranteed.

Mike met a lass in the Cellar who was known to her friends as Coopy. She was a very slim five feet, eight inches tall and was very nimble on her feet. Dave was of the view that 'he'd seen more tits on his father's blackcurrant bush', a comment which caused hilarity among his mates. Mike ignored him and they became very friendly. The first time he took her home, she insisted on introducing him to her mother and father, who was rather taciturn. She had a younger brother and sister, both of whom were very curious to see who she was dating.

Her dad worked in the Yard as a Wages Clerk and had the customary reservations about the motives of Apprentices. It was some weeks before he started to thaw, though there was never much conversation with him. In contrast, her mother was most welcoming and wanted to know as much about him as she could extract. The last member of the household was a malodorous, long-haired and effervescent mongrel bitch, which constantly jumped up at him.

Initially, they only saw each other a couple of nights a week, which suited Mike just fine since, because he didn't want to get 'involved'. As the weeks passed, their meetings became more frequent, though he always ensured that they went out in the company of others. Coopy was not slow to cotton on and she soon suggested that they should go out on their own. Mike did his best to resist and she became increasingly impatient. One evening, she must have thought he had capitulated when they visited a country pub and she was clearly put-out when they were greeted with a loud cheer when they went into the bar. From then on, she steadily applied the pressure and though he still only wanted to be friends, it soon started to get serious. When she invited him to tea on a Sunday afternoon the alarm bells really started to ring.

He couldn't discuss anything of an intimate nature with his mates and when one of them craftily asked him how he they were getting on, he smelt a rat. What Mike didn't know was that the the lad's sister worked with Coopy's best friend and had access to 'intrusive' information. Mike duly held out for some time with a succession of excuses, until the lass finally lost patience with him.

'Aren't we good enough for you, or what?, she asked testily. 'You don't seem to want to come and meet my family properly.'

How the hell do I get out of that? Mike thought gloomily. His only option was to put an end to their relationship, but that took more courage than he had.

'No, it's not that,' he replied lamely, 'it's just that I'm not comfortable in other people's houses.'

It wasn't altogether untrue, but the astute Coopy seized her chance.

'Well mum thinks so,' she said with a catch in her voice, 'and I'm beginning to think that's how it is as well.'

'I'm always polite to her, aren't I?' Mike said irritably. 'I haven't meant to upset her in any way.'

To his later dismay, the daft sod gave in and agreed to visit her home for tea on the following Sunday. On the day, he told his mother he was going for a long bike ride and wouldn't be in for tea and because he didn't dress up, she didn't suspect what he was up to. Having dodged her inquisition, he set out to cycle the eight miles or so to Coopy's house. While he was slowly riding up the long hill out of the other side of Town, the heavens opened and to his dismay, he had left his waterproofs at home. Although soaked to the skin, he decided to finish his journey, apologise for being late and then go home right away. When he knocked at the door, it was opened by her sister and she howled with laughter at his bedraggled appearance. Despite his protests, he was hauled inside and made to strip off. It was all so bloody humiliating.

'We can't have you cycling home, soaking-wet through,' her mother said kindly, 'you'll catch your death of cold.'

She gave him a pair of father's trousers and one of his old shirts, while she set about drying his clothes. She pressed them with an iron, then put them on a clothes horse in front of a sorry-looking coal fire. After an hour of the most dismal time he could remember, he put them on again. Despite saying he was going home when he came down, both mother and daughter insisted that he had to stay to tea.

To say it was 'poor fare' was an understatement. Mike had not known anything like it since the years immediately after the War. Her brother was obviously hungry and Mike couldn't help feeling that he was taking the food out of the lad's mouth. There was a less than amusing exchange across the table near the end, which he ruefully related to his mates the next morning. Coopy's sister, who was twelve years old, was the culprit and when the conversation flagged, she had made a most appalling intervention.

'Are you going to marry our Dinah then Mike?,' she squawked, then dissolved helplessly into fits of shrieking laughter.

There was a round of subdued mirth and a mild admonishment from the two women, which was brought to an abrupt end by Mike's tactless answer.

'Not if I can bloody help it,' he said in some embarrassment. 'Who'd want to be related to you?'

His clumsy attempt at levity went down like a lead brick, as so very many of his jokes often did.

'We don't have swearing in this house,' her father said sternly, 'so I'll thank you to watch your language.'

The visit was not the success Coopy had hoped for and soon after, Mike made good his escape. When they said goodbye, she quietly made her point.

'I wouldn't have expected you to say anything about getting married, but you could have been a little more pleasant. My sister was only joking.'

He had got himself into a tight spot, one that he had to get out of as quickly as possible. The problem was, he didn't have a clue as to how to go about it. It being Sunday, there was nowhere he could get some urgently needed sustenance and the day turned out to be a complete disaster.

The following week, with the weather set fair, the crowd decided that an outing to the seaside was called for and they agreed to meet at the station at half-past ten on the Sunday morning. When he arrived at Coopy's house just after nine, her mother was less than welcoming and abruptly told him she was out. She suggested instead that he could make himself useful by taking the dog for a walk. On going into the local Newsagents for a paper, he was very much taken aback to be served by Coopy. When he came out, the bitch was in the process of being 'mounted' by another mongrel and he untied her and left them to it. He went back to the house and her mother was furious that he had 'lost' her mutt. She went out to look for it and when she returned, she angrily accused him of purposely letting the dog go. While they were arguing, Coopy returned and as it was by then well past mid-day, Mike was absolutely pissed off with her and her family.

When they were alone, he remonstrated with her for not having mentioned her job and it was then that the details of her family's dire financial straits came out. She tearfully told him that up until eighteen months previously, they had been living in a part of the Town that had been scheduled for redevelopment. Their landlord had offered a substantial sum of money to move out and her parents had used it as a deposit for the house on the new estate. In doing so, they had jumped out of the frying-pan into the fire. They had not properly compared their income with the projected outgoings and they had had to supplement their income by all possible means. Her father did odd jobs, such as gardening, decorating etc and her mother took in sewing. The younger children had paper rounds and all but a little of Coopy's pay as a secretary was handed to her mother. She worked in the shop at weekends to increase her contribution still further. She rounded off by shrugging and saying it was no good moaning about it, she just had to put up with it.

When they eventually arrived at the seaside, they walked along the promenade and found their friends on the beach. After suffering some good-natured banter about their tardiness, they went off to find something to eat. A tea shop provided the sorely needed sustenance in the form of high teas and they went back to their friends in a much better frame of mind. What was left of the afternoon was spent on the beach and just after five o'clock, they made their way back to the station. The day had been a disaster, but not as bad as it had first seemed. It confirmed to Mike that he had to bring his friendship with the lass to an early end, because he certainly didn't going to fall into her family's predicament.

Brian, who was an Apprentice in Mike's entry, had organised a week's holiday in a hotel in Ostend and had been let down by his mates and after asking how much it would cost, Mike decided to go. It would be his first real holiday and the prospect of going abroad was very exciting. On the eve of their departure, he stayed at Brian's house overnight and after an uneventful journey by rail and ferry, they duly arrived at their destination. Their room was large, with a double and a single bed and after the evening meal, they made their way into the Town and were well and truly 'oiled' when they made their noisy way back in the early hours. They had met three young ladies from Stockton on Tees in a bar and true to form, Mike had promptly forgotten about Coopy. He got on well with 'his bird' and on the third evening, while cuddling on the dance floor, she asked him the vital question.

'D'you love me? Are you sure? Ee, I think you're a smashing lad, I really do,' she purred and hugged him even more closely.

The lying sod said the right things and their liaison was all the warmer for it, despite the discomfort of snogging in draughty seafront shelters. When he tried to get into her hotel, he was 'slung out on his ear'. Brian, who was engaged to a lovely girl, took no part in his mates' shenanigans, being content to sit quietly sipping his beer, which was much to the disappointment of the third lass. The other lad, Dave, had no inhibitions about enjoying himself and he also gave no thought to the girl he'd left behind. As they were lying in bed, Mike asked him what he thought of his new found love and his reply reduced them to a state of noisy, helpless laughter.

'Not much,' he said laconically. 'She's a flat-faced bastard with glasses.'

His cheek was incredible, because he was no oil painting himself and they were silenced by a furious banging on the wall by an irate neighbour. They were not the most popular residents in the hotel, because every night when they returned, one of them inevitably fell over when climbing the stairs. They surpassed themselves when a plant on the landing was knocked over and the pot broken, which had to be paid for. While their breakfast was sparse, their dinners and evening meals were good. There was a problem with Dave though, which irked both Brian and Mike. By the middle of the week, he was broke and they had to 'bail him out', which was hardly conducive to their camaraderie. At the end of the week, when they were getting ready to leave the hotel, Dave told them he had no money with which to get home and they had to lend him yet more. It took the shine off what had been a pleasant holiday.

On the last evening, Brian had wanted to see the film 'Island in the Sun', which starred Harry Belafonte. The theme was about the racial prejudice which prevailed in West Indian society, when a white woman married a black man. On their way back to the hotel after the show, Brian asked his mates what they had thought of the film and without thinking, Mike replied that he didn't agree with mixed marriages. The bloody fool had unwittingly insulted the lad and his fiancée because the young lady was of Asian origin. Everyone thought she was wonderful and to have upset her or Brian in such a way was unthinkable. There was an angry silence from the lad and when Mike asked Dave later what the problem was, he was mortified when told of his grave offence.

'Bloody hell,' he reflected, 'I had no idea. She's always been one of our crowd and I've never thought of her to be in any way different from the rest of us. I certainly didn't mean to insult her, or Brian either.'

He had effectively brought an end to the friendship of a lad who had always been pleasant to him and he was at a loss as to how to apologise for his stupidity. What was it that Lou had said about 'putting his brain in gear before opening his mouth'? It was an object lesson that he would long remember.

Chapter 16

Another Year Completed

When they returned from their holiday, Mike had finally decided to put an end to his unwanted romance and the opportunity to do so was not long in coming. One evening, Coopy told him at some length about a lad at work for whom she felt so very sorry. His girlfriend had recently 'packed him in' and he was as miserable as could be. For the next few dates, his name regularly came into their conversations, until Mike lost patience and angrily told her that he didn't want to know about the lad or his problems. If she thought so much about him, then she should go out with him, instead of constantly bothering him with his problems. When she angrily accused him of being jealous, his answer was typical, but very much to the point.

'You've got to care to be jealous,' he retorted unkindly.

Tact was not one of his better points, but it effectively ended their courtship. He was almost beside himself with relief on the way home but much to his chagrin, it wasn't quite all over. When he walked into the house the next evening, he found a tearful Coopy talking to his mother. It was the last thing he wanted and while they walked to the bus stop, he made it clear that he had meant what he had said. That was the last he saw of her and he had to endure a lot of flak from his mother, who had thought that she was a lovely girl.

Over the next few weeks, his mates often told him that they had seen her out with a new boyfriend. It was, without doubt, the lad from work who was the new object of her affections. The truth was, he had lost control of their liaison and it had all gone much further than he had intended. Had he learned his lesson? Most definitely not! Like most young men, it wouldn't be long before the lust was surging around his loins and he was back in the proverbial.

One morning, he went across the Yard to apologise to Brian but the lad wouldn't speak to him and their estrangement prevailed for many months after. It was a salutary lesson and he readily accepted that anything which smacked of racial prejudice was wholly wrong. Older people often excuse the inanity of their own early years by saying that one can only learn by one's own mistakes. Lou had also said that 'we all have to learn by our mistakes and, more often than not, the hard way'. A wise man indeed! As it was, Mike deeply regretted the offence that he had given to his erstwhile friends and the outcome was that the crowd, who had enjoyed each other's company for so long, no longer did so. Gone were the jolly evenings in the Cellar Club and the country pubs and his inane crassness came to influence his thinking throughout his adult life.

The last few weeks of the year passed very slowly and the lads only rarely saw the Foreman. When he did come on board, it was only to remind them of the need to keep their heads down. It was an admonishment which wasn't really needed. Their penchant for getting into trouble had become progressively less as the time had passed and gone were the juvenile japes, which had caused them so much grief in their early years. They had become street wise whenever they wandered about the Yard and it was rare for anyone to ask what they were doing. When Mike declined to join their card games, he suffered the usual jibes about being scared of losing and he was quick to reply that he had no experience of the games they were playing. Being cheating buggers, they would soon relieve him of his money.

One Saturday morning, Mike went into the town to meet up with his mates in the King's Head. One of the regulars was a middle-aged lady who was always immaculately turned out, wearing a smart suit, hat, gloves and the most elegant shoes. She was articulate and well informed on most subjects and in her prime, she must have been a beautiful woman. When they had first met her, they had thought her 'a bit snooty', but it hadn't been long before they were chatting amicably.

That morning, Mike told Gwen about the scam his mates had once pulled with the objective of losing their cherries, which she thought was very amusing. She expressed surprise that they had had any such difficulty, being under the impression that modern youngsters were very much more 'forward' than her generation had been. They assured her that it still remained difficult to enjoy the forbidden fruits for the first time.

'They should have come to see me, deary,' the doughty lady replied thoughtfully, 'I would have been only too pleased to sort them out.'

That brought laughter from her listeners and she was quick to put them right.

'Not with me, you silly buggers,' she said, pretending to be cross. 'I meant that I know just the girls who would have been only too happy to oblige them, especially as it was a 'job lot' of inexperienced young men. There was no need for them to go up to London, we could have arranged it down here. Not that I couldn't have done it mind,' she mused. 'There's still life in the old girl yet, I can tell you, and I'm sure I'm more than a match for any of you young sods.'

Mike had often admired a friend of Coopy's, who he had thought was very attractive. When he saw Sylvia in the town, he asked her if she liked jazz and they met up on the following Wednesday evening. They went out on a number of dates in the following weeks and got on very well. He was invited for tea one Sunday afternoon and he reluctantly agreed to go. Her family lived in a large house in the centre of the Town and he was at first a bit over-awed. They welcomed him warmly and while tea was being prepared, he talked to her father, who was a Senior Army Officer. The meal was served in the lounge and the next couple of hours were very pleasant.

Towards the end, Sylvia came in with a plate of jam tarts, which he later described to his mates as 'bloody awful'. Being on his best behaviour, he took a second one when offered and when he thought no one was looking, he offered it to their dog. The mutt sniffed and licked it then moved away, leaving Mike holding a tart that he most definitely didn't want. *Since when did a golden retriever turn down anything to eat?* he thought morosely. He pushed it down the inside of the armchair in which he was sitting and carried on as if nothing had happened. When they went out later, Sylvia told him that her mother had seen what he had done and had retrieved the offending tart. She had been quick to express her displeasure.

'It appears that your young man's manners are not what they should be,' she had said crossly to her daughter.

Sylvia's father had been more understanding, saying that Mike had shown commendable initiative to get out of 'a tricky situation'. Her brother had been more cutting and told Sylvia that she shouldn't have offered the bloody things around.

Mike had become impatient with the lass, because she was always fifteen to twenty minutes late on their dates. The final straw was broken when she kept him waiting for more than half an hour in pouring rain. He was furious as well as very wet and had been on the point of walking away and, when she arrived, she offered neither explanation nor apology. They had missed the train to the concert and so they went into a nearby pub to dry off. He tried to explain that leaving him standing in the rain was not on, but Sylvia was clearly miffed as well. She bluntly told him that if he wished to continue to seeing her, then he had to accept her as she was. Their evening was miserable and an hour or so later, they agreed there was little point in continuing. On reflection, he thought she had been stringing him along, perhaps to make a point on behalf of her friend. One of his mates opined that it was a lady's prerogative to be late, which was hardly the sympathetic answer Mike had expected.

Someone came below one morning to tell the lads that an Aircraft Carrier had come into the Yard and was lying alongside the decommissioning jetty. The biggest ships they had seen up until then had been the large city class Cruisers, which had passed through the locks with little room to spare. The prospect of seeing a different type of Ship was intriguing and they walked over to have a 'butcher's' during the dinner hour. She was what an old Matey knowledgeably described as a 'Woolworth carrier', which had been converted from a merchantman during the War, when the Navy had a chronic shortage of escorts for the North Atlantic convoys. She and others like her had made a significant contribution to the Fleet at a critical stage of the War. They had been 'absolute bitches' in any sort of sea and had pitched and rolled all over the place. The main problem had been that her flight-deck was wooden cladded and despite it being of a lighter construction than a steel deck, she had still been top-heavy and very unstable.

'Couldn't they have lowered her deck to make her more stable?' one of the lads asked the old lad.

'It wasn't as easy as that,' he replied. 'You'd have to go out into the North Atlantic to see the sort of conditions under which she operated and some of the seas would frighten the balls off of you. When we had an urgent need of Escort Carriers, they got on with converting a number of old Liners. There wasn't time for anything fancy and every corner was cut to get them away to sea. They took off the superstructure and put the flight deck on, then ripped out most her innards to make space to stow and maintain the planes. If you get the chance to go on board, you'll see that the Crew's accommodation was basic, even for the Officers. They were what we called 'hard lyers', which was true in every sense of the words. The men that sailed in her were real Sailors, not like today's namby-pamby lot, who enjoy all the comforts of home. Your modern Jack wouldn't put up with what her Crews had to, I can tell you.'

When he'd gone, the lads walked along to the gangway to see if they could go on board, but it was not to be. Anticipating that the Mateys would be curious, the Management had again forbidden unauthorised access. They later learned that she had only recently returned from the Far East and been decommissioned. She had been towed into the Yard to have useful plant and equipment taken off and a couple of weeks later, she was taken away to the breakers. She had given sterling service when it had been so most urgently needed and like all good Ships, she would be broken up with no thought of it.

Soon after, another ship came in and she was a 'Hunt class' destroyer, which had been manned by 'Free Poles' during the War. The same old man was on the jetty and he had another tale to tell. She had recently been returned by the Polish Navy and was in a very run-down state. It was hard to imagine what she'd been like in her prime. Thousands of Poles had come to Britain to fight the Nazis and had endured great hardships in doing so. Their contribution to the War effort had been enormous and they had served in all three Services. To our lasting shame, so very many of their men and women, who had served the Allies so well, were so callously betrayed when it was all over. Instead of being welcomed back in their own country as heroes, very many had been condemned as traitors by the Communist Government. Many were summarily incarcerated and then executed. And the old lad was very bitter about their fate.

One of Britain's newest Submarines also arrived in the Yard and she was berthed at the north-east end of the No. 2 basin. She had been built in a civil Yard and had only recently been handed over to the Royal Navy. She was twice the size of the usual boats and was fitted out with the very latest equipment and weaponry. The security cordon around her was very tight and no one was allowed on board without a special pass. The work to be done remained unknown, because none of the Mateys who were working on her would say anything about it. She was very much part of the new, modern Navy, which was being built to address the military threat posed by our former Allies in the Eastern Bloc. The financial constraints, which had effectively 'hog-tied' the Armed Forces since the War ended were coming to an end and substantial money was being spent to ensure that this Country had both the men and equipment to effectively respond, should the need arise.

The new ships being built were proudly described by the Media as 'the weapons of the future'. However, they were destined to rapidly become obsolete, due to the increasing pace of the technological advances in designs. Not all the old Ships were sent to the breakers, because a number were still being completely modernised. Many of them had been laid-up in the estuaries around the Country and the old sailors took great pleasure when a well-known Ship was brought in for a refit. Despite their many years of service, they still had sound hulls, boilers and main-engines and in their refit, the accommodation spaces, armaments and ancillary equipment were ripped out and replaced. Some, having been completely refitted, were 'mothballed' and put back into reserve, for possible future use in an emergency.

A refitted Warship was perhaps not as impressive as a new vessel, but it was always a red-letter day when she was re-commissioned. It was hard to understand how a Ship, which had been built so long ago, had remained intact, with her hull in very good condition, with little corrosion or degradation. Mike asked a Fitter if the steel used during or before the War was of better quality than that in modern vessels. One would have expected the modern Ships to be of a much superior quality, because of the many advances in steel-making in the intervening years. Their main-engines were often streets ahead, when compared with their modern counterparts, particularly the quality of the main bearings and shafts. The same situation appertained to the steering engines, where those on the old vessels had run for many years without any problems. In contrast, the newer ships regularly suffered breakdowns. He never did get a satisfactory answer to his unending questions.

The lads often discussed how the Ships were operated at sea; the best ones to ask being the old Chief ERAs, who knew all about them from personal experience. They liked to be consulted and were free with their advice and some expressed a preference for a particular type of Ship or a Station on which they had served. They were either 'big' or 'small' Ship men, having served on Battleships and Cruisers or Destroyers and Frigates. The West Indies and the Far East always evoked fond memories, in which the weather was mostly kind, the seas placid and the runs ashore anything but. One old Tar told them lurid tales about the hell of being in a tropical storm and some had sailed in the Arctic convoys and they waxed eloquent about the extreme cold and the physical suffering which they had endured to get supplies through to our Russian Allies. One man would tell them about the friendly, warm-hearted welcome they had received from the Russian people, while others said the complete opposite. The truth will probably never be known.

What was exciting to the old Sweats was not always of interest to the younger generation. However, the 'swinging lights sessions' were mostly enjoyed, because they helped to pass the time. The last few weeks of the year slipped by and the prospect of the forthcoming holiday was eagerly looked forward to. The Yard was no longer closed for a fixed period, though most of the Mateys remained content to take them in the last two weeks in July. Mike was again to remain at home, free from the critical eyes of his parents, who were going down to Cornwall. His intention was not to do anything which could be construed as interfering in their domestic affairs.

Having already taken a week, he would remain at work and have the second one off. While the year had started very badly, his life had greatly improved that by the end of the year, it was far more enjoyable than it had ever been. He no longer had the need to scrimp and save and each week a substantial proportion of his pay remained unspent. Things could only get better, or so he thought!

Book 5: The Fifth Year

Chapter 1

The Final Year

The start of the last year brought the usual changes and after clocking on, Mike went off straightaway to report to his new Foreman. Having endured the usual lecture of 'do's and don'ts', he was told to work with a Mr Harry Grout and he would find him on board the Light Cruiser, which was berthed in the No. 3 basin The painful lesson of the start of the previous year had been well learned and he went right away to report to him. Having worked on a similar Ship before, he duly made his way down below into the boiler-room to report to his new boss and it was not the salubrious billet that he had hoped for. It was sparsely lit by a few runs of temporary lights, which were rigged down the stairways and across the front of the boilers. The atmosphere was very warm and there was an overpowering stench of black oil. His new boss was an old man; perhaps about five feet, six inches tall and he had strikingly blue eyes, which were enlarged by his thick, bottle-bottomed granny glasses.

'Grouty' wore a flat-cap and it was heavily impregnated with fuel oil and while he was talking to Mike, he kept taking it off and scratching his bald, shiny head. He was a Geordie with a very pronounced accent and he had the foulest mouth the lad had ever heard. The volume of his voice indicated that he was deaf and thought everyone else was as well. Everything he said was liberally laced with a broad range of expletives and his profane eloquence was incredible. He and his mate, Harry Cooper, were stripping out the valves in the fuel oil system, which fired the main boilers. They had worked together for many years and as he warmly said, they were very good pals. That apparently entitled him to continually verbally abuse the little chap, who rarely had anything to say, either to him or to anyone else. They were joined shortly after by another Apprentice from Mike's entry called Johnny.

The Fitters and everything about them were liberally covered in the black oil and they stank to high heaven. As mentioned previously, it was an intrusive, noisome substance and no matter how much care one took, it seemed to get everywhere. The Fitter was friendly enough, but he also had a few basic rules which he insisted had to be followed. He didn't want 'muckin' droppin'-in-it' with the bastard Foreman who, to Mike's great amusement, was also called Harry, and he was a 'right grunt'.

'Bloody hell,' Mike said to Johnny. 'There are three old buggers on this job, all called Harry; the Foreman, the Fitter and his Mate. What happens when someone sings out for Harry from 'up-top? Which one do you reckon answers? Not the little fellah, I'll be bound. Perhaps they all make a dash for the stairs, to be the first up to see who's calling who,' he concluded and laughing heartily at his wit, which was obviously not appreciated.

'Why man, that's easy,' interrupted Grouty angrily. 'I'm the senior mucker down here so I answer all the muckin' calls. Now, as I was saying before you so bloody rudely interrupted me, you clever sod, my rules are quite simple. First, the Foreman nearly always comes down to see us between half-past ten and eleven in the morning. You have to be here when the grunt's on board, so just make sure that you bloody well are or he'll cause us no end of muckin' grief. At all other times, you can do what the bloody hell you like, because the job we're doing doesn't amount to much. It's just to keep us muckin' occupied and we can take as long as we like doing it. If you go off the ship, don't get caught, because I don't want it all coming back to me. You can do a bit down here or you needn't bother, that's up to you. Me and my Mate here will get along just fine, if you'd rather be doing something else, like your studies for instance. We'll leave it at that for now.'

Having made the point and for the sake of propriety, we'll continue without further reference to his foul language. Johnny asked him where they could stash their gear and tool boxes, to which he replied that they could go anywhere they liked, as long as they didn't go into the forrad boiler-room and both engine rooms. They were off limits and access was strictly prohibited without special permission. As previously noted, the Cruiser had been in a heavy collision and had suffered extensive damage mid-ships, on her starboard side. Grouty went on to tell them that the hole, which had been left when the two Ships had been pulled apart, had been large enough to accommodate two double-decker buses. How she hadn't sunk, he didn't know and she was now destined for the breakers and would only remain in the Yard until everything of value had been stripped out.

The two lads went back up on deck to look for somewhere to stow their gear and they found a small cubby-hole on the after deck just forward of the Y turret, (i.e. the after-most guns of the main armament). Empty packing cases were found and a further rummage in the mess decks yielded a couple of large leather cushions. When they went below again, the two Harrys were sitting with the old man poring over a drawing. Waving his pipe dramatically, he told them that he had to identify and mark-off each valve as it was taken out and attach a tin tally to the handle. The drawing and identification numbers were to be hard-stamped on it. The valves would then be put into the crates on which they were sitting and they would later be taken away to the Factory. Making the tallies would, he said, be right up their street.

'It's all very simple but,' he stressed, 'the job has to be done right.'

The lads laughed again when he soberly told them that the spillage of oil was a fire hazard which had to be kept to a minimum, even though it was already liberally spread right across the floor plates.

'Whenever a valve or a joint is broken, the oil has to be drained into a bucket, then transferred into the forty-five gallon drum, which has been brought down specially for the purpose. Now then, I want the two of you to make up a good supply of tin tallies', which he pronounced 'din dallies'- 'takin' care to do them right, mind. They must all be three by two inches square, with no sharp edges and the letters and numbers must be exactly as those on the drawing.

'Do you know where these valves will be going? A Mike asked Johnny, again in good humour.

'No,' replied his mate, looking somewhat vacant, as was his wont.

'To the Apprentices' Fitting Shop, where we were in our second year, you daft bugger,' Mike told him with a grin.

'Oh yeah,' said the lad, 'I hadn't thought of that.'

Johnny was a medium-sized young man, with closely cropped blond hair. He was a talented footballer and had already attracted the interested of more than one professional Club. His problem was that he couldn't be bothered with 'all that training and stuff' and when Mike asked him what his plans were for the coming season, he replied that he didn't think he'd be bothering with football any more. He'd recently got engaged and wanted to spend as much time as possible with his fiancée. The Club for which he had signed at the start of the previous season had recently dispensed with his services because he had missed so many training sessions. Most young lads would have given their eye teeth for his talent, but for Johnny, there were more important things in life than getting fit and chasing around after a leather ball.

It was a similar story with regard to athletics. While still at school, he had competed in various County championships and no matter what sport he played, he had always excelled with the minimum of effort. Like so many young lads, the urges in his loins had to be sated and little else was of any importance. In truth, it was very much more than that, as Mike soon found out. Johnny's love of his lass, Debs, was deep and he constantly talked about her. She was the love of his life and she thought the same about him. Ironically, Mike had felt little affection for or commitment to any of the girls that he had known. His dalliance with Moya had been more physical than emotional and while he had missed her when she went away, there had not been a permanent bond between them.

The lads set about making the tin tallies, but there was an immediate problem. The tin snips which Grouty had in his box were old and blunt and the job was a chore. He gruffly maintained that there was nothing wrong with them and bluntly told them that if they didn't want to help, lazy grunts that they were, he would do the job himself. Mike rudely replied that he could do it. Johnny was more positive and went off to look for an alternative and he later returned with an almost new pair of shears, which had obviously been 'liberated'. No doubt their owner was complaining bitterly about 'the thieving sods' around him. Within a day or so, with one lad cutting out the tallies from a sheet of tin-plate and the other hard-stamping them, they had the job under control. Grouty and his mate continued taking the valves out and putting them in the crate.

The Foreman instructed Grouty to retrieve the blow-down valves from the boilers, which he said was just the job for the lads. They were located under the deck-plates and after temporary lights had been installed, they turned-to. Access was not easy and because of the high temperatures to which they had been exposed, most of the fixings were frozen solid. Their release could only be achieved by the use of hammers and cold chisels and late in the afternoon, as Mike was energetically applying himself, he suffered a most painful setback. He was working in a very confined space, with only a single light to illuminate the work. The hammer glanced off of a nearby strut, missed the head of the chisel and connected painfully with his thumb. His loud cries of anguish brought Johnny shuffling across and when he saw what had happened, he could not contain his mirth.

He angrily told Johnny to sod off and then painfully made his way up on deck and off the ship to the first aid post. There, he reported to the first-aider, known to all and sundry as 'Treatment'.

'Come in, sit down and shut-up,' the little man said aggressively, when he knocked at the door. It was his standard greeting to anyone who came to what he grandly called his 'surgery'. The patient did exactly as he was told and 'with no bloody nonsense'.

Treatment was very efficient and he soon put the lad at ease. The thumb was expertly cleaned and bandaged and when he'd finished, he gave Mike a hot, strong cup of tea. He then filled in the accident book with the details. He brooked no nonsense from anyone, but was often the butt of sly comments from the ignorant buggers that he was a bachelor. Whenever there was an accident, which happened with monotonous regularity, those involved were always very pleased when he arrived on the scene. What he lacked in stature, he more than made up for in his expertise and nothing detracted him from his job or caused him any problem in treating the injuries. Mike had not seen him before, but he had no doubt that he was in competent hands. In talking, the man told him that he spent most of his spare time doing charity work. He was a Senior Officer in the St John's Ambulance Brigade and as such, he attended many public functions.

The welcome that he and his colleagues got from the crowd at the local football ground, always gave him a lot of pleasure and when called on to the pitch, they were always given an appreciative round of applause after they had 'fulfilled their duties'. He was one of those unsung' heroes, whose presence was not always appreciated until they were sorely needed. In closing, he told Mike he had to report back every day, until his injury had healed.

'There's nothing broken though you'll have to lay off work for a few days, while we see how it's doing,' he said sternly. 'You must keep it clean and I'll tell you when the dressing can come off. Alright?'

When Mike got back on board, he told Grouty what Treatment had said and the old man's reply was gratifying.

'Quite right too,' he said. 'The man knows well what he's talking about, so just you go and sit somewhere quiet.'

The next morning, after settling comfortably on his packing cases, Grouty filled his pipe with a charge of tobacco and enthusiastically lit it up in clouds of acrid smoke. He then told the lads about his trials and tribulations with his wife. They had already been warned that his stories were always told in great length and detail and with no little drama. His wife, who he described fondly as 'poor old Moll,' had been suffering for some years with acute arthritis and she was constantly in great pain. It was obvious that he loved her dearly.

'She's been so bad lately that the doctors have had to put her on gold injections,' he told them solemnly, with a catch in his throat.

Whether or not he thought it was real gold that was being put into her veins was not clear, but he went on, puffing slowly as he talked.

'They must cost an awful lot of money, but they do help her a lot. Why, she's almost been a new woman since she's been on them and I said to the doctor, can I make a contribution towards the cost of her injections? 'No, Mr Grout,' he replied, 'she'll always have the very best of care from me and I'll see that the hospital does the same and all, so don't you bother yourself.' By lads,' he went on, 'she was a wonderful lass when we were young, always full of life and raring to go. Forty-three years we've been married and it's always been lovely. I couldn't have had a better wife, of that I'm certain. Now, she has to spend most of her time in her bed and it's not much of a life for her. I've said that I'll stop working soon, so that I can look after her better, but she won't hear of it. All she says is that I've got my work to do and that she'll be alright. She seems to worry about me more than herself and that's a fact.'

The poor old bugger had tears running down his cheeks and seeing how upset he was, Mike and Johnny quietly excused themselves and went up top. Over the next few weeks, they had many such poignant sessions and to their credit, they always listened patiently and sympathetically. Forty-three years of marriage was an absolute eternity in their young minds.

While making their way back to the Ship after dinner one day, the lads were larking about, with a lot of pushing and shoving. When Mike broke free and made off smartly down the road. Johnny quickly followed and they were running fast as they neared the brow. He caught up and reached to grab a hold, when Mike turned and gave him a classic rugby hand-off. His mate spun away and went head-first into a heap of sand, which had been dumped on the side of the jetty. Mike ran up the brow but Johnny was apprehended by a policeman, who demanded to know what all the nonsense was about. Having been well 'bollocked', the hapless lad followed his mate on board and loudly complained about having got into trouble. When the Foreman came down, he wanted to know if they had been involved in the sky-larking on the jetty.

'How did you do manage to push me off like that?,' asked Johnny later.

'In rugby, when some bloody great front-row forward is hell-bent on stopping your run for the line, it can sometimes be your only means of getting by,' replied Mike. 'That is, if you don't want to end up under eighteen stones of a bloody great ape, who is intent on pulverising you.'

'I'm going to have to watch you, you lousy sod,' Johnny said ruefully.

He then asked Grouty what the pile of sand was for, which gave the old lad the opportunity for yet another yarn. He sat down and lit up once again to tell them.

'I was in the Merchant Navy during the War,' he said, with the usual, far-away look on his face. 'Most of the time, I was sailing second Engineer on a collier, running up and down the east coast, from the Tyne to London and back. By, we had some hellish trips, and that's no lie. Twice, I had the Ship sunk from under me and was lucky to get out alive. One was an old, clapped-out, natural-draft coal-burner, which should have been scrapped years before and she was mined off Flamborough Head. There was a lot of damage to the hull, with plates sprung all along one side and she was making a lot of water. We worked all night, trying to plug the leaks and put into the Humber. When we were safely at anchor, we had to move some o' the cargo to one side to give the old girl a list and that lifted most of the damaged plates out o' the water. The Chief and me made up cement-boxes for the worst of the leaks and a tug brought out the sand and cement, which we mixed and poured it into the boxes that we'd placed inside the hull. It did the job and we joined a southbound convoy the next day.'

'After many anxious days at sea, we made it into the Pool of London and it was no picnic there either, with the bombs falling all around us. We were more than pleased to sail back north again, I can tell you.

'Have you noticed how this Ship is listing to starboard?' he asked the lads. 'I think she's been making water, like we did all those years ago, so there'll have to be a good few cement boxes made. It's a lot cheaper than putting her into dry-dock an' if she's going to be scrapped anyway and it'll be enough for her to be towed away.'

As the old saying went, 'you learned something new every day'. Mike and Johnny had not heard of cement-boxes before and had been surprised at the old man's explanation about the practical use of them. There was more to Grouty than they had first thought and the fact that he had served in the Merchant Navy during the War impressed them greatly. Like so many of their workmates, they often laughed at the older men, who were often derided and referred to as 'old soldiers'. They were in no doubt that their new boss had definitely 'done his bit', when the chips were down.

Chapter 2

A Dodgy Proposition

A young Fitter, not much older than the lads, came on board and they took to him right away. Geoff was a very large, affable young man who was not long out of his time and like so many young men, he viewed life with a languid attitude of optimistic irresponsibility. He'd been sent to do similar work; to strip the boilers and the associated feed-water system, including the main pumps, of their valves and mountings. The job suited him well and he was soon working away steadily, taking care to mark each piece, before packing it into the specially provided boxes. When asked if he wanted a hand, he declined, saying 'it was up to the Foreman'. What he really meant was, he didn't want them 'horning-in' on his cushy number.

During a morning break, their discussion turned to his impending obligation to 'Queen and Country' and Geoff was adamant that he had no intention of joining up, or going away to sea. Not for him all the poncing about in a shabby uniform, being shouted at and paid a pittance for all the bloody nonsense that conscripts had to endure. 'No thank you very bloody much!,' he said vehemently.

'But how're you going to get out of it?' Mike asked in mock concern.

'Yeah well, that's a bit of a problem,' the young man replied. 'I've had several letters wanting to know when I'm going to be available, but I've managed to fob them off so far. Drastic action may soon be called for 'cos my old man reckons the Military Police will soon come knocking on our door, so I've got to be deciding what to do a bit smartish. Up 'til now, I've had flat-feet, in-growing toe-nails, bad knees, a bad back and Christ knows what, so much so that the bloody doctors have been getting a bit awkward lately. They keep saying there's nothing wrong with me and I should just go and do what 'has to be done. I should cocoa. Not bloody likely.'

'What do you reckon you can do about it?,' asked Johnny.' If there's nothing wrong, you've got to go.'

'Like I say, my old son, I'm working on it,' Geoff replied. 'I ain't beat yet.'

A few days later, he solemnly told them he had a plan. If he explained it to them, they had to treat it in absolute confidence and more important, they were not to laugh. After assuring him that he could rely on them, he settled down to fill them in.

'It's like this,' he said. 'I've been thinking about how I could just disappear, so that nobody would know where I've gone. I've been talking to a bloke in the pub and he reckons it's easy, if you go about it in the right way. You've to go down to one of the sea-side resorts, where there's plenty of casual work and move on every six to eight weeks. Simple, in'it?' he concluded smugly.

'That's all very well,' Mike said, 'but don't forget, you've got to keep clear until you're twenty-six and that won't be easy. I've heard that the MP's are always on the lookout for people who should be in the Services.'

'Yeah, yeah, I know all about that,' replied Geoff impatiently. 'As I've said, I'm still working on it.'

The following week, he came to work in very good humour and told them that he had solved his problem. He didn't want to discuss it with other people around and would give them the 'gen' during the morning break. By then, both Johnny and Mike were beside themselves with curiosity about what he had in mind. They didn't have long to wait before Geoff appeared with his cuppa, sat down and started to explain, after reminding them yet again about the need for absolute secrecy.

'It's like this,' he said earnestly. My mate has given me the lowdown as to how I can dodge the Army and make a lot of money at the same time. There's a lot of old dears in posh places like Bexhill and Brighton and they're always on the lookout for a nice young man to take them to concerts, dances and restaurants and the like. From what I hear, they pay very well and if there's anything else they want,' he went on and winking slyly, 'that will be extra, know what I mean?'

Mike and Johnny knew exactly what he meant and could hardly contain their mirth.

'What, you're going on the game, like a male prozzy?,' Mike blurted out.

'Well, yeah, something like that,' said Geoff, 'but hear me out. It's no good going at it like a bull at a gate and you've got to take it steady at first, until you've made a few contacts, like. Jim says there's a lot of blokes doing it and you have to be a bit careful not to upset anyone. If you meet the right people, then it shouldn't be too difficult. After you've found somewhere cheap to stay, you get yourself a job as a waiter or something in one of the big hotels. You have to have some smart clobber, so as you're well turned out on your 'outings'. The trick is to be particularly attentive and friendly to the ladies, who might be interested in your services. Jim says you'll soon know when you've clicked and after that, it's up to you how you get on.

'He seems to know an awful lot, this Jim,' said Johnny, winking at his mate. 'How come he's not doing it?'

'Oh, Jim's been about a bit, alright,' replied Geoff. 'It all makes good sense to me and providing that I use my noddle, I should be able to keep clear of the army and have a good time as well.'

'What about the physical part, you know, the 'nooky?' asked Mike.

'No problem there, my old son,' came the swift reply. 'I've been going out with the same bird for six months or so and I can assure you everything is in good working order. I'll just give her the elbow, when I'm ready to go. I was wondering like,' he went on and looking intently from one lad to the other 'would either of you like to come with me, down to Bexhill or wherever? We could set it all up as a team effort.'

'You can count me out,' said Johnny earnestly, 'Debs would kill me if she found out I was selling what belonged to her. How about you Mike?'

'Not bloody likely,' Mike replied, still being beside himself with laughter. 'I've never heard anything so bloody daft, that I haven't. By the way, how old are these old ladies you're talking about, Geoff?'

'Oh, about forty to forty-five I should think,' he replied. 'It'd be a waste of time with anyone older.'

That brought more loud laughter and ribald comments from the two lads, so much so that the young man was rather put out.

'You won't be bloody laughing when I've made my fortune,' he said crossly as he got up to go back to work. 'I'll come back to see you buggers in my big flash car one day, you see if I don't.'

The following Saturday evening, Mike and his mates were ensconced in the White Horse pub, before going on to a dance and having been fully briefed about Geoff's hair-brained scheme, Dan suggested they should tell Gwen, who was sitting in her usual place at the bar. He bought her a G & T, then Mike told her about Geoff and his plans. She listened patiently, while gently drawing on her cigarette, which was held in an elegant little ivory holder and obviously, she didn't altogether believe his story and asked him if he was having her on. The lads solemnly assured her it was all kosher.

'Well, that's the best one I've heard for a long time,' she said, laughing out loud. 'One thing's for sure, you young buggers are always up to something or other. Come to think of it though, I know of one or two young gentlemen who are providing the same sort of service round here and they're doing rather well at it. There's quite a demand for discreet escort work, you know and they won't be very pleased to hear they're going to get some competition'.

'Like I said,' Mike interrupted, 'our mate plans to operate somewhere on the south coast, where no one will know him. He needs to drop out of sight so that he can dodge the Army and make a decent living at the same time.'

'He'll have to be very careful,' said Gwen, 'because the Police will be on the lookout for him. If he's to stand any sort of chance, you shouldn't tell anyone else about his plans, because there's always some rotten bugger who'll shop him. Tell you what, I'd like to meet him and maybe I could give him a few pointers, to help him along his way.'

When they discussed it later, they agreed that Gwen had been serious about helping Geoff. The problem was, he had sworn Mike to secrecy and would be very upset that he'd been discussing his plans in a pub. They decided to keep quiet and see how it all turned out. As it happened, it all went pear-shaped anyway and not for the reasons envisaged. When Geoff finished the job on the Boilers, he moved to another Ship and Mike didn't see him again for some months. One Saturday morning, He was in the High Street and who should come by but the veritable Geoffrey. He was accompanied by a po-faced young woman who much to Mike's surprise, he introduced as his wife. Mike smilingly shook her hand but was under the distinct impression that she thought he had crawled out from under something unpleasant. 'I've just got to go into this shop,' she said to Geoff in a flat voice. 'You stay here and don't go away, and no slipping off into the pub with your mate, d'you hear?'

'Bloody hell, Geoff,' said Mike, when she was out of earshot. 'Your wife you say? What happened to all your grand plans to go off and make your fortune?'

'Alright, alright, I know,' said the very downcast young man, 'it all went ape, didn't it? It's all so bloody unfair, because just as I was going to pack her in, she told me she was podded. Now I'm in the shit, right up over my head. I thought of making a run for it, but her old man can be a bit persuasive like and he insisted I made an honest woman of her. To make things worse, I'm going off to join up next week and I can only hope they send me somewhere a long, long way away and the further the better. Bloody hell, here she comes, I've got to go old mate, see you sometime.'

That was the last that Mike saw of Geoff and when he later told Gwen about what had happened to him, she was very sympathetic.

'Oh, I am sorry, dear,' she said. 'I thought from what you told me that he had a lot of promise and would have gone far in his chosen career. You know, it's not always the best thing to marry someone in those circumstances. I know, because I've been married to a right bastard for nearly thirty years. It was the biggest mistake I ever made.

'Not that I was 'in the club' at the time,' she added hastily. 'It's impossible to live happily with someone you don't love, believe me. I've never been able to have children and I don't suppose it would have been any easier if I had, but that's life. You've to take the rough with the smooth. It might have been better for your mate if he had just buggered off, but now that he's made his bed he'll have to lie in it.'

Her reaction didn't surprise the lads, because she was a very discerning person. Geoff's plight strongly reinforced Mike's determination to stay clear of the 'manacles of matrimony', particularly in his last year. Many of the lads in his entry had already taken the plunge and a lot of those who hadn't were well on the way to doing so and like Geoff, some were very unhappy. Young people rarely learn from the mistakes of others and slowly but surely, others would fall by the wayside. Nothing changes.

Johnny and Mike continued working with the Grouty for some weeks and a spell of warm, sunny days made the atmosphere down below unbearably warm. Their working conditions were dreadful but the old man ignored their complaints, because he didn't want to rock the boat with the Foreman. He told them many times that he had a nice little number and he wasn't going to put it at risk for the sake of the two mithering young sods, who were supposed to be working with him. They had not received any payments to compensate for the conditions in which they were working and when they asked him about it, the old bugger just shrugged and carried on with what he was doing.

'You'll have to speak to the Foreman about it,' he said, grinning slyly. 'I don't know what you're griping at; a little bitty oil never hurt nobody. Just get on, the harder you work, the sooner it'll all be finished.'

There was no point in complaining further, because other lads that had worked with him had told them he was a 'tight old scrote'. They decided to slowly withdraw, their co-operation in the hope that he would perhaps do something to help them but, he accepted their lack of interest with equanimity and he and his little Mate carried on in the same relaxed fashion as before. On the fine days, the lads extended their breaks, sitting in the sun on the upper deck and keeping a weather-eye out for the Foreman. On numerous occasions, they were fortunate to just beat him down below and be working steadily when he arrived. He never acknowledged their presence and it was obvious he didn't care what they did either.

An incident happened which could have had serious consequences for Johnny. He had been reading in his paper about the 'big fight', which had taken place in London and in an intense discussion, the old man said that he also liked boxing and, as a young man, he had been quite good at it. Their discussion developed into an argument about whether or not the modern day boxers were as talented as the ones before the War, a point the old man loudly denied. Mike had no interest in their exchanges and couldn't believe his eyes when he saw them squaring up to each other, to emphasise their opposite views. The old man, after doing a natty little bit of footwork, suddenly lashed out at Johnny, completely missed his target and took a hard blow to his body. He crashed to the floor-plates and lay there moaning.

'You bloody fool,' Mike shouted at Johnny, 'look what you've done. You've hurt the poor old sod.'

'I hardly touched him,' replied Johnny, being instantly contrite.

They helped Grouty on to his toolbox and were very concerned when he sat there for the rest of the afternoon. He obviously felt very unwell and groaned loudly from time to time and when he didn't come into work the next day, they were very apprehensive that Johnny was in trouble. The following Monday morning, the old lad came back to work and he looked awful. It was odd but throughout the time he'd been away, his Mate had been absent as well and where he had gone, they didn't know. When Johnny asked the old man if there was anything he could do, he was angrily told to 'leave him alone and go away', or colourful words to that effect.

'I'd have thought you'd done quite enough harm, thank you very much,' the old lad went on. 'You know full well, I've got my poor wife to look after, because she's so seriously ill and your daft antics have stopped me from doing it this past week. I've had to get her sister in to look after her and she's a bloody menace, always grumbling and interfering. I don't want any more messing about, so you can both sod off.'

Gone was the loud old man who had been so full of himself. In its place was a grumpy old sod, with the world on his shoulders. Later, when in a better humour, he told the lads for the 'umpteenth' time about his problems. They had known he had the most onerous burden and despite what had happened, they were sincerely solicitous. He was clearly despondent that the doctors had not been able to do much to alleviate her suffering, but he still made much of their efforts and treatment.

'You can call me an old fool if you like, but when I look at my Molly as she is today, I don't see a broken down old woman. I see her as she was, when we was first married. Aye, she was beautiful, a lovely lass, always smiling and happy and that's how it's stayed for us all through. When so many other people had their problems, our marriage was sound and neither of us had any thought for anyone else. We were more than happy with each other and although we would have liked bairns of our own, none came, so we just had each other.'

Johnny understood what he meant. He thought the world of Debs and in the following Spring they were married. Mike knew, but never admitted that he was missing out on a lot of the benefits of a sound relationship and Johnny tried a number of times to explain how he felt, but was clearly wasting his time. It would be many years before Mike learned that a worthwhile union was a lot more than just 'getting his leg over' and in time, he would come to appreciate that nearly everyone needs someone else to care and be cared for. As many people had told him, nothing worthwhile was free and there always had to be that vital element of 'give and take' in a successful marriage. At the time, he couldn't even begin to understand what they meant. It is one of the follies of youth to be selfish and some people never do learn to respect the needs of others.

A couple of weeks later, the lads were moved on and they were more than pleased to go. Mike was sent to a workshop on the other side of the basin and Johnny went elsewhere. He didn't see him again for quite some time. The conditions in the stoke hold of the old Cruiser, during the warm days of late Summer had been bad enough, but they had changed for the worse as the weeks moved into autumn. As the weather had got colder, so did the boiler-room in which they had been working. Grouty and his little Mate had been moved on as well and no doubt they were glad to be shut of the young buggers.

Chapter 3

A Fool and His Money

The English language is rich in sayings and proverbs, some of which are of great antiquity. Examples like 'There's no fool like an old fool' and 'A fool and his money is soon parted" spring to mind, and the latter would soon apply to Mike.

Since leaving school, he had saved most of the money he'd earned on the Farms during the summer months and throughout the fourth year, he had worked a lot of overtime in the Yard. Whenever warranted, he had never been slow to ask for the additional payments to which he was entitled. His cash had been steadily deposited in the Trustee Savings Bank and he often dreamed of the day when he would strike out on his own. By the beginning of the fifth year, he had over three hundred pounds, which was a considerable sum of money. Only by being tight had he been able to attain that lofty sum and when his fall came, it did so in the most unbelievably naive way.

His bike had served him well through the years but, it was wearing out and had lately become unreliable. Walking home and carrying the machine in the rain was not much fun and he began to think about his options. The buses were regularly unreliable and he lived a mile from the nearest stop. On leaving work, there was always a mad dash to get out of the gate and on a bus into the Town centre. There, he had to change buses and many journeys had been fraught with problems. They were often full and passed the long queues without stopping. Breakdowns and cancellations often made the journey even worse. It was sometimes well after seven o'clock before he arrived home and taking the bus was most definitely not an option, unless it was absolutely necessary.

One evening, he cadged a lift from another lad on his motorbike, but it was not repeated. When he had got off, he'd been a nervous wreck. He had thought of buying a motorbike and had even gone to look at the shining machines in the various agents, but a 'decent' bike, with the necessary protective-clothing and ,tax, insurance etc, would have taken up most of his savings. So what could he do? He either had to continue cycling or find some other means of transport. His most sensible option would have been to get a furnished room or a small flat in the Town but suitable places were difficult to find and the Estate Agents always required references and a large deposit, even though the rental was well within his means.

He had often seen a small, olive-drab car passing through the village and it was always being driven at a cracking rate. It belonged to a Soldier who had recently returned from Germany and was living with his in-laws at the top end of the village. Mike had mentioned to his parents that he was thinking of buying a motorbike, which had provoked a most hostile reaction. They were dangerous and under no circumstance would they have one at their house and that was final! However, it gave them the opportunity to repeat that it was time he moved out anyway. Then, he could do what he liked and if he killed himself, that was his lookout. The argument had gone on until he had dropped the idea.

Not long after, he was talking to Keith one evening and he told him that the Soldier was selling his car. When the lad later confirmed it was for sale, Mike could hardly contain his excitement. He went up the Yard to see Sarge and after listening to the lad's description of the motor, he agreed to have a look at it. When they met Alan, the two men struck up an immediate rapport, having both served in the same Regiment. A bottle was produced and they were soon were happily yarning.

After some time, Mike reminded them that they had come to have a look at the car. That was smilingly answered by Alan, who tossed him the keys and told him to go and have a look at it and they would come out to join him in a few minutes. He went out and his first impressions were positive. The engine started first time and the bodywork had only recently been re-sprayed. It was clean inside and, all in all, it seemed to be in good nick.

When he went back inside, the two squaddies were still talking amicably and it was some minutes before Alan turned to Mike. He asked him what he thought about the motor and perhaps the lad was a little too eager. That gave him the opportunity for which he had been waiting.

'Er, about the asking price,' he said, still smiling broadly, 'I've made a mistake there and have put it a bit low. I shall want another fifty quid for it.'

Mike's face fell, then Sarge said that he would have a look at the car. With Alan loudly extolling its virtues, he looked at various things, then told Mike that it 'seemed alright to him'. Mike shuffled from foot to foot in indecision and if he had had any sense, he would have walked away. To up the asking price at the time of sale was a trick as old as the hills, though with not many cars on the market, the crooks selling them often got away with it. He told Alan that he would think about it and let him know in a day or so. When he tried to discuss the matter with Sarge as they walked down the hill, the man was less than communicative.

'Look,' he said crossly, I've already said it looks alright, haven't I? Whether you buy it or not is up to you.'

Alan must have known he'd hooked a sucker because the next evening, not long after Mike had arrived home, he came knocking at the door to say that he had to speak to him right away.

'Have you made your mind up yet?' he asked and without waiting for an answer, he went on.' If you haven't, I've had someone else come to see me today and he's very interested. He's offered to pay the asking price as well. I've told him I've already got a buyer but he's been a bit insistent and will take it tonight, if you don't want it.'

It was another chance for Mike to back off, but did he take it? No, and how he was to rue it all later.

'Er, well,' he stammered, 'I've got a bit of a problem because you're asking for more money for it than I have in the Bank.'

'That's alright mate,' came the quick reply. 'Just give me what you've got and you can let me have the rest later.'

It wasn't O.K, but Mike didn't have the wit to say so. In fact, he agreed there and then to buy the car and promised to get the money from the Bank the following Saturday morning. Alan went off into the night, having promised to give the car one last 'going over', before he came for it. On Saturday afternoon, Mike went to see him and, fool that he was, he handed over all his hard-earned dosh.

Only the day before, a Fitter had reminded him that before he could take the car on the road, he had to get a provisional driving licence. He would need to buy the necessary insurance and a road-tax disc and he would also have to have a qualified driver with him at all times, until he passed his test. Mike had given no thought to any of them and only then did he appreciate the extra cost involved. Nevertheless, he had still gone ahead. Alan drove the car down to his house and Mike saw right away that the tax-disc on the screen was an old beer bottle label, which meant that the man had been driving the car illegally. It would have to be parked outside the house until he had the necessary funds and he had that first sinking feeling that he'd been 'had'. It was surely going to cost him a lot of time, trouble and effort.

Being in funds, why hadn't he gone to one of the motoring schools for lessons, to pass his driving-test? Why hadn't he noticed that it was a left-hand drive Ford, of German manufacture? The procurement of spare parts was going to be difficult and it was no use blaming Sarge, because he had bought the car 'with his eyes wide open'. His folly brought about an immediate parlous financial situation and his moral sank accordingly. When he had looked into the boot, the spare-tyre was flat and completely worn out. Further inspection of the tyres revealed that two more were in the same condition, with the other two well-worn. Two light-bulbs were blown and the indicators didn't work. In addition to owing Alan more than fifty pounds, he would have to find at least twice that to bring it up to a roadworthy condition.

It was all too much to take in and he went up to Alan's house to discuss all that was wrong with the car. When he came to the door, the warm and friendly greeting, the ready joke and the exudation of goodwill was gone. They were replaced by a scowl and an aggressive attitude, which boded ill for any agreement. When Mike tried to explain the problems, he was quickly silenced with a veiled threat of violence.

'What the naffing hell did you expect for three hundred and fifty quid, a bloody Rolls Royce?' Alan snarled, after closing the door behind him to stop anyone inside hearing what he was saying. 'That's a smashing little runner and you ought to be grateful that I've let you have it so reasonably. All she wants is a little bit of work and she'll be as sweet as a nut.'

Despite Mike's earnest protestations that it was a worn out wreck, Alan had no intention of budging and when the lad asked for his money back, the threat of violence was repeated.

'Go on, clear off, you cheeky bastard,' the squaddy shouted angrily. 'You can forget getting your money back, because I've already spent it. And don't forget, you owe me another fifty quid. I'll be after you until I get it.'

Within a couple of weeks, he was continually knocking at the door demanding his money, despite having agreed that it could be paid 'later'. Mike's parents were aghast at what he had done and he was angrily told to pay the man. In their view, getting into debt was shameful, unlike today when it is a ready means of securing whatever one wants. To avoid further trouble, he duly paid Alan what was owed. His troubles though were far from over and the car went wrong with alarming regularity. The engine was burning oil and something, probably sawdust, had been put into the sump to mask the state of the engine.

In due course, Mike bought the necessary parts and set about stripping the engine down. He made steady progress and was often helped by a German ex-prisoner of war, who had married the girl next door. The piston-rings and bottom-end shells were replaced and the valves re-seated and ground in. With the engine completed, they put it back into the car. His next priority was to obtain replacement tyres and he got them from an Irish lad that he met in the pub, who blithely told him they had come from a write-off. It was best not to ask how he had come by them, but the price was very reasonable. A neighbour's son was an electrician and he checked-out the lighting circuits and within a matter of weeks, the overall condition of the car had been vastly improved.

Sarge turned up one evening, when Mike was re-setting the engine timing and they soon had it ticking-over very nicely and much to the lad's surprise, he described the car as 'a little gem'. His insurance covered him to drive the car and he offered to give Mike a few lessons. A week or so later, Mike bought the cheapest insurance he could find, which covered 'third-party, fire and theft'. With a short-term tax disc on the windscreen, he duly set about learning to drive. It shouldn't have been a problem, but difficulties soon arose. He was headstrong and argumentative because as he had driven tractors, he reckoned he knew how to drive a car. Sarge was at a loss as to how he could get the principles of safe-driving into his thick head and in consequence, he came less often and soon after, he stopped coming altogether. Help came from a neighbour, a Mr Jones, who offered to take him out for the price of a drink 'now and then'.

'We'll just drop the missus off at her sister's, then go back and pick her up later,' was one cunning plan.

'Later' was double-speak for a visit to a pub, to allow him to imbibe a couple of pints and a chaser or two, such as whisky, at Mike's expense. Another ploy was: 'The missus has to pop into the doctors, so we'll just go by the surgery and while she's waiting, we can go for a quick wet.' Also, 'We need a bit of shopping, while we're out and we can stop by for a little wet on the way back.' His regular 'little wets' added significantly to the cost of learning to drive.

Mrs Jones was a very large, unsmiling woman, who continually complained in a monotonous voice, the whole time they were out. Before long, Mike had had enough of them and he told the man he didn't need any more lessons. He was roundly berated as an ungrateful sod and told there was no way he was going to pass his test.

The next person to try to help him was Wilf, a young man from the next village. He had recently completed his National Service, was single and whose sole aim in life was his personal pleasure. After Sarge and Mr Jones, going out with Wilf was a much better option. They were young, red-blooded males and their forays into the surrounding area were full of hilarious incidents, despite Mike's lousy driving. At times, their antics were downright dangerous. An example was after they had visited a jazz club, they'd piled at least three other lads into the car and after nearly turning it over, the passengers loudly yelled for Mike to stop and let them off. They shouted angrily that they were better off walking. Problems with the car came regularly and much to Mike's frustration, Wilf was less than sympathetic.

'It's only an old banger,' he said rudely. 'It ain't as if it's a new motor, with a guarantee.'

He was right, but it still came as a shock when late one night, the bloody car broke down again. When Mike started it, he couldn't get it into gear. They were thirty miles from home and the girls they'd picked up were promptly ejected and told to make their own way home. The car was left in a car park and they made their way to the station to get a train and then walked the four miles home in pouring rain. The next day, when Mike asked Wilf to go with him to pick up the car, he refused, saying he was too busy. The truth was, he didn't care a toss about his mate's predicament. Mike phoned Sarge, but help was not forthcoming there either, although he did identify the probable cause of the problem.

'Like as not, it's the second-gear retaining washer that's gone,' he said. 'If you keep the revs down, you'll probably be able to get it into top gear then, with a bit of care, you'll be able to change down. Try that and see how you get on.'

Mike was pleased to find the car was still in one piece and when he started the engine, he drove down the hill to some traffic lights. They luckily changed to green as he approached and he went bowling down another steep hill towards the junction with the main road. All went well and when he came off it, after a straight run of twenty miles or so, he was nearly home. One last hurdle remained and that was to get the car up the long, steep hill, at the top of which was the lane to his village. By getting up as much speed as he could along the strait, he raced up the top of the hill and he just made it by dropping down into first gear. A few minutes later, he was home and dry and with great relief, he switched the engine off, gave the car a kick and went indoors.

To rectify the fault, he had to disconnect the engine and was again grateful for the help and advice from his neighbour, Heinz. They broke the joint and lifted the gearbox out and with a new retaining washer fitted, they soon had the whole lot boxed up again. Mike had been highly miffed by Wilf's refusal to help him to retrieve the car and much to his annoyance, the lad turned up at his house one evening as if nothing had happened. When asked if they were going out for the evening, It was as much as Mike could do to be civil. However, if he was to drive legally, he needed the lad in the passenger seat. He was being used, but the law clearly stated that he needed a qualified driver with him and it would only be a matter of time before the local bobby came sniffing around.

Chapter 4

Confrontations

The old saying, 'There's none so queer as folk' is as true today as it ever was. Some people can never live in harmony with their neighbours and there is always strife in any community, big or small. The human kind has always had to have the stimulation of acrimony, with someone always ready to have a go at someone else.

The Apprentices were well aware that among the men with whom they were working, there were some very unsavoury characters. If they could 'do the dirty' on a workmate, then he was fair game and it was inevitable that aggro arose. The lads knew that they had constantly to watch their backs and be quick to react if they thought they were being picked on.

Some of the men saw the lads as easy targets and one was a young Fitter called Les and he was often heard loudly stating his dislike of the cocky young sods in the workshop. Due to having been in the Army for three years, he had only recently returned to the Yard. Being a Fitter was in his mind, even though he was still a journeyman, a most definite mark of superiority and he went out of his way to make life difficult for any lad he thought was vulnerable. After all the trials and tribulations he had suffered in the previous four years, Mike was reluctant to get involved with him. The sensible option was not to put up with the nonsense but, discretion certainly had to be the better part of valour.

One Friday morning, there were the usual light-hearted exchanges between the lads at their benches and as had become increasingly regular lately, they chatted about what they were going to do when they finished their time. Sid, who was of a quiet disposition when compared with his mates, said he was dreading having to do his National Service. When he'd registered, it had been so very far off that he'd stated his preference for the Army and that had come back to haunt him. He didn't want to go to sea either and was in a bit of a predicament. Some of the Fitters were clearly unsympathetic, but everything was fine until Les chipped in. He had a nasty habit of casually making snide comments, particularly when excluded from a discussion.

'You lot are 'as green as grass,' he sneered, 'and you're in for a drastic shock when you go to 'get some in'. I was in a crack Regiment for three years and was a Sergeant when I was discharged.'

The lads ignored him, in the vain hope that he would soon tire of his silly nonsense, but he was not to be deterred. He went on needling them and his most offensive comment was completely unacceptable by today's standards. In those days, it could only be described as an insult, which was best ignored.

'Look at him,' he said, pointing at Sid. 'He always comes in to work dressed-up like a pox-doctor's clerk; collar and tie and hair neatly combed. He's like some mother's nancy-boy. You're going to cop it when you join up, I can tell you. You're in for it and no mistake, because they know all about queers like you in the Army.'

It was true, Sid did take a pride in his appearance and each morning, when he arrived in the shop, he changed straightaway into work wear, which he wore underneath his boiler suit. He took his dirty clothes home every Friday and brought them back clean on the Monday morning. Not everyone was as smart as Sid, indeed some of those around him could only be described as 'scruffy buggers'. When he changed, silly remarks were often made by his pals about his skinny legs and that he didn't seem to have much in his pants. He countered by saying that his tackle was all there and in good working order, which always brought a roar of laughter. He was a very pleasant lad and his mates took exception to the offensive comments being made by the mouthy Les. When someone suggested sorting the bastard out, Sid would have none of it.

'No, it's alright,' he said calmly, 'don't bother on my account. He'll soon get tired of picking on me, then it'll be someone else's turn, perhaps one of you ugly lot.'

Unfortunately, his tormentor was a determined sod, who must have thought he had found a 'soft touch'. Over the next week, he subjected Sid to regular verbal abuse, with most of it about him being 'bent'. As the lad had said many times, he had the same lustful urges as anyone else, though had he been that way, it would have been his own business and nothing to do with anyone else. It was a sentiment with which they all agreed and they became increasingly fed up with the unending nonsense.

On the following Monday morning, 'Lousy Les' didn't come in to work and someone casually remarked that he'd been caught up in some bother on Saturday night. Little more was said until he came back to work on Wednesday, when they saw that he had been well and truly 'filled in'. His nose was strapped with sticking-plaster and both eyes were swollen and bruised. Whoever had set about him had done a good job and there was a lot of what is today known as 'schadenfreud' at his misfortune. A few days later, the truth came out when someone noticed that he was no longer picking on Sid. When pressed, Sid admitted responsibility for Les's battered condition and his mates were lost for words. They couldn't believe what had happened.

'Me and my girl were having a good time with our friends at the dance, until Les and his mates came and stood near us,' Sid told them. 'We ignored him, but his comments got worse, with him keeping on about me being queer. I was bloody angry and when the stupid bastard made an insulting remark about Liz, I knew I had to sort it. She insisted we went home and just after the interval, I saw Les going into the cloakroom. I followed him through the door and there he was, on his tod and I asked him what his game was, insulting my girl and all. He just laughed. There he was facing me, fumbling with his flies when I lost it and smacked him one. I must have caught him a purler, 'cause there was blood everywhere. I shoved him into a cubicle, pulled the door to and went out the window. If I'd known it was going to be that easy, I'd have done it long since.'

His mates were stunned, because no one had thought that Sid was so capable of looking after himself. They congratulated him and he was told many times that he had done the right thing, If he'd only hit Les once, how had he done so much damage? The answer was even more amazing.

'When I first started work, my old man said I was a puny little bugger and needed to learn how to look after myself,' he explained. 'He arranged for me to go to Judo classes and surprisingly, I liked it and I've made quite a bit of progress. I've got my brown belt and soon, I'll be ready to go for my black. If my Instructor hears I've been brawling, I'll be well an' truly in it. He's very strict and I wouldn't want to lose out because of that silly sod. My only excuse is that it was in self-defence.'

'Don't worry, my old son,' said one of his mates, 'no one will be any the wiser, being as how you scarpered, after it was over. I can't see Les saying anything, can you lads?'

To his credit, Les approached Sid later in the day and, seeing the young lad flinch, he assured him that he didn't want any more bother. He apologised and said he had been 'well out of order' in baiting him. Sid, being of a more pleasant nature than most of his peers, accepted the apology and that was the end of the matter. Later that day, Les packed up his tools and left the shop without saying 'goodbye' to anyone. When he next came by, the Foreman called everyone together.

'I don't know what's been going on in here and I don't want to either,' he said, looking around balefully. 'What I do know is that one of my Fitters has been damaged, but as it happened outside of work, it's got nothing to do with me. I just want you all to know that if I find out there's been fighting in this shop, I'll sack the buggers involved. Got it? Now get on with your work.'

Sid had resolved his problem and put an end to an endless stream of taunts and insults from his tormentor and there was no come-back, either from the Management or his Judo instructor. The nastiness in the shop also declined, with most of the Fitters keeping well apart from the Apprentices. But it wasn't to last, just because one nasty bugger had gone. The long-term 'bone of contention', between 'the men and the boys' remained and by early December, the situation had deteriorated even further. There were a lot of bad-tempered arguments and it was obvious it would all soon come to a head.

Their predecessors had advised the lads not to get involved with one of the Fitters who, they said, was 'bad news'. Bill had a fearsome reputation and when roused, he was said to be a right 'bad bugger'. In the past, many lads had crossed him and had very much regretted it. He was a very well-built man, of medium height and was probably in his mid- to late-thirties. His method of dealing with what he colourfully described as 'shit' was to administer a prompt beating to the object of his ire and when he blew his top, everyone took cover, including his fellow Fitters.

They, in turn, often used his manic behaviour to bolster their own authority. Although he was not a charge-hand, what Bill said 'went' and given Management's strict intolerance of fighting, it was a puzzle as to how he had got away with his aggression for so long.

The Foreman came into the shop one morning and ordered a general clean-up. As they had not long had one, everyone wanted to know the reason for it. Mike asked his Fitter what was going on, but he said he didn't know. Eventually, one of the men was heard self-consciously clearing his throat, as he broached the subject with the Foreman.

'Er, what's going on then Cyril? Somebody important coming to see us, eh? Usually, we only clear-up once a month,' he added lamely, to cover his embarrassment.

'Yes,' came the immediate reply, 'There's going to be a high-level visit and the Manager wants everything ship-shape by the end of today. Come on you lazy sods,' he said loudly to the Apprentices, 'get on with it.'

Their job was to sweep up and clear away the rubbish and scrap-metal. The Fitters tidied up the machines, such as the air-compressors and generators and also their benches. Despite being pressed, Cyril wouldn't say anything further but when he came back later, everything was to his satisfaction. Early next morning, he again came bustling into the shop to check that all was in order and he then told them what was happening. The visitors were senior officers from the Admiralty in London, together with some German Naval Officers. They would be accompanied by the Captain of the Yard and his staff and would arrive in mid-morning. The Mateys' reaction was rather more than he he'd bargained for, with Bill at the forefront of their angry outcry.

'What the bleeding hell are they coming here for?,' he yelled at the startled Foreman, meaning the German visitors. 'What senseless sod has allowed that to happen? Over my dead body will they come in here, 'cos I'll chin one of the bastards, you see if I don't.'

He then marched out of the shop shouting that he was going to fetch the Shop Steward. Cyril was nonplussed and a number of the men complained loudly in support of their workmate. One stepped forward to express their feelings in a calmer manner.

'You know how it is, Cyril,' he said. 'Along with a lot of others, Bill's family suffered greatly during the War. One of his brothers went down with his ship and another one was a prisoner of war who later died from the ill-treatment. His poor mother has never recovered from the loss of her boys and its little wonder that Bill feels so strongly about it. Look around this Yard and you'll see a heck of a lot of people who lost more than one of their family. Someone in high places has been careless about this visit and we should have been consulted.'

Cyril had a big problem on his hands and he didn't have long to wait before the Steward came marching into the shop and it was clear a confrontation was inevitable. He didn't mince his words and the Foreman was left in no doubt that if the visit went ahead, there would be trouble. Having assured the men of his sympathy, he went off to inform the Manager of the situation. The outcome was that the visit was cancelled and the guests would be taken elsewhere. The men were tersely instructed to resume working and as the Yard was a Defence Establishment, they were under the long-standing obligation to follow strict procedures in all aspects of industrial relations. It came very near to being breached that day and a walk-out was only narrowly avoided.

Just before the dinner break, a Labourer came rushing into the shop shouting that there were 'Gerries' among a large group 'bigwigs' along the jetty. They were looking at an 'A' class Submarine, which was well into a long re-fit. Ignoring the Foreman's loud cries to remain inside, some of the men ran out to see what was going on. Despite his assurances, the visit had gone-ahead and Bill was again apoplectic. It took three of the Fitters to drag him back into the shop and hold him, to prevent him from doing something stupid. Someone must have had the sense to suggest their withdrawal and the party got back into their cars and drove off.

Bill was released and much to the embarrassment of his workmates, he broke down and cried like a child. The emotion of what had transpired had been too much for him to bear and it was some days before he recovered. To some of the lads, his histrionics had been little more than a sham; a cunning ploy to draw attention to himself. Others thought his distress had been genuine and that his outrage had been a true demonstration of his frustration. No one had the courage to say anything to him about it.

Chapter 5

Hard Labour

The shop quickly returned to normal, the Christmas break came and in the New Year, Mike moved on to work in another Fitting Shop. On board the Submarine, there was a most definite air of urgency to complete the refit in good time for the extensive tests, which had to be carried out before she was handed back to the Navy. The Foreman put Mike to work with John, a young Fitter who was working on the torpedo-tubes. His job was to check that all the threaded-holes inside each tube had been properly drilled and tapped in their correct locations. They would then fit new brass guide-rails, which ran along the top and the length of each tube. Eight tubes had to be done; six in the bows and two in the stern. A tube closely accommodated a twenty-one inch diameter torpedo and working inside one was both tight and uncomfortable. With the boat afloat, access was only gained through the rear-end doors.

When Mike asked why the holes had not been checked when the rails were taken out, he was curtly told not to ask silly bloody questions. The problem was, he was claustrophobic and always felt uncomfortable in confined spaces. When he told his new boss, he was abruptly ordered to get on with it. After checking that the doors were tied back securely, Mike crawled inside a tube to make a start. Despite being long and thin, it was a tight space in which to work. Lighting was by a single wandering lead and the thought of it going out, as temporary lights often did, filled him with dread. Lying on his back, he inched himself along the tube and checked that the holes were clear and he then went on to inspect the other tubes. The job took about half an hour in each tube and by the afternoon tea-break, he had inspected them all.

The next day, while they were eating their dinner, the lads discussed the Fitters with whom they were working. Mike said his first impression of John was less than favourable and his mates couldn't resist winding him up. He told them he was not going out of his way to upset him and that brought an immediate reaction.

'Don't you let us down,' one of them said, nudging his mate. 'Like we agreed, we've got to keep the pressure on, otherwise we'll all end up with bugger all. Just make sure that you ask him about what confined-space money you're going to get.'

John was not about when they returned to the shop, so Mike sat down and wrote out his notes on a sheet of paper and when his boss came back, he told him he had found nothing wrong. Providing the rails had been drilled to suit the fixing-holes, there should be no problem in fitting them. John abruptly retorted he would be the best judge of that. In fact, the holes had not been drilled carefully and when Mike had mentioned it, he had touched a soft spot. John went on to say that just as he'd been told, he was 'too bloody clever by half'.

When he went to fit the rails, Mike's suspicions were confirmed. After screwing the first two sections into place, they were clearly all over the place. John was unperturbed and replied that he would sort it. The following day, Mike started bolting the rails into the other tubes, with John watching from the outside. He soon became bored and after the morning break, he said he had other things to do. The lad was left to work on his own in very confined spaces. Later, when they were talking about what had to be done to align the rails, he told Mike that he had had a bright idea and, if he was of a mind to pitch in, it would be appreciated. A suggestion scheme rewarded anyone who came up with a cost-effective solution to a particular problem or devised a better way of doing a job.

John had designed a machine which would cut away the high spots on the rails, instead of having to grind them off by hand. An air-driven, right-angled grinding-machine, fitted with a special cutting-head was to be mounted in a frame. After inserting it into the tube, the excess metal would be milled off by pushing the frame manually through to the outboard end of the tube. Mike would have to operate the machine, because the tubes were too tight for him and it would greatly expedite the work, from the laborious manual chore it was at present. Mike thought the design feasible and was optimistic that in due course, he would be amply rewarded for his contribution. He quietly asked John how much he could expect for his efforts and his temerity brought an immediate, angry response, with a stream of invective about his grasping attitude.

'Do you know, we're all bloody fed up with you lot always trying it on,' John stormed. 'It should be enough that you're working with skilled men and learning from their experience and expertise, without constantly rabbiting on about how much you're going to get out of it. Any extra money that I get is my business, so don't you bloody come it with me, sunshine. If at the end of the job I think you've pulled your weight, then I'll decide how much you should or should not have, whatever the case may be. Now bugger off and don't bother me again.'

Mike was not alone in his frustration and despite all the recent unpleasantness, the Fitters were not going to allow anything to change. Their lads could either 'like it or lump it'. After the problems with their Fitters, the Apprentices had moved their toolboxes into a small annex to sit away from them during the breaks and they quietly discussed how they should go about obtaining a solution. As before, a gradual slow-down of their work-rate was agreed as the most suitable action and given the likely hostile reaction, absolute discretion was vital. They also decided to maintain a passive attitude to their bosses.

Being wise to the wily ways of their charges, it wasn't long before the Fitters 'smelt a rat' and the lads knew they were in for trouble. Who better to sort it all out than the redoubtable Bill and he literally bristled with aggression. He loudly told them he would sort them out once and for all and woe betide the bugger who answered him back. Just after the morning break and led by their champion, most of the Fitters came down the shop and their purpose was quite clear. They were going to put an end to all the rebellious nonsense, which had gone on for so long. Knowing what was going to happen, the lads had expected the confrontation and were determined to stand their ground.

'Right, let's be having you,' shouted Bill. 'Now then, some of you lot is playing silly buggers with us and we're not going to have it, understand? You're here to do a bloody job and that's what you're going to do. You're not going to lay down the bloody law about anything, not while I've got any say in the matter. Anyone who thinks otherwise will have me to deal with and he'll get a smack in the mouth. Come on then, you cocky shower,' he went on and glaring malevolently around, 'who's got something to say? I thought as much, you're all gutless, just like all bloody Apprentices. Now, just you realise,' he said and again looking balefully at each lad in turn, 'we'll have no more piss-taking or else!'

Someone muttered something to the lad standing next to him and Bill heard him. As he moved towards the lad, his mates closed ranks, with most of them having picked up hammers, large spanners or pieces of wood. Bill checked his advance, but the volume and pitch of his invective rose to new heights. It was then that another Fitter intervened, by calling from his workbench across the shop. He told Bill that he'd gone far enough and their ensuing exchange was heated and could have easily got out of hand.

'Who the hell pulled your chain?,' Bill shouted angrily. 'If you ain't got nothing sensible to say, then keep bloody out of it.'

The Fitter had spoken out to stop someone from getting hurt and Bill, if he'd had had a scrap of sense, should have called it a day. However, he didn't and he was confronted, not just by a bunch of angry lads but with another man who was bigger than himself. He was a Scot who had only recently come to work in the shop after completing his service in the Royal Navy and though pleasant enough to talk to, he had mostly kept himself very much to himself up until then. Bill had met his match.

'I think you'd be very wise to back off and cool down a wee bit,' Jock coolly said to him. You look for trouble with me laddie and you'll bloody well get it. I'm fed up with all the angry shouting and it's going to stop, as of now. A man of your age ought to know that you'd do better by talking to the lads about what's bothering them, instead of threatening them with violence all the time.'

Speaking to the rest of the Fitters, he made some other pertinent points, which made a lot of sense.

'Is it any wonder that they are all pissed-off with the way you buggers treat them? You expect them to do as much work as you then, when the job's done, you don't want to give them anything for flogging their bollocks off. If I was one of them, I'd feel exactly the same, so why don't you play the bloody game instead a following this sassy bugger, like a lot of thick sheep?'

Bill backed away from the confrontation, as did the rest of the Fitters and having seen off the object of his ire, Jock then got on with his work. Most of the Fitters, particularly the older men, were shocked by what had happened, but it was by no means the end of the matter.

John had put a lot of time and effort into the design of his brain child and decided to go ahead with its construction. Two brackets, which were mounted on guides inside the frame, firmly held the machine in place. The movement of the cutting-head, which had been made up from five milling-discs, was achieved by rotating a length of endless thread, with a hand-wheel on one end. The frame was held relative to the centre-line of the tube by eight small adjustable wheels, with each one firmly placed in contact with the inside wall. It was a very simple concept but after looking again at the drawing, Mike had doubts about whether or not it would work. John would have none of it and bluntly told him that if he had nothing sensible to say, then he could sod off. The lad should perhaps have been more diplomatic about his boss's pride and joy.

To move the job along, Mike resumed work on the torpedo tubes, using a long straight-edge, a ball of string and some sharpened pieces of hard chalk. He fixed lines along the length of the tube and marked the rails that were out of true, then he took them out and elongated the fixing-holes. He then re-installed them and he did that at least three times, before he was satisfied. Without asking John, he dowelled each rail in place and by the end of the second week, all eight tubes had been finished. John, who had not bothered to check on his progress, was surprised when told that the job had been completed. As Mike wryly commented to his mates, he would be quick to claim the credit for the job.

The next morning, he tried again to explain to John exactly what he meant. The torpedo-tube was of welded fabrication and it was not concentric with its axis, along its full length. He had noted the deviations in each tube, during his close checks with the string-lines. When a torpedo, which was accurately constructed, was loaded into a tube, there was less than an inch of clearance between it and the inside wall. He had seen a working party of Matelots who had been practicing loading and unloading them on another Submarine and had noted the problems they encountered. Many factors could adversely affect the fit, one of which was the trim of the boat. The optimum situation was when she was level, fore and aft and on an even keel.

John was adamant that Mike knew bugger all and he was only knocking the job for the sake it. He would eat his words when the machine was successfully tested. When it was completed, they took it on board the Submarine and by mid-morning it was assembled and all set to go. John's confidence was clearly superficial and he reacted angrily to the levity among his fellow Fitters. He had put up with a lot of snide jibes from them, which he had put down to jealousy. After pushing the machine into the first tube, a hose was connected and the air turned on. He carefully adjusted the guide-wheels to centrally align the cutting head then, after telling everyone to stand back, the operation commenced.

He slowly turned the screw to move it up to the rails, but as soon as it made contact, it abruptly stopped turning. Even when adjusted to barely touch the rails, it deflected and made no impression. The Foreman, who had come down to see the test-run, said nothing but went away again. Despite John's frantic attempts, the machine just didn't work and his disappointment was palpable. After crossly telling Mike to take it out of the tube, he went ashore and when the lad asked what he should do with it, he was abruptly cut off.

'You can throw the whole bloody issue into the dock, for all I care, and don't let me catch you taking the piss,' he cried angrily

When he later asked the Foreman for more time, in which to get his machine to work, his request was denied. There were more pressing jobs to be done and anyway, the job had already been completed by the lad. He hadn't told the boss that Mike had already done it, but some other blighter had!

Their next job was even more difficult. Compressed air provided the means by which the torpedo was ejected from its tube; the reservoirs for which were located beneath the tubes. Because of the very high-pressure, (800 p.s.i), the flanges between the bottles and the connecting pipes were very thick and the joint was made by the judicious and even tightening of large, closely pitched stud-bolts. The flanges were very finely machined, with the bosses evenly grooved across the faces and the copper gasket, to be inserted between them, was half an inch thick. It was essential that it was accurately located and compressed to a calculated final thickness. The nuts were to be tensioned manually with a heavy flogging spanner and feeler gauges would be constantly inserted into the gap, to ensure that it was being evenly compressed.

The four air bottles, which made up the reservoir, were installed under the floor-plates in the forrad compartment and access to them was very tight. The outer bottles were located inside the stiffening webs of the pressure-hull and John turned to with Mike on the first flange to show him how to do the job. He rigged a pull lift to align the flanges and after sliding the joint-ring into place, the stud bolts were inserted and the tightening of the nuts commenced. The boat was cold and dank and Mike made himself comfortable by kneeling on some old sacks. The job took an unconscionable time and when he thought the bolts were near, John inserted the feelers into the gap.

'That's no bloody good,' he said crossly, 'it's got to be compressed a lot more than that.' Then, grinning slyly, he took a small, highly polished plate-gauge, which had been made especially for the job, from his pocket. 'That's exactly how much gap there's got to be between the flanges, to get the correct compression of the ring,' he said, holding it under Mike's nose between forefinger and thumb. 'It's got to be a firm, sliding-fit all round, right?'

The lad took the gauge and resumed flogging the bolts. After a lot of hard work, he eventually completed the job and his Fitter reluctantly agreed it was to his satisfaction. The second joint took half as long to complete and the last two, where access was much better, were completed even more quickly. John was working with a Pipe-fitter and a Rigger on the installation of the up-stream pipework, including valves, which connected with the air compressors. Though care had been taken when dismantling the system, it was impossible to re-erect each piece exactly as before and new sections had to be fabricated and installed. Mike had two similar joints to make under the tubes in the after-end and John had smiled malevolently, when he had reminded him of them. As it turned out, the lad was pleasantly surprised to find that they were more accessible than those forrad and being keen to finish the job, he turned to with a will.

In any Submarine, no matter how large and more so than in any other Naval vessel, there has always been a chronic shortage of space and all the ancillary systems had to be installed as compactly as possible. When it was completed, the air system was hydraulically tested and Mike was both pleased and relieved that all the joints that he had made were sound and signed off. The odd leaks in the rest of the pipework were soon remedied. The bilge pumping pipework was then installed and the floor-platies were laid down and secured, which made for much safer access for everyone.

Chapter 6

Lighter Moments

An old Fitter's Mate often chatted to the lads about his Army service in the First World War and when someone asked him what he had done during Second, he replied that he had been too old for Military Service. Instead, he had been assigned to the fire-watch in the Yard, with his duties additional to his normal work he hastened to add and during the air raids, it had all been a bit hectic.

One morning, he had cause to admonish a lad who unkindly likened him to a pug, a reference to his very battered face. He had taken no notice at first, but when the clown said it again, he objected to his stupidity. He confronted him outside of the shop and told him how he had got 'his ugly mug'.

During the First War, he had been a Lewis gunner on the Somme and after more than a year of living hell, he had been very badly injured and shipped home. A shell had landed in the trench and while his mates had all been killed, he had somehow survived. In the explosion, he had been deafened and some of the bones in his face had been broken.

'What you see is an ugly old bugger with a messed-up face,' he said angrily, 'but you wouldn't have given me any of your lip when I was in my prime, I can tell you. I'll thank you to stop calling me pug, because if you don't, then I'll have to deal with you and that wouldn't be good for either of us.'

The lad was mortified to have caused such distress and he quickly apologised. It was glumly accepted and that was the end of the matter. It was a timely reminder to the lads that not all the old men were so easy to ridicule. They had given their all in a time of great need and deserved respect. However, and as today, not all of the young buggers learned quite so readily.

One morning, Sid was more forthcoming about what he'd been up to in the first couple of years, when he had been happy to amble along, like so many of his mates and had not shown much interest in his studies. At the start of the third year, his father had demanded to know why he wasn't getting on at the Dockyard School and after listening to his lame excuses, they had discussed the matter at some length. They agreed that as he wasn't likely to make much progress there, he would leave and go to the local Technical College instead. He had promised his dad to make more effort and it turned out to be a very wise decision.

Sid had duly registered at the 'College of Knowledge' and in the entirely new surroundings, he had assiduously (no pun intended) attended both day-release and evening classes. At the end of his third year, he had passed his Ordinary National Certificate exams, but had kept schtum about it and his former classmates had had no idea of his achievement. He had then gone on to sail through the first year of the Higher National Certificate (HNC) course. His current problem was that he would not complete the course until he was well into the year after he had finished his Apprenticeship. He had discussed the problem with the Principal and they had agreed it was essential that he finished his studies, before being called-up. He had further advised Sid to seek a further deferment of his National Service without delay.

He duly applied to the appropriate authority and had just heard that his application had been sanctioned. He had thus solved his problem with a modicum of common sense. His father obviously cared about him and when necessary, he had talked to his son in a calm and sensible way. He must have been very proud of his lad's achievements. While they were listening to Sid, one of the lads startled his mates by blaming everyone but himself for his own academic shortcomings. He angrily insisted that he had always tried to work hard, but had been prevented from doing so by all the 'naffing-around' in the classroom. He had a very short memory and several lads reminded him that he had been one of the biggest offenders and had actually contributed to others' failures. People have always blamed others for their own stupidity and Smallman was a classic example. He continued to angrily deny his culpability and the end of the break stopped the argument from getting out of hand.

Like so many of them, Mike had frittered-away his time and he knew that it was no use blaming others; his opportunity had been spurned and he and the other lads involved had only themselves to blame. He reminded them of the Lecturer that they had hounded so cruelly, who had eventually left the College and gone out to Malta. The man had warned them, time and again, of their folly and his words still rang true.

'It's not me that'll suffer,' he had shouted in angry frustration. 'You'll be the ones who'll be sorry.'

During the breaks, most of the lads sat on upturned packing cases playing cards. Their card games were always boisterous, with a lot of noise and from time to time, someone would loudly shout for them to turn it down. Mike took no part and usually, he sat on the top of a storage rack, either reading his paper or quietly snoozing. His lethargy was noticed and his mates were bent on mischief.

During a dinner break, he was rudely awakened by a copious discharge of foul-smelling and dirty water coming out of a rubber hose, which had been craftily positioned above where he was sitting. His outrage and reaction brought a very quick evacuation from the annex, with his tormentors shouting with glee at the success of their stunt. The water had come from a hydraulic testing unit, which was made up of a hand-pump connected to a water tank. The rubber hose had been connected to the outlet and all it had required was a few quick strokes of the pump. Their caper demonstrated the need for care when choosing somewhere quiet to sit during the breaks.

While their juvenile behaviour had very much declined, there were times when someone even embarrassed his mates. Mike's problem was beer, or rather, his inability to hold it. A few pints on a Saturday night turned an amiable lad into a loud-mouthed oaf, who was often bent on trouble. Such was the extent of his problem, if they saw him at a dance, pub or whatever, they gave him a wide berth. His come-uppance was not long in coming. He had been warned many times about his behaviour, but took no notice and no matter what scrape he was involved in, it was never his fault, or so he said. He usually left his bike in an alley along the side the local pub and the first part of his ride home involved free-wheeling down a hill. At the bottom was a small chapel and one evening, he lost control and demolished the paling fence at the front. When he came to, he retrieved his bike and continued on his way. The next morning, he had a sore head and a few bruises, but was none the worse for his accident. Later in the day, members of the chapel came into the village to ask who had damaged their fence.

One Saturday evening, Mike and his mates went to a dance in the social club of a large paper mill. After imbibing freely, they were late arriving and with confusion at the door, they walked in without paying. They were immediately aware of the air of menace in the hall and stood in a group to one side and watched the unfolding drama. The organisers were frantically dashing about, trying to keep order among the potential aggressors. The 'bother' was coming from a large body of Teds, a similar number of local lads and a group of Servicemen. As usual, the girls were haranguing each other, with loud comments about their lack of virtue, appearance or whatever. They were also egging-on their lads to 'get in and sort them out'. The band had upped the volume but, realising the futility of their efforts, they retired to a place of safety and it had all the makings of one hell of a do.

Suddenly, the doors burst open and a large number of Policemen came running into the hall. The confrontation abruptly ceased and the hostile crowd turned as one to face their new adversaries. The 'boys in blue' waded in and there was one heck of a battle for quite a few minutes. Having restored peace, their efforts were undone when another large bunch of peace-keepers arrived, this time the Military Police and without further ado, the fighting was resumed. The squaddies were easily recognised by their haircuts and were immediately targeted by the MPs and without any prompting, the Civvies went to their aid. Had the red-caps not intervened, the fight that followed may have been avoided, but there was complete chaos for some time after.

Mike and his mates had taken no part in the nonsense and had watched the hostilities in some amazement. A nearby Policeman was vigorously assaulted by a yob with a chair and they laughed out loud at his stupidity. Mike suddenly felt a hand on his arm and he and his mates were arrested, taken outside and put in a van. They were taken off to the main Police Station in the Town where they were put in a cell until the following morning, when singly, they were taken out to be interviewed. The Inspector who talked to Mike was in no mood to be reasonable and the lad realised that he was in serious trouble. He was told that he had been arrested for disorderly conduct, with a second charge of assaulting a Police Officer in the execution of his duty. When asked if he had anything to say, he had the good sense to reply politely and quietly.

He explained that he and his mates had arrived late at the dance and the crowd was already out of control when they went in. They had kept well clear of the trouble, by standing to one side and he strenuously denied that they had taken any part in what had followed. They had only been laughing at what was going on when they were arrested.

'So you think assaulting the Police is a laughing matter, do you?,' the Inspector asked angrily. 'One of my officers has said you hit his colleague with a chair and that you could have severely injured him.'

Mike again denied being involved and stated that if he was taken to Court, he would call witnesses to confirm what he had said. He and his mates had stood in front of a group of girls to protect them and he was sure they would bear out what he had said. The Inspector left the room and after what seemed like an eternity, he returned and told Mike that as he had not been positively identified, he was free to go. He was though warned about his future conduct and sternly advised that if he was arrested again, he would certainly be prosecuted. When he walked out of the Station a few minutes later, he found his mates had also been released. They had all told much the same story, due to the fact that they had discussed and agreed on exactly what they would say while in the cell. One lad, who was a Farmer's son, was extremely worried about what his parents were going to say about his arrest.

'What arrest?' Mike asked him. 'All you have to say was that you thought that you'd had too much to drink and couldn't drive home. If your dad asks, I shall confirm that you stayed at my house for the night.'

That they had been incarcerated bore heavily on them and they agreed that to avoid further problems, they would keep clear of the dance halls. It made good sense to revert to the more congenial country pubs on Saturday nights. One last hurdle for Mike was with the local Sergeant who, not long after, stopped and asked him about the trouble. Mike told him the same story as when he was interviewed and insisted that he had taken no part in the disorder. Having listened quietly, the Sergeant reminded him again of the severe recriminations which would follow any future nonsense.

Mike and his mates had favourite a number of watering holes, some of which were a fair distance from their homes. During the week, they often met in a pub by the end of the bridge over the river in the Town and there was always a pleasant atmosphere. The landlord and his wife were very hospitable. It wasn't long though before three young men took to coming in on the same evenings and their intrusion was resented. They had an sullen attitude and often made snide comments about other people. One was adept at latching on to a small group, when a round was being set up and he craftily ensured he was included. It went on until Mike noticed that he never 'put his hand in his pocket'. When he next 'did the honours', he excluded him and was taken to task for doing so. Mike pointedly asked him if there was a problem.

A few nights later, they challenged a lad, who was with his girl outside the pub and the prompt intercession of Mike and his mates saw them off. They had to resolve the problem, before it all got out of hand and he confronted the clown who was causing the trouble. He was warned that any further nonsense would result in a fat lip coming his way. One evening, the landlord announced that his lease was up and that he and Bet were moving on. He thanked everyone for their custom and said that on their last evening, they would have 'a bit of a do'. 'Eats and drinks' would be provided and he hoped they would make it a night to remember. His customers thought highly of them and there was a quick whip-round for a leaving present.

As it happened, Mike had been two-timing his regular girlfriend by seeing another lass at the same time. It was nothing unusual and he duly missed what was later described by one of his mates, as 'all the fun'. On the following Wednesday evening, when he went into the pub to meet the new landlord, he knew right away that something was wrong. He was coldly asked if he was one of the crowd who were regular drinkers in the pub and when he said he was, he was curtly told to 'sling his hook'. They argued for some minutes, until his son came from behind the bar and said that if he didn't go, he would throw him out.

His mates, who were waiting outside when he came out, were grumbling that they had also been banned. They crossed over the bridge and went into another pub, but were surprised when the landlord told them he didn't want their custom either. He had obviously been warned by his 'oppo' in the other pub, who must have seen them walking in his direction. Back out in the street, Mike asked his mates what the hell had been going on. Ted explained that the previous Thursday evening, they had had a very enjoyable party and had given their presents to their hosts, just before closing. Cyril had told them to help themselves to a last drink and while most of his customers had had another pint, a Babycham or Cherry-B, someone had helped himself to a couple of bottles of whisky. That had brought an abrupt end to a most pleasant evening.

'Who the bloody hell pulled a stunt like that?' Mike angrily demanded.

'Who do you think?' replied Ted, who just as irate. 'It was those bastards we've been having trouble with, wasn't it?'

'The lousy buggers,' Mike replied. 'Come on, let's see if we can find them.'

'No, it's all been sorted,' said one of the other lads. 'We caught up with them soon after we left the pub and recovered the bottles and we gave them a belting. We then went back to the pub right away, but the lights were out and it was all locked up. We took the bottles into the new landlord the next day and tried to explain what had happened, but it didn't make any difference, he still slung us out.'

A couple of months of very pleasant evenings, apart from the problems with the other lads, had in the end all gone pear-shaped. Despite seeing each other regularly around the Town, the crowd never did meet up again in the same way.

Chapter 7

Main Engines

The installation of the high-pressure air system on the Submarine progressed well over the next few weeks and a series of pressure tests confirmed the integrity of the completed sections. John was given other work, most of which was in the relative comfort of the workshop, while Mike remained on board to finish the job. He spent some of the time talking to the Engineers about the design parameters of the system and followed the various lines through the length of the hull. It was a valuable experience, which gave him a detailed knowledge of one of the main parts of the Boat. He had still not received any money for the discomfort of working in the torpedo tubes and when he asked John if he was going to get anything, he was bluntly told to bugger off. He pointed out that he had done most of the work and should have received some bonus money, as well.

'It was only paid out last Friday and it was so little, it wasn't worth sharing,' John replied.

'How the hell do you make that out?' demanded Mike. 'I worked bloody hard on that job, yet you say it didn't make anything.'

'Well, Mr Norman deducted some hours,' John explained, 'quite a lot actually, for the time I spent working on the machine. He wasn't very happy when it didn't work.'

It would have been a waste of time going to see the Foreman. Following their confrontation with Bill, the lads had worked normally for a while, in the vain hope that common sense would prevail but it hadn't worked, because most of the Fitters were still pocketing their bonus, with no thought for their lads.

The resolution of the problem was not long in coming and for once, Mike was not at the centre of the agitation. He had gone over to the main canteen and had missed the fun. When he returned, a noisy row was in progress between some of Fitters and their equally irate Apprentices. He had see the Foreman talking to the Manager on the jetty and had meant to warn his mates but, not wanting to be involved in the altercation, he had gone straight over to his bench and was working when the bosses came through the door. The shouting continued for a few seconds until antagonists became aware of their presence and there was an abrupt silence.

'What's going on here?' shouted Mr Norman. 'It's past one o'clock and hardly any of you are working. This bloody nonsense has been going on long enough. There's always bloody trouble in this shop and I'm going to get to the bottom of it.'

Those involved slunk back to their benches and the Foreman called the Charge-hands to go outside with him. There was a lot of bad-tempered muttering from the Fitters, who blamed the lads getting them into trouble. Bill again muttered that he was 'pissed-off with the bolshie young bastards', who were always looking for trouble, instead of doing what they were told. It wasn't long before it was all sorted out and when it was, it was not at all to the Fitters' liking.

The Foreman sent for the men he'd seen arguing and they were warned about their conduct. The following day, he told the lads to choose a Representative to discuss their grievances with the Manager and it gave them the opportunity for which they had been waiting. Soon after, further meetings took place with the Apprentices who were working in other areas.

The outcome was that the bonus scheme was modified. The Fitters would still be given the target hours for a job, but the bonus earned would be apportioned on a seventy-five/twenty-five basis in their favour. The money due to the Apprentice would be paid directly in his pay-packet. After years of acrimony, the Fitters' cynical exploitation of their lads was thus brought to an end. They complained bitterly that a system, which had worked well for so long, had been overturned by a small bunch of troublemakers. The lads were delighted with the new deal and turned to with a will right away. The immediate improvement in moral brought about the resumption of their good-natured banter. However, it had not gone unnoticed that Mike had kept out of the argument with the Fitters in the shop.

In the early years, the lads had played cards for matchsticks or washers but by their fifth year, some of them had the funds with which to gamble. The stakes were gradually raised and even though it was strictly forbidden, significant sums were often wagered. The ones with pressing financial commitments had dropped out and some, like Mike, neither played cards nor gambled in any way. The leading light was our old friend Bud, who had only recently come into the shop. During the breaks, he would deal the cards with great panache and several lads got their fingers burnt. It was unwise to get involved with the serious gamblers and on no account would they play with anyone from outside the shop.

Mike left John and went to work with a fitter called Ted, who was probably in his early sixties. Before starting, Mike spoke to the lad who had been working with him previously and asked the usual questions. 'What was the old boy like?', 'What were his likes and dislikes' etc? Jim had got on very well with his boss and had been sorry to leave him. He was a very placid old fella, but could be a bit pernickety. They had been working together on the installation of the main engines' bearings and crankshafts and that had been followed by the cylinders, housings and the internal lubrication pipework. It had been hard but interesting work and he had learned a lot from the old lad, the experience of which would stand him in good stead in the future. Ted had played the game and had regularly seen that he was paid for confined-space working and uncas. Mike went off to work with him in a much better frame of mind.

When a Submarine came in for a long refit, her main engines were always in need of a complete overhaul and. it was a lengthy process. There were two methods used to do the job, one of which was to remove the pressure-hull plates above them and lift the engines out, either intact or in large pieces, depending on their size. A floating crane was berthed alongside. The alternative was to strip them down, then take the components up through the hatch and lift them on to the jetty. They were then transported over to the Factory for refurbishment. The engines were then rebuilt to an as-new condition, then stripped down again and returned to the 'Sub' for reinstallation. Each piece was hard-stamped with the appropriate reference number. It was considered essential that each item was put back into its designated location.

The main bearings, having been close-fitted to the crankshaft, had already been installed in their stipulated order and orientation in both engines. The pistons were also to be installed in a similar manner, i.e. into the appropriate cylinder and bottom-end. It was a well-worked system and the care taken ensured that when the engine was commissioned, it was in tip-top condition. They were already being shipped aboard, when Mike went down below with his new boss for the first time. The gang was made up of two Fitters, their Apprentices and four Riggers. A shear-legs structure had been erected close to the after access hatch and a runway beam installed on the incline down into and along the centre line of the engine-room. Other beams, which were part of the Submarine's permanent equipment, were rigged above both engines. Trolleys, called 'monkeys' ran along the beams, with 'chain blocks' and pull-lifts hung on them.

The Riggers worked steadily to keep the Fitters supplied with pistons for their respective engines and when Mike commented that most of them must be near retirement, Ted quietly smiled. He must have said something to them, because one of them later pointedly told the lad that 'they weren't due for the knacker's yard just yet'. Working in the unheated engine room was far from pleasant as the hull-plates were very cold to the touch and running with condensation. Everyone was well wrapped-up and wearing additional jumpers, coats and scarves etc. The short times they spent in the warmth of the workshop were luxury indeed. The space in which they worked, particularly behind the engines, were very tight and it had to be the lads who squeezed into them. Wooden planks were cut down to sit on and leant against, which gave them some insulation against the cold.

Temporary lighting ran through the boat from stem to stern and it was at best unreliable. The light provided was sufficient for the work and for the men to go to and fro in relative safety. Blackouts regularly occurred and whenever the lights went out, there was always a loud cheer from those left in the dark. They either sat tight to wait for them to come on again or stumbled through the Boat, up out of the hatch and out on to the deck. The Electricians were already hard at work installing the cable tray, then pulling new cables through the boat and it was followed by the installation of the permanent light fittings and the terminations in the various junction boxes.

Before installing the first piston, Ted had told Mike to look closely through the crank case, to ensure there were no foreign bodies in it. Having confirmed all was in order, the Riggers manipulated it, with its connecting-rod already fitted over the top of the engine. Great care had to be taken, so as not to cause any damage. A ring, which was made up of 'shim-steel', was placed at the top of the cylinder, to protect the rings, when they were compressed as the piston was dropped into the cylinder. Mike was working directly opposite his boss and he became aware of a most noisome smell, which was disgusting in every true sense of the word. Ted, who was short and very fat, suffered from chronic body odour and the stench emanating from him was made infinitely worse by his regular belches of foul breath and loud farts from the other end. Despite the cold, he sweated profusely and continually took great gulps of air and exhaled forcefully from both nose and mouth.

Being absorbed in what he was doing, he must have been either unaware or indifferent to the discomfort he was inflicting on the others. His noisome problem had been a matter of concern for a long time and as someone said to a roar of laughter in the canteen, it had been even worse in the summer. Ted was a fine Engine Fitter and he was fastidious in checking that everything was done properly. Before connecting the bottom-end of a piston to the crankshaft, all the adjacent surfaces were given a final wipe-clean with cotton-waste. A thin smear of engineer's blue was then applied to the journal and strips of thin lead wire we carefully put into the bearing-shells. As they had already been assembled in the works, the installation work should have been straightforward, without further checks being necessary.

When Mike asked him why they were taking so much trouble, Ted explained that he checked everything because he had to ensure that the Engine would perform well when it was run up for the first time. Having 'nipped' the bottom-end on the first piston, they pulled the crank-shaft over, then broke the bearing again. The leads were found to be satisfactory and after he had given each half-shell a few perfunctory scrapes, Ted said he was satisfied. He proudly told Mike that he had never had any 'come-back' about any of the Engines he had assembled over very many years. Some of the other Fitters were not as thorough as him and often made remarks about him being an 'old woman'.

'That's up to them,' he said solemnly. 'I do things my way and they do theirs. If a job's worth doing lad, it's worth doing well. Men's lives depend on us and a bit of pride in your work never goes amiss.'

Mike had heard that before many times since he came afloat and it was said that Ted's Engines always ran like silk, which was how it should be. In a matter of minutes, they had the bearing re-installed, with the securing-bolts tightened-up and the split-pins inserted and opened-out. With everything in order, they then made ready to install the second piston. Again, Mike's task was to finally check the cylinder and crank-case in the same conscientious manner as before.

'That's the way I want it done,' Ted said many times, puffing like an old steam engine. 'There's going to be no half measures here, lad. Everything has to be done right and first time.'

The Riggers were kept busy bringing the other pistons down into the engine-room and they had already left the next one slung ready for dropping into place. Ted and Mike worked steadily along the port engine over the next week and the job was carried through in the same well-ordered manner. After a final and meticulous inspection of the bottom ends and with one last look through the length of the sump, they fitted and closed the crank-case doors. Their next job was to fit the cylinder heads, which was even more difficult, with Ted continually going on about the need for the greatest of care. They were both bulky and heavy and the space in which they had to work was very tight. The Riggers had great difficulty in bringing them down through the hatch and along the space between the Engines and they had even more problems lifting them into position. That was done by the judicious use of the lifting-tackle and with a lot of cursing and swearing.

Due to the close proximity of the pressure-hull bracings, there was only an inch or so in which to edge a head over the stud-bolts. The gasket-ring was secured in its groove and the head was slowly lowered into place and all eight units were installed. The holding-down nuts were then screwed-on to the studs and tightened. Each nut had been matched to its bolt and they were systematically hardened down. Ted sat down, wiped the perspiration from his brow, then he talked to the lads about the next job. It was his responsibility to check the valve clearances and make the final adjustments, which were vital to the smooth running of the engines. Having made his point, the lads were allowed to make a few adjustments, subject to his final tweak, when and as necessary. The 'rocker-covers' were then installed to protect the heads.

The last job was to attach the fluid couplings to the shaft at the front of each engine, which was yet another awkward task, again due to the confined space in which they were working. How on earth the Boat's Engineers managed to strip and repair a faulty engine, while at sea, was a complete mystery. It was the first time that Mike had worked directly with a Charge-hand and he had benefited very much from doing so. For all the snide comments, Ted was greatly respected by his peers and he went about his business in a quiet, methodical way and always calm and collected. In the time that Mike was working with him, he never raised his voice in anger and like so many of the older men, he was highly skilled and his attention to detail and pride in his work was that of a true Craftsman.

With Mike's income having increased to a previously undreamt level, his social life had improved so very much in the past twelve months. He went out for a drink most evenings and despite several near misses, he often didn't bother about having a competent driver with him. One evening, PC Smith pulled him over soon after he'd picked up Wilf and another lad. The Officer regularly stood at the junction where the lane met the main road, usually between seven and eight o'clock and to minimise the risk of apprehension, Wilf usually walked down the hill to meet Mike in a side road. Their ploy worked very well and it saved him from having to walk the mile up to Mike's house. Smithy was clearly disappointed that all was in order and after gruffly advising them to 'take care', they drove off. It was imperative that Mike took another driving test if he was to keep the 'Rozzer' off his back.

On the day he caught the bus into town, having taken the car and parked it outside the Test Office the previous evening. To his dismay when he arrived the next morning, he had forgotten his glasses, which would adversely affect his test. The Examiner's first question was, 'Where was his competent driver?' Mike explained that he and his mate had left the car outside the evening before and it was clear that the man was not satisfied.

'According to the regulations, he should be here with you,' he said crossly. 'Never mind, just read the number plate of that car over there.'

Mike had already checked half a dozen or so of the nearby cars and was able to give him the correct answer and when he asked 'Which was his car?' Mike cheerfully pointed it out.

'But it's a left-hand drive,' the man expostulated, 'I'm not at all happy with that.'

It didn't bode at all well for the test and it was only after some polite persuasion that he allowed him to proceed. Then came the bombshell. After only a few minutes, the Examiner said that he had seen enough and that Mike was clearly not a competent driver. He had made a pig's ear of reversing into a side road and to make things worse, he had also messed up the 'emergency stop'. It was a disaster and he was very upset at having failed the test for the second time. It didn't help later when Wilf laughed and said he knew why.

During the week, the lads often went to The Mill where the beer was well kept, which was not always the case in those days. The bars were usually full of young people and they were often joined by a group of Irish lads, one of whom, Pat, had been very helpful in providing Mike with cheap tyres for his car. When he had told him about the problems with the car and the bugger that had sold it to him, the young man had been very sympathetic and had had subsequently said many times that if he needed anything else, he only had to ask. There was little that 'couldn't be had' on the Site and if it wasn't 'in stock' then it could be 'ordered'. Delivery would be made within a matter of days but, discretion was called for and as long as that was understood, Mike could ask for anything he wanted.

Chapter 8

Pleasant Times

One Saturday evening, after having warmed up in their local, the lads went off to a dance in a village near the Oil Refinery and when they arrived, they were dismayed to see that a stand-off was already in progress, between the local lads and a large group of Irishmen. Mike went up to one of the locals and quietly told him that the Paddies were decent lads, who didn't want any bother and that the real enemy would be arriving shortly, in the form of a large bunch of squaddies. They would almost certainly be 'looking for it', because they had caused no end of trouble in the area in recent months. He suggested it would make good sense to join with the Irish to meet their challenge and to his surprise, his advice was accepted.

When the Army lads arrived, they came into the hall in their normal, aggressive manner and for some of them, paying to get into the dance was an unnecessary expense. Despite the doorman's loud protests, they pushed straight past him. Mike was dismayed to see that Alan was among them and he was actively leading the taunting of the civvies. The Irishmen were usually friendly to everyone they met but, when 'they had the drink taken', they were a formidable foe. They and the locals reacted angrily and for a few minutes, all hell broke loose. Peace returned when the Police arrived and the Sergeant announced that any further disturbance would end the dance and some of them would spend the night in the cells. That brought an end to the hostilities and the dance progressed uneasily but peacefully to the end.

As Mike and his mates were getting into the car, they saw that some of the squaddies had been badly beaten and were being 'helped' into a Police Van. Alan was among them. They had followed the Irish lads outside and how they must have rued their folly. When they next met up in The Mill, it was clear that Pat and his pals had been involved because he was sporting a large bandage on his right hand, which he said was due to a 'h'indushtrial h'accident'. Everyone laughed and it set the tone for the evening. In the next week or so, Mike got some 'funny' looks from Alan's family, but nothing was ever said about what had happened to him.

The folly of driving on his own became more regular and it was incredible that he didn't get caught. No thought was given to his insurance policy, which stated that driving unaccompanied negated the cover. One ploy was to drive up to the top of the hill, and then down over the cart-tracks until he came to a road, which led into the village where he had attended the youth club. He would then go to the pub, have a couple of pints, then go home by the same route. PC Smith was no fool and he regularly kept a close watch out for him. Their relationship had always been strained and getting away with it became much of a game to the lad. Time and again, he escaped by the skin of his teeth. He continued to go out with Wilf, which allowed him to drive past the Officer 'without wetting himself', as he so colourfully put it.

Mike and Bill often went to another Town on a Wednesday evening. The dance hall was in a hotel by the river and it was small, compared to the Town Hall, but the band was good and the atmosphere was always pleasant. One evening, Bill came into the bar smiling broadly and introduced Mike to a young lady called Angela. She was smartly dressed, compared with a lot of the other girls and she was working as a 'Nanny' on a large Farm some miles out of the Town. She was vivacious and friendly and had obviously made a good impression on the lad. At the end of the evening, when Mike asked her how she was going to get home, she replied, 'by Taxi of course'.

'There's no need to go to that expense,' Bill said generously. 'Mike's got his car outside and it's on our way home. We'll give you a lift, won't we, old mate?'

The next evening, she went with them to the jazz club in the same Town and Bill was very taken by the lass. Over the next couple of weeks, they often took her out and she was always dressed up to the nines, even one Sunday afternoon, when they went to a village cricket match. She wore a floral dress, complete with gloves and hat and being very well mannered, she apologised for having to be back by five o'clock, to give the children their tea. Angela was very good company and most unusually, she often bought 'a round', saying that 'she liked to pay her way'.

One Saturday evening, Mike dropped them off at the Farm and drove a short distance up the road, his intention being to give the loving couple a few minutes privacy. As a precaution, the lads had swapped their driving licences and if the Police appeared, it would ensure that his misdemeanour of driving alone would be covered. He had only been there for ten minutes or so when the local Bobby came by on his motorbike and stopped to ask what he was doing. Mike explained that he had dropped his mate and a young lady off at the Farm and was giving them a few minutes alone. The Copper wasn't satisfied and much to Mike's alarm, he decided to check his story.

'Right, follow me down to the yard and we'll see if you're telling the truth,' he retorted briskly

Mike drove down the road with his heart in his mouth and was sure he'd been rumbled. When they entered the yard, the Officer turned without stopping and drove straight out again and, with Mike being so close behind, they nearly collided as he came back out the gate. As he turned around, Mike's head-lights lit up the side of the house and he caught a fleeting glimpse of the reason for the Policeman's hasty retreat. There was Bill, with his trousers around his ankles and the young lady with her skirts hoisted above her waist. Until so rudely interrupted, they had been completely absorbed in the ecstasy of copulation, with Angela's bottom precariously balanced on the top of a milk-churn. The unexpected interruption had caused them no little consternation, not least of which was the loud 'clatter' as the churn had overturned.

Mike followed the Officer back up the road to where he had been parked before and found him highly amused.

'Bloody hell,' he said, 'I've seen some odd things in my time, but nothing like that. I hope I didn't put your mate off his stroke,' he continued, laughing out loud. 'D'you know, I've tried my hardest to talk to that snooty cow whenever I've called at the Farm, but she's always given me the cold shoulder. Now I find she's no different from anyone else.'

Bill came running up the road and not seeing the Copper, he loudly admonished Mike for embarrassing him.

'You lousy bugger,' he stormed, 'Why couldn't you have waited a few more minutes? I was just getting on the 'vinegars', (reaching his climax), and you bloody spoiled it.'

He then that he saw the Copper standing beside the car.

'You can't blame your mate,' he told the indignant lad. 'It was just his bad luck that I was checking him out. Now, he tells me this is your car, so let's be seeing your insurance certificate, shall we?'

He inspected the proffered document and after a number of questions, he was satisfied that everything was in order.

'Right,' he said, 'you've had your fun and I suggest that you buggers get off home. I don't want to see either of you around here in the early hours again. I've got enough to do without chasing a couple of randy sods like you around the countryside so go on, clear off.'

The lads got into the car and when they were well clear, they roared with laughter. It had indeed been a close shave. They agreed that they would have to do as they'd been told, if they were to avoid further trouble with the Bobby. As it happened, when they called for Angela the following Wednesday evening, the Farmer's wife answered the door and coldly told them that she wasn't working there any more.

'She left on Monday morning,' the lady complained, 'without notice or as much as a 'by your leave'. I don't suppose her going off like that has anything to do with you two, has it?,' she asked crossly, looking from one lad to the other.

Bill replied that they didn't know why she'd gone because on Saturday night they'd had a very pleasant evening.

'Wait a minute though,' he said by way of an afterthought. 'She did say that her boss had been bothering her and that she was fed up with it. I offered to sort him out, but she said it was her problem and she'd deal with it herself. If I find out it's true, I'll have something to say to him, that's for sure.'

The woman was shocked at his outburst and with a curt goodbye, she closed the door. When Mike remarked that he didn't seem unduly perturbed by the loss of his new girlfriend, Bill replied that they had known they weren't going anywhere. Angela had already decided to move on because the Farmer had become too much of a nuisance with his amorous advances. She had been hard put to fend him off at times and had threatened to complain to his wife. He had then got stroppy and told her the sooner she went, the better. Bill wondered if she had followed up her threat to write to his wife, to explain what had happened. With a bit of luck, his 'old woman' would give the bastard a hard time, for 'not being able to keep his hands to himself and his dick in his pocket', he commented sagely.

On Sunday evenings, they often went to a cellar beneath a public house in the same Town. Between the hours of seven-thirty and ten, they either danced or just sat and listened to the music which was played by a traditional jazz band. Many of the old favourites such as: 'Basin Street Blues', 'Maryland, My Maryland', 'High Society' and 'Frankie and Johnny' were played to a high standard. A couple of pints and a few games of 'shove halfpenny' upstairs in the interval always set the evening off well. The game required both aptitude and patience, which some of the regulars demonstrated with considerable skill. Someone else who had to be avoided was the landlord's eight year old son, Sid. They often smiled as the crafty little sod set up his victims, and then skilfully relieved them of a few shillings.

His strategy was simple and cunningly applied. He would closely watch them playing, then lead them on by asking questions until they offered to show him how to play. After a few minutes, he would suggest a game, 'but only for sixpence, mind,' because that was all he had. He would purposely lose the game and look so crestfallen that his opponent would offer to play him again for it. Then, the gloves were off and several games would ensue, all of which Sid won easily. He would then say he had to go upstairs, before his dad came to tell him to go to bed and the sucker would then realise he'd been had. Time and again, Sid pulled the stunt and he always got away with it. His father proudly told the lads that the little bugger was as good as a lot of his regulars and had he been older, he would have played in the local league.

Mike's abysmal driving was matched by his dancing in that he had two left feet but when jiving, he was no worse than a lot of the other lads. It demanded little skill and he had already 'picked up the basics' in the Cellar Club. Little effort was needed to twirl a lass around on the same spot. He had first met Jean at a dance in the Hotel and while chatting, she had told him she was very keen on 'trad' music and he had then asked her if she would like to go to the jazz club. It was a membership requirement to 'sign her in' as a guest and he was very surprised when she put the figure 'twenty-six' down as her age. He mentally groaned that he had again picked up an older woman but, as he had recently passed his twenty-first birthday, their age difference wasn't that important. They had a very pleasant evening and at the end, they agreed to meet again at the next dance. A succession of dates followed and Mike became quite fond of her over the ensuing weeks.

At work one morning, he was the object of the day's fun and the routine piss-taking quickly gained momentum. His tormentor was Dan, who had first told him about the jazz club and the nonsense was about Jean. At first, he didn't grasp what the lad was driving at and much to the enjoyment of their mates, the lad spelt it out.

'You're only going out with an old woman,' he said smugly.

'So she's older than me, so bloody what?' Mike asked crossly, knowing that despite his previous determination, he was rising to the bait.

'He's only going out with his granny and he asks, so what?' crowed Dan, with the other lads all laughing loudly. 'How old do you think she is?' he asked.

'Twenty-six,' Mike said lamely, 'that's what she said anyway.'

'And the rest,' said Dan with relish, 'she's at least thirty,' which was probably an exaggeration. From then on, everyone regularly asked Mike 'how his granny was.' And he took it all in good part but, from then on, he looked at Jean in a much different light. One Sunday evening, she asked him if anyone had said anything about her and when he said not, she remarked that she thought he was going off her, which he denied. Later, when they stopped for the usual 'slap and tickle', it became very passionate and much to his embarrassment, he made a bumbling mess of what should have come naturally. She promptly sacked him, saying primly that 'she was not like that'. It was the end of their beautiful friendship and also the end of his visits to the jazz club.

There was unpleasantness in The Mill one evening, which brought an end to his animosity with the Farmers' sons. The problem had in fact declined considerably from the days when their confrontations had often ended in violence. What brought it to a head was when three of them were heard berating another lad as being 'bloody fat and useless'. Their victim, Doug, was the son of a 'Gentleman Farmer' (called such as he owned his land) who had three large Farms. When Mike saw how upset he was, he went across and told them to lay off him and he then invited Doug to join him and his mates, something which was not appreciated by the tormentors. He was an amiable young man and from then on, he regularly accompanied the lads on their jaunts around the countryside.

One evening, he brought a young lady and she was an absolute stunner. Sally's parents were also Farmers and she had enjoyed an expensive education, which had culminated in a finishing school in Switzerland. The term had to be explained to Mike and his mates, because they didn't have a clue as to what it meant. She was a tall, blond and very shapely girl, with a confident and friendly manner and being full of fun, she was soon very much at ease with everyone. She came regularly with Doug for her 'halves of bittah' and the dexterity with which she handled playing cards amused them greatly. Everyone liked Sally and she was obviously very fond of her young man. In due course, they got engaged and the following year, they married.

The Police Sergeant was a very large, affable man and he was highly respected in the community, in direct contrast to his Constables. Closing time was ten-thirty and he often visited the pub on a Friday evening to ostensibly 'turf them out'. He would come into the Saloon Bar, just after time had been called and peremptorily order everyone out. His ill-tempered castigation of the local lads was for the general benefit of the strangers in their midst.

'I've told you buggers about drinking after hours and I'm not in the habit of repeating myself, am I?' he would shout. 'Now get out, before I book the lot of you and don't let me have to tell you again.'

Out everybody would troop and the lads would make as if to either walk off into the night or drive off in their cars. When they were sure the strangers had gone, they would return to the bar through the back door and there, sitting on his stool would be the Sergeant, with a row of beers in front of him.

'Come on lads, I haven't got all night,' he would say 'One for the road eh? then off for your sorely needed beauty sleep. It's your round, Mike,' or whoever's turn it was that time, he would add as an afterthought.

It was the same joke, night after night, but they all laughed, because it kept the Sergeant sweet. The charade went on for some time and ultimately, as happens in so very many pubs, the regulars drifted off to pastures new. A year or so later, the Sergeant retired and emigrated to South Africa, to play some golf and sit in the sun.

Chapter 9

Testing Systems

Having completed his stint of working with the malodorous Ted, Mike was put to work with Jock, the Fitter who had recently confronted the ubiquitous Bill. Like so many others, he liked to reminisce about his life in the Royal Navy and they were soon yarning amicably. He told Mike that he had volunteered, soon after he'd finished his Apprenticeship in a Clydeside Shipyard, on a three year engagement. Like a lot of the other lads, he'd arrived at the training establishment 'bang full' of enthusiasm and thought he knew it all. In fact, he knew bugger all and had soon been, like everyone else, in a severe state of shock. His entry comprised of thirty or so lads and they immediately fell foul of a P.O, three-badge, Physical Training Instructor, (PTI), who was absolutely 'bluidy mental'. He had introduced himself to his callow troops by deliberately enunciating his name in a loud, pronounced cockney accent.

'My name is Attwell, A, double T, double U, E, double L,' he'd yelled. 'You only address me when spoken to and you either call me P.O. or Sir. You obey my orders first time and with no backchat. Shirking will not be tolerated and you will put the maximum effort into everything you do. Anyone who acts the goat will be severely dealt with by my little friend here',' he concluded.

He was tall, rippling with muscles and full of unbridled energy and his predominant feature was his very large aquiline nose, a veritable proboscis. He was instantly nicknamed 'Ichabod' by a wit. His 'little friend' was a short, sturdy cane, the 'cuts' of which most of the entry 'tasted' regularly over the following weeks. Anyone who fell short of what he required, or didn't respond quickly enough to his instructions, suffered painful retribution. Their first morning had been an absolute nightmare, with everyone scared shitless by the screaming banshee, who stood in front of them. He quivered with outraged indignation and emitted a fluent stream of orders, such as 'Stand still', 'Keep silence' and 'move' without apparently stopping for breath and their torment went on for many weeks.

One morning, after energetically warming them up with a series of floor and wall-bar exercises, with innumerable press-ups, sit-ups and running on the spots, he introduced them to 'the skate'. It was a wooden lattice structure, which was suspended from the roof at the far end of the gym and was thirty feet high and wide and made up of equally spaced parallel and vertical bars. Its use was to strengthen their arms and legs and on his command, they would run to it, climb up one side, go over the top, then drop down to the ground as quickly as possible. The last man back would be 'welcomed' by his little friend. If he was the same offender as the time before, he would suffer double punishment. Now that was motivation!

His first shout of 'over the skate' had resulted in an absolute shambles as there were only ten equally spaced 'bays', so the first lads to arrive impeded the second lot and so on. They scrambled up the frame, with no thought for anyone else or their safety. There was an unholy scrum at the bottom, with lads fighting furiously to ensure they weren't going to be the last to finish. The dreaded cry of 'over the skate' came with painful regularity in the days that followed and they got better at it, but it was a painful exercise for a few. Cuts were gleefully administered and they learned the painful lesson that it paid to be always on their toes.

There was method in Ichabod's madness because by the end of the first four weeks, the change in their fitness and spontaneous reaction to his orders was remarkable. They all felt much happier about their lot, both in and outside of the gym and their cross country runs became enjoyable outings, except for the last one 'home'. It was rarely the same lad and Ichabod's little friend gradually came into play less and less. A regular exercise was to jump up and down, with legs apart and legs together and their arms raised and lowered sideways in time to his calls. On his command, they had to jump as high as possible, with legs together and arms held firmly to their sides and anyone deemed not to have jumped high enough was duly chastised. When he shouted 'wait for it', with everyone off the ground, they all fell about laughing. Ichabod gave what passed for a smile and said: 'There now, you didn't know you could enjoy yourselves so much in the gym, did you?'

Jock was moody at times and not always communicative but compared to some Fitters, he was easy to get on with. It was best not to bring women into their conversations, because he was unusually scathing and definite about his dislike for the opposite sex. When he overheard a lad complaining about the problems he was having with his girlfriend, he was quick to point out the dangers of 'getting involved'.

'They're all the bloody same, believe you me,' he told him. 'They take everything you've got, then leave you in the bloody lurch. You'd be well advised to give them a wide berth, laddie, at least until you've had some experience of life and then perhaps, you'll not be so easily taken in by their wily ways.'

He had a deep and genuine love of all things 'Engineering' and was conscientious and thorough in his work. He was often heard trotting out a favourite saying, much to the knowing winks and exaggerated sighs of the other Fitters.

'If a job's worth doing, it's worth doing well and don't you forget it, laddie,' he said many times. 'I've no time for frivolity, so let's get on with it.'

While polite to his workmates, even Bill, he 'tipped his cap' to no one. His main interest was in the main engines and the associated auxiliary machinery in ships. When a machine was brought into the shop, he would go to look at it and discuss what was to be done in a quiet, knowledgeable way. The Foreman had fortuitously come by a Fitter who was clearly outstanding, when compared with most of his other men. In consequence, he was often given the difficult jobs to do and had been set to work on the Boat's HP air distribution system.

Over the next few weeks, they worked on and tested various sections, the last of which were the final connections to the main engines' starters. The Electricians were by that time more numerous on board than the Fitters and the main cable terminations were well in hand, closely followed by the ancillary control systems. Mike had never seen anything like the work they were doing in the control and communications rooms. The cables were multi-cored and they spent weeks with their heads in the large junction-boxes, patiently making-off hundreds of terminations. When they'd finished, it all looked very neat; in the Naval vernacular, 'tiddly'. The commissioning of the main circuits began and increasingly, notices were posted, which advised everyone as the various circuits which had been completed, tested and 'made live'.

Any Ship undergoing a re-fit inevitably accumulates a huge amount of rubbish, which includes all manner of temporary equipment. Riggers were taking down redundant chain and rope blocks, pull-lifts and 'tirfors', which had been put-up on temporary attachments made to the inner hull. Scaffolding, duck-boards, planks and baulks of timber and all manner of detritus was carried ashore. A gang of Labourers systematically worked their way through the various compartments and they often took away parts which were awaiting installation. The Electricians gradually stripped out the redundant temporary lighting and the Boat was regularly plunged into darkness as they gradually changed over to the permanent lighting system. It was chaotic but in a matter of weeks, a measure of order became increasingly apparent.

Increasing numbers of Naval personnel came on board, which gave even more urgency to the work and they were closely involved in testing the live circuits and systems. Jock and his lad were busy installing the many boards, on which would be mounted the pressure and temperature gauges relating to the various machinery functions. If one had to be modified or relocated, a new one was made and the Engineers were often consulted as to their preferred location. The fitting of the gauges followed and the Coppersmiths installed the impulse lines. The Matelots would soon cover them with a thick coating of paint; nothing was more unsightly than copper pipes covered in 'verdigrise'. High humidity was a significant problem on board an operational Submarine. With all the deck-work completed, the casings were replaced and welded on to the outside of the pressure-hull.

One morning, they went forrad to assist the Engineers, who were commissioning the torpedo-tubes' control system. The end-doors operation and interlocks were checked with great care, because some years previously, there had been a serious accident on a Submarine during her sea trials, with consequent great loss of life. The inboard door had to be properly closed, before the bow-door could be opened and vice-versa and ultimately, the doors on all the tubes had been approved and signed off. Each part of the commissioning work was very closely monitored and Jock solemnly warned Mike not to touch anything. Strict control regimes were absolutely imperative and the testing proceeded steadily, with only minor problems and faults, which were fixed as they were found.

The commissioning of the torpedo firing system locally and remotely from the control room was started and the Submarine was ballasted down in the water and the air system pressurised. The bow-door was opened to flood the first tube and the control manifold, which was mounted above and in front of the inboard end, was actuated. A charge of air was released into the tube, which violently expelled the water and the consequent shock sharply lifted the bow of the Boat. The contents of the tube were propelled with some force into the adjacent wall of the basin and a large column of water cascaded down onto the road above. People who had crossed, or were going to cross the bridge between the two basins, were soon complaining about the hazards involved and signs were posted to advise them of the tests.

There was a steady stream of visitors, including Senior Managers and Naval Officers and the Foreman came down in both the morning and the afternoon. A Sailor was sent to the control room to view the 'danger area' through a periscope and he was instructed to telephone the torpedo room, when it was safe to fire. The system worked well, but the opportunity for mischief came when Mike went along to talk to him. He suggested that a judicious firing might lead to a funny situation. The Jolly Jack saw the humour of the plan and had no objection, providing that he was in no way involved. Later, having been caught in the ensuing deluge, Norman arrived on board in a very damp state. He didn't say anything, but when the same thing happened the next morning, he was very much put out.

'I don't know how it happens,' he complained, 'but every time I come over the bridge, you fire a charge and I get an earful.'

The lads could hardly contain their mirth and as the Foreman looked balefully around, he instinctively knew what had been going on.

'Alright you sods,' he said with a wry smile, 'I get it. You've been having a bit of fun at my expense, haven't you?'

Everyone laughed and even he saw the funny side of the prank.

'What I don't see is how you've managed to get it just right each time. Not to worry, I'll soon have my revenge, you see if I don't,' he concluded with a grim smile.

Mike, who had come along to the bulkhead door, decided he had pressing things to do in the workshop. A joke was just that, but one had to tread carefully where the Foreman was concerned.

The Submarine was nearing the end of the refit and access on board was becoming increasingly restricted. Completed areas, such as the control room and accommodation were most definitely off-limits to the Dockyard personnel. The number of Matelots on board had increased substantially and gangs of them were busy throughout the boat. Some were compiling 'punch lists' of outstanding items, which had been completed, but were defective and they were handed to the various Foremen, who passed them on to their men. As each item was completed, it was signed off and the atmosphere on board gradually become a lot more frantic, as the commissioning work progressed.

Barry was very smug about the responsible work he was doing and he crowed that only the most able of Fitters were chosen for the most difficult jobs, so much so that he 'got on the tits' of his workmates. They all thought, or rather hoped that sooner or later, the silly bugger would come a cropper and his demise wasn't long in coming. When he went to replace the fixings of a hull-mounted instrument, which was located under the external casing, he made a complete hash of it. How he fouled up such an easy job was both amusing and a bit of a mystery. Prior to inserting new studs in the hull-mounting plate, he had to first clean up the threads and finding the job harder than it ought to have been, he was horrified to find he had been using the wrong taps. i.e. Whitworth instead of British Standard Fine. He had buggered several threads and was distraught when he went over to the office to report what he had done. The Boat was scheduled to be moved across the basin to commence engine trials and there would be certainly be angry recriminations from the Management if it was delayed.

His gaff couldn't be glossed over and it was decided to fill the damaged holes with weld and grind them off flush with the top of the plate. A crack-detection test ensured that no damage had been caused to the plate. To be absolutely sure, the fitting was rotated by half a hole and the new holes were carefully marked out, drilled and tapped with the correct threads. Hand held electric drills were still scarce in the Yard and most of the drilling was done by means of an air-driven machine, which was mounted in a post arrangement. If no air was available, a hand-ratchet was often used. It was a laborious job, because the bit had to be regularly checked for squareness. Barry carefully tapped-out the threads, closely watched by the Foreman and the Boat's Engineer and the instrument was then installed, connected-up and tested. It was some time before the hapless Barry was allowed to forget his blunder and from then on, any cock-up in the shop was snidely referred to as 'a Barry'. The old adage that 'pride came before a fall' was never more apt.

The changes in the Submarine, which had been brought about in the months that Mike had been working there, were little short of amazing and the chaos, which had been so prevalent for so long, had gone. It clearly demonstrated that the Yard was more than capable of turning out a first-class job. What surprised the lad most was that in the Boat, space was at an absolute premium, with no room to swing the proverbial cat.

Chapter 10

Cold Work

Something had been puzzling Mike for some time and one morning, he asked Jock why Sailors always referred to a Submarine as a 'Boat'. When they referred to any surface Vessel larger than a Motor Torpedo Boat or Gun Boat, they always insisted it was a 'Ship' and were always quick to correct any 'landlubber' who erred on that point. Even the wooden-hulled Minesweepers were referred to as Ships. Some of the Fitters joined in and a lively debate followed as to the reasoning and logic of the matter. Jock thought that the differentiation was very much due to tradition, a relic from when most Naval Vessels were moved by sail. Any Vessel that was square-rigged was referred to as a Ship and anything which could be sailed by a few men and boys was a Boat. He readily admitted that he had no idea as to why Submarines had always been called Boats and nor had anyone else.

Mike and his mates watched the Submarine as she was towed across the basin and double-moored in a flooded dry-dock. The purpose of the move was for her main engines to be run up and tested, to ensure they were in all respects fit for her to be made ready for sea. Mike was called over to the Foreman's office that same afternoon and told he was needed elsewhere and was sent to report to a Test Engineer, who was going to carry out a hull -survey of a Cruiser, which had come in for a short refit.

'This is your chance to learn something new,' Norman told him. 'They've got a new piece of kit which they put on the outside of a hull-plate and it tells them exactly how thick it is. Make sure you pay attention to what's going on, because I shall want to know all about it when you come back.'

Mike walked down the road to the same dry-dock as he had worked in some months before and as then, the weather was cold and wet. His main thoughts were about how he was going to keep warm, while traipsing around the bottom. He looked down at the Ship from the walkway across the top of the caisson for some minutes, and then went along the jetty to the office.

'Ah yes,' the Engineer said in a friendly manner, looking him up and down and taking slow pulls at his pipe, 'I asked for someone to give us a hand. My name is Cyril and I'll be joined shortly by two colleagues and a Technician from Bath, who would be bringing some special equipment with him, which he might find interesting. Know about Ship's hulls, do you?'

Mike replied that he knew nothing about the job, but was very keen to learn and it was what his new boss wanted to hear. He went on to explain in some depth what the job entailed. He was a large, genial man, with thick, horn-rimmed glasses and was probably in his mid to late thirties. Access into the dock would not be available for at least for a couple of days, so there was no hurry to make a start. Cyril commented that his protective clothing was old and shabby and had been hard to get hold of and he regretted that they wouldn't be able to lend Mike any. The lad told him that he already had everything he needed.

When he went over to the amenity block, he was relieved to find his padlock was still intact on the locker door. The problem was, what had he done with the key?, and he went back to the workshop and found it in a tray inside his toolbox. On opening the door, he was pleased to find the contents of the locker were just as he had left them. The heating, which was left on all the year round, provided the warm, dry conditions necessary to keep everything in good order. Finding his wellies, jacket, gloves and socks etc all fit for use, he locked them up again and went back to the office.

The next day, he went back to the shop and came by the more mundane items such as waterproof gloves, a bundle of neck-cloths and a large bag of cotton waste. Cyril was in the office when he returned with his colleagues, one of whom was an ex-Apprentice called Phil, who Mike hadn't seen for a couple of years. Being academically gifted, he had done very well in the Upper School. After their initial 'hello's', he introduced his other colleague; another Apprentice the same age as Mike. The young man was cool-mannered, to say the least and when he asked Phil about him, all he would say was that Mark was rather conceited and abrupt with anyone he thought inferior to himself.

Later that day, a van arrived with their tools, which didn't amount to much. Included were a couple of angle-grinders, an assortment of solid and abrasive wire discs and some coils of rubber air-hose. In addition to being cleaned, some of the plates would have to be ground or buffed-off, to remove imperfections in the surface metal. A visual check would then be made, prior to the tests. While he was elaborating, Phil was rudely interrupted by Mark, who was sitting glumly in a corner. He sarcastically told him he was wasting his breath by explaining things to someone who wouldn't understand what it was all about. Mike bridled at the insult and went out of the office to avoid trouble. Later, Phil told him that he had spoken to Mark about the need to keep a civil tongue in his head.

'I explained that it might lead to a confrontation, which could easily get out of hand and that he shouldn't antagonise you,' he said.

'Thanks for that,' Mike replied. 'You may know I'm on a final warning, so I just have to keep out of trouble.'

Mark was a student Apprentice and his somewhat exalted position had gone to his head. Sooner or later, he would get into serious trouble, unless he pulled it in a bit. The following Saturday evening at the Town Hall, Mike was in the bar with his mates during the interval when they heard a loud voice holding forth a few feet away. Turning around, he saw it was Mark, who was telling a small group of friends about his excellent job. The lads were all ears and couldn't help laughing out loud when he proudly boasted that he was a 'Diagnostician'. Realising he was standing next to some 'herberts', who knew he was bullshitting, he was rather taken aback. He turned angrily to one of the buggers laughing at him.

'What do you know?' he demanded angrily. 'You're only a common Apprentice who doesn't know one end of a Ship from the other.'

'Enough to know what you are, my old son,' came the prompt reply from Ernie, who was completely unabashed at being confronted.

Turning to one of the young ladies, he explained very politely that he had to put the record straight.

'You shouldn't take any notice of Mark, because he's no different from the rest of us. 'He's only working with a Test Engineer as his 'gofor', nothing more.'

He was interrupted by another lass, who wanted to know what a gofor was.

'It's like this,' he replied with a smile. 'Whenever his boss needs something, it's 'Mark, go for this or go for that.' I've even seen him making his tea,' (which the lying sod hadn't, but who knew otherwise?_ 'If there's a dirty job to be done, he does it, ain't that right lads?,' he asked. 'Yeh, that's what he is, a gofor.'

Ernie had very much exaggerated, because everyone knew that Mark was a very able lad. However, his superior attitude was deeply resented by a lot of his fellow Apprentices. No one doubted that he had a bright future, but many of them would have done anything to take him down a peg or two. At that point, the girl with Mark must have sensed there was going to be trouble and told him she wanted to go back into the dance. Ernie had to have the last word.

'That's it love,' he said as they moved off, 'take him away, before one of these common buggers teaches him some manners.'

Back in the dance hall, Mike saw the young woman who had asked what a gofor was, standing on her own. She was very pleasant when he went over and asked her to dance. As it happened, her name was Leslie and she was Mark's sister and apparently, he and his girlfriend had gone home and left her 'on her Tod'. They had most of the ensuing dances, during which she told Mike that she was older than her brother and was working in London as a Solicitor. He still treated her like a little girl, instead of an adult and independent woman. He had been trying to impress his new girlfriend and had gone a bit over the top. After the dance, Mike gave her a lift home and as she was returning to London the next day, a date wasn't possible. It was agreed that they 'might' meet again, when she next came down to see her parents. Her last comment was that she would remember to use the word 'gofor' whenever Mark was being pompous.

Soon after they arrived at work on Monday morning, Mark angrily demanded to know what Mike had been up to with his sister.

'I don't think it's any of your business,' he replied huffily.

'You and your bloody mates spoiled our evening,' the lad said hotly. 'We were having a private conversation in the bar and you lot had to butt in. We paid good money for the tickets and we didn't get a refund when we left early. Now my girlfriend doesn't want go to the Town Hall again. Why couldn't you have minded your own business?'

Being confronted in such an aggressive manner, Mike stood up and asked if he wanted to make anything of it.

'No I don't,' replied Mark, stepping back hastily. 'I just wanted to make the point that you spoiled our evening.'

Just then, the Engineers came into the office and sensing that there was trouble, Cyril asked what the problem was.

'There's no problem,' said Mike. 'We were just discussing the dance at the Town Hall on Saturday night.'

'Well come on then,' Cyril replied, 'we've got work to do.'

Their first task was to identify and mark the plates to be surveyed. Cyril picked up the relevant drawings, then went out and headed towards the stairway down into the dock. Mike went off to change and when he returned, he was suitably attired for the conditions in which they would be working. A large, wheeled, scaffolded-platform had been provided, which would easily be moved, thus providing safe access to each plate. While the engineers identified them, the Apprentices cleaned and marked them off with their definitive numbers. It was a cold but dry day and not as bad as Mike had feared. Good progress was made during the morning shift, with most of the port-side plates having been identified. The starboard side was completed by the end of the day.

A small, bald-headed man called Charles arrived next morning, with a brand-new ultra-sonic scanner and Mike had neither seen nor heard of anything like it before. It was about twelve inches square by six inches thick and was contained in a canvass bag with a shoulder-strap attached. A sensing-head, cable and socket were stowed in pockets on the sides. On the top was a small screen, three inches square and also a number of buttons and knobs. Charles was dressed like the other Engineers in grubby overalls, a donkey jacket and was wearing a pair of wellies which were several sizes too big. With a flourish, he made to test the machine in the office, before taking it down into the dock, but it was dead. After he had switched it on and off a few times, Mike asked Charles how it was powered and when told it was by a battery, he asked where it was. For once, he wasn't being clever.

'Oh bloody hell,' the little man exclaimed, 'I've left it in the office.'

Cyril and the other engineer looked at each other in dismay and went off to the Test House to find a suitable replacement. In the meantime, Mike had improved his relations with Mark because while they were waiting, he had complained about his kit and had looked at Mike's with some envy. Like his peers, his coat was old and torn and his wellies had seen better days and weren't watertight. His overalls had been worn by countless others, who had not thought to send them to the laundry. Knowing that many of the lockers in the amenity-block contained better kit, Mike took Mark and Phil over to there to see what they could find. After opening several lockers, he was able to provide them with suitable replacements, on condition that everything had to be returned when the job was completed.

The only thing Mike was unable to provide was some form of headgear. He had previously worn a beret, to guard against the insanitary habits of the dirty buggers who were working on the Ship. It was not unusual for someone to 'slash' over the side, rather than go ashore to the bogs and he advised them to get something similar. When Cyril returned, he saw that some skulduggery had taken place but, being keen to get on, he ignored it. Over the next week, their work was regularly interrupted by rain and a small number of plates required further polishing, to abrade the minor faults which impeded the smooth movement of the sensing-head across the surface. Initially, the box of tricks was solely operated by Charles, but that soon changed. Within days, both Cyril and the Phil did the job, while the boffin 'took a breather'.

The data on the screen was not easy to read, due to its size and it was illegible in anything less than deep shadow. The set often had to be re-calibrated by twiddling various knobs and Cyril became increasingly frustrated with the time that the job was taking. Mike hadn't found the conditions in the dock unduly hard, but the Engineers certainly had and they regularly went up 'for a warm'. It wasn't long before Phil and Mark were doing most of the work for them. Try as he might, Mike couldn't grasp the technique of reading the screen, though the others seemed to have little difficulty so, he was happy to do the wire-brushing and grinding work on his own.

The following day, Cyril and his team went away to assess the data and write-up their report. With Mike at a loose end, the Dock Foreman attached him to the gang which was removing the starboard inner and outer screws from the same Ship. As before, scaffolding around the stern provided the safe means of access and the space in which to work. Chain blocks had been rigged off brackets welded on to the hull and after having loosened the screws the gang drew them off their shafts. The discomfort of working in the dock was sweetened by the overtime they were working and as each screw was freed, the hook from the dockside crane was attached to the slings and gradually, the weight was transferred. It was then lifted up on to the jetty. And soon after, both screws were loaded on to trailers and taken off to the Factory.

In this modern age, the technology available greatly eases the decision making and evolutionary process in every aspect of Engineering. In 1958, things were much different and it was some days before the Management decided to pull the tail-shafts out as well. With normal usage, they gave many years of service, though the bearings which supported them often required renewal. The frequency of such maintenance very much depended on how well the Ship was handled and as the cruiser had been aground, there was no option but to take them out for straightening. It was odds on that it wasn't the first time it had happened.

Chapter 11

Under Pressure

There is usually someone, in any group of workers, who can tell a tale and is never short of a humorous quip. Joe was a brash 'Tyke', i.e. a Yorkshireman, who had travelled the world and been to places that most of his listeners had never even heard of. He often reminisced about his service in the Merchant Navy and like so many of the Mateys, he regularly indulged in denigrating the Royal Navy. His favourite observation nearly always brought a laugh from his workmates.

'While I was in the Merchant, I got some real sea-time in,' he would say, speaking loudly enough for the nearby Jacks to hear. 'Not like that lot over there, who spend most of their time tied-up at a jetty, after getting lost and hitting something on the way in.'

While awaiting instructions, the gang stood on the dock-bottom and sensing his mischief, everyone was curious about what Joe was up to. A party of RN Officers came down the steps, all smartly dressed in snow-white overalls and when they had walked around under the hull, he nonchalantly sidled over to listen to their discussion. One of them was the Engineer Captain of the Yard and he was making much of how the damage they'd seen was a 'pretty poor show' and that the Ship was urgently needed in the Fleet. There was a lot of self-conscious coughing and embarrassed looks between some members of his party. The First Lieutenant, (or 'Jimmy the one' as he was known), appeared to be bearing the brunt of the bollocking and after some minutes, the party turned to go back up out of the dock.

As they neared the foot of the steps, the Captain stopped abruptly, turned and sternly took the watching Mateys to task.

'I say you chaps, 'chop-chop,'' he said, in that languid, drawling voice that they knew so well. 'Let's be getting on with it, shall we? We've got to get this Ship back to sea as quickly as possible.'

No doubt feeling pleased to have scored a point in castigating 'those lazy bloody Mateys', he ran up the first few steps with a spring in his step. Some of the Officers remained below and gloomily mooched around the dock bottom for a few minutes more, pretending to look again at the hull. When they thought the coast was clear, they made for the steps and Joe pounced.

'By heck, Skipper,' he said, addressing the Senior Officer with a deadpan expression, 'you've made a right good job of that, haven't you?'

He got no further.

'You cheeky sod!', stormed the incensed Officer. 'Since when were we answerable to you lot? You stand around making silly bloody comments about a most serious situation and what's worse, you laugh about it. It's not funny you know and don't call me 'Skipper'. Skippers command trawlers, not Her Majesty's Ships.'

Completely unabashed and clearly delighted that his inanity had struck home, Joe continued with his inanity.

'Oh, I'm very sorry, Sir,' came the innocent reply. 'I didn't know that, did you lads? Anyhow, if you're responsible for all this lot, then you're well in the 'rattle' (Naval parlance for 'in trouble'). Her Majesty isn't going to be very pleased, when she hears what you've done to her nice ship. It looks as though she's been firmly ashore to me,' he concluded, nodding pointedly and winking slyly at his mates.

The Officer shouted furiously that he was an insolent bastard and demanded his name, but he was quickly ushered away and up out of the dock by his fellow Officers, very much to the amusement of the watching Mateys.

'Hey Joe, you ain't half going to cop it,' someone said laconically.

The Mateys followed them up on to the jetty and within a matter of minutes, what had gone on had spread among the other gangs. Later, a friendly Matelot told Mike that the argument among the Officers had continued for some time, with loud recriminations on all sides. The Crew had been warned not to talk to the Mateys, but that didn't stop him from blabbing and at some length. Apparently, the Ship had been coming into the Yard for a boiler-clean and had touched bottom, while negotiating a long curve in the river. It had happened to the delight of the Crew and the great consternation of her Officers on the bridge.

'It's an ill wind, as they say,' said the Jolly Jack. 'It was going to be in and out, quick as you like, clean the boilers, store and bunker, then back out into the river, ammunition-up and away again to God knows where. No time for a few days leave or anything; just one big rush. Then this lot happens. Now, we shall all get a chance to go home to our nearest and dearest, with a few days of well-earned rest and carnal contentment, if you know what I mean. Lovely grub,' he concluded, rubbing his hands together.

Having marked up the drawings, Cyril came down for a further look at the hull plates, before compiling his list of the ones to be replaced. Some of them warranted further investigation and there was also work to be done at the base of the stem. The toe and an adjacent plate had been 'stove-in' and the ship must have been making water when she was afloat. The resultant works were added to the list and the main problem was the acute shortage of time. Overall, he was of the view that the hull was in pretty good nick, though it would take approximately three weeks to complete all the remedial work. The survey had also revealed that the starboard outer tail-shaft had been damaged. The inboard one had been put slightly out of true and it would also be taken out for straightening.

The work started at a cracking rate and both shafts were pulled out, lifted up out of the dock and taken away. When Mike went over to the Factory to see the inner one being checked, his old pal Lou was in the process of re-aligning it, by the judicious application of a hydraulic jack, which was mounted on the large lathe. They went over again a few days later to see the repairs being done on the screws and it had gone very well. The inboard one had already been completed and was in the process of being dynamically balanced, again in the big lathe.

The damage to the outer shaft was more serious than initially thought and a replacement had already been secured. The work was duly completed and the they were soon on their way back to the dock. The gang set to work to move the inboard one in through the A-frame and stern tube bearings and into the hull. The bearings had been renewed, while the shafts were in the Factory and a problem had been found with a muff-coupling, which connected the inboard end to the next section of the shaft. It had taken an inordinate amount of time to dismantle and was in very poor condition. Everyone pulled his weight and the shafts were back in place and connected up by the end of the following week. The rigs were altered to re-fit the screws and as someone aptly remarked, it was all go and no notion.

Another week of hard graft passed, before everything was finally fully boxed up'. By then, most of the damaged hull-plates had been replaced and there was a rush to get 'a lick o' paint' over the hull. Gangs of Matelots were also energetically slapping it on the upper works, from precarious platforms rigged off the deck and they gleefully splashed large globs on to the Mateys in the dock below, much to their annoyance. When it was completed in the immediate area, the quarter-deck was uncovered and every blemish removed from the wooden-decking. Her deck furniture was then restored and the brass-work polished to the normal mirror-finish. Everyone agreed that the old girl was 'looking as good as new and she bore no comparison to the state she'd been in when she had come in only a few weeks previously.

The 'lazy bloody Mateys' had come up trumps at a time of great urgency and to their surprise, their work had not gone unnoticed. The Engineer Captain, who had been regularly in the area throughout, told the Foreman he would be sending his thanks to his Manager. The Ship's Officers were also very complimentary about their efforts; even the Commander who had been so very angry in the early stages. He surprised everyone by loudly proclaiming what a superb job had been done and he also wrote to express his thanks and satisfaction. Turning to Joe, who he had seen standing nearby, he walked over and shook him by the hand and apologised for the rough way he had spoken to him. The crafty bugger should have been taken aback but no, he surprised his mates even more by the smarmy way in which he replied.

'Please don't apologise, Sir,' he said humbly. 'I was well out of order speaking to you in the way I did and I'm sorry for any offence. I meant no disrespect to you personally and, thinking about it, I spoke out of turn. You were right to give me a bollocking. I know from my own time at sea how, at times like this, we all have to pull together.'

His mates were dumbstruck at his audacity. However, with the apologies freely given and graciously accepted, that was how it was left. When the lads went back to the Workshop and sat down for their 'cups o' char', Joe was roundly taken to task for his 'bloody cheek'.

'You snivelling bastard,' said Bert indignantly. He'd been in the Navy for many years and had long since been fed up with Joe's stupid remarks about the Andrew. 'How you had the bare-faced gall to speak to the Officer like that, I don't know. 'Yes Sir, no Sir, three bags full Sir.' It makes me want to puke. If truth be known, he wasn't even on board when she touched bottom. The Skipper probably left the Ship as soon as she came in and the man you spoke to was the Jimmy's replacement. You blamed the wrong man, you stupid sod and the first apology should have come from you, not him. All you did was upset him in front of his Officers. Mark my words, one day, you'll get your bloody desserts and find yourself out the gate, you smarmy sod.'

'Yeah, well,' said Joe, smiling ruefully, though completely unabashed, 'I just thought it would be more appropriate to say a few words of appreciation, what with everybody so happy like.'

That was greeted with yet more jeers and laughter. The Engineer Captain was true to his word and one morning, the Manager came down to thank them personally for a job well done. As someone remarked, it was nice to be appreciated for once, given the normal fraught relations between the two camps. No doubt, the goodwill was soon forgotten and things returned to normal.

After being re-floated, the cruiser was taken down to the No. 1 Basin to be made ready for sea. She bunkered and raised steam and Mike walked down one dinner time to see her go out through the locks. At the time, the river was in flood, at a higher level than normal and the basins were being freshened up. At high-tide, both lock gates were opened and the Cruiser and two other ships left the Yard in quick succession. Someone remarked that there must have been 'a bit of a flap on' somewhere. Just as she cleared the seaward end of the lock, she nudged the jetty and the paintwork, which had been so carefully applied on only a few days earlier, was badly scuffed. The gates were closed, probably to the great relief of the Manager.

When Mike asked Nobby what would have happened if he had not been able to close either of them, he was told he should have known the answer.

'Didn't I tell you before?,' Nobby said with some relish, pointing to a caisson which was lying alongside the jetty. The stand-by tug would have quickly pushed her into position and she would have been flooded down to seal off the basin in a matter of minutes. 'What could be more simple, eh?'

The locks were also infrequently dredged of the mud and silt, which had accumulated in them over the years and as with the decommissioning berth, the spoil was loaded into railway trucks and taken away for disposal. The sea-ward caissons were operated remotely, on the principle of a fine balance between floating and settling into position and when ballasted down, they provided an effective seal from the river. When light, they were pulled open or pushed shut by means of the hydraulic system, with the motive power boing provided by the big engine in the pump house. It was a simple, efficient means of working, which had been in operation for very many years. When it was necessary to carry out maintenance at either end of a lock, the stand-by caisson was often used to provide the necessary isolation.

When Mike went back to the Fitting shop, Jock was overhauling a small air compressor; a hand-cranked, diesel-driven machine which was contained in a sturdy skid-frame. It had been lying for some months in the Annex, with the components stashed in a couple of wooden crates. Bill gruffly asked Jock what he was doing, but he was bluntly told to mind his own business. He'd not been anything like his old aggressive self for some time and he walked away with his dignity dented yet again. When he complained to the Foreman, he was told that Jock had used his initiative to do something useful, something that he would do well to emulate. As it happened, Norman had forgotten about the compressor and was only too pleased to order the parts needed for its refurbishment.

A few days later, he interrupted the job when a similar machine required urgent attention on a Frigate. Having been on patrol in the North Atlantic, she had come in for emergency repairs and was already set down in the dock. Jock went over to speak to the Chief ERA and while they were looking down on her, before going on board, he shook his head.

'You know laddie, this Ship's been through hell', he commented knowingly, 'look at all the damage to the upper works. Like all her class,' he went on, 'she rolls like a bastard and ships 'green-yins' every few minutes, in anything like a seaway. I sailed on one just like her, so I know full well how her Crew must have suffered. Everything on the mess-decks is soaking wet through and no matter how securely you stow your kit, it all comes shooting out of the lockers. We'll see for ourselves what a fine old state she's in when we go on board, so no clever comments, eh? We'll just get on and do something useful for a change.'

They went below to the Engineer's office and were told that the Chief was in the Engine-room. Someone went to find him and when he eventually came up he looked at Jock closely for a few seconds, then said he was sure that he knew him. Jock confirmed that they had served together some years previously and after yarning about the old days for a few minutes, they got round to discussing the problems with a compressor. The RN always seemed to know if a Matey was ex-Andrew and Jock was keen to assist his former colleagues. There was rarely any of the aloofness and cynical disdain, which was the norm with what were considered 'lesser mortals'.

Chapter 12

Perversity

The Chief explained at some length about the problems they'd had with the compressor, which had been playing up for some weeks, before it had broken down altogether. They had tried to repair it, but due to the appalling weather and a lack of spares, they had been unable to do so. He then took them up on deck to see the machine, which was lying aft on the port side by the brow. They must have walked right past it when they had come on board.

'I'm bloody glad to see you, I can tell you,' said the Chief with some feeling because that bloody compressor has been a pain in the arse for as long as I can remember. It's only a small part of our equipment, but we like to keep everything in order and running smoothly.'

After looking at it for a couple of minutes, Jock told him that he would get it taken up to the workshop right away.

'We'll soon be able to fix this wee job for you,' he said. 'Spares won't be a problem and a week will see her back in full working order. Can you wait that long?,' he asked blandly.

It was a loaded question. The crafty bugger had sensed an opportunity for a 'wee bit of ovies' and perhaps even a weekend, if he played his cards right.

'Well,' said the Chief, playing along, 'we should have been going back out to sea pretty smartish, but some hull-plates have been bent and will have to be fixed. Tell you what, I'll tell the Engineer the sooner it's back on board, the better. It'll be something less for us to worry about and I'm sure he won't disagree and in return, I'd like a bit of effort on this one. I'll get our lads to move it up on to the jetty for you.'

'It's alright Chief,' Mike said brightly, 'I'll get a crane-driver to lift it off. It'll only take a couple of minutes and we'll take it to the workshop right away.'

Jock was all smiles and after again assuring the Chief of their best efforts, they went ashore. He went off to report to the Foreman and after 'humming and ha-ing,' Norman told him to start work right away. He would order the parts for a complete refit. A start was made in stripping it down and it was soon apparent it had suffered serious damage. Some of the moving parts were completely knackered and Jock set about writing up a list of what he required. He had made a similar list for the shop machine only a few days before and most of what was wanted was delivered the next day. As their workmates were getting ready to go home, he and his lad were subjected to snide comments, the object being to arouse Bill again. Comments like 'lucky sods' and 'snivelling gits' were called out to stir things up, but were ignored.

Bill was still hopping mad that Jock had horned-in on his job and he had good reason to be upset because, soon after he had started the job, he'd been given more pressing work to do. He'd also forgotten about it, though he wouldn't admit it. He loudly complained that Jock should have discussed it with him, before doing anything on 'his machine'. His nose remained well out of joint, particularly now the bugger was going to benefit financially and all he could do was to grumble about the unfairness of it all. There was little sympathy, because anyone who could upset him was O K with the other Fitters..

As noted previously, the cynicism in the workplace, both to Management one's peers, has not changed in the last fifty years and what has always been called 'shit-stirring' or 'back-stabbing' has always been the norm. Rarely is it enough to score a harmless point over a vulnerable workmate and given the opportunity for mischief, the 'rat' is always ready to do the dirty on him or her. He or she will be quick to inform the Management of a misdemeanour and obtain get great satisfaction from doing so. The case of the poor old sod who had worked way past his retirement date, when Mike was in his fourth year, amply demonstrates the point. A fallacy, which has prevailed for many years, is that a 'true Brit' never hurts a workmate, which is fallacious nonsense. We are as bad as any other Nation where troublemaking is concerned and for that very reason, we can rarely be at peace with each other. An old saying went that the only person you could trust was your mother and even that was often said with tongue in cheek.

Such anti-social behaviour regularly occurred in the shop and the Foreman often heard about an offence with incredible speed. One of the worst ones for telling tales was a small, very thin, elderly Labourer, who was known as Benny. Everyone knew he couldn't be trusted and nothing of a confidential nature could be discussed when he was nearby. His demeanour to the Foreman was always obsequious, with a fawning obeisance as he stood beside the boss and gazed up at him with a dog-like look of devotion. He was often taken to task about it, but he ignored the contempt of his workmates and anyone who came to work in the shop was soon made aware of his predilection. The stupid little bugger couldn't tell the difference between the ones that were vulnerable and those that were not.

Jock was most certainly not one of the former and when the Foreman spoke to him one morning about some minor point, he knew right away from whom he'd got his information. Later that day, everyone was highly amused to see the Benny getting his 'just deserts' from the irate Scot. Having been hoisted off the ground by his shirt front, he was squealing like a stuck pig and protesting loudly about his innocence.

'I ain't done nothin' wrong,' he cried, while pleading to be put down.

'You tell tales on me and I'll teach you a lesson you'll not forget, you wee bastard,' shouted Jock furiously. 'Do it again and you'll end up in the bloody dock, just see if you don't.'

He then tossed the hapless the little man aside and Benny scrambled away to put a safe distance between himself and his tormentor. He stood for a moment by the sliding double-door and had to have the last word.

'You can't blame me for something I ain't done,' he shouted shrilly. 'I'm go straight over to the office to make a complaint.'

With the enraged Scot bearing down on him, he ran off and it was the last they saw of him for the rest of the day. Jock knew that the little man was not alone in his perfidy and glaring balefully at the watching crowd, he made his point.

'If I find out he's been telling the truth and one of you has dropped me in it, I'll beat the shite out of him so just be warned, 'cos I'll not tell you again.'

Jock and Mike worked steadily in fitting the new components in the compressor and took care that everything was done properly. Three days later and well within the promised time, the machine was ready for testing. The Chief and his P.O. came into the shop and while he was filling the sumps, Jock told him that the wrong grade of oil had previously been used in the engine. It was later confirmed, when the Chief found a near-empty five-gallon oil drum on board. After a final inspection, it was taken outside and given a test run and with everything in order, the Chief told his Stokers to take it straightaway back to the Ship. When Jock and Mike went along later, the Chief was 'laying down the law' about its correct maintenance, to ensure that the previous mistakes wouldn't be made again.

Jock spoke briefly to the sailors, his main points being that the oil-levels had to be checked before starting up and the correct grade of lubricating-oil used. It was just as bad to overfill a sump, as it was to let it run low and if they looked after the machine properly, they would get the best out of it. He also mentioned the specific instructions in the operating and maintenance manual, even though it hadn't been used very often in the past. When Mike commented, he was quietly told that they would discuss it later. Jock then handed over the oil which remained in the drum from which he had filled the sump. The Matelots had listened intently to what he'd said, which perhaps indicated that they had not previously had much training for that particular piece of kit.

'Don't judge them any the less for that,' Jock said as they walked back to the shop. 'As I said earlier, they've had a rough time lately and, with the shit regularly hitting the fan, training is not a priority. You asked about the manual', he went on, 'well, some Engineers like to keep them in pristine condition and don't let them out of the office. If anyone has a query, he might be allowed to have a decko, with the Chief looking over his shoulder.'

There wasn't much to do until the second set of spares arrived and when they came, they made an immediate start on reassembling the shop compressor. Only a few weeks before, the shop had been busy, but that had changed and interesting jobs were few and far between. In consequence, moral had dipped and there was a lot of bickering, which often led to noisy rows. The Foreman relied on the Charge-hands to keep order and the Fitters' tenuous hold on their Apprentices slackened. Whoever said that idle hands made mischief certainly knew a thing or two.

An S-Class submarine had just come in for a refit and Norman gave Jock a list of key items of equipment, which had to be taken from her before the Mateys descended on her en-masse to start work. He was sent aboard with strict instructions to get on with it. The lighting system had been connected to a temporary supply and they spent nearly an hour walking through the Boat, with Jock explaining the various systems. Having retrieved the listed items and it not being long before dinner, they sat comfortably in the control room. Mike recalled what Sam had said in that if one was fortunate enough to be first aboard a newly paid-off Vessel, a search of the various spaces could yield interesting pickings. They made their way aft again to have a look under the plates in the engine-room.

Jock found a carton of two hundred cigarettes, neatly wrapped in oil-cloth, while Mike found two spanners, a small ball-peen hammer and an Engineer's torch. Sam had also warned him about the need for care in taking contraband ashore, because it could have been planted by someone hoping to catch the finder red-handed. Jock thanked the lad for mentioning it and he went back to the control room to stash his fags. No more than a few minutes later, they heard other people coming on board and it was uncanny how a vessel, which was tied up alongside, could be so eerily silent. The noise of men coming down through the main hatch echoed loudly through the Boat and it was three Customs Officers, who were very surprised to see two Mateys ostensibly working on a piece of equipment.

'What are you doing on this Ship?,' asked one of them crossly. He had two stripes on his epaulets and was apparently in charge. 'We haven't given our clearance yet and until we do, no Dockyard personnel are allowed on board.'

'Ah good morning gentlemen,' replied Jock affably. 'We've been sent over on an urgent message. Is there a problem I can help you with perhaps?'

'I've already said, nobody is supposed to come on this Ship until we've cleared it,' the man replied haughtily. Looking even more cross and to emphasise his authority, he went on. 'I must ask you to leave right away and not to come back until I say so.'

Jock and Mike picked up their bags and the boxes of fittings and made to leave.

'Just a minute,' the Officer said, 'we'll just have a look in your tool bags, if you don't mind.'

Mike smiled inwardly, knowing that the officious bugger was going to do so whether they minded it or not. Sam had been right when he'd said that Customs men were always antagonistic to anyone who crossed their paths.

'Of course, Officer,' replied Jock. 'Put your bag down alongside mine, Mike, so he can have a wee look, a'fore we go. Oh, and while I think of it, it's called a Boat, not a Ship' he informed the man.

The few small items which they had found in the bags were of no interest and he was clearly disappointed to have found nothing untoward.

'I'm still not satisfied that you have any business on board this 'Boat' as you call it,' he said sniffily. 'How do I know you're not up to some mischief or other? Have you anything to confirm your presence on board?'

'Certainly, sir,' said Jock, now not quite so affable as before and rolling his 'rrr's to good effect. 'Here's my job-card and the list of the items to be collected.'

The man looked disinterestedly at the proffered documents, then brusquely handed them back. 'Alright, you can go,' he said, 'but remember, don't come back on board this Ship – I mean Boat – again until I say so. You can leave those bits and pieces where they are for now.'

'I'm sorry to have to tell you that these fittings are most urgently required for another Submarine, which is tied-up alongside our workshop', Jock interjected. She's to be moved to the commissioning berth later today and I was specifically told to get them over to her as quickly as possible. Are you telling me I can't take them away?'

It had all the makings of a bloody good argument, with Jock craftily manoeuvring the Officer into a corner. However, it was not to be.

'Is everything there according to your list?,' said the man, pointing at the boxes.

'Aye, it is,' replied our worthy. 'It's all there.'

'Right you two,' he said to his colleagues, 'help them with those boxes and see them off the Ship, Boat I mean. Bloody hell!'

And so a few minutes later, the reprobates walked down the road with the fittings. They could hardly contain their mirth, though Jock sternly told Mike not to laugh or even look back. When they got back to the shop, they burst out laughing and a number of their workmates came to see what all the noise was about. Jock told them about their brush with the Customs Officers, which everyone thought was hilarious, though he made no mention of their 'finds', being very aware of the big ears in their midst. He later went over to see Norman to ask what he wanted done with the equipment and was told to 'just clean them up and put them in the store for the time being'. So much for the urgency of the job!

Chapter 13

Interesting Jobs

One morning, Jock noticed that Mike was frequently taking off his glasses and rubbing his eyes and he knew right away what the problem was. The lad had suffered a 'flash' which he stressed, was not due to a welder 'exposing' himself. His eyes had been damaged by the intense light which emanated from an electric arc.

'You've surely been warned not to watch welders working,' he said. 'I thought everybody knew that.'

'No I haven't,' Mike replied. 'I can't understand how it's happened, because I'm always very careful not to watch them.'

'You've been caught unawares then,' said Jock more sympathetically. 'Get yourself off to the first aider right away and he'll put some drops in your eyes.'

When Mike arrived at the surgery, it was all shut up and he was told that Treatment had not been seen for some time. The problem didn't merit the long ride up to the main medical centre and he thought that the discomfort would decline in a few days. It didn't and, for some time after, he suffered regular, painful reactions. When asked what it was like, he could only describe it as like having sand in his eyes. The discomfort would suddenly become acute and his eyes would water copiously, which temporarily blinded him. He had been foolish indeed not seeking medical help.

One evening, when cycling through the High Street, he was passing a couple of buses at a stop when he had an attack. As luck would have it, a middle-aged woman suddenly appeared from between the buses, pushing a small child out in front of her to cross the road. Mike braked but couldn't avoid hitting her. A Policeman, who had seen what had happened, came running across to help the woman, who was lying dazed in the road. She quickly came to and having ascertained that she was not badly hurt, the Officer turned to Mike who was standing nearby with tears streaming down his face.

'It's alright lad, there's no need to be so upset,' he said kindly. 'The lady's not badly hurt; she's just a bit shook up, that's all.'

He told Mike to take his bike to the Police Station and report to the Duty Sergeant. There, he told the Officer about the accident, how the woman with the child hadn't looked his way before crossing the road and he made no mention of the problem with his eyes. After the Sergeant had examined his bicycle and pronounced it in good order, he took the lad inside again to make a formal statement. A couple of days later, Mike called again at the Station and the Sergeant confirmed that no real harm had been done. He asked him if he should go to her home and apologise to the woman, but was advised not to do so.

'My Constable saw what happened and has made a report of the incident,' he said. 'The lady caused it by not looking where she was going and she'll be only too glad that you didn't hit the child. Just leave it at that, because if you admit anything, her family will blame you. Just go home and forget about it.'

That was the last that Mike heard about it and a week or so later, his eye problem had cleared up.

Not long after their escapade with the Customs men on the Submarine, Jock remarked that he had been impressed with the way Mike had performed, when they'd been confronted.

'I must say you did very well. Contrary to the opinions of others, you've learned a lot from your Apprenticeship. What did you say your man's name was? Sam was it? I'd be pleased to shake his hand, because he made a bloody good job of training you, that's for sure.'

'One thing that puzzles me,' Mike replied, 'is that usually when someone speaks to you, you reply in your normal Scottish accent. When talking to those customs men, you could easily have come from the roughest part of Glasgow. How come?'

'Och well, it was all a wee bit of play-acting, wasn't it?,' Jock replied. 'It wouldn't have done to have acted too bright with those bastards. Never underestimate them. The senior man will have had many years' experience in dealing with the likes of us and only let us go after weighing up all the pro's and con's. If we've any sense, we'll keep clear of that bugger, because sure as hell, he'll be looking out for us, especially when he found his ciggies were gone!.'

A couple of days later, Jock was contentedly puffing on a 'tailor-made', and seeing the lad looking, he smiled archly and asked what his problem was.

'Oh, it's nothing,' replied Mike.

His boss pressed him to say what it was and before doing so, he walked around the bench and out of the hearing of the other men.

'I couldn't help noticing your smoke is of better quality than normal,' he said.

'Aye well, there's no mystery in that laddie. When the Customs men arrived, I'd just finished putting my carton in of one of the boxes, under the fittings, then one of the daft buggers took it up out of the Boat and put it in the hand-cart for me. There's no substitute for a bit of help when it's sorely needed,' he added lugubriously and the ciggies were 'export quality'.

'You crafty sod,' said Mike, 'I'd never have had the nerve to do that.'

'Now, then laddie,' said Jock, 'your Dad smokes eh? Well, here's a couple of packets for him in recognition of your help and I hope he enjoys them.'

The cigarettes languished in Mike's toolbox for some weeks, before he eventually plucked up the courage to take them home. As he was walking out of the gate, he remembered one of the Chaplain's sermons when still at school. A young lad called Bill Stickers had committed a minor indiscretion and while on his way home on a train, he had been mortified to see notices, writ in large letters and posted at successive stations. They read that 'Bill Stickers will be prosecuted.' By the time he reached his destination, he was convinced that he had been 'rumbled' and was going to be punished. The moral of the sermon had been that conscience invariably plays a great part in our lives. Mike had thought that someone might have found out about their crime and that every Policeman who was standing at the gate was looking at him.

When the duo had gone down to the Submarine to recover further items of equipment, they had taken another surreptitious look through the various compartments and with other Mateys on board, they had to be more careful than previously. In the galley store, Mike had found an unopened, seven-pound, 'Admiralty issue' tin of apricots in syrup and after checking that it had not been interfered with, he put it into his tool bag. When back in the shop, there was an immediate problem as no one had a tin-opener, which was odd, given the Mateys liking for condensed milk.

The next day, the opening of the tin was delayed until the dinner break and when the top was taken off to reveal the succulent contents, they were found in perfect condition. Generous portions were doled out into dirty mugs and with no little relish, the contents were greedily consumed. While most of the lads were satisfied with their portions, one gutsy oaf finished off the inch or so of syrup remaining in the tin. Much to the delight of his mates a few minutes later, he rushed for the door and having only just made it outside, he was violently sick. For some time after, he was regularly teased with loud 'honking' sounds.

Mike's work with Jock was again interrupted, when the Foreman sent him again to help the Test Engineers in the dock. They were working on the same Frigate as previously and she had come back into the Yard with further problems. Cyril dolefully shook his head as he explained that some of the plates were very doubtful and they were going to re-survey parts of the hull, because a re-appraisal of the previous data had given grave cause for concern. It was a bit of a mystery as the problems had come about, despite the Ship having been regularly dry-docked.

The main problem stemmed from the poor quality of the steel used in her construction in that extensive laminations, porosity and slag-inclusions in the fabric of the metal were clearly evident. No doubt, the quality of the plate was markedly inferior to that which had been made in the pre-War years. The old Cruiser which had recently been surveyed had been built in the late thirties and the Frigate in the early fifties. British Shipyards were having serious financial problems and were trapped in an ever-increasing spiral of decline. They could no longer compete on price, quality or the time taken to do a job and their foreign competitors had all but taken over their previously dominant share of the World markets.

It was a sad situation, which had been brought about by a combination of circumstances, which Cyril dolefully listed: a fallacious opinion, based on a long-held conceit that 'British was best'; a militant, unproductive workforce, which thought that the World owed it a living; and apathetic Management, particularly in the development of modern designs and building techniques.

Phil had tried many times to explain to Mike how the 'box of tricks' worked, but Mike had not been able to take it in. The nonsense with Mark had gone and when he ruefully admitted he would never make a diagnostician, they laughed aloud. With the weather again wet and cold, the job was just as unpleasant as before and when it was finished, Mike went to see the Foreman to ask for condition payments. He was both very surprised and gratified when he was given twenty hours of both uncas and height money. Norman told him that he could have it, because it was coming out of Cyril's budget!

When the overhaul of the compressor was finished, Mike and two of the other lads were set to work on overhauling the valves in the workshop air system and when they had done, it was pressure-tested and deemed fit for service. The next day, Jock connected the compressor to the system, started it up and made an adjustment to the cut-in, cut-out mechanism.

The system was then put back into service and there were immediate complaints about the noise and that it smelled horrible. The Foreman was asked if the compressor could be moved outside or, failing that, into the annex but Norman said he'd think about it and, as everyone expected, that was how it was left. It remained in the shop and within a few days, everyone had got used to it anyway.

The lads who were intent on joining the Merchant Navy at the end of their time were already writing to the various Shipping Companies and some had already received positive replies. They kept their own counsel and only shared the good news with their friends. Junior Engineer's jobs were not easy to obtain, due to the very large number of young men who were completing their Apprenticeships at the same time. Mike had long since concluded that the Royal Navy, which was the only other sensible option, was not what it was made out to be, though Jock disagreed.

'It's as good a way to see the World as any,' he said on numerous occasions. 'What could be better than visiting places you'd never see in any other job and being well paid for doing it? Everything is provided, good food and a comfortable berth to boot.'

Mike's brother had long since dissuaded him about the merits of the Andrew. He had joined as an Apprentice at sixteen years of age and had been constantly 'dripping' (complaining) about it ever since. Having been promoted to Chief Ordnance Artificer at the age of twenty four, he should have been more settled but he had consistently maintained he was desperate to 'buy himself out' and would even borrow the money to do so. While working on the various Ships, Mike had seen that the Crew's accommodation was inevitably cramped and even junior Officers shared small cabins. The Chiefs and P.Os had their own messes, in which they lived literally on top of each other and in a submarine, the problem was infinitely worse.

In contrast, most Merchant Navy Companies looked after their Officers and in comparison, their lives were comfortable. Though the juniors' cabins were much smaller than their seniors', they at least enjoyed some measure of privacy, which was impossible in the highly-manned RN Ships. It was an incentive for them to buckle down and get on and as one 'went up the ladder', the space and comfort provided improved substantially. On the Liners, the certificated Officers lived luxurious accommodation. Jock told Mike that if he was worried about a 'wee bit of discomfort', he'd be as well going elsewhere but, he could only speak from experience and the Andrew had suited him down to the ground. In fact, he had been thinking a lot recently about re-joining.

One evening in the pub, Bill told his mates he was going to buy a car and with Mike's jalopy causing continual problems, they understood why. He had recently started going steady with a lass from the Town and the need for his own transport had become increasingly pressing. A car would, he thought, give them a little bit of comfort and privacy for the physical side of their courting. A few evenings later, he announced that an old lady, who lived in the next village, had a 'Standard Eight' for sale, which was only two years old and in very good condition. He was going to have a look at it on Friday evening and if it was all it was said to be and the price was right, he would probably buy it. On the following Saturday night, Bill and Mike knew right away that their mate's purchase had not gone ahead as planned.

'Come on, you bugger, don't keep us all in suspense,' said Mike. 'How did you get on?'

'Don't ask,' replied the clearly dispirited lad. 'I didn't buy it, did I?'

He had gone to see the lady and after only a few minutes, she had suggested a price which was a lot cheaper than he had envisaged. The car had a low mileage on the clock and it had been regularly serviced since new and it had all seemed to be too good to be true, when she took him out to the garage. Despite not having been used for some months, it started first time and he brought it out to give it the once over. Everything was in good working order; the only thing was that the back seat squab was missing. Then the truth came out. She tearfully told him that her husband had committed suicide in the car and that the seat had been heavily stained. She had not been able to replace it. Having quickly put the vehicle back in the garage, Bill 'gently' told her he couldn't buy it. His mates were less than sympathetic about his lack of willingness to help the 'poor old girl' out.

'It's all very well for you to talk', he replied huffily, 'but you weren't there. I couldn't get out of there quick enough, I can tell you.'

That was not quite the end of the matter. When Bill bought his motor from a dealer some weeks later, it was a Standard Eight and the same colour as the lady's car!

Chapter 14

Getting Some In

The prospect of their impending National Service was increasingly weighing on some of the lads' minds and as noted earlier, there was no shortage of ex-conscripts who were willing to elucidate at length as to how it had affected them personally. Their tales were interesting and they always had an audience when 'holding forth'. Some gave graphic accounts of the poor lot of a conscript, with bad pay and living conditions being a particular 'bitch' and the discipline had been particularly 'ball-aching' for some. Others had enjoyed the completely different way of life and said it was the best thing that had ever happened to them in that they had travelled to exotic parts of the World. For some, their living conditions had been rough and their food had often been plain and unappetising. On a lighter note, many of them had not had three square meals a day before and some of them had even enjoyed being on active service, with all the dangers that that had entailed.

If a young man was good at sport, he was given the opportunity to play at a consistently high level and in excellent facilities. With regular physical training and skilled coaching, some conscripts achieved very high standards. If one played for the Fleet, Regiment, Command or the Combined Services, then life could be very enjoyable indeed. A good example was a lad who had played hockey at County level during his Apprenticeship and when he was posted to an RAF station near his home, he was only rarely required on Camp at weekends. His presence on the field was more important than on mundane guard duties. Many sallow, unhealthy looking youths who were poor physical specimens on entry, were transformed into strapping young men. They were confident and full of vitality, with a zest for life when they came out again. The strict discipline, coupled with the educational and vocational training that they received, stood them in very good stead for the rest of their lives.

Rob had been a devoted born-again Christian during his Apprenticeship and hadn't drunk alcohol, gambled or had anything to do with women. He had been a quiet, well-mannered lad, who was often teased by his workmates, but had steadfastly held to his principles and remained a paragon of virtue. When called up, he had joined the Royal Air Force and from then on, it was all downhill. One Saturday night, perhaps eighteen months later, he staggered on to the last bus waiting by the Town Hall and he was in a most dreadful state of drunkenness. It was only with great difficulty that two of his erstwhile mates persuaded the conductor to allow him on board. Rob was very noisy and with incredible fluency, he was 'swearing like a trooper'. Whilst his National Service could not be totally responsible for his fall from grace, it had certainly had something to do with it.

Another lad had been indentured to a printing firm and had interrupted his Apprenticeship to do his duty. After his basic training, he had served most of his two years in Cyprus during the EOKA insurgency. The Greek Cypriots had long aspired to political union with Greece and had not only fought the British Military, but the Turkish Cypriots as well. Their absolute intention was to force both parties to leave what they considered to be their island. Like all civil wars it was cruel and bloody, with great suffering on all sides. A large number of Servicemen didn't come back and others never fully recovered from the stress they suffered. Whether or not the Government was justified in sacrificing so many of its reluctant conscripts remains a matter of opinion. The lad however was not one to complain about his lot and with some pride he told his listeners that he had manfully 'stuck it out'.

When he came home, he was a totally different person from when he had joined up. His had been an exciting experience and he couldn't understand why so few of his mates didn't want to hear about his exploits. He'd enjoyed it so much that he had even thought of volunteering for an additional period of service. Common sense had prevailed, because of the pressing need to complete his Apprenticeship. Like so many other young men, the benefits he had received stood him in very good stead in his career, which was very successful indeed.

On completing his time, an Apprentice had to move quickly if he wanted to avoid conscription. There was little possibility of being rejected on health grounds if he was in any way 'normal and a most definite stigma was attached to any rejection, which was due to an illogical sense of patriotism that demanded that everyone 'did his bit'. Anyone thought to have dodged the call to duty was quickly reminded of the need to serve his Country. Conscripts, even the married ones, were paid a pittance, when compared with the regular Servicemen, who themselves were not exactly well-paid. As a time-served Tradesman, there was usually an option to sign on for a three-year or longer engagement, which brought enhanced chances of promotion and the extra pay that went with it.

Luckily, those who were not of a mind to go down that road had the option of joining the Merchant Navy. However, the Ship owners took cynical advantage of the young men who were so very keen to get away to sea. A Junior Engineer was poorly paid, compared to what he would have earned as a Fitter. He did, of course, have 'his keep thrown in', when standing by a Ship or at sea, but he was very much the 'lowest of the low' until he had got some sea-time in. Many of the senior Engineers suspected that the new juniors were 'Army dodgers', an accusation which had to be quietly denied, even if it was true.

As we have noted, the bane of the conscripts was almost inevitably their non-commissioned officers, (NCOs). Little in their previous lives could have prepared them for the shock to which they were subjected when they arrived in the barracks. The perceived advice was that no matter what the provocation or outrage, which they would surely suffer, they should not under any circumstance even try to be clever or complain. It was most definitely a no-win situation and the only sensible thing to do was to grin and bear it. To protest or to disobey an order would bring the 'wrath of the Gods' down on anyone daft enough to step out of line.

The NCOs had to turn a disparate bunch of youths into smart, efficient Soldiers, Sailors or Airmen in a very short time. There were a lot of tales about the suffering at the hands of so many mean-minded bastards and it was tempting to laugh at the raconteurs in the belief that no one could be so stupid and offensive. Bert met up with his mates one evening during his first leave after training and his account of the trauma he had suffered was eagerly listened to. His father was an ex-regular Royal Marine and what was more, he had been in the RM Cadets for some years. He had thought he was well prepared for the demands which were inevitably the lot of the National Serviceman.

'Don't think you know anything about the Royal Marines,' his father had solemnly warned him. 'They've got a job to do and not much time in which to do it and there are golden rules, which you break at your peril. You always stand up straight, chin in, chest out when called to attention and you must always listen carefully to your Instructor because, like as not, he will not repeat himself. When given an order, jump to it right away and always show willing and above all, respect. Your personal cleanliness is essential because a smart soldier will get a lot less bother from his NCOs, than some scruffy bugger who knows it all. Do something useful before turning in, like going over your kit. You'll be very glad you've done it the following morning. Fold your clothes properly and stow them away before getting into bed. You never know when an inspection may come, so be one step ahead of the rest. Keep your nose clean and it'll pay off in the end, my lad.'

When he arrived at the barracks, Bert had found himself among thirty or so new recruits and right from the start, their Instructors had treated them like imbeciles. What he had quickly found very useful was his knowledge of caring for his kit. For many years, he had watched how his father had brushed and pressed his uniforms, ironed his shirts, and cleaned his boots and brasses. A lot of the other lads hadn't got a clue and he had made quite a few bob by showing them how to do it. He thus came by the funds to buy a few pints of what he acerbically described as 'the weak piss' that passed for beer in the NAAFI. Despite his father's warnings, his initial training had been much worse than anticipated, though he had come out of it well. He had not suffered anywhere near as much as some of the other lads.

For the first few weeks the relentless demands of their Instructors had been exhausting. The Lee Enfield 303 rifle, which was used in their drills, had been cumbersome and heavy and it had taken weeks to get used to it but, eventually, he had handled it well. Everything his dad had told him had been sound advice indeed, though even so, he had suffered a small number of extra drills and fatigues. He had completed his square-bashing as the best recruit and the outdoor training, regular meals and hard exercise had had the desired result. He and his fellows had gained both strength and physical condition and Her Majesty's Royal Marines had suited them very well.

Bert finished his account with a tale about someone called Milburn, who hadn't known his left from his right and how he had been sent to the Royal Marines was a mystery. He was a tall, well-made lad from the North East and had previously worked as an Electrician in a Tyneside Shipyard. Having not expressed a particular preference for any Service when he had registered, Jacky, as he was known, had not been unduly concerned about being sent for a 'boot-neck'. He was an amiable, easy going lad, but his 'deficiency', which was exposed almost right away, caused him no end of grief. The orders were clear and only one other lad had the same problem. Everyone else had soon got the hang of it, but not Jacky and the other lad. They were singled out by the NCOs and their victimisation went on for some time.

The Instructors must have thought that they were being messed about and it brought all hell down on their heads. No one doubted that Jacky's problem was genuine, but it looked like the other lad was indeed 'acting the crack'. From the first day, he had tried to give the impression that he was both clever and witty and when Bert warned him about 'being funny' with the NCOs, he had bluntly told him to mind his own business. While they were all sorry for Jacky, no one was for Stone, as the stupid sod was called. The NCOs soon 'rumbled' him and he was off 'doubling' around the parade ground, sometimes long after the working day had ended. Jacky's moral though had slumped badly and his mates decided to help him. They had patiently showed their disconsolate mate how to resolve his problem, aided by a piece of string, which was tied around his left thumb. He had soon got the message.

One final hurdle had to be cleared with the Corporal, who had seen them practicing the drill with the lad. Bert explained that Jacky was genuinely upset about his problem and a little bit of coaching had done the trick, to which the Corporal bluntly told him that it was 'his bloody job' to sort things out. However, after Jacky had demonstrated that he had indeed 'got it right', he softened somewhat, although his final comment was very much to the point.

'If you lot have got a problem, come to me. That's what I'm here for.'

Just to be sure, Jackie kept his piece of string around his thumb for a good few weeks after. Bert had been the instigator in the early days of pulling the platoon together and he had warned them of the risk of upsetting their Corporal. They had taken his advice. The attitude of the platoon had not been in any way out of line, though it could have gone badly wrong. In speaking about the need to always act sensibly and with respect, he had made a final point.

'We should make maximum effort for our Corporal,' he had said loudly, knowing that the stalwart was listening nearby. 'We're up against the other platoons and if we come out on top, it will be very much to his credit, so let's do our best, eh lads?'

From then on, all but the one lad was always seen to be performing well and for some odd reason, their lot had eased significantly.

Chapter 15

More Domestic Problems

Despite having been financially secure for some time, Mike had still not left home and his mother regularly told him that as he was earning such good money, he should pay more into the family budget. She maintained that he had a debt of gratitude to pay, to make up for all the years that they had 'gone short' in keeping him and it was pay-back time. Though he resisted her incessant demands, he knew that there was some merit in her argument. The problem was, despite the extra cash he gave her, it was never enough; she always wanted more and of late, she had become even more demanding. His efforts to avoid the confrontations and rows had failed miserably and he had long since ceased complaining to his mates. They had problems of their own and compared with some, his were of little consequence.

One morning, Mike told Jock about the pressure he had recently come under to settle-down and marry a nice girl, instead of gallivanting around and getting into trouble. The previous Friday evening, after he had finished his tea, his mother had announced that she had spoken to a neighbour who had a twenty year old daughter called Maureen. His first reaction was 'Bloody hell, not again', but to keep the peace, he didn't say so. She went on to describe their discussion over a nice cup of tea and she had promised to speak to him when he came home. His answer had been promised for the following day.

All this sounds a bit far-fetched, but as said earlier, match-making was still very much a part of village life, though whether it still happens now is not known. As it was, Mike was appalled and he couldn't contain his anger.

'What the hell have you done that for?' he replied angrily. 'I would have thought that after the last time, you'd have known better than to pull that stunt again.'

His mother was unabashed and the situation quickly developed into a blazing row. His father weighed in with his 'two-penn'oth' and his brother, who was at home on leave, jeered at his brother's outrage.

'Don't speak to your mother like that, you ignorant sod,' the old man shouted at Mike. 'And you can bloody well shut up as well,' he said, glaring angrily at the older lad. 'Every bloody time we sit down to eat, there's trouble and I'm sick of it.'

'I don't want her interfering in my life,' Mike retorted. 'Why can't she mind her own business? If I want to speak to a girl about marriage, I'll do it without help from anyone else.'

'I only want what's best for him and was only trying to help,' wailed his mother, with copious tears to add to the drama. 'Everyone else his age is either married or engaged and its time he did something about it. I want him to settle down with a nice girl before I go,' she concluded by sniffing loudly to emphasise her point.

'I was married at twenty,' his brother chipped in and, before he could get any farther, Mike cut him off.

'Yes and we all know bloody why,' he angrily retorted. 'You only got married because you had put the stupid cow up the duff. You're hardly the best example of male virtue, you lousy sod.'

That was the signal for chaos, with the brothers both intent on combat. The ensuing commotion brought a couple of neighbours running in and the two protagonists were pulled apart. A few minutes later, their father ended the argument by angrily shouting that he didn't care what Mike did. One thing was for sure, he was leaving at the end of his Apprenticeship and that was final. He had said it so very many times before that Mike saw no point in replying. After nodding at his brother towards the back door, a challenge which wasn't accepted, he left the house. Despite his best intentions, he had been involved in yet another row. It was, as he told Jock, all so bloody frustrating and he would be glad when he went off to sea.

'You're right, laddie,' his mentor said, 'but believe me, if you've no notion of getting married, then don't bloody do it. It's a rocky road at the best of times and if you've any doubts at all, walk away and give it a miss. If you don't mind me saying, while you were right to object to your mother's interference, you shouldn't have reacted in the way you did. You'd have done far better to have said a most definite no and then no more about it. Put it down to the impetuosity of youth and know better next time, eh?

'As for your brother, it sounds as if you'll have to settle it with him sooner or later. I know because I had a similar situation before I left home.'

He then told Mike about the failure of his marriage. While away on a long commission, the letters from his wife had gradually come less frequently. During his last leave, their relationship had become strained. They'd had problems before but, after thinking about it, he had tried to improve matters. She was not on the jetty when he returned, as she had always been previously. The flat was locked up when he arrived home and when he got in, it was empty.

Still hoping to put things right, he had tracked her down and found she was living with another man. When he had asked to see his daughter, she had bluntly told him that as he was not her father, so he had no right to see her. He had lost his temper and when the other man intervened, he had 'punched the shite out of him'. That was the last he'd seen of her and they were now going through the messy process of divorce.

'D'you know what?,' he asked the bemused Mike. 'She even had the bloody cheek to ask me if I would agree to admitting adultery, for the sake of the child. I told her to piss-off.'

'Bloody hell, Jock,' said Mike soberly. 'I thought I had problems.'

'Well, I hope you'll keep what I've just told you to yourself. I don't want this bloody lot knowing my business,' he said, nodding towards the other men. 'Life's bad enough, without having the piss taken out of me by some other clown.'

431

'You can count on me,' replied Mike. 'I'm only too grateful that you listened to my problems in the first place.'

'If you don't mind me saying,' Jock replied, 'You'd do well to steer well clear of any more confrontations at home. Believe me, it's a lonely life without your family. I might as well tell you one last thing, again in confidence mind. I've just heard from the Navy that they're going to have me back. I'll have the same rank and after a short stint of retraining, I'll be going back to sea. I'll be among my own kind and set well to make a new life for myself. I'll be leaving at the end of the month.'

Jock's tale made Mike even more determined to avoid the perils of matrimony. Bearing in mind his boss's misfortune, getting tied down was most definitely not to be taken lightly. Many of his mates had got themselves into a right mess, which had come about from a few minutes of unbridled, carnal pleasure. When he arrived home, he couldn't believe his ears. Despite the row of the previous evening, his mother had continued with her nonsense. Ignoring the old man's advice to 'drop it', she tore into Mike as soon as he came through the door and, being mindful of his mentor's advice, he didn't react.

'I've had Mrs Pearce round again this morning, she said angrily, 'and she wants to know your answer. Now then, what are you going to do?'

'You can tell her whatever you like,' he replied quietly. 'I've nothing more to say, either to her, or her daft daughter.'

'I can't tell her that,' his mother retorted and getting even more agitated. 'She'll want a proper answer, so I'll ask you again, what are you going to do?'

'I've told you, the answer's no and that's final. You've got yourself into a mess and you're going to have to get out of it.

'Take no notice of the ignorant sod,' intervened his father. 'As I've said before, he thinks he's much too good for a village girl. Just tell her he's already got someone you didn't know about, then perhaps we'll hear no more about it.

A few minutes later, with his mother out of the room, Mike spoke directly to his father, which he hadn't done for a very long time.

'It's not about me being better than anyone else,' he said. 'When I finish my time, I'll go off to sea. There's no point getting married only to leave my wife for months on end. I'm going off to see the world; to Australia and New Zealand and other interesting places. From what I've been told, it's no life for a married man.'

'Why the bloody hell didn't you say so?,' the old man responded angrily, 'then we could have done without all this bloody argument. I don't want to hear any more about it. As I've said many times, the sooner you're gone from this house, the better.'

But the nonsense had still not run its course. The following day, his mother informed him that she had told the woman that he wasn't interested and as expected, she had taken offence at his snub to her family. Because of his lack of consideration, Mrs Pearce wouldn't be speaking to her again. Mike bore with the incessant nagging, but was shocked when she said that the woman had asked her if there was something wrong with him, which he took to mean, 'was he queer?' He was astounded at the very suggestion and decided to speak to 'the cheeky cow' at the first opportunity. His chance came over the following weekend and he went straightaway to set the record straight.

'I'd just like you to know that there's nothing wrong with me, queer or otherwise,' he told her angrily, 'and if there was, it wouldn't have been any of your business, would it? I like girls as much as anyone else, but ones that are not one quite as ugly as yours. OK?'

That really was unkind and the poor woman, who had been taken aback at being so angrily confronted, was clearly very upset. Mike knew right away that he had overstepped the mark and he quickly apologised, saying that he hadn't meant what he said. The woman's husband came on the scene and told him to clear off in no uncertain terms and while he didn't take kindly to being spoken to in that way, he walked away without further comment. A couple of weeks later, he saw Maureen at a dance and again apologised for being rude to her mother.

'It's alright, really,' she said brightly. 'When I heard what had been going on, I was just as angry as you. I told mum straight that she had no business discussing me with your mother and that I'll choose my own husband when the time comes. How could she even think I'd be interested in a slob like you? I'm not that desperate.'

They both laughed and went into the bar for a drink. When Mike told his mates about the latest intrigue, it led to the usual piss-taking. Most of them were tied down and were often contemptuous, superior even, to the lads that were unattached. They tended to moralise, saying smugly that sooner or later, they would get their come-uppance. The truth was, they envied their mates' freedom to come and go and spend their money as they pleased. Mike told them, with tongue in cheek, that he could see no point in buying food, only to have some other bugger sharing it. It was a cynical sentiment which brought the desired reaction. One of the lads replied that he had a bloody awful attitude to women and it was little wonder he was still single. His prompt answer was a reference to the most personal and precious male spherical objects, which led to the usual cheers and jeers.

What his mother hadn't known was that he was going steady with Val, a lass from over the other side of Town. As she lived so far away, he only saw her at the weekends and it suited them both. Neither questioned what the other did during the week. She was a large, buxom lass, with long brown hair and she loved dancing and was full of fun. At first, Mike's two left feet hadn't seemed to matter but as the time passed, what was at first a minor irritation became more of an issue. Knowing he would be going away soon, which he didn't mention, he ignored her increasing frustration. Apart from that, they got on well. Their necking sessions, while at times passionate, didn't get out of hand and lead to any complications. She must have wondered why, but he made no effort to tell her. He was determined not to fall on the last lap.

Late in the afternoon of the last Friday of the month, Mike watched as his boss cleared his drawer and put his tools into a hold-all. It was the end of his employment in the Yard and in the following week, Jock was off to re-join the Navy. As they walked up the road, he told Mike that the last impediment to his departure had been removed. He had reached agreement with his wife about their divorce, which had saddened him greatly, despite all that had gone on behind his back. Once outside the Yard, they shook hands and wished each other luck and with a last admonition to 'take care', Jock walked over the road to his bus. It was the last that Mike saw of a man that he had come to both like and respect.

When he arrived home on the following Monday evening, a man was waiting for him by the front door. As he had declined to state his business with her son, his mother had refused to let him into the house. Four weeks previously, Mike had filled in a football coupon and handed the collector a pound for four weeks' entry, using the same numbers. He had forgotten all about it and when the man said that he was from the Pools Company, he knew right away that he had won a substantial sum of money. They moved along the terrace, away from prying eyes and ears and the extent of his win was more than Mike had ever dreamed of. After he had explained the circumstances of his home life, the Rep agreed to meet him the next day, in a Hotel in the Town.

When he went into the house, his mother immediately demanded to know who the man was and what he wanted. Mike told her that he was an insurance agent and that he was thinking of buying life insurance, before he went off to sea. His refusal to discuss it further led to what was probably the worst row that they'd ever had. It all got out of hand when he angrily told her that she would in no way be a beneficiary in the event of his demise. The old man furiously told him that they wanted nothing from him and that he should pack his bags and get out. The fog of anger cleared from Mike's mind and he calmly said that he would do so the next morning, on the clear understanding that they would have no further claim on each other. The long awaited breach was final. The old man said that was fine by him and that was how it was left.

Throughout the morning, Mike didn't know if he was coming or going. He duly arrived at the King's Head and with everything in order, the Rep duly gave him his cheque. Having thought it over through what had been a sleepless night, he had decided to deposit the money in a Bank and leave it untouched until such times as his future became clear. A brief interview with the Manager opened the account and the passbook was withheld in the branch for safe-keeping. He booked into the Hotel for the rest of his time and then went back to work the next morning as if nothing had happened. His torment was at long last at an end.

Chapter 16

The Last Lap

With the end of his Apprenticeship nigh, Mike made his last move. He went to work on a large, modern Destroyer which was nearing the end of her refit. His job was to survey and refurbish the valves in the fire main systems on the upper deck and down below. As he was opening up the first valve, he was confronted by a scowling fourth year Apprentice, who sullenly informed him that he had been told to work with him. He was clearly unimpressed to be working under another Apprentice, even one who was nearing the end of his time. Jed was a small, stocky lad and he made it clear that he had no intention of doing any work and Mike could either 'like it or lump it'. Mike shrugged and told him he could do as he liked. Having kept out of trouble for so long, there was no way he was going to get involved in any aggro with the stroppy little bugger.

Working on the valves was not a demanding job – almost every one was in good condition and needed little doing to it. The overall system was made up of a number of ring mains and he went along to see the ship's Engineer. A large drawing had been taped to the bulkhead in his office and parts of the system had already been marked off as completed. It would be fully tested during the running-up of the ancillary machinery, in the final stages of the refit. In talking to Mike, the Lieutenant told him that the Navy was short of Engineers and asked if he had thought of joining up. The lad replied that he was going to join the Merchant Navy. What he didn't tell him was that he had frittered away his time when he should have been studying and was in no way qualified to serve as an Engineer Officer. In the ensuing weeks, they got on well and often chatted when Freddie was doing his rounds.

One morning, the Foreman came by and seeing Mike was working alone, he asked where 'the lad' was. Mike replied that he didn't know, but said he must be somewhere on board. Jed had in fact been spending most of his time in the Seamen's' mess, playing cards with other disaffected youths.

'I'll somewhere the lazy sod when I find him,' grumbled the Foreman. 'He's completely bloody idle that one and when you came aboard, I thought you would be just the bloke to sort him out.'

Mike wasn't best pleased to hear that, but it gave him the chance to make his feelings known where Jed was concerned.

'I've got enough problems without having to wet-nurse a bolshie Apprentice,' he said, with a smile. 'Mr George, you can't expect me to do your dirty work for you.'

'You're right,' came the prompt reply. 'I'll go and have a look about and when I find him, he'll get a right bollocking.'

That should have been the end of it, but soon after, Mike was again confronted by the furious Jed and this time, he was backed up by his pals.

'You've dropped me right in it, you lousy bastard,' he howled. 'Now I've got the bloody Foreman on my back because of you.'

'Hang about,' replied Mike with equal venom, 'I haven't done anything of the kind. When Mr George came on board about half an hour ago, he asked me where you were and I said I didn't know. That's all there was to it.'

The stream of invective from the angry lad continued until eventually, Mike lost his temper. Other men had stopped working and were listening to the altercation, which he didn't appreciate at all.

'Right, bastard,' he said, 'I've told you how it was and if it isn't good enough, then you can piss off before I give you a slap. Go on, get lost you horrible little git.'

Jed wisely did as he was told, but then had the audacity to say that he was going to see the Foreman to demand to work with someone else. He wasn't going to be threatened by the likes of him. Mike had the last word.

'While you're at it, tell him what a lazy, good for nothing little swine you are as well. How, instead of working, you skive off and play cards all day. I'll come with you if you like.'

It had the desired effect. Mike had got shut of the lad and from then on, he got on with the job on his own. When he later saw the Foreman, he told him that he had heard about the angry exchange. Obviously, the ship's bulkheads had ears! He smiled wryly and told him not to worry about it. He had a number of dirty jobs lined up for Jed and his mates and he'd be keeping a very close eye on them in future. The discord didn't end there though. From time to time, Mike had to put up with snide comments from the other lads and at times, he was hard-pressed to ignore them. The irony of the situation was not lost on Mike, given his own attitude problems in the past few years.

Due to the drastic change in his financial circumstances, his social life was hectic and it was imperative to do something about his driving. Having had a lot of practice and despite his mates' poor opinion about his ability, he applied to retake his test. He still didn't have much of a grasp of driving safely and there were a lot of knowing looks when they discussed his shortcomings. One lad took the time off to come with him to the test centre and after checking his documents, the examiner took him outside. As before, he strongly objected to the left-hand drive vehicle. Mike really should have known better. The driving part of the test went without any problems and Mike thought he answered all his questions correctly. He was then devastated to be told that he had failed, this time due to inadequate use of the mirror. To fail his first test had been disappointing enough, but having failed the second was a disaster.

He was convinced that he had been treated unfairly and wouldn't listen to any advice, however well meant. He became even more careless about driving unaccompanied and on a number of occasions was lucky not to have been apprehended. One evening, while driving through the Town, a Police car followed him and despite making numerous turns, the Rozzers remained on his tail. Eventually, he turned into a cul-de-sac, stopped and got out, then made to go into a house. One of the Officers called him over and said that one of his indicators was not working properly.

'That's strange,' said Mike, acting the innocent. 'When I checked earlier, they were both working. I'll just have a look.'

He got back into the car, switched on the ignition and operated the suspect indicator a few times, noting with relief that the one in question was working normally.

'It seems to be alright, officer,' he said. 'Perhaps it's just damp or dirty, I'll give it a wipe to see if I can improve it.

The copper nodded and to Mike's great relief, he got back into his car and drove off. He left the car in the street and went into a nearby pub for a well-needed drink and later, he drove home without any further problem. For a week or so, he was careful about driving alone, but was soon doing it again. He knew his mates were taking advantage and they rarely made a contribution towards the cost of the journeys they made. They expected to be collected and taken back to their homes and were 'miffed' when he didn't oblige them. One evening, he was again very fortunate. He had driven over to near where he used to live, parked the car in a side road, crossed the field and looked over the hedge. P. C. Smith was standing at the T-junction and Mike knew he was waiting for him.

He left the car where it was and walked up the hill to The Mill. He had only been inside for a few minutes when the officer came in and said that he wanted a word with him. There was a sarcastic cheer from his mates as he followed him out through the door.

'Right,' said Smithy, 'I thought you'd be here. I've had a look in the car park and can't see your car, but I know that you're out driving on your own. I want to know where you've left it.'

'I don't know what you're talking about,' replied Mike, feigning indignation. 'You want to get your facts right before you go about making accusations. If you must know, I came on my bike,' he said, pointing to it a machine leaning against the wall. 'I don't like being hauled out of the pub in front of everybody for no good reason. I suggest you find something better to do than chase around after me.'

It was a stupid thing to say, but his outburst took the Officer aback.

'I know you're up to no good,' he retorted angrily and sooner or later, you'll slip up. When you do, I'll be waiting.'

He then got on his motorcycle and rode off back down the hill.

Mike didn't always think about the seriousness of what he was doing. One Friday morning, he took the car into work to show off, but there was also a degree of laziness involved. Compared with cycling, the car was luxury indeed. No matter which gate he used, the Dockyard Police could stop him, so the risk of apprehension was just as real as on the public highway. What actually stopped him from doing it again was something quite different. Mac had looked at the car during the dinner- hour and had warmly complimented him on his wheels. Mike should have been suspicious, because nearly five years of animosity could not have ended that easily. Their conversation culminated in a request for a lift home at the end of the day and, fundamental orifice that he was, Mike agreed.

After clocking off, they drove out the gate and Mac was very chatty as they went through the town. Due to the heavy traffic, their journey was very slow. On Monday morning, Mike cycled in to the Yard and after clocking on, he made ready to start work. Within minutes, he was subjected to a tirade of abuse from the very bugger he had gone out of his way to oblige. The slob loudly described how he had driven so slowly that he could have made the journey quicker by bus. He went on and on until Mike lost his temper and just as he was moving to chastise his critic, the Foreman appeared.

Many of the lads had written to the Shipping Companies, but job opportunities for Junior Engineers were still few and far between. They mostly tended to take applicants with qualifications. The favourites were the Companies that sailed to the more attractive parts of the World, such as Australia, New Zealand, North America and South Africa. Some had large, refrigerated cargo Vessels, which carried up to one hundred and twenty passengers and, with a bit of luck, a lad could secure a berth on one of them. There were numerous companies which plied their trade in specific Countries and though they were not so particular, it was still not easy to get a job with them. The Tankers compared well with the general cargo vessels, in that they were better paid, but the living conditions on their ships could be basic. One could also be away for a year or more. Very much at the bottom of the deep-sea list were the Tramp Steamers, which traded all over the World.

One morning, a Fitter told Mike about a Tramp Ship he had sailed on. She was what was known as a 'hard Ship', with demanding work, indifferent accommodation and food. During his twenty-one months on board, his pay had been substantially enhanced by two promotions, first to Fourth and then to Third Engineer and he had eventually come home with a large sum of money, including a bonus, which had been paid tax-free. Another Fitter had sailed on 'Coasters'; small vessels which traded around the ports of the UK and Europe. He had earned less than he would have got 'deep sea', but the Ships had spent a lot of their time in port and more important, had come home regularly. The general consensus was that you very much took your chance, with the various Ship owners. There was no guarantee that anyone would like the life and there was only one way to find out.

With National Service a definite non-starter and his time almost completed, it was imperative to get set-up as soon as possible. Out of the dozen or so letters he had sent, Mike received five replies, which was a good return. Two were outright rejections and two invited him for interview. One was from a company that traded in the Far East and was discarded. The other one was from a South American line, which had been highly recommended by an old sea dog. When Mike telephoned the Engineer Superintendent, he was dismayed to be told that their need was immediate, with the Ship sailing in the following week. He wouldn't be available until after the end of July, which was more than four weeks away. The man abruptly put the phone down, after telling him he was wasting his time.

Fortunately, another letter came a few days later, which invited him for interview on a specific date and he lost no time in replying. When he arrived in the office for interview, two other lads were also waiting. One was a Welshman, the other a Geordie and they had both served their time in Shipyards. Mike was called in first and the Superintendent told him that his Company traded down the West African coast. He then spent about twenty minutes questioning him about his training and the work he had done in his Apprenticeship. He was then sent to an office in the city to register as a Seaman and get his MN identity card and discharge book. He then reported back to the office and was given his expenses, which covered his travel costs, a meal and an overnight stop in the Mission to Seamen. He didn't see the other lads again. Early the following week, confirmation came that he had been accepted and he was instructed to return to Liverpool, with his kit, on the Monday following the end of his Apprenticeship.

All but a few of the lads had secured employment, but those that hadn't showed little concern. The noisy discussions in the canteen were jolly and relaxed, which as usual were irksome to the men sitting nearby. Most of them kept the details of where they were going to themselves, but Mike had no such inhibitions. He was so relieved that his search for a berth had been successful. One afternoon, he cycled down to the Locks to see Nobby and with Manchester having retired, his erstwhile mentor was firmly ensconced in the Foreman's chair, no doubt very much to the disgust of the men working under him. He was very pleased that Mike had taken the trouble to come down to say goodbye.

'Just remember, lad,' he intoned solemnly, 'life on board Ship is not for the faint-hearted and it will be bloody hard work, far worse at times than you could ever have expected. Don't think for one moment that you know anything about Engineering, just because you've finished your time. You'll soon realise you now bugger all and the only thing to do is to buckle-down and keep your trap shut. If I can give you one bit of advice, it's to learn all you can about your Ship. An inquiring mind is an active one and for your own safety and that of everyone else, you must know how everything works and exactly what it does.'

After taking his leave, Mike went back to the his job. He was gratified that Nobby had still taken an interest in him and had been so very helpful with his advice. The last week came and little work was done by any of the lads who were leaving. Their tools were collected up and returned to the stores, boiler-suits were handed in and final goodbyes said. Arrangements were made to take their toolboxes out of the Yard, with the necessary passes being obtained from the Foreman. On the last Friday afternoon, they duly reported to the Manager's office to be formally handed their indentures. It was a most valuable piece of paper, which confirmed that the owner had successfully completed his Apprenticeship.

He then made his way to the gate, handed in his pass and left the Yard for the last time. As he made his way back to the Hotel, he was very aware that an important part of his life had come to an end. His relationship with Val, which he had thought of as 'a comfortable companionship', had not endured. She had finally lost patience with his poor dancing and on the last Saturday evening they had their one and only 'tiff'. The cha-cha was all the rage and she did it very well, but Mike's efforts were disjointed and clumsy. After he had stood on her feet (yet again), the lass stormed off the floor, leaving him very annoyed. When they arrived at her home, Mike had abruptly said 'good night' and driven away, something which he later regretted. He should have made the effort to make up or at least have been honest about his intentions. Not for the first time, he had lacked courage and had shown no sensitivity for her feelings. He didn't see her again.

Over the past five years, there had been many times when he had regretted entering the Dockyard. Somehow, he had stuck it out and at the end, he knew he had been right to have done so. The innumerable rows at home had resulted in a complete breach with his parents, which would never be healed. Despite that, he had to admit that his father had been right to insist that 'you've got to have a trade'. He was now a Tradesman, albeit a journeyman and had learned what was needed to earn a living as a Fitter. He looked forward to the future with confidence and was full of optimism about his forthcoming career at sea. However, there was a final twist to the tale, which he had not even thought of.

He was homeless and all set to join the Merchant Navy on the following Monday morning. He had had no inclination to buy or rent a flat or house but, all was not lost. On the Saturday evening, he was talking to an old couple in a pub and they offered to keep his toolbox in their garden shed. They would also be pleased to put him up, whenever he was in the area and would let him park his car beside their garage until he could find a buyer. Their generosity was greatly appreciated.

It brought an end to what could only be described as a long haul. He'd had had his ups and downs with many trials and tribulations, many of which had been resultant from his own failings. Now, he was making a fresh start and he was determined to do as well as he could. Time would tell if he had the ability to make a success of his life, but he was under no illusions on that score. He was on his own and, whatever happened, only he could control his destiny.